The Last King of Shang

The Last King of Shang

Based on Investiture of the Gods

By Jeff Pepper

IMAGIN8
PRESS

This is a work of fiction. Names, characters, organizations, places, events, locales, and incidents are either the products of the author's imagination or used in a fictitious manner. Any resemblance to actual persons, living or dead, or actual events is purely coincidental.

Copyright © 2024 by Imagin8 Press LLC, all rights reserved.

Published in the United States by Imagin8 Press LLC, Verona, PA 15147 USA. For information, contact us via email at info@imagin8press.com, or visit www.imagin8press.com.

Our books may be purchased directly in quantity at a reduced price. Visit www.imagin8press.com for details.

Imagin8 Press, the Imagin8 logo and the sail image are all trademarks of Imagin8 Press LLC.

Written by Jeff Pepper

Based on the original 16th century Chinese novel by Xu Zhonglin

ISBN: 978-1959043614
Version 1.1

Contents

Acknowledgements 9
Introduction 11
Cast of Characters 15
Chapter 1 The King and the Goddess 23
Chapter 2 The Rebellion of Su Hu 29
Chapter 3 Daji is Given to the King 34
Chapter 4 The Fox Demon Kills Daji 39
Chapter 5 The Master of the Clouds 43
Chapter 6 The Burning Pillar 47
Chapter 7 Fei Zhong Plots Against the Queen 51
Chapter 8 Princes Flee from Zhaoge 56
Chapter 9 The Death of the Prime Minister 62
Chapter 10 Ji Chang Finds Thunderbolt 66
Chapter 11 The Deaths of the Grand Dukes 70
Chapter 12 The Birth of Nezha 74
Chapter 13 Two Immortals Fight 78
Chapter 14 Nezha Returns to Life 83
Chapter 15 Jiang Ziya Leaves Mount Kunlun 88
Chapter 16 The Jade Lute Demon 92
Chapter 17 The Snake Pit 98
Chapter 18 Flight from Zhaoge 102
Chapter 19 Gifts for the King 107
Chapter 20 San Yisheng Bribes the Ministers 113
Chapter 21 Flight Through Five Passes 118
Chapter 22 The Grand Duke Returns 121
Chapter 23 Dream of a Flying Bear 126
Chapter 24 From Fisherman to Prime Minister 131
Chapter 25 A Feast for Demons 137
Chapter 26 Daji Plots Revenge 142

Chapter 27 The Grand Tutor Returns..148

Chapter 28 Punishing the North Grand Dukedom....................154

Chapter 29 Death of Two Grand Dukes..159

Chapter 30 Huang Feihu's Rebellion..165

Chapter 31 Flight and Pursuit..172

Chapter 32 Huang Tianhua Meets His Father..............................177

Chapter 33 The Battle at the Pass...182

Chapter 34 The Rebel Meets the Prime Minister......................187

Chapter 35 Two Generals Join West Qi..191

Chapter 36 The First Attack on West Qi...196

Chapter 37 Jiang Ziya Returns to Mount Kunlun......................201

Chapter 38 Four Monks in West Qi...207

Chapter 39 Jiang Ziya Freezes Mount Qi.......................................213

Chapter 40 The Shang Army Surrounds West Qi City...........218

Chapter 41 Grand Tutor Wen Goes to West Qi.........................224

Chapter 42 The Bandit Chiefs Join Grand Tutor Wen............229

Chapter 43 Grand Tutor Wen is Defeated....................................234

Chapter 44 Jiang Ziya's Soul Floats to Mount Kunlun............238

Chapter 45 The First Battle of the Traps.......................................244

Chapter 46 The Second Battle of the Traps................................250

Chapter 47 Zhao Gongming Helps the Grand Tutor..............254

Chapter 48 The Illness of Zhao Gongming..................................260

Chapter 49 Ji Fa in the Red Sand Trap...265

Chapter 50 The Yellow River Trap...270

Chapter 51 The Defeat of Grand Tutor Wen...............................276

Chapter 52 The Death of Grand Tutor Wen................................281

Chapter 53 Deng Jiugong Attacks West Qi..................................286

Chapter 54 Earth Traveler Sun Attacks West Qi........................292

Chapter 55 Earth Traveler Sun is Captured.................................297

Chapter 56 The Betrayal of Deng Jiugong....................................301

Chapter 57 Su Hu Fights Against West Qi....................................308

Chapter 58 Lu Yue, The God of Plague 313
Chapter 59 The Second Prince Returns 318
Chapter 60 Ma Yuan Helps the Shang Army 323
Chapter 61 The Death of the Second Prince 328
Chapter 62 The Arrival of Winged Celestial 332
Chapter 63 Yin Jiao Returns 337
Chapter 64 The Burning of West Qi City 343
Chapter 65 The Crown Prince is Captured 348
Chapter 66 The Sorcerer Hong Jin 353
Chapter 67 Jiang Ziya, Commander of the Army 357
Chapter 68 Two Daoists Stop the Army 363
Chapter 69 Trouble at Golden Chicken Mountains 367
Chapter 70 The Mystery of the Five Lights 371
Chapter 71 The Battle of Three Passes 375
Chapter 72 The Immortals Argue 379
Chapter 73 The Earthworm 384
Chapter 74 The Battle of Green Dragon Pass 388
Chapter 75 The Little Man Steals a Camel 393
Chapter 76 The Zhou Army Captures Sishui Pass 399
Chapter 77 Laozi Brings Three Immortals 404
Chapter 78 Breaking the Trap 409
Chapter 79 Four Generals Are Captured 414
Chapter 80 Breaking the Plague Trap 419
Chapter 81 The God of Plague 425
Chapter 82 The Last Trap 431
Chapter 83 Lion, Elephant and Tiger 435
Chapter 84 Two Religions Come Together 440
Chapter 85 The Rebellion of Two Generals 445
Chapter 86 Generals and Princes Fall 451
Chapter 87 Death of Earth Traveler Sun and Deng Chanyu . 455
Chapter 88 Crossing the Yellow River 459

Chapter 89 The King Cuts Open Pregnant Women 464
Chapter 90 The Defeat of Two Demons 469
Chapter 91 The Giant Attacks 473
Chapter 92 Yang Jian Defeats Demons 478
Chapter 93 Jinzha Captures the Pass 483
Chapter 94 Death of the Messenger 488
Chapter 95 The King's Ten Crimes 493
Chapter 96 Daji Flees 498
Chapter 97 Death of the Tyrant 502
Chapter 98 The New King Gives Food 507
Chapter 99 The Naming of the Gods 512
Chapter 100 King Wu Gives Gifts 524
About the Authors 527

Acknowledgements

We are grateful to the original authors of this story and to the scholars who have translated the book into English before us.

In writing this book we have referred to the original Chinese text in *The Project Gutenberg eBook of Feng Shen Yan Yi*[1], as well as an English translation, *Creation of the Gods,* translated by Gu Zhizhong[2].

These books are both available free online. See the footnotes for tinyurl.com shortcut links to their websites. These shortcut links are safe and do not use any tracking software.

Thanks to my writing partner Xiao Hui Wang, who has translated my English back into Chinese for the books in our *Last King of Shang* series, and has worked with me on so many other fun projects.

Also, many thanks to Yu Jin and his team of artists at Next Mars Media for their terrific cover artwork, Tzu Yang for her help in translating the poems at the beginning of each chapter, and Jean Agapoff for her careful proofreading.

---

[1] Lu, Xi Xing, *The Project Gutenberg eBook of Feng Shen Yan Yi*, Publisher unknown. 2007-2021. Shortcut link www.tinyurl.com/FengShenBang-01 resolves to www.gutenberg.org/files/23910/23910-h/23910-h.htm.

[2] Zhizhong, Gu (translator), *Creation of the Gods I, II, III and IV by Xu Zhonglin*. New World Press, Foreign Languages Press and Hunan People's Publishing House, 1002. Shortcut link www.tinyurl.com/FengShenBang-02 resolves to journeytothewestresearch.com/wp-content/uploads/2020/05/fsyy-en-cn.pdf.

Introduction

This book is loosely based on the historical events that led to the overthrow in 1066 B.C. of King Di Xin, the 31st in a line of Shang kings going back seventeen generations and six centuries.

The king's name in his lifetime was Di Xin of Shang (商帝辛, shāng dì xīn). After his death he was mockingly referred to as King Zhou (zhòu wáng), because zhòu (紂) is Chinese for "crupper," the rear strap on a saddle that goes under the horse's tail and is most likely to be soiled by the horse. For this reason, some translations refer to him as King Zhou. We call him Di Xin, because the name Zhou (紂, zhòu) is confusingly similar to the name of the Zhou (周, zhōu) Dynasty that succeeded Shang.

Di Xin, also known as King Zhou of Shang.

Unlike most of his predecessors, Di Xin was a tyrannical despot who, encouraged by his favorite concubine Daji, enjoyed inventing creative ways to torture and execute people who displeased him. Not surprisingly, he was despised by his subjects.

According to the concept of "mandate of heaven" (tiānmìng), heaven gives its mandate to a just ruler, the so-called "son of heaven." If the ruler loses his mandate, the people have the right to overthrow him. In fact, if a ruler is overthrown, that can be taken as proof that he was unworthy and had lost heaven's mandate.

In the case of Di Xin, there were many indications that he had lost heaven's mandate. One poem said that "Heaven has sent down death and disorder; famine comes repeatedly[1]." This was partly caused by his mismanagement of the kingdom's resources, but also the result of a long-term cooling climate which caused crops to fail. To make matters worse, there were two disturbing portents in the sky. The five known planets all appeared tightly clustered together in the constellation of Cancer. And a few months later, Halley's comet blazed in the sky. Taken

---

[1] Chittick, Andrew (2003). "The life and legacy of Liu Biao: governor, warlord, and imperial pretender in late Han China". Journal of Asian History. Harrassowitz Verlag.

together, many believed that Di Xin had lost the mandate of heaven and needed to be toppled from the throne.

Matters came to a head in January of 1066 B.C., when Ji Fa, the leader of Zhou and Overlord of the West (a title given to him by Di Xin) dispatched a large army which arrived in the capital city of Zhaoge the following month. To defend the capital, Di Xin had gathered 530,000 soldiers and conscripted another 170,000 slaves. But the slaves refused to fight, and many of the soldiers turned their spears upside down or defected to the Zhou side. The Zhou army quickly overthrew Di Xin in the Battle of Muyi, described by a historian as "like crushing dry weeds and smashing rotten wood." Ji Fa became King Wu, founding the Zhou Dynasty which lasted for almost 800 years.

The overthrow of the king of Shang by a mere provincial governor was considered a disturbing precedent by the kings and emperors who followed. They didn't like the idea that their subjects might decide that they were unhappy with their ruler and should take matters into their own hands. For a local official to presume to go against his king was seen later as "a monstrous crime of insubordination and a violation of Confucian ethics," even though Confucius wasn't born until 500 years after these events.

For centuries, philosophers struggled to resolve this contradiction. The great philosopher Confucius taught that officials should be loyal to their king, just as a child should be loyal to their parents. But what if the king fails in his duties and doesn't care for his people? When the Confucian philosopher Mencius was asked about this, he replied that a king should be benevolent and merciful, but if he is not, then he is not a king but a tyrant, and tyrants must be punished. Speaking of the overthrow of Di Xin, he wrote[1], "We heard that the tyrant was punished; not that the king was murdered."

Twenty-four centuries later, Zhu Yuanzhang, the founder of the Ming Dynasty, was also fond of creative methods of torture and execution. He was worried about the precedent set by the popular uprising against the king of Shang. So in the year 1393 he ordered all mention of this historical event deleted from *Mencius*, a classic book written by Mencius and his disciples. This resulted in the disappearance of about a third of the book, and what was left became known as the *Abridged Essays of Mencius*.

The book you are about to read is not just a chronicle of the depraved actions of a bewitched king. It also examines the life-and-death decisions faced by his ministers and generals. Should they remain loyal

---

[1] Mencius, *Mencius, Liang Hui Wang* (second part)

to the king, despite the awful things he does and says? Or should they conclude that the king has lost the mandate of heaven and must be removed? There is no middle ground. And as you'll see, each individual needs to decide where their loyalties lie.

~ ~ ~

The original Chinese title of this book is 封神演义 (fēng shén yǎnyì), although it is commonly known as just 封神榜 (fēng shén bǎng). The closest word-for-word translations of these titles would be "Romance of the Naming of the Gods" and "The Granting of the Names of the Gods."

Because these are awkward in English, translators over the years have come up with many different titles for the book, including *Investiture of the Gods*, *Canonisation of the Gods*, *Creation of the Gods*, *The Legend of Deification*, *The Story of Chinese Gods*, and even *Chronicles of the God's Order*. But we have chosen to break with tradition completely and call this book *The Last King of Shang*. Of course, this doesn't match the original title at all. But we feel it best captures the theme of the book, which is the corruption and decay of the Shang dynasty and the difficult choices faced by his ministers and generals as they try to decide what to do with their incompetent and deluded king.

~ ~ ~

The original novel *Investiture of the Gods* was published sometime between 1567 and 1619, roughly 2,650 years after the historical events it's based on. It is one of the great examples of what is now called shenmo fiction (神魔小说; shénmó xiǎoshuō), a genre of Chinese fiction that revolves around mythical deities, immortals, demons and monsters. *Journey to the West* and *Investiture of the Gods* are the two best known examples of classical shenmo fiction.

No one knows for certain who wrote the book. The best clue lies in a 20-volume woodblock print of the book that was published during the Ming Dynasty and is now in the Library of the Japanese Cabinet in Japan. On the cover is an inscription saying that the book was carved by Shu Congfu in the Jinkai Bookstore. No author is listed. However, in the second volume it mentions that the book was edited by "Xu Zhonglin, a hermit (or 'leisure man') of Zhongshan." Nothing more is known about him. Since he is referred to as the editor, we don't know how much was actually written by him and how much he collected from other authors and storytellers.

In the book's preface, the publisher claims that the book was purchased in Chu, and that he, Li Yunxiang, "daringly continued the writing, by deleting its absurd parts and the vulgar slang... Now the book is finished and it is up to the readers to decide if it is credible or not[1]."

Investiture of the Gods is one of the great novels of classical Chinese literature, along with *Journey to the West, Water Margin, Romance of the Three Kingdoms,* and *Dream of the Red Chamber.* But of these, *Investiture of the Gods* probably has had the most impact on the daily lives and language of the people. Many of the episodes in the book have become deeply embedded in Chinese culture. Nearly everyone in China is familiar with the main characters of the novel, and there are many popular idioms that come from episodes in the book.

For example, "Jiang Taigong is here, the gods avoid" refers to the power of Jiang Ziya (called Jiang Taigong after he becomes a god at the end) to review the behavior of all the gods and punish them as needed. Traditionally, when Chinese people build houses they put up banners or write the idiom on a wooden beam (see figure at right), hoping to intimidate any evil demons and keep them away from the new home.

Another popular idiom, "Jiang Taigong fishes, and those who wish to take the bait" is based on the unusual fishing method used by Jiang Ziya in the book. His fishing rod and line were very short, the hook was straight, and he used no bait. He would say to himself, "Fish, if you don't want to live anymore, come and swallow the hook yourself." Today, people use this idiom to describe someone who willingly falls into a trap or ignores the consequences of their actions.

---

[1] Shuofang Xu and Qiuke Sun, *A History of Literature in the Ming Dynasty,* translated by Li Ma, Springer Nature Singapore Ptc Ltd., 2018.

Cast of Characters

The original Chinese novel *Investiture of the Gods* had over 450 different named characters[1]. To simplify things, we have avoided giving names to the minor characters. Here are the important ones who are named in the book. If a character defects from one side to another over the course of the story, they are listed according to their original allegiance.

The numbers in brackets indicate the chapter where the character first appears.

Shang Royal Family

- Di Xin – the last king of Shang [1]
- Ji Zi – uncle of the King of Shang [6]
- Jiang – queen of Shang, daughter of Jiang Huanchu [1]
- Su Daji – daughter of Marquis Su Hu, the king's chief concubine and then queen, possessed by a fox demon [1]
- Yin Hong – younger son of the king and Queen Jiang [1]
- Yin Jiao – Crown Prince, elder son of the king and Queen Jiang [1]

Shang Leaders and Ministers

- Bi Gan – Vice Prime Minister, uncle of the King [2]
- Chong Heihu – Marquis of Caozhou, known as Black Tiger, brother of Chong Houhu, [3]
- Chong Houhu – the cruel Grand Duke of the North [1]
- Du Yuanxian – Chief Minister of the Observatory [6]
- E Chongyu – Grand Duke of the South [1]
- Fei Zhong – a minion courtier [1]
- Ji Chang – the virtuous Grand Duke of the West, later titled Prince Wen of West Qi [1]
- Jiang Huanchu – Grand Duke of the East [1]
- Jiao Ge – Supreme Minister [11]
- Mei Bo – Supreme Minister [1]
- Shang Rong – Prime Minister [1]
- Su Hu – Marquis of Jizhou, father of Daji [2]
- Su Quanzhong – son of Su Hu [2]
- Yang Ren – Supreme Minister, later a disciple of Virtue of the Pure

---

[1] For a complete list of all named characters in the original novel, except for characters like Laozi who already existed, see "Creation of the Gods: A Somewhat Less Than Critical Listing of Characters in Order of Appearance" in www.poisonpie.com/words/others/somewhat/creation/text/characters.html.

Void [7]
- You Hun – a minion courtier [1]
- Zhao Qi – Supreme Minister [9]

Shang Military
- Bian Ji – son of a Shang general [84]
- Chao Lei – a palace general of Zhaoge [7]
- Chao Tian – a palace general of Zhaoge [7]
- Chen Qi – a sorcerer and supply officer at Green Dragon Pass [73]
- Chen Tong – commander of Tongguan Pass [31]
- Chen Wu – commander of Chuanyun Pass, brother of Chen Tong [32]
- Chong Yingbiao – son of Chong Houhu, a general at Jizhou [2]
- Deng Chanyu – daughter of Deng Jiugong, married Earth Traveler Sun [41]
- Deng Jiugong – commander of Sanshang Pass [18]
- Dou Rong – general opposing Jiang Wenhuan at Youhun Pass [14]
- Fang Bi – Chief of Guards, later a ferryman [8]
- Fang Xiang – Chief of Guards, later a ferryman [8]
- Feng Lin – general under Zhang Guifang [36]
- Gao Jineng – general with a bag full of centipedes and bees [69]
- Gao Lanying – wife of Zhang Kui [86]
- Guo Chen – general under Lu Renjie at Zhaoge [94]
- Han Rong – commander of Sishui Pass [19]
- Han Sheng – elder son of Han Rong [19]
- Hong Jin – commander of Sanshang Pass and a powerful sorcerer [62]
- Huang Feibiao – brother of Huang Feihu [30]
- Huang Feihu – the head of military affairs [1]
- Huang Gun – commander of Jiepai Pass, father of Huang Feihu and Concubine Huang [30]
- Huang Ming – palace general, brother of Huang Feihu [8]
- Huang Tianhua – disciple of Master Pure Void Virtue, son of Huang, raised by Master Pure Void Virtue [31]
- Kong Xuan – powerful magician, commander of Sanshan Pass [53]
- Li Jing – commander of Chentang Pass, disciple of Burning Lamp, father of Nezha, Jinzha and Muzha [12]
- Long Anji – general at Chuanyun Pass [59]
- Lu Xiong – elderly general of Zhaoge, led attack against Jizhou [2]
- Lu Ya – a powerful magician from Mount Kunlun [48]
- Ma Shan – bandit who joined the Shang [63]
- Madame Dou – wife of Dou Rong [93]
- Mo Lihai – guard at Jiameng Pass [31]
- Mo Lihong – guard at Jiameng Pass [31]

- Mo Liqing – guard at Jiameng Pass [31]
- Mo Lishou – guard at Jiameng Pass [31]
- Ouyang Chun – commander of Lintong Pass [84]
- Peng Zun – general and magician at Jiepai Pass [78]
- Qiu Yin – commander of Green Dragon Pass [36]
- Rui Ji – general at Lintong Pass, joined Zhou [85]
- Tai Luan – general with a face like a crab [53]
- Wen Zhong – titled Grand Tutor Wen, head of civil affairs for the King of Shang [1]
- Winged Celestial – immortal from Penglai Island [62]
- Xiao Yin – general at Longtong Pass [31]
- Xin Huan – former bandit chief [41]
- Xu Fang – commander of Chuanyun Pass, younger brother of Xu Gai [79]
- Xu Gai – commander of Jiepai Pass [78]
- Yu Da – eldest son of Yu Hualong [81]
- Yu De – youngest son of Yu Hualong [81]
- Yu Guang – third son of Yu Hualong [81]
- Yu Hua – the Seven Headed General, sorcerer for Han Rong at Sishui Pass [33]
- Yu Hualong – commander of Tongguan Pass [81]
- Yu Xian – fourth son of Yu Hualong [81]
- Yu Zhao – second son of Yu Hualong [81]
- Zhang Feng – commander of Longtong Pass, sworn brother of Huang Feihu's father
- Zhang Guifang – commander at Lintong Pass [18]
- Zhang Kui – commander in Mianchi County [31]
- Zhang Shan – commander of Sanshang Pass [62]
- Zheng Lun – general under Su Hu at Jizhou, leader of the Black Crow army [3]

Shang-Aligned Gods, Immortals and Demons

- Black Cloud – disciple of Grand Master of Heaven [72]
- Celestial Lotus – powerful magician from Golden Turtle Island [43]
- Chang Hao – snake demon from Mount Plum [87]
- Chen Geng – friend of Lu Yue, leader of 3,000 soldiers [69]
- Cloud Firmament – sister of Zhao Gongming, from Three Immortals Island [47]
- Dai Li – dog demon under Yuan Hong [92]
- Ding Ce – general under Lu Renjie at Zhaoge [94]
- Dragon Head – disciple of Grand Master of Heaven [72]
- Fa Jie – Daoist monk, master of Peng Zun [76]
- Gao Youqian – Daoist immortal, friend of Grand Tutor Wen [38]

- Grand Master of Heaven – leader of Jie Daoism [72]
- Green Firmament – sister of Zhao Gongming, a hermit on Three Immortals Island [47]
- Jade Firmament – sister of Zhao Gongming, a hermit on Three Immortals Island [47]
- Lady of Golden Light – Daoist master, friend of Grand Tutor Wen [43]
- Lady Pretty Cloud – magician, a friend of Shen Gongbao [49]
- Li Ping – friend of Lu Yue [80]
- Li Xingba – Daoist immortal, friend of Grand Tutor Wen [38]
- Long Ears – disciple of Grand Master of Heaven [77]
- Lu Renjie – general under Yuan Hong at Mengjin [87]
- Lu Yue – immortal from Nine Dragon Island [57]
- Luo Xuan – Burning Flame Immortal, the master of fire [64]
- Ma Sui – disciple of Grand Master of Heaven [82]
- Ma Yuan – immortal from Skeleton Mountain [60]
- Many Treasures – disciple of Grand Master of Heaven [73]
- Mother Fiery Spirit – Daoist, master of Hu Lei [71]
- Mother Golden Light – disciple of Grand Master of Heaven [43]
- Mother Golden Spirit – Daoist, master of Yu Yuan [72]
- Pretty Cloud – a magician, friend of Shen Gongbao [49]
- Qin Wan – Daoist master, builder of the Heavenly Destruction trap [43]
- Shen Gongbao – untrustworthy disciple of Heavenly Primogenitor [37]
- Spiritual Teeth – disciple of Grand Master of Heaven [77]
- Spiritual Tortoise – disciple of Grand Master of Heaven [72]
- Wang Mo – Daoist immortal, friend of Grand Tutor Wen [38]
- Wu Long – centipede demon from Mount Plum [87]
- Wu Wenhua – giant under Yuan Hong at Mengjin [91]
- Yang Sen – Daoist immortal, friend of Grand Tutor Wen [38]
- Yang Xian – goat demon under Yuan Hong [92]
- Yao – Daoist master, builder of the Captured Soul trap [44]
- Yu Yuan – immortal from Penglai Island [75]
- Yuan Hong – white ape demon from Mount Plum [87]
- Zhang – trap-building immortal [44]
- Zhao Gongming – powerful magician from Mount Emei [46]
- Zhu Zizhen – pig demon under Yuan Hong [92]
- The 28 Constellations: Wood Insect, Wood Dragon, Wood Wolf, Wood Elk, Fire Tiger, Fire Pig, Fire Snake, Fire Monkey, Golden Ox, Golden Goat, Golden Dog, Golden Dragon, Water Leopard, Water Ape, Water Worm, Water Beaver, Earth Bat, Earth Pheasant, Earth Buck, Earth Jackal, Sun Horse, Sun Rooster, Sun Rat, Sun

Rabbit, Moon Crow, Moon Swallow, Moon Fox, and Moon Deer [83]

Shang Others

- Hu Ximei – nine-headed female pheasant sprite, concubine to Shang king, friend of Daji [1]
- Huang – one of the Shang king's concubines, younger sister of General Huang Feihu [1]
- Wang – one of the Shang king's concubines [1]
- Yang – one of the Shang king's concubines [1]

Zhou Leaders and Ministers

- Bo Yikao – elder son of Ji Chang [10]
- Ji Fa – younger son of Ji Chang, later titled King Wu [10]
- Jiang Wenhua – son of East Grand Duke [7]
- Jiang Ziya – Prime Minister of West Qi, disciple of Heavenly Primogenitor, leader of the Zhou army [11]
- King Wen – former king of West Qi, previously known as Ji Chang, the West Grand Duke [1]
- King Wu – king of West Qi, son of Ji Chang, previously known as Ji Fa [10]
- San Yisheng – Supreme Minister of West Qi [3]

Zhou Military

- Bai Jian – deceased general under Xuanyuan, brought back to life by Jiang Ziya, builder of the Terrace of Creation [37]
- Deng Kun – Shang general at Lintong Pass, joined Zhou Army [85]
- Hu Lei – general guarding Green Dragon Pass [71]
- Huang Feihu – general of Zhaoge [1]
- Huang Tianjue – youngest son of Huang Feihu [30]
- Huang Tianlu – eldest son of Huang Feihu [30]
- Huang Tianxiang – fourth son of Huang Feihu [30]
- Nangong Kuo – general of West Qi, West Grand Duke's minister of external affairs [10]
- Wei Ben – general on a black horse, fought Nangong Kuo [68]

Zhou-Aligned Gods, Immortals and Demons

- Burning Lamp – leader of all the immortals, disciple of the Buddha [14]
- Deng Hua – an immortal from Mount Kunlun [45]
- Dragon Beard Tiger – immortal, disciple of Jiang Ziya [38]
- Earth Traveler Sun – dwarf, disciple of Krakucchanda, married to Deng Chanyu [52]

- Fairy Primordial – immortal, master of Nezha, from Qianyuan Mountain [11]
- Grand Completion – immortal, rescues the Shang King's sons [9]
- Heavenly Master Manjusri – immortal, master of Jinzha [12]
- Heavenly Master of Divine Virtue – master of Wei Hu [40]
- Heavenly Master of Outstanding Culture – master of Jinzha [12]
- Heavenly Primogenitor – grand master of Chan Daoism, master of Jiang Ziya and Shen Gongbao [15]
- Immortal of the South Pole – Daoist immortal [15]
- Jade Tripod – master of Yang Jian [40]
- Jinzha – disciple of Heavenly Master Manjusri, first son of Li Jing, brother of Nezha [12]
- Kakusandha – a Buddha [45]
- Krakucchanda – immortal [44]
- Laozi – Grand Master of Heaven, founder of Daoism, brother of Heavenly Primogenitor [44]
- Long Ji – princess, daughter of Haotian and Golden Mother of Jade Pond [55]
- Master Grand Completion – immortal [9]
- Master of Clouds – immortal from Mt. Zhongnan, raised Thunderbolt [5]
- Master Pure Essence – immortal, disciple of Heavenly Primogenitor [9]
- Merciful Navigation – immortal [44]
- Muzha – second son of Li Jing, brother of Nezha [12]
- Nezha – third son of Li Jing, a powerful immortal, disciple of Fairy Primordial [12]
- Pure Essence – immortal from Nine Immortals Mountain [9]
- Pure Void Virtue – lives on Green Peak Mountain, master of Yang Ren and Huang Tianhua [18]
- Thunderbolt – found as a baby by Ji Chang, raised by Master of the Clouds [10]
- Universal Virtue – Daoist, master of Muzha [12]
- Wei Hu – disciple of Heavenly Master of Divine Virtue [59]
- Woe Evading Sage – immortal from West Kunlun Mountain, spiritual master of Li Jing [12]
- Wu Ji – woodcutter, saved by Jiang Ziya, later a general under Prince Wen [23]
- Yang Jian – immortal, disciple of Jade Tripod [40]
- Yellow Dragon – immortal, aids Jiang Ziya [44]
- Zheng Lun – leader of the Black Crow army [3]
- Zhunti – bodhisattva [65]

Non-Aligned Ancients, Gods and Demons

- Ao Bing – Ao Guang's third son [12]
- Ao Guang – Dragon King of the Eastern Ocean [12]
- Blue Cloud Boy – disciple of Fairy Rock [13]
- Chang'e – goddess of the moon [26]
- Chen Tang – King Tang, an ancient king [22]
- Daoist of Extreme Purity – one of the Three Pure Ones [77]
- Daoist of Jade Purity – one of the Three Pure Ones [77]
- Daoist of Upper Purity – one of the Three Pure Ones [77]
- Emperor Earth – master visited by Yang Jian [58]
- Emperor Heaven – master visited by Yang Jian [58]
- Emperor Humanity – master visited by Yang Jian [58]
- Empress Shiji – powerful immortal on Skeleton Mountain [13]
- Fuxi – mythical king, born around 2600 B.C. [81]
- Gaozong – temple name of ancient emperor Wu Ding [24]
- Golden Mother of Jade Pond – mother of Princess Long Ji [55]
- Heavenly Matchmaker – god of marriage and love [67]
- Hong Jun – master of Grand Master of Heaven [84]
- Jade Emperor – Emperor of Heaven [5]
- Jade Lute – demon, friend of Daji's demon Thousand Year Old Fox [1]
- King Cheng – son of King Wu [100]
- Nüwa – the Mother of Earth [1]
- Pretty Cloud Boy – disciple of Fairy Rock [13]
- Shen Nong – mythical king, reigned after Fuxi, cured smallpox [1]
- Shun – ancient emperor [28]
- Thousand Year Old Fox – demon controlling Daji [1]
- Xuanyuan – ancient emperor [13]
- Yao – ancient emperor [24]
- Yellow Emperor – ancient emperor [13]
- Yi Yin – ancient farmer, minister to King Tang [24]

Others

- Jiang Huan – criminal, servant of Fei Zhong [7]
- Lady Jia – wife of Huang Feihu [30]
- Madame Ma – wife of Jiang Ziya [15]
- Madame Yin – wife of Li Jing [12]
- Song Yiren – merchant, Jiang Ziya's sworn brother [15]
- Xia Zhao – a young Confucian scholar [27]
- Yao Fu – palace servant [10]

Chapter 1
The King and the Goddess

In the beginning, Pangu split the world in two;
Then came yin and yang, then the stars in the sky
After the sky came the ground, then people;
Youchao taught them to build homes and stay safe

Suiren taught them to use fire to cook food,
Fuxi showed them the ways of yin and yang
Shennong gave them medicine;
Xuanyuan gave them culture and family

Under the five emperors people prospered;
Yu the Great stopped the floods
Xia gave them five hundred years of peace;
But King Jie came and turned day into night

Every day he drank wine and played with his concubines;
Until King Chen Tang came to cleanse the palace
The cruel king lived but fled to the south;
The clouds and rain passed and the nation prospered again

Thirty-one kings later, Yin Zhou takes the throne;
The Shang family breaks like a string
The palace is in chaos, wife and sons are killed;
While the foolish king listens only to his evil advisors

Daji fills the palace with dirt and chaos;
Her snake pit and burning pillar bring pain to the loyal
The Deer Terrace brings pain to the people;
Their anger covers the entire sky

Loyal ministers lose their hearts or die on the burning pillar;
Mothers see their babies die; farmers' feet are cut off

The king trusts evil ministers and forgets to care for the country;
He fights for no reason and removes good ministers

The ways of religion are forgotten,
Now there is only black magic and trickery
The king's friends are evil, he does not fear God;
He drinks all the time, he is like a wild animal

Ji Chang comes to the capital but is imprisoned in Youli;
His son escapes in a dust cloud and wait for the right time
Even God in heaven is angry and sends disasters
That cover everything like an endless ocean

Life is difficult in the nation, the people cry out;
Then Jiang Ziya appears, a god among men
He sits and fishes, not for fish but for a wise master;
The flying bear comes to him in a dream

Ji Chang brings Ziya back to Zhou in his carriage;
Ziya stays by his side and gives him two thirds of the nation
Ji Chang does not live to see the final victory;
His son takes the throne and works hard every day

Eight hundred marquises come together;
They make a plan to destroy the cruel and evil
At dawn the two armies come together in Muye;
But the king's armies turn and attack Shang

The people kowtow in fear like wounded beasts;
Blood flows like a river and covers the pillars
The new king dons the robe of heaven;
Now the nation is at peace with King Tang on the throne

The war horses return to Mount Hua as the war ends;
The Zhou family begins eight hundred years of rule

The dead king is hung on a white flag;
The souls of the dead soldiers can finally rest

Master Jiang Ziya was born a wise man;
He put everything in the correct place
This is the great story of Shang and Zhou;
It is passed down to this day from parent to child

≡ ≡ ≡

In the beginning, the King of Shang was a good man.

His name was Di Xin. His father was the twenty-seventh king of the Shang Dynasty. When the old king died after ruling for thirty years, Di Xin became the twenty-eighth king. He did not know that he would be the last.

Di Xin married a beautiful woman named Jiang, who was the daughter of a powerful grand duke. The king also had two concubines named Huang and Yang.

For seven years the country was peaceful. Heaven brought wind and rain at the right times, and the people were never hungry.

The trouble started one day when the prime minister, a man named Shang Rong, stepped forward in court. Shang Rong told the king, "Your Majesty, tomorrow is the fifteenth day of the third month. It is the birthday of the goddess Nüwa. Do you know the story of how she saved our country?"

The king smiled and said, "Yes, but please tell us the story again."

"Many years ago, Buzhou Mountain held up the sky. Two powerful gods were fighting. One of the gods was losing the fight, so he smashed his own head against Buzhou Mountain and destroyed it. The sky started to fall. There were fires and floods. Dangerous animals came to our kingdom and ate the people. When Goddess Nüwa heard about this, she immediately came to help us. First, she cut the legs off a giant tortoise and used the legs to hold up the sky again. Then she used colored stones to repair the sky. But she could not completely repair the sky. That is why even today, the sun and moon move from east to west, and the stars move from southeast to northwest."

"That is a good story," said the king. "What else did Nüwa do?"

"The ancients say that when the world was young, Nüwa was all alone. There were no animals and no people. So on the first day she created chickens. On the second day she created dogs. On the third day she created sheep. On the fourth day she created pigs. On the fifth day she created cows. On the sixth day she created horses. On the seventh day she started creating people from yellow clay. She made the people one at a time. But it took a long time and she got tired. She dipped a rope in yellow clay and swung it around. Bits of yellow clay fell everywhere, and each bit became a person."

"And now?"

"Even now, Nüwa takes care of our people. She brings wind and rain at the right times, so the people are never hungry. You should worship her by going to her temple tomorrow on her birthday."

"You are right," said the king. "We will go."

The next day, the king left the palace through the south gate. It was a warm sunny day. He rode for several *li* to the temple in his royal carriage. Three thousand soldiers on horses rode with him, along all the ministers of the court. Leading the army was General Huang Feihu, the brother of Concubine Huang.

When the king arrived at the temple, he walked into the main hall. He burned incense, bowed low, and prayed to Nüwa. Then he took a little time to look around the temple. While walking around the temple, he saw a statue of Nüwa hidden behind a curtain. Just as he was looking at the statue, a strong wind came in through a nearby window. It blew the curtain aside, and the king saw Nüwa. She was the most beautiful woman he had ever seen. She was more beautiful than flowers in springtime, more beautiful than the moon in the sky.

The king's body became hot with desire. He said to himself, "We have a beautiful queen and we have concubines, but none are as beautiful as this goddess. We must have her!" He told his attendants to bring him brush and ink. Without thinking he wrote a love poem to the goddess right on the wall of the temple. This is the poem:

> *There are phoenixes and dragons*
> *But they are like dirt to us*
> *You are like a beautiful fruit tree in the rain*
> *You are like flowers in the mist*
> *Please come alive, O beautiful goddess*

> *Come to us, come down from your temple*
> *We will bring you to my palace!*[1]

The Prime Minister saw the poem. His eyes grew big. He said to the king, "Your Majesty, Nüwa has been a great friend to our people. You came to her temple to thank her. But now you have insulted her. Please, I beg you, wash this poem off the wall!"

The king replied angrily, "We see no problem here. We saw the goddess and thought she was beautiful. Be quiet. Don't forget that We are the king." And he returned to the palace, to enjoy time with his queen and his concubines.

That evening, Goddess Nüwa returned to her temple after visiting with some friends. She saw the poem written in black ink on the wall of her temple. When she read the poem, she became very angry. She said, "This king is evil. He writes dirty poems on the wall of my temple. He does not know how to show respect to the gods. I will make sure he is the last king of Shang!"

She called for her phoenix and rode it to the capital city of Zhaoge. She was looking for the king. She looked down from the sky and saw the king. But when she saw him, she knew that it was the will of heaven that he would live for another twenty-eight years.

Still angry, she returned to her temple. She told her servants to bring her a magic gourd called the Demon Summoning Gourd. She placed the gourd on the ground. She opened it and pointed to it with her finger. A beam of bright white light came from the gourd and rose into the sky. All the demons in the area saw the light and came to her temple. Dark clouds appeared in the sky. A cold wind began to blow.

Nüwa waited for all the demons to arrive. Then she told all of them to go home except for three female demons: Thousand-Year-Old Fox, Nine Headed Pheasant, and Jade Lute. Nüwa said to them, "Listen carefully to me. I have heard the singing of the phoenix in the west. It tells me that a new king has been born in the province of Qi. I want to destroy King Di Xin, but it is Heaven's will that he will live for another twenty-eight years. So I will destroy him while he lives. I want you three to change into beautiful women. You must enter the palace, and do

---

[1] This may not seem like an insulting poem, but the king's suggestion that the goddess leave her temple and join him in the royal palace made it vulgar, or even obscene, at the time this novel was written.

whatever is needed to stop the king from attending to affairs of state. In time this will end the Shang Dynasty and bring in the new one. Now go!" The three demons turned into winds and blew away.

Back in the palace, the king thought could think of nothing but the beautiful goddess. He did not eat, drink or sleep. He found no pleasure with his queen or his concubines. He did not care about affairs of state. He did not know what to do. Finally, he called one of his ministers, an evil man named Fei Zhong. He knew that Fei Zhong would say anything and do anything to make him happy.

The king said to Fei Zhong, "We cannot think of anything except the goddess Nüwa. We don't care about our queen or our concubines or the affairs of state. What can we do?"

Fei Zhong gave the king a big smile. He said, "Your Majesty, you are the most powerful man in the world. You can have anything you want. If you want a beautiful woman, that is no problem. Just tell each of the four grand dukes to send you a hundred of the most beautiful girls in their region. Soon you will have four hundred girls to look at. I'm sure you will find one as beautiful as the goddess."

The king thought this was a wonderful idea.

Chapter 2
The Rebellion of Su Hu

The Prime Minister in his golden carriage speaks to the king;
In all the kingdom, who is as loyal and wise?

If he knew that the marquises were coming,
He would not have poured ink on sunflower paper

The king was pleased with the report;
He read it and then returned to the palace;

The evening came and then the morning;
The next day, ministers came and praised the foolish king

≡ ≡ ≡

The kingdom of Shang was quite large. To help him rule the kingdom the king had four grand dukes. Each grand duke ruled about a quarter of the country. Each grand duke had about two hundred marquises, and each marquis ruled a small city or village.

The next morning, the king told his attendants to send letters to each of the four grand dukes. The letters told each of them to bring a hundred beautiful young women to the palace. But Prime Minister Shang Rong heard about this. He said to the king, "Your Majesty, this is a bad idea. Please think about this. Right now, the people are happy in their work and they obey you. But if you do this, they will become unhappy. They will not want you as their king. If you spend your days listening to music, playing with your concubines, drinking wine and hunting, you will not be king for long. I have been a minister for your grandfather, your father, and now you. And I tell you, do not forget the affairs of state and seek only a life of pleasure!"

The king sat quietly for a long time. Then he said, "You are right. We will not do this." He left the hall and went to his chambers to play with his concubines for a while.

The months passed, but the king never forgot about the beautiful goddess Nüwa. The next summer, the four grand dukes and all eight hundred marquises came to Zhaoge. During this time, the evil minister Fei Zhong had become more powerful. He demanded bribes and gifts from each grand duke and marquis. Most of them gave him gifts, but Su Hu, the marquis of Jizhou, did not. Su Hu was a good man, and he disliked Fei Zhong.

Fei Zhong wanted revenge. He waited until the king was not busy. Then he said to the king, "You were right to not ask the four grand dukes to send those beautiful young women last year. But I have heard that the marquis Su Hu has a daughter named Daji. It is said that she is as beautiful as the goddess Nüwa. Perhaps you should bring her to the palace."

The king liked this idea, and started to think about being with Daji. He ordered Su Hu to come to the palace to see him. Su Hu arrived a short time later. He kneeled in front of the king and waited for him to speak.

The king said, "We have heard that your daughter is a fine young woman. We want her to serve us in the palace. If we do this, this will be good for you. You will become part of the royal family. You will also become rich and powerful. How do you feel about this?"

Su Hu replied, "Your Majesty, I think someone has given you bad information. Why would you want my daughter? You already have a lovely queen and many concubines. My daughter is not beautiful. In fact, she knows nothing and has an ugly face."

The king laughed loudly. He said, "You are a fool, Su Hu. Your daughter would be treated like a queen. And you would become part of the royal family."

Forgetting to be careful when speaking to the king, Su Hu stood up and shouted, "You are a terrible king. You care nothing for affairs of state. You spend all your time drinking and playing with women. Change your ways, or your dynasty will end soon!"

The king shouted to his soldiers, "Arrest this fool and throw him out of Zhaoge!" The soldiers took Su Hu away. They took him to the north gate of the city and told him to go back to Jizhou and never return.

Su Hu returned to Jizhou. When he arrived, his ministers asked him what happened during his visit to Zhaoge. Su Hu told them, "That idiot king wanted my daughter as a concubine. What should I do? If I refuse, he will send an army here. But if I agree, he will continue to ignore the affairs of state, and people will say that I helped him to go down that road."

One of the ministers replied, "The ancients say that if a king is bad, his ministers may leave him. Our king only cares for women and pleasure. We should leave him and try to save our country."

Su Hu agreed. He called for a large brush and ink. Then he rode his horse back to Zhaoge. He walked up to the main gate. He held a large brush in one hand and ink pot in the other. He quickly wrote this poem on the wall:

> *You have no respect for your ministers*
> *You have forgotten the five virtues*
> *And so Su Hu, the marquis of Jizhou*
> *Will no longer serve the king of Shang*

A soldier at the gate saw this. He ran back to the palace, kneeled before the king, and told him about the poem on the wall. The king was furious. He called Fei Zhong and told him how angry he was. He said, "It is time to destroy the city of Jizhou. Who should lead our army?"

Fei Zhong thought about this for a few minutes. He said to the king, "Jizhou is in the north. I suggest that the Grand Duke of the North should destroy the city." Fei Zhong knew that the Grand Duke of the North was a cruel man named Chong Houhu.

Prime Minister Shang Rong heard about this. He was worried about what the cruel general might do. So he went to the king and said, "Your Majesty, Chong Houhu is the Grand Duke of the North, but the people do not like him. It may be difficult for him to do this job. Perhaps you should use the Grand Duke of the West, Ji Chang, instead. He is a good man, the people trust him."

The king listened to this. Then he said, "We will send both of them. They will lead the army together."

The two grand dukes, Chong Houhu and Ji Chang, sat down to discuss their plan to attack Jizhou. They agreed that Chong Houhu would lead the army and would arrive first at the city of Jizhou, and Ji Chang would follow shortly afterwards.

Back at Jizhou, Su Hu met with his own generals. They knew that the city of Jizhou was in great danger. They prepared their army to fight against the king's army.

A few days later, Su Hu heard that the king's army had arrived at Jizhou.

The king's army had 50,000 soldiers with spears and swords. "Who is leading this army?" asked Su Hu.

"Chong Houhu, the Grand Duke of the North," one of his ministers replied.

"That man is evil and cruel," said Su Hu. "But I will talk with him anyway." He led his soldiers out of the city. The army of Su Hu stood facing the army of the king. Su Hu was in front. He shouted, "Let me talk with your general!"

Chong Houhu came out to meet him. He rode on a big horse. He wore bright golden armor, a red robe and a jade belt. He held a long sword in his hand. Behind him were his son and two other generals.

Su Hu bowed to Chong Houhu. He said, "How are you, Grand Duke. I'm sorry we have to meet like this. But you know that our king has become a bad ruler. He treats his ministers badly, and he cares nothing for affairs of state. He only wants women and wine. And now he wants my daughter as a concubine."

Chong Houhu replied angrily, "None of that matters. You are a traitor. His Majesty the King has ordered me to kill you. You should kneel before me, but instead, you stand there with your armor and sword." He turned to his men and said, "Who will kill this traitor for me?"

One of Chong Houhu's generals shouted, "I will!" He rode his horse forward and attacked Su Hu. But before he could get close, Su Hu's son Su Quanzhong rode forward on his horse. The two fought, sword against sword, for twenty rounds. Finally, Su Quanzhong killed the general.

Su Hu gave the order for his army to attack. All the soldiers on both sides ran forward, holding their swords high. There was a huge battle. When it was over, the ground was covered with the blood of dead and dying soldiers. Chong Houhu's army was defeated. They fled from the city.

Later that night, Su Hu's army returned and attacked Chong Houhu's army again. They attacked like hungry tigers. Su Hu saw Chong Houhu and shouted, "Chong Houhu! Get down off your horse, I will bring you back as a prisoner to Jizhou!" Chong Houhu saw that his army was losing and that he could not win against Su Hu. So he turned and fled like a dog, as fast as he could.

A few hours later Su Hu's army attacked for a third time. Su Quanzhong saw Chong Houhu and shouted, "I have been waiting for you. Drop your sword, get down off your horse, and prepare to die!" Two of Chong Houhu's generals rushed forward, and all three of them fought with Su Quanzhong. Su Quanzhong fought like a dragon in the sea. He struck the three generals with his sword, killing one and injuring another. Chong Houhu and his army ran away, defeated for the third time. Su Hu's army returned to Jizhou.

The next morning, Su Hu met with his generals and ministers. He asked his son, "Did you capture that dog Chong Houhu?"

"No," replied Su Quanzhong. "Our soldiers fought like tigers. I myself killed one of their generals and injured another. But Chong Houhu and his army ran away. It was dark and I did not want to ride after them."

Su Hu was happy to hear that his army had won the battle. He said, "Chong Houhu was lucky. Now rest, my son."

Chapter 3
Daji is Given to the King

The king ordered Chong to attack the ministers;
But he had little wisdom and could not make a good plan

The failed battle started in the morning;
By evening he had lost and had to flee the camp

From the beginning of time, lust has led to the fall of kingdoms;
Since ancient days, the evil done by ministers never ends

This is not about the king's lust for Daji;
It is heaven's will that Zhou will rule the kingdom

☰ ☰ ☰

Chong Houhu and his army fled from Jizhou as fast as they could. Only one in ten of his soldiers survived, and many of those had terrible injuries.

Chong Houhu said to his generals, "We had to fight against the army of Su Hu all alone. Where was the Grand Duke of the West and his army? His Majesty told him to help us, but he did not come. He is a traitor."

Just then, a soldier rushed in and told him that a huge army was approaching. Chong Houhu did not know if they were friends or enemies. He jumped up on his horse and rode out to see. He saw a general leading thousands of soldiers. The general's face was as black as the bottom of a cooking pot. He had a red beard, golden eyes, and wore a long red robe. He rode a fire-eyed monster. In each of his hands he held a golden axe. On his back he carried a strange red gourd. Chong Houhu knew this man. It was his own brother, the Marquis of Caozhou, known to everyone as Black Tiger.

"I heard that your army was defeated," Black Tiger said to Chong Houhu, "so I got here as quickly as I could. It is good to see you again!"

"How many soldiers do you have?" asked Chong Houhu.

"I have three thousand Flying Tiger soldiers, and another twenty thousand are coming soon." The two armies joined together and marched towards Jizhou. They stopped just a few *li* from the city.

In Jizhou, someone told Su Hu that the Black Tiger had arrived. "This is bad," said Su Hu. "Black Tiger is a very good fighter. Also, he has studied magic. I have heard that he can cut off someone's head as easily as taking a stone out of a bag."

His son Su Quanzhong replied, "Father, do not talk like that. You are only making him stronger and yourself weaker. I am not afraid. I will go and fight Black Tiger myself!" Before anyone could stop him, he jumped on his horse and ran out to meet Black Tiger.

Now Su Quanzhong did not know that his father and Black Tiger were good friends, and sworn brothers. When Black Tiger heard that Su Hu's son was coming, he shouted, "My young friend! Please go back and tell your father to come and see me."

Su Quanzhong shouted, "Forget that! We are enemies. Leave this place right now, or you will die!" He attacked Black Tiger with his sword. Black Tiger fought with his two golden axes. They fought for a long time but neither could win. Then Black Tiger turned and rode away quickly. Su Quanzhong rode after him.

As he rode, Black Tiger pulled the lid off his magic gourd. He said some magic words. Suddenly a cloud of black smoke came out of the gourd. A dozen huge eagles came down from the sky. They attacked Su Quanzhong and his horse. Su Quanzhong fought off the eagles with his sword, but the eagles attacked the horse. The horse fell to the ground. Su Quanzhong was thrown to the ground and was taken prisoner by Black Tiger's soldiers.

Su Hu heard this bad news. He said to himself, "My son did not listen to me, and now he is a prisoner. There are many soldiers out there. Soon Jizhou will lose the war. What have I done to cause this? Maybe it is because I have a daughter. If I had no daughter, the king would not want her as a concubine, and my city would not be attacked by the king's army. I cannot let my family be captured by the king's army. It is better that I kill everyone in my family before the king's soldiers come here." He picked up his sword and rushed into the room where his family was.

Daji saw him. She smiled and said, "Dear father, why are you here, and why are you holding that big sword?"

Su Hu stopped. He could not kill his daughter.

Outside the city, Chong Houhu wanted to use all of the soldiers from both armies to attack Jizhou. But Black Tiger said, "Please wait. We don't need to attack the city. Let's surround the city. They will have no food or water, and soon they will not be able to fight. Also, the Grand Duke of the West's army will be coming soon."

The soldiers surrounded the city of Jizhou. Several weeks went by. No food or water could come into the city. The people were very hungry and weak. Finally, one of the generals, a man named Zheng Lun, came to see Su Hu. He said, "Sir, please let me go and fight Black Tiger. I will try to take him prisoner and bring him back here. If I fail, they can cut off my head."

Zheng Lun picked up his two Demon Subduing Clubs, jumped up on his horse, and led 3,000 soldiers out of the city. His soldiers were all dressed in black, making his army look like a black cloud moving across the ground. He got close to the enemy and shouted, "Come out and fight me, Black Tiger!"

Black Tiger came out, surrounded by his Flying Tiger soldiers. "Who is the man who wants to fight me?" he shouted.

"I am General Zheng Lun of Jizhou. You must be Black Tiger. You are holding a prisoner. He is the son of my marquis. Give him to me right now, or I will turn you into dust!"

Black Tiger did not reply. He rode his horse forward, striking at Zheng Lun with his golden axes. Zheng Lun fought back with his two clubs. They fought for a long time, but neither one could win.

As they fought, Zheng Lun saw the red gourd on Black Tiger's back. He knew it was a magic gourd. But he had his own magic. He raised his clubs in the air and said some magic words. Two beams of bright light came out of Zheng Lun's nose. They hit Black Tiger in the face. Black Tiger became dizzy. He fell off his horse. The soldiers grabbed him and tied him up as a prisoner.

Zheng Lun's soldiers carried Black Tiger back to the city of Jizhou. Zheng Lun watched as they threw him down on the ground in front of the gate to Su Hu's palace. When Su Hu saw this, he ran forward. He told his soldiers to untie Black Tiger. Then Su Hu bowed to him. He said, "My brother, please forgive me. Zheng Lun treated you badly. I am so sorry." Then he ordered Zheng Lun and the other generals to come and bow to Black Tiger.

Black Tiger replied, "Thank you, my brother. Please understand that I am trying to help you, not kill you. Let's talk about how we can get you out of trouble and also keep our king happy."

Meanwhile, Chong Houhu was angry that he still had heard nothing from Ji Chang, the Grand Duke of the West. One of Ji Chang's ministers arrived at the camp. Chong Houhu said to him, "Why does your grand duke ignore our king's orders? He rests in his palace while we must come here and fight!"

The minister replied, "My grand duke always says, 'War is a terrible thing, one should fight only when there is no other way.' He has sent me here with a letter for Su Hu. The letter asks Su Hu to stop fighting and give his daughter to the king. If he does that, he can remain the Marquis of Jizhou. If not, he will die."

Chong Houhu laughed loudly. He said, "I think Ji Chang is just afraid to fight. Well, go ahead, give Su Hu the letter, let's see what happens."

The minister left Chong Houhu's camp. He rode up to the city wall of Jizhou. He called out, "Here is a minister of the Grand Duke of the West, with a letter for your marquis." The city gates opened, and he was taken inside.

Su Hu and Black Tiger were having dinner together. They looked up when the minister entered the room. The minister said, "I have a letter for you from Ji Chang, the Grand Duke of the West." Then he handed the letter to Su Hu. It said:

I know you are a good man and you want to serve your king. Please listen to my words. If you send your daughter to the king, you will become part of the king's family. You will become wealthy and powerful. Jizhou will be safe, your family will be safe, your people will be safe, and your soldiers will live. But if you do not send your daughter, Jizhou will be destroyed, your entire family will be killed, and many people and soldiers will also die. You and I are both ministers of the Shang Dynasty. Please think about this and do the right thing.

Su Hu did not say a word. He handed the letter to Black Tiger. Black Tiger read the letter. Then he said, "The Grand Duke of the West is a good man. You should send your daughter to the king as soon as possible. This will show your loyalty to the Shang Dynasty."

Su Hu told the minister to eat dinner with them and stay in the palace overnight. The next day, Su Hu met with the minister. He said that he would bring his daughter to the king's palace. Truly, one letter was more powerful than a hundred thousand soldiers!

Su Hu and Black Tiger drank cups of wine together and smiled. They thought that their troubles were finished.

Chapter 4
The Fox Demon Kills Daji

The world is at war, fighting is everywhere;
The nation is flooded by evil words

The king would not listen to the loyal Shang Rong;
But he listened to the evil minister Fei Zhong

Lust made the king marry the fox and sleep with her;
While cruel monsters ruled the nation and the phoenix flew away

If the fox can bring down the kingdom,
The goddess will give him a bit of incense[1]

≡ ≡ ≡

Black Tiger left Jizhou. He returned to Chong Houhu and told him that Su Hu would give Daji to the king. Chong Houhu said, "Brother, I cannot understand how your letter could win this battle, when my fifty thousand men could not."

Black Tiger replied coldly to his brother, "The ancients say, 'One tree may have both sweet and sour fruit; sons of the same mother may be good or bad.' You should never have attacked Jizhou. Many soldiers have died because of you. I am leaving now. I never want to see you again."

Black Tiger then ordered Su Quanzhong be released and sent back to Jizhou. Then he and his army returned to Caozhou. A day later, Chong Houhu led his own army back to Zhaoge. This was the end of the attack on Jizhou.

Su Hu told his daughter that she would become a concubine of the king. She cried for hours. He told his son Su Quanzhong that he must take care of affairs of state while he was in Zhaoge. He told his wife that he would be gone for a long time. And he said goodbye to his elderly

---

[1] "A bit of incense" is a metaphor for a reward obtained in the human world. In this case, it's the reward given to the fox demon by the goddess Nüwa in return for destroying the Shang king.

mother.

The next day, Su Hu and Daji left Jizhou and began the long journey to Zhaoge. Three thousand soldiers traveled with them. Su Hu rode close to Daji's carriage to protect her.

After traveling for several days, they arrived at a courier station about halfway between Jizhou and Zhaoge. Su Hu told the station officer to prepare a room for Daji.

The station officer said, "Sir, this is not a good place for you. Three years ago, a demon arrived here. Since then, not a single person has wanted to stay here overnight. I think you should keep traveling and not stop here."

Su Hu replied, "I am a marquis of the king of Shang, do you think I am afraid of a demon? We are not leaving. Prepare the room now!"

When the room was ready, Daji entered it. Three thousand soldiers surrounded the room to protect her. And Su Hu himself sat outside the door to her room. He did not sleep that night. He read a book by candle light, but every couple of hours he looked in Daji's room to see if she was all right.

Around the time of the third watch[1], a cold wind blew in through an open window. It felt like a wild animal had come into the room. Someone shouted, "A ghost! A ghost!"

Su Hu ran into Daji's room and woke her up. "Are you all right, my dear?" he asked. "Did you see a ghost?"

She smiled and said, "No, father, I was sleeping and saw nothing. Please don't worry about me."

Su Hu thought that he was talking with his daughter. But he was really talking to Thousand-Year-Old Fox Demon sent by Nüwa. The fox demon had eaten Daji's soul and taken her body.

The next morning, they continued on their journey to Zhaoge. A few days later they arrived at the capital. General Huang Feihu told Su Hu to leave his three thousand soldiers outside the city, and to come in alone with Daji.

The evil minister Fei Zhong heard that Su Hu had returned. He was

---

[1] The night is divided into several two-hour periods or watches. First watch starts at 7:00 pm, second watch at 9:00, third watch at 11:00, and so on.

unhappy to hear that Su Hu had not been killed by the king's soldiers. He told the king that Su Hu had returned.

"That fool!" shouted the king. "We wanted to kill him once, but you told us to let him live. Then he wrote that poem on the wall. We will kill him tomorrow. You just wait and see."

Fei Zhong nodded his head and said, "Your Majesty is right. The laws of the kingdom are for everyone, even marquises."

A little while later, Su Hu came in to the main hall. Instead of wearing his red robe, he just wore the clothing of a prisoner. He bowed and said, "The criminal Su Hu is here. He deserves to die."

The king replied, "Yes, it is time for you to die. We should have done this a long time ago." Then he shouted for his soldiers to take Su Hu away and cut off his head.

But Fei Zhong said, "Your Majesty, please let go of your anger for a little while. Look at Su Hu's daughter. If you are pleased with her, you can take her as your concubine and let Su Hu go. But if you are not pleased with her, then cut off both of their heads. This will show the people that you are strong."

The king replied, "You are right as always, Fei Zhong. All right, bring in the girl."

Daji slowly entered the main hall. She knelt down and said, "Long live the King! Long live the King!"

The king looked carefully at Daji. Her hair was as black as night, her lips were like red fruit, her face was as beautiful as a peach blossom. Her body was as slim as a willow tree. She looked like an immortal from the Ninth Heaven or a visitor from the moon. When she spoke, her breath was like sweet incense. She said softly, "The daughter of your criminal servant wishes Your Majesty to live for ten thousand years!"

The king looked at Daji. He felt dizzy and his soul left his body. His ears became hot, and he could not see. After a minute he was able to stand up. He said to Daji, "Please stand up, our beauty!" He told his servants to bring her to the Immortal Long Life Palace. Then he said to everyone, "Su Hu's family is now part of our family. Su Hu will receive 2,000 piculs of rice every month. He will stay here as our guest for three days. Then five of our ministers will take him back to Jizhou."

Then the king stood up and left the main hall. He and Daji had a long dinner together, with plenty of wine. Then they spent the night together. The next day he stayed in bed with Daji all day.

The king fell in love with Daji. He forgot all about affairs of state. He gave no orders. None of the grand dukes or marquises were able to meet with him. All across the kingdom, trouble started, but the king did not care at all.

Chapter 5
The Master of the Clouds

Colorful spring flowers grow here under a peaceful blue sky;
White clouds and rain fly over distant southern mountains

Purple fog surrounds a golden pavilion;
Youthful immortals drink jade and eat pears

Flowers sing songs of heaven to welcome the gods;
The blue phoenix dances, its green hair flying

This is a place where immortals live, far from the human world;
But then a demonic power breaks down the gates

≡ ≡ ≡

A Daoist immortal named Master of the Clouds lived on Mount Zhongnan[1]. He had lived there for several thousand years.

One day, Master of the Clouds went for a walk. He carried a flower basket in one hand while he picked medicinal herbs. Looking to the southeast, he saw a dark cloud over the city of Zhaoge. "Ah," he said, "it looks like an ancient fox demon is in Zhaoge. She is probably causing trouble in the palace of the king[2]. I'd better do something about this."

He picked up a pine branch, then he used his knife to make a slender wooden sword. He put the sword in the flower basket. Then he rode on a cloud to the king's palace.

Things were not going well in Zhaoge. The king was spending all his time in bed, playing with his beautiful concubine Daji. It had been ten months since he last came to the main hall. His ministers were becoming very worried. They decided to call all the ministers and

---

[1] For centuries the Zhongnan mountains, just south of Chang'an (modern-day Xi'an), have been home to many Daoist hermits and Buddhist monks. The Daoist sage Laozi is believed to have lived there when he wrote the *Dao De Jing*.
[2] Fox demons, both male and female, are common in Chinese folklore. They seduce humans with their beauty and sexual skills, then suck the life force from their victims. The older the fox demon, the more powerful it is.

generals to a meeting, and invite the king to see them.

The king was lying in bed with Daji, drinking wine and talking. A servant came in and said, "Your Majesty is requested to come to the main hall." The king stood up, told Daji that he would be back soon, then he put on his robe and went to the main hall.

When he got there, he saw that all of his ministers and generals waiting for him. He did not want to talk with any of them. He did not want to read their reports. All he wanted was to go back to bed with Daji. "What is going on?" he asked.

Shang Rong said to him, "Your Majesty, we have not seen you for a long time. Where have you been? We ask you to please take care of the affairs of state, and spend less time with your concubines. If you don't, we are afraid that heaven will become angry and will bring trouble to our kingdom."

The king was not interested in this. He replied, "Everything is fine in the kingdom. We have heard that there is a little bit of trouble at the North Sea, but Grand Tutor Wen Zhong is taking care of that. As for the rest, we're not interested in any of it. You are our ministers. If you do your jobs well, we don't need to do anything!"

While the king was arguing with his ministers, the doors to the main hall opened and Master of the Clouds walked in. He wore a long robe with wide sleeves. In his right hand he held a dust whisk, and in his left hand he held the flower basket. When he walked, the earth trembled. Tigers kowtowed to him and dragons knelt before him.

Master of the Clouds said to the king, "Your Majesty, this poor Daoist greets you."

The king was a little bit unhappy because the Daoist did not bow to him. But he just said, "Sir, where do you come from?"

"I come from the clouds and rivers. My heart is as free as the white clouds, and my mind is as clear as water."

The king smiled. "And where will you go if the sky becomes clear and the waters run dry?"

"When the sky becomes clear, a bright moon appears. When the rivers run dry, a bright pearl appears."

The king was pleased by this. He invited the Daoist to sit down beside him. The Daoist said, "You know that there is Daoism, Buddhism and

Confucianism. Of these, Daoism is the highest."

"And why is that?"

"A Daoist bows to nobody and wants nothing. He is not interested in money or fame. He finds happiness in forests and mountains. He sings and dances in the sunlight, he sleeps under the stars when he is tired. He spends time with his friends, he writes poetry, and he drinks wine."

The king was delighted by this. He said, "That sounds wonderful!"

"The years pass, but he lives forever by understanding *yin* and *yang*. He helps people when he can. He rides on a green phoenix, and he visits with the Jade Emperor himself."

"And why have you come to see us today?"

"Earlier today I was walking on Mount Zhongnan. I saw a dark cloud over your city. I think there is an evil demon here. So I have come here to help you get rid of the demon. Here is a short poem I have written about it,

> *She is beautiful, she wants to be your lover*
> *But she will drink your spirit and make you weak*
> *If you find her before it's too late*
> *You will save your people from a terrible fate*

The king said, "We don't believe there is a demon in this palace. But if there is, how can we get rid of it?"

Master of the Clouds put his hand in the flower basket and picked up the pine sword. He gave it to the king, saying, "This is a magic pine sword. Hang it in the main tower and wait. It will kill any demon within three days."

The king ordered his servants to do as the Master of the Clouds said. Then he said, "Thank you for coming here and telling us about spirits and demons. Please stay here and protect us. You will have a high rank, you will wear fine clothing, and you will be famous throughout the kingdom."

"Thank you, but I am a simple man. I know nothing about ruling a nation. I sleep late in the morning and I walk barefoot in the mountains. I have no need of fine robes because I only wear old clothing. I want nothing, except maybe an invitation to the Feast of the Immortal Peaches in heaven. Thank you for listening to me, but now I must go." And with that, he turned and walked out of the main hall.

After the Daoist left, the king had no interest in talking with his ministers. He also left and returned to see Daji and tell her about his meeting with the Daoist. But Daji was lying in her bed. She looked very ill.

"Oh, my dear!" cried the king. "You looked so healthy a few hours ago. Now you are so ill. What is wrong?"

Daji looked up at him, smiling sweetly. She said, "Your Majesty, just now I was outside taking a walk. When I came to the Central Palace Tower, I saw a strange wooden sword hanging there. As soon as I saw it, I began to feel very ill. Now I am so ill that I cannot have sex with you. I'm very sorry, Your Majesty!" And she began to cry.

The king was angry. "That Daoist tricked us! He told us that there was an evil demon in the palace. But instead, he wanted to hurt our lovely Daji." Turning to his servants, he said, "Take down that wooden sword. Burn it immediately!"

The king stayed with Daji all night. The next day she felt better. But the Shang Dynasty's troubles kept getting worse.

Chapter 6
The Burning Pillar

Now the Shang king is killing the loyal and the wise;
So much cruelty, even the gods in heaven know of it.

Loyal and brave warriors are burned to ashes;
Evil demons surround the palace of the king

In the morning, beautiful songs are played on a guqin;
But in the evening, dragon's saliva and green glowing jade[1]

One by one, good people die on the burning pillar;
The souls of old men have no way to return home

≡ ≡ ≡

The Master of the Clouds stayed in Zhaoge for a while to see what would happen. He saw that the sword was burned, and there was still a black cloud over the city. He said to himself, "Now I understand what will happen. The Shang Dynasty will end. The Zhou Dynasty will replace it. And new gods will be created. I must try to tell the people about this." Before returning to Mount Zhongnan, he stopped to write this poem on the wall in the marketplace:

A demon cloud is over the king's palace
A new hope rises in the West.
Before many years pass
Zhaoge will see blood and war

People in the marketplace saw the poem but they did not understand it. Then Du Yuanxian, the Chief Minister of the Observatory, came riding through the marketplace on his horse. He stopped and read the poem. He said to himself, "I have also seen this demon cloud over the king's palace. Things are bad there. I must write a letter to the king."

He stayed up all night writing the letter. Then he gave it to the Prime

---

[1] These are symbols of extreme luxury and decadence. In Chinese lore, dragon saliva was used to create very expensive perfume that would last for decades without evaporating. Green glowing jade was embedded in expensive furniture and other décor.

Minister Shang Rong, asking him to give it to the king.

A little while later, Shang Rong was allowed to enter the king's private chambers. The king was, as usual, in bed with Daji. He had been drinking wine. "What do you want?" asked the king.

Shang Rong replied, "Your Majesty, I have a letter from Du Yuanxian, the Chief Minister of the Observatory. I want nothing for myself here, I am just doing my job as your prime minister. You can cut off my head for doing this, if you want."

The king read the letter. It said:

> *Your servant is the Chief Minister of the Observatory. My job is to study the sky. Recently I have seen a dark cloud over the royal palace. As you know, demons and dark clouds appear when the nation is in trouble. A few days ago, a Daoist gave you a wooden sword to get rid of the dark cloud, but you burned the sword. Now the cloud is bigger and stronger. It can even be seen in the Ninth Heaven.*
>
> *I have been thinking about this. This cloud appeared at the same time that Su Hu brought his daughter into the palace. Since then, you have forgotten about affairs of state. While you lie in bed with your woman, dust has covered your desk, and grass has grown on the steps to the main hall. It is my job to tell you of these things, even though you may cut off my head for it.*

The king read the letter. Then he gave it to Daji, saying to her, "Du Yuanxian sent us this letter. What do you think about it?"

Daji fell to her knees. She said to the king, "We know that the Daoist is an evil man. Now we know that Du Yuanxian is helping him. You must have him killed."

"You are right, my dear. We must stop Du Yuanxian before other people start listening to him and causing trouble." The king ordered his soldiers to grab Du Yuanxian, take off his fine clothing, and bring him to the palace gate.

When the soldiers were bringing Du Yuanxian to the palace gate, they passed the supreme minister Mei Bo and the Prime Minister Shang Rong. They both saw this, and rushed to see the king. The king was not happy to see them. He shouted, "What do you want? Why do you bother us like this?"

Mei Bo asked, "Your Majesty, may I ask why you want to have Du Yuanxian killed?"

"He is telling crazy stories about a black cloud over the palace. This is frightening the people and causing trouble in the city. He is a traitor to the kingdom."

Mei Bo said, "Your Majesty, you have not been in the main hall for half a year. You drink all day, and spend every night with your concubine. You care nothing for the people or the kingdom. You do not listen to your ministers. Now if you have Du Yuanxian killed, it will be like bringing down a house by smashing its pillars. Please, let Du Yuanxian live!"

The king was furious. He ordered his guards to seize Mei Bo and kill him at once. But Daji stepped forward. She said, "Wait! Your Majesty, I have an idea."

"What is it, my love?" asked the king.

"Mei Bo is not an ordinary criminal. So you should not punish him in an ordinary way."

"What do you think we should do?"

"I have an idea. I think you will like it. Make a pillar of brass, twenty feet high and eight feet across. Put three fire doors in it, at the top, middle and bottom. Strip Mei Bo of his clothing and tie him to the pillar, with his face against the brass. In a few seconds he will die and become a cloud of smoke."

The king smiled at his lover. "That is a wonderful idea, my dear!" He told his attendants to order some workers to build the burning pillar as Daji had said.

Shang Rong heard all this. He wanted to cry. He said to the king, "Your Majesty, I am an old man now, in the evening of my life. I am tired and would like to go home, to spend my last few years with my family. May I go?" The king agreed, and Shang Rong left the palace, never to return.

For the next few days, workers built the burning pillar while the king spent all his time drinking and having sex with Daji. Finally, the burning pillar was ready. Daji looked at it carefully, and said that it was good. The king saw it and laughed. He said to Daji, "My love, you are very smart! Let's use this on Mei Bo tomorrow."

The next day, the burning pillar was brought to the courtyard outside the main hall. Servants put wood inside the pillar and started a fire. Soon the pillar was red hot.

Soldiers brought Mei Bo in front of the king. He was wearing prisoner's clothing. The king said, "Do you know what this is?"

"No."

"You fool. You know how to tell lies, but you don't know what this is. We built it just for you. We will use it to roast you, so everyone will know you are a traitor to your kingdom."

Mei Bo shouted at him, "I am not afraid of death and I am not afraid of you. I have served three kings. Now it looks like the Shang Dynasty will end soon. I am glad that I will not see it."

The king ordered Mei Bo stripped and tied to the red hot pillar. As soon as his body touched the pillar he screamed. Then his body turned to smoke and ash. A terrible smell filled the courtyard.

The king was in a good mood as he left the courtyard with Daji. But his ministers stayed and talked among themselves. Huang Feihu said, "My friends, this burning pillar did not just kill Mei Bo. It also killed the Shang Dynasty. Our nation will become just a cloud of smoke and ash. It will disappear from the earth."

That night, the king ordered a feast for himself and Daji. Music filled the air. The wind carried the sound of music to Queen Jiang's bedroom. She asked her servants, "What is that music?"

They replied, "His Majesty and Lady Su are drinking and eating together."

The queen said, "Get my carriage ready. I must go and see the king at once."

Chapter 7
Fei Zhong Plots Against the Queen

The king loves to have beautiful girls day and night;
He can never get enough drinking and lust;

The moon has gone down, the wine still flows;
The song ends, the guqin starts to play

Becoming even more cruel, he forgets the five virtues;
This brings much killing and great sadness

Loyal ministers cannot turn back the evil;
To this day, it is locked inside the western tower

≡ ≡ ≡

Queen Jiang arrived at the king's palace. When the king saw her, he commanded Daji to sing and dance for the queen. The queen sat down on the right side of the king. Daji danced and sang for the queen. She danced so beautifully, it looked like her feet never touched the ground. But the queen never even looked at her and did not smile.

When she was finished, the king said to the queen, "My dear, life is short. The years pass by like water. We have little time to enjoy life. Why don't you enjoy Daji's dance?"

She queen replied, "There is nothing beautiful in that woman's dance. And there is nothing good about your rule. A good king cares for his people and stays away from evil ministers. A good king does not drink too much wine and he does not spend too much time with concubines. But all you want is sex and wine. You kill your loyal ministers and you forget about the affairs of state. Change your ways or this will be the end of the Shang Dynasty." She waited for a moment, then added, "I am just a woman, please forgive me if I have said too much." Then she stood up and walked out of the palace.

The king watched her go. He drank more wine. Then he said to Daji, "We don't know what's wrong with that woman. We had you dance and sing for her, but she didn't even look at you. Her words have made us angry. Please dance again, it would make us feel happy again."

Daji replied, "I am sorry, Your Majesty. I cannot sing and dance again for you. Her Majesty said that my singing and dancing will bring the end of the Shang Dynasty. Now I am very worried. I want to serve you, but Her Majesty says I am making you a poor king. I do not want to cause such trouble!" Then she started to cry.

The king put his arms around her. He said, "Don't worry, my dear. We know what to do with that woman." Then they continued drinking and lovemaking.

Daji was very angry at the queen. She thought about this for a few days. Then she sent a secret letter to the evil minister Fei Zhong ordering him to help her get revenge against the queen.

Fei Zhong thought to himself, "This is a difficult situation. The queen's father is the Grand Duke of the East. He has hundreds of thousands of soldiers. He can easily have me killed if I do something against his daughter. But if I don't help Daji, she only has to say a few words to the king while they're in bed, and that will be the end of my life. What can I do?"

He was thinking about his problem, walking back and forth in front of his home. Just then, he saw a big man walking by. He asked the man, "What is your name?"

The big man knelt in front of the minister and replied, "My name is Jiang Huan."

Fei Zhong realized that this man had the same surname as the queen. He said to the man, "What do you do here?"

"I am one of your servants. I work in the gardens. I have been here for five years. Please forgive me for getting in your way."

Fei Zhong smiled and said, "Jiang Huan, I have a job for you. If you do this for me, I will make you a wealthy and powerful man."

"Sir, I do not care about wealth and power. I only want to serve you." And then the two men began to talk quietly about the job that Fei Zhong had for him.

A few days later, Daji said to the king, "Your Majesty, your love for me has caused you to be gone from the main hall for over ten months. Perhaps it's time for you to go there and take care of the affairs of state." The king agreed and said he would go the next day.

The next day the king rode in his carriage to the main hall. Suddenly a large man jumped out in front of the carriage. He held a long sword in his hand. He shouted, "You are a terrible king. You spend all your days drinking and playing with your girlfriend while the kingdom is dying. My mistress has ordered me to kill you so her father can become king!" Then he attacked the king with his sword. He was quickly surrounded by the king's soldiers. They tied him up and threw him to the ground.

The king's carriage continued on its way to the main hall. When he got there, he told his ministers about the attack. "Who will question this criminal for us?" he asked.

Fei Zhong stepped forward. "Though this servant has no skill, I will do it." The big man was brought to Fei Zhong. After being questioned, the big man said that the queen commanded him to kill the king.

Fei Zhong returned to the king. He said, "Your Majesty, I will tell you what I found out, but only if you agree not to punish me for telling you what he said."

"Of course, we will not punish you," the king replied. "Out with it."

"The criminal's name is Jiang Huan. He is a relative of Jiang Huanchu, the Grand Duke of the East. So of course he is also a relative of your queen, Lady Jiang. The criminal says that the queen ordered him to kill you so that Jiang Huanchu could take your place as king. Thanks to the gods that you were not injured! Now I hope you will discuss this with your ministers and decide what to do with this criminal."

The king said, "Madame Jiang is our wife and the queen. How could she do this to us?" Then he ordered Concubine Huang to judge whether or not the queen was guilty of this crime.

A servant told the queen what the criminal said, and that Concubine Huang would be the judge. The queen rushed to the West Palace where Huang lived. She kneeled before Huang and said, "Heaven and earth know that I did not do this. You know me. You know that I am a good woman. I hope you will tell the king that I did not do this."

Huang replied, "Jiang Huan says that you told him to kill the king, so that your father would become the new king. If this is found to be true, you and your entire family will be killed."

The queen said, "Please listen to me! My father is already a very powerful man. He rules 200 marquises and is a member of the royal family. He has no reason to want to be king. Also, think about my son, Yin Jiao. He is the Crown Prince. If the king dies, my son will be the new king. But if my father takes the throne my son will never be king. Please, tell these things to His Majesty."

Concubine Huang returned to the king and told him everything that Lady Jiang said. He thought about it. He said to himself, "The queen makes some good points." He did not know what to do. But he saw that Daji had a cold smile on her face. "What is it, my love?" he asked her.

"I think the queen told Concubine Huang a fairy tale, and now Huang is confused. You know that Jiang Huan confessed that he was working for Jiang Huanchu and the queen. That criminal did not mention anyone else. I think the queen must be tortured until she tells the truth."

Concubine Huang said, "Don't talk like that, Su Daji. You know that the queen is the wife of the king. She is also the first lady of our kingdom. A queen must never be injured or killed, and certainly she must never be tortured."

Daji replied, "Everyone is the same under the law, even the king and the queen. We all know that the queen commanded Jiang Huan to attack the king. She must confess. If she does not, she must lose an eye."

The king smiled sweetly at Daji and said, "You are quite right, my dear."

Concubine Huang left and returned to the West Palace to see the queen. Crying, she said, "Your Majesty, that evil woman Daji wants to gouge out one of your eyes if you don't confess! Please, save yourself!"

The queen replied, "Sister, how could I confess to something that I did not do? I have been a good woman all my life, now I will not say something that would make my father a criminal. It does not matter if they take out one of my eyes or cut me into a thousand pieces. I will not confess to this."

Just then, several of the king's soldiers arrived. One of them held a dagger in his hand. "Quickly, Your Majesty," cried Huang, "confess!"

"I would rather die!" cried the queen.

The soldiers grabbed the queen. One of them used a dagger to gouge out one of her eyes. Blood ran onto the floor. The queen fainted. The soldiers picked up the eye, put it on a plate, and brought it to the king. Huang followed them.

The king looked at the eye, then he looked at Huang. "Did she confess?"

he asked.

"No," replied Huang. "She would rather die than confess to something that she did not do."

The king said nothing for a little while. Then he turned to Daji and said, "We listened to you and removed her eye. Now what do we do?"

Daji replied, "If she does not confess, her father might bring his army here to Zhaoge. He has a hundred thousand soldiers. So we must make her confess. Tell Huang to prepare some burning charcoal. If the queen does not confess, Huang must put her hands in the burning charcoal. That will make her confess."

"But Huang says that the queen has done nothing wrong. If we continue to torture her, I'm afraid that my ministers will become angry. That could bring trouble."

"Your Majesty, we cannot stop now. We are riding on the back of an angry tiger. If we get off, we will be killed and eaten! We must keep going."

"All right," said the king. Then he said to his soldiers, "If she still does not confess, put her hands in the fire."

Huang and the soldiers returned to the queen's palace. The queen was lying in a pool of her own blood. Huang said to her, "Your Majesty! What did you do in a previous lifetime, that you should have to suffer like this now? That stupid king still wants you to confess. If you do not, your hands will be put into burning charcoal!"

The queen said, "I am not afraid of death. And I will not confess!"

The soldiers grabbed the queen's hands and put them in burning charcoal. Instantly her hands burned and were turned into smoke and ash. The queen fainted. Huang fell to the ground, crying.

A little while later, Huang returned to the king. She said to him, "The queen has been tortured again and again, and she still says that she did not do this. Do you think that perhaps someone else is the criminal, and is trying to make it look like the queen did it?"

Before the king could say anything, Daji said, "Don't worry, Your Majesty. Remember that we have the criminal Jiang Huan. Bring him and the queen here and question them both at the same time. That will make the queen confess."

The king said, "That's a very good idea, my dear!"

Chapter 8
Princes Flee from Zhaoge

A beautiful woman brings disaster to the nation;
Thousands die, and many more are sent away

The king obeys his concubine and kills his own wife;
Then he kills his son, ending the line of kings

Great men try to leave but many still die;
The wise ones try to stay out of sight if they can

No one stands with the king, even the army leaves;
They drop their armor and weapons in the dust

☰ ☰ ☰

Several soldiers brought the criminal Jiang Huan to the West Palace. The queen looked at Jiang Huan with her one eye and said, "Who gave you money to tell lies about me? Heaven will punish you for this!"

Jiang Huan looked at the queen and replied, "You are the one who told me to attack the king. Don't you remember?"

"You are lying!" she shouted.

While the queen and the criminal were waiting to be questioned, a servant ran to the East Palace, the home of the king's two sons, Yin Jiao and Yin Hong. Yin Jiao was fourteen years old, and his brother was twelve. They were playing chess when the servant came in.

He cried, "Your Highnesses, stop your game and come quickly! Someone tried to kill your father the king. The criminal said that the queen told him to do this. His Majesty the king is now very angry. He ordered his soldiers to gouge out one of the queen's eyes, and to burn her hands to ashes. You must help her!"

The two boys ran to the West Palace. They saw their mother lying in her own blood. They cried when they saw her. She said to them, "My sons, look at your mother. Daji told the king that I ordered Jiang Huan to attack him. This was a lie. But the king had me tortured. Please, I beg you, avenge my death!" Then she closed her eye and died.

The crown prince Yin Jiao grabbed his sword and shouted, "Where is the man named Jiang Huan?"

Concubine Huang pointed to the criminal and said, "There he is." Yin Jiao grabbed his sword, ran over to Jiang Huan and cut him in two. Then he shouted, "Where is Daji? I will cut off her head." Then he ran towards the Immortal Longevity Palace to find Daji and kill her.

As the boy was leaving, Huang called after him, "Wait! I have something important to tell you!" He stopped and turned around. She continued, "Dear boy, you have killed Jiang Huan. Now we cannot torture him to learn the truth. And soon the king will hear about what you have done. You are in great danger!" Yin Jiao returned to the palace.

A little while later, two of the king's generals ran up to the West Palace, swords in their hands. They said, "His Majesty has commanded us to cut off the heads of the two princes."

Huang stood in the doorway. She said to them, "You fools! The boys are not here. I think you just want to come in and look at the pretty concubines. Go and look for the boys in the East Palace. That is where they live."

As soon as the generals left, Huang told the boys to go quickly to the Fragrant Palace where Concubine Yang lived. They ran to the other palace and told Yang everything that had happened. "Come in quickly!" she said to them. The boys went inside the palace.

A few minutes later, the two generals arrived at the Fragrant Palace. Yang shouted, "Stop! You cannot enter this palace." Frightened, the two generals turned around and left. After they were gone, Yang went inside and told the boys that it was too dangerous for them to stay in Zhaoge. She told them to go quickly to the Grand Hall and talk with some of the senior ministers.

The boys left the palace. Yang sat down and cried. She was in a terrible situation. She knew that the king and Daji would soon find out that she had helped the boys. Once they found out, they would torture Yang until she died. She said to herself, "Oh, this is a dark day for me and for the kingdom. The bonds between father and son, between husband and wife, and between king and ministers, all are broken. The kingdom is in great danger, and my life is over." Then she went into her bedroom and hanged herself.

The boys ran to the Grand Hall. When they entered, they saw many ministers and officials. They ran to General Huang Feihu and grabbed onto his robes, crying. Yin Jiao cried out, "Please save, us, General! My father has tortured my mother. I saw her die. Seeking revenge, I killed Jiang Huan with my sword. Now the king has ordered that my brother and I be killed. Please, save our lives so that the Shang Dynasty can live!"

Two ministers, Fang Bi and Fang Xiang, were brothers. They said to the other ministers, "The king has killed his queen. He has tried to kill his sons. He has tortured and killed a good minister with the Burning Pillar. But what do we do? We stand around talking like a bunch of old women in the marketplace. We say that our king should no longer rule our nation. We should all leave Zhaoge and find a new king."

Then the two Fang brothers picked up the two princes. Fang Bi picked up Yin Jiao, and Fang Xiang picked up Yin Hong. They carried the boys out of the Grand Hall and left the city through the south gate.

Huang Feihu said to the other ministers, "There are many ministers here, but only those two have shown true loyalty to the kingdom. If the king sends soldiers after them, they will probably die."

In the Immortal Longevity Palace, the king was angry. "Where are the princes?" he asked his generals.

They replied, "We have looked in the East Palace, the West Palace, and the Fragrant Palace, but could not find them."

The king said, "They must be in the Grand Hall. Go there, find them, and put them to death."

The two generals ran over to the Grand Hall. They shouted, "Where are the two young princes?" Huang Feihu told them that the Fang brothers had taken them out of the city already. The two generals returned to the king and told him.

The king shouted, "Go and tell Huang Feihu to find the Fang brothers and the two princes, and kill them all right away."

Huang Feihu was told of the king's command. He got on his ox and rode quickly out of the city. Soon he saw Fang brothers and the princes walking on the road. He rode up to them and got off his ox. Then he threw himself onto the ground and said to the princes, "His Majesty commanded me to come here and kill you. I cannot do that, but I must obey the king's command. Please, take your own lives."

Yin Jiao kneeled and said, "Oh please, general, let us live."

"I cannot do that. My king has commanded me."

"All right. Then kill me, but let my younger brother live."

Yin Hong said, "No, that is wrong. My brother is the Crown Prince, and I am just a young boy with no talents. Cut off my head and let him live."

The two boys cried and argued, and the three men listened. Finally, Huang Feihu said, "All right, stop crying. We must save our kingdom, no matter the cost. I have an idea, but you must not tell anyone about this. If the king hears about my plan, it will bring death to me and my family. Fang Bi, you take the boys to Jiang Huanchu, he is their maternal grandfather and the Grand Duke of the East. Tell him to gather a large army. Fang Xiang, you go to see E Chongyu, the Grand Duke of the South. Tell him to also gather a large army. Together, they should attack Zhaoge and get rid of this evil king."

Then Huang Feihu turned around and rode back to Zhaoge. He told the king, "Your Majesty, I tried to catch up to the princes, but I could not find them. I asked many people but nobody had seen them."

The king nodded his head. Then Daji said to the king, "Your Majesty, I am afraid that the two princes will meet up with their grandfather and gather a powerful army. You must stop them. Send an army of three thousand soldiers on horses after them right away!" The king ordered Huang Feihu to do that.

Huang Feihu said to one of his generals, "The king has told me to gather three thousand soldiers on horseback. Go and gather three thousand soldiers, but only take those who are old and sick. That will be the king's army."

The next morning, the army of old and sick soldiers started slowly after the two princes. But the Fang brothers and the two princes had already been traveling for two days.

The Fang brothers and the two princes came to a fork in the road. One road went east to the lands of Jiang Huanchu, who was the Grand Duke of the East and the princes' grandfather. The other road went south to the lands of E Chongyu, who was the Grand Duke of the South. The Fang brothers decided that it would be safer for the two princes to travel by themselves. So Yin Jiao took the road to the east, while Yin

Hong took the road to the south. The Fang brothers went back towards Zhaoge, leaving the boys to travel alone.

The two young princes had lived their entire lives in the palace. They did not know how difficult it was to walk on a road for days, without a comfortable bed or good food. They both became tired and hungry, and they walked slowly.

Around midday, Yin Hong came to a small house near the road. He walked into the house. Seeing the family eating dinner, he said loudly, "Bring food for the prince!" The family jumped up, led him to a seat, and brought him rice and other food. They asked him his name. "I am Yin Hong, the younger son of the king," he replied. The family all kowtowed to him. Yin Hong ate his meal. When he was finished he thanked the family, then continued walking south. As nighttime came, he was in a place without any houses or inns. But he saw an ancient temple in the forest. He pushed the door open, lay down, and quickly fell asleep on the floor.

Meanwhile, his older brother Yin Jiao was walking east. He was also very tired and hungry. When nighttime came, he saw a large house. He opened the door and called out, "Is anyone home?"

"Who is there?" said a voice from the darkness.

"I am a traveler, just passing through. It is getting late. Would you please let me stay here for the night?"

"Your voice sounds like you are from Zhaoge. Is that true?"

"Yes sir, I am from Zhaoge."

"Come in, come in."

Yin Jiao walked into the house. He looked into the darkness and saw an old man. Looking closer, he saw that the man was none other than Shang Rong, the prime minister. Shang Rong saw Yin Jiao. He immediately knelt down before the prince. He asked, "Why are you here, Your Highness? Why are you traveling all alone?"

Yin Jiao told him about the torture and death of his mother, the king's order to kill the two princes, and the other terrible things that the king had done. Shang Rong listened to his story. When the prince was finished, Shang Rong said, "That king has broken the bonds between husband and wife, between father and sons, and between king and ministers. He must go. Your Highness, I will return to Zhaoge with you.

I will ask the king to change his ways, before the kingdom falls."

Back on the road, the three thousand soldiers finally reached the fork in the road where one road went south the other went east. The generals knew that the army was traveling too slowly to catch the princes. So one general took fifty of the strongest soldiers and went on the east road. The other general took another fifty soldiers and went on the south road. The rest of the soldiers were told to wait there for the two generals to return.

Chapter 9
The Death of the Prime Minister

The loyal minister speaks to the king to help the nation;
Wake up, he says, and rule your kingdom wisely

He does not want to join the others in death;
But he thinks, is this my last day on earth?

His mind cannot be moved, it is like gold or stone;
Even the gods in the jade capital are listening now

But he does not succeed and his head is smashed;
The others see it, their tears flow like rivers

≡ ≡ ≡

The two groups of fifty soldiers headed east and south in search of the two princes. They marched all day and into the night without stopping. In the middle of the night the eastbound soldiers came to the ancient temple where Yin Hong was sleeping. They entered the temple. In the torchlight they saw the sleeping prince. The general cried, "Your Highness! Your Highness! We are here to take you back to the palace!"

Yin Hong replied, "General, I will go with you, even if it means going to my death. But I am so tired that I cannot walk." The general helped the young prince onto his own horse, and he walked beside the horse. They marched back to the fork in the road.

Meanwhile, the eastbound soldiers came to the home of Prime Minister Shang Rong. The general entered the home. He saw the Prime Minister sitting with Yin Jiao. The general said, "Your Highness! Prime Minister! His Majesty the King asks that you return to the palace."

Yin Jiao looked up and saw the general. He said, "All right, I will return to the palace with you. But I have little hope that I will live much longer. Perhaps my younger brother will live longer than me, so he can avenge the death of our mother."

The general said to Shang Rong, "Prime Minister, I will take Yin Jiao back to the palace. You should wait a little while before returning, so nobody thinks that we were planning something together." He kowtowed to the Prime Minister, then he left with Yin Jiao.

The group of soldiers with Yin Jiao marched back towards the fork in the road. There they met the group of soldiers with Yin Hong, and the rest of the three thousand soldiers who were waiting there. Together they all returned to Zhaoge.

When they came to the gates of the royal palace, the two young princes saw General Huang Feihu and a large group of ministers standing there waiting for them. Yin Jiao said to them, "Ministers, General, you all know that my brother and I have done nothing wrong. Please help the Shang Dynasty and save us from death!"

"Don't worry," said the ministers. "We will speak up for you."

The two generals who had brought back the princes went to see the king. They told him that the two princes were now back in Zhaoge. The king said to them, "We don't need to see them. Just cut off their heads and bury their bodies."

"Your Majesty," said one of the generals, "how can we kill them without a written order from you?"

Without saying a word, the king picked up a brush and ink. He wrote on a piece of paper, "Kill the princes." He handed the paper to the generals.

The generals returned to the gate, carrying the king's order. But when they got there, one of the ministers grabbed the king's order and tore it to pieces, saying, "The king is doing terrible things, and you fools are helping him! Do you really plan to kill the two princes right here at the city gate? That would be a disaster. Let's all go to the Grand Hall. We will ask the king to come and talk with us about this matter." They all walked to the Grand Hall. As they walked, several of the generals surrounded the two princes to protect them.

When they all reached the Grand Hall, the ministers struck the bells and banged the drums to tell the king that they wanted to meet with him. In the Immortal Longevity Palace, the king was with Daji, drinking and talking. They heard the bells and drums. The king said to Daji, "The ministers want to talk with us. They probably want us to let the princes live. What should we do?"

Daji replied, "Order that the princes be killed today, and that anything else can be discussed tomorrow." The king picked up brush and ink. He wrote, "Kill the princes today. If you have questions, we can talk about it tomorrow." He handed the order to a servant, telling him to carry it to the main hall.

But the two princes were not fated to die that day. An immortal named Pure Essence was from Taihua Mountain. Another immortal, Grand Completion, was from Nine Immortals Mountain. The two immortals had nothing to do, so they were traveling together. They were just passing through Zhaoge when they saw two bright red beams of light coming up from the princes to the sky. Looking more closely, they saw a dark cloud of death over the royal palace. They understood that the Shang Dynasty was going to end soon, but that the two princes needed to live. Grand Completion said, "Let's save the two princes."

The two immortals brought a great wind. The wind picked up dust and moved rocks. It blocked the sun and turned day to night. Darkness fell over the palace. Thunder and lightning filled the sky. All the ministers in the Grand Hall fell to the ground, covering their heads with their arms. When the wind stopped, they looked around. The two young princes were gone.

The ministers said to each other, "Heaven will not harm those who have done nothing wrong. And earth will not cut off the life blood of the Shang Dynasty."

Around this time, Prime Minister Shang Rong arrived at Zhaoge. He walked into the Grand Hall. He said to the other ministers, "My friends, I have been living a quiet life in the forest. I did not know that the king would kill his wife, try to kill his sons, and spend all his days playing with his concubine. While this is going on, you have been living the good life and have done nothing to help the nation!"

"What could we do?" they replied. "The king spends every day with Daji. We never see him."

Shang Rong said to them, "I will go and see the king, though it will surely mean my death. I will tell him the truth. That is the only way that I can face the kings of ancient times when I meet them after I die." Then he told the guards to strike the bells and beat the drums, to call the king.

The king was angry when he heard the bells and drums, but he got up and rode in his carriage to the Grand Hall. Walking into the hall, he saw a man kneeling on the floor. "Who is that man?" he asked.

"The man once called the Prime Minister dares to give you my report," said Shang Rong. And without looking up, he handed his report to one of the ministers, who put it on the desk in front of the king.

In the report, Shang Rong started off by telling the king that in the beginning, the king served the people and the nation well. But, he said, recently the king has listened to traitors, spent his days drinking and playing with concubines, tortured and killed his own queen, and ordered the death of his own children. He told the king that it was time for him to change his ways. He must kill Daji and the other evil ministers. This, said Shang Rong, was the only way to return the nation to health and happiness.

The king turned red with anger. He shouted to his guards, "Take this fool out to the palace gate and beat him to death with a golden hammer."

As the guards moved towards Shang Rong, the old Prime Minster shouted, "I have served three kings. I have taken care of this nation as if it was a motherless child. Everyone can see that this dynasty will soon fall. What will you say to your ancestors when you meet them after you die?"

"Kill that old man at once!" roared the king.

"I am not afraid to die!" said Shang Rong. "What about you?" Then he threw himself against a stone pillar. His head crashed against the stone. Blood poured from his head as he fell to the ground and died.

The ministers watched this but dared not speak. The king ordered that Shang Rong's body be taken out of the city and thrown into a field.

Chapter 10
Ji Chang Finds Thunderbolt

Heavenly mist surrounds Mount Qi;
Thunder in the southeast is carried on the morning wind

The sound of thunder awakens dreaming butterflies;
Lightning comes from the shadows and stirs up the dust

Three of five show the way to Qi's success[1];
Now a hundred sons are in the Zhou capital

The dynasty has little time left, soon dragons and tigers will come;
They will kill the old king and bring the new days of Zhou

☰ ☰ ☰

One of the ministers, a man named Zhao Qi, stepped forward. He said to the other ministers, "My friends, I am willing to give up my life and join the Prime Minister in the underworld." Then turning to the king, he said, "You are a criminal! You have killed your wife and the Prime Minister. You don't listen to your ministers or dukes. You only listen to Daji and the evil minister Fei Zhong. Your rule is like a tree without roots. It will fall soon!"

The king shouted at him, "How dare you say this to us!" Then turning to his guards, he said, "Put this criminal on the Burning Pillar!"

Zhao Qi said, "Death is nothing to me, because I have lived a good life. But you are a criminal. You will lose your throne and will suffer for ten thousand years!"

The guards had already started a fire inside the Burning Pillar. Now it was red hot. They took off Zhao Qi's clothing and tied him to the Burning Pillar. In a few seconds he was turned to ash. A cloud of smoke was all that was left of him.

The king turned and walked out of the Grand Hall. He got in his

---

[1] "three of five," or three fifths, often refers to something powerful, influential, or significant. Here, it is the discovery of Ji Chang's hundredth son, Thunderbolt.

carriage and rode back to the Immortal Longevity Palace. There he sat down with Daji and drank a cup of wine with her. He said to Daji, "Today Shang Rong killed himself, and we put Zhao Qi on the Burning Pillar. But no matter how many of these fools we kill, the rest of them still insult us. Also, we are worried about Jiang Huanchu. When he hears of his daughter's death, he might bring an army and attack us. How can we stop this?"

Daji smiled sweetly and said, "Your Majesty, I am only a woman. I know nothing of these things. Perhaps you should ask Fei Zhong, he always has good ideas."

The king called for Fei Zhong. After the king told him what happened, the evil minister knelt and said, "Your Majesty, you are right, the four dukes could start trouble. Perhaps you could bring all of them to Zhaoge and cut off their heads. Then the eight hundred marquises will be like a dragon without a head, or a tiger without teeth."

The king was delighted to hear this. He sent orders for the four grand dukes to come to Zhaoge.

One of the messengers came to see Ji Chang, the Grand Duke of the West. He handed the king's order to the duke. Ji Chang read the order and thanked the messenger. Then he said to his eldest son, "My son, I have been ordered to go to Zhaoge. I have divined that I will be there for seven years. This is the will of heaven. Do not try to visit me. While I am gone, you will rule in my place. Take care of the people, always follow the law, and listen to your elders. I will return after seven years."

Then he said goodbye to his mother, his wife, his concubines, and the rest of his ninety-nine sons. He set out on the road to Zhaoge with fifty men.

After they had traveled about seventy *li*, Ji Chang said to his men, "Find a safe place for us to stay during the rain storm."

The men said to each other, "The sky is clear. How can it rain?" But a few minutes later the sky grew dark, there was thunder and lightning, and heavy rain began to fall.

After a few minutes the rain stopped and a bright light appeared in the sky. Ji Chang said, "A bright light after a rain storm means a great warrior has arrived. Go and find him." The men did not understand this, but they did as he ordered. They heard a baby crying. Coming closer, they saw it was a baby boy. They picked up the baby and brought it to Ji Chang.

Ji Chang said, "I have ninety-nine sons. If I make this boy my son, that will be one hundred."

As he looked at the baby boy, a tall Daoist appeared. He said, "My name is Master of the Clouds. I am looking for the great warrior who just arrived." Ji Chang bowed to the Daoist, and told his men to give the baby boy to him.

The Daoist said to Ji Chang, "This baby's name is Thunderbolt. Please let me take this baby to Mount Zhongnan. I will be his teacher. Later, I will give him back to you." Ji Chang bowed his head. The Daoist turned and walked away, carrying the baby boy.

Ji Chang and his fifty men traveled for several more days. They finally arrived in Zhaoge. Ji Chang met with the three other grand dukes. None of them knew why they had been called to Zhaoge. They sat together for several hours. They talked, they drank wine, and they argued. After a few hours Chong Houhu was tired so he went to bed. The other three stayed there, talking. Around the second watch, they heard one of the attendants quietly, "Tonight you are drinking and laughing, but tomorrow your blood will be on the ground."

Ji Chang said, "Who said that?" None of the attendants said anything. Ji Chang asked again, but still, none of the attendants would speak. Angrily, Ji Chang called to the guards, "Take all of them outside and cut their heads off!"

When they heard this, the attendants all pushed one of them, a man named Yao Fu, forward. Ji Chang told the rest of the attendants to leave. Then he turned to Yao Fu and said, "Why did you say that? Tell me the truth and you will be rewarded. Otherwise, you will lose your head."

Yao Fu replied, "Sir, I work in the home of a royal messenger. The messenger told me that after the king killed the queen, he was afraid of the four grand dukes. Daji told the king to bring you all here, so that he could cut your heads off. Watching you drinking so happily, it hurt me to think of your deaths tomorrow."

Jiang Huanchu asked the attendant how his daughter, the queen, had died. Yao Fu told him about the torture. Jiang Huanchu fell to the floor, crying. "I will go to see the king tomorrow!" he said.

Back at the Immortal Longevity Palace, Fei Zhong told the king that the four dukes were in Zhaoge. He said to the king, "Tomorrow the dukes will come to give you their reports. Don't bother reading the reports. Just tell the guards to tie them up and cut off their heads."

The next day, the four dukes came to see the king. Jiang Huanchu was the first to give his report to the king. The king did not even look at the report. He said to the duke, "You and your daughter planned to kill us and take our throne. This crime is as great as a mountain." He said to his guards, "Take this criminal out and cut him into a thousand pieces!"

As he was dragged away, Jiang Huanchu shouted, "You fool! I have been a good servant of the nation. But you are an evil tyrant. You killed the queen and even tried to kill your own children. You listen only to your evil concubine and your evil ministers. I am not afraid of you or of death itself!"

Chapter 11
The Deaths of the Grand Dukes

How can you tell the secrets of heaven,
When the king harms loyal ministers and gives power to evil

If not for the loyal ministers,
We would have seen blood and flesh flying

Remember the ancient king imprisoned for seven years,
He studied the words of Fuxi and gave us the Eight Trigrams[1]

Since ancient times, fate has favored a wise king;
And right now the sun is shining on Mount Qi

☰ ☰ ☰

The three other dukes watched, frightened, as the guards dragged Jiang Huanchu away. One of them said, "Your Majesty, the king is the nation's head but his ministers are his arms and legs. If you kill Jiang Huanchu without even reading his report, it will destroy the bond between king and ministers. Please think about this!"

Then, still frightened, they handed their report to the king. The king read the report, growing more and more angry as he read it. Finally he tore it up, pounded his desk with his fist, and shouted, "Take these traitors away and cut off their heads!"

Fei Zhong was pleased with this, but he did not want his friend Chong Houhu to be killed with the others. He knelt before the king and said, "Your Majesty, all four of the dukes are criminals, but some are worse than others. Certainly, Jiang Huanchu should die for trying to kill his king. E Chongyu and Ji Chang have said bad things to you or about you. But as I see it, Chong Houhu's only crime was in following the others. He has served you well in the past. We beg you to spare him so that he

---

[1] King Wen of Zhou (1099 – 1050 BCE), a wise and fair king, visited the court of the Shang king Jou the Terrible, who threw him in prison for seven years. While in prison, King Wen reflected on the ancient Eight Trigrams developed by Emperor Fuxi 1800 years earlier. He decided to arrange the eight trigrams to form an eight-sided ring. This arrangement is called the post-heaven Bagua circle.

can serve you in the future."

The king agreed to spare Chong Houhu, but said that the other three must die. Then Huang Feihu and several other ministers came forward and knelt before the king. They said that the three dukes were all good men who had served the king well. But the king said to them, "They are all traitors who have planned to kill us or said terrible things to us. How can you ask us to spare them?"

The ministers replied, "Your Majesty, these three dukes have large and powerful armies. If you kill them, wouldn't those armies rise up and start a war?"

The king thought about this. He said, "All right, we will spare Ji Chang. But the other two must die immediately! And if you continue to try to have them spared, we will do the same to you!"

Several guards came forward and dragged two of the dukes out of the Grand Hall. One of them drew his sword and cut off E Chongyu's head. Several others tied Jiang Huanchu's hands and feet to a pillar, and cut him into a thousand pieces. The king returned to the Immortal Longevity Palace. That night, the attendants of the two dead dukes left the city and rode back to their homes as quickly as they could.

The next day, Fei Zhong came before the king. He said, "Your Majesty, you must be careful with Ji Chang. He says one thing but thinks another. If you let him return home, he will join with the armies in the south and east, and we will have war. It will be like sending the dragon back to the ocean, or the tiger back to the forest. Too dangerous!"

The king replied, "We have already spared him. What can we do?"

"Leave it to me," smiled Fei Zhong.

The next day, Ji Chang left the city with his attendants. He rode about ten *li*. There, several other ministers were waiting for him. They said, "We heard that you were leaving today. We have food and wine for you. Please eat and drink with us before you go home."

Ji Chang was pleased to join them. They ate and drank and talked for a while. Then Fei Zhong rode towards them, bringing more wine. The other ministers saw him. None of them liked Fei Zhong. So they quickly said goodbye to Ji Chang and returned to the city.

Fei Zhong sat down with Ji Chang. They drank a large amount of wine together. Ji Chang had already drunk a lot of wine, so he became careless with his words. Fei Zhong said, "Duke, it is said that you can see the future. Is this true?"

He replied, "Of course. I throw gold coins and I read them with the I Ching. This method never fails."

"We both know that His Majesty is having trouble ruling the nation. Can you see the fate of this dynasty?"

Foolishly, Ji Chang said, "The future is dark. I have seen that our king will be the last king in the Shang Dynasty."

"When will the dynasty end?"

"In a few decades, no more."

Fei Zhong nodded. "And can you see my fate also?"

"Yes. Your fate is strange. Some people die from illness, others from the actions of others. But I see your fate is to die from being frozen in ice."

Fei Zhong laughed. "And what of your own fate, duke?"

"I will die happily, in my old age."

They talked and drank for a while longer. Then Fei Zhong said that he had things to do in Zhaoge and had to return. He rode back to the palace and went to see the king. He said, "Ji Chang is a terrible man. He says that the Shang Dynasty will end with your death, in a few decades. He says that I will die frozen in ice. But he says that his own death will be from old age."

The king hit his desk with his fist. He said, "That old fool! We spared him, and now he talks like this! Send some soldiers to bring him back here. We will cut off his head!"

Meanwhile, Ji Chang and his men rode westward. He knew that he had drunk too much wine and said the wrong things to Fei Zhong. Also, he knew that his fate was to remain in Zhaoge for seven years, so it was too soon for him to return home. He looked to the east and saw a general and several soldiers riding towards him. The general said, "Grand Duke, His Majesty orders you to return to Zhaoge immediately."

"I know," he replied. He told his men to continue riding home. He said, "I will return home in seven years. Tell my son to listen to his mother, live in peace with his brothers, and take care of the people." Then he followed the general back to Zhaoge.

The general brought Ji Chang before the king. The king was still angry. "You old fool!" he said. "We spared your life, but now you speak lies about us and the dynasty. We should cut off your head right now."

"Your Majesty, I am a fool. But I know that there is heaven above, earth below, and the king in the middle. How can I tell lies about you?"

"You talked about our fate, but you spoke nothing but lies!"

"I only used the gold coins and the I Ching to see your fate. This method has been used for many centuries. It does not fail."

"Oh? We will show you that it fails. You predicted you will live a long life, but we will have you killed right now. Guards, take him outside and cut off his head!"

But before the guards could take him away, Huang Feihu and five ministers came into the Grand Hall. Huang Feihu said, "Your Majesty, we care only about the fate of the nation. The people love Ji Chang. There will be trouble if you kill him. Also, his method of seeing the future is a good one. Please, order him to see the immediate future and tell you what tomorrow will bring."

The king laughed. "All right. Ji Chang, what will happen tomorrow?"

Ji Chang threw some gold coins on the floor and looked at them. Then he looked at the king. "Your Majesty! Tomorrow at noon the Ancestral Temple will catch fire and burn to the ground. Quick, do something!"

But the king said to his guards, "Lock up this old fool. We will see what happens tomorrow at noon."

The next day, the ministers were all at Huang Feihu's home, watching the Ancestral Temple. The weather was beautiful, without a cloud in the sky. But exactly at noon, a huge bolt of lightning came down from the sky. It struck the Ancestral Temple, setting it on fire. Then a strong wind came and made the fire bigger and hotter. In a short time, the entire temple was turned to ashes.

The ministers rushed to see the king. They said, "Your Majesty, the Ancestral Temple has burned to the ground, just as Ji Chang said it would! Now we all know that he is a great sage. You must set him free!"

The king replied, "All right, we will spare his life. But we will not let him return home to cause trouble. He will stay here in Zhaoge until the kingdom is at peace again. Take him to Youli."

And so, Ji Chang lived quietly for several years in Youli. In his heart he had no anger towards the king or anyone else.

Chapter 12
The Birth of Nezha

A rare treasure is hidden in the cave of golden light;
It was put on earth to help the virtuous

The Zhou Dynasty has started to prosper;
But it's the beginning of the end for the Shang Dynasty

Since ancient days, the will of heaven brings help;
But even so, disasters will come

Time runs in a circle, dynasties rise and fall;
The king, the ministers, the people, all turn to dust

≡ ≡ ≡

When the attendants of the dead Grand Dukes of the South and East returned home, they told the marquises in their regions what had happened to the two dukes. Soon afterwards, 400 marquises gathered their armies. A huge army of 600,000 soldiers attacked two mountain passes that led to Zhaoge. But the king's soldiers were already guarding the mountain passes and they stopped the army.

A third mountain pass, Chentang Pass, was guarded by a general named Li Jing. He was a Daoist who had studied for many years with an immortal named Woe Evading Sage.

Li Jing had two sons. His wife had been pregnant with a third child for three and a half years but had not given birth yet. Li Jing and his wife thought that because the baby was so late, it must be a demon or a monster.

But one night, Madame Li had a dream. In her dream, a Daoist came into her bedroom and told her, "Hurry Madame, your excellent baby is coming!" Then the Daoist threw something at her. When she woke up, she felt the baby coming. A little while later, a strange baby was born. It looked like a ball rolling around on the floor. Frightened, Li Jing struck it with his sword. The ball split in two and a beautiful baby came out. His face was white as the moon. He wore a gold bracelet on his right wrist and a piece of red silk on his belly. Li Jing picked up the baby and held it in his arms.

The next day, a Daoist came to see him. He said to Li Jing, "My name is Fairy Primordial. I live on Qianyuan Mountain. May I please see the child?"

Li Jing picked up the baby and handed it to the Daoist. The Daoist looked carefully at the baby. He said, "This is no ordinary boy. He is really an immortal named Pearl Spirit, sent down from heaven. You should call him Nezha."

"I will. Thank you very much," replied Li Jing.

"Would you please allow me to teach this boy?"

"We would be very happy."

The Daoist thanked him. Li Jing invited him to stay for dinner, but the Daoist said he had things to do on Qianyuan Mountain. He stood up and left.

Nezha began to study Daoism with Fairy Primordial. Seven years passed. Now the boy was already taller than most men. One day he went for a walk beyond Chentang Pass. It was a hot day. Nezha saw Nine Bend River nearby. He took off his shirt. Then he put the red silk in the water so he could wash himself. Every time he put the red silk in the water, the river water turned red and the ground shook.

Ao Guang, the Dragon King of the Eastern Ocean, noticed that the ground was shaking. He sent a yaksa, a nature spirit, to find out why. The yaksa went to Nine Bend River. He saw the tall boy putting his red silk in the water and shaking the ground. He came out of the water and said, "Boy! Why are you turning the water red and shaking the ground?"

Nezha looked up. He saw a large beast with blue face, red hair, a big mouth, and holding a large axe in his hand. "What kind of beast are you?" he asked.

"Who are you calling a beast?" replied the yaksa angrily. He rushed at Nezha and tried to hit him with the axe. Nezha had no weapons, but he hit the yaksa on the head. The yaksa fell to the ground, dead.

One of Ao Guang's soldiers saw this. He ran to Ao Guang and said, "Your Majesty! A young boy has killed your yaksa!"

Ao Guang was very angry. He stood up and prepared to go and fight with the young boy. But before he could leave, his third son, Ao Bing, came in. He said to his father, "Relax, Father. You don't need to do this. I will go and catch this criminal for you."

Ao Bing and a group of dragon soldiers rushed out of the palace and towards Nine Bend River. They came to the place where Nezha was standing. Ao Bing said, "Are you the boy who killed my father's yaksa? Tell me your name and where you are from."

"Yes, it was me," replied Nezha. "I am Nezha. I am the third son of Li Jing, the general of Chentang Pass. I came here to bathe in the river. Your yaksa attacked me for no reason, so of course I killed him. And who are you?"

"I am Ao Bing, third son of Ao Guang, the Dragon King of the Eastern Ocean." Then Ao Bing attacked Nezha. But Nezha just laughed. He threw his red silk up in the air. Thousands of fire balls appeared and fell down on Ao Bing. Ao Bing fell to the ground. Nezha went over to him and hit him on the head, killing him instantly.

Nezha thought that he should give his father a gift. So he removed a tendon from the dragon's dead body, thinking that it would make a fine belt for his father to wear. Then he returned home, carrying the tendon in his hand.

The soldiers returned to Ao Guang. They told him that the boy was the son of Li Jing, and that the boy had just killed Ao Guang's third son. Ao Guang was very unhappy and very angry. He changed into an old scholar and went to see Li Jing.

Li Jing heard that Ao Guang was coming. He was very happy, because the two of them were good friends and bond brothers. He came outside to greet his old friend. But Ao Guang said to him coldly, "Brother, one of your sons was bathing in Nine Bend River today. He used a magic weapon to turn the water red and make the ground tremble. Then he killed one of my yaksas. I sent my son to see what had happened, and your son killed him too. Even worse, your son took a tendon from my son's body!"

Li Jing said, "My good friend, this cannot be true. I don't think my son was away from my house today. Please wait here. I will ask him." He went to find Nezha. Nezha told him the story of what happened at the river.

Li Jing cried and said, "Oh my son, you have caused great trouble for me and our family. Come and tell your uncle what you just told me."

The two of them went to see Ao Guang. Nezha said to him, "Uncle, I am sorry I killed your son. I did not mean to do it. I still have the tendon. You can have it back if you want it."

This made Ao Guang even more angry. He shouted to Li Jing, "You have a terrible son! My yaksa was appointed by the Jade Emperor himself, and my son was the god of rain. Your son killed both of them! Tomorrow I will go see the Jade Emperor. He will know what to do with you." Then he turned and stormed out of the house.

Li Jing and his wife cried, thinking that the Jade Emperor would kill their entire family. Nezha kneeled before them and said, "Father, Mother, remember that I am a disciple of Fairy Primordial. I will go and see him right away. He will surely help us."

Nezha picked up a handful of dirt and threw it in the air. Then he used his magic powers to fly on the dirt to Qianyuan Mountain. He went to Fairy Primordial and knelt before him. He told his master everything that had happened, and he asked for help.

Fairy Primordial said to Nezha, "Come over here. Open your shirt." Nezha opened his shirt. The immortal used his finger to draw an invisibility spell on Nezha's chest. Then he said, "Go to the Palace of Heaven. Find the Precious Virtue Gate and wait there for Ao Guang to arrive." Then he told Nezha what to do when Ao Guang arrived. He finished by saying, "And if you have any trouble, come back and see me. And don't worry about your parents, they will be fine."

Nezha went to the Palace of Heaven. He found the Precious Virtue Gate. The gate had four huge pillars. Wrapped around each pillar was a red-bearded dragon whose job was to gather clouds and make rain. Inside the palace were thirty-six smaller palaces and seventy-two huge halls. Everywhere there were beautiful gardens filled with colorful flowers and grasses. There were many ministers and attendants in the palace, all wearing colorful robes. Pretty birds flew in the sky above them.

Nezha waited there. Soon Ao Guang arrived, but he could not see Nezha because the boy was invisible. Nezha ran up to Ao Guang and hit him on the back. Ao Guang fell to the ground. Nezha raised his fist, ready to kill Ao Guang.

Chapter 13
Two Immortals Fight

Even Shiji can become wise;
Her spirit waited inside a stone for ten thousand years

She took energy from the moon, the stars, and the earth
She spent years learning about Li, Kan, and the Heavenly Stems[1]

Look at the clouds forming, watch the mist rising;
Listen to the songs of dragons and the roar of tigers

Use fire to face disaster and win;
The dark cannot fight against the light

≡ ≡ ≡

Ao Guang looked up from the ground. He saw Nezha holding him down and ready to kill him. He said, "So, it's you! First you kill my yaksa. Then you kill my third son. And now you dare to attack me, the god of rain, right here in the Palace of Heaven! You are a criminal, and you will pay for this!"

Nezha replied, "Shut up or I'll kill you too. You don't know that I am an immortal. My real name is Pearl Spirit. I'm a disciple of Fairy Primordial. Heaven sent me to be the son of Li Jing, so that I can serve as a general in the coming war between Shang and Zhou. I was taking a bath in Nine Bends River when those two came and insulted me, so of course I had to kill both of them. Now you want to tell the Jade Emperor about it? He will just laugh at you."

Then Nezha started to pull off Ao Guang's dragon scales, one by one. Blood came from the places where the scales had been. He said, "Now, I want you to forget about talking to the Jade Emperor. Come with me to Chentang Pass, or I will finish killing you."

---

[1] Li and Kan are two of the Eight Trigrams, where each trigram is a combination of three solid or broken lines that symbolizes different natural phenomena and aspects of life. The Heavenly Stems are part of the 60-year calendar cycle, said to have been invented by the Yellow Emperor in 2700 B.C.

Ao Guang had no choice. He agreed. Nezha started to let him get up. But then he stopped and said, "I have heard that dragons can become very large or very small. I don't want you to fly away from me. Change into a small snake. I will carry you to Chentang Pass." Again, Ao Guang had no choice. He changed into a small snake. Nezha picked him up and put him inside the sleeve of his robe. Then he flew down to Chentang Pass.

Li Jing met his son. "Where have you been?" he asked.

"I went to the Palace of Heaven to ask my uncle Ao Guang to not talk to the Jade Emperor about me. Here he is." He reached into his sleeve, took out the small snake, and threw it on the ground.

The snake changed into human form. It was Ao Guang. He said angrily to Li Jing, "You son is an evil beast! He killed my yaksa, he killed my son, then he pulled off my scales. Look!" He showed Li Jing where the scales had been pulled off. He continued, "I am going to call the dragon kings of the four oceans. Together we will go and see the Jade Emperor about this!" And with that, he changed to a gust of wind and blew away.

Li Jing and his wife watched the dragon king fly away. They were both worried, but they knew that their son was extremely powerful. His wife said to the boy, "Nezha, please go and play outside for a while."

Nezha went outside. He walked past the mountain pass. He saw a stone tower. Walking up inside the tower, he saw a large bow and three arrows. He said to himself, "My master told me that I will a general in a war against the Shang Dynasty. Perhaps I should learn how to use a bow and arrow." He picked up the bow and one of the arrows, and shot the arrow towards the southwest. It flew through the air, all the way to a cave on Skeleton Mountain.

This cave was the home of a powerful immortal named Empress Shiji, who had two disciples named Blue Cloud Boy and Pretty Cloud Boy. The arrow hit Blue Cloud Boy, killing him instantly. Pretty Cloud Boy saw it. He ran to tell Empress Shiji. Empress Shiji pulled the arrow out of Blue Cloud Boy. Looking at it, she said, "I know this arrow. It is Sky Shocking Arrow. It should be at Chentang Pass. Li Jing must have shot it, killing my disciple."

She mounted her phoenix and rode quickly through the air until she arrived at Chentang Pass. She called out, "Li Jing! Come out here now!"

Li Jing ran out to see her. He kowtowed and said, "Your disciple kneels before you. What brings you here?"

"Don't say those nice words to me." She showed him the arrow and told him that it had just killed one of her disciples.

Li Jing said, "I know this arrow. This is the Sky Shocking Arrow. This was left here by the great Emperor Xuanyuan. It is a treasure of Chentang Pass. Nobody has been able to use this bow and arrow since ancient times! Please, give me a few minutes so I can find out who did this."

He went back to his house, thinking that perhaps his immortal son was the one who shot the arrow. He called Nezha to come and see him. When the boy arrived, he said, "My son, I think it's time for you to learn how to use a bow and arrow."

Nezha replied, "Yes Father, I want to learn! In fact, just a few minutes ago I found a bow and three arrows in a stone tower. I shot one of the arrows but I don't know what happened to it."

His father shouted, "You unfilial boy[1]! You keep causing more and more trouble for this family." And he told the boy what the arrow had done.

Nezha said, "Father, please don't be angry. Please take me to see this immortal on Skeleton Mountain." The two of them flew quickly to Skeleton Mountain. They were met by Pretty Cloud Boy. Nezha thought that a fight was going to start, so he hit the boy as hard as he could. Pretty Cloud Boy fell to the ground. Empress Shiji rushed out of her cave and saw her second disciple lying on the ground. "You monster!" she screamed. Nezha threw the red silk into the air to try to wrap up Empress Shiji. But Empress Shiji just opened the sleeve of her robe, pulling the red silk inside. Nezha had no other weapons. He turned and flew away as fast as he could.

Empress Shiji said to Li Jing, "This has nothing to do with you, you can go home now." Then she flew after Nezha.

Nezha flew to Qianyuan Mountain and knelt in front of his master. He said, "Master! Empress Shiji thinks I killed her disciple. Now she's trying to kill me. Please save me!"

Fairy Primordial replied, "Go and hide in the garden. I will deal with her."

---

[1] Filial piety is the obligation that a child has to their parents.

He waited. Soon Empress Shiji arrived at his cave. "Brother," she said, "your disciple has killed one of my disciples and hurt the other one. He also attacked me. Tell him to come out right now."

Fairy Primordial smiled and said, "Sister, please let go of your anger. Listen to me. We both have studied the Way. We know that a great war is coming. The Shang Dynasty will fall soon. The Zhou Dynasty will rise in its place. And an immortal named Jiang Ziya will create many gods. To prepare for the coming war, my Grand Master told me to send all my disciples down to the human world to join in the fight. Nezha is one of my disciples. He will help Jiang Ziya establish the new Zhou Dynasty. Now, I am sorry that your disciple has died. But don't worry, your disciple will become a god when the war is over."

Empress Shiji was still angry. She replied, "Though we have both studied the Way, we must find out who is the stronger."

Fairy Primordial began to tell Empress Shiji why he was stronger. But Empress Shiji would not let him finish speaking. She attacked him with her sword.

Fairy Primordial quickly ran into his cave. He kowtowed towards Kunlun Mountain and said, "Master, please forgive me. Your disciple must disobey your order not to kill anyone." Then he came out of the cave and began fighting with Empress Shiji. They fought with swords for a few rounds. Then Empress Shiji threw her magic handkerchief at him. He said a few magic words and pointed at the handkerchief. It fell to the ground.

He took the Nine Dragon Divine Fire Coverlet out of his sleeve and threw it at Empress Shiji. It landed on her head. He turned and saw that Nezha was watching the fight with great interest. He said to Nezha, "You must go home right now. The four dragon kings have already met with the Jade Emperor. The emperor has sent his guards to arrest your parents. Go and save them!" Then, seeing the look on Nezha's face, he added, "And no, you cannot have my Nine Dragon Divine Fire Coverlet."

Then he turned to face Empress Shiji. He clapped his hands. The Nine Dragon Divine Fire Coverlet caught on fire. Nine fire dragons appeared. They wrapped around Empress Shiji and burned her until she changed into her true form, a large uncarved rock[1].

Nezha flew home. The four Dragon Kings were already there, ready to kill his parents. Nezha said to them, "I am the one you want, not my parents. I will pay with my life." Then he used his sword to cut off his own left arm. Then he cut open his own belly. Then he broke all of his own bones.

Nezha died. His soul floated on the wind until it reached Qianyuan Mountain.

---

[1] Shiji was a Daoist. In the *Dao De Jing*, an "uncarved block of wood" refers to a person's original nature, unaffected by cleverness. It is the simple and natural state that one should return to. The Daoist classic *Zhuangzi* says, "If you were to meet someone who understands great plainness, who subscribes to nonaction and returns to the simplicity of the uncarved block... you would really be surprised!"

Chapter 14
Nezha Returns to Life

Who knows the power of immortals;
They can even bring the dead back to life

Just one grain of cinnabar awakens the dead;
A soup made of lotus leaves heals the soul

Nezha was not of this world, he did not need flesh and bones;
But he needed incense to become an immortal

From now on he must conquer the land and give it to the true king;
And help the Zhou of West Qi to expand their empire

≡ ≡ ≡

Fairy Primordial was sitting in his cave on Qianyuan Mountain. Looked up, he saw Nezha's soul floating towards him. He said, "You cannot stay here. Go back to your home at Chentang Pass. Visit your mother in a dream. Tell her to build a temple for you. If people worship you for three years you will be able to return to human form. Now go!"

Nezha's soul returned home. He waited until night when his mother was sleeping. Then he entered her dream and said, "Mother, it's me, your son Nezha. I am dead. I have no place to rest my soul. Please build a temple for me where people can worship me. Only then will I be able to go to Heaven."

Madam Yin woke up from her dream. She told her husband what she had seen. But Li Jing said angrily, "Forget about Nezha. That boy has caused enough trouble already."

But the next night Nezha came to his mother again in her dream. He came again, night after night. After a week he said to her, "Mother, if you don't do as I ask, I will cause a lot of trouble for the family."

Madam Yin did not want to argue with her husband. So she quietly told a few of her servants to go into the forest and build the temple. It was a beautiful temple deep in the forest, with high white walls. In the center was a golden statue of Nezha surrounded by attendants and guards.

People started coming to the temple. They prayed to Nezha, and Nezha always answered their prayers.

Li Jing did not know about the temple. But one day he was returning with his army from a trip to another mountain. He saw a large number of people visiting a strange temple in the forest. "What is this?" he asked some of his men.

The soldier replied, "This temple appeared about six months ago. There is a god inside, and he answers the peoples' prayers."

"And who is this god?"

"God Nezha."

Li Jing was furious. He went inside and saw the gold statue of his son. He kicked it, knocking down the statue and breaking it. Then he went outside and told his soldiers to burn down the temple.

Nezha's soul was not in the temple at that time. But later that evening he returned to the temple. He saw nothing but smoke and ashes. One of his attendants told him that Li Jing had destroyed the temple. "Oh Father," he cried, "How could you do this to your son?" He did not know what to do. So he went to see his master on Qianyuan Mountain. He knelt before his master and asked him what to do.

Fairy Primordial said, "There isn't much time. Soon Jiang Ziya will come. You must be ready to help him." He told one of his attendants to bring him two lotus flowers and three lotus leaves. He tore the flowers into three hundred little pieces; these were for the three hundred bones in the human body. He put the pieces on the ground. Then he placed the three lotus leaves on the pieces; these were for heaven, earth and man. Then he put a little bit of golden elixir in the center and pushed some of his own *qi* into it. Finally, he grabbed Nezha's soul and threw it into the center. There was a tremendous bang, and a human young man jumped up. He was big and strong.

Nezha kowtowed to Fairy Primordial. He said, "Thank you, Master. Now I must take revenge on my father."

"First, come with me to the garden," said Fairy Primordial. They walked into the garden. Fairy Primordial gave Nezha several magic weapons. There was a Fire Tip Lance for fighting, two Wind Fire Wheels for traveling fast, a piece of red silk to replace the one he had lost, a Universal Ring for fighting, and a gold brick. "Now go back to Chentang

Pass," he said.

Nezha used the Wind Fire Wheel to return quickly to Chentang Pass. "Father, come out right now!" he shouted.

Li Jing came out and said, "You evil beast! You brought trouble before your death. Now that you have returned to life, you have brought even more trouble!"

"You destroyed my temple!" shouted Nezha, and he attacked his father with the Fire Tip Lance. They fought for several rounds. Li Jing knew he could not win against his immortal son, so he turned and rode away on his horse to the southeast. Nezha followed on his Wind Fire Wheels. He quickly caught up to his father. But just then, they saw a young Daoist walking. It was Muzha, the second son of Li Jing.

Muzha said to his younger brother, "Nezha, stop this now. You must not kill your own father!"

Nezha said, "Elder brother, this is not your fight. You don't know the situation." Then he told Muzha everything that had happened. "So, who is right, Li Jing or me?"

Muzha replied, "Parents are always right in matters of their children."

Nezha said, "That man is no longer my father." This made Muzha very angry. He attacked Nezha. Nezha fought back. After a few rounds, he threw his gold brick at his brother, knocking him to the ground. Then he started chasing Li Jing again.

Li Jing knew he could not move as fast or fight as well as Nezha. He thought that maybe he should just kill himself so he would not have to lose a fight to Nezha. But just then, he heard a voice singing,

> *Warm winds blow through the forest*
> *Beautiful petals float on the water*
> *Where do I live, you ask*
> *Far away among the white clouds*

This was Heavenly Master Manjusri, the master of Li Jing's son. "Save me, Master!" cried Li Jing.

"Go and wait in my cave," replied the master. Li Jing went into the cave.

A few minutes later, Nezha arrived on his Wind Fire Wheels. He saw Heavenly Master Manjusri standing there. "Have you seen General Li Jing?" he asked.

"Yes, he is in my cave. And who are you, young man?"

"I am Nezha, a disciple of Fairy Primordial. Tell Li Jing to come out right now."

"I have never heard of you. Now go away and stop causing trouble here." Nezha attacked Heavenly Master Manjusri, but the master took out his weapon, the Dragon Bound Stake, from his sleeve and threw it in the air. Strong winds blew, fog filled the air, and Nezha began to feel confused. A moment later he found himself tied tightly to a golden stake, with golden rings surrounding his body. He could not move.

Heavenly Master Manjusri called out, "Jinzha!" This was Nezha's eldest brother. "Beat this young man for me." Jinzha began hitting Nezha. After a while Heavenly Master Manjusri said, "All right, that's enough. You can stop now."

A few minutes later, Fairy Primordial arrived. Heavenly Master Manjusri smiled and said to him, "I have been teaching your disciple a little lesson. Now, set him free and bring him here." Fairy Primordial went up to Nezha, waving his hand. The golden rings fell off Nezha's body. He said to Nezha, "Come with me. Kneel down and kowtow to your uncle!"

Nezha had no choice. He kowtowed to Heavenly Master Manjusri and said, "Master, thank you for the beating."

Heavenly Master Manjusri replied, "From this day forward, there must be no anger between father and son." He turned to Li Jing and told him he could leave. Then he told Nezha that he could also leave.

But Nezha was still very angry. He started chasing his father again. Li Jing looked back and saw Nezha coming after him. "What do I do now?" he thought.

Just then, he saw another Daoist. "Please, help me!" shouted Li Jing.

"What seems to be the problem?" asked the Daoist.

"Nezha is coming. He wants to kill me!"

Just then, Nezha arrived on his Wind Fire Wheels. The Daoist turned to Li Jing. He hit Li Jing on the back and spat on him. Then he said, "Go and fight the boy. I will watch you."

Li Jing knew he could not win against his immortal son. But he started fighting anyway. The fight began. Nezha thought that he would win easily, but his father was very strong and fought very well. "I think that Daoist is helping him," he thought. He turned and attacked the Daoist with his lance.

The Daoist spat a white lotus flower. It stopped Nezha's magic lance. He said to Nezha, "Why are you attacking me?"

Nezha replied, "Because you are helping Li Jing!" And he attacked the Daoist again. The Daoist lifted his arms towards the sky. A beautiful pagoda fell down from the sky and landed on top of Nezha, trapping him inside. A fire started inside the pagoda. Nezha began to burn. The pain was terrible.

The Daoist said, "Now will you make peace with your father?"

"All right, I will," replied Nezha.

The Daoist put out the fire and said, "Call him 'father' and kowtow to him." Nezha had no choice, he did what the Daoist ordered. Then the Daoist said to Li Jing, "I give this pagoda to you. Any time Nezha gives you trouble, you can put this pagoda on him and burn him. Now, the two of you must live in peace together. Forget about the past, and help the Zhou king in his war against Shang. Nezha, you can leave now."

Nezha left and returned to Qianyuan Mountain.

Li Jing said to the Daoist, "Master, may I know your honorable name?"

The Daoist replied, "I am Master Burning Lamp. It is time for you to give up wealth and fame. You must go into the mountains and become a hermit. As you know, the king of Shang is evil and must be destroyed. Soon, the king of Zhou will need your help in the coming war. When that happens, you may leave the mountains and join the fight."

Li Jing kowtowed to Master Burning Lamp. He went home, quit his job as general of Chentang Pass, and became a hermit in the mountains.

Chapter 15
Jiang Ziya Leaves Mount Kunlun

Ziya has returned to the human world;
His hair is grey, he looks like a wild man

He is too old and too slow to work;
He tries to make money but people just see a fool

The river was not in the flying bear dream;
But the river knows that prosperity is coming soon

Soon it will be time for Ziya to begin a new empire;
It will bring eight hundred years of prosperity

☰ ☰ ☰

Heavenly Primogenitor was the grand master of Daoism. He lived in a great palace on Mount Kunlun.

He was worried about the coming fall of the Shang Dynasty. So he called all the leaders of Daoism and Confucianism to meet with him. They talked for a long time. The leaders decided to create 365 new gods. To create these new gods, they would use people who would die in the coming war between Shang and Zhou. Those people would be changed into gods of thunder, fire, stars, mountains, clouds, rain, and other things.

The leaders needed someone in the human world to select the 365 people and change them into gods. Jiang Ziya, one of Heavenly Primogenitor's disciples, was to be that person.

So Heavenly Primogenitor sat on his golden throne and called Jiang Ziya to come and see him. Jiang Ziya came and kowtowed before his master.

"How long have you been here on Kunlun Mountain?" asked the master.

"Master," said Jiang Ziya, "I came here at age thirty-two. I am now seventy-two."

"The Shang Dynasty will end soon, and the Zhou Dynasty will rise. New gods must be created. I want you to leave this mountain and go to live in the human world. You will help the new king of Zhou as his general and prime minister. Here is your fate:

> *You will be poor for twenty years*
> *While fishing at the river, a wise man will find you*
> *And make you prime minister to the king*
> *You will be a general at ninety-three*
> *Powerful men will create a new dynasty*
> *And you will name new gods at ninety-eight."*

Jiang Ziya did not want to leave Kunlun Mountain. He had been studying the Way for forty years but had failed to become an immortal. He still had much to learn. He told his master he did not want to go. But his master said, "This is your fate. You must do this." So sadly, Jiang Ziya picked up his things and left Kunlun Mountain.

He knew nothing of the human world. But he remembered that he had a sworn brother named Song Yiren who lived in Zhaoge. He decided to go see his brother.

Song Yiren was a wealthy man with a large house and many servants. He came out to greet Jiang Ziya. "Brother," he said, "I have not seen you for many years. I am so happy to see you today!"

The two brothers sat down and had a vegetarian meal with wine. Song Yiren asked, "What have you been doing in heaven these past forty years?"

"I have learned many things. I know how to carry water, to care for the trees, to make a fire, and to make magic elixirs."

His brother replied, "Those jobs are for servants. You are no servant. You should start a business. And also, you need a wife."

The next day, Song Yiren went to see an old friend named Ma who had an unmarried daughter. He gave the friend four *taels* of silver as a gift, and the friend agreed to let his daughter marry Jiang Ziya.

Song Yiren went back to tell Jiang Ziya that he'd found a wife for him. He said, "You will like her. She has a good education. She has never been with a man. And she is sixty-eight years old, so she will be a good match for you."

They were married soon after. But Jiang Ziya was really not interested in married life. He kept thinking about his earlier life on Mount Kunlun.

He wanted to study the Way and had no interest in his wife or in starting a business.

One day Ma said to him, "We are living a good life here with your brother. But what if he dies? We should have a business, so that we will always have money for a good life."

"You are right," he replied. "But what can I do? I know nothing of business. All I can do is make rakes."

"All right, let's start a rake business. There are many bamboo trees nearby. Cut down some trees, make some rakes, then bring them to the marketplace in Zhaoge and sell them. It's easy. It will bring us a little bit of money, and that's better than no money at all."

So Jiang Ziya made some rakes. Then he carried them thirty-five *li* to the Zhaoge marketplace. He spent all day there but did not sell a single rake. He walked back home, carrying the rakes on his back. He told his wife, "Nobody in Zhaoge needs a rake."

She replied, "You old fool! Everyone needs a rake. You just don't know how to sell them." They started shouting at each other.

Song Yiren heard the shouting. He ran over and said, "Please don't argue! There are other ways to make money. We have a lot of wheat here. I'll ask my servants to turn the wheat into flour. You can take the flour to the marketplace and sell it there."

When the flour was ready and put into bags, Jiang Ziya carried the bags to the Zhaoge marketplace. He went to several different places but nobody wanted to buy his flour. Finally, a man stopped and asked for a penny's worth of flour. Jiang Ziya put the flour bags on the ground and started to take out a small amount of flour for the man.

But just then, a frightened horse came galloping down the road. Jiang Ziya and the man jumped out of the way, but the horse's legs caught on the flour bags. The bags went flying every direction, and all the flour blew away. The man left without buying any flour, and Jiang Ziya walked home with no money and empty bags.

When he got home, his wife was happy to see the empty bags of flour. "This is wonderful!" she said. But then Jiang Ziya told her what happened. She started shouting at him again, and before long they were arguing loudly.

Song Yiren came over and stopped them from arguing. "Don't worry about a little bit of flour," he said. "I have another idea. I own several restaurants in Zhaoge. One of them is a large restaurant near the city's south gate. You can go there and be the boss."

But that did not work either. People went to Jiang Ziya's restaurant, but they were frightened of him and did not stay to eat any food. He had to return home and tell Song Yiren that he could not be a restaurant boss either.

"All right, let's try one more thing," said Song Yiren. "I'll give you fifty *taels* of silver. Go buy some pigs and sheep. Take them to the marketplace in Zhaoge and sell them. That should be easy."

But that did not go well either. Heaven was angry at the King of Shang, so there had been no rain for many weeks. The king had told the people to pray for rain. And during this time, nobody was allowed to kill any animals. Jiang Ziya did not know this. So when he brought his pigs and sheep to the marketplace, the guards took all his animals. They wanted to arrest Jiang Ziya, but he left the animals and ran away.

He returned home with no money and no animals. Sadly, he told Song Yiren what had happened. "I am a terrible businessman," he said. "I have lost your money. I don't know what to do."

But Song Yiren just said, "Don't worry, it's just a few *taels* of silver. Come, let's go into the garden and have some wine."

Chapter 16
The Jade Lute Demon

Demons keep coming, the fate of the nation is dark;
The will of heaven brings suffering to the capital

Strange energy did not harm the stars in the sky;
It was evil spirits that killed the loyal ministers

A thousand years of work is lost
To gain a single day of happiness

If not for Ziya's wisdom,
No one would see the pipa demon in the fire

≡ ≡ ≡

Jiang Ziya sat in the garden with his bond brother, drinking wine and enjoying the fine weather. He saw goldfish in the pond, and he heard birds singing in the trees. He looked around. Smiling, he said to Song Yiren, "This would be a good place to build a tower."

"Why would I build a tower here?" replied Song Yiren.

"It will bring you good fortune. If you build a tower here, your family will have thirty-six jade belted ministers and also several gold belted ministers.[1]"

"It's interesting that you tell me this. I have tried to build here several times, but each time I build something, it burns down. I don't even try anymore."

"That's because there are evil spirits here. But don't worry. You build the tower, and I will take care of the evil spirits."

Song Yiren gathered several workers. They started to build the tower. After several days of work, they were ready to raise the main beam. That night, Jiang Ziya sat quietly in the garden, watching. At midnight a

---

[1] In ancient China, leather belts with sheets of ornamentation, called *dàikuǎ*, were worn by officials as indicators of their rank. The highest ranking wore jade, and the second highest wore gold.

strong wind came, sending clouds of dust into the air. A fire started in the new building. Jiang Ziya looked inside and saw five evil spirits in the tower. Fire came from their mouths. The wind made the fire so hot that the earth turned red.

Jiang Ziya drew his sword. He walked through the fire towards the five spirits and said, "Come out, demons! You have already caused too much trouble. Now you must die!"

A loud bolt of thunder shook the earth, causing the spirits to fall to their knees. "Lord!" they cried, "please spare our lives. We used to be animals, but we have studied the Way for many years. Now we are spirits. If you kill us, all of our work will be for nothing. We are sorry we caused you trouble."

"All right," he replied. "Leave this place and go to Mount Qi. Wait for me there. Don't cause any trouble. Later I will need your help with something." The five spirits kowtowed to him, then flew away to Mount Qi.

While he was talking to the spirits, Madame Ma and Song Yiren's wife were watching him. They could not see or hear the spirits, so they thought Jiang Ziya was just talking to himself. "Old man, who are you talking to?" asked Madame Ma.

"Oh, I was just getting rid of some evil spirits," he replied.

"You can talk to spirits?"

"Yes. And I am also a fortuneteller." Just then Song Yiren came to find out what was happening. Jiang Ziya told him the story.

Madame Ma said to Song Yiren, "My husband is a fortune teller. We should give him a shop in the city so he can start a fortunetelling business."

Soon after, Song Yiren gave his brother a nice little shop near the south gate of Zhaoge. Jiang Ziya put up a few small signs. On the left was a sign saying, "Speak only of the Dao." On the right was a sign saying, "Always speak the truth." On the back wall was a third sign saying "Inside the sleeves are the sky and earth, inside the jug are the sun and moon." He opened the shop and sat down to wait for customers. He went to the shop every day for four months, but no customers came in.

Finally, a woodcutter came into the shop. He was a big man who lived in the forest. He dropped his firewood on the floor and looked down at

Jiang Ziya. He pointed to the sign on the back wall and asked, "What does that mean?"

Jiang Ziya replied, "It means that I know the past, the future, and everything in heaven and earth. Also, I will live forever."

The woodcutter said, "Big words, old man. If you know the past and the future, you should be able to tell my future. If you are right, I'll give you twenty coppers. If you are wrong, I'll beat you up and destroy your shop."

"This is my first customer, and he is a very bad man!" thought Jiang Ziya. But he said, "That is no problem. I will write three sentences on a piece of paper. You must do exactly what is on the paper. Ok?"

The woodcutter agreed. Jiang Ziya wrote three sentences on the paper. The woodcutter read it:

> *Walk south.*
> *You will find an old man sitting under a tree.*
> *He will give you 120 copper coins, four plates of food, and two bowls of wine.*

The woodcutter thought this could not possibly be right, because nobody had ever given him that much money in twenty years. But he picked up his firewood and started walking south. Soon he saw an old man sitting under a tree. The old man shouted, "Woodcutter! Come over here!"

The woodcutter walked over to him.

"Your firewood looks good," said the old man. "I will buy all of it for 100 copper coins." The woodcutter was happy to sell the firewood. He was also happy that the man was giving him 100 coppers instead of 120, because he did not want to pay the fortuneteller. He gave the firewood to the man. While the man went in his house to get the money, the woodcutter swept the ground clean.

A few minutes later, a young servant came out. He carried four plates of food, a pot of wine, and a bowl. "Please, eat and drink," said the servant. The woodcutter poured all of the wine from the pot into the bowl, so it would be one bowl of wine instead of two. But after he drank the wine in the bowl, he saw that the pot was full of wine again. He poured that wine into the bowl and drank it too. Then he ate the four plates of food.

The man came out of his house carrying a bag of coins. He said, "I was going to give you 100 copper coins. But I see that you have swept the ground clean in front of my house. So I'll give you another 20 coins. Go and buy yourself some wine."

The woodcutter ran back to Jiang Ziya's fortunetelling shop, shouting, "There is an immortal in Zhaoge! There is an immortal in Zhaoge!"

He arrived at the fortunetelling shop and said to Jiang Ziya, "You really are an immortal, sir! Now the people of Zhaoge will be happy and have no more trouble."

"Fine, fine. Give me my twenty copper coins," replied Jiang Ziya.

"I must do something more for you," said the woodcutter. Then he ran outside and looked around. He saw a wealthy looking man. The woodcutter grabbed the man and pulled him towards the shop.

"What are you doing?" said the man. "I have business in the city and I don't have time for this."

"Come with me. You have to meet this fortuneteller."

"No, I don't. Let go of me."

"If you don't come with me, I will throw both of us into the river and end our lives." The rich man had no choice, so he went with the woodcutter into Jiang Ziya's shop.

Jiang Ziya told the rich man's fortune. He told the rich man that he would collect 103 silver *taels* that day. The man walked out of the shop, laughing and shaking his head. As he left, the woodcutter shouted to him, "If the fortuneteller is correct, you must pay him half a *tael* of silver." The rich man just waved him away and kept walking. A crowd of people had gathered to watch this.

Two hours later, the rich man returned. He said loudly so that everyone in the crowd could hear, "This fortuneteller is truly an immortal sent from heaven! I collected 103 silver *taels*, just as he said!"

This made Jiang Ziya famous throughout Zhaoge. Everyone wanted him to tell their fortune, and they were all happy to pay him a half *tael* of silver. He brought home a lot of silver, and this made his wife very happy.

Jiang Ziya's fame spread far and wide. It even reached the demon named Jade Lute who lived in a graveyard several *li* south of Zhaoge. Jade Lute was one of the three demons who was called by Nüwa seven years earlier. She was a friend of the thousand-year-old fox demon who had killed Daji and taken her body. She would often go to visit Daji at night. Whenever she visited Daji she would stop to eat one or two of the palace maids.

One morning she was leaving the palace after visiting Daji. Flying over the city, she looked down and saw a crowd of people surrounding Jiang Ziya's fortunetelling shop. "I wonder if he can tell my fortune," she said to herself. So she came down to earth, changed into a beautiful young woman, and walked through the crowd to Jiang Ziya's shop. She said, "Sir, can you tell my fortune?"

Jiang Ziya saw her. He knew immediately that she was a demon. "Of course, madam," he said to her. Then he grabbed her hand and would not let go.

"How dare you!" she shouted, so everyone could hear. "I am a lady. Let go of me at once!"

People in the crowd shouted at Jiang Ziya, telling him that he was an old man and should not touch a lady like that. But he said to them, "My friends, this is no lady. This is an evil demon."

She tried to get away from him. Jiang Ziya grabbed a brick and hit her on the head. She fell down and blood ran onto the ground. "The fortuneteller has killed a lady!" shouted the people.

Just then, Prime Minister Bi Gan rode past on his horse. He stopped and asked what was happening. Someone said, "There is a fortuneteller here named Jiang Ziya. A woman asked him to tell her fortune. He grabbed her. She fought back. He hit her head with a brick and killed her!"

The Prime Minister ordered his guards to arrest Jiang Ziya. They dragged him to the Prime Minister, but still he would not let go of the woman's hand. "What are you doing to that woman?" he asked.

"Sir," replied Jiang Ziya, "I am no criminal. This is an evil demon. You know that there is evil in Zhaoge these days. I think perhaps this demon is the reason for it."

Bi Gan said, "I will bring you to the king. He will decide what to do with you." So they all went to the palace to see the king.

When they arrived at the palace, the king was sitting with Daji. The king looked at them and said, "This looks like a woman, not a demon."

Jiang Ziya replied, "Your Majesty, if you put her in the fire, you will see her true form."

The king agreed. So the guards gathered a large amount of firewood. They lit it and waited for the fire to become big and hot. Then threw the woman's body into it. They watched for four hours, but the woman's body was not burned at all. Finally, the king said, "Four hours in the fire is enough. The fortuneteller is right. She is a demon."

Chapter 17
The Snake Pit

The snake pit is full of evil, its spirit fills the sky;
It is filled with palace maids' blood and flesh

So many pretty bones, no place to bury them;
Their smell lingers near their souls

Once they dreamed of home, now they sing empty songs to the moon;
Sad and lonely, they cannot rest

Their air of sadness fills the heavens;
But it also helps to bring the Zhou to power

≡ ≡ ≡

Jiang Ziya watched the evil demon's body lying in the fire, not burning. He wanted to see the demon's true form. So he brought out magic fire from his mouth, nose and eyes. The magic fire flew towards the demon's body. The demon opened its eyes and sat up. It looked at Jiang Ziya and said, "Why are you doing this to me?"

The king and his ministers saw and heard this. They could not believe that the dead body was sitting up and talking. "Your Majesty," said Jiang Ziya, "please go inside. A big storm is coming." And just then, a huge bolt of lightning came down from the sky. The ground shook. The fire went out. When the smoke blew away, the demon's body was gone. And a jade lute was lying on the ground.

Daji was very angry that her good friend Jade Lute had been killed. She thought to herself, "Sister, don't worry. I will have my revenge on Jiang Ziya. He and I cannot both live." Although she was very angry, she smiled at the king and said, "Your Majesty, I would like to have that jade lute. I can play it for you day and night. Also, it looks like Jiang Ziya is a wise and powerful man. You should give him a job here in the palace."

"Good idea, my love," said the king. He ordered his attendants to put the jade lute in the Star Picking Mansion. Then he gave Jiang Ziya the position of Director of the Imperial Observatory.

The next day, Daji went to the Star Picking Mansion. She picked up the jade lute and moved it to the very top of the building. She knew that if the jade lute gathered qi[1] from heaven, earth, sun and moon for five years, her friend would return to life and become a demon again.

A few days later, Daji was playing the jade lute and dancing for the king. All the concubines were smiling and watching. But in the back of the room, about seventy palace maids were crying. Daji asked who they were. A servant told her that they were maids of the dead queen.

Daji went to the king. She told him about the seventy maids. She said to him, "Those maids will cause trouble for us. They must all die."

"Of course, my dear," smiled the king. "We will have them killed right away."

"No, please wait. I have a better idea. You should dig a hole in front of the Star Picking Mansion. Make the hole 50 feet deep and 240 feet around. Put thousands of snakes in the pit. Then strip the maids and throw them into the pit."

The king liked this idea, but he did not have enough snakes. So he commanded his people to bring snakes to the palace. All the snakes in Zhaoge were brought to the palace. When there were no more snakes in Zhaoge, the people went out into the countryside to find more.

Jiao Ge, the king's Supreme Minister, did not know why the king wanted so many snakes. He asked the leader of the king's guards what the snakes were for. The guard leader replied, "The king wants all of the queen's palace maids to be killed. They are to be thrown into a large hole in front of the Star Picking Tower. Then the snakes will bite and kill the maids."

Jiao Ge and the other ministers ran to the Star Picking Tower. They saw a group of palace maids standing near the large hole. They were stripped, tied up with rope, and crying with fear.

Jiao Ge went to see the king. He knelt before the king and said, "Your Majesty, these maids have done nothing wrong. But you are going to kill them in a terrible way. No king has ever done anything like this before!"

The king just replied, "These palace maids are evil. We must deal with

---

[1] qi is spiritual energy.

them."

Jiao Ge said angrily, "The king should be a good father to the people. But you care nothing for the people. You do not listen to your ministers. You killed two of the grand dukes, and you used the Burning Pillar to kill other good people. And now you want to kill these maids who have done nothing wrong. I tell you, stop spending all your days playing with your concubine Daji. Stop listening to Daji and that evil minister Fei Zhong. Only then can you save this kingdom and bring peace to the land."

The king jumped up and shouted, "How dare you speak to us like this! Guards, strip this fool and throw him into the snake pit!"

But before the guards could grab him, Jiao Ge shouted, "You are a tyrant, and death will come for you soon enough." He jumped out of a window and smashed into the ground, dead.

"Throw that body into the snake pit!" roared the king. "And throw the palace maids in after him!"

The king's guards grabbed each of the palace maids and threw them into the pit. The snakes surrounded them, bit them, and started to eat their bodies. The king and Daji watched this for a while. Then the king patted Daji on the arm and said, "My dear, this is really too wonderful for words."

Daji smiled and said, "Your Majesty, I have another good idea. You can dig two more holes. Put trees in one of the holes, then hang strips of meat on the tree branches. This will be the 'Meat Forest.' Fill the other hole with wine and call it the 'Wine Pool.' Your Majesty will be the only one to use the Meat Forest and the Wine Pool."

"Wonderful!" said the king. He told his servants to dig two more holes and create the Meat Forest and Wine Pool. When they were finished, the king and Daji had a nice dinner.

"I have another idea for you, Your Majesty. I think you should have the palace maids fight with the eunuchs. It will be fun to watch. Let the winners drink from the Wine Pool. But the losers should be killed and their bodies thrown into the Meat Forest." The king liked this idea, and ordered his servants to do as Daji said.

Now, Daji had her own reasons for wanting all these people to be killed. She was really a fox spirit, of course. Late every night, while the king was sleeping, the fox spirit changed back to its original form. Then the fox spirit drank the blood and ate the flesh of the dead bodies.

Daji was not finished doing evil things. She still wanted to have revenge on Jiang Ziya for killing her friend, the demon Jade Lute. One day when she and the king were drinking wine, she asked him to build a new building. She wanted it to be forty-nine feet high, with a huge terrace on top. She called it the Deer Terrace. "Your Majesty," she said, "if you build this, it will show everyone how powerful you are. It will be like one of the palaces in heaven. Immortals will come down from heaven to visit with you. They will kowtow before you and call you 'Great King.' You and I will live together forever."

"Of course, my dear," said the king, who had drunk too much wine. "But who could build this for us?"

"I think Jiang Ziya is the best person for the job," she replied. "He is a wise man, and he understands *yin* and *yang*." So the king called for Jiang Ziya to come and see him.

Jiang Ziya did not know why the king was calling him. So he did a divination and saw that great danger was coming. He said to Bi Gan, "Good bye, my friend. Thank you for helping me. I don't know if we will see each other again." Then he went to the palace.

When Jiang Ziya arrived, the king said, "We have an idea for a new building. We call it the Deer Terrace." Then he showed Jiang Ziya the designs for the Deer Terrace and said, "We want you to build this for us. It's a big job, but we know you can do it."

Jiang Ziya looked at the designs for the Deer Terrace. He thought to himself, "This building cannot be built. Daji and the king are out to get me. I'd better get out of Zhaoge, and quickly!"

Chapter 18
Flight from Zhaoge

Day and night,
the Wei River flows

Ziya sits alone fishing,
his hook above the water

Even before the dream of the flying bear,
he waited at the riverbank

As the sun falls slowly behind him,
he thinks of his white hair

☰ ☰ ☰

The king showed Jiang Ziya the designs for the Deer Terrace. He said, "We want you to build this for us. It's a big job, but we know you can do it."

Jiang Ziya looked at the designs. The king waited for a few minutes. Then he looked at Jiang Ziya and said, "I want you to build this. How long will it take?"

Jiang Ziya studied the designs for the Deer Terrace. He thought about it. Then he replied, "This is a huge project, Your Majesty. It will take thirty-five years, maybe longer."

The king turned to Daji to ask her what she thought. She said, "Your Majesty, what good is the Deer Terrace if it's not ready until we are both too old to enjoy it? I do not trust this man. He is just a poor magician who knows nothing about how to build anything."

"You are right, my dear," said the king. Turning to his guards, he said, "Take this magician away. Execute him using the Burning Pillar."

"Your Majesty," said Jiang Ziya quickly, "please wait and listen to me. Building the Deer Terrace will need many workers and a huge amount of money. But the kingdom has no money anymore. The people are hungry, the country is at war, and you spend all your time in bed with your concubine. Please do not continue on this path. It will destroy you and the kingdom."

The king was enraged. He shouted to his guards, "Seize this fool! Cut him into little pieces!" But before the guards could grab him, Jiang Ziya ran out of the palace. He ran to the Nine Dragon Bridge, jumped off the bridge, and disappeared under the water. The guards ran after him. When they got to the bridge, they looked down at the water but they could not see him. They thought he had drowned, but in fact, Jiang Ziya had flown away on an invisible water cloud.

A few minutes later, Supreme Minister Yang Ren came to the bridge. The king had named him Supreme Minister after the previous Supreme Minister, Mei Bo, was executed on the Burning Pillar. Yang Ren saw four guards on the bridge looking down at the water. He asked them what they were looking at. They told him that Jiang Ziya had jumped off the bridge.

"Why did he do that?" asked Yang Ren.

The leader of the guards replied, "His Majesty told him to oversee the building of a huge new building called Deer Terrace. Jiang Ziya spoke against the king. So of course, the king became angry. He ordered us to kill him by cutting him into many pieces. That's why Jiang Ziya jumped off the bridge."

"What is this Deer Terrace?" asked Yang Ren. The leader of the guards told him.

Yang Ren was unhappy about this situation. He went to see the king, who was at the Star Picking Mansion with Daji. He kneeled before the king and said, "Your Majesty, our nation has three big problems right now. In the east, the son of the late Grand Duke Jiang Huanchu is fighting against us. In the south, the son of the late Grand Duke E Chongyu is also fighting against us. And in the north, Grand Tutor Wen Zhong has been fighting at the North Sea for ten years but has not won the war yet. Many good people have died in these three wars, and it has been very expensive. We have no more people and no more money. Please, Your Majesty, stop this foolish project."

But the king did not want to hear this. He told his guards, "Take this traitor out of here and remove both of his eyes." The guards did as they were ordered. They gouged out Yang Ren's eyes, then they brought the eyes back to the king on a plate.

Even though the king took both of Yang Ren's eyes, the Supreme Minister continued to do his job and help the king. In the heavens, a Daoist immortal named Master Pure Void Virtue saw this. He told one of his disciples to bring Yang Ren to his cave in the sky. The disciple flew to Star Picking Mansion. Then he created a big dust storm and took Yang Ren's body while it was hidden by the dust.

The king's servants told the king what had happened. He said to Daji, "The same thing happened when I was about to execute the two princes. It looks like this is happening a lot these days. It's nothing to worry about. But now we need someone else to oversee the building of the Deer Terrace." He selected Chong Houhu, the cruel Grand Duke of the North.

The disciple brought Yang Ren's body to the Daoist's cave. The Daoist poured a little bit of magic elixir into both eye sockets. Then he blew a magic breath. "Rise up, Yang Ren!" he cried. Yang Ren sat up. In each eye socket there was now a tiny hand. In the palm of each hand was a tiny eye. Now Yang Ren could see again, but he could also use his new eyes to see all the secrets of heaven and earth.

He looked around and saw the Daoist. He bowed and said, "Thank you, Sir. Please take me as your disciple and let me serve you for the rest of my life." The Daoist agreed. Yang Ren stayed with Master Pure Void Virtue for several years.

Back at Zhaoge, Chong Houhu brought thousands of workers from all parts of the kingdom. He worked them day and night. Many of the workers, mostly the young and old, died while working there. Their bodies were thrown into the foundations of the Deer Terrace. Many others tried to flee the country.

Jiang Ziya flew back to his home on the water cloud. His wife met him and said, "Welcome home, husband and minister!"

He told her that he was no longer a minister of the king, and that the king had tried to kill him. He said, "We need to leave Zhaoge. Let's go to West Qi. We can wait there until it is time for me to help the new king."

But his wife was not happy. She said, "Husband, you should have obeyed His Majesty and built this Deer Terrace. We would have had lots of money. Why did you argue with the king like that, when everyone else knows which way the wind is blowing? You are nothing but a poor magician, and you are a fool. I will not follow you to Qi."

"A wife must follow her husband. We will have a good life in West Qi, and you will have money and happiness there."

"No, I am a native of Zhaoge, and I will not leave. Our marriage is over. Give me a divorce."

Jiang Ziya wrote a letter of divorce and held it in his hand. He said to his wife, "As long as this letter is in my hand, we are still husband and wife." Without waiting even a second, she reached out her hand and grabbed the letter. He said quietly, "The bite of a snake and the sting of a wasp are nothing compared to this woman's heart."

Jiang Ziya packed up his things and left the house. He traveled west towards the province of West Qi. He crossed many rivers and mountains. Finally, he came to Lintong Pass. There he saw hundreds of people. They were sitting on the ground, crying.

"Who are you and why are you here?" he asked.

One of them replied, "We are all from Zhaoge. The king has named Chong Houhu to oversee the Deer Terrace project. He has ordered that two out of every three men must work on the project. Tens of thousands have already died. If we go there, we will probably die too. So we left Zhaoge. But now we cannot get through the pass because the commander will not let us through."

"Don't worry," he said, "I will take care of this." He put down his luggage and went to see the commander. The commander heard that an official from Zhaoge was here to see him, so he let Jiang Ziya in. But after he heard what Jiang Ziya had to say, he became angry.

He said, "You are not a court official, you are just a poor magician. The king gave you wealth and power, but you turned your back on him. You say that you want to help these people, but all I see are a bunch of traitors and cowards. The law says that I should arrest you and send you back to Zhaoge. But this is the first time we have met, so I will be kind and let you go. Now get out of here."

Jiang Ziya returned to the crowd of people. He told them what the commander had said. They all began to cry. "Please don't cry," he told them. "I can help you but you must do exactly what I tell you. Wait until night comes. Then close your eyes. You may hear the sound of wind. Don't worry about that. And do not open your eyes. If you do, you will die."

When night came, the people all closed their eyes and waited. Jiang Ziya kowtowed towards Mount Kunlun. Then he began to say some magic words. A strong wind came. It picked up all the people. The wind carried them across Linton Pass, across several other passes and mountains, all the way to Golden Chicken Mountain. Then the wind placed them safely on the ground. Jiang Ziya told them, "You can open your eyes now. You are at Golden Chicken Mountain in the province of West Qi. You can go now."

The province of West Qi was governed by the Grand Duke of the West, Ji Chang. But Ji Chang was a prisoner, forced to live in Youli by the king's order. So the province was governed by Ji Chang's eldest son Bo Yikao.

Bo Yikao took good care of the hundreds of people. He gave them food and homes and jobs. He also talked with the people, and they told him everything that was happening in Zhaoge.

Bo Yikao said to his ministers, "My father has been a prisoner for seven years. Nobody from his family has gone to see him. What good are his ninety-nine sons if we cannot help him? I must go and see him. I will take the family's three great treasures and give them to the king. Perhaps then the king will let my father return home."

Chapter 19
Gifts for the King

The loyal minister's son dies
Because of the king's fox demon

The evil king plays with his concubine
And ignores his ministers

Better for him to die from ten thousand knife cuts
While keeping his honor

History will tell his sad story;
Tears fall like pearls

≡ ≡ ≡

Bo Yikao said goodbye to his mother. Then he went to see his younger brother Ji Fa and said, "Guard the province while I am in Zhaoge. Don't change anything, and take care of your brothers."

Then he set out on the journey to Zhaoge. He passed quickly over five mountain passes and across the Yellow River. Finally, he arrived at Zhaoge and stayed overnight at a hostel.

The next day he went to the palace. He waited all day but nobody came to let him inside. He did not dare to enter on his own. So he returned to the hostel. He went back on the second, third and fourth days but was still not invited into the palace. Finally on the fifth day, while he was waiting at the gate, he saw the Prime Minister Bi Gan coming on horseback. He knelt before the Prime Minister.

"Who is kneeling before me?" asked Bi Gan.

"I am Bo Yikao, son of the criminal Ji Chang."

Bi Gan got off his horse and raised the young man up, saying, "Please get up, Prince. Why are you here?"

"Sir, when my father offended His Majesty, you saved his life by speaking to the king. My family will never forget this. Now my father has been a prisoner for seven years, living in Youli. We are worried about him. I have come here to ask His Majesty to let my father return to his home. In return, I have brought the king valuable gifts."

"What are these gifts?"

"I have brought four gifts. First, I have brought a magic carriage that comes from the ancient Yellow Emperor. It can go wherever the rider wants to go, without need of driver or horses. Second, I have brought a magic carpet that makes any drunk person sober as soon as he lays down on it. Third, I have brought a white-faced monkey that sings and dances. It knows three thousand eight hundred songs. And finally, I have brought ten beautiful young women for the king's harem."

"These are wonderful gifts, but I'm afraid His Majesty is too far gone to change his ways. In fact, these gifts might make things worse. However, I will tell him and we will see what he does."

Bi Gan went to the palace and told the king that Ji Chang's son had come to see him. The king ordered the young man to enter the palace. Bo Yikao entered, fell to his knees, then he walked on his knees until he was close to the throne. Without looking up from the floor he said to the king, "The son of your criminal minister wishes to speak with you, Your Majesty."

"Speak, young man," said the king.

"Our family is grateful that you have allowed my father to live. I now ask you to let him return to his family so that he may live the last few years of his life at home. If you do this, your kindness will be remembered for ten thousand years."

While he was speaking, Daji stood behind a curtain secretly looking at him. She liked what she saw. The young man was tall, strong and handsome. She came out from behind the curtain and walked until she was standing next to the king. She said to the king, "Your Majesty, I have heard that this young man is a great musician, a master at playing the guqin[1]." Turning to Bo Yikao, she smiled sweetly and said, "I have heard that you play the guqin very well. Would you play a song for me?"

Still looking at the floor, Bo Yikao said to the king, "Please, Your Majesty, my father has suffered for seven years. My heart is broken.

---

[1] The guqin is a plucked seven string instrument, similar to a zither, that according to legend has been played in China for five thousand years. In 1977 a recording of guqin music was included on the Golden Record that was sent out to interstellar space on the Voyager 1 and 2 spacecrafts.

How can I take pleasure in music at a time like this?"

"Yikao," replied the king, "play us a song. If we like it, we will set you and your father free."

This made Bo Yikao happy. He thanked the king. Servants brought in a guqin. He sat on the floor, put the guqin on his knees, and began to play this song:

> Willows move in the morning breeze
> Peach blossoms glow in the sun
> Without care for carriages running east and west
> The grass covers the earth like a green blanket

Music came from Bo Yikao's fingers like the tinkling of jade, like the sound of pine trees in the forest. The king loved the music. He said to Daji, "You are right, this young man plays beautifully."

Daji also enjoyed the music. But what she really wanted was to enjoy Bo Yikao. She though he was very handsome and strong. Then she looked at the king and thought he was old and weak. She said to herself, "I must keep this handsome young man here. I will find a way to get him into my bed. I think he will be a lot more fun than that old king."

She said to the king, "Your Highness, I have an idea. You can let Ji Chang go home, as we have no need for him. But keep Bo Yikao here. He can teach me to play the guqin, and he can play for you anytime you want."

"That is a wonderful idea," said the foolish king, and he agreed.

Daji ordered the palace servants to prepare a feast. During the feast she raised her golden cup of wine and toasted the king again and again and again, until the king was too drunk to even sit up. When he fell asleep, she told the servants to put him to bed. Then she asked Bo Yikao to teach her how to play the guqin.

The two of them sat on the floor, each one with a guqin on their knees. Bo Yikao told her about the guqin: when to play it, when to not play it, how to hold it, how to use one's hands to play the strings, and so on. Daji listened, giving him smiles and warm looks with her eyes.

Bo Yikao knew that Daji was trying to seduce him, but he knew that it would be a terrible mistake for him to go along with her. So he kept his heart like ice. He did not even look at Daji during the lesson.

Daji saw that she was not getting anywhere with the young man. She ordered another feast, and told Bo Yikao to sit next to her. He replied, "I am the son of a criminal. I would not dare sit next to the queen. If I did, I should die ten thousand deaths!" He remained sitting on the floor, not even looking up at her.

Daji had one more idea. She told the servants to clear away the feast. Then she said to him, "Let's continue with the lesson. But you are too far away from me. I cannot learn like this. I will sit on your lap. You can put your arms around me and hold my hands. That way you can teach my hands how to play the strings. I will learn much more quickly."

Bo Yikao was in trouble now. He said to himself, "I think it is my fate to die here. But I would rather be an honorable ghost than a dishonorable man." Then he said to her, "Your Majesty, if I did as you ask, I would be no better than a beast. You are the queen, the mother to the country, honored by all. Please do not lower yourself like this. If the people learned about this, they would never honor you again."

Now Daji was furious at Bo Yikao. She ordered him to leave the palace. Later that night, in bed, the king asked her how the lesson went. She replied, "I must tell you, that young man was not interested in teaching me to play the guqin. He only wanted to use my body for his own enjoyment. When I saw what he was trying to do, I sent him away."

The next morning, the king ordered his servants to bring Bo Yikao back to the palace. He said, "Why did you give the queen such a bad lesson yesterday? She still cannot play the guqin."

The young man replied, "Your Majesty, it takes time to learn to play the guqin."

The king did not want to say anything about the seduction. He said, "Play us another song, young man." Bo Yikao sat on the floor and played this song:

> My loyalty reaches to the heavens
> May His Majesty live forever!
> May the rain and wind come at the proper time
> May the kingdom be strong and last forever

The king liked this song and could not find anything wrong with it. When Daji saw this, she said, "Your Majesty, I have heard that the white-faced monkey can sing very well. Let's hear it sing."

The servants brought out the monkey. Bo Yikao gave it two wooden clappers that it could use to play while it sang. The monkey sang a beautiful song. As the king listened to the song, he forgot his anger. As Daji listened, all evil thoughts left her body. She even forgot who she was. The fox spirit floated out of her body.

Daji did not know that the monkey was more than just a monkey. It was a powerful spirit who had studied the Way for a thousand years. It saw the fox spirit. Dropping the clappers, it attacked Daji. The queen jumped backwards. The king hit the monkey and killed it with one blow from his fist.

Daji started to cry, saying, "That young man tried to use the monkey to kill me!"

"I did not do anything!" cried Bo Yikao.

"How can you say that?" shouted the king. "Everyone saw your monkey try to kill the queen!"

"Your Highness, monkeys are wild animals. They do not always do as they are told. This one likes to eat fruit. When he saw the fruit in front of the queen, it tried to grab some of it. Besides, how could a little monkey harm a person? It had no weapons of any kind."

The king thought about this for a while. Gradually his anger left him. He said to Daji, "This young man's words make sense. The monkey was a wild animal."

Daji said, "Your Majesty, you have been kind to this man. Let him play another song. But if there is any anger or criticism at all, then you must execute him."

"Of course, my dear," said the king.

Now Bo Yikao saw that he could not escape the net thrown by Daji. He sat on the floor to play one more song.

> *A king is always good to his people*
> *He will never be cruel to them*
> *Hot pillars turn flesh to ash*
> *Long snakes feast on bellies*
> *The sea is full of blood*
> *The forest is full of corpses*
> *The people are hungry*
> *But the Deer Terrace is full*
> *The farms are dying*

> But the king eats well
> May the king remove evil ministers
> And bring peace to the nation

The king shouted, "Guards, grab that traitor and execute him!"

But Bo Yikao said, "Wait! I am not finished with the song." Then he sang,

> May the king let go of his lust
> May he get rid of the evil queen
> When the evil is gone
> The ministers will gladly obey
> When the lust is gone
> The kingdom will be at peace
> I am not afraid of death
> But you must kill evil Daji

Then he stood up and threw the guqin straight at Daji's head. The queen jumped out of the way and fell to the floor.

"Guards!" shouted the king. "Trying to kill the queen with a guqin is a terrible crime. Throw him in the pit of snakes!"

"Wait," said Daji, getting up from the floor. "Give him to me. I will deal with him." She told the soldiers to nail his feet and hands to planks of wood. Then she ordered the soldiers to cut off his flesh, bit by bit. Bo Yikao continued to shout at her until he died.

When he was dead, Daji said to the king, "I have an idea. Let's cut up the flesh into little pieces. Then we will make meat pies out of it and give them to Ji Chang. If he eats the pies, that means he is just an ordinary man and you can let him go home. But if he refuses, that means that he is a sage, and you should kill him to prevent trouble."

The king agreed. Bo Yikao's flesh was sent to the kitchen, where it was made into meat pies. Then he ordered the meat pies to be sent to Ji Chang in Youli.

Chapter 20
San Yisheng Bribes the Ministers

Since ancient times, evil ministers love wealth;
They harm the loyal and virtuous

To spare a life, they demand that gold and silver be put in their bag[1]

They think only of themselves;
They don't care about the pain of their country

But everything can change in a second;
They don't know that the sword is already coming down

≡ ≡ ≡

During the seven years that Ji Chang was a prisoner in Youli he never spoke in public and never caused any trouble. He spent his time studying divination. He wrote a book that would later be called the Book of Changes (I Ching). He also relaxed by playing the guqin.

One day while playing the guqin, he heard an unhappy sound coming from the lowest string. The sound was like death. He stopped playing and did a divination using gold coins. This is how he learned that his son had died. The divination also told him that the king wanted to give him his son's flesh to eat.

Soon after that, a messenger arrived carrying a plate of meat pies. The messenger told Ji Chang, "His Majesty is worried about your health. He went hunting yesterday and killed a deer, so he ordered the kitchen to make the deer meat into pies for you."

Ji Chang knew that this was a trap. If he refused to eat the pies, the king would know that he was a powerful magician and would have him killed. So he said to the messenger, "How kind is our king! Even though he was tired from hunting all day, he still found time to think of his criminal minister. Long live His Majesty!"

---

[1] In the original Chinese poem, the ministers demanded that coins be put in a *jīn chán*, a special purse made of rich brocade that was used as a tip jar for performers in ancient times.

He ate one of the meat pies. Then he ate another, then one more. The messenger watched him eat the pies but said nothing. Then he left and returned to Zhaoge. He went to the palace and said to the king, "The criminal Ji Chang thanked you many times for the meat pies. He ate three of them. Then he kowtowed and said, 'Long live His Majesty!' He kowtowed again and asked me to deliver his words to you."

The king smiled and said to Fei Zhong, "So, Ji Chang has eaten the flesh of his own son. It looks like he is not a powerful magician at all, just an ordinary man. I think there is no danger if let him return home."

Fei Zhong replied, "Your Majesty, please be careful. I think Ji Chang is trying to trick you. He knew that you would kill him if he refused to eat the pies. It would be dangerous to allow him to return home. There is already trouble in the west, you don't want any more!"

The king said, "No man, not even a sage, could eat his own son's flesh. But maybe you are right. I will keep him in Youli."

Meanwhile, the soldiers and servants who had traveled with Bo Yikao to Zhaoge heard that their master had been killed. That night they all fled back to Qi. When they arrived home they told Ji Fa, the younger brother of Bo Yikao, what had happened to his older brother.

Ji Fa cried and said, "How could the king do such a thing? Even though my father has been a prisoner for seven years we have remained loyal to the king. But now the king has killed my older brother. The bond between king and his people has been broken."

Then one of Ji Fa's generals stood up and shouted, "It is time for us to fight! We must send an army to Zhaoge, get rid of this evil king, and bring peace to our country!"

But the Prime Minister, a man named San Yisheng, stood up and said, "Master, you should cut off that man's head. He is a fool and will cause us great trouble."

Ji Fa replied, "Why should I cut off the head of my general?"

San Yisheng said, "Think of your father Ji Chang. He has been a prisoner for seven years, but he remains loyal to the king and he is alive. If you send an army to Zhaoge, the king will execute him before our army even reaches the city."

The room grew quiet as the ministers thought about this. Then San Yisheng continued, "You know that Ji Chang did a divination and told us he would be a prisoner for seven years. He told us not to send anyone to save him. But your older brother did not listen, and now he is dead. He should not have gone to Zhaoge. And he should have done things differently. He should have bribed the evil minister Fei Zhong. That way Fei Zhong would have spoken to the king and helped to free Ji Chang. Once Ji Chang was free, we could have raised an army and attacked the king."

Ji Fa said to San Yisheng, "You speak well, Prime Minister. Tell me what should we do now?"

"Send two of your best ministers. Have them wear the clothing of merchants. One of them should give valuable gifts to Fei Zhong. The other one should give valuable gifts to another minister, a man named You Hun. Both of them have the ear of the king. By bribing them both, you will make sure that the king does what we want."

Ji Fa agreed. Two of his ministers were given valuable gifts to bring to Zhaoge. They traveled over five passes and across the Yellow River and arrived at Zhaoge. They did not stay in the hostel used by ministers. Instead, they stayed at a small inn that was used by merchants.

The next evening, one of the ministers went to see Fei Zhong. Fei Zhong said to him, "Who are you and why are you here at this late hour?"

The minister replied, "Sir, please forgive me for coming here so late in the evening. You have been very good to us and you have saved the life of our master Ji Chang. We are grateful to you. I have some small gifts for you. I also bring a letter from San Yisheng, the Prime Minister of West Qi."

The minister handed San Yisheng's letter to Fei Zhong. It said,

> *Supreme Minister Fei Zhong. I am sorry that I have never met you. But all of us in West Qi thank you for your help. Our master Ji Chang foolishly said some things which angered His Majesty. But because of your help, he is still alive and living in Youli. Please accept these small gifts as our way of thanking you. Also, please think about our master, who is old and sick and wishes to return home. If you could speak to the king about this, we would remember your kindness for ten thousand years.*

Fei Zhong looked at the gifts, which included 2,400 taels of gold and two pairs of white jade coins. "These gifts are very valuable!" he thought to himself. He told the minister to return to West Qi. He said he needed a bit of time to him think about how to help get Ji Chang released.

Meanwhile, the other minister had a similar meeting with You Hun. Satisfied, the two ministers returned to West Qi.

Fei Zhong and You Hun were both very happy with the bribes, but of course they did not say anything to each other about the meetings or the bribes.

A few days later, the king was relaxing, playing chess with Fei Zhong and You Hun. The king won all the games. Afterwards they had a feast. The king said, "I heard that Ji Chang ate the flesh of his son. So of course, he is no magician."

Fei Zhong said, "Your Majesty, you know that I have never trusted Ji Chang. However, I sent some of my men to Youli to keep an eye on him. They tell me that Ji Chang is loyal to you. He burns incense for you on the first and the fifteenth of every month. He prays for your health and for peace in the kingdom. He has never said anything bad about you in seven years."

The king turned to You Hun and asked, "And what do you think of Ji Chang?"

You Hun had listened to Fei Zhong's words. Now he knew that Fei Zhong had also received bribes. He knew that he needed to do something more in order to earn the bribes that he had just received. So he said to the king, "I have also heard that Ji Chang has been loyal to Your Majesty. In seven years, he has done nothing to harm the country. Moreover, I think that Ji Chang could help us to win the wars that we are fighting in the east and south. Perhaps you could give him the title of Prince and put him in command of the dukes' armies. Once the rebels in the east and south hear of this, they will put down their weapons and go home."

The king was pleased to hear that his two most trusted ministers both agreed on this. He gave the order that Ji Chang be freed and should come to see him. A messenger went to Youli to tell Ji Chang.

Ji Chang said goodbye to the people of Youli and traveled to Zhaoge to see the king. He entered the palace, dressed in white because he was a criminal. He kowtowed to the king, saying, "The criminal Ji Chang should be executed for his crimes, but Your Majesty has chosen to let me go home to see my family again. May you live for ten thousand years!"

The king replied, "Ji Chang, you have been a prisoner for seven years but have never said a word against me. You are a loyal minister. I am letting you go home. I am also naming you prince[1], the leader of all the dukes, so you can use their armies to protect the kingdom. There will be a great feast in your honor. After the feast, you may parade through the streets for three days." Ji Chang kowtowed again.

For the next two days, Ji Chang paraded through the streets. Late on the second day, he saw a large group of men on horseback coming from the other directions. He saw that it was General Huang Feihu riding on his huge ox. Ji Chang dismounted and bowed to Huang Feihu. Huang Feihu dismounted from his ox, bowed to Ji Chang, and invited him to come to his home later that evening.

The two men ate and drank for a while. Then Huang Feihu said to Ji Chang, "My friend, I can see that you are happy today. But you must see what is happening! Our king spends all his days drinking and talking with evil ministers like Fei Zhong. He spends all his nights playing with his concubines. He has executed many loyal ministers. He has thrown people into the pit of snakes. You must do something about this! Stop parading through the streets. Go back to Qi immediately and do something to help your country!"

Ji Chang felt like he had just awakened from a dream. He bowed and thanked Huang Feihu. He said, "Thank you, my friend. I will leave right away. But how can I get home?"

Huang Feihu replied, "I can help you. Put on the clothes of an army officer. Take these tiger tallies[2]," and he handed him some tallies. "You will be able to go through the five mountain passes with no trouble."

Ji Chang again bowed and thanked Huang Feihu. That night, Huang Feihu ordered his men to open the gates of the city. Ji Chang and a small group of soldiers left the city under cover of darkness.

---

[1] Now that the king has named Ji Chang as a prince, the original book sometimes refers to him as Prince Wen. But we will continue to call him Ji Chang.
[2] Tiger tallies, called *hǔfú*, were used in ancient China as a way for kings and emperors to authorize and delegate the power to generals to command and dispatch an army. The tiger was a symbol of courage.

Chapter 21
Flight Through Five Passes

Huang saved Ji Chang, he gave him a tally;
This allowed him to leave the king's land

You and Fei asked the king to stop him,
Help came from the clouds for the Qi lord

Good people usually don't live long in this world,
Now the flying dragon brings auspicious news

Ji Chang vomited his son's flesh,
But sweet fragrance remains in his mouth

≡ ≡ ≡

Ji Chang did not return to his hostel that night. The officials at the hostel waited for him. When he did not appear, they went to tell Fei Zhong.

Fei Zhong went to see the king, but he was very afraid. He went to the Star Picking Mansion and kowtowed again and again before the king. Then he said, "Your Majesty, I must tell you that Ji Chang only finished two days of parading through the city streets. Now he is gone. Nobody knows where he is, but I think he has left the city."

The king was very angry. He said, "You told me that I should name him Prince and forgive his crimes!"

Fei Zhong continued to kowtow. Without raising his head, he said, "Your Majesty, who can understand the human heart? You know the saying, 'When the sea dries up you can see the bottom, but even when a man dies nobody can know what was in his heart.' The criminal Ji Chang has been gone for less than a day. There is still time to catch him. You can send soldiers to bring him back to Zhaoge, then you can cut off his head."

The king sent an army of three thousand soldiers on horses with orders to catch Ji Chang. The soldiers left the city through the west gate.

Ji Chang was in no hurry. He had crossed the Yellow River and was riding towards the first mountain pass. He rode slowly west, enjoying the beautiful weather. Suddenly he heard the sound of many horses behind him. Turning around, he saw a cloud of dust rising in to the air. "Oh no!" he said to himself. "I have been very foolish. That must be the king's army. If they capture me, I will be a dead man." Then he began riding westward as fast as he could, with the king's army close behind him.

Meanwhile, on Mount Zhongnan, the Master of Clouds was sitting outside his cave. He looked down and saw the army chasing Ji Chang. Quickly he called one of his disciples and told him to fetch Thunderbolt. A few minutes later Thunderbolt arrived and kowtowed to his master.

"Disciple," said Master of Clouds, "your father is in danger. You must go quickly and save him!"

"My father? Who is that?" asked Thunderbolt.

"Don't you remember? It is Ji Chang, the Grand Duke of the West. Go quickly to Tiger Cliff to find a weapon, then come back here to see me."

Thunderbolt left the cave and went to Tiger Cliff. He looked around but did not see any weapons. He was about to leave when he smelled something delicious. He followed the smell. He came to a little stream running down the mountain. It was a beautiful place. All around were trees and grasses. Foxes and deer wandered through the trees, and birds flew overhead. Looking up, he saw two red apricots hanging from a tree branch. He reached up and pulled the two apricots off the branch.

"I will eat one and give the other to my master," he thought. But when he ate one, it was so delicious that before he could stop himself he ate both of them.

A moment later, there was a loud "Pop" and a long wing suddenly appeared under his left arm. Then there was another loud "Pop" and another wing appeared under his right arm. Then his body began to change. His face turned a dark blue, his hair turned red, his teeth grew long and his eyes grew large. His body became twenty feet tall.

He stood there with no idea what was happening. Just then, the disciple came up to him and said, "Brother, our master orders you to come immediately to see him."

Thunderbolt walked back to his master's cave. His head was down and his long wings dragged on the ground. Master of Clouds saw him. "Wonderful, wonderful!" he said. "Come with me."

They walked together to a nearby peach garden. Master of Clouds picked up a large golden cudgel. He handed it to Thunderbolt and started to teach him how to use it. Thunderbolt learned how to move the cudgel up and down, left and right, how to turn like a tiger of the forest, and how to rise like a dragon from the sea. The cudgel flew through the air, filling the air with bright light.

When he was finished, Master of Clouds wrote the word "Wind" on his left wing and "Thunder" on his right wing. Then he told his disciple, "These two words will let you fly through the heavens. Now go quickly and help your father get away from the soldiers. Help him go through the five passes. But you must not hurt any of the soldiers. When you are finished, return here so you can finish your studies."

Thunderbolt flew quickly down to earth. He saw a man in a black shirt on a galloping horse, with thousands of soldiers chasing him. He shouted to the man, "Are you the Grand Duke of the West?"

Ji Chang looked up and saw a huge bird holding a golden cudgel. He was terrified, but he shouted back, "Who are you? How do you know my name?"

Thunderbolt came down to the ground and kowtowed. "Forgive me, Father, I did not mean to frighten you."

Ji Chang had many sons, but none of them looked like this. He replied, "Why do you call me Father? I don't know you."

"My name is Thunderbolt. You found me in the forest seven years ago and made me your son. Now you are in danger. I can help you get through the five mountain passes and return safely to West Qi."

"All right. But you must not hurt or kill any of the soldiers. I am already in a lot of trouble; I don't want you to make it worse."

"Of course. My master told me the same thing." Then Thunderbolt flew into the sky. He flew back towards the army and came down to earth right in front of them. Waving the golden cudgel, he shouted, "Stop right there!"

The soldiers stopped. Some of them turned back. But the two generals shouted, "Attack!" and charged towards Thunderbolt.

Chapter 22
The Grand Duke Returns

Ji Chang returns home after eating his son;
His tears never dry

This do not change who he is;
He is still loyal to his king

No one can say what heaven has written;
But crimes always bring blood and ashes

It does not matter what happens on earth;
Heaven always decides who must leave and when

☰ ☰ ☰

Thunderbolt saw the two generals coming towards him. He held up his golden cudgel and said to them, "My friends, please stop. My name is Thunderbolt. I am the hundredth and youngest son of Ji Chang, the Grand Duke of the West. He has been a loyal minister for his whole life. He is filial to his parents, he is loyal to his friends, he upholds the law and does his best to be a good subject of the king. But the king made him a prisoner for seven years. Recently the king set him free and allowed him to return home. So why are you chasing him and trying to capture him? My friends, you do not need to show your courage. Go back home and leave us in peace."

One of the generals laughed loudly and said, "You ugly beast! Your words are the words of a fool!" Then he rushed towards Thunderbolt, attacking him with his sword.

Thunderbolt easily blocked the sword with his golden cudgel. Then he said, "Please stop. I would enjoy fighting you, but my master and my father both told me not to hurt your or any of your soldiers. Before you attack me again, watch this."

While the generals watched, Thunderbolt jumped up into the sky. He landed on a side of a nearby mountain. He swung his golden cudgel at another mountain. With a loud roar the mountain split in half. He said to the generals, "Do you think your heads are stronger than that mountain?"

That was all the generals needed to see and hear. They turned and led their soldiers back to Zhaoge. Thunderbolt returned to his father and said, "I spoke with the generals and asked them to go home to Zhaoge. They are leaving now. Now it's time for me to take you home to West Qi."

"Thank you," said Ji Chang. "But what about my horse? He has been my loyal servant for seven years."

"Father, the horse is not important. Let it go."

Sadly, Ji Chang patted the horse on its head. He said, "I don't want to leave you here, but the soldiers might come back again. Go now and find yourself another master." Then he climbed on Thunderbolt's back and closed his eyes. He felt the wind on his face as Thunderbolt jumped into the sky and flew quickly through the air. After a few minutes they had flown over all five mountain passes and arrived at Golden Chicken Mountain. Thunderbolt came down to earth and said, "Father, we have arrived. I must leave you here. Take care. I will see you again."

Ji Chang looked around. He said, "But son, we are not at West Qi City yet. We are still in the mountains far from the city. Why are you leaving me here?"

Thunderbolt replied, "I must leave you here, Father. My master ordered me to only take you beyond the five mountain passes. You must travel the rest of the way by yourself. I will join you later, when my magic is more powerful." He knelt down and kowtowed to his father. Then he jumped into the sky and flew back to Mount Zhongnan.

Having no horse to ride, Ji Chang turned and began walking west. He walked all day. He was an old man and was exhausted by the end of the day. Stopping at an inn by the side of the road, he ate some dinner and went to bed. But in the morning, he realized that he was not carrying any money. He could not pay for his food and his room.

The clerk, a young man, was very angry. He said, "How can you stay here and eat our food, then not pay for it?"

Ji Chang replied, "I am sorry, young man, but I have no money with me. All my money is in West Qi City. Please let me leave. I will be happy to pay you later."

The clerk said angrily, "You may not know this, but you are in the province of West Qi. Nobody here will steal from another person. The Grand Duke of the West rules with kindness and fairness. Everyone here lives in peace and happiness. Now you need to pay what you owe, or I will take you to see the Supreme Minister."

Just then, the innkeeper came to see why the two people were arguing. He looked carefully at the visitor and saw he was Ji Chang, the Grand Duke of the West. The innkeeper kowtowed and said, "Please forgive us, Your Highness. We had eyes but did not see you. I am the owner of this small inn. It has been in my family for over a hundred years. Please sit down and have some tea."

Ji Chang was happy. He said, "Sir, I am glad to meet you. Do you have a horse that I can ride to the city? I will of course pay you for it when I return."

"Your Highness, we are not wealthy people, we have no horses. But we have an old donkey. You can ride the donkey, and I will go with you to make sure you arrive safely at the city."

Ji Chang was pleased to hear this. Soon he and the innkeeper left the inn and began traveling west. They traveled for several days until they reached West Qi City. It was late autumn. The trees were turning from green to red, and cold winds blew. Ji Chang had been gone for seven years, and he missed his family.

In West Qi City, Ji Chang's mother was sitting at home. She felt a strange wind come in through the window. She did a divination and learned that her son was returning. Quickly she told her grandchildren and the ministers. They all came out of the city and waited in the road for Ji Chang to arrive.

Soon Ji Chang arrived, riding the innkeeper's donkey. His eldest son Ji Fa stepped forward. He said, "Father, you were a prisoner for seven years. Your children did nothing to help you. We are no better than criminals. Please forgive us. We are overjoyed to see you again!"

Ji Chang began to cry. He said, "My friends, my sons, I never thought that I would come home and see you again! I am very happy, but I can't help but feel a bit sad at the same time."

Supreme Minister San Yisheng stepped forward and said, "In ancient days, King Tang was also made a prisoner. He was kept in Xiatai for many years. When he was finally freed, he united the entire country and became the first king of the Shang Dynasty[1]. Now that you are home again, perhaps you will be like King Tang, and your years at Youli will be like his years in Xiatai."

But Ji Chang said, "Your words have no meaning for me. A loyal subject of the king would never do such a thing. I am a criminal, but His Majesty was kind to me and only imprisoned me for seven years. Now he has set me free, named me a prince, and ordered me to fight the rebels. I will never turn against our king. And I ask you to never speak like that again."

He returned to his home to see his wife and his mother, then he put on his official robes. He rode his coach through the streets, greeting the people of West Qi City. Everyone in the city came out to see him. They sang, danced and shouted his name.

As he looked at the people, he thought of his son Bo Yikao. He remembered eating his son's flesh. He fell to the ground, screaming. His face turned as white as paper. Then his belly made a strange sound. He opened his mouth and vomited up a piece of meat. The meat fell onto the ground. Then it grew four feet and two long ears, turning into a rabbit. The rabbit ran towards the west and disappeared[2].

Ji Chang saw the rabbit run away. Then he vomited up three more pieces of meat. They also turned into rabbits and ran away towards the west.

The ministers took him to see his doctors, who told him to rest for a few days. After resting, he met with his ministers and told them the whole story of his imprisonment, his release by the king, and his escape back to West Qi with the help of Thunderbolt and the innkeeper. "Please make sure that the innkeeper is given a good amount of money to thank him for helping me," he said.

Then Supreme Minister San Yisheng tried one more time to get Ji Chang to rebel against the king. He said, "Master, two thirds of the kingdom and four hundred marquises are now in rebellion against the

---

[1] King Jie was the last ruler of the Xia Dynasty, which was the first dynasty in China. It was said that he drank day and night with his concubines and made a lake of wine large enough to float full sized boats. Chen Tang led an uprising against Jie. Tang was exiled to Xiatai but was later released, He then led an army that deposed Jie and established the Shang dynasty in the 16th century B.C.

[2] The *Book of Documents*, one of the five classics of ancient Chinese literature, says that when Ji Chang vomited up his son's flesh, he created rabbits on earth. The Chinese words for rabbit (兔) and vomit (吐) are both pronounced *tù*.

king. Now you have returned home like a dragon returning to the sea or a tiger returning to the mountain. This is the time for us to act."

One of his generals spoke up, saying, "My Lord, we need to act now. We have 400,000 soldiers and sixty generals. We should attack the mountain passes, surround Zhaoge, and cut off the heads of Daji and Fei Zhong. We can name a new king and bring peace to the kingdom."

But again, Ji Chang refused to turn against the king. He said, "You both have been loyal subjects, but now you both speak like criminals. How can you forget that the king is the head of the kingdom? A minister must be loyal to the king, just like a son must be filial to his father. Without thinking I spoke words against the king, and the king was right to punish me as he did. Now I am grateful to the king for letting me return home. I wish that the rebels would put down their weapons. Please stop this talk, and I hope I never hear you speak like this again."

The general replied, "What of your son Bo Yikao? He only went to Zhaoge to help you, and you know what the king did to him. We must have a new king!"

"No, my son caused his own death. I told him that I would be a prisoner for seven years, and I told him not to come and see me. He disobeyed my orders. He did not understand the situation. That is why he lost his life. Now that I have returned, my job is to help the people of West Qi to have a better life, not to start a war."

San Yisheng and the general listened to his words. They kowtowed to Ji Chang.

"Now," continued Ji Chang, "I want to build a new building, south of the city, to be called The Spiritual Terrace. It will be used for divination, to see the future. This will help the people of West Qi. But I'm afraid it will be too expensive."

"Please don't worry about that," said San Yisheng. "You have been good to the people. They are grateful to you and would be happy to help build it. And if want, you can pay them with silver and let them come and go as they wish."

This made Ji Chang very happy. He sat down and wrote the notice that would be put up on the gates of the city.

Chapter 23
Dream of a Flying Bear

Ji Chang is the king's loyal servant;
His loyal subjects are happy to work for him

They build the Spiritual Terrace;
He puts money in their pockets

West Qi stands on a strong foundation;
The king's empire drowns under the sea

No need to discuss the fate of Mengjin;
Everything is in the dream of the flying bear

☰ ☰ ☰

Ji Chang's notice read:

> West Qi is a peaceful land, but from time to time we have had floods and droughts here. We need a way to learn what the weather will be. For this reason, I wish to build a Spiritual Terrace in a place just west of the city. Many workers are needed for this project. If anyone wishes to work on this project, I will pay you one tenth of a tael of silver for each day of work. You may start and leave whenever you wish. If you do not want to work on this project, I will not order you or anyone else to do this.

The people of the city read the notice. They were happy to learn that the Spiritual Terrace would be built, and they were even happier to learn that they would be paid in silver to work on the project. Many workers stepped forward, and in just ten months the project was finished.

After the Spiritual Terrace was built, Ji Chang saw that the *yin* and *yang* were not quite correct. The terrace needed a pool of water on one side. He told this to San Yisheng. A short time later, a group of workers started to dig a hole for the pool. As they were digging, they found a skeleton buried in the ground. They told Ji Chang about the skeleton. He told the workers to go and bury the skeleton somewhere else.

By this time, it was late in the day. Ji Chang ate dinner on the Spiritual Terrace, then he decided to spend that night in a room on the terrace instead of returning to the palace.

That night he had a strange dream. In the dream, a big white tiger flew in from the southeast. It crashed into the room where Ji Chang was sleeping. Then there was a loud "Boom!" at the back of the terrace, and a bright white light shot into the sky.

Ji Chang woke up from the dream. He thought about it but he did not know what it meant. In the morning he asked San Yisheng about the dream.

"Your Highness," said San Yisheng, "this is a very good dream. The animal in your dream was not a tiger. It was a flying bear. This means that a great minister will soon come here and enter your service. The bright white light is the future peace and happiness of West Qi."

Ji Chang thanked him. Then he returned to his palace, thinking about who the great minister might be.

Meanwhile, let's return to Jiang Ziya. After he helped the people who were trying to leave Zhaoge, he went to live in a small hut in the forest. There was a river near the hut. Every day he sat on the ground, his back against a willow tree, and he fished. As he fished, he recited Daoist scriptures, and his mind was always on the Dao.

One day, as he was reciting Daoist scriptures and fishing, he heard a man nearby. The man was singing this song:

> *Over the hills and across the mountains*
> *The air is filled with the sound of my axe*
> *The axe is with me all the time*
> *I use it to cut away vines*
> *Rabbits run across the fields*
> *Birds sing in the trees*
> *I am just a happy woodcutter*
> *I have no money but I don't care*
> *I sell my wood to buy food*
> *I have rice, vegetables and good wine*
> *At night I sleep beneath the trees*
> *My life is good, I have no worries at all*[1]

---

[1] This song is strikingly similar to the song of the woodcutter who Sun Wukong meets in Chapter

When the song was finished, the woodcutter walked up to Jiang Ziya. He dropped his firewood on the ground and sat down. He said, "Sir, I often see you fishing here. May I have a little chat with you?"

Jiang Ziya replied, "Yes, of course! A chat between a fisherman and a woodcutter, just like in the old stories![1]"

The woodcutter said, "Sir, my name is Wu Ji. Please tell me, what is your honorable name, and where do you come from?"

"My name is Jiang Ziya, but sometimes I am called Flying Bear."

Wu Ji laughed loudly. "My friend, great sages have two names. But you are nobody. You are just an old man who sits and fishes all day. You remind me of the man who waits all day for a rabbit to run into a tree and knock himself out. You don't look like a great sage to me."

Then the woodcutter looked closely at Jiang Ziya's fishing line. He laughed again and said, "My friend, you look old, but you have learned nothing in your years. Look at this fishing hook!" He held up the fishing hook in his hand. It was just a straight needle. "You may fish for a hundred years but you won't catch anything. Let me tell you what to do. First, make this needle red hot and bend it into a hook. Then put a bit of meat on it. Wait for a fish to bite, then quickly pull the fish out of the water."

Jiang Ziya just smiled at the woodcutter. He said, "You only know half of the story, my friend. I don't care about catching fish. I am waiting to catch a duke, or perhaps a king."

"So, you want to be a duke or a king? You look like a monkey to me."

"Well, I may not look like a duke or a king. But your face doesn't look very good either. Your left eye is a little bit green and your right eye is a little bit red. That tells me that you will kill a man in the city today."

Wu Ji stood up. He said, "We were just having a friendly chat. Why did you suddenly say such a terrible thing to me?" Then he picked up his firewood, turned, and walked away.

---

1 of *Journey to the West* (see our book, *The Rise of the Monkey King*).

[1] This conversation is very similar to the one between the fisherman and the woodcutter in Chapter 10 of *Journey to the West* (see our book, *The Emperor in Hell*). There are many stories and songs in Chinese folklore about a fisherman and a woodcutter discussing the meaning of life. Education was valued in ancient China, but Daoism stressed the value of living in simplicity and harmony with nature. Thus, educated people may talk at length without getting anywhere, but simple people such as these can quickly get to the heart of the matter.

The woodcutter arrived at the city. He walked through the marketplace, trying to sell his firewood. Just then, Ji Chang was traveling through the marketplace on his way to the Spiritual Terrace. Guards rode ahead of him, shouting, "Get out of the way! Get out of the way!" Wu Ji turned quickly to get out of the way. He still had his load of firewood on his back. One long piece of firewood had a sharp end. As Wu Ji turned around, the firewood struck a city guard in the head, killing him instantly.

Other guards quickly arrested the woodcutter. Ji Chang stopped his horse. He looked down and asked the woodcutter, "Why did you do that?"

Wu Ji said, "I did not mean to kill that guard. I was trying to get out of the way. My wood swung around and hit the guard."

"I am sorry, but you killed a man. Now you must pay with your life. That is the law here in West Qi."

He ordered his men to draw a large circle on the ground. He ordered Wu Ji to stay inside the circle and wait there until it was time for his execution. This was the custom in West Qi. Since Ji Chang could know everything through divination, nobody, not even a criminal, would dare to try and escape the circle. They knew that they would be captured, and things would be much worse for them.

Wu Ji waited inside the circle for three days. He thought of his mother, who was waiting for him at home. He started to cry. Just then, San Yisheng passed by and saw the woodcutter crying. He said, "Why are you crying? It is the custom in West Qi for a killer to pay with his life. Crying will not change that."

Wu Ji replied, "Please forgive me, sir. I know that I must pay with my life. That is not why I am crying. I am thinking of my poor mother who is waiting for me at home. When I am executed there will be nobody to take care of her. She will die at home and her bones will remain unburied. Thinking about this breaks my heart."

San Yisheng thought about this. Then he said, "Don't cry. I will talk to His Highness about this. Perhaps you can go home, take care of your mother for a while, then come back later for your execution." Wu Ji kowtowed in thanks.

San Yisheng went to the Spiritual Terrace and talked with Ji Chang about the matter. Ji Chang agreed to let the woodcutter return home for a while. Wu Ji was allowed to leave the city and go home.

When he got home, his mother said, "My dear boy! Where have you been? I was afraid that a tiger had killed you on the mountain. I have not been able to eat or sleep for several days."

Wu Ji told her what had happened. He told her about meeting the old man who fished with a straight needle. Then he told her about the old man's divination, and the killing in the marketplace.

She said to him, "My boy, that was no ordinary fisherman. He was a great sage. You must go back to him and beg him to save your life."

Wu Ji thanked his mother. Then he went looking for Jiang Ziya.

Chapter 24
From Fisherman to Prime Minister

Jiang Ziya left busy Zhaoge to rest here,
where green waters surround the hills

He reads Daoist books to pass the time;
Three golden fish smile at him

Birdsong fills the air;
He listens to the sound of the stream

The garden is covered with morning dew;
It waits for the arrival of Ji Chang

≡ ≡ ≡

Wu Ji went to the stream where he had seen the fisherman earlier. There, sitting under a tree, was Jiang Ziya. Wu Ji walked up quietly behind him. Without turning around, Jiang Ziya said, "Aren't you the woodcutter I met a few days ago?"

"Yes sir," said Wu Ji, "I am."

"Did you kill someone that day?"

Wu Ji threw himself down on the ground and cried. He told Jiang Ziya everything that had happened in the city that day. Then he said, "When autumn comes, I must go back to the city. I will be executed for killing that man. There will not be anyone left to care for my mother, and I fear that she will die soon afterwards. I beg you, please save us!"

Jiang Ziya said, "This is your fate. Fate is hard to change. You killed a man, so now you must pay with your life. What can I do?" But Wu Ji continued to cry. Finally, Jiang Ziya said, "All right, I will save you. But you must become my disciple."

Wu Ji kowtowed and agreed. Jiang Ziya continued, "Now that you are my disciple, I must help you. Go home and dig a hole next to your bed. Make it four feet deep. Sleep in it tonight. Tell your mother to throw a few grains of rice on top of you. That's it. You will have no more trouble."

Wu Ji ran home and told his mother. "We must do as the sage commands!" she said. Wu Ji dug the hole as his master had ordered him to, his mother threw some rice on top of him, and he slept in the hole that night. That same night, Jiang Ziya said some magic words to cover up Wu Ji's star so that nobody could see it in heaven.

The next day, Wu Ji returned. Jiang Ziya said, "I don't want you to spend all your time cutting wood. Every afternoon you must study military strategy. If you do this, you will become a minister. Remember what the ancients say: 'No one is born a general or minister; a person must work hard to get ahead in life.' "

Meanwhile, San Yisheng was thinking about the woodcutter. He said to Ji Chang, "Do you remember that woodcutter, the one who killed the guard? I let him go home to care for his mother. But he has not returned. I wonder what happened to him."

Ji Chang did a divination. He said, "Ah, I see. The woodcutter threw himself into a deep pool of water and drowned. So he is dead. There's nothing else we need to do now."

Winter came and went, and spring arrived. One day Ji Chang said that he wanted to get out of the city and enjoy the beautiful weather. He rode out of the east gate on his horse, accompanied by his ministers and hundreds of soldiers. As they rode, they saw colorful flowers, tall grasses, and beautiful birds. Farmers worked in the fields, and young girls picked tea leaves.

After a while they came to a hill. Ji Chang saw that his soldiers had arrived there before him and had killed a large number of deer, foxes and tigers. The ground was red with their blood. Ji Chang was very unhappy when he saw this. He said to his prime minister, "This is not right. You know that the ancient emperor Fuxi did not eat meat[1]. Fuxi said, 'People eat meat when they are hungry, they drink blood when they are thirsty. But I only eat grain because I want all creatures to live in peace.' Here we are, enjoying the beautiful weather. How can we enjoy ourselves when animals suffer because of us?"

San Yisheng bowed. He told the soldiers to stop killing animals.

---

[1] Fuxi is a mythical emperor, the brother and husband of the goddess Nüwa. It is said that he created humanity and invented music, hunting, fishing and cooking.

A little while later, they saw some people sitting by a stream, drinking and singing. Some of them were singing this song:

> Remember King Tang[1] who killed the tyrant
> It was the will of heaven and the people
> King Tang brought peace to the land
> Six hundred years ago
> Today we have another tyrant
> He loves wine, women and killing
> While his people go hungry
> Deer Terrace is covered with blood
> I wash my ears clean of power and money
> Every day I sit by the stream and fish
> Every night I study the stars
> I will live with no worries at all
> Until my hair turns white

"That is a well written song!" said Ji Chang. "Go find out who wrote it." One of his generals rode his horse over to the group of singers and asked them who wrote the song.

One of them told him, "The song was written by an old fisherman. He lives about thirty-five *li* from here, next to a stream. He fishes there every day. We heard him singing the song there."

Ji Chang said to San Yisheng, "Did you hear the words, 'I wash my ears clean of power and money'? It reminds me of a story about the ancient emperor Yao. He had a son but the son was worthless. So he searched for a good man to be the next emperor. One day he found a man sitting by a stream and playing with a golden ladle in the water. He asked the man what he was doing. The man said, 'I have walked away from fame, money and family. I only want to live here in the forest.' Yao said, 'Sir, I am the emperor. I see you are a good man. I do not want my worthless son to be the next emperor. Would you please take this job?' The man immediately jumped into the stream and started washing his ears in the water."

San Yisheng laughed, and the two men continued riding and enjoying the weather. Soon they came to a group of woodcutters singing this song:

---

[1] This is Cheng Tang, the first king of the Shang Dynasty and mentioned in Chapter 22. He overthrew King Jie, a tyrant and the last king of the Xiao Dynasty.

> *When dragons rise in the air, clouds appear*
> *When tigers come, the wind blows*
> *But no one comes to see me*
> *Remember Yi Yin who worked in the fields*[1]
> *He waited for King Tang to find him*
> *Remember Fu Yue, poor and forgotten*[2]
> *He waited for King Gaozong to dream of him*
> *Since ancient times, some people become famous*
> *While others remain forgotten and poor*
> *I spend my life here by the stream*
> *Resting under the sunshine*
> *While kings and dukes fall*
> *I look to the heavens and smile*
> *While waiting for a wise ruler*

Once again, Ji Chang though this was a good song. He sent his general to ask who wrote it. The woodcutters told the general that the song was written by an old fisherman who lived by a nearby stream.

"We should go and see this old fisherman," said Ji Chang. But just then, a woodcutter came. He was carrying firewood and singing this song:

> *In the spring, waters flow without end*
> *In the spring, grasses are beautiful*
> *The goldfish have never seen Yinpan River*
> *The world does not know me*
> *They think I am just a fisherman*
> *Sitting by the stream all day*

"This must be the sage we were looking for!" said Ji Chang.

But San Yisheng looked at the woodcutter and said, "Your Highness, this is no sage. This is Wu Ji, the man who killed your guard in the marketplace last year."

Ji Chang said, "It cannot be. My divination said that the woodcutter killed himself last year." But he agreed that the man was Wu Ji. He ordered the woodcutter arrested. Then he said angrily, "How dare you

---

[1] According to legend, Yi Yin was a farmer living in obscurity. King Tang had to ask him five times to join his government. He became a high official in Tang's government.

[2] Gaozong was the temple name of Emperor Wu Ding of the Shang Dynasty. He dreamed that he would meet a sage named Yue, and sent officials throughout the land to find him. Fu Yue was discovered in a woodshed and became Chancellor in Wu Ding's government.

run away and try to escape your fate!"

Wu Ji threw himself on the ground and kowtowed to Ji Chang. He said, "Your Highness, I have always been a good man. When you set me free, I went to see an old fisherman named Jiang Ziya. They also call him Flying Bear. He took me as his disciple and let me live and work without fear. Sir, even ants and worms try to live as long as they can. Shouldn't men do the same?"

Ji Chang discussed the matter with San Yisheng. Then he let Wu Ji go and asked him to take them to meet the old fisherman. They all rode to the stream, but when they arrived the old fisherman was not there. They went to his small house nearby, but the servant boy said that the old fisherman was not at home and he did not know when his master would return.

San Yisheng said to Ji Chang, "Your Highness, I think we are doing this wrong. You know that when the ancient emperors went to meet great sages, they did not just go. They selected a good day, they washed, and they did not eat meat. We should go home and do these things correctly."

Ji Chang agreed with this plan. They returned to the city. Ji Chang ordered his ministers to spend three days preparing for their second visit to the stream. On the fourth day, they put on their best robes and returned to the stream. Ji Chang rode in his carriage.

When they got close to the stream, Ji Chang told everyone to stop and wait. He got down from his carriage and walked quietly to the stream. He saw Jiang Ziya sitting by the stream, fishing. Ji Chang stood quietly behind him. Jiang Ziya was singing this song:

> *The wind blows from the west*
> *White clouds fly in the sky*
> *Where will I be at the year's end?*
> *Five phoenixes sing as my master comes*
> *Few men truly know who I am*

When he stopped singing, Ji Chang said softly, "Are you truly happy?"

Jiang Ziya turned around and saw the prince. He threw himself to the ground and said, "Please forgive me, Your Highness, I did not know you were here."

Ji Chang helped him to stand up and said, "I have been looking for you.

I was here once before, but I was not prepared to meet you. Now I have prepared, and here you are. I am very happy to meet you."

"Your Highness, I am an old man. I know nothing of how to be a minister or a general. You should not have wasted your time coming to see me."

San Yisheng said, "These days, the nation is troubled. Our king spends his days drinking wine and playing with his concubines. He treats his people worse than dogs. He has killed two of the four Grand Dukes. Many of the marquises have risen up against him. My master has come today with gifts, hoping that you will help him rule the nation." Then he put the gifts on the ground in front of Jiang Ziya. "Please," he said, "get onto His Highness's carriage and come with us back to the palace."

But Jiang Ziya would not get into the carriage. He said, "I am a man of low rank, how could I possibly ride in His Highness's carriage?"

Ji Chang and San Yisheng tried to get him to ride the carriage, but he refused. Finally, they asked if Jiang Ziya would ride on the horse that pulled the carriage. He agreed. In that way they all rode back to the palace.

When they arrived at the palace, Ji Chang named Jiang Ziya prime minister of West Qi. Jiang Ziya was eighty years old when he began his work as prime minister. He did his job well. West Qi was peaceful and the people were happy.

News of Jiang Ziya's new job reached the commander of one of the nearby mountain passes. He sent a messenger to Zhaoge to tell the king what was happening in West Qi.

Chapter 25
A Feast for Demons

The Deer Terrace was built for the gods;
Only demons came to the feast

Ordinary people cannot escape the ordinary world[1];
How can a mortal mind see past the mortal trap?

If you try to trick a wise man,
Your evil actions will only make things worse

Only a fool like this king would obey evil Daji
And kill the virtuous

≡ ≡ ≡

The messenger rode for several days until he arrived at the capital city. He gave his report to Bi Gan, the Prime Minister and the king's uncle. Bi Gan went immediately to see the king in the Star Picking Mansion.

"Your Majesty," said Bi Gan, "I have just heard that Ji Chang, the Grand Duke of the West, has named Jiang Ziya as his prime minister. This is bad. You know that the Grand Duke of the East and the Grand Duke of the South are already rebelling against us. In the north, Grand Tutor Wen is busy fighting rebels there. If Ji Chang also rises up against us, we will be in serious trouble."

The king listened. But before he could say anything, an attendant came in to tell the king that Chong Houhu, the Grand Duke of the North, wanted to see him. The king told the attendant to bring him in.

"Your Majesty," said Chong Houhu, "you ordered me to build the Deer Terrace. I am happy to tell you that after two years and four months, the project is finished."

"That is wonderful!" said the king. "As long as you are here, we have to

---

[1] In the original poem, this line reads "Muddy bones cannot escape the muddy world." Muddy bones means an ordinary person, as opposed to a saintly person who is clear and beyond worldly things.

tell you something. We just heard that Ji Chang has named Jiang Ziya as the prime minister of West Qi. What should I do about that?"

Chong Houhu laughed. "Don't worry about him, Your Majesty. I know that man. He is like a frog at the bottom of a well[1]. He knows very little and he can do nothing to harm us. If you sent your army to fight him, all the marquises would just laugh at you."

"You are right of course," said the king. "Now, we would like to take a look at the Deer Terrace. We will take the queen to go and see it. You and Bi Gan may join us there."

A short time later, the king and Daji rode in the royal carriage to the Deer Terrace, followed by dozens of servants and maids. It really was a beautiful building. The towers were tall and covered with blue tile roofs. Inside the building were several halls. Each hall had bright white pearls set into the ceiling, so it looked like a night sky full of stars. Everything in the halls was made of jade and gold.

The king loved it. But Bi Gan thought only about the huge cost of the project, and all the workers who had died building it. He thought, "The paintings on the walls are made from the blood of the people, and the halls are built from the spirits of the dead."

The king ordered a big feast with music and dancing. He said to Daji, "My love, do you remember what you said to us? You said that when the Deer Terrace was finished, immortals would come down from heaven to visit us there. Now the Deer Terrace is finished. When do you think the immortals will come?"

Of course, Daji knew nothing at all about immortals, and she had no idea how to call them. She had just said this to trick the king into building the Deer Terrace. She needed some time to come up with a plan. "Your Majesty," she said to him, "the immortals cannot come now. They will come when the moon is full and the sky is clear."

"There will be a full moon in five days," he replied. "Let's come back then and meet the immortals." He was hungry for Daji, so he took her to their bed and played with her the rest of the night.

For the next four days Daji thought about how to trick the king into

---

[1] There is a well known Chinese folk tale of a conceited frog who lived at the bottom of a well. The frog thought he knew everything about the world, but in fact he only knew what little he could see by looking up at the sky from the well.

thinking that immortals were coming to visit. On the fourth night she gave the king a lot of wine. He fell asleep. As soon as he was asleep the fox demon came out of Daji's body. It flew on a gust of wind to the cemetery where the grave of Emperor Xuanyuan was, thirty-five *li* outside of the city. Dozens of powerful demons lived there.

One of the demons, Nine Headed Pheasant Demon, greeted her. It said, "My dear, why are you coming to visit us here? I thought you were enjoying life in the royal palace and had forgotten all about us."

"My old friend," replied the fox demon, "I have not forgotten about you. The king has built a Deer Terrace and wants to meet immortals there. I would like you and the other demons to change your appearance so you look like immortals. Then come to the Deer Terrace when the moon is full tomorrow night."

Nine Headed Pheasant Demon said, "I am sorry but I cannot come tomorrow night, I have to do some other things. However, thirty-nine of the demons here are powerful enough to change their appearance. They will all come to your Deer Terrace tomorrow night."

Daji thanked her and returned to the palace. In the morning she told the king, "Your Majesty, tonight is the full moon. Thirty-nine immortals will come to the Deer Terrace. If you meet them, you will have a long and happy life."

The king was pleased to hear this. He told Bi Gan to come to the Deer Terrace that night. Bi Gan thought this was a stupid idea, but he said he would come.

That night, the king, Daji and Bi Gan came to the Deer Terrace, accompanied by dozens of servants and maids. A great feast was prepared. They sat and waited in the cool evening with the stars shining overhead. Finally, the moon rose in the eastern sky. A great wind began to blow, thick clouds covered the sky, and the earth became cold from heavy fog. Then up in the sky, thirty-nine immortals appeared. Of course, they were not really immortals; they were demons. Some of them were hundreds of years old. These demons had eaten the *qi* of heaven, earth, sun and moon, and had the ability to change their appearance. Now they all looked like Daoist sages. They wore robes of blue, yellow, red, white and black.

One of the demons called out, "Today we are honored to come to this feast given by the King of Shang. May his dynasty last a thousand years!"

The king told Bi Gan to walk out onto the terrace and serve them wine. Bi Gan saw thirty-nine Daoist sages sitting in chairs, in three rows of thirteen chairs each. "How strange!" he thought. "They really do look like immortals."

He greeted the demons and offered them wine from a golden pitcher. They looked beautiful. But although they could change their appearance, they could not change their smell. They smelled bad, like foxes. Bi Gan smelled them and thought, "Immortals are beautiful and smell clean. These are beautiful but they smell terrible. I think these might be demons."

He gave each of the demons more wine to drink. The fox demons had never tasted the king's wine before, and it was very strong. As they drank the wine, they became drunk. They began to lose their ability to change their appearance. Their fox tails reappeared and could be seen hanging out of their robes. Bi Gan saw this. "Oh no," he thought, "here I am serving wine to a bunch of fox demons." He finished serving the wine. Then as quickly as he could, he left the Deer Terrace and mounted his horse. Two attendants rode ahead of him, holding red lanterns to light the way.

As he rode away from the terrace, he met general Huang Feihu riding towards him. He told Huang Feihu, "My friend, I was just on the Deer Terrace with His Majesty and Daji. I was serving wine to thirty-nine immortals. But then I learned that they were not immortals at all, but evil demons. I could see their fox tails by the light of the moon. What should I do?"

"Don't worry," replied Huang Feihu, "I will take care of this matter. You go home and go to bed."

Huang Feihu ordered his men to watch the gates leading out of the city. He told them to watch for demons walking or flying away from the Deer Terrace. If they saw any, they were to follow them to see where they were going.

A short time later, the feast was over and the fox demons all left the Deer Terrace. They were very drunk and had difficulty flying. Several of them fell to the ground. They walked slowly, in groups of three and five, back to their home at the grave of Emperor Xuanyuan. The soldiers saw this and reported it back to Huang Feihu.

The next morning, Huang Feihu ordered three hundred of his soldiers to carry firewood to the grave, and to build a big fire at the hole where the fox demons had gone. They lit the fire and watched as it burned. When the fire had burned out, the soldiers pulled out the bodies of the dead fox spirits. The air was filled with smoke and the smell of burned flesh.

Huang Feihu told his men to collect the dead foxes that did not have any burns on them. He told them to skin them and make a fur robe for the king. He thought, "This will make the king happy because it will show that we are loyal. It will also be a warning to Daji."

But there is an old saying, "Mind your own business and you will have no trouble, but your nose into other people's business and disaster will follow."

Chapter 26
Daji Plots Revenge

On a windy and snowy night,
Bi Gan tried to give a gift and change the king's mind

He wanted to remove evil from the king's heart,
But now he is the demon's next target

The heart of Daji's demon is as cold as ice;
People will speak of its evil for ten thousand years

Too bad the Shang dynasty has come to this;
It has become like rain lost in springtime's flowing river

≡ ≡ ≡

Winter had arrived. Strong winds came from the north, and heavy snow covered the capital city of Zhaoge like a blanket of silver pearls. The wealthy sat around their stoves, eating hot soup and keeping warm. The poor had no rice to eat and no firewood for their stoves.

The king and Daji were sitting together in the Deer Terrace, drinking wine. An attendant arrived, saying, "Bi Gan is here. He wants to see you."

The king told the attendant to bring him in. When Bi Gan came into the room, the king said, "Uncle, it is cold and snowing. Why don't you stay home where it is warm?"

"Your Majesty," said Bi Gan, "the Deer Terrace is so high that it reaches all the way to heaven. It must be cold here. I brought you something to keep you warm." Then he gave the king the fox skin robe. The king put it on.

"Thank you, uncle," he said. "We have never seen such a beautiful robe." Then he invited Bi Gan to have some wine and enjoy the Deer Terrace with him.

When Daji saw the robe that was made from the skins of the fox demons, she felt like a sword had been pushed into her heart. She thought, "I will kill you, Bi Gan, you old bastard." But she did not show her anger to the king. Instead, she smiled at him and said, "Your Majesty, you are a great king, the dragon of this land. How can you wear a robe made from such a low animal as a fox?"

"You are right, my dear," replied the king. He took off the robe and gave it to his attendants.

Daji thought for several days about how to have her revenge on Bi Gan. Then one day she had an idea. While she was with the king, drinking wine, she changed her appearance so that she was not as beautiful as before. The king looked at her with a confused look on his face. Daji looked up at him and asked, "Why are you looking at me like that?"

The king said, "Because you are as lovely as flowers and as beautiful as jade. We want to hold you in our arms and never let you go." But he did not mean these words. He really was wondering why his concubine was now so unattractive.

"Oh, Your Majesty, I am not beautiful. But you should meet my sworn younger sister, Hu Ximei. She is a hundred times more beautiful than I am."

"Oh, I would like to meet her!" said the king.

"She is a nun. She has spent years in a mountain cave studying the Way. She lives at the Purple Sky Nunnery. I remember that she once told me, 'If you ever want to see me, just burn some incense and speak my name. I will come to you right away.'"

"Please, my dear, burn some incense and bring her here!"

"We must do this correctly, Your Majesty. Tomorrow night I will wash my body, then I will put out tea and fruit on a table in the moonlight. Then I will burn the incense."

Later that night, during the fourth watch while the king was asleep, the fox demon slipped out of Daji's body. It went to the grave of Emperor Xuanyuan to meet Nine Headed Pheasant.

When Nine Headed Pheasant saw the Thousand Year Old Fox Demon, she was very angry. "You asked my sisters to come to your Deer Terrace, and I helped you. That night they were all killed! This is your fault."

Thousand Year Old Fox Demon cried with her and said, "I am so sorry, my sister. But don't worry, we will have our revenge." Then she told

Nine Headed Pheasant her plan. Nine Headed Pheasant listened and agreed to the plan.

The next day, the king could not think of anything but meeting Daji's beautiful sister. He waited all day. Finally, the moon rose in the sky. He and Daji went up to the Deer Terrace. Daji said to the king, "Your Majesty, please understand that my sister is an immortal and also a nun. If she comes here and sees you, she might be frightened. Please go and wait in another room."

The king agreed. Daji washed her hands. Then she burned some incense and called out the name of her sister. Soon the wind began to blow, dark clouds covered the moon, and fog filled the air. It became very cold. Then they heard a sound like the tinkling of jade. "Here comes Hu Ximei, riding on the wind and the clouds!" cried Daji.

The king waited in the next room, watching through the curtains. The clouds disappeared and the moon came out again. In the moonlight he saw a Daoist nun. She wore a pink robe, a silk belt, and shoes made of hemp. Her face was as white as snow, her mouth was small and red, her cheeks were like peaches. She was the most beautiful woman the king had ever seen. The king thought that Daji was pretty, but Hu Ximei was like a goddess from heaven, like Chang'e come from the Palace of the Moon. His heart beat fast and he felt hot. "If I could sleep with Hu Ximei, I would be happy to give up my throne," he thought.

The two women were talking and sipping tea. Daji ordered a vegetarian feast, and the two of them ate together. They knew that the king was watching and listening, so Hu Ximei did everything she could to increase the king's desire for her. Watching her, the king could not sit still. Finally, he coughed to tell Daji that he could not wait any longer.

"Dear sister," said Daji, "I must ask you something. Please don't be angry with me."

"Of course, my dear," replied Hu Ximei.

"I have told His Majesty of your great virtue. He would like to meet you. But he wanted me to ask you first, to see if that was all right with you."

"Oh, sister," said Hu Ximei, "I don't think I could meet him. I am a nun, as you know. It would be against the rules for me to sit at the same table with him."

"No," said Daji. "You are not just a nun, you are now an immortal. You have moved beyond the rules of the three realms[1]. Besides, our king is the Son of Heaven. He has the right to meet with anyone he wants to. And remember, you and I are sworn sisters, so the king is really your brother-in-law. There's nothing wrong with meeting with a close relative!"

Hu Ximei nodded her head and said, "Then I will do as you ask."

As soon as he heard this, the king came out. He bowed to her. They greeted each other. Then he sat down, giving Daji and Hu Ximei the seats of honor. He stared at Hu Ximei, and she looked back at him, a hungry look in her eyes.

Daji knew that the king was drunk with desire. She stood up and said, "Your Majesty, please excuse me. I must go and change my clothes. Please keep my sister company for a while."

After Daji left, the king poured wine for Hu Ximei. He gave her the cup. She said softly, "You are too kind, Your Majesty."

The king felt like he was on fire. He asked her to take a walk with him on the terrace. She agreed. They walked out in the moonlight, with Hu Ximei's hand on the king's arm. She leaned her body against him, and he could feel the heat from her body.

"My dear," said the king, "leave that nunnery and live here in the palace with your sister! Life is short, and you will be very happy here. You will have wealth, power, and pleasure." She said nothing, but continued to keep her body close to his.

Seeing no resistance, the king picked her up and carried her to a nearby room. He set her down gently on a bed and took off her clothes. Then the clouds and rain came[2].

Afterwards, as they put their clothes back on, Daji came in. She smiled and said to them, "Well, what have you two been doing?"

"We just made love," said the king. "This was fated by heaven. From now on, the two of you will live here with me." He ordered another

---

[1] The three realms as defined in Buddhism are the realm of sensuous desire (*kāma*), the realm of the material world (*rūpa-dhāt*), and the realm of formlessness (*rūpa-dhātu*).

[2] According to legend, the lady Yaoji died unmarried, was buried at Wushan and became a goddess. Later, the king of Song was traveling through the area. He dozed off under a canopy and dreamed of her sharing a pillow with him. She left him with this poem: "Dawn is the clouds, dusk is the rain, day and night, under the canopy." Over time, "clouds and rain" became a metaphor for lovemaking.

feast. After they finished, he made love to both of them again.

For days, the king did not leave the room where he lay with Daji and her sister. They spent every day making love, singing, and drinking wine.

But one day, Daji cried out. She fell to the floor, spitting up blood. The king said to Hu Ximei, "I have never seen this before. What is going on?"

"Oh, her old illness has come back. When we were together in Jizhou, she had an illness of the heart. She almost died. The doctor helped her by giving her a special soup, made from a human heart that had seven openings."

"We must do that," said the king. "But where can we find someone who has a heart with seven openings?"

"Your Majesty, I can find out by divination."

"Do it at once!" said the king.

Hu Ximei moved her fingers as if she was doing a divination. After a minute she said, "Your Majesty, there is only one person in Zhaoge with this kind of heart, but I don't think he will want to give it up. It is your minister, Bi Gan."

"That is wonderful! Bi Gan is my uncle. He should be happy to give up a bit of his heart to let my queen live." He ordered Bi Gan to come see him immediately.

Bi Gan was at home when a messenger arrived to order him to come to the palace. "That's strange," he said to himself. "There is nothing going on in court. Why does the king want to see me?" Then another messenger arrived, and another. Finally, when the sixth messenger arrived, Bi Gan asked him what was going on. The messenger explained about the arrival of Hu Ximei, Daji's strange illness, and the divination.

Bi Gan was frightened. He went to say goodbye to his wife. "My dear," he said, "the evil concubine Daji is ill, and the idiot king wants to use my heart to cure her. I don't think you will see me alive again."

"Husband," said his wife, crying, "you have never done anything to cause the king to want you dead. How can he send you to such a cruel death?"

His son came in. He was also crying. He said, "Father, don't worry. Jiang

Ziya knew that this would happen. He left a note for you." Then he handed the note to his father.

Bi Gan read the note. Then he burned the note and mixed the ashes with water. He drank it. Then he put on his official robes and rode his horse to the palace.

When he arrived at the palace, the other ministers asked him what was going on. He replied that the king needed his heart, but that he did not understand the real reason. Then he went up to the Deer Terrace to meet with the king.

The king said, "Uncle! Our queen is very ill. She can only be cured by drinking soup made from a special heart, one with seven openings. You are the only one in the kingdom with such a heart. Please give us a small piece of it."

Bi Gan said, "How can I live if my heart is damaged? You are a foolish dog and you are not thinking clearly. Too much wine and too much sex, I think. If you kill me, that will be the end of your dynasty!"

The king shouted at him, "If the king demands your death, you must die. Now do as I command, or I will have my guards remove your heart!"

Bi Gan asked one of the guards for a sword. He said to the king, "When I die, I will meet the ancient kings in heaven. I have nothing to fear from them. Can you say the same?" He kowtowed towards the Ancestral Temple. Then he opened up his official robe. He pushed the sword into his own chest, making a large hole. He reached into the hole, pulled out his own heart, and threw it on the ground. Not a single drop of blood came from the wound.

Everyone stared at him. He stood up straight, closed up his robe, and left the terrace without saying another word.

As he walked out of the Deer Terrace, the other ministers shouted, "Bi Gan, how did it go with the king?" But he did not reply. He walked past them, mounted his horse, and rode towards the north gate of the capital city.

Chapter 27
The Grand Tutor Returns

The dynasty's birth and death are already written;
Nothing can change its fate

One minute the ministers discuss peace,
The next minute the armies start fighting again

Mortals try but they cannot change fate;
The gods decide the direction their lives will go

Evildoers are always punished in the end;
They try to escape but heaven does not listen

☰ ☰ ☰

Bi Gan rode away from the city quickly, the wind whistling past his ears. After riding for a few *li*, he heard a woman selling cabbages by the side of the road. She called out, "Tasty cabbages, sir. They have no heart!"

Bi Gan stopped his horse. He said to her, "But what if a man has no heart?"

"A man with no heart will die at once!" she replied. As soon as Bi Gan heard this, he cried out and fell from his horse. Blood poured out from his chest. The woman ran away as fast as she could.

What happened here? Bi Gan was alive because of the magic in the note that Jiang Ziya had written. The magic protected Bi Gan from harm, but the magic only worked if Bi Gan believed that it would work. If the cabbage selling woman had said something like, "A man can live even without a heart," Bi Gan would have continued to live. But she said that he would die. He believed her, and he died.

A few minutes later, two generals arrived. They had been sent by Huang Feihu, who had ordered them to follow Bi Gan. They saw Bi Gan's dead body on the ground. They turned around and rode as fast as they could to tell Huang Feihu and the other ministers what had happened.

One of the ministers, a young Confucian scholar named Xiao Zhao, was furious. "That tyrant killed his own uncle!" he cried. "That goes against the law and everything that is right. I am going to see him right now." He ran right into the Deer Terrace, not even asking permission.

The king was in the Deer Terrace, waiting for Daji's heart soup to be prepared. He looked up and saw Xiao Zhao. "What do you want?" he asked.

The young scholar said, "I am here to kill you!"

The king laughed. "I don't think a junior minister is permitted to kill a king."

"Oh, and is a king permitted to kill his own uncle in order to make soup? Bi Gan was your uncle, the younger brother of your father. You and that bitch Daji have broken the law. You are an evil tyrant, and I am going to kill you now!"

He grabbed a sword and ran towards the king. But the king was a very good fighter. He easily stepped aside, and Xiao Zhao's sword only stabbed the air. The king's guards ran towards Xiao Zhao. But before they could grab him, Xiao Zhao ran to the edge of the terrace and jumped to his death.

Meanwhile, Bi Gan's body was brought back to the city. Funeral preparations were made.

At the same time, the great general Grand Tutor Wen was returning to the city, riding his great black unicorn. He had just finally defeated the rebels at the North Sea. As he approached the city, he saw the flags of a funeral procession. "Whose funeral is this?" he asked.

"Bi Gan," said someone.

Grand Tutor Wen entered the city. He looked around. He saw the huge Deer Terrace. He saw the two tall yellow pillars. Then he entered the Grand Hall of the palace and saw the dust on the king's desk. "Everything has changed around here!" he said. "What are those yellow pillars?"

Huang Feihu replied, "They are called burning pillars. They are hollow and made of brass. If anyone does something that the king does not like, a great fire is built inside the pillars. When the pillars are red hot, the prisoner is tied against the pillars, face first. They are quickly burned to ash. In this way, many good men have died, and many more have left the city."

Grand Tutor Wen has furious. He had a third eye in his forehead. All three of his eyes became bright with anger, and a white light came out of his third eye. He shouted, "Strike the bells and ask His Majesty to come to the main hall!"

Back at the Deer Terrace, the king was resting with Daji. She had drunk the heart soup and appeared to quickly recover from her illness. An attendant came in and said, "Your Majesty, Grand Tutor has returned from the North Sea. He wants you to come to the main hall."

The king was silent for a minute. Then he said, "I will come."

An hour later, the king entered the main hall. He said to Grand Tutor, "You have defeated the rebels at North Sea. We are truly grateful to you."

"Thank you, Your Majesty," Grand Tutor Wen replied. "For fifteen years I have fought monsters, demons, rebels and thieves. You know that I will do anything to serve my king and my country. But I have heard that there is trouble here in Zhaoge. I have also heard that several dukedoms have rebelled. This worried me, and that's why I have returned. Please tell me what's going on."

"Two of the grand dukes, Jiang Huanchu and E Chongyu, were working together to kill me and take the throne. So I had them executed. Now their sons have risen up in rebellion."

"Who else heard Jiang Huanchu and E Chongyu saying that they wanted to kill you?" The king had no answer to this.

"What are those yellow pillars?"

"We use them when ministers are disloyal."

"What is that huge new building?"

"We go up there in the heat of summer. It is cool there and we have a nice view of the city."

Grand Tutor Wen became angry. He said, "Now I understand why the dukedoms are rebelling against you. You have failed in your duty to the nation. You do not listen to good ministers. You spend all your time playing with your concubines and plotting with evil ministers. You have spent the nation's money on foolish projects like the Deer Terrace and those brass pillars."

Grand Tutor Wen continued, "I remember when your father was king.

The people were happy and our borders were peaceful. Now there is trouble everywhere. I need to think about this. I will give you a report in a few days."

The king got up and returned to the Deer Terrace. Grand Tutor Wen went to see the other ministers. He said, "Please, tell me everything."

Huang Feihu bowed and began to speak. He told Grand Tutor Wen everything that had happened since Daji arrived at Zhaoge. When he was finished, Grand Tutor Wen said, "This is all my fault. I have been away from Zhaoge for too long and I have allowed this to happen. Now I must do something. In four days, I will give my report to the king."

The ministers all went to their homes. Grand Tutor Wen stayed in his house for three days, writing a memorial to the king. On the fourth day, he went to see the king. He said, "Your Majesty, I have a memorial for you." Then he laid the memorial on the desk in front of the king. The king read it. The memorial started off by discussing the king's failures. Then it made ten proposals:

1. Destroy the Deer Terrace.
2. Destroy the Burning Pillars.
3. Fill in the Pit of Snakes.
4. Fill in the Wine Pool and destroy the Meat Forest.
5. Banish Daji from the capital.
6. Cut off the heads of Fei Zhong and You Hun.
7. Open the granaries to feed the hungry people.
8. Send ministers to the East and South dukedoms to discuss peace.
9. Search the mountains and forests for wise sages.
10. Encourage the people to speak freely without fear.

When the king was finished reading, Grand Tutor Wen handed him an ink brush. He said, "Your Majesty, please sign your name."

The king replied, "We must think about the first item. The Deer Terrace is a beautiful building, and we spent much time and money building it. As for the fifth item, we will not send Daji away, because she is a good queen with many virtues. And as for the sixth item, we do not want to execute Fei Zhong and You Hun, they have served us well and committed no crimes. So, I approve all your proposals except for the first, fifth and sixth."

Grand Tutor Wen told the king that all ten proposals were important.

"The people are very unhappy about the Deer Terrace. The ghosts of the dead are weeping because of Daji. And the gods in heaven are angry because of Fei Zhong and You Hun. You must do all ten of these things, to save the nation."

The king stood up. "That's enough for now. You and I must discuss this again later. I will agree to seven of these proposals, but not all ten of them."

As the king started to leave, Fei Zhong and You Hun came into the room. They did not realize what was happening. Fei Zhong tried to speak to the king, but Grand Tutor Wen stepped in between them, saying, "Who are you?"

"I am Fei Zhong."

Grand Tutor Wen said, "Ah, so you are the one who has turned the king against his own people!" And he smashed his fist into Fei Zhong's face, knocking him to the floor.

"What did you do?" cried You Hun.

"And who are you?" asked Grand Tutor Wen.

"I am You Hun."

"So! The two of you are working together to make yourselves rich and powerful, while the nation suffers!" And with that, he raised his fist and knocked You Hun to the floor. He called to the guards, "Seize these two traitors and hold them for execution!"

The king said, "Those two have insulted you, but that is not bad enough to have them executed. They both will be tried according to law, and we will see what punishment they receive."

Grand Tutor Wen thought that he may have gone too far. He knelt before the king and said, "Your Majesty, I only want happiness for the people and peace for the nation. I want nothing else."

That was the end of the meeting. But shortly afterwards, a messenger arrived to tell Grand Tutor Wen that there was a new rebellion in the East Sea district.

Grand Tutor Wen went to see the king. He said, "There is a new rebellion in the East Sea district. I must deal with this. I need to go there with 200,000 soldiers. We can continue discussing the memorial when I return."

The king was very happy to learn that Grand Tutor Wen was leaving the capital. He quickly approved the plan.

A couple of days later, the army was ready to leave. The king went outside the east gate with Grand Tutor Wen and General Huang Feihu. The king raised a cup of wine to Grand Tutor Wen. But Grand Tutor Wen gave the cup to Huang Feihu. He said, "Let General Huang drink this wine. General, you must take care of the state while I am gone. Don't be afraid to do what must be done."

Then he turned to the king and said, "I hope you will take better care of the nation. Listen to your loyal ministers and don't do anything to make things worse. I will be back in a year, maybe less." Then he rode his horse to the front of the huge army, and they rode eastward.

Chapter 28
Punishing the North Grand Dukedom

The Grand Tutor returns in victory,
But he knows nothing of the evil in the kingdom

The king has failed in his duty;
The nation is broken and falls into chaos

The Grand Tutor offers ten proposals to save the kingdom;
He wants to remove all the evil ministers

The nation should be happy and prosperous;
He makes plans but knows that nothing will happen quickly

≡ ≡ ≡

Of course, the king was delighted when he found out that Grand Tutor Wen was leaving the capital. He immediately ordered that Fei Zhong and You Hun be released from prison and given their jobs back. Then he ordered a party for himself and invited all of his ministers to come to the royal garden.

It was a beautiful spring day. The garden was filled with flowers and birds. Green water flowed underneath a golden bridge into a blue pool full of goldfish. There was a white stone path through the garden, with two carved stone dragons on either side. Lovely palace maids walked through the garden bringing food and drinks.

The king sat in the library, with Daji and Hu Ximei sitting on either side of him. The other ministers were in the garden. As he ate, Huang Feihu said to the ministers, "I'm sorry but I cannot enjoy this banquet. The country is being torn apart by rebellions, how can I enjoy the flowers? The king must change his ways, or I'm afraid this dynasty will end soon." The other ministers nodded their heads in agreement.

The banquet ended at noon. But when the ministers went into the library to thank the king, he said, "It is such a beautiful spring day, why are you leaving? Stay, and I will come and drink with you." The ministers had no choice, they had to remain.

The drinking, singing and dancing continued. When darkness fell, the king ordered that candles be lit. In the library, Daji and Hu Ximei had become drunk from too much wine. The two women fell asleep. Then the fox demon inside Daji flew out of her body. It flew away on a gust of cold wind, looking for human flesh.

Everyone in the party felt the cold wind. Someone called out, "A demon is coming! A demon is coming!" Huang Feihu was half drunk, but he jumped up. He saw the fox demon coming towards him. In the darkness he saw that it had eyes like golden lamps, a long tail and very sharp claws. Huang Feihu had no weapon, so he broke off a piece of wood from the pavilion railing and swung it at the demon. He missed, and the demon attacked him.

"Fetch my hunting hawk!" shouted Huang Feihu. His guards went and got the hunting hawk, which was large and had golden eyes. The hawk flew up in the sky. It saw the fox demon and attacked it with its claws. The fox demon cried out and dove under some rocks in a nearby hillside.

The king saw this. He ordered his attendants to dig out the rocks to get to the fox demon. They dug down two or three feet into the hillside. They did not find the fox demon, but they found a huge pile of human bones. The king saw the pile. He said, "The Daoist sage told me that there was an air of evil in the palace, but I did not believe it. But now I see that he was right."

That was the end of the party. The ministers thanked the king and went home. Daji was still in bed, but she had bad scratches on her face. In the morning the king saw her face and asked what happened. "Your Majesty," she said, "last night after you left to drink with your ministers, I went for a walk in the garden. I walked into a tree branch and got these scratches on my face."

"My dear, you should be more careful!" said the king. "There are fox demons in the palace." Then he told her the story of what happened. But he did not realize that he was telling the story to a fox demon, and he did not know that he had been sleeping with that fox demon for the past several years.

Meanwhile, Jiang Ziya was serving as the prime minister for Ji Chang. One day he read a report that there was another rebellion against the king, and that Grand Tutor Wen had been sent to stop the rebellion. Then another report came, saying that the king had ordered Bi Gan's heart to be cut out of his body to be made into a medicinal soup for Daji. Then a third report came, saying that Chong Houhu was plotting with Fei Zhong and You Hun, and was making himself wealthy while the people went hungry.

Jiang Ziya went to see Ji Chang and told him everything he had learned recently. He said, "In my opinion, we must get rid of Chong Houhu. If he stays at His Majesty's side, disaster will follow. As you know, His Majesty gave you the power to fight traitors and rebels. Well, Chong Houhu is a traitor. If you get rid of him, you will help His Majesty be a great ruler again."

Ji Chang replied, "Tell me, if we send an army against Chong Houhu, who will lead it?"

"I shall serve you like a dog or a horse."

Ji Chang was happy to hear this, but he was also afraid that Jiang Ziya might be too eager to attack the city. So he said, "Good. But I will go with you, so we can discuss important matters together."

They gathered an army of 100,000 soldiers. Ji Chang carried an ox-tail hammer and a yellow axe, both given to him by the king to show that he had the authority to fight traitors and rebels. The Zhou army left West Qi City with the cheers of the people ringing in their ears.

A few days later, the Zhou army reached Chong City and set up a large camp just outside the city. Chong Houhu was not there, but the city was under the command of his son Chong Yingbao. Chong Yingbao said to his generals, "Ji Chang has decided to attack us. You remember that he fled Zhaoge a few years ago. Now he attacks us for no reason. Well, if he wants to throw away his life, that's fine with me." Then he told his generals to capture Ji Chang and bring him to Zhaoge.

The first fight was between one of Ji Chang's generals, a man named Nangong Kuo, and a general of the Flying Tiger army. The two of them fought on horseback, horses circling and swords flying. The Flying Tiger general was strong, but Nangong Kuo was stronger. They fought for thirty rounds. Then Nangong Kuo knocked the other man from his horse. Some Zhou soldiers ran up and cut the man's head off. They brought the head back to their camp and gave it to Jiang Ziya.

Chong Yingbiao saw this, and he was furious. He hit his desk with his fist and shouted, "Get the entire army ready. Tomorrow we will fight!"

The next day, the gates of Chong City opened and a huge army rushed out. They rushed towards the other army, then stopped a short distance away. They saw an old Daoist riding his horse towards the front lines. He had white hair and a long silver beard. He wore a gold hat and a robe tied with a silk belt, and he carried a sword in his hand. It was Jiang Ziya.

Jiang Ziya shouted, "Commander of the Chong army! Meet me at once!"

Chong Yingbao rode his horse forward. He wore gold armor over a red robe. He shouted, "Who dares to attack my city?"

"I am prime minister Jiang Ziya. You and your father are as evil as the sea is deep. You have taken the people's wealth like hungry tigers, and you have harmed them like wild wolves. You are not loyal to His Majesty. Now my master, Ji Chang, is doing the job that His Majesty has given him."

Then Ji Chang rode up next to Jiang Ziya and shouted, "Chong Yingbao! Get down off your horse and come with us. We will bring you back to West Qi and execute you and your father. There is no need for your soldiers to die for you."

Chong Yingbao shouted back, "Jiang Ziya, you speak big words but you are just a weak and foolish old man. And Ji Chang, you are a traitor to our nation!" Then he turned to his generals and asked, "Who will remove these fools for me?"

One general from Chong City rode forward, swinging his axe. He could not defeat either of his opponents, so Chong Yingbao sent two more generals into the fight. Jiang Ziya saw the situation and ordered six of his dukes to join the battle. Outnumbered, Chong Yingbao rode forward himself and joined the battle.

They fought for twenty rounds. Two of Chong Yingbao's generals were killed. Seeing that he was badly outnumbered, Chong Yingbao fled back to the city with the generals and the rest of his army. They closed the city gates. Chong Yingbao sat down with his generals to decide how to fight the Zhou army.

On the Zhou side, Jiang Ziya wanted to attack the city immediately. But Ji Chang said, "If we attack the city, jade and stone will be burned together[1]. Many people will die. We have no reason to kill the people of the city; we want to rescue them."

Jiang Ziya thought to himself, "My master is as virtuous as Yao and Shun[2]." So he decided to wait. He sent Nangong Kuo to Caozhou with a letter for the Marquis of Caozhou, the brother of Chong Houhu and the man known as Black Tiger. He hoped that Black Tiger would come and help them. Then he waited.

---

[1] "Burn both jade and stone" is a Chinese idiom meaning to destroy indiscriminately.
[2] Emperor Yao was born around 2717 BC. He was one of the first emperors of China, and is revered for his wisdom and fairness. He had nine sons but did not feel any of them were worthy to take his place, so he selected a brilliant young man named Shun to be the next emperor.

Chapter 29
Death of Two Grand Dukes

Chong Houhu is cruel and greedy;
He takes the people's wealth and makes it his own

He meets the king and wants to control him;
He uses a thousand different tricks to help himself

He works the people almost to death,
Then he makes plans to remove the king

Jiang Ziya has virtue, though his king has none;
He knows the dynasty will fall and many people will die

≡ ≡ ≡

Nangong Kuo left for Caozhou. He spent the night in a hostel, and the next day he went to see Chong Heihu.

"What brings you here to see me?" asked Chong Heihu.

"My lord, I have a letter for you. It's from prime minister Jiang Ziya."

Chong Heihu opened the letter and began to read.

Dear Chong Heihu,

A minister should be loyal to his king, helping him so that the people and the state will benefit. But if the king is evil, or if the king does things that are harmful to the people and the state, then a minister must not help him. You know that your brother has been doing evil. His crimes are as great as a mountain. For that, he is hated by the gods and the people.

My master, the Grand Duke of the West, has the authority to punish your brother. But if he does this, may people might die. So I ask you to do the right thing. Arrest Chong Houhu and bring him to the Zhou camp.

If you do this, you will be known as a virtuous and courageous man.

If not, people will think you are the same as your brother. They will not be able to tell the difference between jade and stone. Please think about this and give us your reply as soon as possible.

Jiang Ziya, Prime Minister

Chong Heihu read the letter, then he read it again. He sat and thought about it. Then he said quietly, talking to himself, "Jiang Ziya is correct. Even a filial brother should know when to do the right thing. If I arrest my brother, I will save the Chong clan from certain death. If this is unfilial, then I will apologize to my parents after my death." Then he looked up at Nangong Kuo and said, "I will do as your prime minister asks. There is no need for me to reply to this letter. Tell Jiang Ziya that I will arrest my brother and bring him to the Zhou camp."

The next day he left for Chong City with 3,000 Flying Tiger soldiers. When he arrived at the city, his nephew Chong Yingbao came out to meet him.

"Forgive me, uncle!" he said. "I am wearing armor so I cannot give you a proper bow."

"Dear nephew, I heard that Chong City is being attacked. I bring 3,000 of my best soldiers to help you defend the city. But tell me, why is Ji Chang attacking the city?"

"I don't know, uncle. But I am certainly happy that you are here to help us!"

At dawn the next day, Chong Heihu led his Flying Tiger soldiers out of the city to face the Zhou army. He was wearing golden armor over a red dragon robe, and he rode a fire-eyed monster. His face was as black as the bottom of a pot, he had yellow eyebrows, golden eyes, and a long red beard. Jiang Ziya saw him, and he understood what was happening. He sent Nangong Kuo out to face him.

"Chong Heihu," shouted Nangong Kuo. "Your brother is a criminal. He has harmed many good people. We have the right to arrest him!" Then he raised his sword and attacked Chong Heihu. They began fighting. The two of them were close to each other, slashing with their weapons. They fought for twenty rounds. Then Chong Heihu said quietly, "Let's stop fighting now. I'll see you again when I have arrested my brother."

Nangong Kuo slashed at his opponent one more time, then he turned his horse and retreated, calling out, "Chong Heihu, you are too strong.

Please don't come after me!"

Chong Heihu turned and rode back to the city. Chong Yingbao had been watching the fight. He asked Chong Heihu, "Uncle, when your enemy ran away, why didn't you use your magic eagle?"

Chong Heihu replied, "My dear nephew, you forgot that Jiang Ziya is a powerful magician from Kunlun Mountain. He would have killed my eagle. But don't worry, we won the fight. Now we must make plans. We need your father here. Please send a messenger to him and tell him to return here immediately."

Chong Yingbao sent a messenger to Zhaoge, telling Chong Houhu of the situation and asking him to return to Chong City.

Chong Houhu read the letter. He immediately went to the king and said, "Your Majesty, we are having problems with Ji Chang. He does not wish to live in peace. He has brought a large army to Chong City and he has attacked my brother. Please, I beg you to help!"

"Ji Chang is a criminal," replied the king. "Go to Chong City right away. Take three thousand men and seize that traitor."

A few days later, Chong Heihu saw his brother approaching the city with his army of three thousand soldiers. He said to one of his soldiers, "Take twenty men and wait just inside the city gate. When you hear me rattling my sword, arrest Chong Houhu and take him to the Zhou camp." Then he said to another soldier, "As soon as I leave the city, arrest Chong Houhu's family. Take them to the Zhou camp." Then he rode out of the city to Chong Houhu's camp.

Chong Houhu saw his brother approaching the camp. He came out to greet his brother. Chong Yingbao was also there and he came out to greet his uncle. Then the three of them rode back together to the city. As soon as they rode through the gate, Chong Heihu pulled his sword halfway out of its scabbard, then he pushed it back in and gave it a loud rattle. Immediately, twenty soldiers ran out. They seized Chong Houhu and his son Chong Yingbao.

"Dear brother," cried Chong Houhu, "what are you doing?"

Chong Heihu replied, "Brother, you are not a good minister. You have caused the people great suffering. You have made yourself wealthy while the people go hungry. But our Grand Duke is wise. He can tell the difference between good and bad. As for me, I would rather offend our ancestors than see our clan destroyed. I must arrest you."

Chong Houhu and his son were brought to the Zhou camp, where his wife and daughter were already waiting for him. He said to her, "Ah, my brother is so cruel to me. Who would have thought he would do something like this?"

Chong Heihu also entered the camp. He dismounted and went to see Jiang Ziya and Ji Chang.

"Chong Heihu," said Jiang Ziya, "you are a loyal minister. You have placed the well-being of the people above your own family. You are truly a hero."

But Ji Chang looked at Chong Heihu in surprise. He asked, "What are you doing here?"

Chong Heihu replied, "My brother has committed crimes against heaven. I have brought him here for trial."

"But he is your older brother!"

Jiang Ziya spoke up. He said to Ji Chang, "The people hate Chong Houhu. Even little children hate him. But now they know that Chong Heihu is a virtuous man, and much better than his brother."

Then he ordered Chong Houhu and Chong Yingbao to be brought in. The two of them kneeled in front of Ji Chang, Jiang Ziya and Chong Heihu. Jiang Ziya said, "Chong Houhu, you have committed so many crimes, I cannot list them all. It is time for you to be punished by heaven. Guards! Take them outside and cut off their heads."

Ji Chang was too surprised to say anything. The guards grabbed the two prisoners and took them outside. A few minutes later, the guards returned, holding two heads in their hands. Ji Chang had never seen a head cut off like that. He covered his eyes with his sleeve and cried out, "This is terrible! I will surely die because of this."

Later, after Chong Houhu's family was released, Ji Chang returned to his home in West Qi. He felt sick. He could not eat or drink anything. Every time he closed his eyes, he saw Chong Houhu standing before him, crying out to Ji Chang to give him his life back. Doctors came to see him, but their medicines did not help him at all.

All the lands that were ruled by Chong Houhu were now ruled by Chong Heihu. They became a separate country, not under the control of the king in Zhaoge. The king learned of this and was furious. He ordered his army to go to West Qi and arrest Ji Chong and Chong Heihu.

But his ministers knelt before him and said, "Your Majesty, please think about this. Many people hated Chong Houhu and thought he was cruel and greedy. They are happy that he has been arrested and killed. Perhaps this is not be a good time for you to take action." The king agreed to wait.

Ji Chang's health continued to worsen day by day. He called Jiang Ziya to his bedside. Jiang Ziya came in and kneeled by the bedside. Ji Chang said to him, "I must tell you something important. I am grateful to His Majesty for making me Grand Duke of the West. I should have remained loyal to him. I was wrong to allow the deaths of Chong Houhu and Chong Yingbao. He and I were the same rank, so I did not have the authority to execute him. Now I hear him weeping all the time. When I close my eyes, I see him standing by my bed. I don't think I can live much longer."

He continued, "After I die, you must not rise up against the king. If you do, it will be a difficult situation for you to meet me after you die."

Tears ran down Jiang Ziya's face. He said, "It was you who made me prime minister. I dare not disobey you now."

Just then, Ji Fa came in. Ji Chang said to him, "My dear son, you must take my place after I die. You are young. Do not listen to anyone who says anything against our king. It is true that our king has no virtue, but he is still our king, and we must be loyal to him. Now, kneel before the prime minister and accept him as your father."

Ji Fa knelt down and kowtowed to Jiang Ziya.

Ji Chang continued, "My dear son, remember to love your brothers, and be kind and helpful to the people. If you do as I say, I can die in peace." Ji Fa kowtowed to him.

Then Ji Chang said, "His Majesty was kind to me. I am sad to think that I will never see his royal face again. And I will not be able to go back to Youli and help the people there." Then he died. He was 97 years old. It was the twentieth year of the reign of King Di Xin of the Shang Dynasty.

After the funeral, Jiang Ziya proposed that Ji Fa become the new Grand Duke of the West, with the title of King Wu[1]. Ji Fa's first order was to

---

[1] This means "The Military King."

increase the rank of all officials by one grade. All 200 marquises and all the tribal leaders came to the city and kowtowed to him.

News of this reached the palace secretary in Zhaoge. He decided that he needed to tell His Majesty that there was a new king in West Qi. He went to the Star Picking Mansion to see the king.

Chapter 30
Huang Feihu's Rebellion

When the king tries to play with the minister's wife,
he weakens the throne and lets evil triumph

He listens only to the demon Daji;
he turns away from the wise words of Lady Huang

This virtuous woman stands tall;
while the foolish king brings disaster to all

Now the rebels push against the strong pillars of heaven;
they want the save the kingdom from the king

≡ ≡ ≡

The king's guards let the palace secretary into the Star Picking Mansion. The secretary kowtowed to the king. He said, "Your Majesty, I have bad news. Ji Chang is dead. His son, Ji Fa, is now calling himself King Wu. This could be a big problem. I suggest that you send an army to punish him immediately."

The king laughed and said, "Ji Fa just recently stopped drinking his mother's milk. What can he do to us?"

"Yes, he is young. But remember that he is getting help from Jiang Ziya, San Yisheng, and Nangong Kuo. Together, they are dangerous."

"Jiang Ziya? He is just a sorcerer, nothing more."

The palace secretary bowed and left the mansion. He said to himself, "This king is a fool. I'm afraid the dynasty will end soon."

Time flew by. Soon it was New Year's Day, the twenty-first anniversary of the start of the king's reign. All the ministers came to greet the king, and their wives came to greet Queen Daji. This is when trouble started.

Lady Jia was the wife of Huang Feihu. She came to greet Queen Daji. When Daji heard that Jia was coming, she thought, "So, Huang Feihu, you sent your eagle to kill me. Now your pretty little wife comes to see me. She will walk right into my trap!"

Daji's palace maids brought Lady Jia in to see her. Daji said, "My dear Lady Jia, it is so good to meet you! You are a few years older than I am. You should become my sworn sister."

Jia replied, "Oh, Your Majesty, how could I? You are a queen, but I am just an ordinary woman. It would be like a pheasant in the woods becoming the sister of a beautiful phoenix."

Daji said, "Oh no, my dear. I am just the daughter of a marquis. But you are the wife of a prince, a relative of His Majesty."

The two of them sat and drank a few cups of wine. Then a palace maid entered and said, "His Majesty is coming."

"Oh no!" cried Jia. "It is not right for me to meet him here. I am a minister's wife. This would be a violation of the law. Where can I hide?"

Daji smiled and said, "Don't worry, sister. Go there," and she pointed to the rear of the hall. Jia ran and hid in the rear of the hall. Then the king came in. He saw cups and plates on the table.

He said to Daji, "Who were you drinking with, dear?"

"I was sitting and talking with Lady Jia, the wife of Prince Huang Feihu. Have you ever seen her, Your Majesty?"

"Of course not. We cannot visit with the wife of our minister. That would be a violation of the law."

"But Your Majesty, remember that Huang Feihu's sister is your concubine. So, Lady Jia is actually your relative. You may see her without violating the law." The king thought about this. Then Daji continued, "She is really quite beautiful. I think you would really like her. Please allow me to bring her up to the Star Picking Mansion. Then you can go there and surprise her."

The king was excited about seeing the beautiful Jia. So he left to wait. Daji went to find Jia. She saw that Jia was uncomfortable and wanted to leave, so she said, "Sister, please don't leave yet. Come with me to the Star Picking Mansion. You can see the entire kingdom from up there!"

Jia had no choice, so she followed Daji to the top of the Star Picking Mansion. Looking down, she saw a pit. The pit was filled with piles of human bones and thousands of snakes.

"What is that?" she asked.

Daji replied, "That is the pit of snakes. It is difficult to keep evil people out of the palace. So, if we find any evil people here, they are stripped and thrown into the pit to feed the snakes." Daji saw that Jia was frightened, but she just smiled and told the palace maids to bring wine.

While they were drinking, a palace maid came and told the two women that the king was coming. Daji said to Jia, "Don't worry, sister. Go over there," she pointed to the railing, "and wait for me."

The king came in. He sat down next to Daji. Then he looked to where the beautiful Lady Jia was standing by the railing. "Who is that?" he asked.

"That is the wife of Prince Huang Feihu," said Daji. Jia had no choice. She turned and bowed to the king. The king looked at her with desire in his eyes.

"Please sit down," he said to her.

Jia remained standing. Daji said to her, "You are my sister-in-law. There is nothing wrong with you sitting with us."

Now Lady Jia saw the trap. She became frightened, but she said to the king, "Your Majesty, I came here to visit with my sister. Now please allow me to obey the law and leave at once."

The king smiled at her and said, "Please sit. If you don't sit down, we will have to stand up." He poured a cup of wine and handed it to her.

Now Jia saw that she was trapped. She knew that she would not be able to leave the Star Picking Mansion alive. She took the cup of wine and threw it in the king's face. She shouted, "Idiot king! My husband has been your loyal servant. But instead of thanking him, you insult me and violate all the laws of heaven and earth. You and your evil queen will soon meet your deaths!"

The king shouted to his guards to seize Lady Jia. But before they could grab her, she ran to the railing. She shouted, "Dear husband, I will protect our honor with my life. Please take care of our children!" Then she jumped to her death.

Soon, news of Jia's death reached Concubine Huang, the sister of Huang Feihu and the sister-in-law of Lady Jia. She ran to the Star Picking Mansion and went upstairs to find the king. She pointed her finger at him and said, "You damned tyrant! You owe your life to my brother. He has fought pirates on the eastern ocean. He has fought rebels in the south. Every member of my family has been loyal to you. Today, Lady

Jia came to greet your queen. But you could not control your queen or your own lust. Now my sister-in-law is dead. Years from now, when people tell the story of our kingdom, your name will be dirt!"

Then she turned to Daji and said, "And you, you bitch. You have poisoned the king's mind and brought chaos to our kingdom. And now you have brought death to my sister-in-law!" She ran over and punched Daji in the face, as hard as she could. Daji fell to the ground. Concubine Huang hit her twenty or thirty more times.

Now, Daji was really a fox demon and could have easily fought back against Huang. But she knew that the king was watching. She cried, "Help me, help me, Your Majesty!"

The king ran over and pulled Huang off Daji. But Huang, blind with rage, turned and hit the king in the face. "You tyrant!" she shouted, "How can you defend that bitch. I'll make her pay for killing my sister!"

Now the king was angry. With one hand he grabbed her hair; with the other hand he grabbed the front of her robe. Then he picked her up and threw her over the railing. She fell to the ground and died instantly.

The king looked down from the railing. He saw Huang's broken body, lying next to Jia's body. He felt bad about what he'd done, but he did not say anything to Daji.

Lady Jia's attendants were still waiting for her in a nearby hall. A couple of palace maids came and told them what had happened. The attendants ran to General Huang Feihu, who was enjoying a feast with his brothers and generals. They cried, "Disaster, Your Highness! Disaster!" Then they told him that Lady Jia threw herself from the railing of the Star Picking Mansion, and that the king had then thrown Concubine Huang to her death.

Huang Feihu heard their words but could not think of anything to say. His brother, Huang Ming, jumped up and said, "Brother, I think I know what happened. The king saw your wife's beauty and wanted her for himself. Your wife had no choice but to jump to her death. Concubine Huang probably heard of this and argued with the king, causing him to throw her off the Star Picking Mansion."

He continued, "You know that the sages say, 'If the king does not rule properly, the people may seek a new king.' We are all loyal to the kingdom. We have fought for our country in the north, south, east and west. But now we are no longer loyal to this tyrant. We must rebel!" He and the others jumped up, holding their swords in their hands.

Huang Feihu said, "Stop! What does the death of my wife have to do with you? Remember, the Huang family has served the kingdom for seven generations. How can you rebel against the king now, just because a woman has died?"

The others stood still, surprised at this. They did not know what to do. Then Huang Ming laughed and said, "You're right, brother. This has nothing to do with us at all. Why be angry?" Then he and the others went back to eating, drinking and talking.

Huang Feihu was still angry. He said to them, "Why are you all laughing?"

One of the generals looked at him coldly and replied, "To tell you the truth, brother, we are all laughing at you." Huang Feihu was speechless. The general continued, "We all know that you have earned your rank as the top general in the kingdom. But other people, who knows what they think? They might think that your high rank is because the king really liked your wife."

Now Huang Feihu was turning red from rage. He shouted, "Enough! We are leaving Zhaoge!" Then he paused and added, "But where should we go?"

Huang Ming replied, "You know what the ancients say, 'A good man chooses a good master.' The king of West Qi already controls two thirds of the kingdom. He is a good man. Let's go there."

Then Huang Ming thought, "My brother might change his mind. I'd better make sure that doesn't happen." He said to his brother, "We should get our revenge now and not wait until later. Let's fight the king right now."

The men all rode to the king's palace. Huang Feihu rode his ox while the other men rode their horses. They all wore armor and held swords in their hands. They arrived at the palace gate just as the sun was coming up. One of the generals shouted, "Tell the tyrant to come out right away. Otherwise, we will smash the gate and come in anyway!"

The king was sitting alone in the palace, thinking about what had happened the previous night. A guard ran in and told him that Huang Feihu and his men were waiting outside, swords in hand. The king put on his armor and rode out on his horse to meet them.

One of the generals raised his sword and shouted, "Tyrant! You have insulted the wife of your minister!" Then he rushed at the king, slashing with his sword. The king easily blocked the blow. Then Huang Ming rode forward and also attacked with his sword. Seeing this, Huang Feihu rode his ox forward and joined the fight.

The king was big and strong and a good fighter, but he could not win against three opponents. It was like a dragon fighting three wild tigers. He fought for thirty rounds, then turned and rode back through the palace gate. His guards closed the gate and locked it.

Huang Feihu and his men turned around. They rode out of Zhaoge through the west gate. There, they met up with their families, and together they rode towards Mengjin[1].

The king sat in his court, saying nothing. His ministers came in to find out what was happening. They asked him, "Your Majesty, why did Huang Feihu rebel against you?"

The king replied, "Lady Jia insulted our queen. Then she felt guilty, so she threw herself over the railing. Concubine Huang arrived and also insulted our queen. While they were arguing, she accidentally fell over the railing." He did not explain why he was fighting with Huang Feihu and his men.

The ministers did not know what to say about this. The story sounded false, but of course they could not say that to the king. Then Grand Tutor Wen arrived. He had just returned from the Eastern Sea district. He also asked what was going on. The king told him the same story that he'd just told the ministers.

Grand Tutor Wen said, "I know Huang Feihu. He is a good man, loyal to you and to the kingdom. He and his wife came to the palace because it was New Years Day. But the Star Picking Palace is your private home, not part of the main palace. Why was Lady Jia there?"

The king did not answer. Grand Tutor Wen continued, "Then Concubine Huang must have heard of her sister in law's death and come here. But I think you were angry at her and threw her off the balcony. These deaths were not the fault of Jia and Huang. They are

---

[1] Today, Mengjin (pronounced *mèngjīn*) is a district in the city of Luoyang. In ancient times it was a ferry crossing for the Yellow River. It is believed that King Wu of Zhou and his allies crossed the Yellow River here on their way to Zhaoge, leading to the theory that the original name was actually *Méngjīn*, which means "ferry crossing of the alliance."

your fault! You know what the ancients say, 'If the king rules badly, the people may seek a new king.' I am not surprised that Huang Feihu rose up against you. Your Majesty, you should forgive him. I will go and find him, and ask him to return."

One of the ministers spoke up. He said, "Grand Tutor Wen, you are right that His Majesty should have treated Madam Jia and Concubine Huang better. But on the other hand, Huang Feihu was wrong to attack the king."

Grand Tutor Wen thought about it. Then he said, "Perhaps you are right. Send messengers quickly to the commanders at the mountain passes. Tell them to close their gates and not allow the rebels to pass through. That will give me time to catch up to them."

Chapter 31
Flight and Pursuit

The loyal and virtuous depart;
There is no rain and the people are hungry

The wise Grand Tutor quickly takes control,
While evil ministers continue to bring misery to the people

Don't even think about crossing the three passes;
The enemy is approaching from all four directions

The enemy chases the army but it disappears in the bright sun; Don't worry, their fate is already written

☰ ☰ ☰

Huang Feihu and his men left Zhaoge through the west gate. They passed through Mengjin, crossed the Yellow River, and rode until they were close to Lintong Pass. Huang Feihu heard sounds of shouting and saw a cloud of dust rising into the air. Looking back, he saw a great army approaching. Then he looked to his right and left and saw two more armies coming from both sides. Then he looked backwards and saw that yet another army was coming towards him from Lintong Pass.

He sighed deeply and thought, "How can I fight all four of these armies? All I can do is wait for death for myself and my family."

In heaven, the immortals had nothing to do. In the past, the Daoist masters had enjoyed going to listen to lectures at the Jade Palace. But these days there were no lectures. Everything was on hold until Jiang Ziya finished creating the new gods. So the immortals passed the time touring the nearby mountains and picking flowers.

One of the immortals, Master Pure Void Virtue, was traveling over Lintong Pass when he heard the sounds of sadness coming from a man on earth. Looking down, he saw Huang Feihu and his men surrounded by four armies. "Well," he thought, "it looks like someone needs to rescue these people." He told one of his servants, a genie, to wrap up the men in a flag and hide them deep in the mountains. The genie did as he was ordered.

Grand Tutor Wen led his army towards the place where Huang Feihu had been. He looked around but did not see anyone. He met with the generals who were leading the other three armies, and they said that they had not seen Huang Feihu's men either. Wen thought, "This is strange. I was told that Huang Feihu crossed the Yellow River and was headed towards Lintong Pass. We came at him from all four directions, but he is not here. Where is he?"

Master Pure Void Virtue saw that Wen had stopped. He thought, "I have to make these soldiers go away, so that Huang Feihu can continue through the pass." He took a handful of magic sand out of his robe and threw it towards the southeast. The sand turned into a group of men riding fast towards Zhaoge. Grand Tutor Wen saw them and sent all four of the armies in pursuit. The armies rode all the way to Mengjin, but they never caught up.

When the armies had gone, Master Pure Void Virtue ordered his genie to return Huang Feihu and his men to the road. The men looked around, confused. They saw that the armies had disappeared. "Heaven has surely helped us!" said Huang Ming.

But they still had to get through Lington Pass. The pass was guarded by a group of soldiers led by Zhang Feng, an older man who was a sworn brother of Huang Feihu's father.

Huang Feihu led his men up to the gate of Lington Pass. Zhang Feng came out, leading a group of soldiers. "Listen to me," he said, "Your father and I are sworn brothers, and you are a loyal subject of the king. Do not bring shame to your ancestors. Get down from your ox and let me take you back to Zhaoge. Perhaps some ministers will speak up for you, and you and your family will not have to be executed."

Huang Feihu replied, "Uncle, you know that our king spends all of his time drinking and playing with his concubines. He listens to evil men, he does not listen to his loyal ministers, he ignores affairs of state, and he is cruel to the people. I have done hundreds of things to help him, yet he forgets all that and insults me. How can I remain loyal to him? Please, let us pass through."

When he heard these words, Zhang Feng became angry. "Traitor!" he shouted. He slashed at Huang Feihu with his sword, but Huang Feihu blocked the blow. He struck again. Now Huang Feihu became angry and attacked. They fought for thirty rounds. Zhang Feng was a good fighter but he was an old man. He became tired and could not fight anymore. He turned around and rode away on his horse.

Zhang Feng looked back and saw that Huang Feihu was chasing him. He put away his sword. He reached into his robe and threw a stringed hammer[1] at his pursuer. But Huang Feihu knew about this weapon. As the hammer flew towards him, he slashed upwards with his sword, cutting the string. Then he grabbed the flying hammer with his other hand.

Seeing this, Zhang Feng fled back to the pass. The soldiers locked the gate behind him. He sat down, breathing heavily. He thought for a while about what to do next. Then he ordered General Xiao Yin to come see him.

Xiao Yin came in and awaited his orders. Zhang Feng said, "We cannot beat Huang Feihu in a fight. So tonight, I want you to take three thousand men with bows and arrows. Surround his camp. Then have all your men shoot their arrows at the same time. Kill every one of the rebels, then cut off their heads and bring them to me."

Xiao Yin left. But he remembered that several years earlier, he served in the army under Huang Feihu and was promoted to general. He did not want to repay this kindness by killing Huang Feihu and his family. Secretly he went to Huang Feihu's camp and met with the rebel leader.

"Sir," he said, "you remember that I served under you several years ago. You made me a general. I must tell you that Zhang Feng has ordered me to kill all of you tonight with bows and arrows. I cannot do that. It would be a crime against heaven."

Huang Feihu replied, "I cannot thank you enough for coming and telling me this. If not for you, my entire family would die tonight. Tell me, though, is there anything you can do to help us get out of here?"

"Wait a few minutes for me to return to the pass. Then attack as soon as you can. I will open the gates for you."

Huang Feihu immediately gathered his men. They rode towards the pass, shouting and waving their swords. The gates opened and they rushed through.

---

[1] This is a small hammer or mallet with a rope attached, making it possible for the user to throw it, then retrieve it afterwards.

Zhang Feng heard the sound of galloping horses. He saw what happened, and set off to chase Huang Feihu. But as he passed through the gate, he did not see Xiao Yin standing on the other side. Xiao Yin slashed at him with his sword. Zhang Feng fell from his horse, dead.

"Thank you!" Huang Feihu shouted to Xiao Yin as he rode away. "I don't know when I can repay you for what you did today."

They rode about eighty *li* and stopped when they got to the next pass, Tongguan Pass. The commander of this pass was Chen Tong. This man also knew Huang Feihu. Several years earlier, he had served under Huang Feihu in the army. He disobeyed a command and was sentenced to death. But several other generals asked Huang Feihu to show mercy, so he was not executed. Still, Chen Tong disliked Huang Feihu and was happy to have a chance to punish him now.

He put on his armor and prepared for battle.

When he saw Huang Feihu he shouted, "Hello, General! You used to be a high ranking general, but now you are just another criminal on the run. Grand Tutor Wen told me that you would be coming here. Get down off your ox. I will take you back to Zhaoge. There is nothing else you can do."

Huang Feihu replied, "You are wrong, General. Once you were under my command and I treated you like my own brother. You disobeyed my orders, but I showed you mercy and did not execute you. But even after that, you insult me. Very well. Get down off your horse and fight me now. If you win, I will go with you to Zhaoge."

Then Huang Feihu attacked with his sword. Chen Tong blocked with his own sword, and they fought for more than twenty rounds. Huang Feihu was the stronger fighter, though, so Chen Tong turned, jumped up on his horse, and rode away as fast as he could.

Huang Feihu chased him. But then Chen Tong pulled out a magic javelin. This javelin had been given to him by an immortal. It never missed its target. He threw it. Huang Feihu was struck in the chest. He cried out and fell to the ground.

Huang Ming and another general saw this. They rushed forward to attack Chen Tong. But Chen Tong threw the javelin again and killed the other general. Then, not wanting to fight Huang Ming, he turned around and fled.

The men in Huang Feihu's camp were filled with sadness when they saw the two dead fighters. They had no leader, no plan, no place to go towards, no place to return to.

In heaven, Master Pure Void Virtue was on Mount Green Peak, meditating on his green cloud. Suddenly his heart jumped. He looked down and saw that Huang Feihu had been killed. Immediately he called for one of his disciples to come and see him.

The disciple was a young man, nine feet tall, with smooth skin, bright eyes and a body that was as strong as a tiger. He wore a robe with a hemp belt, and simple straw sandals. "What can I do for you, Master?" he asked.

"Your father needs your help," replied Master Pure Void Virtue.

"Who is my father?"

"He is Huang Feihu, a prince of Shang. He has been killed by a magic javelin. Bring him back from the dead. Then introduce yourself. You will serve together in the battle that is to come."

"I don't understand, Master. How can this man be my father?"

"Thirteen years ago, I was riding a cloud. Suddenly I saw a bright beam of light. I looked down and saw that the light was coming from your head. You were only three years old at the time. I knew immediately that you had a bright future, so I brought you here to be my disciple. Your name is Huang Tianhua."

Then Master Pure Void Virtue gave the boy a sword and a flower basket, and told him how to bring his father back from the dead. The boy kowtowed to his master. Then he picked up a handful of dust, threw it in the air, and rode it swiftly to Tongguan Pass.

Chapter 32
Huang Tianhua Meets His Father

Using the power of the five Dao¹,
You can become like air and be carried far on the wind

You can travel through the lands of the living and the dead,
And fly high over Mount Tai and Mount Mang

Don't fail to save your father even if it is difficult;
Have a strong heart and don't fear the wolves

Father and son meet at Tongguan Pass;
They are both pillars of virtue for Qi and Zhou

≡ ≡ ≡

Huang Tianhua flew down from Mount Green Peak. He arrived at the Huang camp around five in the afternoon. Nearby a group of men and horses stood around a lamp. The men saw him and reached for their swords. "Who are you?" they called.

Tianhua replied, "This poor Daoist is from Mount Green Peak. I have heard that His Majesty is in trouble. I can help him. Bring me to him quickly!"

The men looked at him carefully. He had long black hair that was coiled up on top of his head. He wore a long robe with big sleeves that fluttered in the wind. In one hand he held a strange flower basket, and he had a sword tied on his back. He looked like a powerful tiger.

They led him to Huang Feibao, the brother of the dead general Huang Feihu. Huang Feibao could immediately see that the boy looked a lot like his own brother. He said to the boy, "Can you bring my brother back from the dead? If you can, you would be like a father or mother who brings new life into the world."

---

¹ Daoists believe that everything in the material universe is made from five elements: wood, fire, earth, metal and water. These five elements are associated with the five directions, five colors, five bodily tissues, five fluids, five solid organs, and five hollow organs.

The boy was led to the back of the camp. There he saw Huang Feihu lying on the ground, cold and dead. His face was white and his eyes were closed. Next to him was another body. "Who's that?" he asked.

"That is our sworn brother. Both of them were killed by Chen Tong's magic javelin."

"Bring me some water," said Huang Tianhua. When the water arrived, he took some elixir out of his flower basket and mixed it with the water. He opened up Huang Heihu's mouth and poured the liquid into his mouth. The liquid ran into the dead man's body, reaching all his internal organs and all 84,000 hairs on his body.

"Now we wait," said Huang Tianhua. They waited for an hour or two. Then the dead man cried out in pain and opened his eyes.

"Where am I?" asked Huang Feihu, looking around. "Is this the land of the dead? Why are you all here with me?" The others told him what happened. Huang Feihu stood up and thanked the boy.

The boy knelt down and said, "Father, don't you know me? I am your son, Huang Tianhua! You remember that when I was just three years old, you sent me away to study with Master Pure Void Virtue on Mount Green Peak. I have been there for thirteen years." His father looked at him and cried with joy.

Tianhua looked around and saw his two uncles and his three brothers. But he did not see his mother. "Father, why didn't you bring my mother with you? If the tyrant king captures her, it will be a terrible day for our family!"

Huang Feihu began to cry. He told his son how his mother had jumped from the Star Picking Mansion to stop the king from dishonoring her. Then he told the boy that the king had also thrown his aunt from the Star Picking Mansion. When the boy heard this, he said, "Father, I will not go back to Mount Green Peak. I will stay here on earth and take revenge for my mother's death!"

Just then, a messenger rushed in to tell them that Chen Tong was outside the camp, calling for a fight. Huang Feihu was so frightened that his face turned the color of ash. But his son said, "Father, don't worry. Go and fight him. I will protect you."

Huang Feihu put on his armor and rode his ox out to meet Chen Tong. Chen Tong was surprised to see the man who he thought was dead.

Huang Feihu shouted, "You hit me with your javelin, but heaven did not want me to die." Then he attacked Chen Tong. The two of them began to fight. After fifteen rounds, Chen Tong turned and rode away.

Huang Feihu followed him. Suddenly Chen Tong turned and threw another magic javelin at him. But Huang Tianhua pointed his flower basket at the javelin. The javelin turned in mid-air and fell into the basket. Chen Tong threw more javelins, but each one was captured by the flower basket.

Chen Tong saw that the Daoist boy was capturing all his javelins. He raised his sword and charged towards the boy. But Tianhua pointed his own sword at Chen Tong. A beam of starlight flew from the tip of the sword towards Chen Tong. When it hit Chen Tong, his head flew off his body and rolled onto the ground.

"Chen Tong is dead!" shouted the Zhou soldiers. They charged towards the gate. They broke open the gate and rushed through to the other side.

Tianhua stopped and called out, "Father, I must return to Mount Green Peak to talk with my master. But we will meet again. I will see you in West Qi. Be careful!"

Huang Feihu was sad to see his son leave. But he continued with his men, riding towards the next pass. This was Chuanyun Pass and it was guarded by Chen Wu, the brother of Chen Tong.

When Huang Feihu and his men arrived at the pass, Chen Wu came out to meet them. He wore no armor and carried no weapons. "Welcome, Your Highness!" he called out.

"Greetings," replied Huang Feihu. "We have committed a crime against the king and are fleeing from Zhaoge. I am sorry to say that your brother died yesterday when he tried to stop us from passing through Tongguan Pass."

Chen Wu replied, "Your family has been loyal to the king for many, many years. But we all know that this king is a tyrant and has treated you badly. My brother did not understand the situation. He deserved his death. You may pass through with no problem. But won't you please come in and rest with us for a little bit."

Huang Feihu did not know that Chen Wu already knew of his brother's death. When he heard that his brother had died, Chen Wu was so angry that he spouted smoke from his seven orifices[1].

The men dismounted from their horses and went through the gate. Chen Wu invited them to come into the main hall and have something to eat. When they'd finished eating, Huang Feihu said, "Thank you, my friend. Now we must be going. Would you please open the other gate and let us pass."

"Of course," Chen Wu replied. "But we have prepared some wine for you. Please join us and have a few drinks." Huang Feihu could not refuse, so he and his men sat down again and drank some wine. They sat and talked for hours. Soon it was evening.

"Please don't go yet," said Chen Wu. "You have been traveling for many days, you must be very tired. We would be happy to give you and your men beds for the night."

Huang Feihu was not comfortable with this, but he could not find a reason to say no. So he and his men brought the luggage inside, then they all went to bed. The men fell asleep right away. But Huang Feihu could not sleep. He kept thinking about the many years that his family had served the kings of Shang. "Who would have thought that we would now be rebels against the king!" he thought.

First watch came, then second watch, then third watch. Still Huang Feihu could not sleep. He thought, "I used to have power and wealth. Now here I am, fleeing for my life!"

Suddenly a cold wind came into the room. The candle blew out, leaving the room in darkness. A voice called softly, "My lord, don't be afraid. It's your wife, Lady Jia. You are in great danger! Your hosts are preparing a fire that will burn all of you to death. Get up and get out of there immediately! Now I must return to the land of the dead."

Huang Feihu jumped up. He woke up the others. They ran to the door but found that it was locked from the other side. They smashed the door. They saw that the other side of the door was piled high with firewood. Quickly they pushed their luggage out of the building, jumped on their horses, and left the building. As they rode away, they looked back. They saw Chen Wu and his generals running towards the building, holding burning torches.

---

[1] This is a Chinese idiom meaning that someone is seething with anger. The seven apertures of the human head are the two eyes, two ears, two nostrils, and the mouth.

Chen Wu saw that he was too late. He and his men jumped on their horses and rode towards Huang Feihu and his men. He shouted, "You rebel! I was hoping to kill you and your whole family. You are still alive for now, but you will not escape my net!"

The two groups of fighters came together, and they battled hand to hand, sword to sword. Huang Feihu fought against Chen Wu. After a few rounds, he stabbed Chen Wu in the heart, killing him.

The other fighting soon ended. Chen Wu's men were defeated. Some were killed, the rest returned to Chuanyun Pass.

The next pass was Jiepai Pass, eighty *li* away. "Well, at least we won't have to fight at Jiepai Pass," said Huang Ming to Huang Feihu. "The commander there is your father, old Huang Gun."

At Jiepai Pass, Huang Gun waited for his son to arrive. He was very angry when he heard that his son had rebelled against the king and killed so many generals and soldiers. He ordered three thousand soldiers to arrest his son and the others. He also prepared ten prison carts to carry them back to Zhaoge.

Chapter 33
The Battle at the Pass

Evil ministers have evil hearts;
They bring a hundred problems and a thousand disasters

They talk about their powerful magic,
But they don't know that all their plots will fail

Yu Hua tried to succeed but failed;
Han Rong's new rank is nothing compared to my dream

Heaven's will is already set;
When I think of the naming of the gods my heart fills with tears

☰ ☰ ☰

Huang Feihu and his men approached Jiepai Pass. They saw thousands of soldiers waiting for them, and they saw the prison carts. "Things don't look good," said one of the generals.

When Huang Feihu rode his ox close to the gate, he said to Huang Gun, "Father, your worthless son begs your pardon, I cannot kowtow to you."

"Who are you?" asked Huang Gun.

"I am your eldest son. How can you ask a question like that?"

Huang Gun shouted, "This family has been loyal to the king for seven generations. Never have we done anything evil, never have we committed treason. But now you have left your king because of a woman. You have cut off the precious jade from your waist. You are a rebel. You have dishonored your ancestors and your father. I don't know how you can even face me."

Tears came to Huang Feihu's eyes. He could not speak. Huang Gun continued, "If you want to be a filial sun, get down off your ox. I will take you to Zhaoge. You will die an honorable death as a true minister of the king. Or if you are truly unfilial, just go ahead and kill me. Then you can do what you wish, and I will not have to see or hear any of it."

By now, Huang Feihu was crying. He said, "Don't say anything more,

Father. Take me to Zhaoge now." Then he prepared to get down from his ox. But before he could get down, his younger brother Huang Ming spoke.

"Brother, don't do it!" he said. "The king is a tyrant. Why should we be loyal to a tyrant? And why are you willing to commit suicide just because of what this old man says?"

Now Huang Feihu did not know what to do. He just sat on his ox, thinking but not speaking. Huang Ming turned to Huang Gun and said, "General, listen to me. You are wrong. Even a tiger would never kill its own child. Don't you know that the tyrant killed your daughter and made your daughter-in-law commit suicide? Don't you care about them, don't you want to avenge their deaths? The ancients say, 'If a ruler is evil, the people may seek a new ruler. If a father is unkind, his sons may leave him.'"

Hearing these words, Huang Gun became furious. He attacked Huang Ming, slashing at him with his sword. Huang Ming blocked his blows. He shouted to Huang Feihu, "Brother, I am keeping your father busy. Get out of the pass now, as fast as you can."

Huang Feihu and the others rushed out of the pass. When Huang Gun saw this, he jumped off his horse. He was so upset that he tried to kill himself with his sword. But Huang Ming jumped off his horse and grabbed him. He said, "Sir, please wait and listen to me. Your son Huang Feihu has made me very angry. He has insulted me and has tried to kill me several times. I could not say anything to you, because I was afraid he would hear me. But now that he is gone, I can speak freely. I have a plan."

"What is your plan?" asked Huang Gun.

"Go quickly and catch up to your son. Tell him that I was right, and a tiger would never kill its child. Invite him to come back and have dinner with you. Tell him you will go with him to West Qi. But as soon as he comes back, have your soldiers take their weapons. You can then put them all in the prison carts and take them to Zhaoge. As for me, I just hope that you and the king will forgive me."

Huang Gun said, "Huang Ming, you are a good man. I will do as you say." He jumped on his horse and went to catch up with Huang Feihu. He called out, "My son, I have decided to come with you to West Qi after all. Please come back. We can all eat some food and drink some wine, then we will go to West Qi."

Huang Feihu did not know why his father changed his mind. But he came back to the pass. He kowtowed to his father. Then they all sat down to eat and drink.

While they were eating dinner, two of Huang Feihu's men set fire to the buildings that held all the grain. Huang Gun saw the fire and ran outside. Immediately, Huang Feihu and the others rode out of the gate. "I've been fooled!" said Huang Gun.

"Father," said Huang Ming, "I must tell you the truth now. The king is an evil tyrant. But Ji Chang is a wise and good ruler. We are going to West Qi to join up with him and his army. You are welcome to join us."

He waited for a few seconds to let the old man think about this. Then he said, "Of course, we have just burned all your grain. If you don't join us, you won't be able to pay your taxes and you will certainly be executed by the king."

Huang Gun thought about it. Then he said, "All right. My family has been loyal for seven generations. But we are all rebels now." He kowtowed to Zhaoge eight times. Then he left Jiepai Pass, taking all his soldiers and guards with him.

Huang Gun said to Huang Ming, "I hope you know that you are leading the whole Huang family to its death. The next pass is Sishui Pass. There is a magician there named Yu Hua. They call him the seven-headed general. He has never lost a battle. If I'd taken you to Zhaoge I might have lived. But now it looks like we will all die at Sishui Pass."

They rode for about eighty *li*, and they reached Sishui Pass late in the afternoon. The commander of the pass, a man named Han Rong, blocked the gate and prepared for battle.

The next day, the magician Yu Hua came out, shouting that he was ready to fight. Huang Feihu rode forward on his ox, saying, "I will fight him."

Yu Hua had a golden face, red hair and beard, and two golden eyes. He wore a tiger-skin robe under his armor, and a jade belt. "Who are you?" he shouted to Huang Feihu.

"I am prince Huang Feihu. I am rebelling against the wicked tyrant. We are going to West Qi to join up with the sage ruler there. Who are you?"

"I am Yu Hua. I'm sorry we have never met before. Tell me, why are you rebelling against our king?"

"It's a long story. But the short story is this: the king is a cruel tyrant who does not care about the people. But the leader of West Qi is a good and wise man, and he already controls two thirds of the Shang kingdom. It is the will of heaven that the king will fall. Now, will you please let us through?"

"Your Highness, I cannot possibly let you through. You are trying to climb a tree to catch a fish[1]. You are rebelling against the king, and that makes us enemies. Dismount now. I will take you back to Zhaoge and the king can decide what to do with you. There is no way that you will get through this pass."

"I have already gotten through four passes. Yours is the last one. Let's see if you can stop me!" And with that, Huang Feihu raised his sword and attacked. He was a very good fighter. His sword was like a silver snake coiling around Yu Hua. Yu Hua could not fight back. He turned and fled. But as he fled, he turned and raised his Soul Killing Flag. A black cloud came out of it. It wrapped around Huang Feihu and threw him to the ground. The soldiers grabbed him and took him prisoner.

Huang Gun saw this. He said, "You fool! You did not listen to me. Now these men will get the reward for capturing you, instead of me."

The next day, Yu Hua came out again, ready for battle. Huang Ming and another general rode out to meet him. They fought for about twenty rounds. Then, just as before, Yu Hua rode away. Then he turned around and raised his Soul Killing Flag. The two men were surrounded by black smoke. They fell off their horses and were taken prisoner.

The next day, two more general fought Yu Hua. Both were surrounded by black smoke and were captured. And the day after that, the last two Huang generals more met the same fate. Now Yu Hua had seven prisoners. Huang Gun was alone with his three young grandsons.

Yu Hua came out once more, ready for battle. One of the three grandsons went out to fight him. The grandson was able to stab Yu Hua in the leg, but then he also was captured.

Huang Gun could not wait any longer. The old general took off his armor, then his jade belt and his robe. He put on white robes of mourning. Then he walked with his two grandsons to the gate. He said

---

[1] In other words, you are attempting the impossible.

to the guard, "Please tell your commander that Huang Gun wishes to see him."

Then Huang Gun knelt at the gate and waited.

Chapter 34
The Rebel Meets the Prime Minister

There is chaos by the side of the road,
Because a foolish king causes trouble

The king is ruled by lust and does not care about his duties;
And so the nation suffers

Generals and ministers decide to serve a virtuous ruler;
Why does Han Rong try to stop them?

Nezha stands in the middle of the road;
Be careful when he picks up his gold brick!

≡ ≡ ≡

Huang Gun saw Han Rong coming out. Generals stood on the commander's right and left sides. Huang Gun said, "Sir, this criminal kowtows to you. The Huang family has committed many crimes, and we must be punished. But I beg you to please spare the life of my seven-year-old grandson. If you let him live, the Huang family will survive. Would you please consider this, General?"

Han Rong replied, "General, I cannot do that. I am the commander here and I must obey the law. Your family enjoyed great wealth and honor, yet you chose to rebel against the king. Now I must send all of you, including your grandsons, to Zhaoge. The court will decide who is a criminal and who is not. If I did as you ask, I would be a rebel just as much as you."

"Your Excellency," cried Huang Gun, "how can there be harm in sparing a small child? The ancients say, 'If you can help someone but you don't, it's like returning from a treasure mountain with empty hands.' I beg you to show mercy to this small child."

But still Han Rong refused. He put Huang Gun and his grandsons in prison along with the rest of the Huang family.

Afterwards, Han Rong sat down for a banquet with Yu Hua and the other generals. He said, "Yu Hua, I want you to go with the prisoners to

Zhaoge. Only then will I be sure that they will arrive with no trouble."

The next day, Yu Hua took three thousand soldiers and left for Zhaoge with his eleven prisoners.

Meanwhile, on Qianyuan Mountain, the immortal named Fairy Primordial was sitting on his bed. Suddenly his heart began to beat rapidly. He did not know why. He did a divination and saw that Huang Feihu and his family were in danger.

He called for his disciple Nezha. He said, "Disciple, I see that Huang Feihu and his family are in danger. Go and help them to get past Sishui Pass. When you are finished, come back here at once."

Nezha was very happy to get this order. He picked up his Fire Tip Lance and flew away on his magic wheels to just outside Chuanyun Pass. There he waited until he saw an army coming towards him. There was a great cloud of dust. Flags fluttered in the wind, and swords shone in the sun.

Nezha stood on his magic wheels in the middle of the road and began to sing:

> *I have lived so long, I don't know my age*
> *I obey my master, I do not fear heaven*
> *No matter who comes this way*
> *They must pay me in gold*

A soldier rode up to Yu Hua and said, "General, there's a strange man standing in the middle of the road. He is singing."

Yu Hua told his men to stop. He rode forward towards the man. "Who are you?" he shouted.

"You don't need to know my name. I have lived here for a long time. Anyone who passes by must pay me in gold. It does not matter if you are a king or a common man, you still must pay."

Yu Hua laughed and said, "I am a general, taking prisoners to Zhaoge. Get out of my way if you want to live."

"Fine. Just pay me ten gold coins and you can pass."

Yu Hua was furious. He attacked the man, not knowing that he was attacking an immortal. Nezha easily blocked his sword. Unable to win, Yu Hua fled. Then he turned and waved his Soul Killing Flag. But Nezha just laughed. He waved his hand and the flag flew into his hand. He put it in his bag. "Do you have any more of these?" he laughed.

Yu Hua came back and attacked Nezha again. Nezha threw his gold brick into the air. It came down, hitting Yu Hua on the head. The general almost fell off his horse. He rode away. Nezha threw the gold brick in the air again. All of Yu Hua's soldiers turned and rode away as fast as they could.

Nezha went over to the prison carts. He looked at the tired and dirty men in the carts. He said, "I am Li Nezha, disciple of Fairy Primordial. My master saw that you were in trouble and sent me to help you." Then he used his gold brick to smash open the prison carts, freeing the men. He continued, "I will go back to Sishui Pass and open the gates. You can go through with no problem." Huang Feihu and the other men fell to the ground and kowtowed to Nezha.

At Sishui Pass, Han Rong was drinking with his generals when Yu Hua returned. "What are you doing here?" he asked. Yu Hua told him about his fight with the immortal. Han Rong said, "We must bring those rebels back to Zhaoge. If we don't, the king will never forgive me."

A few minutes later, a soldier rushed in and said, "There's a man outside the gate. He is riding on a pair of wheels. He wants to fight the seven-headed general."

"That's the man who beat me!" cried Yu Hua. They all went out to see.

"Who are you?" asked Han Rong.

"I am Li Nezha, disciple of Fairy Primordial. My master sent me to help Huang Feihu. The Shang dynasty will fall soon, and Heaven has decided that the Huang family should help the new dynasty. I am here to help them get to West Qi. Why would you act against the will of heaven?"

Han Rong and his soldiers attacked Nezha, but Nezha was as strong as a dragon and as fast as lightning. Many soldiers fell from their horses. The rest of them fled for their lives.

Yu Hua mounted his monster and attacked Nezha. Nezha blocked his blows. Then he hit Yu Hua, breaking his arm. Yu Hua turned and fled.

That was the end of the battle. Sishui Pass was now open. Huang Feihu and his men passed through the gates and continued towards West Qi. They thanked Nezha, who said, "Take care of yourselves. We will meet again." Then Nezha returned to Qianyuan Mountain.

The Huang family and their army continued towards West Qi. They climbed many mountains and crossed many rivers. They stopped just outside West Qi City and set up camp.

Huang Feihu went alone into the city. He saw that the people in the city were healthy, wore good clothes, and were polite. There was lots of food in the marketplaces. He asked where the prime minister's mansion was. A man pointed to a gold-colored bridge and told him that the mansion was on the other side of the bridge.

He walked up to the mansion gate and told the guard that he was there to see the prime minister. A short time later, Jiang Ziya came out to meet him. "Please forgive me for not riding out to meet you," he said.

"I am a refugee now," replied Huang Feihu. "I am like a bird who has lost its nest. Would you be so kind as to take me in?"

"Of course. But tell me, why did you turn against the Shang Dynasty?" Huang Feihu told him everything that happened, and why became a rebel.

Jiang Ziya said, "Our king would be happy to have you here. Please rest a while. I need to talk with him."

Jiang Ziya went to the king's palace to meet with Ji Fa. He explained what had happened. Ji Fa was happy to hear the news. He asked that Huang Feihu be brought to see him.

The next day, Huang Feihu was brought in to see Ji Fa. He said, "Your Majesty, I am not alone. I am with my father, my brothers, my sons, my sworn brothers, a thousand guards, and three thousand soldiers. They are all waiting at Mount Qi. Please tell me what to do with them."

"Bring them all to the city," replied Ji Fa. "Each will keep their old rank, with no changes." Huang Feihu thanked him. His family and his army entered West Qi City, and they all became part of West Qi.

But soon war threatened the whole land.

Chapter 35
Two Generals Join West Qi

The Huang family travels west like flying hawks;
They hope to reach West Qi, no matter how long the journey

In the silent land the army travels through five passes;
The bleeding from battles never stops

Ziya makes clever plans to save the Zhou dynasty;
But Grand Tutor Wen cannot change the king's evil ways

The army is strong but has lost its virtue;
Chao Tian travels alone through the wind and fog of war

≡ ≡ ≡

Grand Tutor Wen was angry. He had just tried to capture Huang Feihu, only to learn that he was chasing the wind. He had been tricked by the immortal Pure Void Virtue. As soon as he realized what had happened, he rushed back to Zhaoge to protect the king and the palace.

He met with the king's ministers and told them what happened. "We don't need to worry about Huang Feihu," he told them. "There are five mountain passes between here and West Qi. The passes are guarded by loyal commanders and many soldiers. Even if Huang Feihu had wings, he could not cross those five passes and get to West Qi."

But soon, messengers began to arrive with bad news. First, a messenger said that Huang Feihu had killed the commander of Linton Pass and gotten through. Then a second messenger arrived to say that Huang Feihu had killed the commander of Tongguan Pass and gotten through that too. A third messenger reported that Huang Feihu had gotten through Chuanyun Pass. And then a fourth messenger reported that the commander of Jiepai Pass had quit his job and gone to West Qi.

Finally, a messenger came and said that Han Rong, the commander of Sishui Pass, needed more soldiers immediately. Wen said, "I told the late king that I would protect his son. But I did not think this king would be such a terrible ruler. The Grand Dukes of the East and South have risen up against the king. And now we have lost Huang Feihu. I don't know if we can win this battle, or if the dynasty will fall. However, I told the late king that I would protect his son. So that is what I must do."

He called his generals to come and discuss the matter with him. One of the generals said, "We don't need to worry about the rebels in West Qi. There are five mountain passes between them and us. Also, we don't have enough money to fight a new war. Let's just ignore West Qi."

Wen replied, "Remember the old saying, 'When you are dying of thirst, it's too late to dig a well.' We must prepare now to fight against West Qi."

"We need to learn more," said a general named Chao Tian. "I will go to West Qi. And I will fight them if I must."

The next day, Chao Tiao, his brother Chao Lei, and 30,000 soldiers left Zhaoge. They crossed the Yellow River and all five mountain passes, then set up camp outside the west gate of West Qi City. They waited for a while. Then Chao Lei rode forward on his horse towards the gate.

He shouted, "This is General Chao Lei. I am the leader of the king's army. We do not want your soldiers to die, so I am willing to fight one man from West Qi. Who will fight me?"

General Nangong Kuo, the leader of the Flying Tiger army, rode out of the gate. He shouted, "General Chao, why have you brought this army to our city?"

Chao Lei replied, "I have come here to arrest Ji Fa. He calls himself a king, but His Majesty does not approve of this. Also, he has taken in the rebel Huang Feihu. You must go back inside, tie up Ji Fa and Huang Feihu, and bring them out to me. If you don't, you and your people will suffer."

Nangong Kuo smiled and said, "Chao Lei, your king is an evil tyrant. He cuts his ministers into little pieces. He burns them on hot pillars. He feeds them to snakes. He took his own uncle's heart and fed it to his concubine Daji. He has killed many people who did nothing wrong. But here in West Qi, my king rules with kindness and wisdom. The people love him, and they are happy. Why don't you join us?"

Chao Lei did not answer. He rode forward to meet Nangong Kuo. Two horses met, two swords were raised, and two men began to fight. After about thirty rounds Chao Lei grew tired. Nangong Kuo knocked him off his horse. Soldiers tied him up and they took him into the city.

When he was brought before Jiang Ziya, Chao Lei refused to kneel. "Why don't you ask for mercy?" asked Jiang Ziya.

"I am a minister of heaven," replied Chao Lei. "You are just a small man who sells noodles and makes baskets. Why would I kneel before someone like you?"

When he said this, the other generals in the room could not stop themselves from smiling. Jiang Ziya understood why they smiled. He said to them, "This man is telling the truth. We know that in the past, Yi Yin was once a poor farmer, but he became prime minister to the first king of Shang[1]. This is fate. Some achieve greatness early, some late, some not at all." Then he pointed his finger at Chao Lei and said, "Take him outside and cut off his head."

The soldiers took Chao Lei outside. Quickly, Huang Feihu said, "Prime Minister, please let me talk with him. Maybe I can bring him over to our side. He could be useful to us."

Jiang Ziya agreed. Huang Feihu went outside, where he found Chao Lei kneeling on the ground and waiting for the sword. He said, "General! Look around you. Your king is on the throne now, but it is like a few cold days in the spring. You know that it will not last. And you know that our king is a good man, just like Yao and Shun in ancient days. I have spoken to the prime minister. He will let you live and keep your old rank. Please think about this!"

Chao Lei said, "Thank you. But I have insulted your prime minister. Why would he let me live?"

"Let me take care of this." Together, they went back to see Jiang Ziya.

Chao Lei knelt. He said, "I have insulted you and I deserve to be executed. I am grateful to you for letting me live."

Jiang Ziya replied, "You have agreed to join us. We are now all part of the same government. You may live. Bring your troops in now."

"My brother is still out there. Let me go and talk with him. I will try to bring him over to our side." Jiang Ziya agreed, and Chao Lei left the

---

[1] According to legend, Yi Yin was a slave. When his master's daughter married the king of Tang, he became the king's slave. He was a good cook, so the king made him his chef. While serving meals to the king, he often offered his advice. He earned the king's trust, was named a high-ranking minister, and ruled for several years as regent after his death.

city.

When he got to his brother's tent, Chao Tian asked him how he managed to escape from the city. Chao Lei replied, "They brought me before Jiang Ziya. I did not kneel. I insulted him. But then I talked with Huang Feihu, and now I believe we should join West Qi. Let's go back to the city together!"

"You fool!" shouted Chao Tian. "Don't you remember that our families are all in Zhaoge? Don't you care about your parents, your wife, your children? They will all be killed."

"Then what should we do?" The two brothers talked for a while. Then Chao Lei returned to the city to meet with Jiang Ziya. He said, "My brother is willing to join us. But he is a general appointed by the king. He wants you to send a high-ranking general to meet with him."

"That's no problem," replied Jiang Ziya. Looking at Huang Feihu, he said, "Go and see him. Bring him back here." Huang Feihu left immediately. But after he left, Jiang Ziya spoke to Nangong Kuo and two other generals and gave them secret orders.

Huang Feihu arrived at the gate of the Shang camp. Chao Tian met him. "Come in, come in!" he said, smiling. But as soon as Huang Feihu entered the camp, soldiers jumped out from the right and left sides. They grabbed Huang Feihu and tied him up.

Huang Feihu shouted and fought, but the soldiers would not let go. Chao Tian said to him, "It's just like the old saying, 'You wore out your iron shoes searching for something, then it arrived with no effort at the right time.' Now we have you. We will take you back to Zhaoge."

The two Chao brothers left the camp immediately and headed back towards Zhaoge, bringing Huang Feihu who was bound with ropes and tied to a horse. They'd traveled about thirty-five *li* and it was getting dark when they suddenly found their road blocked by two generals. One of them said, "Release General Huang Feihu at once!"

Chao Tian shouted, "How dare you!" and attacked them with his sword. They began to fight. Then the other West Qi general rode forward and began to fight with Chao Lei. The fighting went on for a while. Chao Lei became tired, so he turned his horse around and fled. The two West Qi generals captured Chao Tian, then they freed Huang Feihu. They tried to find Chao Lei, but he was already gone.

Chao Lei had escaped from the two West Qi generals, but he did not know the area and he soon became lost. He turned around several times but could not find his way. Around midnight he came to a road. On the road was a small group of soldiers carrying lanterns. In the middle of the group was Nangong Kuo.

Chao Lei tried to fight Nangong Kuo, but he was not as strong and not as good a fighter. Nangong Kuo easily defeated him. Chao Lei was tied up and brought back to West Qi City.

Just before dawn, the two Chao brothers were brought before Jiang Ziya. Huang Feihu said to him, "Thank you, prime minister! You saved my life."

Jiang Ziya said, "I became suspicious when I heard that Chao Tian wanted you to go to their camp. So I sent three generals to wait for you. Things happened exactly as I thought they would."

Then he turned to the Chao brothers. He said coldly, "You are liars and traitors. But you could not trick me. Guards, take them outside and cut off their heads."

As they were being dragged out, Chao Lei cried, "Prime minister, please wait a minute!" Jiang Ziya held up his hand to stop the guards.

"I am listening," he said.

"Prime minister, everyone knows that the king of West Qi is a good man. We would love to join you. But our parents, wives and children are all still in Zhaoge. If we join you, they will all be executed!"

"You have the heart of a wolf. Why didn't you tell me this earlier?"

Chao Lei began to cry. "We are stupid and we did not think. We should have told you."

Jiang Ziya asked Huang Feihu if this story was true. Huang Feihu said that yes, their families were still in Zhaoge and were in great danger.

"All right," said Jiang Ziya. "Chao Tian will be kept here as a hostage. Chao Lei may return to the capital with my secret instructions. He will bring both of your families back here to West Qi."

Both brothers kowtowed to Jiang Ziya. Then Chao Lei set out for the capital.

Chapter 36
The First Attack on West Qi

Heading west by imperial decree, jade split in half[1];
Flags flutter in the air throughout the long journey

Surprised to see painted battle axes turn into leopards;
Even more surprised to see ice flowers turn into Buddha's swords

Zhang Guifang captures the enemy and receives a new title;
His skills are like jewels as he fights in wind and forest

Although wise and clever he is still defeated;
Helpless against the tyrant and the will of heaven

≡ ≡ ≡

Chao Lei traveled for several days, crossing mountains and rivers. When he arrived at the capital, he immediately went to see Grand Tutor Wen.

"What is the situation in West Qi, General?" asked Wen.

Chao Lei replied, "First, I fought against Nangong Kuo. We fought for thirty rounds but neither of us could win. The next day, my brother fought another general and defeated him. After that there were several days with more fights and more battles. But now we have almost no food left. Han Rong has not come to help us. The army is hungry and cannot fight. We need your help."

Grand Tutor Wen said, "I don't know why Han Rong has not given you the food you need. All right. Take three thousand soldiers and bring a thousand piculs of rice back to your army."

Chao Lei did as he was told. But without telling Grand Tutor Wen, he also brought his family and Chao Tian's family with him back to West Qi. He kowtowed to Jiang Ziya and told him, "I have brought our families from Zhaoge to West Qi City. Thank you, prime minister. We

---

[1] In ancient China, a piece of jade would be split in half and shared by two parties to document a contract, an agreement, a royal declaration, or (in this case) a declaration of war.

will never forget this."

Three days later, Grand Tutor Wen began to feel uneasy. He did not understand why Han Rong didn't give food to Chao's soldiers. He burned incense and did a divination. From this, he learned that Chao Lei had tricked him. Furious, he sent another of his generals, a man named Zhang Guifang, to West Qi. He put a hundred thousand soldiers under his command.

Zhang Guifang and his army traveled for several days. They arrived at West Qi City and camped a few *li* outside the south gate.

Inside the city, Huang Feihu said to Jiang Ziya, "I know this Zhang Guifang. He is a sorcerer. As you know, before a one-on-one fight, the fighters tell each other their names. When Zhang Guifang learns the name of his opponent, he shouts the name and says, 'Why don't you get down off your horse?' The man falls from his horse and is captured. We must be careful not to tell him our names."

The other generals heard this but they laughed, not believing it.

The next day there was a fight between one of Zhang Guifang's generals and Ji Chang's twelfth son. The son was killed in the fight.

The day after that, Zhang Guifang shouted that he wanted to fight Jiang Ziya. Jiang Ziya said, "If you want to capture the tiger, you must go into his cave." He rode out of the city to fight Zhang Guifang. He was dressed as a Daoist, with a white robe and a long white beard. He carried two swords and rode a black horse. His generals rode on his right and left sides. His soldiers followed behind them, wearing helmets of silver and gold.

On the opposite side, Zhang Guifang waited for him. He wore white robes, silver armor, and a silver helmet. He rode a white horse. He looked like a statue carved from ice.

Zhang Guifang rode forward. He said, "Jiang Ziya, how can you rebel against your king? You deserve to die. Get down off your horse and give yourself up. If you don't, I will smash your city. I don't care if jade is destroyed along with stone."

Jiang Ziya laughed. He said, "General, you are on the wrong side. Don't you know that a good minister serves a good master? You are a loyal general, but don't close your eyes to your king's foolish ways. Here we follow the law, but your king follows evil. Take my advice. Turn around and go back to Zhaoge."

Zhang Guifang ordered one of his generals to attack Jiang Ziya. The general rode forward and blocked the attack. While they were fighting, Zhang Guifang rode forward and attacked Huang Feihu who was on his great ox. They fought for fifteen rounds. Then Zhang Guifang called out, "Huang Feihu, get down from your ox!" Huang Feihu fell down from his ox. Some of Zhang Guifang soldiers tried to capture him, but two of Jiang Ziya's men fought them off and brought Huang Feihu back to their side.

The battle continued for a while. Zhang Guifang captured Nangong Kuo and another general, then they returned to their camp. They put the two prisoners in wooden carts, to be returned to Zhaoge.

The next day, Zhang Guifang called out again to Jiang Ziya to fight him. But Jiang Ziya would not come out. He hung up a sign declaring a truce. When Zhang Guifang saw the sign, he smiled and said, "Good. Let's enjoy a short rest."

Meanwhile, Fairy Primordial was sitting in his cave when he felt something strange in his heart. He did a divination to find out what was happening. Then he told his disciple to bring Nezha to see him. Nezha arrived and kowtowed to his master.

Fairy Primordial said to Nezha, "Your uncle, Jiang Ziya, needs your help. West Qi is in trouble. They will face thirty-six invasions. Go there now and see how you can help them."

Nezha kowtowed again. Then he picked up his weapons, jumped up on his Wind Fire Wheels, and went to see his uncle the prime minister. He knelt down before Jiang Ziya.

"Who are you and where do you come from?" asked Jiang Ziya.

"This poor disciple's name is Li Nezha. My master, Fairy Primordial, has commanded me to come and serve you. What can I do to help you?"

"You have come just in time. We are being attacked by one of the king's generals, a man named Zhang Guifang. He is a great sorcerer. He has already captured two of our best generals. We have had to hang the truce sign."

Nezha said, "Uncle, it is time to end the truce. I will meet this sorcerer and take him captive."

Jiang Ziya ordered the sign of truce to be taken down. Almost immediately, Zhang Guifang called for a fight. Nezha said that he wanted to fight Zhang Guifang. "Be careful," said Jiang Ziya. "This sorcerer can make you fall just by calling your name."

"Don't worry, Uncle," said Nezha. Then he mounted his Wind Fire Wheels and rode out of the city.

He saw a large and very ugly man waiting for him. The man had a blue face, red hair, and long teeth. In each hand he held a wolf-teeth club.

Nezha said, "I don't know who you are. But get out of my way. I want to fight Zhang Guifang." The man, whose name was Feng Lin, became angry. He attacked Nezha. They fought for twenty rounds. Then Feng Lin rode away on his horse like a strong wind blowing away a leaf. Nezha chased him like heavy rain hitting a flower. Suddenly Feng Lin turned around and spat out a cloud of black smoke. In the cloud was a red ball. It flew right towards Nezha's face.

Nezha said to himself, "This is not the way of the Dao. This is sorcery." He waved his hand at the smoke and the ball, and they both disappeared. Feng Lin turned around angrily to fight Nezha. But Nezha threw his Universal Ring at the man. It hit him and broke his shoulder bone. Injured and unable to fight, Feng Lin rode slowly back to his camp.

When Zhang Guifang heard what happened, he became very angry. He mounted his horse and rode out to meet Nezha. "So," he said, looking at the man standing on the Wind Fire Wheels, "you are Nezha."

"Of course," replied Nezha. "Are you the fool who calls out peoples' names to make them fall?"

This made Zhang Guifang even more angry. He attacked Nezha. They fought for a long time, maybe thirty or forty rounds. One fought for his king and country, the other fought for the entire world. Both were very good fighters. But Nezha was an immortal. Zhang became tired. He tried to use sorcery, calling out, "Nezha, get down from your wheels!"

Nezha heard the magic words. His feet wanted to move, but he stopped them. His body did not move.

Zhang tried again and again, using the same words. Finally, Nezha said, "What a fool you are! You can see that I am not going to get down from my wheels. Why do you keep barking at me like an old dog?"

Zhang attacked Nezha again, but he could not hit him with his swords. After a while, Nezha grabbed his Universal Ring and threw it, hard, right at Zhang's head.

Chapter 37
Jiang Ziya Returns to Mount Kunlun

Jiang Ziya returns to the palace for the first time;
The mist parts before the jade tower as he approaches

Earthly dreams float away on green waters;
Green mountains watch the death of wise rulers

The army and the people meet disaster as the war begins;
Generals and soldiers die from strange magic

Their fate is to endure the investiture of the gods;
A new tower rises on Mount Qi

☰ ☰ ☰

Nezha's Universal Ring flew through the air. It hit Zhang, breaking his left arm. Zhang was able to stay on his horse, but he could not fight, so he turned and fled. He sent a message to Grand Tutor Wen in Zhaoge, asking for more soldiers.

Nezha returned to West Qi City and met with Jiang Ziya.

"What happened?" asked Jiang Ziya. "Did that sorcerer call your name?"

Nezha replied, "I threw my Universal Ring at him and broke his arm. He called my name three times, but I just ignored him."

How could Nezha just ignore Zhang Guifang's magic? Anyone who is born from essence and blood has three souls and seven spirits[1]. When Zhang Guifang calls their name, these souls and spirits are sent away from their body, in all directions. But Nezha was born from lotus flowers and had no soul or spirit. That is why the magic could not touch him.

Jiang Ziya was worried. He did not know what he would do if the king sent a larger army. He bathed, put on clean robes, and went to see Ji Fa.

---

[1] A person has three *hún*, the "spiritual soul" which goes to heaven and can leave the body, and also seven *pò*, the animal soul which is attached to the body and goes to earth at the time of death. These are often translated as just "soul" and "spirit."

He said, "Your Highness, I must go to Mount Kunlun to see my master."

"Don't be long," replied Ji Fa. "We need you here."

"I will return in two or three days."

Jiang Ziya bowed to Ji Fa, then flew to Mount Kunlun on a dust cloud. He looked around. He had not seen this place for ten years, and everything looked new. The sun was shining. Thousands of trees covered the mountains in a green blanket. Grasses and colorful flowers filled the air with a sweet fragrance. Phoenixes flew through the sky, black monkeys rested in the trees. Blue lions and white elephants could be seen on the mountainside. It was more beautiful than heaven.

Jiang Ziya entered the palace and knelt before his master, and said, "Your disciple wishes the teacher to live forever!"

Heavenly Primogenitor said, "I am happy that you have come to see me. I have a job for you. You must go to Mount Qi and build a Terrace of Creation. Here is an important paper, it is the Feng Shen Bang[1]. Hang it up in the terrace. This will be the most important work of your life."

Jiang Ziya took the Feng Shen Bang. Then he said, "Master, please help me. A powerful sorcerer named Zhang Guifang is attacking West Qi. I am a weak disciple with no knowledge or power to use against him. Can you help me?"

But Heavenly Primogenitor said, "Must I help you with every little thing? You are prime minister now, with great wealth and great power. Your ruler is a good and wise man. You will get help from other people when you need it. You don't need my help. Now go."

Jiang Ziya got up and started to leave. But Heavenly Primogenitor held up his hand. He said, "Wait. One more thing. After you leave here, do not answer anyone who calls you from behind. If you do, West Qi will be invaded thirty-six times."

Jiang Ziya walked out of the palace, holding the Feng Shen Bang in his hand. As he walked, he heard someone behind him calling, "Jiang Ziya! Jiang Ziya!"

Of course, Jiang Ziya did not turn around because he remembered what his master had just told him. He kept walking. He heard the voice say,

---

[1] This document lists the names of all the mortals and immortals who are fated to be elevated to gods. It is called *fēng shén bǎng*, which is also the popular title of this book.

"Jiang Ziya! How can you forget your old friends? We were together in this palace for over forty years. But now that you are a prime minister, you don't even bother to talk with me anymore?"

Jiang Ziya turned around. He saw his old friend Shen Gongbao, who was also a disciple of Heavenly Primogenitor. The man wore a long silk robe and a blue scarf. There were clouds and fog under his straw sandals. He held a bright metal sword in his hand.

Jiang Ziya said, "Brother, I did not know it was you. I'm sorry if I offended you."

"What's that in your hand?" asked Shen Gongbao.

"It's the Feng Shen Bang. Master asked me to put it in a new terrace that I must build on Mount Qi."

"Tell me, brother. Which side are you on?"

"What a strange question! Our master asked me to help Ji Fa, the king of West Qi, to bring about the end of the Shang Dynasty. Now I am the prime minister of West Qi. This is heaven's plan."

"We will see about that. I am leaving right now. I am going to Zhaoge to help protect the Shang Dynasty and the king. You must help me if we are to remain friends."

"But brother, we must follow our master's orders!"

"No, I want you to protect the Shang Dynasty. Look, you are nothing compared to me. You have only studied for forty years. But I am much more powerful than you. I can move mountains and oceans. I can defeat dragons and tigers. I can fly on a crane to the ninth heaven, and I can ride on a beam of light for a thousand years."

"You have powers, but so do I," said Jiang Ziya.

"Your little powers are nothing. If you cut off my head, it can fly for a thousand miles on a red cloud. When it returns to my neck, I become whole again. Can you do that?"

Jiang Ziya laughed. He said, "Brother, let me cut off your head and throw it in the air. If you can live after that, I will burn the Feng Shen Bang and follow you to Zhaoge."

"Do you promise?"

"Of course. A man's words are as heavy as Mount Tai."

Shen Gongbao took off his scarf. He pulled up his hair with his left hand. With his right hand he swung his sword, cutting off his own head. His left hand threw his head up into the air. It flew up and up and up, until it disappeared in the sky.

A friend of Heavenly Primogenitor, the Immortal of the South Pole, was watching this. He saw the two men arguing. Then he saw Shen Gongbao cut off his own head. He saw the head flying up into the air. "Oh, Jiang Ziya," he said, "you have been tricked." Then he called to one of his disciples. "Quick. Change yourself into a white crane. Fly up, grab that head, and take it to the South Sea." The disciple did as he was told.

Then the Immortal of the South Pole came over to Jiang Ziya. He said, "You are a fool. Don't you know that Shen Gongbao is a sorcerer? He tricked you. Your master told you not to turn around if someone called you, but you did not obey him. Now you will have to deal with thirty-six invasions."

Jiang Ziya could not say anything. He just looked at the ground. The Immortal of the South Pole continued, "I told my disciple to take his head. If the head does not return in three hours, Shen Gongbao will die. Then you will be out of trouble."

Jiang Ziya said, "Please, brother, don't do this. Daoism teaches us kindness and mercy. It does not matter what Shen Gongbao did. You must show mercy to him."

"All right," said the Immortal of the South Pole. He waved his hand. The white crane opened its mouth. The head fell onto Shen Gongbao's neck. The man opened his eyes and looked around. He saw that his head was backwards on his neck. He lifted up his head, turned it around, and put it on his neck again.

The Immortal of the South Pole said to him, "How dare you try to trick Jiang Ziya like that! Get out of here right now."

Shen Gongbao said to Jiang Ziya, "Just wait. I will turn West Qi into an ocean of blood and a mountain of bones." Then he left.

Jiang Ziya also left. Holding the Feng Shen Bang in his hand, he headed towards West Qi City. As he flew over a mountain, he saw a great sea. Huge waves crashed against the shore. Black clouds filled the sky and a powerful wind blew through the trees. Then a naked man walked out of the waves. Jiang Ziya flew down to meet the man.

The man said, "Great immortal! I have been trapped here for a thousand years. A few days ago, a master named Pure Void Virtue came to see me. He said that soon I would meet a great master and that I should serve him. Please release me from this place, and I will be your servant!"

"Who are you?" asked Jiang Ziya.

"My name is Bai Jian. I was a general under the great emperor Xuanyuan. I was killed in battle and have been trapped here ever since."

"All right," said Jiang Ziya. He held out his hand. A bolt of lightning came from each finger. The lightning flew towards the sea, releasing Bai Jian.

He said, "Bai Jian, you must come with me and serve West Qi." Bai Jian fell to his knees and kowtowed.

The two of them continued towards West Qi City. Soon Jiang Ziya saw five gods waiting to meet him. They all cried, "We are here to serve you, prime minister!"

"All right," said Jiang Ziya. "Go to Mount Qi. Start building the Terrace of Creation. This man, Bai Jian, will supervise the work. When the terrace is finished, I will come back."

The five gods and Bai Jian went to Mount Qi and began to work on building the terrace. Jiang Ziya continued on his journey back to West Qi City.

He reached West Qi City. He met with Ji Fa, but he did not tell him everything that happened, because the will of heaven must be kept secret.

That night, he ordered a night attack on Zhang Guifang's camp. The attack was a complete surprise. Nezha and the West Qi soldiers fought well. Soon they reached Nangong Kuo, freeing him from his prison cart.

Zhang Guifang and the few surviving Shang soldiers fled to Mount Qi. He quickly wrote a report and sent it to Zhaoge, requesting more soldiers and supplies.

The report reached Grand Tutor Wen. He read it, and his eyes grew big. "What? I gave Zhang Guifang a large army, but he could not win the battle. It looks like this old man must go to West Qi and take care of this matter himself."

One of his generals said, "Sir, please think again. We need you here in Zhaoge. You have many powerful Daoist friends in the mountains. Ask them to help us!"

This seemed like a good idea. But it caused the deaths of four great Daoist masters.

Chapter 38
Four Monks in West Qi

Since ancient times the king's way has always been kindness;
Foolish war leads to defeat and death

Soldiers rush forward seeking fame;
They find only disaster and are cut off from the gods

Great skills and rare treasures, who has them?
Fighting for victory, what is real?

Better to close your eyes and sit in the mountains;
Find joy and return to your natural state

≡ ≡ ≡

Grand Tutor Wen clapped his hands and said, "That is a wonderful idea! I have been so busy, I'd forgotten all about my old Daoist friends." Then he turned to his generals and said, "I will be gone for a few days."

He went outside and mounted his unicorn. Together they rose up into the sky. They rode on the clouds and the wind until they arrived at Nine Dragon Island in the western sea. He landed near a large cave. A young man came out of the cave.

"Is your master here?" asked Wen.

"Yes," said the young man. "He is playing chess with his friends."

"Please tell him that Grand Tutor Wen is here to see him."

The young man went back into the cave. A few minutes later, four old Daoists came out. "Brother Wen," said one of them, "it is good to see you!"

Wen said, "I have come to ask for your help. Jiang Ziya, a Daoist immortal from Mount Kunlun, has been helping Ji Fa to rebel against the king. I sent Zhang Guifang to stop him, but he could not win. I cannot go myself, because I am needed in the capital. I am asking the four of you to help me."

"Of course," they said, "we will be happy to help you. Please return to Zhaoge. We will meet you there soon."

The next day, the four Daoists flew to Zhaoge on a water cloud. The people of the city saw them and were frightened. The four Daoists were all around sixteen feet tall and quite ugly. The first one, Wang Mo, had a face as round as the moon. He wore a grey robe and a long scarf. The second, Yang Sen, had a black face, a red beard, and yellow eyebrows. He wore a purple robe. The third, Gao Youqian, had long red hair and had long fangs that stuck out from the top and bottom of his mouth. He wore a scarlet robe. The fourth Li Xingba, had a dark brown face and a long beard. He wore a golden crown and a yellow robe.

The four Daoists soon found the home of Grand Tutor Wen. Wen brought them to the palace to meet the king, who was quite frightened by their appearance. After that, the four Daoists left the city and flew to West Qi.

They found the Shang soldiers hiding on Mount Qi, about seventy *li* from the city. They were met by Zhang Guifang and Feng Lin. Both of the generals had trouble walking. "Are you injured?" asked Wang Mo.

Feng Lin told them about the recent battles. Wang Mo took some medicine from his sleeve, crushed it between his teeth, and put it on their wounds. The wounds healed immediately.

Wang Mo told the generals to bring their army back to West Qi City. Then he told Zhang Guifang to challenge Jiang Ziya to a fight.

Yang Sen gave magic charms to the two generals. He said, "Put these charms on your horses. It will stop them from being frightened when they see our beasts."

Zhang Guifang rode towards the city gate, alone. He shouted to Jiang Ziya to come out and fight him. Soon Jiang Ziya came out, followed by hundreds of soldiers. He rode a big black horse and carried a sword. He said, "Zhang Guifang, you were defeated once already. Why are you here again?"

Zhang Guifang replied, "Victory and defeat, this is the fate of a warrior. But now things have changed. Look!"

Four strange animals appeared behind Zhang Guifang. Wang Mo rode a monster. Yang Sen rode a lion. Gao Youqian rode a leopard. And Li Xingba rode a unicorn.

The horses of the West Qi army saw these strange animals. They reared up in fright, throwing Jiang Ziya and his generals to the ground. Only Nezha remained on his wind fire wheels.

The four Daoists looked down at Jiang Ziya and laughed. They said, "Get up slowly, old man!"

Jiang Ziya stood up and straightened his hat and robes. He bowed to the four Daoists and said, "Hello, brothers. Who are you, where do you come from, and what can I do for you?"

Wang Mo said, "We are four Daoists like yourself. We come from Nine Dragon Island. Grand Tutor Wen asked us to come and help you. We have three proposals for you."

"If your proposals are good, you can give me thirty of them. Please tell me what they are!" replied Jiang Ziya.

"First, your king Ji Fa must agree that he is a subject of the Shang Dynasty."

"Brother, our king has always been a loyal subject. That is no problem."

"Second, you must give away all the treasure in West Qi to the Shang soldiers. And third, you must give us Huang Feihu."

Jiang Ziya said, "I see no problem with your three proposals. Please allow me to return to the city and write a letter to His Majesty. And please thank His Majesty for his kindness towards us."

The two sides returned to their own camps. Huang Feihu said to Jiang Ziya, "Prime minister, I do not want our king or our city to suffer because of me. Please give me to them, so they can take me as a prisoner to Zhaoge."

"Don't worry," replied Jiang Ziya. "I do not plan to accept their three proposals. But we could not fight with all of our generals lying on the ground. I needed some time to think about what to do next."

Jiang Ziya bathed, then he traveled again to Mount Kunlun to see his master. Before he could say anything, Heavenly Primogenitor held up his hand and said, "I know that there are four Daoists causing trouble in West Qi. They are riding four beasts from ancient times." Then he turned to his servant and told him, "Bring my beast."

A short time later, the boy returned with the beast. It had the head of a unicorn, the body of a dragon, and the tail of a wolf. The master said, "I have chosen you to create the new gods. Now I give you my own beast, so you can meet those four beasts without fear."

Then he gave a long wooden staff to Jiang Ziya. He said, "Go to the northern sea. Someone will be waiting for you there. Protect yourself with this staff. It has a note hidden inside. If you run into trouble, take out the note and read it. You will know what to do."

Jiang Ziya kowtowed to his master. Then he took the staff, mounted the beast and flew to the northern sea. The beast brought him down on a mountain near an island in the sea. The mountainside was covered with beautiful flowers, tall bamboos and large pine trees. He could hear the sound of the sea below.

Suddenly dark clouds appeared. Then a very strange creature came out of the clouds. It had the body of a fish but a head like a camel. It had hands with sharp claws, and one foot that looked like a tiger's foot.

The creature shouted, "Jiang Ziya! Give me a piece of your flesh!"

Jiang Ziya said, "Why? We are not enemies."

"You cannot escape. Give me a piece of your flesh right now!"

Jiang Ziya did not know what to do. He pulled the note out of the staff and read it. Now he knew what to do. He said, "Do you want to eat me? Just pull this staff out of the ground. If you can do that, I will let you eat me." Then he pushed the end of the staff into the ground.

The staff grew to be about twenty feet long. The beast tried to pull it out of the ground, but it did not move. He kept trying, but he could not move it. Then Jiang Ziya held his hands up to the sky. Lightning and thunder came from each of his fingers. The beast tried to let go of the staff, but his hands were stuck. "Eat my sword!" shouted Jiang Ziya.

"Great immortal," cried the beast, "please have mercy on me! I did not know who you were. This was all Shen Gongbao's fault."

"What?" replied Jiang Ziya. "What does Shen Gongbao have to do with this?"

"Oh great one, I am Dragon Beard Tiger. I have lived here for many years by eating the essence of the sun and moon. Two days ago, Shen Gongbao came to see me. He said that you would be coming here today. He said that if I ate a piece of your flesh, I would live for ten thousand years. I was a fool to believe him. Please have mercy on me."

"I will let you live, but only if you become my disciple."

"I will."

Jiang Ziya told him to close his eyes. Then he sent a huge thunderbolt, and Dragon Beard Tiger found that he could move his hands again. He knelt before his new master. Jiang Ziya pulled the staff out of the ground, and the two of them went to West Qi City. He said to his generals, "This is Dragon Beard Tiger from the northern sea. He is my new disciple."

Days passed. Nobody came out of West Qi City to bring Huang Feihu to the Shang army. After eight days, Yang Sen said to Wang Mo, "Brother, it has been eight days. Jiang Ziya has not brought the prisoner out. Let's ask him why."

The Shang army, led by Feng Lin and the four Daoists, marched to the city wall. They shouted for Jiang Ziya to come out. Soon Jiang Ziya came out, riding his black horse. Nezha, Dragon Beard Tiger and Huang Feihu were with him.

The battle started with Wang Mo shouting and attacking Jiang Ziya with his sword. Nezha rode forward on his Wind Fire Wheels and fought against Wang Mo.

Next, Yang Sen rode forward and threw a magic pearl at Nezha, knocking him off his magic wheels. Wang Mo tried to cut off Nezha's head but Huang Feihu stopped him.

Yang Sen threw another magic pearl, this time at Huang Feihu, knocking him off his ox. But Dragon Beard Tiger ran forward and attacked Wang Mo. Quickly, Gao Youqian threw one of his own magic pearls, hitting Dragon Beard Tiger on the neck.

With three of his generals wounded, Jiang Ziya was fighting alone. Li Xingba threw a magic pearl and hit him in the heart. He cried out in pain, turned around, and fled towards the northern sea. He saw Wang Mo chasing him. So he told his beast to fly into the air. But Wang Mo shouted, "Don't you know, any Daoist can fly through the clouds!" He told his monster to follow Jiang Ziya.

As they flew through the air, Wang Mo threw a magic pearl. It hit Jiang Ziya on the back, knocking him off his beast and onto the ground. Wang Mo got off his monster. He stood over Jiang Ziya, preparing to cut off his head. But just then, he heard someone singing:

Soft winds blow through the willow trees
Flower petals fall onto the water
If someone askes me where I live
My home is deep in the white clouds

Wang Mo looked around, and saw that it was the Heavenly Master Manjusri. "What are you doing here, brother?" asked Wang Mo.

The master replied, "Dear friend, don't hurt him. I have come here to tell you that Heaven has decided several things. First, the Shang Dynasty will end. Second, a new king has been born in West Qi. Third, Chan Daoism must break the rule against killing. Fourth, Jiang Ziya will enjoy wealth and power in the world. Fifth, he will create new gods. My friend, listen to me. Go back to your cave while you can. Soon it will be too late."

Wang Mo did not want to hear all this. He raised his sword and started to attack the Heavenly Master Manjusri. But just then, a young Daoist in a yellow robe stepped out from behind the master. He said, "Stop, Wang Mo. I am Jinzha, disciple of the Heavenly Master."

Wang Mo and Jinzha began to fight, sword against sword. While they were fighting, Heavenly Master Manjusri pulled out a stake[1] from his sleeve. He threw it in the air. When it came down on Wang Mo, it held him tightly with three golden rings. One ring was around his neck, one around his waist, and one around his feet. He could not move.

Jinzha raised his sword and aimed it at Wang Mo's neck.

---

[1] Manjusri's weapon is a *dùn lóng zhuāng*, a pillar-like rod with three golden rings, and dragons wrapped around it.

Chapter 39
Jiang Ziya Freezes Mount Qi

The four immortals fight heaven for no good reason;
They use their strange skills to turn things upside down

Men come from the west with the List of Creation;
Going north, they will know immortality

How many great people have disappeared in this land;
Many evil deeds have led to those crimes

A thousand feet of snow falls in July;
You and Fei die and travel to the land of Nine Springs[1]

≡ ≡ ≡

With one blow, Jinzha's sword cut off Wang Mo's head. Wang Mo's soul left his body and flew to the Terrace of Creation.

Jiang Ziya was still lying on the ground, badly injured. Heavenly Master Manjusri poured a little bit of magic elixir into his mouth. Soon Jiang Ziya opened his eyes. He saw Heavenly Master Manjusri and said, "Brother, why are you here?"

Heavenly Master Manjusri smiled and said, "It is the will of heaven." Then he turned to Jinzha and said, "Help your uncle return to West Qi." After they departed, Heavenly Master Manjusri dug a grave and buried Wang Mo's body. Then he returned to his own home.

Jiang Ziya and Jinzha returned to West Qi. The king and all his generals welcomed them. "Where were you?" asked Ji Fa. "We were all worried about you."

"If it were not for Jinzha and his master, I would not be alive today," Jiang Ziya replied.

In the Shang camp, the three Daoist masters were very worried. They had all seen Wang Mo chasing Jiang Ziya across the sky, but Wang Mo

---

[1] The underworld is said to consist of nine wells, one after the other, giving rise to the term *jiǔquán zhī xià*, "under the nine springs."

had not returned yet. Yang Sen did a divination with his fingers. Then he cried out, "Oh no! For thousands of years our brother studied the Way, but now he has died on Five Dragon Mountain."

The next morning, the three Daoists rode to the gate of West Qi City, demanding that Jiang Ziya come out and meet them. Jiang Ziya was still weak from his injuries, but he rode out anyway, accompanied by Nezha and Jinzha.

The three Daoists shouted, "Jiang Ziya, you monster! You killed our brother. Now we cannot let you live!"

They rushed forward to attack Jiang Ziya. Nezha and Jinzha rushed to block them. The six warriors battled, sword against sword. Red clouds filled the sky. Then Jiang Ziya threw his magic staff in the air. There was a flash of lightning and a roar of thunder. The staff came down and hit Gao Youqian on the head. He died instantly, and his soul flew to the Terrace of Creation.

Yang Sen, blind with rage, charged at Jiang Ziya. But Nezha threw his universal ring at him. As the Daoist tried to catch the ring, Jinzha used his magic stake to capture him, three rings wrapping around his body. Then Jinzha cut him in half with his sword. Yang Sen's soul also flew to the Terrace of Creation.

Now there was only one of the four Daoist masters left, Li Xingba. He rushed into the fight, along with Zhang Guifang and Feng Lin. During the fight, Feng Lin was killed by one of Huang Feihu's sons. His soul also flew to the Terrace of Creation.

Zhang Guifang saw that they could not win the battle, so he returned to the Shang camp along with Li Xingba. He sent a message to Grand Tutor Wen in Zhaoge asking for more soldiers.

The next day, Jiang Ziya rode out of the city and demanded to see Zhang Guifang. The two men began to fight. One fought to protect his king, the other fought to save his country. After thirty rounds neither could win. Jiang Ziya ordered that the drums be beaten, ordering his entire army to attack. Dozens of men on horses surrounded Zhang Guifang, who fought like a wild tiger.

Jinzha and his brother Nezha fought against Li Xingba. Li Xingba could not fight both of them. He flew away on his beast.

Now Zhang Guifang was fighting alone, with all his generals dead or defeated. He knew he could not get out alive. He shouted, "My king, I cannot serve you any longer!" Then he stabbed himself with his short sword. His soul flew to the Terrace of Creation.

Li Xingba flew far from the battle. After a while he arrived at a mountain side and dismounted from his beast. Exhausted, he lay down to rest. A little while later he heard the sound of someone singing. Looking up, he saw a young Daoist coming towards him. The young man bowed and said, "Greetings, brother! Who are you and where do you come from?"

"I am Li Xingba, a Daoist master from Nine Dragon Island. I was fighting in a great battle, but our side was defeated. I came here to rest a bit."

"How wonderful to meet you! I am Muzha. My master sent me to help my uncle Jiang Ziya. My master told me that if I met a man named Li Xingba, I should capture him and bring him to Jiang Ziya."

Li Xingba laughed and said, "You foolish boy. How dare you insult me like this!" He got up and slashed at Muzha with his sword. They fought up and down the mountain side. Li Xingba was a powerful fighter, but Muzha carried two magic swords on his back, one female and one male. He shook his left shoulder. The male sword flew into the air, dropped down on Li Xingba and cut off his head. Li Xingba's soul flew to the Terrace of Creation to join the others.

Back in Zhaoge, Grand Tutor Wen received a report. He read it and learned that Feng Lin and all four of the Daoists had been killed. He immediately called for a meeting with all of his generals to discuss how to help Zhang Guifang. He did not know that Zhang Guifang had also been killed.

An elderly general named Lu Xiong stepped forward. He said, "I would like to go and help Zhang Guifang."

Wen smiled and said to the white haired general, "Thank you, my old friend. But you have lived for many years. This might be difficult for you."

The old man replied, "Grand Tutor, youth is not as important as you might think. A good general must understand the situation. He must bring together his soldiers to fight as one. He must know how to make a weak army strong. He must know when to attack and when to retreat. He must turn danger into safety, and defeat into victory. Give me a couple of good advisors and I will bring you victory."

Wen was very happy to hear these words. He said, "Wonderful. I will give you two of our king's best advisors." Then he ordered the two evil ministers Fei Zhong and You Hun to come see him immediately.

When they arrived, Wen told them, "We need your help. Feng Lin has been killed and Zhang Guifang has been defeated. You are to go with General Lu and help him turn this defeat into victory."

The two ministers were terrified. Fei Zhong said, "Grand Tutor, we know nothing about war. We are ministers, not soldiers! We cannot help you."

"Both of you are clever. You know what to do when the situation changes. That is what we need right now. No more discussion. Go now!"

Fei Zhong and You Hun had no choice, they had to agree to go. Soon they marched off to war, with General Lu and fifty thousand soldiers.

It was summer. The weather was very hot. The sky was cloudless and there was no wind. The soldiers and horses had no water. They suffered badly in the hot weather. Then a message arrived that Zhang Guifang had been killed. General Lu decided to wait before going to West Qi City. He brought his army into the forest near Mount Qi to wait for instructions from Zhaoge.

In West Qi City, Jiang Ziya heard that there was a large army camped near Mount Qi. He sent Nangong Kuo and a small army of five thousand men to Mount Qi to keep an eye on the Shang army.

The next day, they received an order from Jiang Ziya. They were to march to near the top of Mount Qi. "We will die if we try to do this!" said one of the generals.

Nangong Kuo replied, "We cannot disobey an order." They began marching up the mountain. There was no water for drinking or cooking. It was so hot and dry that the trees were dying and birds were falling dead from the sky. The Shang soldiers saw them marching up the mountain, and laughed at their foolishness.

Soon Jiang Ziya arrived with another three thousand men. And then carts arrived carrying loads of heavy jackets and hats. "What are these for?" asked the soldiers. "If we put these on, we will just die faster."

That night, Jiang Ziya went alone to the top of the mountain. He took out his sword and bowed to Mount Kunlun. Then he spoke some magic words and poured some magic water on the ground. Soon, a strong wind blew through the forest. The air began to get cool.

The Shang general Lu Xiong smiled and said, "This weather is much better for fighting!" But the wind kept blowing, and the weather kept getting colder and colder. For three days the wind blew and the weather got colder. On the fourth day it began to snow.

The Shang soldiers were wearing thin clothes and metal armor. They began to suffer badly from the cold. The elderly general Lu Xiong was nearly frozen to death. But at the top of the mountain, the Zhou soldiers put on the warm clothing and were quite comfortable.

The snow kept falling. Near the top of the mountain there was only two feet of snow, but lower down it was four or five feet deep.

Then Jiang Ziya went to the top of the mountain again. He began to recite different magic words. The snow stopped. The hot sun returned. The snow began to melt. The water rushed down the side of the mountain in fast-flowing rivers.

Then Jiang Ziya recited more magic words. The weather turned very cold. The water turned to ice. Soon, the side of the mountain was covered by a frozen sea of ice.

Jiang Ziya selected twenty of his men and told them, "Go down the mountain side into the Shang camp. Capture the officers." The Zhou soldiers went into the Shang camp. They found everyone frozen in ice. They easily captured General Lu, Fei Zhong, and You Hun. They brought the three prisoners up the mountain to face Jiang Ziya.

Chapter 40
The Shang Army Surrounds West Qi City

The four Mo brothers are called heavenly kings;
Only the Green Cloud Sword is special

When the pipa plays, soldiers die;
When the magic umbrella opens, light turns to darkness

Don't speak of how fire can burn;
Speak of how the magic fox can eat the strong

Even if you have many treasures of the world;
Once you meet Huang Tianhua, you are fated to die

≡ ≡ ≡

When the three prisoners were brought to the Zhou camp, Fei Zhong and You Hun fell to their knees and begged for mercy. But General Lu Xiong stayed on his feet and said nothing.

Jiang Ziya ignored the two kneeling ministers. To Lu Xiong he said, "General, you must learn how to tell truth from lies. Everyone knows that your king is evil. Two thirds of the country knows this, and they now follow us. Why do you continue to act against the will of heaven?"

"There is no need for all this talk," replied Lu Xiong. "I fight for His Majesty. Now I will die for him."

Jiang Ziya told his soldiers to execute the three prisoners. Then he went back up to the top of Mount Qi and recited some magic words. The clouds disappeared and the sun returned to the sky. Soon the ice melted. Two or three thousand Shang soldiers had died in the ice, but the rest all fled back to Zhaoge.

In Zhaoge, Grand Tutor Wen did not know what to do. His best generals had been killed, and also his four Daoist friends. "Who should we send to West Qi now?" he asked.

One of his generals replied, "Grand Tutor, the situation is serious. Everyone we send to West Qi has failed. Now it is time to send the Mo brothers."

Wen agreed at once. He sent a letter to the four Mo brothers, telling them about the situation in West Qi and ordering them to go. The Mo brothers read the order and laughed. One of them said, "Why is he so worried about Jiang Ziya and Huang Feihu? This will be easy for us. It's like using a great sword to kill a small chicken."

The Mo brothers gathered a hundred thousand soldiers. They traveled over mountains and across rivers and camped outside West Qi City.

Inside the city, Huang Feihu met with Jiang Ziya. He said, "Prime Minister, these brothers are very powerful. I was their commander when we fought at the eastern sea."

"Tell me about them," said Jiang Ziya.

"The eldest is Mo Liqing. He has a magic sword. It creates a dark wind filled with thousands of swords that kills anyone who is caught inside the wind. It also creates fire and smoke that burn anyone near it. Next is Mo Lihong. He has a magic umbrella. When it's opened, it covers the earth in darkness. When he turns the umbrella, it makes the earth tremble. Third is Mo Lihai. He has a magic pipa[1]. When he plays the pipa, fire and wind come and kill everyone nearby. And the youngest is Mo Lishou. He has a magic white fox that he carries in a bag. When he lets the fox out, it turns into a white flying elephant that eats everyone in its path."

When he heard that the Mo brothers were calling for him, Jiang Ziya was worried. But Muzha, Jinzha and Nezha all said, "Don't be afraid, uncle! Heaven is on our side!" Jiang Ziya went out the city gate to meet them.

He bowed politely and said, "Are you the four Mo brothers?"

Mo Liqing said, "Jiang Ziya, you are creating trouble everywhere. You have cut off the heads of our generals, and you don't obey the orders of His Majesty. Put down your weapons and give up. If you don't, we will destroy your city."

"You are wrong, sir. We obey all of His Majesty's laws, and we have not sent a single soldier over the five passes."

"This is nonsense!" shouted Mo Liqing. All four Mo brothers rushed

---

[1] The pipa is a traditional Chinese stringed instrument.

forward to attack Jiang Ziya. The Zhou generals fought back. The battle lasted for hours.

The magic of the Mo brothers was very powerful. The magic umbrella captured Nezha's universal ring and Jinzha's magic stake. Jiang Ziya tried to use his magic staff, but it did not work against the Mo brothers and it was also taken by the umbrella.

The battle turned against the Zhou. Fire and smoke and thousands of swords poured out from Mo Liqing's magic sword, killing many of the Zhou soldiers. Mo Lihong opened his magic umbrella, turning the sky black. More soldiers died when Mo Lihai played his pipa. Finally, Mo Lishou released his fox. It changed into a huge white elephant that killed many more soldiers. Nine Zhou generals were killed, and most of the soldiers were killed or injured. The army turned and fled back to the city.

The Shang army was pleased with their victory. There was singing and dancing in the Shang camp. The four Mo brothers met to discuss their next moves. They agreed to surround the city, attack the walls and gates, and try to capture Jiang Ziya and Ji Fa. They thought they could defeat the city in a single day.

The next day, the Shang army surrounded the city and called for Jiang Ziya to come out. Jiang Ziya did not want to fight them. He stayed inside the city and hung up a truce sign. But the Shang paid no attention to the truce sign. They put ladders up against the wall and began to climb the ladders.

The Zhou army fought to keep the Shang soldiers from entering the city. They used lime bottles[1], stone balls, burning arrows, and long spears. The Shang army tried for three days but could not climb over the walls and enter the city.

The Mo brothers told their soldiers to pull back. They decided to wait until West Qi City ran out of food and water. But after two months the city still had enough to eat and drink. They decided to try their magic weapons instead.

That night, a strange wind blew across West Qi City. Jiang Ziya became worried. He did a divination with gold coins and saw that the Mo

---

[1] In the 12th century A.D., Chinese navies filled thin bottles with poison, lime and iron pickles and flung them onto opposing ships. When they broke on the decks, sailors could not open their eyes and could not fight. Sometimes the lime was mixed with explosives.

brothers were starting to use their magic weapons. Quickly he bathed, changed to clean clothes, and kowtowed towards Mount Kunlun. Then he used powerful magic to pick up the whole northern sea and hang it above the city to protect it.

The Mo brothers began to use their powerful weapons. They used their magic swords, magic umbrella, magic pipa, and the fox. Dark clouds covered the sky, cold fog covered the earth.

But the city was not touched by the magic. At dawn, Jiang Ziya sent the northern sea back to where it had come from. The Mo brothers looked at the city and saw that it was not touched by the magic at all.

The Mo brothers did not try their magic again. They waited for two more months, hoping that West Qi City would run out of food. The city was almost out of food, it had only enough for a few more days. Even the birds and animals became hungry and left the city. But then two young Daoists came to the city. One was dressed in red and the other was dressed in blue. They asked to meet with Jiang Ziya.

"Where do you come from, and why are you here?" asked Jiang Ziya.

"We are disciples of Heavenly Master of Divine Virtue. Our master has sent us here to give you some food."

"That is wonderful. Where is it?"

One of the young men took a small bowl of rice out of his bag and held it in his hand. The generals looked at it and tried not to laugh. But Jiang Ziya told one of his aides to take the rice to the city's three rice warehouses. Two hours later, the aide returned and said, "Sir, all the warehouses are now full of rice!"

Now they had enough food to eat and enough soldiers to defend the city, but they still could not defeat the Mo brothers. Jiang Ziya waited. The Shang army continued to surround the city.

Two months later, another Daoist arrived at the city gate. He was tall and thin. He wore a long robe with a silk belt, a rising-to-heaven hat, and straw shoes. Jiang Ziya greeted him. The Daoist said, "This disciple's name is Yang Jian. My master has sent me here to help you. Tell me, where are the generals who are attacking your city?"

Jiang Ziya told him about the four Mo brothers. Yang Jian said, "I need to know more about them. Take down the sign of truce. I will meet them outside the city gates."

Some soldiers took down the sign of truce. Immediately the Mo brothers demanded that Jiang Ziya come out and fight. But Yang Jian and Nezha came out instead.

Mo Liqing looked at the tall Daoist but did not recognize him. "Who are you?" he asked.

"I am Yang Jian. The prime minister is my uncle. How dare you use your evil magic here. I will teach you a lesson. Then you will die and no one will bury your bodies!"

The Mo brothers rushed forward. Yang Jian and Nezha began to fight them. Mo Lishou released his fox. It changed into a huge white elephant. The elephant had a large mouth and teeth like sharp knives. It ate Yang Jian with one bite. Seeing this, Nezha ran back inside the city walls. He told Jiang Ziya that the elephant had eaten the Daoist.

The Mo brothers were delighted. They drank together. They decided that they would send the fox into the city to eat Jiang Ziya and Ji Fa. Mo Lishou took the fox out of the bag, released it, and told it what to do. The fox flew towards the city. But Yang Jian had made himself very small and was hiding in its belly. As the fox flew, Yang Jian reached up and squeezes the fox's heart, killing it. Then he made himself larger again. He returned to Jiang Ziya.

"You were killed in battle. How are you still alive?" asked Jiang Ziya.

"I can change my size, and I know seventy-two transformations. I can change into any animal that I wish. Just now, I was hiding in the belly of the fox. When the Mo brothers sent the fox to kill you, I killed it."

"With your great powers, we have nothing to fear!" said Jiang Ziya. "Why don't you change into a fox, go back to the Shang camp, and steal the Mo brothers' weapons?"

Yang Jian changed into a fox and flew to the Shang camp. The Mo brothers looked at it. One of them said, "It looks like our fox did not eat anyone." Then they put the fox in its bag. They drank some wine and fell asleep. While they were sleeping Yang Jian crawled out of the bag, changed into human form, grabbed the magic weapons, and carried them back to Jiang Ziya. Then he returned to the Shang camp and crawled back into the bag.

In the morning, the Mo brothers saw that their weapons were gone. They looked everywhere in the camp but could not find them. Mo Lihong said, "We need those weapons to defeat the Zhou. What will we do now?"

Meanwhile, on Mount Green Peak, Master Pure Void Virtue called for his disciple, Huang Tianhua. He said to his disciple, "You must go to West Qi. Help your father Huang Feihu and your king Ji Fa." Then he gave Huang Tianhua two hammers, a jade unicorn, and a magic javelin.

Huang Tianhua flew on the unicorn, arriving at West Qi City. He immediately went to see his father. That night, he gave up his vegetarian diet and ate meat for dinner. The next day, he took off his Daoist robes. He put on golden armor over a scarlet robe, and went to see Jiang Ziya.

Jiang Ziya saw him and said, "Young man, you are a Daoist. Why do you dress like a soldier?"

Huang Tianhua replied, "I came here to fight the Mo brothers, so I have to dress as a general."

"All right, but don't forget that you are a Daoist. At least, put on this silk belt." He handed a silk belt to Huang Tianhua, who put it on. "Now be careful!"

"Don't worry. My master told me what to do. I am not afraid of these Mo brothers at all." Then he mounted his jade unicorn and rode out of the city, with the two hammers in his hand.

Chapter 41
Grand Tutor Wen Goes to West Qi

Grand Tutor Wen leads his army out of the capital city;
The west wind comes from the setting sun

The people suffer from the king's poor leadership;
While loyal ministers lose their lives

We know the date of departure, not the date of return;
We only know the times of growth, not the times of death

The four generals follow their leader and fight in the west;
In their hearts the people remember the first king of Zhou

≡ ≡ ≡

The four Mo brothers walked towards the gate of West Qi City. They saw a young general coming out to meet them. He was riding a jade unicorn. He wore a gold helmet and a scarlet robe covered by gold armor. He held two silver hammers.

The young man called out, "I am Huang Tianhua, eldest son of Prince Huang Feihu. I have been ordered by my king to take you all prisoner."

Mo Liqing laughed and ran towards the young man. The two began to fight, one long sword against two silver hammers. After twenty rounds, Mo Liqing threw his jade ring at Huang Tianhua, hitting him in the back and knocking him off his unicorn. He lay on the ground, not moving. Mo Liqing raised his sword to cut off Huang Tianhua's head.

Nezha saw this. Shouting, "Don't hurt my brother!" he rushed forward on his Wind Fire Wheels to fight Mo Liqing. Another of the Mo brothers rushed forward. Not wanting to fight both of them, Nezha turned and rode back to the city.

Some Zhou soldiers came out to collect Huang Tianhua's body and bring it back to the city. Huang Feihu saw the body of his son and cried. Then he brought the body to Jiang Ziya to be buried. But a young Daoist boy came to the city gate and asked to see Jiang Ziya. Coming into the hall, the boy said, "I am a disciple of Master Pure Void Virtue.

He told me to bring the body of my elder brother back to the mountain."

Jiang Ziya agreed. The boy carried the body back to Mount Green Peak. There, Master Pure Void Virtue opened up the mouth of the dead man and poured in some magic elixir. An hour later, Huang Tianhua opened his eyes.

"Master, what happened?" asked Huang Tianhua.

"You fool!" snapped the master. "I sent you to West Qi but you forgot that you were a Daoist! First you ate meat instead of vegetarian food. And then you took off your Daoist robes. What were you thinking? I only brought you back to life because Jiang Ziya needs your help."

Huang Tianhua could not say anything. He kowtowed again and again to his master. The master continued, "Now go back to West Qi and try again. This time, use this weapon." And he gave something to Huang Tianhua.

The next day, Huang Tianhua rode out again to fight the Mo generals. "I will fight you all, to the death!" he shouted at them.

Mo Liqing attacked him first. They fought for a few rounds. Then Huang Tianhua turned and rode away. As his enemy chased him, he put away his silver hammers. Then he reached inside a bag and took out a shining magic nail, seven and a half inches long. He threw it at Mo Liqing. The nail went through his heart, killing him instantly. Then the nail returned to the bag.

Next, Mo Lihong rushed at him. Huang Tianhua grabbed the nail and quickly threw it at him. His enemy had no time to move away from the nail. It went right through his heart, killing him.

Mo Lihai shouted, "You beast, I will kill you!" and attacked Huang Tianhua. But in just a few minutes he was also dead from the magic nail.

There was just one brother left, Mo Lishou. He reached into his bag to release his magic white fox. But he did not know that the fox was really Yang Jian. The fox bit his hand off. Mo Lishou screamed in pain. Quickly, Huang Tianhua threw the nail again, and the fourth Mo brother died.

With all four Mo brothers dead, Huang Tianhua returned to the city, along with Yang Jian and Nezha.

A few days later, news of the battle and the deaths of the four Mo brothers reached Grand Tutor Wen in Zhaoge. "What a demon you are, Jiang Ziya!" he said. "Enough of this. Tomorrow I will ask His Majesty to allow me to go to West Qi myself. That is the only way we will win this war."

He went to see the king, who agreed to let him go to West Qi. Grand Tutor Wen said carefully, "Your Majesty, this old minister will try to defeat the rebels and bring peace. While I am gone, I hope that Your Majesty will listen to his ministers. I will be back in a few months."

Grand Tutor Wen mounted his black unicorn. But the unicorn screamed and reared up, throwing him to the ground. As he picked himself off the ground and straightened his hat and robes, one of the younger ministers said, "Grand Tutor, this is a bad omen. Perhaps you should not go."

But Grand Tutor Wen replied, "A soldier does his job without thinking of his home, his health or his life. It is nothing to a soldier to be injured or even killed. Please say no more about this."

He got back on his unicorn, and led his army of 300,000 men out of Zhaoge. After several days they came to Yellow Flower Mountain. This was a beautiful place. The hillsides were covered with tall pine trees. Flowers made the ground look like it was made of jade and emerald. Small streams flowed down the hillsides, and birds sang in the trees.

Grand Tutor Wen ordered his army to stop and make camp. He rode his unicorn a short distance away. He looked at the mountain's beauty and said to himself, "Ah, if Zhaoge ever becomes peaceful some day, I would love to live here!"

Then he saw a man on a black horse. The man wore gold armor over a red robe and was leading a large group of bandits. The bandit chief shouted, "Who are you, and what are you doing here?"

Grand Tutor Wen smiled and replied, "I like this place. I wish I could live here, and spend my days resting and reading Daoist books. Is that all right with you?"

"You Daoist demon!" shouted the man, and attacked.

The two fought, Grand Tutor Wen using his two golden staffs, the other man using his axe. Wen was a very good fighter and he had no trouble blocking the man's blows. He stopped fighting and rode away on his unicorn. The bandit chief followed on his horse. As soon as Wen saw that the man was following him, he pointed to the ground with one of his golden staffs. A high golden wall appeared all around the man, trapping him inside. Wen stopped, got off his unicorn, and sat down to wait and see what would happen next.

Soon two more bandit chiefs appeared. As they came closer, one of them shouted, "Who are you? And what have you done to our elder brother?"

Grand Tutor Wen said, "Who? That fool over there? I asked him to give me this mountain. He started to argue with me, so I killed him."

The two men shouted and rushed at Wen. Again, Wen rode away, then turned and pointed at the ground. One of the men was surrounded by water. The other man was surrounded by a thick forest. Happy with his work, Wen got off his unicorn and sat on the ground.

There was one more bandit chief. When he heard that his three brothers had all been killed, he flew into the air. From high in the sky he shouted down to Wen, "You are a monster! How can I let you live after you have killed my three brothers?" Then he flew down and attacked Wen with two large hammers.

Wen liked this man. He easily blocked the man's blows, then rode away. "Don't run away from me, you damned Daoist!" cried the man, and rode after him. Quickly, Wen called a local nature spirit and told him to drop a large rock on the bandit chief.

Wen walked over to the man, who was lying under the large rock. As he raised his golden staff, the man cried, "Great Daoist master, I am sorry if I offended you. I would be grateful to you if you let me live."

"Tell me your name," said Wen.

"I am Xin Huan."

Wen replied, "I am no Daoist. I am Grand Tutor Wen of Zhaoge. I was just passing through this region. Your brothers attacked me for no reason. Now, I will let you live if you become my disciple and help me defeat West Qi. If you do well, you will become a high-ranking minister. Make your decision."

Xin Huan said, "I am certainly willing to become your disciple," replied the bandit chief. "And I beg you to let my three brothers live. They will also be happy to help you."

Wen told the local nature spirit to lift the heavy rock off the bandit chief. The man tried to stand up, but he was weak and fell to the ground. Wen helped him to stand up. Then Wen said, "You should move away a little bit." Xin Huan moved away.

Grand Tutor Wen opened his hand. A great clap of thunder shot from his hand, shaking the mountain. The other three bandit chiefs were freed from their prisons of metal, water and wood.

The chiefs looked around. They saw their brother standing next to Wen. The three of them shouted, "Grab that Daoist demon!" and raising their weapons, they all rushed towards Wen.

Chapter 42
The Bandit Chiefs Join Grand Tutor Wen

Disasters come in strange ways;
Gods from heaven join the battle

Their magic is powerful but still they are defeated;
Mortals and gods are unafraid but all are injured

Once, the country prospered under the King of Shang;
But then came chaos, defeat, and a new king

Strong generals are found at Yellow Flower Mountain;
Together they travel to the land of Mount Qi

≡ ≡ ≡

Before the three bandit chiefs reached Grand Tutor Wen, Xin Huan held up his hand. He said "Brothers, please let go of your anger. This is my master, Grand Tutor Wen."

Immediately the other three bandit chiefs got down from their horses. They knelt and kowtowed to Grand Tutor Wen. They said, "Grand Tutor, we have heard wonderful things about you. We thank heaven for bringing you to our mountain. We are sorry if we offended you."

They led Grand Tutor Wen to their camp. They told him that they did not want to be bandits, but there was so much trouble in the kingdom that they came to the mountain to seek peace.

"Come and join me," said Grand Tutor Wen. "If you help me win the battle at West Qi, you will all become ministers in the government."

"If you will have us, we are happy to come with you."

"How many men do you have?"

"Just over ten thousand."

"We will take everyone who wants to come with us. If they don't want to come, we will give them money and food and they can return home."

The men were happy to hear this. Seven thousand agreed to join Grand

Tutor Wen's army.

They traveled for several days. One day they saw a stone sign at the side of the road, reading "Dragon Extinction Mountain." Grand Tutor Wen read the sign. He stopped, sitting silently for a long time.

"What's the matter?" asked Xin Huan.

"I studied with an immortal for fifty years. When I was finished with my studies, my teacher sent me down to help the Shang Dynasty. She told me, 'If you ever see the word "extinction," disaster will follow.' Now I see that word and I am a bit afraid."

The others laughed. One said, "Grand Tutor, heaven favors the good. Words have nothing to do with it. You are a great general, you will surely succeed." But Grand Tutor Wen said nothing and he did not smile.

A few days later, the Shang army arrived and set up camp just outside the city wall. Grand Tutor Wen gave Xin Huan a letter and told him to bring it to Jiang Ziya. Xin Huan entered the city, went to the palace, and handed the letter to Jiang Ziya.

The letter read,

> *Wen Zhong, Grand Tutor of the Shang Dynasty and commander of His Majesty's army, greets Prime Minister Jiang Ziya.*
>
> *You know that is a crime against heaven to rise up against the king. His Majesty has sent armies to stop you, but you refused their orders. Instead, you fought His Majesty's armies, killed his generals, and hung their heads on the city wall.*
>
> *By order of His Majesty, I have come to put down your rebellion. If you care about the people of your city, come out now and receive your punishment. If you don't, your city will be destroyed.*

Jiang Ziya read the letter. Then he said to Xin Huan, "Please give my best wishes to Grand Tutor Wen. Here is my reply: 'We will meet in battle in three days time.' "

Three days later, Grand Tutor Wen looked out from the Shang camp. He heard the roar of cannons. Then he saw a formation of soldiers coming out of the gate. They were dressed in green robes and carried four green flags. They carried swords and spears. The formation looked like a city made of iron.

At the second roar of cannons, another formation of soldiers came out. They wore red robes, carried red flags, and carried bows and arrows.

At the third roar of cannons, another formation of soldiers came out. They wore white robes and carried white flags. They carried cutlasses.

At the fourth roar of cannons, soldiers dressed in purple robes and carrying purple flags came out, led by generals wearing black. The soldiers carried axes.

At the fifth and final roar of cannons, a formation of men on horses and other animals came out. Jiang Ziya was in the center, riding his huge beast. Huang Feihu rode beside him on a five colored ox. With him were Nezha, Jinzha, Muzha, Yang Jian, Huang Tianhua, and several more generals. They wore yellow and carried yellow flags.

Grand Tutor Wen rode forward on his black unicorn to meet them. His face was pale gold, and he had a long beard. The four bandit chiefs were at his sides. They stopped a short distance from Jiang Ziya.

Jiang Ziya rode forward. He said, "Grand Tutor Wen! Please pardon me for not being able to greet you properly[1]."

Grand Tutor Wen replied, "Prime Minister Jiang, you studied for many years on Mount Kunlun. How can you be so foolish as to not understand what you are doing?"

Jiang Ziya replied, "How can you say that I am foolish? Yes, I am a disciple of Mount Kunlun. I have never disobeyed the will of heaven, and I always obey the law. We have never led an army against His Majesty, and we have never gone over the five passes. Here in West Qi, our king is a good man, and the people are happy."

"You are a criminal. You have insulted His Majesty by naming your own king. You have cut off the heads of our generals. You have taken in the traitor Huang Feihu. How dare you fight me instead of giving yourself up!"

"You are wrong, Grand Tutor. Everyone knows that the king in Zhaoge is no longer fit to rule this kingdom. A minister may leave if his king is no longer fit to rule. That is why Huang Feihu and nearly all the dukes and marquises have joined us. Are they all traitors? As for your generals,

---

[1] A soldier in full armor cannot bow.

they lost their lives because they came here to attack us. Grand Tutor, you are a good man, admired by all. I don't know why you came here. Think twice before you attack us. You don't want to disobey the law of heaven and damage your reputation forever."

Grand Tutor Wen could not answer this. His face turned red. But then he saw Huang Feihu and he grew angry. He said, "You rebel, Huang! Come here at once!" When Huang did not move, Grand Tutor Wen turned to his generals and shouted, "Who will kill this traitor for me?"

Three of the bandit chiefs rushed forward. They were met by Huang Feihu and two other generals. As they fought, Xin Huan flew up into the air and came down on Jiang Ziya, swinging his two hammers. Before he could hit the prime minister, Huang Tianhua rode forward and blocked him.

Grand Tutor Wen rode forward on his unicorn and attacked Jiang Ziya. They fought fiercely. Grand Tutor Wen threw one of his staffs. It hit Jiang Ziya's shoulder, knocking him off his beast. Nezha rode forward on his magic wheels and attacked Grand Tutor Wen. Grand Tutor Wen knocked Nezha off his wheels. Jinzha and Muzha rushed forward, but both were struck by Grand Tutor Wen's magic staffs.

Yang Jian rode forward and joined the fight. Grand Tutor Wen threw his staffs but they just bounced off Yang Jian. Grand Tutor Wen said to himself, "What a powerful warrior he is!"

The battle became even more fierce. Generals on both sides all used their magic weapons. Sharp spears and arrows flew through the air. The sky grew dark. The wind blew dust and stones across the ground. The soldiers could not stand up in the strong wind, and they could not tell east from west.

The magic was too much for the soldiers of West Qi. They dropped their weapons and flags, and fled back to the city. Behind them, bodies of dead men and horses covered the ground. The West Qi army was defeated.

The Shang army returned to their camp, having won a great victory.

Jiang Ziya decided to wait a few days, then attack again. Three days later, his army came out again. This time, Jiang Ziya was ready for the enemy's magic. When Grand Tutor Wen threw one of his staffs, Jiang Ziya used his own magic staff to break it in two.

"Jiang Ziya, you monster. How dare you break my magic weapon!" shouted Grand Tutor Wen. But Jiang Ziya attacked again, knocking Grand Tutor Wen off his unicorn. With the enemy army confused, the soldiers of West Qi killed thousands of them. This battle was a great victory for West Qi.

Jiang Ziya met with his generals. They decided to attack again, that same evening. They planned to attack the Shang camp from three sides at the same time. Meanwhile, Yang Jian would enter the camp and burn the Shang grain supplies.

But in the Shang camp, Grand Tutor Wen felt something strange in the air. He burned incense and did a divination. He saw that Jiang Ziya was planning a surprise attack that night. He smiled. Then he met with his generals and began to prepare for the attack.

At nightfall, Jiang Ziya's soldiers left the city quietly and came close to the Shang camp. Suddenly the cannons roared, and they attacked the Shang camp on three sides.

Chapter 43
Grand Tutor Wen is Defeated

Great danger comes when fighting at night;
Soldiers run away, throwing away their armor

In smoke and fire, they try to return to the path;
Their spirits drift away as they search for home

How many brave men die for nothing?
How many soldiers die in their dreams?

Who knew that Ji Li's[1] words would live so long;
They bring the gods to the northern mountains[2]

≡ ≡ ≡

The battle was over quickly. Nezha and Huang Tianhua led an attack on the front of the camp. Huang Feihu led an attack on the left while Nangong Kuo attacked from the right. Jinzha and Muzha waited a few minutes, then rushed in to join the attack. While they were fighting the Shang soldiers, Yang Jian entered the camp and used his magic fire to burn the grain warehouse. Yellow fire rose high in the sky like golden snakes. Smoke filled the air. In the dark and smoke, the Shang soldiers could not tell friend from enemy. Grand Tutor Wen mounted his unicorn and tried to fight back, but he could not stop the Zhou army. The Zhou ran through the Shang camp, killing many Shang soldiers.

Grand Tutor Wen saw that the battle was lost. He fled back to Mount Qi with his generals, with Xin Huan circling high overhead to protect them from attack.

High on Mount Zhongnan, Master of the Clouds watched the battle from his cave. He decided that it was time to send his disciple Thunderbolt to help the Zhou. He called Thunderbolt and told him,

---

[1] Ji Li is a minor character in the story, a general and a disciple of Grand Tutor Wen, later killed by Nezha.
[2] The Northern Mountain is where immortals gather, ceremonies take place, and important events unfold. It is believed to be the final resting place for many emperors.

"Go now, see your elder brother Ji Fa and your uncle Jiang Ziya. Watch out for a person with wings."

Thunderbolt opened his wings and flew quickly to Mount Qi. He saw Grand Tutor Wen and his army fleeing from the battle. He decided to attack the soldiers.

Grand Tutor Wen saw the flying man. Quickly he called to Xin Huan and told him to fly up to protect the fleeing army. Xin Huan flew up, holding his two hammers. Thunderbolt attacked with his golden cudgel. They fought in the sky three thousand feet above the ground. Thunderbolt was stronger, so after a few rounds Xin Huan flew away, defeated.

Thunderbolt decided not to chase him. Instead, he flew to West Qi City. He entered the palace and bowed to Jiang Ziya, saying, "Greetings, Uncle."

"Who are you?" asked Jiang Ziya.

"My name is Thunderbolt. I am a disciple of Master of the Clouds. My father was Ji Chang. When I was seven years old, I helped my father escape from danger at the five passes. Now my master has sent me here to help you."

Jiang Ziya brought the young man to meet his elder brother, the king Ji Fa. He greeted the king. The king replied, "Dear brother, I am so happy to meet you. Our father told me about you many times." The two brothers talked for a long time.

Meanwhile, Grand Tutor Wen gathered his army and set up camp on Mount Qi. He was very unhappy. He had lost over twenty thousand soldiers in the battle. This was the worst defeat of his life. He sat on the ground, thinking about his defeat and the deaths of so many soldiers.

One of his generals said, "Grand Tutor, do not give up hope. Don't you know, there are many holy men living in caves in the mountains. Some of them have great powers. Perhaps you could ask them for help."

Grand Tutor Wen stood up and said, "That is a very good idea! I had completely forgotten about my friends on Golden Turtle Island." He told his generals that he would be gone for a few days.

He mounted his unicorn and flew into the air. Soon he arrived at Golden Turtle Island in the eastern sea. He looked around. Huge ocean waves crashed against the shore. He heard peacocks singing, and he saw a unicorn sleeping in the grass. Deer and foxes walked through the forest. Peaches hung from tree branches. Above, white clouds floated through the sky.

He walked around the beautiful island, but saw no one. He was about to leave when he heard a voice calling out to him, "Brother Wen, where are you going?"

He turned around. It was the Celestial Lotus, a Daoist master and an old friend. "Greetings, Celestial Lotus!" he said. "I am looking for you and the others."

She said, "A few days ago, Shen Gongbao came here. He asked us to help you. So we are all working on building ten death traps. Go to White Deer Island and you will meet the others."

Grand Tutor Wen thanked her. He flew to White Deer Island. He saw his other friends there. They told him that nine of the traps were ready, and that they could leave for West Qi as soon as Lady of Golden Light finished her trap.

Soon Lady of Golden Light finished her work and joined them. They all flew to the Shang camp on Mount Qi. They met with the Shang generals and told them about the ten traps. Then they all marched the seventy *li* to West Qi City, accompanied by the Shang army.

In West Qi City, Jiang Ziya heard the sound of the returning Shang army. He climbed the city wall with Nezha and Yang Jian and looked out. They saw that the Shang camp was hidden by dark clouds and cold fog. A dozen columns of thick black smoke rose through the air. Jiang Ziya looked at this but he did not understand what was happening in the Shang camp.

The next day, Grand Tutor Wen marched out of the Shang camp and called for Jiang Ziya to come out.

Jiang Ziya came out with his generals and five formations of soldiers. He saw ten ugly Daoists standing behind Grand Tutor Wen. They all rode deer. Their faces were many colors: green, red, yellow, white and pink.

One of the Daoists, Master Qin, rode forward. He bowed and said, "Greetings, Jiang Ziya!"

Jiang Ziya also bowed, saying, "Greetings, brother. Who are you and where do you come from?"

"My name is Master Qin. My brothers and I come from Golden Turtle Island. We are Jie Daoists and you are a Chan Daoist[1]. So we are all brothers. Why do you insult us?"

"What do you mean, brother?" asked Jiang Ziya.

"You killed the four Mo brothers. Isn't that an insult?"

"Brother, you know that His Majesty is an evil tyrant and does not have heaven on his side anymore. There is a new ruler here in West Qi. And you know that the phoenix has sung on Mount Qi. You should respect the will of heaven. How can you not see the truth of this?"

"If what you say is true, then heaven wants Ji Fa to be the new king. But what of us? Isn't it heaven's will that we are here to defend His Majesty? Jiang Ziya, we should not fight, because that would be against the will of heaven. But we have created ten death traps. I'd like you to come and take a look at them."

"If that is what you wish, I dare not argue."

Two hours later, Jiang Ziya entered the Shang camp. Four of his generals were with him. Master Qin led them around the camp and showed them the ten traps. They were: Heaven's Punishment, Earth's Anger, Roaring Wind, Cold Ice, Golden Light, Flowing Blood, Bright Flame, Captured Soul, Red Water and Red Sand.

"What do you think, Jiang Ziya?" asked Master Qin after they had seen all ten traps.

"This is no problem," he replied. "I know all of these, and I can defeat them all."

Jiang Ziya left the Shang camp and returned to the city with his generals. He was very worried. Yang Jian asked him, "Can you really break those ten traps?"

Jiang Ziya just sat and shook his head. "How can I? These traps are full of mystery and Jie Daoist magic. I don't understand them." He thought for a minute. Then he added, "I don't even recognize their names."

---

[1] Jie Daoism does not really exist. In this book, it is supposedly a sect of Daoism founded by Heavenly Master Manjusri. The other sect mentioned in the book, Chan Daoism, is real and is known in the west as Zen.

Chapter 44
Jiang Ziya's Soul Floats to Mount Kunlun

Dark magic and demons make matters difficult;
Ghosts and curses pass from ancient times to today

You don't need a flying sword of the gods to harm others;
You don't need a letter of fate[1] to find their soul

How many heroes have left this world?
If they leave, others will take their place

The will of heaven is written by fate;
A single thread of souls departs and then returns

≡ ≡ ≡

"Tell me about these traps," said Grand Tutor Wen, sitting in the Shang camp with the ten Jie Daoists.

One by one, each of the Daoists told him about their traps.

The first one said, "The Heaven's Punishment trap was made by my master using power from before the world was born. It has three flags, for heaven, earth, and people. This trap turns mortals to ash, and it smashes immortals into little pieces."

The second one said, "The Earth's Fury trap contains all the power of the earth. It appears, then disappears, then appears again. It has a red flag. The flag brings thunder above and fire below. No mortal or immortal can survive it."

The third one said, "The Roaring Wind trap brings magic wind and fire that was made before the world was born. Inside the wind and fire are millions of sharp swords. Mortals and immortals are cut into small pieces. None can survive."

The fourth one said, "The Cold Ice trap is actually a mountain of

---

[1] In Chinese folklore, *qǔ mìng jiān* ("letter of fate") is a letter or card that contains information about a person's fate or life path. A person can consult their letter of fate to see the future or understand coming events.

swords. In the middle is wind and thunder. Above is a mountain of ice like wolves' teeth. Below is a lake of ice like sharp swords. When the ice on top and the ice on bottom smash together, they kill anyone who is inside, even if they have magic powers."

The fifth one said, "The Golden Light trap is made from the power of the sun, moon, heaven and earth. Inside are twenty-one magic mirrors, each one hanging from a tall pole. If any mortal or immortal is inside, golden light comes out of the mirrors. The light turns into a stream of blood. No one can survive."

The sixth one said, "The Flowing Blood trap also contains wind and thunder, but it also has a lot of black sand. If anyone is inside, the wind blows the sand towards them. When the sand hits them, it turns their bodies into blood, killing them."

The seventh one said, "The Bright Flame trap has three kinds of fire: the fire of air, the fire of rock, and the fire that immortals make in their bellies. There are three red flags. If anyone is inside, the fires burn them to ashes. It does not matter if they are immortals who know magic, they will still die."

The eighth one, a man named Yao, said, "The Captured Soul trap closes the gates of life and opens the windows of death. It has a white flag. If anyone is inside, their soul is taken away and the person dies immediately."

The ninth one said, "The Red Water trap has a terrace inside with three gourds on it. If anyone is inside, red water comes out of the gourds like a great flood. When the water touches a person, it turns to blood and they die."

The tenth and last one said, "The Red Sand trap has three parts: one for heaven, one for earth, and one for humans. There is red sand in each part. Each grain of sand is really a sharp sword that can turn the bones of any mortal or immortal into dust. No one can escape."

Grand Tutor Wen was very happy to hear this. He said, "This is wonderful. We will defeat West Qi in just a few days!"

But Yao said, "Wait, my friends. We don't need to use all of these traps. Jiang Ziya is weak and West Qi's army is small. I can easily kill him in just twenty-one days by using my Captured Soul trap. Then West Qi will be like a snake without a head. It will die quickly."

Grand Tutor Wen and the others agreed with this plan. Yao walked over to his Captured Soul trap. He made an effigy of Jiang Ziya out of straw and wrote "Jiang Ziya" on it. On the effigy's head he put three small lamps, one for each of Jiang Ziya's souls. At its feet he put seven small lamps, one for each of his spirits. Then he recited some magic spells. He said the magic spells every day, three times a day.

After three days, Jiang Ziya began to feel weak. He could not eat or sleep. He did not speak in meetings with his generals. Everyone became worried about him.

After seven more days, he had lost one of his three souls and three of his seven spirits. He lay in bed, not speaking.

A week later, he had lost another soul and three more spirits. His eyes were closed and he slept all day. His generals began to think that Daoist magic was involved. They pulled him out of bed and brought him to a meeting, but he did not speak or open his eyes.

A week after that, Jiang Ziya lost his third soul and his seventh spirit. He stopped breathing and appeared to be dead. His generals stood over his body, crying. But Yang Jian put his hand on the body and said, "Wait! It's still warm. He might still be alive. Let's wait and see what happens."

Jiang Ziya's souls and spirits had all left his body. Because he had spent forty years studying on Mount Kunlun, that is where his last soul and spirit flew. On the side of Mount Kunlun, the Immortal of the South Pole was taking a walk when he saw the soul and spirit floating through the air. Quickly he grabbed them, put them into a gourd, and closed the gourd.

Immortal of the South Pole wanted to take the souls and spirits to his master, Heavenly Primogenitor. But he ran into another immortal, Pure Essence. Pure Essence said that he would be happy to take care of the matter. So the Immortal of the South Pole gave him the gourd.

Pure Essence carried the gourd down to West Qi City. He met with Ji Fa and said, "I came here to help Jiang Ziya. Where is his body?" Ji Fa brought him to the room where Jiang Ziya was lying. Pure Essence looked at the body. Then he said, "Don't worry, my friends. Jiang Ziya will wake up as soon as I get his souls and spirits back into his body. Now I must go to the Captured Soul trap."

Pure Essence left the city and flew to the Shang camp. He saw black smoke, cold fog and flying ghosts in the air above the ten traps. When he approached the Captured Soul trap, he saw Yao walking in circles, reciting Daoist magic words. Every few minutes, Yao stopped and used a stick to hit the ground next to the effigy. Every time he hit the ground the lamps were extinguished, but then they lit again. No matter how many times Yao hit the ground, the lamps would not stay extinguished. Jiang Ziya would not die.

Quickly, Pure Essence ran in and tried to grab the effigy. But before he could grab it, one of the other Jie Daoists saw him. The Daoist shouted, "Pure Essence, how dare you come in here!" and threw some black sand at him. Pure Essence flew away as fast as he could, then he returned to the city.

He told Ji Fa to keep an eye on the body, because he still had work to do. Then he flew back to Mount Kunlun. Seeing the Immortal of the South Pole, he said, "Brother, this is more difficult than I expected. I have to go and see our master, Heavenly Primogenitor."

But his master told him, "I am sorry, I cannot do anything about this. You must go and see my elder brother."

"Who is that?" asked Pure Essence.

"Laozi.[1]"

Pure Essence flew all the way to Mount Xuandu, the home of Laozi. It was a beautiful place. The ground was covered with colorful flowers and green grasses. He saw many immortals. Some were talking quietly, some were meditating, some were playing chess. He heard the singing of dragons and phoenixes.

He waited outside Laozi's cave for a while. A priest came out. Pure Essence told the priest why he had come. A short time later, the priest brought him in to the cave. Pure Essence entered, knelt down, and said to Laozi, "May you live forever!"

Laozi said, "Your problem has been fated by heaven. When the Daoists made the Captured Soul trap, they used my magic map of the Eight Trigrams." He handed the map to Pure Essence and said, "Here is the map. Take it and use it to rescue Jiang Ziya. Now go."

Pure Essence returned to West Qi City. He waited until the third watch. Then he flew to the Shang camp. He opened the map. It turned into a

---

[1] This is the great saint known in the west as Lao Tzu, author of the *Dao De Jing* and considered one of the founders of Daoism.

many-colored bridge made of gold. The bridge protected him as he ran across it into the Captured Soul trap. He grabbed the effigy. He flew into the air and left the camp as quickly as he could. But Yao saw him. He threw some black sand at Pure Essence. The sand hit him, causing him to cry out in fright and drop the magic map. Yao grabbed the map. Pure Essence held on to the effigy and flew back to the city.

When he returned to the city, he told Ji Fa and the generals what he had done. "I grabbed the effigy and Jiang Ziya's souls and spirits," he said, "but I lost Laozi's magic map." He opened the gourd and poured the souls and spirits from the effigy into the gourd. Then he put the gourd up against Jiang Ziya's head. He hit the gourd three times. The souls and spirits entered Jiang Ziya's body.

Jiang Ziya opened his eyes and sat up. Looking around, he saw Pure Essence. "Brother, thank you for saving my life! But how did you do it?" Pure Essence told him everything that had happened.

"How will we get the map back?" asked Jiang Ziya, worried.

"Rest for a few days, then we can talk about it," replied the immortal.

A few days later, they all met to discuss what to do next. As they were talking, Yang Jian came in and said, "We have a visitor. Yellow Dragon has arrived." They all stood up to welcome the immortal.

The Daoist master named Yellow Dragon said to them, "I have come to help you with the ten traps. Many immortals will also come to help us. But these immortals are coming from heaven and they will not enter a place like this. So you must build a clean new pavilion for them. Make it out of straw, and hang lanterns and flowers on the walls. Put clean carpets on the floor."

Within a day, the new pavilion was ready. Jiang Ziya and the generals went to the pavilion to wait for the immortals. Soon they began to arrive. Master Grand Completion was there. So was Master Pure Essence, Yellow Dragon Immortal, Fairy Primordial, Heavenly Master Manjusri, Master Pure Void, and many other immortals.

When they all had arrived, Master Grand Completion said, "My friends, now that you are here, it is time to help the good and bring down the evil. Jiang Ziya, you must destroy the ten traps."

"What, me?" asked Jiang Ziya. "Dear brothers, I have only studied on Mount Kunlun for forty years. My powers are not strong. Would one of you do this instead of me?"

None of the other immortals wanted to take his place. But just then, they heard the cry of a deer in the sky, and the air was filled with a sweet fragrance.

Chapter 45
The First Battle of the Traps

The Heaven's Punishment trap is very dangerous;
But the Earth's Fury trap is even worse

Everything in Qin Wan's life is written by fate;
But Yuan Jiao's death comes from his greed[1]

Two immortals are killed by fire and thunder;
But three more have not been taken away yet

The ten traps have done nothing;
But names have been written on the List of Creation

☰ ☰ ☰

Everybody looked up. An immortal was slowly floating down from the clouds. It was Immortal Burning Lamp, the leader of all the immortals and disciple of the Buddha himself. All the immortals came out to greet him.

"Sorry I have arrived late," said Burning Lamp. "Please forgive me. I have seen these ten traps. They are all very powerful. We must fight them. I will be your commander, and I will lead you in this battle." Jiang Ziya was only too happy to give up command of the immortals.

Just then, a messenger arrived from the Shang camp with a letter from Grand Tutor Wen to Jiang Ziya. Jiang Ziya read the letter. Then he wrote on the bottom, "We will meet you in battle three days from today." He gave the note back to the Shang messenger, who brought it back to Grand Tutor Wen.

Grand Tutor Wen looked at the Zhou camp. He saw colorful clouds and golden lanterns floating in the sky above the camp. He said, "It looks like a great many immortals have come from Mount Kunlun to help the Zhou." The ten Daoist magicians also saw this. There was nothing they

---

[1] The Daoist immortal Yuan Jiao made the Cold Ice trap, and Qin Wán made the Heaven's Punishment trap.

could do, so they just had to wait.

On the morning of the third day, everyone in the Shang camp heard the Zhou army firing their cannons. The ten Daoists came out of the Shang camp. They placed their ten traps in a row in front of the camp.

Then the Zhou generals came out. Nezha and Huang Tianhua were in front. A dozen or more immortals and human generals were just behind them, led by Immortal Burning Lamp.

The first battle was in front of the Heaven's Punishment Trap. A Daoist magician stood in front of the trap. One of the Zhou immortals, a man named Deng Hua, rushed forward. He shouted at the Daoist, "Don't think that you are so powerful. I am Deng Hua, an immortal from Mount Kunlun!" He attacked the Daoist with his sword.

The Daoist magician blocked the sword, then turned and ran into the trap. Deng Hua followed close behind. The Daoist picked up the three flags and threw them into the air. When the flags came down to the ground there was a great crash of thunder. Deng Hua fell to the ground, dead. The Daoist ran over to him, cut off his head, and lifted it up in the air. He shouted, "You immortals from Mount Kunlun! Look what happened to your friend. Who else dares to come into my trap?"

Immortal Burning Lamp looked around. He saw Heavenly Master Manjusri. "Go and take care of that Daoist!" he shouted.

Heavenly Master Manjusri smiled. As he walked forward, he sang:

> *I dare to use my sharp sword*
> *The jade dragon cries out in fear*
> *Purple clouds rise from my hand*
> *White clouds cover my head*
> *I used to grow peaches in the jade palace*
> *I used to discuss the Dao in the golden tower*
> *But now I have left my heavenly home*
> *I've come to the human world, singing this song*

Then he said to the Daoist, "My brother, why have you brought these evil traps here to harm people? I have been commanded to destroy your trap, and so I must kill you. I'm sorry, but this is the law."

The Daoist laughed and said, "You know nothing about my trap. You are the one who will die here."

The Daoist struck at Heavenly Master Manjusri, but his blows were blocked. He turned and ran inside his trap. Heavenly Master Manjusri carefully and slowly entered the trap. He pointed his finger at the ground and two large lotus flowers appeared. He stepped on the flowers and rode them into the trap. Then he held out his left hand. Five beams of white light shot out from his fingers. At the end of each beam of light, a white lotus flower appeared. Each flower held five golden lanterns.

The Daoist picked up the three flags and threw them into the air. They fell to the ground, but nothing happened. The lotus flowers were protecting Heavenly Master Manjusri.

Heavenly Master Manjusri threw his sword into the air. Instantly three rings surrounded the Daoist, holding him tight. Heavenly Master Manjusri turned to Mount Kunlun, bowed his head, and said, "Your disciple is sorry but he must kill today." Then he swung his sword, cutting off the Daoist's head. Then he walked out of the now-powerless trap.

Grand Tutor Wen saw what happened. He shouted angrily, "Don't leave, Heavenly Master. I'm coming for you!" But Heavenly Master Manjusri didn't even look at him. He was not afraid of the Shang general at all.

There were still nine more traps. One of the Daoist magicians shouted, "Who dares to enter my Earth's Fury trap?" A Zhou general, a mortal man, rode his horse into the trap. Strange clouds came, followed by thunder and fire. The young general was turned into dust, and his soul flew to the Terrace of Creation.

The Daoist said, "Why do you send mortals into my trap? Killing them is too easy. Send someone with magic powers!"

Burning Lamp called another one of his immortals, a man named Kakusandha[1], to come forward. Kakusandha carefully entered the trap. When he saw the danger inside the trap, he opened a small door at the top of his head. Magic clouds floated out to protect him. He ordered his yellow-scarved genie to tie up the Daoist and throw him on the ground. The Daoist landed so hard that fire came out of his seven orifices. He was still alive, but the Earth's Fury trap was destroyed. The Zhou

---

[1] Kakusandha Buddha is the first of the five Buddhas of the present kalpa (age). He was born in India. His father was a brahmin priest. He led a family life for four thousand years and had a wife and son. Then he renounced family life, and after only eight months of study he achieved enlightenment. He lived for 40,000 years.

soldiers took him prisoner.

Grand Tutor Wen was even more angry now that the second trap was destroyed. He shouted at Kakusandha, "Don't go away, I am coming for you!"

But one of the Zhou immortals said, "Think about your words, Grand Tutor Wen. We are not fighting with physical strength, but with magical skill. You should not act like this." Grand Tutor Wen stopped, shamed into silence.

The two armies went back to their camps. In the Zhou camp, some of the immortals asked Burning Lamp what they should do next. He replied, "The next trap is Roaring Wind. But to destroy this trap, we need the Wind Stopping Pearl."

"Where do we find this pearl?" they asked.

"My friend, Woe Evading Sage[1], has it. I will write him a note. Jiang Ziya, send two people to his cave. Give him my note, and I hope he will give you the magic pearl."

Jiang Ziya selected San Yisheng and General Chao Tian to go and get the pearl. They took a ferry boat across the Yellow River. They traveled for several days, finally arriving at the immortal's cave high on a mountaintop. The mountain was covered with tall ancient pines that looked like dragons.

They waited outside the cave until a young man told them they could enter. San Yisheng gave the note to Woe Evading Sage. The immortal read the note. Then he said, "Of course I will give you the pearl. But be very careful with it. Don't lose it."

San Yisheng took the pearl, then the two men rode as fast as they could. But when they got to the Yellow River, they could not find any ferry to take them across. "This is strange!" said San Yisheng. "A few days ago there were many ferries, now there are none at all."

For two days they rode up and down the riverbank, looking for a way to cross the river. They did not see a single ferry. Finally, they asked a local man where they could find a ferry. The man replied, "Recently two evil men came to this region. They were very tall and very strong. They told all the ferrymen to leave. Everyone was afraid of them, so

---

[1] Earlier in the story, Woe Evading Sage is mentioned as the spiritual master of Li Jing, a Shang general who was the father of the immortal Nezha and his brothers Muzha and Jinzha.

they left. Now there is only one ferry, it's about five *li* from here. You can take that ferry, but I think it will be very expensive."

They rode to the ferry. They saw two very large men there. These two men were not using boats. They used a raft which they pulled across the river using heavy ropes. Looking closely, they saw that the two men were Fang Bi and Fang Xiang. These were the two Shang generals who had saved the lives of the king's two sons several years before.

"Hello, brother!" said Fang Bi. "Where are you going and why?"

Chao Tian replied, "Would you please take us across the river? As you know, the King of Shang is an evil tyrant. We have decided to help the sage ruler of West Qi. There is a great battle going on near West Qi City, and we have a magic pearl that we plan to use to help us win the battle."

"A magic pearl?" said Fang Bi. "I've never seen one of those. Can I see it?" Chao Tian took it out of his robe. Fang Bi quickly grabbed the pearl and put it in his own robe. "This will pay for your ride across the river," he said.

Chao Tian could not fight Fang Bi, because the man was more than twice as tall as he was. San Yisheng was so upset about losing the pearl that he tried to drown himself in the river. But Chao Tian stopped him. He said, "My friend, don't kill yourself. If we die here, Jiang Ziya will never know what happened. We must return and tell him the story. Better for him to kill us than for us to dishonorably kill ourselves."

San Yisheng agreed that they should return to West Qi City. The two of them rode their horses towards the city. After a little while they came upon a large group of soldiers and carts moving slowly in the same direction. Looking closely, they saw that it was General Huang Feihu bringing grain to West Qi.

San Yisheng got off his horse. Huang Feihu got down off his huge ox and asked him, "Where are you going?"

San Yisheng began to cry. He told the story of how they had lost the magic pearl. "Don't worry," said Huang Feihu. "Wait here, I will get the pearl back for you." Then he mounted his ox and rode away as fast as the wind.

After an hour or two he saw the Fang brothers walking down the road. When they heard him coming, the Fang brothers turned around. They immediately knelt and said, "Your Highness! Where are you going?"

"I am looking for you. I heard that you have a magic pearl. Give it to me at once." Fang Bi did not argue. He pulled the pearl out of his robe and handed it to Huang Feihu.

Huang Feihu said, "I must tell you that I no longer serve the tyrant king of Shang. There is now a sage ruler in West Qi. He rules two thirds of the kingdom. Since the two of you are homeless, you should come with me and serve the ruler of West Qi. You will be given a high rank, I'm sure."

The Fang brothers agreed. The three of them rode back and met up with San Yisheng and Chao Tian. Huang Feihu gave them the pearl and told them to return to the Zhou camp as fast as they could.

When they reached the Zhou camp, they gave the pearl to Jiang Ziya and told him the whole story. The prime minister gave the pearl to Burning Lamp.

"Now that we have the pearl," said Burning Lamp, "we can deal with this Roaring Wind Trap. We can do that tomorrow. Let's rest tonight."

Chapter 46
The Second Battle of the Traps

Immortals and Buddhas don't often complain;
Complaints bring trouble in this world

Use strength instead of wisdom, lose a thousand years of study;
Fight, and you will pay for ten thousand kalpas[1]

How often do we look to the past with sadness;
Thinking of who harmed us long ago?

This is the day of the Investiture of the Gods;
Together we wander through the world of dreams[2]

☰ ☰ ☰

The next morning, one of the Shang immortals rode out of their camp, on a huge deer. He held a sword in each of his hands. He shouted to the Zhou army to come out and fight.

Burning Lamp looked around, but he did not see anyone whose fate it was to enter the Roaring Wind trap. But just then, Huang Feihu returned to the camp with the two Fang brothers. "They just joined us," said Huang Feihu. "They are good fighters."

Burning Lamp looked at them and knew their fate. But he had no choice. "Fang Bi," he said, "go and break that Roaring Wind trap."

Fang Bi was a good fighter but he had no knowledge of magic. The Shang immortal looked at him, then turned and rode his deer back inside the Roaring Wind trap. Fang Bi followed him into the trap. The

---

[1] A kalpa is a measure of time. A regular kalpa is 16,798,000 years. The longest, a maha kalpa, is described this way by Buddha: "Imagine a huge empty cube sixteen miles in each side. Once every hundred years, you drop a tiny mustard seed into the cube. The cube will be filled before the kalpa ends."

[2] In the original Chinese poem, this line refers to *nán kē mèng*, the South Kuo Dream. This is a dreamlike world where events are not as they seem. In the classic novel *Dream of the Red Chamber* the character Xue Baochai has a dream in which she visits South Kuo and learns of the impermanence and fleeting nature of life, as and that the world is not always what it appears to be.

immortal picked up a black flag and started waving it. A powerful wind came up. The wind turned into thousands of sharp swords. Fang Bi was instantly cut into pieces, and his soul flew to the Terrace of Creation.

"You should be ashamed!" shouted the immortal. "You sent an ordinary mortal into my trap? Send someone who knows magic!"

Burning Lamp gave the Wind Stopping Pearl to one of the Zhou immortals, a man named Merciful Navigation.

Merciful Navigation walked up to the trap and shouted, "My friend, why do you seek your own death? Your own master told you not to come here."

The Shang immortal replied, "You think your magic is stronger than mine? I don't think so. Better you should leave now and let someone else do the fighting."

Then the Shang immortal swung his swords at Merciful Navigation. They fought for a few rounds, then the immortal ran back inside the trap. Merciful Navigation followed him with the magic pearl on his head. The immortal waved the black flag. Nothing happened. The wind did not come. Then Merciful Navigation threw his magic gourd in the air. A black cloud came out of the gourd. The Shang immortal was sucked inside the gourd.

Merciful Navigation walked out of the trap, carrying the gourd. He turned it over. The Shang immortal's clothing fell out on to the ground. The immortal was dead, and his soul had already floated to the Terrace of Creation.

Seeing this, Grand Tutor Wen rode forward on his unicorn, ready to fight. But Burning Lamp said to him, "Grand Tutor Wen, why are you so angry? We have only broken three of your traps. You have seven more."

Another Shang immortal stepped forward. This was the immortal who had the Cold Ice trap. The same things happened. The Shang immortal shouted for someone to come out and fight him. Burning Lamp sent a mortal soldier to fight him. The two of them fought for a few rounds. The immortal ran inside his trap. The soldier followed. This time, the immortal waved a purple flag. A mountain of ice came down from the sky and crashed onto a pile of ice as sharp as wolves' teeth. The soldier was smashed and his soul flew to the Terrace of Creation. A Zhou immortal ran forward. Bright white light came from his fingers, melting the ice. He cut off the head of the Shang immortal, sending his soul to the Terrace of Creation.

Now there were just six traps left.

Another Shang immortal, a woman, stepped forward in front of the Golden Light trap. A mortal soldier came out to fight her. The two of them fought for a few rounds. The immortal turned and ran inside her trap. The soldier followed. The immortal pulled a rope, shaking the magic mirrors. A golden light shot out. It killed the soldier and sent his soul to the Terrace of Creation. A Zhou immortal, Master Grand Completion, ran forward. He spread out his magic robe, blocking the golden light. Then he used his magic to break all the mirrors. He threw a rock, hitting the Shang immortal on the head and killing her instantly. Her soul floated to the Terrace of Creation.

Now there were just five traps left.

The next battle occurred in front of the Flowing Blood trap. A soldier entered the trap and was turned into a stream of blood by a storm of black sand. This time, Fairy Primordial stepped forward on the Zhou side. Fairy Primordial rode into the trap on two green lotus flowers. He pointed to the sky and brought down a beam of white light that protected his body. The black sand could not touch him. Fairy Primordial threw his Nine Dragon Divine Fire Coverlet[1] at the immortal. He clapped his hands. The Nine Dragon Divine Fire Coverlet caught on fire. Nine fire dragons appeared. They wrapped around the Shang immortal and burned him to ashes. His soul flew to the Terrace of Creation.

Now there were just four traps left. Grand Tutor Wen was so angry that white light shot from his third eye and his hair stood straight up. He said to the four remaining Daoist masters, "I am willing to give up my life for my king. But I never wanted to send six of my friends to their deaths! Please, all of you, go home and leave me here. I will fight Jiang Ziya myself."

The four Daoist masters left him sitting alone. He tried to think of a way to defeat Jiang Ziya and the Zhou army. Suddenly he remembered his old friend, the powerful magician Zhao Gongming[2]. "If anyone can help

---

[1] This is the same weapon that Fairy Primordial used in Chapter 13 to defeat Princess Shiji.
[2] The character Zhao Gongming appeared for the first time in this story, and later become known as *Cái Shén*, the God of Money. In Chinese folklore he can control thunder and lightning, ward off plagues and disasters, bring happiness, and chase away criminals.

me, it's him!" he thought.

He told two of his generals to guard the camp. He mounted his unicorn and flew to the mountain cave where Zhao Gongming lived. He banged on the wooden door to the cave. A young man came out.

"Is your master in? Please tell him that Grand Tutor Wen from Zhaoge is here to see him."

The young man went inside. A few minutes later, Zhao Gongming came out. He smiled and said, "Brother Wen, what brings you here? You are a wealthy and powerful man in Zhaoge. I thought you had forgotten me."

They walked together inside the cave and sat down. Grand Tutor Wen told him about the battles and the deaths of the six immortals. "I don't know what to do," he said. "Can you help me?"

Zhao Gongming replied, "Of course. You should have come here earlier. Now go back to West Qi. I will join you there shortly."

Grand Tutor Wen thanked him and left on his unicorn. Zhao Gongming and two of his two disciples began walking down the mountain. Suddenly two tigers came out of the woods. One of them, a black tiger, ran towards him. "Welcome, my friend!" said Zhao Gongming. "I need your help." Then he put his hand on the tiger's neck and spoke a magic spell. He got on the tiger and together they flew through the air, all the way to West Qi.

When he arrived at the Shang camp, the soldiers were very afraid of the flying black tiger. But Grand Tutor Wen came out, saying, "Don't be afraid, my friends. This is Zhao Gongming. He's here to help us."

Then Grand Tutor Wen on his unicorn, and Zhao Gongming on his black tiger, rode out of the camp. They called to Jiang Ziya to come out and fight.

Chapter 47
Zhao Gongming Helps the Grand Tutor

There are many treasures, but don't show them to others;
Remember that they are not all the same

The dynasty is ending but still they still speak of victory;
But when they meet their enemy, they must think about defeat

One cannot ride a tiger, that is just a dream;
But one can defeat a dragon even without a plan

Sadly, the King of Shang's rule is nearly finished;
And the people closest to him cannot help him

☰ ☰ ☰

"Come out, Jiang Ziya! Come out and fight me!" shouted Zhao Gongming.

Nezha went inside to tell Jiang Ziya about the man shouting outside. "Be careful," said Burning Lamp. "This is Zhao Gongming from Mount Emei. He is a very powerful magician."

Jiang Ziya rode out of his camp. Just behind him were Nezha, Thunderbolt, Huang Tianhua, Yang Jian, Jinzha and Muzha. He saw apricot-yellow flags fluttering, and a tall Daoist riding a black tiger. He rode forward and bowed. "Friend, who are you and where do you come from?" he asked.

"I am Zhao Gongming, from Mount Emei. You have broken six of our traps and killed six of my friends. I know that you are a disciple of Heavenly Primogenitor from Mount Kunlun. Today we will fight to see who is stronger."

Without waiting for an answer, he slashed his sword at Jiang Ziya. They fought for a few rounds. Then Zhao Gongming threw his sword up into the air. It came down and hit Jiang Ziya on the back, killing him. The others joined the fight, attacking from all sides. There were too many for Zhao Gongming to fight, so he turned and rode his tiger back to the Shang camp. He had a few injuries, but he used his magic elixir to quickly heal himself.

Jiang Ziya, however, was dead. Jinzha carried the body back to Ji Fa's mansion. They put the body on the bed. It was cold and lifeless. The face was white. Ji Fa and the others looked at the body, not knowing what to do.

Then Master Grand Completion entered the room. He said to the others, "Don't worry, it was his fate to die." He put some magic elixir in a cup of water, opened Jiang Ziya's mouth, and poured the medicine into him. Then they waited.

About two hours later, Jiang Ziya opened his eyes and sat up. "Oh, what pain!" he cried.

Master Grand Completion smiled and said, "Just rest here for a while. I will go and find out what Zhao Gongming is planning to do next."

The next morning, Zhao Gongming rode his black tiger out of the Shang camp. Burning Lamp was waiting for him. Zhao Gongming said, "Brother, we should not fight like this. Buddhists, Daoists and Confucians are all one family. Red flowers, white roots and green leaves are all part of the same lotus."

Burning Lamp replied, "Brother, we are here by the will of heaven. If you fight us, you will only make a fool of yourself. Why do you look for trouble?"

Zhao Gongming said, "Do you think I am less powerful or less wise than you? I can stop the sun and I can move the moon. How dare you think of fighting me!"

Just then, Yellow Dragon stepped forward. He said, "Zhao Gongming, you are here. That means your name is on the list at the Terrace of Creation. And that means you are fated to die here."

This made Zhao Gongming very angry, because he knew that Yellow Dragon's words were true. He threw a magic rope around Yellow Dragon and tied him up.

The other Zhou immortals rushed at Zhao Gongming, using their magic weapons. Zhao Gongming threw his string of twenty-four magic pearls into the air. While they flew through the air, the pearls gave off light of five different colors. Then the pearls came down, hitting Master Pure Essence and knocking him to the ground. Zhao Gongming threw the string of pearls into the air again, hitting Master Grand Completion and knocking him to the ground too. He kept throwing the string of pearls, and knocked down three more of the Zhou immortals.

Finally, he picked up Yellow Dragon and carried him back to the Shang camp. Grand Tutor Wen told his soldiers to hang Yellow Dragon from a tall flagpole, so the Zhou side could see him. He put a magic charm on Yellow Dragon to prevent him from escaping.

The Zhou fighters returned to their camp. Later that night Yang Jian turned himself into a flying ant. He flew across to the Shang camp and up to Yellow Dragon. He whispered in his ear, "Uncle, your disciple Yang Jian is here to set you free. What should I do?"

Yellow Dragon replied, "Just take the magic charm off me." Yang Jian found the charm and pulled it off Yellow Dragon's body. Yellow Dragon flew back to the Zhou camp, followed by Yang Jian.

The next morning, Zhao Gongming came out again, shouting for Burning Lamp. As soon as Burning Lamp came out, Zhao Gongming struck at him with his sword. Then he threw his string of magic pearls into the air. Burning Lamp was ready for this. He used his third eye to look up at the pearls. He saw them but did not know what they were. Before the pearls could come back down to the ground, Burning Lamp rode quicky away to the southwest on his deer. Zhao Gongming chased after him.

They rode for a few *li*. Then Burning Lamp came upon two men. One wore green clothes and had a black face, the other wore red clothes and had a white face. They were playing chess. They asked Burning Lamp why he was riding so quickly. Burning Lamp told them about the battle between Shang and Zhou, and about Zhao Gongming's attack.

"Oh, don't worry about him!" they said. Burning Lamp said goodbye and rode away.

A few minutes later, Zhao Gongming arrived on his black tiger. "Who are you two?" he shouted.

One of the men said, "Ah, you must be Zhao Gongming! I will tell you,

> *We live here among the beautiful clouds*
> *We grow the golden lotus in our hands*
> *We enjoy drinking wine*
> *We cook dinner over a fire*
> *We ride a dragon to see the blue sea*

The night is quiet, the flowers are asleep

If you must know, we are hermits from Mount Wuyi. We are not happy at all to hear that you are attacking our friend Burning Lamp. This is an act against heaven."

Zhao Gongming shouted at them and attacked with his sword. They began to fight. Soon Zhao Gongming threw his magic rope in the air. But the man in red had a magic gold coin called the Treasure Catching Gold Coin. He took the coin out of a tiger skin bag and threw it into the air. The coin rose in the air, then came down. The magic rope followed the coin like a dog following its master. Zhao Gongming saw it fall to the ground and he cried out in anger. He threw his string of magic pearls into the air, but again, the man in red threw his gold coin and captured the pearls.

With no magic weapons left, Zhao Gongming threw his sword high in the air. The man in red threw his gold coin again, but because the sword was an ordinary sword and not magical, the coin could do nothing about it. The sword came down and hit the man in red. He died and his soul flew to the Terrace of Creation.

The man's brother shouted in anger and attacked Zhao Gongming. Burning Lamp had stopped to watch the fight. Now he returned and threw a rock at Zhao Gongming. The rock hit Zhao Gongming and almost knocked him off his tiger. Howling in pain, Zhao Gongming rode away to the south.

Burning Lamp approached the man wearing green. He said, "Sir, I am so sorry that your friend was killed trying to help me. Please tell me, what was that gold coin that the man in red threw in the air?"

The man replied, "That is the Treasure Catching Gold Coin. Here, take a look." And he handed the coin to Burning Lamp. He also showed him the magic rope and the magic pearls.

"Oh, how wonderful!" said Burning Lamp. "When the earth was first created, these pearls shone on Mount Xuandu. But then they disappeared and no one has seen them since. I am so happy to see that you have them now."

"These pearls are of no use to me. Please, just take them."

Burning Lamp thanked him. He took the pearls back to the Zhou camp and showed them to the others.

Back in the Shang camp, Zhao Gongming told Grand Tutor Wen and the others about his defeat, and how he had lost the magic rope and the magic pearls. "I must get these weapons back. To do that, I need to visit Three Immortals Island. My three sisters live there. They can help me."

He jumped on his black tiger and flew swiftly to Three Immortals Island. He came to a cave, and waited politely at the door until the three sisters came to see him. The oldest was Cloud Firmament, the second was Jade Firmament, and the youngest was Green Firmament.

They invited him to come in and sit down. He told them the story of how he lost his treasures. Then he asked for their help.

Cloud Firmament shook her head. "I'm sorry, brother, but we cannot help you. All of us were all in the room when the three religions got together and made the list of names at the Terrace of Creation. You know that the phoenix sang on Mount Qi, telling the world that a new sage ruler was born there. Now we must wait for Jiang Ziya to create the new gods. As soon as that happens, I will get your pearls back for you. But for now, we cannot help you."

"What? You won't help your own brother?" cried Zhao Gongming.

"I want to, but I cannot. Please, go back to your mountain and wait. The new gods will be created soon."

Zhao Gongming stood up angrily and walked out of the cave. He walked about two *li* when he heard someone shouting behind him. He turned around and saw a Daoist woman. Her black hair, which was coiled on her head, was filled with a powerful magic. It was his old friend, the powerful magician named Celestial Lotus.

"Where are you going, my friend?" she asked.

Zhao Gongming told her the story. She said to him, "Are you telling me that your own sisters would not help you? Let's go back and talk with them again."

They returned to the cave together. After they sat down, Celestial Lotus said to the sisters, "You are all from the same family. How can you refuse to help your brother? You know that the Zhou now have his magic rope and magic pearls. He must get them back! Think of your shame if you don't help your brother, and someone else does. Like me."

Green Firmament said, "Sister, just give him the Golden Dragon Scissors."

Cloud Firmament thought about it for a while. Then she said to Zhao Gongming, "All right, take these magic scissors. Go to Burning Lamp. Tell him, 'Give me back the magic pearls. If you say no, I will use these magic scissors and make a great deal of trouble for you.' He will give you back the pearls. I tell you, though, you must be very careful in this situation."

Zhao Gongming took the scissors and agreed to follow his sister's command. He left the island quickly. Celestial Lotus said to him, "I will join you as soon as my weapon is ready."

Zhao Gongming returned to the Shang camp. He showed the scissors to Grand Tutor Wen and told him about his visit to Three Immortals Island.

The next morning, Grand Tutor Wen rode his unicorn and Zhao Gongming rode his black tiger out of the Shang camp. They shouted for Burning Lamp to come out.

In the Zhou camp, Burning Lamp already knew about the magic scissors. He told everyone to wait indoors, then he rode his deer out to meet the enemy alone.

Zhao Gongming shouted, "Burning Lamp! Give me back my magic pearls! If you do, I will have no quarrel with you and our fight will be over."

Burning Lamp replied, "These pearls are a Buddhist treasure. You cannot have them. Don't even dream of getting them back."

"Then there is nothing more to say," shouted Zhao Gongming. He rode forward on his black tiger. The two of them began to fight. Then Zhao Gongming took out the magic scissors and threw them in the air.

Chapter 48
The Illness of Zhao Gongming

The House of Zhou rules with the mandate of heaven;
Why fear treasure if they have heaven's blessing?

Lu Ya wrote how to shoot shadowy arrows;
Zhao Gongming cannot protect his own head

Many immortals can change their appearance;
No one believes that a cruel tyrant can survive against them

Grand Tutor Wen fights against the will of heaven;
His heart is loyal to the king, the son of heaven

≡ ≡ ≡

The Golden Dragon Scissors was made from a pair of dragons that lived on the spirit of heaven, earth, sun and moon. When they were thrown into the air, the two dragon tails locked together. Their bodies could cut anything in two, like scissors cutting a piece of paper.

Burning Lamp saw the scissors coming down towards him. He jumped off his deer and ran away. But the scissors hit the deer and instantly cut it in two.

Burning Lamp returned to the Zhou camp. He told everyone about the magic scissors. They were all very frightened. As they were talking, a man walked into the room. He was short, with a long beard, and was dressed in a red robe. Nobody knew who he was. Burning Lamp asked him, "Who are you and where do you come from, my friend?"

The man replied, "My name is Lu Ya. I live in a cave on Mount Kunlun. I have heard that Zhao Gongming is here and that he has the golden dragon scissors. I can make the scissors useless, and I can kill Zhao Gongming."

The others listened but said nothing. They did not know if he was telling the truth or not. But they let him stay in the camp.

The next morning Zhao Gongming rode out again on his black tiger. He shouted for Burning Lamp to come out. But Lu Ya came out instead.

"Who are you?" asked Zhao Gongming.

"How could you know me? I am not a Daoist and I am not a sage. My name is Lu Ya of Kunlun Mountain. Here is my story:

> I am like the clouds, my mind is like the wind
> I float wherever I want to
> I float on a bright moon on the eastern sea
> I ride a dragon on the southern sea
> I sit on a tiger in the mountains
> I have no wealth, I have no power
> Nobody knows my name
> I do not care about long life peaches[1]
> Three cups of wine and I am happy
> I sit quietly on the rocks listening to the deer
> I play chess with my friends
> I write poems for heaven to enjoy
> Your work of many years will be gone soon
> I am here to kill you, Zhao Gongming!"

Hearing this, Zhao Gongming rushed towards him on his black tiger. Lu Ya attacked with his sword. After a few rounds of fighting, Zhao Gongming threw the scissors up into the air. But Lu Ya just laughed and said, "Ah, I knew you would do that!" He turned into a rainbow and easily escaped.

When Lu Ya returned to the Zhou camp, he said, "I know how to defeat Zhao Gongming. But I will need help from Jiang Ziya."

"Of course I will help you," said Jiang Ziya. "Tell me what you want me to do."

Lu Ya handed him a piece of paper with magic spells written on it. He said, "Go to Mount Qi and build a platform there. Make a straw effigy and write 'Zhao Gongming' on it. Put one lamp on its head and another one at its feet. Then pray to the statue three times a day, saying the spells that are on this paper. Do this for twenty-one days. Then we will

---

[1] In Chinese mythology, the Jade Emperor and his wife Xi Wangmu gave their guests peaches of immortality at the annual Peach Festival. In *The Immortal Peaches*, Book 3 of the *Journey to the West* series, the monkey king Sun Wukong stole some of these peaches and ended up in serious trouble.

kill him."

Jiang Ziya did what Lu Ya had told him. He went to Mount Qi with three thousand soldiers. They built the platform and made the effigy. Every day, Jiang Ziya walked around the effigy three times and said the prayers.

After a few days of this, Zhao Gongming began to feel uncomfortable. He felt like his heart was burning up. He walked back and forth but could not get comfortable.

Grand Tutor Wen was worried about Zhao Gongming, and wanted to let him rest. But one of the Daoist immortals said to him, "Grand Tutor, we cannot just sit and wait. How will we ever win? Now is the time for me to use my Bright Flame trap." And without waiting for Grand Tutor Wen, he rode out of the Shang camp on his deer, shouting to the Zhou to come out and fight.

The Zhou immortals heard him shouting. None of them wanted to go out, but finally Lu Ya said, "I will go." He walked out of the camp, smiling and singing a song.

"Who are you?" asked the immortal from the Shang camp.

"My name is Lu Ya. Thank you for preparing this trap. I would like to see it."

The Daoist immortal became angry and attacked Lu Ya with a sword. After a few rounds of fighting, he retreated back into the trap. Lu Ya followed him. Instantly he was surrounded by fires from the sky, from the ground, and from the human world. But Lu Ya could not be touched by fire. For four hours, Lu Ya stood in the fire, singing and smiling. Then he reached into his robe and took out a gourd. A beam of light came from the gourd and shot thirty feet into the air. At the top of the beam were two eyes. A white light came down from the eyes. It hit the Daoist immortal's head. The head fell to the ground, and his soul flew to the Terrace of Creation.

Lu Ya put the gourd back in his robe. He turned around to walk out of the trap. But then Yao, another immortal from the Shang camp, ran up to him. He had a golden face, a red beard, and long fangs coming from his mouth. His voice was like thunder. He shouted at Lu Ya, "Don't run away! Come into my Captured Soul Trap." This was a very powerful trap. It closes the gates of life and opens the windows of death. This is the trap that Yao had used earlier, when he tried to kill Jiang Ziya.

Before Lu Ya could respond, Pure Essence ran forward and entered the trap. He knew all about the trap, because he'd been inside it once before. As soon as he entered the trap he was hit by a powerful flying cloud of black sand. But Pure Essence took a mirror from his robe and held it up. The black sand turned around and hit Yao. Yao fell down. Pure Essence walked up to him and cut off his head, sending Yao's soul to the Terrace of Creation.

These two traps were destroyed, so there were only two traps left in the Shang camp. Grand Tutor Wen was worried about that. But he was also worried about Zhao Gongming, who was tired and only wanted to sleep.

Grand Tutor Wen did not know why Zhao Gongming was sleeping all the time. He did a divination with gold coins and learned that Jiang Ziya's prayers at the effigy had weakened Zhao Gongming's spirit and brought him close to death. He said, "Soon Lu Ya will shoot arrows into the effigy, and that will be Zhao Gongming's death! What can we do?"

He decided to send two of his immortals to Mount Qi, to steal the effigy. Soon after that, Lu Ya felt something strange in his heart. He did a divination and learned of Grand Tutor Wen's plan.

Quickly he sent Yang Jian and Nezha to Mount Qi. Nezha rode quickly on his Wind Fire Wheels, while Yang Jian rode his horse.

The two Shang immortals flew through the air towards Mount Qi. Looking down, they saw Jiang Ziya walking around the effigy with his head down, saying prayers and burning incense. The two immortals flew down, grabbed the effigy, and flew away like the wind.

Jiang Ziya did not see them, but he heard something. He looked up and saw that the effigy was gone. He looked around but did not see it anywhere. Just then, Nezha arrived. Nezha said, "Be careful, Jiang Ziya! Someone is coming to steal the effigy!"

Jiang Ziya replied, "You are too late! I was kowtowing just now when I heard a noise. I looked up and saw that the effigy was gone. Quick, get it back. If you don't, we all will die!"

Nezha turned and rode his Wind Fire Wheels back towards the Shang camp. Soon, Yang Jian arrived on his horse. When he heard what had happened, he knew that he could not catch the thieves. So he picked up a handful of dirt and threw it in the air. Then he sat down to wait.

Back at the Shang camp, the two immortals saw Grand Tutor Wen sitting in a chair. They gave him the effigy. Immediately, the camp disappeared, and the two immortals found that they were standing in a field all by themselves.

Yang Jian rode his horse towards them, swinging his sword. Then Nezha arrived on his Wind Fire Wheels. The fight was over quickly. The two immortals were killed, and their souls flew to the Terrace of Creation.

"Where is the effigy?" asked Nezha.

"I have it," replied Yang Jian. "When I heard that those two had stolen the effigy, I changed myself to look like Grand Tutor Wen. I told them to give me the effigy. Now those two thieves are dead and we can bring the effigy back to Mount Qi." They returned to Mount Qi and gave the effigy to Jiang Ziya.

Back at the Shang camp, Grand Tutor Wen heard about the failure of his plan. He sat down and cried. A little while later he went to see Zhao Gongming, who was sleeping in his bed. He said, "Dear brother, wake up!" Then he told Zhao Gongming about what happened.

"Oh, I am finished!" said Zhao Gongming. "Why didn't I listen to my sisters? Dear brother Wen, it looks like I will die soon. I became an immortal many years ago, during the time of the Jade Emperor[1]. Who would have thought that I would die now, at the hands of Lu Ya? After I die, please wrap up the Golden Dragon Scissors in my robe and give them back to my three sisters." He began to cry and could not speak anymore.

Now there were only two Daoist immortals left at the Shang camp. One of them had the Red Water trap. He ran out of the camp and shouted towards the Zhou camp, "Which of you will meet me at the Red Water trap?"

Burning Lamp said to Master Pure Void Virtue, "Go and break that trap." Master Pure Void Virtue stepped forward.

---

[1] The mythical Jade Emperor was born the crown prince of the kingdom of Pure Felicity and Majestic Heavenly Lights and Ornaments. After his father died, he ascended the throne. He was a good and wise king. He then decided to cultivate his Dao. He attained Golden Immortality after 1,750 eons of study, each eon lasting for 129,600 years. A hundred million years after that, he finally became the Jade Emperor.

Chapter 49
Ji Fa in the Red Sand Trap

A single thought brings understanding, all things come to rest;
Do without doing[1], make without making, no need to worry

White jade is in my heart, most people cannot understand;
The gold of this world means nothing to me

On the rocky shore, the river speaks to me in Sanskrit;
The mountain's colors cover the cool water

Sometimes I sit by the riverside;
The moon hangs low in the sky like a fishing hook

☰ ☰ ☰

Master Pure Void Virtue raised his sword, ran forward, and attacked the Daoist immortal. The immortal turned and ran into the Red Water trap. Master Pure Void Virtue followed him.

When he stepped inside the trap, he saw that it was full of red water. He took a white lotus flower out of his sleeve and dropped it onto the water. Then he stepped on to the flower. He floated there for two hours, untouched by the red water.

The Daoist immortal knew that he had lost the fight. He tried to run away. But Master Pure Void Virtue took out his magic fan. It was called the Five Fire and Seven Bird Fan, because it produced five kinds of fire and it was made from the wings of seven different kinds of birds. The fan was so powerful that it could burn rocks to dust, and turn an ocean dry. He waved the fan once at the Daoist immortal. The immortal cried out once, then turned into red ash and died. Master Pure Void Virtue and the others returned to the Zhou camp.

The next morning, Lu Ya met with Jiang Ziya. He said, "Zhao Gongming will die at noon today. And the Red Water trap has been broken."

---

[1] *Wéi wú wéi*, "doing without doing," is one of the key principles of Daoist living.

He took a small bow and arrow out of his flower basket and handed them to Jiang Ziya. He said, "Go back to Mount Qi. Shoot the effigy with this bow and arrows. Shoot the left eye first, then the right eye, then the heart."

Jiang Ziya returned to Mount Qi and shot an arrow into the effigy's left eye. In the Shang camp, Zhao Gongming cried out in pain and closed his left eye. Jiang Ziya shot the right eye, and Zhao Gongming cried out again. Then Jiang Ziya shot the heart, and Zhao Gongming died.

Jiang Ziya returned to the Zhou camp. When he arrived, Burning Lamp told him, "There is one trap left. It is the Red Sand trap, the most powerful and evil of all. We need someone blessed by heaven to break this trap."

"Who should we send?" asked Jiang Ziya.

"It must be our king, Ji Fa. Anyone else will fail."

Jiang Ziya sent someone to talk with Ji Fa and ask him to come to the camp. A short time later, Ji Fa arrived. "Master," he said to Jiang Ziya, "what do you want me to do?"

"Your highness, we have broken nine of the ten traps. Only the Red Sand trap remains. You are the only one who can break it. Will you help us?"

"You are all here because of your love for the people. How can I say no to you?"

Burning Lamp said to him, "Your Highness, please remove your robe." Ji Fa removed his robe. Burning Lamp used his finger to draw some magic words on the king's chest and back. After the king put his robe back on, Burning Lamp drew more magic words inside the king's crown. Then he told Nezha and Thunderbolt to protect the king when he entered the trap.

The three of them walked towards the Shang camp. A Daoist immortal rode out on a deer out to meet them. He had a face as cold as ice, a long red beard, and carried two swords. "Who will fight me?" he shouted. Then he attacked.

Nezha stepped forward and blocked his swords. The immortal turned and ran into his trap. Nezha, Thunderbolt and Ji Fa followed him. The immortal grabbed a handful of red sand and threw it at them. The sand hit Ji Fa, sending him and his horse down into a deep pit. The sand also hit Nezha and Thunderbolt, and they both fell into the pit.

Back at the Zhou camp, they saw black smoke coming up from the trap. "Don't worry," said Burning Lamp. "They will all be released in a hundred days."

Jiang Ziya replied, "But Ji Fa is a mortal man, how can he live in that trap for a hundred days?"

"Trust heaven and don't worry."

In the Shang camp, Grand Tutor Wen was deeply unhappy because of Zhao Gongming's death. Every day he walked into the trap and threw handfuls of red sand down on Ji Fa. The red sand was supposed to cause great pain. But because of the magic words on Ji Fa's body, he was not harmed by the sand.

Meanwhile, Shen Gongbao went to see Zhao Gongming's sisters on Three Immortals Island. Shen Gongbao was an old friend of Jiang Ziya and also a disciple of Heavenly Primogenitor, but he was fighting on the side of the Shang king.

Shen Gongbao told the sisters that their brother was dead, shot by Jiang Ziya's arrows. The sisters all began to cry. Shen Gongbao said to them, "Your brother told me to tell you that he was sorry he did not follow your advice."

The oldest sister, Cloud Firmament, replied, "We cannot leave this island. If we do, heaven says that we will die and our souls will fly to the Terrace of Creation. Our brother did not listen, and that's why he is dead."

But Jade Firmament said, "Sister, what are you saying? Do you have no heart? We must go and see his body, even if it means that we will die. After all, we are of the same blood."

And with that, Jade Firmament and Green Firmament flew away towards West Qi. Cloud Firmament said to herself, "I must go with them to make sure they don't get into trouble." And she mounted her phoenix and flew after them.

They heard a voice calling, "Wait for me!" Turning around, they saw Celestial Lotus. "I am going with you to West Qi," she said.

A short time later, they heard another voice calling, "Wait for me, sisters!" They turned and saw another woman, named Lady Pretty Cloud. She said, "Shen Gongbao said I should travel with you to West

Qi. I am happy to meet you all! Let's go together."

A short time later, the five women arrived at the Shang camp. They told a guard to tell Grand Tutor Wen that they had arrived. The Grand Tutor came out to meet them. They all sat down.

Cloud Firmament said to him, "My brother left his home on Three Immortals Island to help you. Now he is dead, killed by Jiang Ziya's arrow. We are here to get his body and bring it home. Will you please tell us where it is?"

Grand Tutor Wen replied, "Before he died, Zhao Gongming told me, 'I am sorry I did not listen to my sisters. I have caused my own death.' Then he asked me to give you the Golden Dragon Scissors and his robe. Here they are." He handed the scissors and robe to her. Then he began to cry, and the five women cried with him.

"Show us his body," said Cloud Firmament. They followed Grand Tutor Wen to the back of the camp. Seeing the blood on his body, they could not control their anger. Green Firmament said, "Sisters, let's catch the killer and shoot him with three arrows too!"

Cloud Firmament said, "Yes, and let's not forget Lu Ya. We will kill him too. Then we will have our revenge."

The next day, the five women and Grand Tutor Wen rode out towards the Zhou camp. Cloud Firmament shouted, "Lu Ya, come out and meet me!"

Lu Ya picked up his sword and ran out of the camp to meet her. His sleeves were blowing in the wind. He bowed to the women. Cloud Firmament said to him, "So, you are Lu Ya?"

"Yes, I am."

"Why did you kill my brother, Zhao Gongming?"

"I will tell you everything, if you will listen to me."

"I will listen."

"The only path to wisdom is to follow the Dao. I studied and followed the Dao for many years, and I became an immortal during the time of the Heavenly Emperor. But your brother made a terrible mistake. He sided with a cruel tyrant. He used his magic powers for evil instead of for good. He acted against the will of heaven, and that's why heaven sent me to kill him. My friends, can't you see that this is not the place for you? Here you will only find mountains of weapons and oceans of fire. If you stay here, I'm afraid you will die."

Cloud Firmament looked down at the ground and said nothing. But Jade Firmament shouted, "You brute! How dare you tell us these lies. You killed my brother, now I will have my revenge!" And with that, she picked up her sword and rushed at Lu Ya.

Lu Ya fought back, and they battled for several rounds. Then Green Firmament threw a magic weapon into the air. This was the Universe Muddling Dipper, a very powerful weapon. It caught Lu Ya and threw him to the ground. Green Firmament jumped on him, tied him up, wrote magic words on his body, and hung him from a flag pole.

She said to the others, "Lu Ya killed my brother with a bow and arrow. Now we will kill him the same way." Five hundred men with bows and arrows came. Arrows fell like rain on Lu Ya, but as they came near, they turned to ashes and fell to the ground.

"Sorry, ladies, but I have to go now," said Lu Ya. Then he changed into a rainbow and disappeared.

Cloud Firmament was very angry. The next day she went out with the four other women and shouted for Jiang Ziya to come and see her. Jiang Ziya came out, with disciples on his right and left. He bowed to her, saying, "Greetings my Daoist friends!"

"Jiang Ziya!" she shouted. "Yes, we are Daoists. We care nothing for the things of this world. We are only here because our brother was killed by your magic arrows. Now you must pay for what you did."

"No, you are wrong. Your brother came here against the wishes of his master, and caused trouble. He brought disaster on himself."

"How dare you say these lies!" shouted Jade Firmament. She attacked him with his sword. Jiang Ziya fought back. Huang Tianhua and Yang Jian joined the fight. Green Firmament, Cloud Firmament and Pretty Cloud Lady all rushed forward to fight them.

Chapter 50
The Yellow River Trap

The Yellow River's evil follows the Three Realms;
In this disaster even the gods will suffer

The river curves ninety-nine times to hide its nature;
Its thirty-three bays hide wind and thunder

People who study Dao speak carelessly about the heavenly garden;
Who can claim to understand the soul and the holy child?

In this situation, you must completely change your bones;
Then you'll see that dark magic does not lead to a good life

≡ ≡ ≡

What a battle! It started when Pretty Cloud Lady threw a magic pearl at Huang Tianhua. The pearl hit him in the eyes, knocking him off his unicorn and onto the ground. Jinzha rushed forward, picked him up, and carried him away.

Jiang Ziya threw his magic staff into the air. It hit Cloud Firmament and knocked her off her phoenix. Then Yang Jian sent his heavenly dog to attack Jade Firmament. The dog bit her on the shoulder, tearing her robe.

Celestial Lotus sent a powerful black wind towards the Zhou fighters. It turned the sky dark and made the mountains shake. Pretty Cloud threw another magic pearl, hitting Jiang Ziya in the eyes.

Yang Jian fought off Jade Firmament and carried Jiang Ziya back to the camp. There, Burning Lamp gave elixir pills to Jiang Ziya and Huang Tianhua, curing them both.

The battle ended. But Cloud Firmament was angry. She had been injured by Jiang Ziya's staff, and her sister Green Firmament had been bitten by the dog.

She told Grand Tutor Wen, "Give me six hundred of your strongest soldiers. I will make the most powerful trap." Then she went to the back of the camp. She picked up a piece of chalk and drew a picture of a large building. It had many doors and windows, and there were arrows showing where to advance and where to retreat. The soldiers went to work building the trap.

Half a month later the trap was ready. Grand Tutor Wen looked at it and said to her, "Please explain how this trap works."

"It uses the powers of heaven, earth, and man. It contains all the secrets of gods and immortals. If an immortal enters, they become mortal. If a mortal enters, they die. The trap takes away their spirits, their souls, their energy, and their life. No one can escape, not even the leaders of the three great religions."

Grand Tutor Wen liked what he saw. He rode his black unicorn out of the camp with the five women and called out to Jiang Ziya to meet him. When Jiang Ziya came out, Cloud Firmament said, "Jiang Ziya! You and I both have great powers. We both can move mountains and seas. But now I have a trap that is more powerful than anything you have ever seen. Try to break it. If you break it, we will leave West Qi and not trouble you anymore. But if you cannot break it, you will all die."

Yang Jian answered her, saying, "Ladies, we will be happy to take a look at your new trap. But please do not try to trick us when we go inside to look at it."

"Of course," replied Cloud Firmament. "We will not do anything to you, as long as you don't attack us with your dog. Now go and take a look."

Yang Jian, Jiang Ziya and the others walked into the trap. They saw a small sign reading, "Nine Bends of the Yellow River Trap." They saw several hundred soldiers carrying five-color banners. There was a cold wind and dark fog. After a while they turned and walked out of the trap.

When they were outside the trap, Green Firmament cried out, "What? Are you going to attack us with your heavenly dog again?" Quickly, Cloud Firmament threw her Universe Muddling Dipper into the air. It captured Yang Jian and threw him into the trap.

Jinzha shouted in anger and attacked Jade Firmament with his sword. Cloud Firmament just laughed at him, threw the Universe Muddling Dipper into the air. The dipper threw Jinzha into the trap.

Muzha was next. He shouted, "How dare you take my brother!" He threw his weapon, called the Hooks of Wu, at her.

Cloud Firmament just said, "These aren't even magic!" Then she used the Universe Muddling Dipper to throw Muzha into the trap with his brother.

Next, she attacked Jiang Ziya with her swords, then she threw the Universe Muddling Dipper into the air. But Jiang Ziya was ready for her. He waved a magic yellow flag. Golden flowers came out of the flag, blocking the path of the dipper. The dipper turned over and over in the sky but could not come down.

Jiang Ziya was not harmed by the Universe Muddling Dipper. He returned to the Zhou camp. But now three men were in the Red Sand trap and three more were in the Yellow River trap. In the Shang camp, Grand Tutor Wen ordered a great feast.

The next day, the five women rode out and called for Burning Lamp. When he came out, Cloud Firmament said to him, "Burning Lamp! You have insulted us. That's why I created the Yellow River trap. See if you can break it. You should send someone with great power."

Burning Lamp replied, "My Daoist friend, don't do this. You were there when the List of Creation was made. How can you not understand what is happening here? Zhao Gongming was not destined to be an immortal, so his fate was to die."

Cloud Firmament did not reply. She threw the Universe Muddling Dipper into the air. Master Pure Essence ran forward to fight her. The Universe Muddling Dipper caught Master Pure Essence and threw him into the trap. Immediately he became like a drunken man. A thousand years of studying the Dao were turned to dust.

Master Grand Completion saw this. He said to Cloud Firmament, "How can you use your Daoist powers for evil like this?" He began to fight with Cloud Firmament. But while they were fighting, Jade Firmament picked up the dipper and threw in the air. It captured Master Grand Completion and threw him into the trap with the others.

Quickly the sisters used their magic dipper to capture nine more immortals from the Zhou side, including Fairy Primordial, Merciful Navigation and Master Pure Void Virtue. In a few minutes, all twelve immortals lost the wisdom they had gained during a thousand years of studying the Dao.

There were only two immortals left: Burning Lamp and Jiang Ziya. The sisters tried to capture Burning Lamp with the dipper, but he quickly changed into a gust of wind and disappeared. The sisters returned to the Shang camp, and Grand Tutor Wen ordered another great feast.

In the Zhou camp, Burning Lamp said to Jiang Ziya, "Our brothers will not be killed, but all of their wisdom has been lost. We cannot fight these women. I must go to Mount Kunlun and get help."

He flew to Mount Kunlun to meet with his master, Heavenly Primogenitor. But when he got there, a disciple told him that Heavenly Primogenitor was already preparing to go to West Qi. The disciple said, "Go back and prepare a place to meet him."

Burning Lamp returned to the Zhou camp. He and Jiang Ziya bathed, burned incense, and waited for their master. Soon Heavenly Primogenitor arrived. He rode in his Nine Dragon Carriage. Burning Lamp and Jiang Ziya kowtowed to him.

Heavenly Primogenitor entered the room that was prepared for him. Jiang Ziya kowtowed again and said, "Many of your disciples are in the Yellow River trap. Please, save them from this terrible fate."

Heavenly Primogenitor replied, "This is their fate and nobody can change it. Say no more." The three of them sat in silence for a long time. At midnight, a bright colorful cloud appeared in the sky. Thousands of burning lamps floated up above the camp.

The next morning, Heavenly Primogenitor said, "Now that I am here, I want to see the trap." He rode in his Nine Dragon Carriage. Burning Lamp led the way and Jiang Ziya followed behind. When they got to the Shang camp, a disciple shouted, "Cloud Firmament! Come out and meet Heavenly Primogenitor."

Cloud Firmament came out, with her sisters on her left and right. They bowed to Heavenly Primogenitor and said, "Uncle! Please forgive us for our rudeness."

"It is my disciples' fate that they suffer. But still, even I do not go against the will of heaven. Why do you ignore heaven's will?"

Then without waiting for a reply, Heavenly Primogenitor rode his Nine Dragon Carriage into the Yellow River trap. His carriage floated two feet above the ground on a colorful cloud. He looked around and saw his twelve disciples lying on the ground. Their eyes were closed. "Ah," he said to himself, "they could not let go of their desire. Now they have lost everything."

Just as he turned to leave, Pretty Cloud threw a magic pearl at him. But the pearl turned to dust before it reached him. Cloud Firmament saw this. Her face turned pale but she said nothing.

When Heavenly Primogenitor returned to the Zhou camp, Burning Lamp asked him how the twelve immortals were doing. He replied, "They have lost their divine flowers, and their divine gates are closed. They are just mortals now."

"Can you rescue them?"

"I must consult with my elder brother." Then he smiled and looked up towards the sky. "Ah, here he comes now."

They all went outside to meet Laozi. As the master came down from the sky, Heavenly Primogenitor said to him, "I know that you will be here to help me throughout the eight hundred years of the new Zhou Dynasty."

"Here I am," replied Laozi, smiling. Then he asked, "Have you looked at the trap yet?"

"Yes. It was just as we thought. I have been waiting for you."

"You should have destroyed it, no need to wait for me." Then the two of them sat in silence for the rest of the day and all night.

The next day, Laozi said to his younger brother, "Let's go and break the trap. We should not stay in the red dust of this world[1] any longer than we need to." Heavenly Primogenitor agreed.

Heavenly Primogenitor rode his carriage and Laozi rode his blue ox. A red fog appeared, and the smell of incense filled the air. Together they went to the Yellow River trap.

Laozi called out, "You three sisters, come out and meet us!"

The three sisters came out from the trap. But they did not bow and they did not greet their visitors.

"How dare you!" said Laozi. "Even your master would bow when meeting us."

Green Firmament replied, "We have our own master. And since you

---

[1] Red dust (hóng chén) refers to the bustle and activity of human affairs. It comes from a poem "Ode to the Western Capital" by Ban Gu, a writer and historian of the Eastern Han Dynasty. It refers to the flying dust raised by horses and carriages on busy roads.

don't show us any respect, we will not show you respect."

Laozi said, "Well, you are a brave little beast, aren't you?" Then the three sisters turned and walked into the trap. Laozi and Heavenly Primogenitor followed.

What will happen inside the trap? And what will become of the three sisters and the immortals trapped inside? If you want to know, you will have to read the next book.

Chapter 51
The Defeat of Grand Tutor Wen

The prime minister led his army into battle
But now his fate will not bring him praise

The storm comes like a wave and the enemy flees
Dragons and tigers fall like flowers to the ground

The Yellow River army conquered the enemy
But still, we weep for the people

Don't stay too long in the land of the dragons
Let's go together to the Terrace of Creation

☰ ☰ ☰

Inside the Yellow River trap, Laozi looked around. He saw many of his disciples. Some were lying asleep on the ground. Others walked around like drunks. A few were dead. "Ah," he said to himself, "a thousand years of study, all gone."

Jade Firmament saw him walking around. Quickly she threw the Golden Dragon Scissors into the air. Laozi saw the scissors go up into the air and start to come down. He held out one of his sleeves. The scissors fell into the sleeve and disappeared.

Next, Green Firmament threw the Universe Muddling Dipper into the air. But Laozi told his genie to grab the dipper and take it back to his home in heaven.

"Stop stealing our weapons!" cried the three sisters. They attacked Laozi and Heavenly Primogenitor with their swords. But the two Daoist masters did not want to lower themselves to fighting like that. Laozi told his genie to capture High Firmament and trap her beneath a mountain. Heavenly Primogenitor told his disciple to throw his staff in the air; it came down and smashed Jade Firmament's head. Then Heavenly Primogenitor opened up a small box. Green Firmament fell into the box and was turned into a pool of blood. In less than a minute, all three sisters were dead. Their souls flew to the Terrace of Creation.

Laozi pointed his finger to the ground. A loud clap of thunder came, and immediately all the disciples were free from the evil magic. They all kowtowed to Laozi and Heavenly Primogenitor.

Heavenly Primogenitor said to them, "It's too bad that you have lost the wisdom you got from a thousand years of study. But this was your fate, and fate is difficult to avoid. Now you must help Jiang Ziya in the coming battles. Use all the weapons that we took from the three sisters. Now we must leave you and return home." Laozi and Heavenly Primogenitor flew away.

Pretty Cloud and Celestial Lotus were still alive. They returned to Grand Tutor Wen to tell him about the death of the three sisters.

There was still one trap left, the Red Sand Trap. The next day, the Immortal of the South Pole went out of the Zhao camp. He shouted, "I am here to smash the Red Sand Trap!"

The last of the trap-building immortals, a man named Zhang, came out. He said, "Brother, you are a good man, but you are not powerful enough to break this trap. You will die if you enter it!"

Zhang turned and ran into the Red Sand Trap. The Immortal of the South Pole followed him. Inside the trap, Zhang picked up some red sand and threw it. But the Immortal of the South Pole just waved his fan, blowing away the sand. He shouted, "Zhang, you will not be able to escape today!" Then he swung his sword, cutting off Zhang's head. Zhang's soul flew to the Terrace of Creation.

The trap had no more power. The Immortal of the South Pole looked around inside the trap. He saw Nezha, Thunderbolt and King Wu. He released a bolt of thunder. Nezha and Thunderbolt jumped up. But King Wu[1] lay on the ground. He was dead.

Jiang Ziya cried when he heard of King Wu's death. But the Immortal of the South Pole told him, "Don't worry, it was his fate to suffer for a hundred days. Now I will bring him back to life." He took some elixir out of his robe, put it in water, then poured it into King Wu's mouth.

Two hours later, King Wu opened his eyes. He said to Jiang Ziya and the others, "How happy we are to see you all again!"

Now all the immortals were gathered together. Burning Lamp said to them, "We have broken all ten of the traps. Our work is almost done.

---

[1] This is Ji Fa, which is the name we used for him in the previous book. But he took the name King Wu when he was named king of West Qi.

Grand Completion, you must stop Grand Tutor Wen from entering the Good Dream pass. Pure Essence, you must stop him from entering the other five passes. Merciful Navigation, you stay here. The rest of you can go."

When the immortals had gone, Jiang Ziya gathered his generals together. He told them that a big battle was coming the next day. The generals left to prepare their soldiers.

Back at the Shang camp, Grand Tutor Wen was talking with Pretty Cloud and Celestial Lotus. He knew the battle was coming soon. He was waiting for more soldiers to arrive from Zhaoge. Just then, he heard the thunder of cannons and the shouting of many men. A messenger ran in, telling him that Jiang Ziya was outside, wanting to talk with him. He mounted his black unicorn and rode out to meet him.

Jiang Ziya said, "Grand Tutor Wen! You have been here for three years but you still have not won. Do you have any more traps for us?" Then he told his soldiers to bring out the immortal who had made the Earth's Fury Trap and had been taken prisoner. When the man was brought out, Jiang Ziya took out a sword and chopped off his head.

This was too much for Grand Tutor Wen. He shouted and rushed forward, trying to kill Jiang Ziya. Huang Tianhua blocked him. The two immortal women, Celestial Lotus and Pretty Cloud, both rushed forward, but they were blocked by Yang Jian and Nezha. All the other immortals, generals and soldiers rushed forward and a huge battle began. The two sides fought like lions and tigers.

Several of the immortals began to use magic. Celestial Lotus sent an evil black wind, but Merciful Navigation stopped the wind with a magic pearl. Jiang Ziya threw his magic staff in the air. It came down on Celestial Lotus's head, killing her. Pretty Cloud heard the sound. She turned to look and was stabbed to death by Nezha. The two souls flew to the Terrace of Creation.

Grand Tutor Wen saw the death of the two female immortals. He lost heart, turned and ran back to the Shang camp. His generals and soldiers followed close behind.

Jiang Ziya prepared his army to continue the attack that night. He told Huang Tianhua, Nezha and Thunderbolt to attack from three different directions. He told Yang Jian to burn all the grain in the Shang camp. He told Huang Feihu to attack on the left with five thousand soldiers, and Nangong Kuo to attack on the right with five thousand soldiers.

Then he told several generals that they should bring three thousand soldiers right up to the front gate of the Shang camp and shout, "If you continue to support the tyrant, you will die. If you want to live, join us."

Grand Tutor Wen saw with his third eye that a big attack was coming. He told his generals to guard the right, left and rear of the camp. He went to the front gate to guard it himself.

When night came, Jiang Ziya told his army to move quietly to their places. Then, with a thunder of cannons, they all attacked the Shang camp at once. There was fighting everywhere. Immortals, generals and soldiers all fought for their lives. At the front gate, Grand Tutor Wen tried to keep the Zhou soldiers back. Jiang Ziya saw him and threw his magic staff up into the air. Grand Tutor Wen could not move away fast enough, and the staff struck him on the left shoulder, hurting him badly.

The Shang soldiers could not hold back the Zhou army. The Zhou rushed forward and encircled the Shang camp. The grain stores burned, sending clouds of black smoke into the air.

The Zhou soldiers shouted, "Why would you give up your lives for the tyrant? Join us and live in happiness!" Half of the Shang soldiers threw down their weapons and crossed over to the Zhou side. Most of the rest turned and left the camp to return to their homes. Grand Tutor Wen's army, which once was 300,000 men, was now only one tenth of that size.

"Where should we go now?" one of the generals asked Grand Tutor Wen.

Grand Tutor Wen looked around. He saw a road leading away from the camp. "Where does this road lead to?" he asked.

"Good Dream Pass."

"Then that is where we will go."

Grand Tutor Wen and his army moved slowly down the road towards Good Dream Pass. After a while they came to a small mountain. On the mountain was a yellow flag. Under the flag stood a Daoist. It was Master Grand Completion.

"Master Grand Completion, what are you doing here?" asked Grand Tutor Wen.

"I am waiting for you. Don't you know that you are acting against the will of heaven? You have helped the tyrant and hurt many good people. I cannot let you enter Good Dream Pass. Please turn around and go away."

"How dare you speak to me like this!" shouted Grand Tutor Wen. He rushed forward on his unicorn, attacking Grand Completion. They fought for a while, sword against sword. Then Grand Completion threw something into the air. Grand Tutor Wen knew that it was a magic seal[1], and he could not fight against it. He turned his unicorn around and fled to the west.

"Why did you turn around?" asked one of his generals.

"We cannot fight against that seal. Let's try to go through the five passes and return to Zhaoge."

They traveled for several days, until they saw the first of the five passes. But just before the pass they saw another yellow flag. Under that flag stood Master Pure Essence.

"Grand Tutor Wen," said Master Pure Essence, "you must not go through these passes. I have been ordered by Burning Lamp to stop you. Please turn around and go back."

Grand Tutor Wen was so angry that black smoke came out of his nose and fire came from his mouth and ears. He shouted, "Pure Essence! You and I are both Daoists, how can you say this to me? I will not turn around!"

He rode his unicorn forward and attacked Pure Essence. But Pure Essence took out his magic mirror, ready to use it against his enemy.

---

[1] A Chinese seal stamp (yìnzhāng) is used to mark a document or object to show who owns it or created it. It's used by pressing the carved lower surface into red or black ink, and then stamping it. Wen's weapon is a "magic overturning seal."

Chapter 52
The Death of Grand Tutor Wen

False news of victory comes often to the capital
The tyrant king only lusts with his women

No one speaks wise words in court anymore
In the mountains, autumn leaves fall like tears

Listen to the monkeys crying in the moonlight
The war is over for him, but his worried soul stays behind

Even with a loyal heart, he remains in the past
Like Duyu, who thinks of home and cries in the east wind[1]

≡ ≡ ≡

Grand Tutor Wen knew that if the magic mirror shone red, it would cause his death, so he quickly rode his black unicorn away. He decided to take his army towards Green Dragon Pass. But after a half day of walking, they came to another army. They heard the thunder of cannons and saw red flags waving in the air. Then Nezha rode up on his Wind Fire Wheels.

"Grand Tutor Wen," he shouted, "you cannot return home this way. Here is where you will meet your death!"

Grand Tutor Wen and four of his generals surrounded Nezha and attacked him. Nezha killed two of them. The others retreated along with their soldiers, but Nezha blocked their retreat, shouting, "Put down your weapons and save yourselves."

"We will follow your king!" shouted most of the soldiers, and put down their weapons. Nezha returned to West Qi with his own army and twenty thousand Shang soldiers.

Grand Tutor Wen sat in his tent, thinking about his defeat. "I have never been defeated like this," he said.

---

[1] Dùyǔ was an emperor in ancient China. According to folklore he turned into a cuckoo after he died, and cried out to his people in sadness.

"Don't worry," said one of his generals. "Victory and defeat are both common in the life of a soldier. Let's return to Zhaoge and plan our next attack."

But the next day, things got worse. As they walked down the road, another army stood in front of them. In front of the army was Huang Tianhua. He called out, "By order of Prime Minister Jiang Ziya, I am here to stop you. You have lost many men. There is nothing you can do. Please just surrender."

Grand Tutor Wen became angry when he heard this. With two of his generals beside him, he attacked Huang Tianhua. In the fight, both of the generals were killed. Grand Tutor Wen retreated with his army. He saw that the Zhou army did not chase them, so they marched slowly until they found a place to rest at the base of a mountain. They had dinner and lay down to rest for the night.

But in the middle of the night, they were awakened by the thunder of cannons. Looking up, Wen saw King Wu and Jiang Ziya sitting on top of the mountain, drinking and laughing. Grand Tutor Wen mounted his unicorn and rushed up the mountain to fight them. But when he got there, there was a crash of thunder, and the two men disappeared. He looked around, but even with his third eye he could not see anyone.

Then he heard another sound of cannons. Looking down, he saw a great army surrounding the mountain. He rushed down to fight them, but again they disappeared. A third time he heard cannons, and again he looked up and saw King Wu and Jiang Ziya on top of the mountain, laughing at him.

He rushed up the mountain again to fight them. This time, Thunderbolt flew at him and swung his huge cudgel. Wen moved out of the way, but the cudgel hit his unicorn and cut the animal in two. Then Thunderbolt flew away, leaving Grand Tutor Wen alone with the dead unicorn.

He turned his face up to the sky and said, "Heaven has turned its back on the Shang Dynasty. I have been loyal but I cannot change things." Then he gathered the few soldiers who still were with him, and began to walk towards Zhaoge. They had no food, and all of them were tired and hungry.

Soon they came upon a small village. Grand Tutor Wen asked his soldiers to go and beg for food. One of the villagers invited Grand Tutor Wen to come into his house. He brought food and tea for the general. After Grand Tutor Wen had eaten, the man invited the other soldiers to come in and have something to eat. Grand Tutor Wen asked the man his name, and told him that he would tell the king of the man's kindness.

Feeling a bit better, Grand Tutor Wen and his men left the village. They started walking towards Zhaoge but soon lost their way. They heard the sound of wood being cut nearby. Seeing a woodcutter, Grand Tutor Wen asked him how to get to Zhaoge. The woodcutter replied, "Go southwest about fifteen li. There you will find the road to Zhaoge."

They did not know that the woodcutter was really Yang Jian, who had changed his appearance so that Grand Tutor Wen and his soldiers would go the wrong way.

They walked for more than twenty li. They found themselves in a dangerous place. All around them were high mountains, steep cliffs, and fast flowing rivers. They thought they saw evil spirits in the grasses and wild animals looking at them from caves.

Grand Tutor Wen heard a sound. He looked up and saw a Daoist standing nearby. He recognized Master of the Clouds, and asked him, "Brother, what are you doing here?"

"I am here by order of Burning Lamp," the immortal replied. "This is Dragon Extinction Mountain. You will die here."

Grand Tutor Wen remembered that many years earlier, his teacher had told him, "If you ever see the word 'extinction,' disaster will follow." He was worried, but he put on a brave face. He replied, "Do you think I am a baby? You and I both know how to travel by using the five elements. What can you do to me?"

Without replying, Master of the Clouds sent a bolt of lightning from his hand into the ground. Eight pillars of fire came up from the ground, encircling Grand Tutor Wen. Each pillar was ten feet across and thirty feet high.

Grand Tutor Wen smiled and said, "Do you think this childish magic will stop me?" He made a magic sign with his hand, to protect him from the fire.

Master of the Clouds sent another bolt of lightning from his hand. Forty-nine fire dragons jumped out of each fire pillar. But Grand Tutor Wen said, "Your magic is quite ordinary. I will go now."

He jumped straight up in the air. But when he got to the top of the pillars, he smashed into a huge purple-gold bowl that was upside-down on the top of the pillars. His hat fell off his head and he fell to the ground. Master of the Clouds sent more lightning from his hand, making the fire hotter and hotter. Soon Grand Tutor Wen was nothing but ashes on the ground.

Even so, he was not quite dead yet. His soul flew to the king's palace in Zhaoge. The king was drinking with Daji. Suddenly the king became very sleepy. He fell asleep at the table. In his dream, he saw Grand Tutor Wen standing before him.

Grand Tutor Wen said, "Your Majesty, by your order I went to West Qi with a great army. But I was defeated and lost my life. Please, be kind to the people, listen to your loyal ministers, and stay away from wine and evil women. Obey the will of heaven. Now I must go, because if I stay longer, it will be difficult for me to reach the Terrace of Creation." Then his soul flew to the Terrace of Creation. His soul was welcomed by Bai Jian, the man who had been ordered by Jiang Ziya to build the terrace.

The king woke up, remembered his dream, and told it to Daji. But Daji just said, "Your Majesty, dreams come from the mind. You are just worried about the battles in West Qi. I'm sure Grand Tutor Wen is doing fine and has not lost any battles."

The king replied, "You are right, my queen!" And he put the dream out of his mind.

This was the end of the great battle of West Qi. But the war was not over. Shen Gongbao heard about the death of Grand Tutor Wen. He decided to search for immortals and magicians who could help defeat West Qi.

One day he saw a young man playing on the side of a mountain. The young man was small, perhaps four feet tall, and his face was the color of earth. Shen Gongbao said to the young man, "Who are you and where do you come from?"

The young man replied, "I am Earth Traveler Sun."

"How long have you studied the Way?"

"About a hundred years."

Shen Gongbao smiled down at him and said, "You cannot become an immortal, but you might become rich and powerful in the human world."

"How can I do that?"

"Leave this mountain and go to Sanshang Pass. I will give you a letter. Take it and give it to the commander of the pass. He will give you a job there."

"Thank you!" said the young man.

"Tell me, do you know any magic?"

"I can travel a thousand *li* a day under ground."

"Show me!"

Earth Traveler Sun twisted his body and disappeared into the ground. Then he came up from the ground a short distance away.

"Wonderful!" said Shen Gongbao. "Go and steal some magic ropes and five jars of elixir from your master. Then go to Sanshang Pass." Earth Traveler Sun did as he was ordered.

Chapter 53
Deng Jiugong Attacks West Qi

The Wei River flows day and night
When will the war in West Qi come to an end?

Tigers and leopards have left their caves
And the pixiu[1] lives at the top of the enemy's tower

Good people cry over the bones of the dead
While minions write foolish poems about wine

Who knows the will of heaven?
The weapons of war are used again and again

≡ ≡ ≡

Grand Tutor Wen's army was now only a few hundred men. They fled to Sishui Pass. When they arrived at the pass, they told the commander that their leader had died. The commander sent a messenger to Zhaoge to tell the king.

When the king heard the news, he said to his ministers, "How strange! Just a few days ago I had a dream. In my dream, Grand Tutor Wen told me that he had died on Dragon Extinction Peak! And now I hear that he is dead. What should I do now?"

One of the ministers said, "Your Majesty, the commander of Sanshan Pass is a man named Deng Jiugong. He is a great warrior. If you want to defeat West Qi, he is the only one who can do it." The king agreed. He ordered that the white scepter and yellow axe be given to Deng Jiugong[2].

A messenger brought the scepter and axe to Deng Jiugong. Deng Jiugong named a new commander for the pass, then he met with his

---

[1] The píxiū is a Chinese mythical creature, similar to a winged lion. They are protectors of the dead. According to legend, the pixiu defecated on the floor of heaven. The Jade Emperor was angry and spanked the creature so hard that its anus was permanently sealed. The Emperor then declared that from then on, the Pixiu could only eat gold, silver, and jewels.
[2] In ancient China, the scepter was a symbol of the king's authority, and the axe symbolizes the king's military might and ability to implement justice.

generals to plan the attack on West Qi. His daughter, Deng Chanyu, was a very skilled fighter. She sat in the meeting with the generals.

The next day, a very small young man came to the main gate of the pass. It was Earth Traveler Sun. He asked to see Deng Jiugong. When he was brought in to see Deng Jiugong, the young man gave him Shen Gongbao's letter.

Deng Jiugong did not know what to do with this young man. He did not look like a fighter or a leader. He thought about it, then said, "Earth Traveler Sun, I see that Shen Gongbao wants me to give you a job. All right. You will be the supervisor of the food supplies for our army."

Soon after, the army set off towards West Qi. It took them about a month to reach the enemy city. When they arrived, they set up camp just outside the main gate of the city.

Jiang Ziya saw the army setting up camp. A messenger told him that Deng Jiugong was leading that army.

"What do you know about this Deng Jiugong?" he asked his generals.

Huang Feihu replied, "He is a very skilled general."

Jiang Ziya smiled and said, "It is easier to beat a great general than a great magician."

Nangong Kuo said, "I will go and meet them." He rode out to meet the Shang army. A general was waiting for him. He had a long yellow beard and had a face like a crab.

"Who are you?" shouted Nangong Kuo.

"I am General Tai Luan. Now get down from your horse and surrender. If you don't, things will go very badly for you."

Nangong Kuo just laughed and said, "Tai Luan, don't you know what happened to Grand Tutor Wen, and the four Mo brothers, and all the other Shang generals? Some lost their heads, and others were turned to ash and dust. You are like little insects that fly around but have no strength. Go home while you still can."

This made Tai Luan very angry. He rushed forward on his brown horse, slashing at Nangong Kuo with his sword. Nangong Kuo fought back. They battled for several rounds. Tai Luan was very strong. He slashed at Nangong Kuo, cutting off the armor from his shoulder. Nangong Kuo was frightened, so he turned and rode back to the city.

"Don't worry," Jiang Ziya told him. "Victory and defeat are common in war. A general must know how to read the situation, so he can decide what to do next."

The next day, Deng Jiugong brought his entire army out of the camp. They stood in five square formations, facing West Qi City. He shouted for Jiang Ziya to come out.

Jiang Ziya was ready. His cannons fired three times. The left side of the army came out behind two green flags and a general wearing green armor. The cannons fired again, and the right side of the army came out behind two white banners and a general wearing white armor. Then a third formation came out behind two black banners and a general wearing black. Then the fourth formation came out behind two orange banners and a general wearing orange.

Finally, two rows of generals came out. They all wore gold helmets and gold armor over red robes. In the middle, on his huge horse, was Jiang Ziya, his long white hair flowing in the wind.

Deng Jiugong watched all this. He said, "It is not surprising that Jiang Ziya has defeated so many other generals. He is a powerful leader." He rode forward on his horse and shouted, "Greetings, Jiang Ziya!"

Jiang Ziya bowed as much as his armor would let him, and replied, "Commander Deng, I am pleased to meet you."

"Jiang Ziya, your leader King Wu is evil. But you are a wise Daoist. How can you be so foolish as to help him? You have fought against our king, and you have gone against the law of the nation. You will lose this war and lose your life, and many people of your city will die for nothing. Get down from your horse and surrender now."

"General Deng! You talk like a fool. Almost the entire country supports King Wu. You have only two hundred thousand soldiers and perhaps ten generals. You are like a lamb fighting a tiger, or an egg fighting a stone. You will lose. Turn around, go back to Zhaoge, and tell your king that West Qi does not want to fight against him. Let both sides live in peace. If you don't, you will meet the same fate as Grand Tutor Wen."

Deng Jiugong turned to his generals and said, "This man is just a flour seller and a fortuneteller from Zhaoge. How dare he talk like that to me!" He rushed forward, sword in hand. But Huang Feihu rushed forward and blocked his attack. The two of them fought back and forth. Then other generals from both sides rushed forward to join the fight.

Soon a dozen generals were fighting hand to hand and sword to sword, beneath the walls of West Qi City.

After a few rounds, the Zhou army rushed forward. Deng Jiugong saw that they could not win the fight. He turned and rode back to his camp, followed by his generals and soldiers. Jiang Ziya and his men rode back to West Qi City.

Back in the Shang camp, Deng Chanyu saw that her father was badly hurt. She said, "Papa, take care of yourself. I will go out there and get revenge for you."

"Be careful, my child!" said Deng Jiugong.

Deng Chanyu rode out to the city wall and shouted for someone to come and fight her. Jiang Ziya heard this. He was worried. He said to his generals, "There are three things to be afraid of in war: Daoists, Buddhists, and women. Many are powerful magicians. We must be very, very careful."

Nezha replied, "Your disciple will go and meet her, Master." Jiang Ziya agreed to let him go.

He rode out on his Wind Fire Wheels. He saw a beautiful young woman riding towards him, her sword raised in the air and her long black hair flying in the wind. She shouted at him, "Who are you?"

"I am Nezha. And you are just a young girl. How dare you try to fight me! You may know something about war, but you cannot win against me. Go back to your camp and find someone stronger to fight me."

She attacked Nezha with her sword. Nezha fought back. After a few rounds, she shouted, "You are too strong for me!" and turned to ride away.

Nezha smiled and followed her. He said to himself, "Of course, she's just a girl."

Deng Chanyu rode away, chased by Nezha. When she saw that he was getting close, she put away her sword. She grabbed a small stone from her robe, turned and threw it at Nezha. It hit him on the nose. His face covered with blood, Nezha turned around and rode back to the city.

When he returned, Huang Tianhua laughed and said, "A general should look in all directions and be prepared for everything. How could you be defeated by a small stone?"

Deng Chanyu returned to her father. She told him that she had defeated Nezha by hitting him with a stone. He was delighted to hear this.

The next day, Deng Chanyu went out again and called for someone to fight her. Nezha said to Huang Tianhua, "I think you should fight her. Show us how to do it!"

"Be very careful," said Jiang Ziya to Huang Tianhua.

Huang Tianhua mounted his jade unicorn and rode out to meet the girl. "Who are you?" shouted Deng Chanyu.

"I am Huang Tianhua, the eldest son of Prince Huang Feihu. Are you the foolish girl who hit my brother with a stone yesterday? I will make you pay for that!"

He attacked her with his two hammers. She fought back with her sword, then turned and rode away, shouting, "Do you dare to follow me?" Huang Tianhua rode after her. After a short chase, the girl grabbed another stone from her robe, turned, and threw it at Huang Tianhua. It hit him in the face. Bleeding heavily, he fled back to the city.

When he returned to the city, Nezha was waiting for him. He said, "I have heard that a general should always know what is happening all around him. It looks like you have been defeated by a young woman. And your nose is broken. You know, the top of the nose is like the root of a mountain. If you break it, you will have a hundred years of bad luck."

These words made Huang Tianhua angry. The two of them started to shout at each other. Finally, Jiang Ziya heard the shouting. He said to them, "Stop it! You were both hurt while serving our king. There is no need to fight each other."

The next day, Deng Chanyu rode out to the city again, shouting for someone to fight her. This time Dragon Beard Tiger came out. This strange creature had the body of a fish but a head like a camel. He had hands with sharp claws, and one foot that looked like a tiger's foot. Deng Chanyu saw him and cried, "What kind of creature are you?"

The creature replied, "You foolish girl, I am Dragon Beard Tiger. I am a disciple of Prime Minister Jiang Ziya. By order of my master, I am here to fight you."

Before she could say anything, Dragon Beard Tiger opened his claws.

Clouds of small stones came out from each of his claws. They flew at her like a thousand angry birds. She turned and rode away on her horse, with the stones flying towards her. She threw a stone at Dragon Beard Tiger. The creature moved his head away, but the pebble hit him on the neck. She threw another stone, which knocked the creature to the ground. She saw him fall. She turned around and rode back towards him, holding her sword high and preparing to cut off his head.

Chapter 54
Earth Traveler Sun Attacks West Qi

The world is at war, fighting is everywhere;
The nation is flooded by evil words

The king would not listen to the loyal Shang Rong;
But he listened to the evil minister Fei Zhong

Lust made the king marry the fox and sleep with her;
While cruel monsters ruled the nation and the phoenix flew away

If the fox can bring down the kingdom,
The goddess will give him a bit of incense[1]

☰ ☰ ☰

Just as Deng Chanyu was about to cut off the head of the tiger creature, she heard someone shout, "Wait!" She turned and saw Yang Jian running towards her. She turned to fight him, but he was a very good fighter. She ran away, then she turned again and threw two stones at him. The stones did not hurt him at all.

Then Yang Jian sent his heavenly dog to attack her. The dog jumped up and bit her on the neck. Crying in pain and bleeding, she rode her horse back to the Shang camp.

Earth Traveler Sun saw that Deng Jiugong and Deng Chanyu were both badly wounded. But he had the magic elixir that he had stolen from his master. He put one of the magic pills into a gourd and added some water. Then he used a feather to put the medicine on Deng Juigong's wound. Immediately his pain and the wound both disappeared.

Then he did the same thing to Deng Chanyu, putting the medicine on her neck. Immediately her wound also disappeared.

Later that night, Deng Jiugong gave a banquet for Earth Traveler Sun and all the generals. Earth Traveler Sun asked him, "Sir, how many

---

[1] "A bit of incense" is a metaphor for a reward obtained in the human world. In this case, it's the reward given to the fox demon by the goddess Nüwa in return for destroying the Shang king.

times have you fought against Jiang Ziya?"

"We have fought him several times, but we have never defeated him."

"If you had made me commander, you would have defeated West Qi long ago."

Deng Jiugong thought about this. The next day, he named Earth Traveler Sun the commander of the Shang army. Immediately, the young man led the Shang army to the gates of West Qi City. He shouted, "Come out and fight me, Nezha!"

Nezha heard the young man calling him. He rode out on his Wind Fire Wheels. He looked around but could not see any great general waiting for him. Finally, he looked down and saw a little man standing there. He said, "Who are you, little man, and why are you making such a big noise?"

"I am Earth Traveler Sun, and I am the commander of this army. Get down off your horse and surrender to me right now."

Nezha laughed, and slashed downward with his sword. Earth Traveler Sun blocked it with his cudgel. Nezha had trouble fighting the little man because he was so small and moved so quickly. He got down off his Wind Fire Wheels so he could see the little man better. But Earth Traveler Sun threw his magic rope, the one that he had stolen from his master. Nezha was instantly tied up. He lay on the ground, not moving. Earth Traveler Sun brought Nezha back to the Shang camp as his prisoner.

Deng Jiugong asked, "How did you capture him?"

"I have my own methods," replied the little man.

Deng Jiugong ordered the prisoner to be held in the back of the camp, to be sent later to the king in Zhaoge.

The next day, Earth Traveler Sun went out again and shouted for Huang Tianhua to come out. After a short fight, Earth Traveler Sun used his magic rope to capture him too.

Deng Jiugong was very happy. That night he had dinner with Earth Traveler Sun. They both drank a great deal of wine. Earth Traveler Sun told him, "Sir, if you had named me commander earlier, this war would be over now, and you would defeat West Qi."

Without thinking, Deng Jiugong said, "General, if you can defeat West

Qi, I will give you my daughter to be your wife."

This made the little man very happy. He could not sleep at all that night, thinking about having Deng Chanyu as his wife. The next day he went out again to the gate of the city, this time calling for Jiang Ziya to come out. They fought. Earth Traveler Sun threw his magic rope in the air. It hit Jiang Ziya, who fell off his horse and lay on the ground. But before the little man could capture him, some Zhou soldiers grabbed him and carried him back to the city.

In the prime minister's mansion, Jiang Ziya lay on the floor, tied up tight. His generals tried to remove the magic rope. But every time they touched it, the rope became tighter. Finally, he said, "Don't touch the rope. Just leave it."

Yang Jian looked closely at the rope. He said, "I know this rope. I have seen it before. I saw it when we were fighting the ten traps. It was used in the Bright Flame Trap, which was made by a Daoist immortal named Krakucchanda."

Jiang Ziya said, "I know Krakucchanda. He would not do anything like this."

As they were talking, a messenger came in, saying that a young Daoist boy was at the city gate and wanted to see Jiang Ziya. They let him come in. The boy entered the room. He said, "Sir, by order of my master, I have come to release you from this magic rope." Then he pointed his finger at Jiang Ziya and said a few magic words. The rope fell away from Jiang Ziya. Without another word, the boy turned and walked out.

"Let me fight this little man," said Yang Jian. Jiang Ziya agreed. And so, the next day, Yang Jian went out to fight Earth Traveler Sun. They started to fight. The little man threw the magic rope, but Yang Jian used his own magic. The rope wrapped around a large rock instead of the immortal. Then Yang Jian sent his heavenly dog to attack Earth Traveler Sun. But before the dog could get to him, the little man jumped down into the earth and disappeared.

Earth Traveler Sun came up out of the earth inside the Shang camp. He said to Deng Jiugong, "Tonight I will win this war. I will go under the earth and enter West Qi City. I will kill their king and Jiang Ziya. With the two leaders dead, the war will end quickly."

That night in West Qi City, a strange and powerful wind began to blow.

Doors and windows flew to the ground, small houses were smashed, trees fell down, and flagpoles broke in half. Jiang Ziya knew that something strange was happening. He quickly burned some incense and did a divination. "Oh no!" he said. "The little man will come to the city tonight and try to kill us!"

Jiang Ziya did not tell King Wu about the plan to kill him. But he asked the king to spend that night in a secret room, surrounded by four generals.

Earth Traveler Sun traveled underground and came up inside the palace in West Qi City. He looked around and saw that he was in the king's bedroom. He said to himself, "I have worn out my iron shoes, but now I have it[1]!" He saw the king with one of his concubines, they were eating dinner and playing music. He heard the king say, "My dear, we have had fun, but now we should go to sleep." They took off their clothes, and soon he saw that they were both asleep.

Quietly, he crept over to the bed. He stood over the sleeping king. Then he took out his knife and cut off the king's head. It fell to the floor. He did not know that this was a false king created by Yang Jian.

The concubine did not wake up. He looked at her. Her face was as beautiful as a peach blossom. He was filled with desire. He wanted the lovely concubine. He said loudly, "Who are you and why are you still asleep?"

The concubine woke up. She looked at him and asked, "Who are you? Have you been here all night?"

"I am Earth Traveler Sun. I am a general in the Shang camp. I just killed the king. Do you want to live or die?"

"Sir, I am just a weak woman. Please don't kill me. If you think that I am not too ugly, I will serve you."

Earth Traveler Sun said, "All right. Have sex with me and I will let you live." She smiled at him. He took off his clothes and jumped into the bed. He put his arms around the beautiful concubine. She put her arms around him. But the concubine's arms were very, very strong. Earth Traveler Sun could not breathe.

---

[1] The proverb tàpò tiě xié wú mì chù means "I wore out my iron shoes but got it without effort." In other words, one searches for so long that they wear out their iron shoes, but when they stop looking for it, they come upon it with no effort.

"My dear, please don't hold me so tightly!" he said.

"You fool!" she shouted. "Look who you are in bed with!" He looked at her face, and saw it was not a beautiful concubine. It was Yang Jian. He tried to escape, but Yang Jian picked him up and started to carry him out of the palace.

Yang Jian carried the naked little man to Jiang Ziya. He asked, "What should we do with him?"

Jiang Ziya said, "Take him outside and chop off his head."

Yang Jian carried the little man outside. He moved the little man from his right hand to his left hand so he could grab his sword. When he did that, Earth Traveler Sun reached down with his foot and touched the ground. Instantly he disappeared into the earth.

Yang Jian went back to tell Jiang Ziya that the little man had escaped. He said, "Sir, I need to go and see Krakucchanda. He can tell us about the little man and the magic rope."

Jiang Ziya replied, "All right. Come back as soon as you can. We need you here if the little man returns."

Yang Jian flew away from West Qi City towards the mountain where Krakucchanda lived.

Chapter 55
Earth Traveler Sun is Captured

It is never good to hide oneself
Everything falls into place, why do you do these things?

You lose your innocence and are driven by greed
You turn away from your teacher and now go to war

After thousands of tricks, return to truth at the end
Yang Jian's skills are not of this world

At last, two come together as one
They accept the marriage made by the matchmaker god

≡ ≡ ≡

Yang Jian did not know how to find the mountain where Krakucchanda lived. He flew for a while, but then he came down on the wrong mountain. What was there?

He sees trees as high as the sky
He hears the cry of monkeys in the green fog
He hears the song of cranes in the green shade
The green water is clear, the scent of pines is in the air
Pretty birds and large insects fly back and forth
Deer jump through the trees
He stands on the green grass but sees no one
It is more beautiful than Mount Penglai[1].

Yang Jian walked through the forest, enjoying the beauty all around him. Soon he came to a large mansion.

He stood under a pine tree looking at the mansion. The front gate

---

[1] In Chinese mythology, Mount Penglai is the home of the Eight Immortals. Everything there is pure white, its palaces are made from gold and silver, and jewels grow on trees. The rice bowls and wine glasses never become empty no matter how much people eat or drink from them; and there are enchanted fruits that can heal any ailment, grant eternal youth, and even resurrect the dead.

opened and a beautiful lady walked out. She wore a red silk robe. Two young men walked in front of her carrying fans and flags, and eight young women walked beside her. He hid behind the tree.

The lady pointed to the tree where Yang Jian was. She to her servants, "Go over there. Find out who that man is."

As soon as he heard this, Yang Jian stepped forward. He said, "Please forgive me. My name is Yang Jian. By order of Prime Minister Jiang Ziya I am traveling to see the Daoist master Krakucchanda, but I do not know where he lives."

"Why are you looking for him?" asked the lady.

"A little man named Earth Traveler Sun is making trouble for us in West Qi City. He tried to kill our Prime Minister and our king. I think he is a disciple of Krakucchanda."

The lady replied, "You are right, he is a disciple of Krakucchanda. You should go and see him immediately." Then she told him where to find the Daoist's mountain.

"May I ask you your honorable name?" he asked.

"I am Princess Long Ji. My father is Haotian, the Supreme God of Heaven[1], and my mother is the Golden Mother of Jade Pond. I was ordered to serve wine at the Peach Festival but I did it poorly. My father has punished me by sending me to live on this mountain."

Yang Jian bowed to her, then he jumped up in the air to fly to Krakucchanda's mountain. He arrived at the mountain, entered the Daoist's cave, and knelt before him. "Greetings, Uncle!" he said.

"Greetings to you also," replied Krakucchanda. "What brings you to see me?"

"Tell me, Uncle, are your magic ropes missing?"

Krakucchanda jumped up and looked around. He did not see his magic ropes anywhere. He said, "Yes! But how did you know?"

"A little man named Earth Traveler Sun is helping the Shang army attack West Qi City. He has used your magic ropes to capture several of

---

[1] Her father, Hàotiān Shàngdì, is the Supreme God of Heaven, the Ruler of the Three Realms. He was the supreme deity until the Creation of the Gods that occurs at the end of this book, when the Jade Emperor appears.

our generals, and he even tried to capture our Prime Minster."

"That beast!" shouted Krakucchanda. "How dare he steal my treasures! Thank you, Yang Jian. Now go back to West Qi City. I will be there soon and I will take care of this matter."

Yang Jian returned to West Qi City. A few hours later, Krakucchanda arrived on a golden beam of light. He entered the Prime Minister's mansion and bowed to Jiang Ziya. Jiang Ziya returned the bow, and they sat down together.

Krakucchanda said, "I have not looked at my treasures in a long time. I never thought that that little beast would steal them. But no matter, I can easily capture him and get my magic ropes back."

The next morning, Jiang Ziya rode out of the city gate alone on his horse. A messenger ran to tell Deng Jiugong. Earth Traveler Sun heard this. He said, "Commander, don't worry. I will capture him, and we will have our victory today."

He rushed out of the Shang camp, attacking Jiang Ziya with his cudgel. Jiang Ziya fought back, and they fought for several rounds. Then Jiang Ziya rode away. Earth Traveler Sun chased him. He threw one of the magic ropes in the air. It did not come down. But the little man did not think anything of this, because all he could think of was the beautiful Deng Chanyu. He knew that if he won the war, the young woman would be his wife.

He threw another magic rope in the air, then another. None of them came down. Finally, he had no magic ropes left in his bag.

Jiang Ziya turned to face him, shouting, "Little man! Fight me now, without those magic ropes!"

Earth Traveler Sun knew that he could not win against Jiang Ziya. He started to stamp his foot on the ground so he could escape through the earth. But he heard a voice from the clouds saying, "Where are you going, Earth Traveler Sun?" Krakucchanda pointed his finger to the ground. Instantly the ground became like iron. Earth Traveler Sun stamped his foot, but the ground did not open for him.

Krakucchanda waved his hand. One of the magic ropes wrapped around Earth Traveler Sun, binding him tightly. The master said to him, "You beast! I never thought you would steal my treasures! Tell me, why did you do it?"

"Master, I met a Daoist riding on a tiger. He told me his name was Shen Gongbao. He said I could never become an immortal, but I could have wealth and fame here in the human world. He told me to steal your magic ropes and elixir, and go to Sanshan Pass to offer help to Deng Jiugong. Please forgive me, Master!"

Jiang Ziya turned to Krakucchanda and said, "Brother, he is a damned beast. He tried to kill me and also tried to kill our king. He is no use to us. You should just cut off his head."

Krakucchanda heard this. He jumped up and said to the little man, "What? Why would you try to kill Jiang Ziya and the king? What did they ever do to you?"

Earth Traveler Sun replied, "Master, please listen. I captured two of the Zhou generals. This made Deng Jiugong very happy. He told me I could marry his daughter if I defeated West Qi and won the war. So, I entered the city, hoping to kill those two and give victory to Deng Jiugong."

Krakucchanda listened to this. Then he lowered his head and did a divination. He said to Jiang Ziya, "This beast is fated to marry Deng Chanyu. But I think that might be good for us. Let's help to make this happen. Pick a good man, a scholar, to be the matchmaker. Send him over to the Shang camp."

"I will send San Yisheng," replied Jiang Ziya. He went to see San Yisheng and told him to go to the Shang camp and discuss the marriage with Deng Jiugong.

Chapter 56
The Betrayal of Deng Jiugong

Marriages are really made in heaven
Red thread connects the two people

Enemies come together
Anger is past, two birds now fly together[1]

Ziya's plan is hard to understand
The matchmaker god's plan is clever

Heaven's plan is a mystery
The tyrant king does not have heaven's blessing

≡ ≡ ≡

San Yisheng walked up to the gate of the Shang camp. He told the guards that he wanted to meet with Commander Deng. A guard told Deng. At first, Deng did not want to meet with an enemy general, but then he decided that it would do no harm for him to hear what San Yisheng had to say. He told the guard to bring San Yisheng to meet him.

San Yisheng was brought to Deng Juigong's tent. They greeted each other and sat down together.

"Commander," said San Yisheng, "I have come to discuss a matter of great importance. Yesterday we captured one of your generals. We were surprised to learn that he is your son-in-law."

"What? Who is this son-in-law?"

"Commander, you know him of course. It's Earth Traveler Sun. He is your daughter's husband."

"My daughter has no husband. She is like a pearl to me. Many young men have asked for her hand, but none are good enough for her."

San Yisheng could see that the commander was becoming angry. He

---

[1] In Chinese folklore, marriages are fated before birth. An invisible red thread is thought to connect the feet of two people that are supposed to be married.

replied, "Please let go of your anger, Commander, and listen to me. Earth Traveler Sun is a good man. He is a Daoist, a disciple of Krakucchanda. He was deceived by Shen Gongbao, and is also in love with your daughter. Trying to win her hand, he entered our city and tried to kill our king and Jiang Ziya. We captured him. We were planning to kill him, but he begged us to let him live so he could marry your daughter. I discussed this with Jiang Ziya. Together, we agreed to let him go free and return to you, so he can marry the girl he loves."

Deng Jiugong replied, "Minister, let me tell you the truth. This Earth Traveler Sun is a good fighter and knows some magic, so I made him a general. He captured Nezha and Huang Tianhua, and he almost captured Jiang Ziya. I had dinner with him. I drank too much. Foolishly, I told him that if he defeated West Qi, he could marry my daughter. But he was captured, so he failed to defeat you. The matter is finished."

"Commander, you know that a man's words are as heavy as Mount Tai. Once words are spoken you cannot take them back. Everyone knows that you offered your daughter's hand to Earth Traveler Sun. If you change your mind, what would people think of you?"

Deng Jiugong thought about this. Then Tai Luan walked over and spoke some words quietly in his ear.

Deng Jiugong smiled. He said to San Yisheng, "I understand, minister. Please give me some time to discuss this with my daughter."

San Yisheng thanked him and returned to West Qi City. He told Jiang Ziya about the meeting. Jiang Ziya laughed and said, "If he thinks he can trick me like that, he is truly a fool."

The next day, Tai Luan left the Shang camp and entered West Qi City. He was allowed to enter the city and meet with Jiang Ziya and Krakucchanda. Tai Luan bowed and said, "I am only a soldier, yet you show me such respect. I should kowtow to you."

Jiang Ziya replied, "You are here to speak for your army, and so you are our guest. Please sit down and tell us why you are here."

Tai Luan said, "My commander asked me to tell you that he was drunk when he promised his daughter to Earth Traveler Sun. He loves his daughter, but he understands that a promise is a promise. So, he will allow her to marry Earth Traveler Sun. He has selected the day after tomorrow as the most auspicious day for the wedding. He would be greatly honored if you and San Yisheng bring the young man to the wedding. Afterwards, he would be happy to discuss other matters with you."

Jiang Ziya agreed, and Tai Luan returned to the Shang camp. He told Deng Jiugong about the meeting. Deng Jiugong smiled and said, "Good. Tomorrow will be the end of Jiang Ziya and West Qi. Select three hundred of your best soldiers. Give them daggers and put them just outside the tent. When I drop a wine cup on the ground, all of them should rush in and cut Jiang Ziya and his generals into little pieces. Also, put a large group of soldiers on the right side of the camp, and another large group on the left side. When they hear the sound of cannon, they should attack."

Two days later, the wedding day arrived. Jiang Ziya ordered fifty strong soldiers to carry the wedding gifts. He told Thunderbolt and Nangong Kuo to be ready to attack from the left and right. And he prepared the rest of his army to attack the Shang camp.

Deng Jiugong prepared the camp for the wedding. He laid carpets on the ground and hung lanterns and banners. At noon, San Yisheng entered the gate of the Shang camp. Tai Luan and Deng Jiugong both came out to meet him.

San Yisheng said, "We are happy that you have agreed to the marriage. Prime Minister Jiang Ziya will be here soon. He will bring your son-in-law and the wedding gifts."

"Thank you," replied Deng Jiugong. "Let's wait here for the prime minister."

A short time later, Jiang Ziya and Krakucchanda arrived. Jiang Ziya greeted his enemies. Then they all entered the commander's tent. Flowers and silks were everywhere, but he could also feel that death was in the air.

"Bring in the gifts," ordered Jiang Ziya. The fifty soldiers started to carry in the gifts. One of the Zhou generals was standing next to a large box. Inside the box was a cannon. The general lit the fuse. The cannon roared. The earth shook. Immediately the fifty Zhou soldiers dropped the gifts and took out their weapons. Deng Jiugong and Tai Luan were surprised by this. They ran out of the tent.

Thousands of Zhou soldiers rushed into the camp. They easily defeated the three hundred Shang soldiers. The Shang armies on the left and right tried to advance, but they could not defeat Thunderbolt, Nangong

Kuo, and the Zhou army.

Deng Chanyu saw the Shang army being defeated. She turned to run away. But Earth Traveler Sun saw her. He knew that she could throw stones, so he used his magic ropes and tied her up. He picked her up and carried her back to West Qi City.

Deng Jiugong and his army fled. The Zhou army chased them for fifty li, then they turned and headed back to West Qi City.

Jiang Ziya and his generals met at his mansion to discuss the day's battle. It was a great victory for the Zhou army. He said to Earth Traveler Sun, "This is the auspicious day for you and Deng Chanyu to be married. Today you will be husband and wife. Go. I will talk with you tomorrow." Then Jiang Ziya and his generals went off to enjoy a wedding feast.

Earth Traveler Sun entered the room where Den Chanyu was waiting. He smiled at her. But she shouted at him, "You pig! You turned against your commander. You are a traitor. And now you want me to be your wife? What kind of man are you?"

Earth Traveler Sun replied quietly, "I am no ordinary man. And you should know that San Yisheng spoke with your father two days ago. Your father agreed that we would marry today. That has not changed."

"My father only said that to trick the prime minister. He failed. Now I am prepared to meet my death."

"Words once spoken cannot be taken back. A promise is a promise. And I tell you, the only reason I entered West Qi City and tried to kill the king was that I was in love with you. I wanted to have you as my wife. Jiang Ziya and Krakucchanda understood this. That's why they let me go. Also, Krakucchanda did a divination and learned that it was our fate to be married. Dear sister, the whole army knows that you are my wife. Please think about it!"

Deng Chanyu could not say anything. She lowered her head. Earth Traveler Sun said, "My dear, you are like a beautiful heavenly flower. I am lucky to be your husband now."

He tried to pull her towards him, but she pushed him away. "You might be right," she said. "But I need to talk with my father about this. We can become husband and wife tomorrow."

Earth Traveler Sun was filled with desire for her. He pulled her again, and tried to kiss her. She cried, "If you force me, I will fight you to the death!"

He kept trying to kiss her and pull off her clothes. She kept fighting him. Finally, he said, "All right. I won't force you. But I hope you won't change your mind after you speak with your father."

She said, "I am already your wife. How could I change my mind?"

"All right," he said. He reached down to help her stand up. She stood up. Suddenly, he grabbed her around the waist and picked her up. He put her over his shoulder, so she could not fight him. She said, "General, you tricked me. How can you treat your wife like this?"

"Dear wife, if I didn't, you would never stop fighting me." She smiled at this.

He removed her clothes and carried her to the bed. They spent the rest of the night making love.

In the morning, they washed and dressed. Then they went to see Jiang Ziya. The prime minister said, "Deng Chanyu, you are now a Zhou general. But your father is still our enemy. I do not want to fight him. What should we do?"

Deng Chanyu knelt before Jiang Ziya and replied, "I belong to Zhou now. Please trust me. I will talk with my father and ask him to surrender."

"I trust you. But your father may not agree with you. Take an army with you." Deng Chanyu thanked him. Soon afterwards, she left the city leading a large army.

Fifty *li* outside the city, Deng Jiugong had made camp with his generals and soldiers. He was meeting with his generals. He told them, "This was a terrible defeat. Now we are like a deer caught in a fence. We cannot go forward and we cannot go back. What should we do now?"

Just then, a guard ran up and told him that his daughter was at the camp gate with an army flying Zhou banners. Deng Jiugong told the guard to let her enter.

She came in and knelt before her father. He reached down and helped her to stand. "What do you want to tell me, dear daughter?" he asked.

"Father, you got drunk and promised me to Earth Traveler Sun. Then you tried to trick Jiang Ziya by inviting him to come to your camp. Now

I am Sun's wife and a general in the Zhou army. You must know that most of the kingdom has already joined West Qi. We can all see that this is the will of heaven. Even Grand Tutor Wen could not go against heaven."

Her father said nothing. She continued, "Father, do you think the king of Shang will let you live after this defeat? Please, stop fighting for that evil tyrant. It's time for you to serve a wise and good king."

Deng Jiugong thought about this for a while. Then he said, "My child, you are right. But I cannot just ride into West Qi City and kneel before Jiang Ziya."

"That is no problem, Father. I will go first and ask him to come out and meet you."

She returned to West Qi City and told Jiang Ziya of her father's decision. Jiang Ziya gathered a small army and marched about one *li* from the city. He waited for Deng Jiugong. Soon Deng Jiugong approached, riding at the head of his army.

Jiang Ziya rode forward. He said, "Greetings, Commander."

Deng Jiugong bowed and said, "Prime Minister, I am here to surrender to you. Will you forgive me?"

Jiang Ziya smiled and replied, "We are now both ministers in the same court. There's no need to speak like that." Then they rode side by side back to West Qi City. Their two armies followed, marching together as one.

A few days later, news of Deng Juigong's surrender reached the Shang king in Zhaoge. The king was furious. He called his ministers together. He told them, "I ordered Deng Jiugong to attack West Qi City. He failed to defeat the enemy. He let his daughter marry an enemy general. And then he became a traitor and joined the Zhou army. He must be punished. How can we do this?"

One of his ministers stepped forward. He said, "Your Majesty, if a general is defeated in battle, he may be afraid that you will punish or kill him. So, he will surrender. Perhaps you could find a general who is a close relative. He will fight hard and will not surrender if things go badly for him."

"Do you have someone in mind?" asked the king.

"Your Majesty, perhaps you could use Su Hu. He is the Marquis of

Jizhou, one of the most important marquises in the kingdom. And he is a relative of yours, as his daughter is your queen."

"That is an excellent idea!" said the king. He sent a messenger to order Su Hu to be the new commander of the Shang army.

Chapter 57
Su Hu Fights Against West Qi

Su Hu wants to join the Zhou
The Shang kingdom is drifting in the sea

The red sun is setting behind the mountains
The flowers fall and float away on the water

The people want to follow a wise ruler
The wind has turned the boat around

The royal family and officials have all left
The lonely one sleeps alone in the red chamber[1]

≡ ≡ ≡

When Su Hu heard the king's order, he was delighted. He did not want to fight for the king, and he saw this as a way to show his loyalty to the people.

Later that night, he ate dinner with his son Su Quanzhong and his wife. He told them, "I never thought that Daji would forget what we taught her, and be such a cruel queen. Because of her, many marquises are angry with me. But now I can show them what kind of man I am. I will take this army and surrender to the king of West Qi. Then I will join the other marquises in defeating the king of Shang!"

The next day, Su Hu called his generals together. He told them to prepare to lead their army to West Qi. And so, with banners flying, the army of a hundred thousand soldiers left Jizhou and headed towards West Qi. They traveled for several days until they saw the city. They stopped and set up camp.

A messenger told Jiang Ziya that Su Hu's army had arrived. He gathered his generals to discuss the matter. "What do you think of him?" he asked.

Huang Feihu replied, "Su Hu is a good man. He speaks his mind. He has

---

[1] The "lonely one" refers to the king, in this case, the king of Shang. "Red chamber" is a symbol of wasteful luxury.

sent me several letters telling me that he is unhappy about the Shang king. He wants to join us."

But three days passed, and Su Hu remained in his camp. Jiang Ziya did not understand why. Finally, he told Huang Feihu to go and see him. Huang Feihu mounted his five-colored ox and left the city, with cannons roaring. He rode to the gate of Su Hu's camp and shouted, "Will General Su Hu please come out and see me?"

Su Hu did not come out. Instead, one of his generals came out, riding on his war horse. He shouted to Huang Feihu, "I have orders to arrest you. Get down off that ox right now."

Huang Feihu just laughed. He said, "General, you are not good enough to fight me. Go back to your camp and tell your commander to come out."

The general shouted, "How dare you!" Then he surprised Huang Feihu by attacking him fiercely. They fought for twenty rounds. Then Huang Feihu captured the general. He tied him up and brought him back to see Jiang Ziya.

The general refused to kneel before Jiang Ziya. "Just kill me," he said. "There is no need to discuss anything else." But Jiang Ziya ordered the general to be put in jail.

The next day, another general came out of the Shang camp. This was Zheng Lun, a black-faced magician with two Demon Subduing Clubs and the ability to shoot white fire from his nose.

Huang Feihu came out again. He saw the black-faced magician and said, "Who are you?"

"I am Zheng Lun, and you are a traitor! Lay down your weapons and surrender right now."

"Don't be a fool. Go back and tell your commander to come out and see me. I have something important to tell him."

Zheng Lun did not answer. He swung his clubs at Huang Feihu, and the two began to fight. After a few rounds, the magician shot two beams of white fire from his nose. The beams hit Huang Feihu, making him fall off his horse. Several Shang soldiers ran up, captured the general, and carried him back to the Shang camp. Su Hu put him in jail.

The next day, Huang Feihu's son Huang Tianhua asked permission to fight Zheng Lun. He mounted his jade unicorn and rode out to battle. But he was also captured and put in jail with his father.

Jiang Ziya did not understand what was happening. "I thought Su Hu came here to surrender!" he said. "Why has he attacked and captured two of my best generals?"

The next day, Zheng Lun came out of the Shang camp again and shouted a challenge. Earth Traveler Sun said to Jiang Ziya, "Commander, I have not done anything to help you yet. Please let me go out and fight this magician."

Jiang Ziya agreed. As the little man was getting ready to leave, his wife Deng Chanyu begged for permission to go with him. Jiang Ziya let her go with him.

With cannons roaring, Earth Traveler Sun and Deng Chanyu rode out towards the camp gate. Zheng Lun was waiting there on his jade unicorn. He saw a woman and a very short man. He laughed and said, "Well, who are you?"

Earth Traveler Sun replied, "By order of our prime minister, I am here to capture you."

"You want to capture me? You look like a baby still drinking his mother's milk."

"You damned fool, how dare you insult me!" shouted Earth Traveler Sun. He jumped off his horse, rolled on the ground, and struck the unicorn's leg with his cudgel. Zheng Lun tried to hit the little man with his clubs but he could not reach him. Finally, he shot two beams of white light from his nose. Earth Traveler Sun fell to the ground and was captured by some Shang soldiers.

This infuriated Deng Chanyu. She rode up to the magician, her long hair flying in the wind, and slashed at him with her sword. He swung his clubs at her, just missing her face. She turned and rode away. Then she stopped, turned, and threw a small stone. The flying stone hit Zheng Lun in the face. Bleeding and in pain, he fled back to his camp.

In the Shang camp, Earth Traveler Sun was brought before Su Hu. Su Hu looked down at him and said, "What use is this little man? Take him out and cut off his head."

"No, wait!" said Earth Traveler Sun. "Let me go back and report to my commander. Then I will return and you can cut off my head."

Su Hu and his generals laughed when they heard this. "He really is a fool," said Su Hu. "Cut off his head now."

"All right, if you won't let me go, I will go anyway," said Sun. Then he twisted his body and disappeared down into the earth.

Su Hu saw this. He turned to his generals and said, "West Qi has many talented people. That is why we have not defeated them."

The next day, Zheng Lun wanted to fight Deng Chanyu again, so he called for her to come out and fight him. But Jiang Ziya decided to send Nezha instead. Nezha rode out on his Wind Fire Wheels. Without saying a word, he attacked the magician with his lance. He was a powerful fighter and soon began to gain the upper hand against Zheng Lun. The magician shot white fire from his nose. But Nezha had no soul, so the white fire did not affect him at all.

Zheng Lun tried again, then again. Nezha laughed and said, "You fool. What sickness do you have that makes that stuff come out of your nose?"

Zheng Lun attacked again, and they fought for thirty rounds. Finally, Nezha threw his Universal Ring up in the air. It came down on Zheng Lun's back, injuring him badly. He almost fell off his horse, but he managed to return to his camp.

Su Hu met with Zheng Lun. He said, "General, this is the will of heaven. Most of the marquises are now supporting Zhou. Soon they will gather together to attack the king of Shang in Zhaoge. Everyone knows that the Shang king is an evil man and must be removed from the throne. You know what the ancients say, 'A good bird rests in a good tree, and a good minister serves a good master.' Let's join Zhou together. What do you think?"

Zheng Lun replied, "Commander, I cannot agree with you and I cannot follow you. I am loyal to our king. If I die in the morning, you can go to Zhou in the morning. If I die in the afternoon, you can go to Zhou in the afternoon. My heart will not change."

Su Hu left the room and thought about this. Later, he ordered Huang Feihu and his son to be freed, and he invited them to have dinner with him. He told them, "My friends, I need to explain the situation. For a long time, I have wished to join Zhou. But I have spoken with Zheng Lun about this, and he remains loyal to the king. It will be very difficult for me to come over to Zhou."

Huang Feihu replied, "If you want to join Zhou, do it now. Don't worry about Zheng Lun, we will deal with him. You must do what is in your heart, and not worry about what other people think."

Su Hu got up and led the two prisoners to the back gate of the camp. "Please go and tell the prime minister what I have said." The two men left the camp. They returned to West Qi City and reported everything to Jiang Ziya.

Meanwhile, Zheng Lun was in terrible pain from his injury. He could not sleep. He lay awake in his bed, thinking of his commander getting ready to surrender.

The next day, a stranger came to the Shang camp. He had three eyes and was dressed as a Daoist. He was allowed into the camp and was brought before Su Hu. He said, "Sir, I have come here to help you defeat the rebels."

"Who are you and where do you come from?" asked Su Hu.

"My name is Lu Yue. I have come from Nine Dragon Island, but I do not need a boat to travel across the water. My soul can move without anyone seeing it. I was told by Shen Gongbao to come here."

Just then, he heard someone crying out in pain. "Who is that?" he asked.

Su Hu told him, "That is General Zheng Lun. He was injured in battle."

"Please bring him out so I can see him." When Zheng Lun was carried out, the Daoist looked at him. He said, "This injury is from the Universal Ring. I can take care of it." He took a pill out of his robe and mixed it with water in a gourd. Then he put some of it on the wound. Immediately the pain was gone and the wound was healed. Zheng Lun bowed to Lu Yue and accepted him as his master. This did not make Su Hu happy.

Su Hu thought that Lu Yue would go out right away to challenge the Zhou. But he did not. He just waited. Several days later, four more Daoists arrived. Their faces were green, yellow, red and black, and they wore colorful robes. They were very tall, probably sixteen or seventeen feet tall, and they looked as fierce as tigers or wolves.

Su Hu was unhappy to see these four warriors come into his camp. Without asking Su Hu's permission, Lu Yue said to them, "Which of you would like to fight the first battle?"

The green-faced Daoist replied, "I will!" He ran out of the Shang camp and shouted a challenge.

Chapter 58
Lu Yue, The God of Plague

Plagues come again and again
But Jiang Ziya has great skills

He builds the foundation for a strong nation
To protect the people from disasters

Gods and ghosts cry out as disaster comes
Soldiers and common people suffer from war

When will the day of peace come?
When auspicious clouds cover the Long-Life Palace

≡ ≡ ≡

Jiang Ziya saw the Daoist. He ordered Jinzha to go out and meet him. When Jinza got close, he saw that the man had a green face, red hair, long teeth and golden eyes. The Daoist said, "My brothers and I are from Nine Dragon Island. You think you are better than us, so I have come to see who is stronger."

They began to fight, sword against sword. After a few rounds, the Daoist ran away. Jinzha chased after him. Suddenly the Daoist took his Headache Rock out from his robe and struck it three times. Jinza felt dizzy. His head started to hurt and his face turned pale. He fled back to the prime minister's mansion, crying in pain.

The next day, Jiang Ziya sent Jinzha's brother Muzha to fight. He saw a Daoist with a yellow face as round as the moon, with a long beard and a yellow robe. "Are you the demon who gave my brother a headache?" asked Muzha.

"No," replied the Daoist, "but I am also a disciple of Lu Yue."

"It does not matter," replied Muzha. "You are all sorcerers." He rushed at the Daoist with his sword raised high. They fought for several rounds. The yellow-faced Daoist ran away, then he turned and waved a flag several times. Muzha felt like he was on fire. He took off his clothes and ran back to the prime minister's mansion, shouting, "I feel like I am going to burn up!"

On the third day, another Daoist came out of the Shang camp, shouting "Who will fight me?" He had a red face and huge eyes. Thunderbolt came out of the Zhou camp. He jumped in the air and slashed at the Daoist. The Daoist ran away, then turned and pointed his sword. Thunderbolt fell to the ground. Then he slowly got up and walked back to the prime minister's mansion, in great pain.

On the fourth day, Lu Yue ordered the fourth Daoist to challenge the Zhou. This one had a black face and wore a black robe.

Jiang Ziya was worried. It seemed like there was no end to the number of Daoist magicians who were fighting them. It reminded him of the ten traps, and he wondered if there were going to be ten Daoist magicians. He sent Dragon Beard Tiger out to face the Daoist.

Dragon Beard Tiger did not have a sword. Instead, he threw stones at the Daoist magician. But the Daoist took out a whip and waved it. Dragon Beard Tiger dropped his stones. He turned and slowly walked back to the prime minister's mansion, white saliva coming from his mouth.

Jiang Ziya did not know what to do. He did not know that these four Daoists were all carriers of plague. One of them brought plague to the east using the Headache Rock, one in the west using the Fever Flag, one in the south using the Sword of Sleep, and one in the north using the Plague Spreading Whip.

Soon after, a messenger told Jiang Ziya that a Daoist with three eyes had just come out of the Shang camp and was demanding to see him. This was Lu Yue, the master of the four other Daoists.

The Zhou cannons roared, and Jiang Ziya rode out of the city gate. He saw a tall Daoist with a greenish-blue face. The man wore a red robe and rode on a camel. The Daoist said, "Are you Jiang Ziya?"

"Yes," replied the prime minister. "Tell me, where do you come from, and why are you hurting my disciples? Don't you know that the king of Shang is a tyrant? You must have heard that the phoenix has sung on Mount Qi, many great men have joined together with us, and heaven is on our side. You may have won a few rounds, but you will lose in the end."

The Daoist said, "My name is Lu Yue, and I come from Nine Dragon

Island. You have already met four of my disciples. Now it is time for me to show you my power. Your death is near, Jiang Ziya!"

But the prime minister just laughed at him. "I have heard these same words from many other magicians and sorcerers. All have gone with the wind. Now you will join them."

Lu Yue shouted and attacked. Immediately, the battle was joined by Yang Jian, Nezha, Huang Tianhua and Earth Traveler Sun. The five of them surrounded the Daoist. Zheng Lun came up to help his master, but there were still five Zhou against two Shang.

Lu Yue shook himself. He turned into a creature with a green face, long fangs, three heads and six arms. Each hand held a different weapon. He attacked Jiang Ziya. The prime minister retreated. All the Zhou fighters turned to Lu Yue and attacked him at the same time, knocking him off his camel. Injured, he ran back to his camp. Then Nezha stabbed Zheng Lun in the shoulder, and he also ran back to the Shang camp. The fight was over.

In the Shang camp, Lu Yue used his magic elixir to heal himself and Zheng Lun. He smiled and said, "Jiang Ziya, you think you have won the fight. But you cannot escape your fate!"

That night, Lu Yue ordered his four disciples to secretly enter the Zhou camp. Each one carried a gourd full of plague pills. They put the plague pills in the rivers, ponds and wells. Then they returned to the Shang camp. Lu Yue said to Su Hu, "See? There is no need for swords or fighting. Everyone in West Qi City will be dead in six days. You will win your war, and I can go back to my island home."

The next day, people drank the water and became sick. The streets were empty, and the air was filled with the cries of people in pain. The only people not sick were Nezha, because he was reborn from lotus flowers, and Yang Jian, who was able to change his body as he wished.

Zheng Lun decided this was a good time to attack the city. Yang Jian saw him approaching the city. He threw two handfuls of dirt in the air and shouted some magic words. Instantly, many tall warriors appeared on the city walls. Zheng Lun saw the warriors and dared not approach the city.

Yang Jian knew that his magic would only last a few hours. He was worried and did not know what to do next. But just then, he saw a bright golden light. It was his master, Jade Tripod. Yang Jian kowtowed to his master, who said, "Yang Jian! You must go to Fire Cloud Cave. There you will see three great masters. Beg them to give you elixirs to help your people!"

Without waiting even a second, Yang Jian jumped into the air and flew to Fire Cloud Cave. It was a beautiful place covered with ancient pine trees and fragrant grasses. Green phoenixes flew over distant mountains, and dragons rested in cool streams. He walked up to the cave and waited.

After a while, a young man came out. Yang Jian bowed and said, "I am Yang Jian, a disciple of Jade Tripod. My master has ordered me to come and see the three masters."

The young man said, "Do you know who the three masters are?"

"I am sorry, I don't know."

"They are Emperor Heaven, Emperor Earth, and Emperor Humanity. Come with me."

The young man led him into the cave. Yang Jian saw three men sitting in the cave. The one in the middle had two horns on his head. The on the left wore a tiger skin and a robe made of leaves. The one on the right was dressed like an emperor.

Yang Jian bowed to them. He said, "My master Jade Tripod has commanded me to come here and see you. My king and his people have become sick from a plague brought by the magician Lu Yue. Many are near death. I beg you, please save them!"

The man on the left stood up. He said, "The people of Shang lived in peace and happiness for many years. But now the dynasty is ending, and there is war throughout the country. Shen Gongbao is going against the will of heaven and is bringing sorcerers to help the tyrant king." Then he walked to the back of the cave, picked up something, and brought it back to Yang Jian.

"Take this," he said. "There are three pills here. Give one to your king and his ministers. Give one to Jiang Ziya and his disciples. Put the third one in the city's water supply for the people."

Yang Jian took the pills, bowed, and turned to leave.

"Wait," said the master. "Come with me." Together they walked outside. The master bent down and picked some herbs. He handed the herbs to Yang Jian and said, "This is Sickle-Leaved Rabbit Ear. If boiled in water, it will cure any illness."

Yang Jian brought the pills and the herb back to West Qi City. Everyone did as the master had told them, and soon all the people in the city were healthy again.

Lu Yue did not know about the elixirs, of course. He waited eight days, until he was sure that everyone in the city was dead. Then he told his disciples and Su Hu that they had won the war.

But Su Hu wanted to see for himself. He secretly went to West Qi City. Looking inside the city gate, he saw many people in the streets, and many soldiers. He returned and told Lu Yue, "Your magic has failed. How dare you try to trick me like this?"

Lu Yue was surprised and angry. He did a divination, then said to Su Hu, "Ah. Jade Tripod sent his disciple to get elixirs from Fire Cloud Cave!" He immediately ordered an attack on the city from all four sides. Su Hu gave him twelve thousand soldiers for the attack.

Yellow Dragon Immortal saw the soldiers coming. "Open all the city gates!" he ordered. "We will deal with the soldiers when they are inside the city."

Chapter 59
The Second Prince Returns

The crimes of the Shang king are too great
His dynasty cannot continue

Shen Gongbao could try to take the throne
But it is heaven's will that the Shang dynasty end

Four generals are fated to die
They lose their souls when they face three disasters

It was the disciple's fate to turn into ashes
Cries come from the Tower of Creation

≡ ≡ ≡

The Shang army attacked the city, with three thousand soldiers coming in at each of the four city gates. Yang Jian was waiting for them at the east gate, Nezha at the west gate, Jade Tripod at the south gate, and Yellow Dragon Immortal at the north gate.

At the east gate, Yang Jian ordered his dog to attack the Daoist leading the attack. As the Daoist fought against the huge dog, Yang Jian cut him in two with his sword. The Daoist's soul flew to the Terrace of Creation. The soldiers attacking the east gate turned and fled for their lives.

At the west gate, Nezha defeated the Daoist general by stabbing him with his sword. At the south gate, Jade Tripod cut off his opponent's head. The souls of the two defeated generals flew to the Terrace of Creation and their soldiers fled.

But at the north gate, the powerful sorcerer Lu Yue was leading the Shang soldiers. He fought against Yellow Dragon Immortal and was close to defeating him. The other Zhou immortals surrounded him, fighting furiously. Muzha threw one of his hooks, cutting off Lu Yue's left arm. The sorcerer fled on his camel. He could not get to the Shang camp, so he and his last disciple rode into a nearby field and sat down on a rock.

As they sat on the rock, resting, they heard the sound of a man singing nearby. Looking up, they saw a tall man. The man wore a Daoist robe but a warrior's helmet on his head. He carried a large club in his hand. "Who are you?" asked Lu Yue.

"I am Wei Hu," replied the man. "I am a disciple of the Heavenly Master of Divine Virtue. My master has commanded me to help Jiang Ziya defeat the sorcerer, Lu Yue."

"How dare you!" shouted Lu Yue's disciple, attacking the man.

"Well, I am a lucky man!" said Wei Hu. "It seems that I have found the sorcerer that I am looking for!" The two of them started to fight. After a few rounds, Wei Hu threw his club in the air. It came down on the disciple's head, killing him instantly. His soul flew to the Terrace of Creation, to join the other three disciples.

Lu Yue tried to fight Wei Hu using his one hand, but could not get past his club. When Wei Hu threw his club in the air, Lu Yue flew away on a beam of yellow light.

Far away in a mountain cave, Master Pure Essence was sitting quietly. A messenger entered the cave and told him that he must go to Mount Kunlun to attend a ceremony honoring Jiang Ziya. The master called his disciple, Yin Hong, the second son of the king of Shang.

"Disciple, the war is going well. Soon Jiang Ziya will cross the five mountain passes and meet the other marquises in Mengjin. Go to him now and see if you can help him." Then the master said, "There is just one problem. You are the son of the king of Shang. How do you feel about fighting against him?"

"Master!" cried the young man, "I am the son of the king, but he is also my enemy. My father listened to Daji, then he gouged out my mother's eyes and burned her hands until she died. He also ordered the deaths of my brother and me. I am ready to avenge my mother's death, even if it kills me."

"Are you sure you will not change your mind later?" asked the master.

"I dare not do anything against your wishes," Yin Hong replied.

"Good. Go to Good Dream Pass and meet Mother Fire Spirit. You will not be able to see her, but she will see you. Take these weapons." He handed the boy a sword, a robe, and a small mirror. "This sword will protect you. Wear this robe and no one will be able to hurt you. As for the mirror, you see that it is white on one side and red on the other. If you flash the white side to someone, they will die. But if you flash the red side to them, they will return to life. Go now."

Yin Hong turned and started to walk out of the cave. The master shouted, "Wait a moment!" The young man turned around. The master said, "Never forget what I've told you, and do not forget your promise!"

"If I change my mind, may I be burned to ashes!" the young man replied. The master nodded, and Yin Hong left the cave.

Yin Hong set off for West Qi. After a while he stopped to rest in a beautiful forest on a mountainside. Suddenly a man rode toward him. He had a long red beard, yellow eyebrows, and golden eyes. He wore a black robe and rode a black horse. He attacked Yin Hong. The young man fought back with his sword.

Then a second man came, riding a yellow horse, and joined the fight. Yin Hong could not fight against the two of them, so he took out his mirror and flashed the white side at the two men. They both fell off their horses and lay on the ground without moving.

Two more men rode towards him, waving their swords. Yin Hong flashed the mirror at one of them, who fell off his horse and lay on the ground.

The second man, seeing this, stopped his horse. He got off, kowtowed to Yin Hong, and said, "Forgive us, great immortal!"

"I am no great immortal. I am Prince Yin Hong, son of the king of Shang." The man continued to kowtow and beg forgiveness. "I will not hurt you or your friends," said the prince.

He flashed the red side of the mirror at the three other men. They woke up, as if from a dream. Before they could attack, the fourth man said, "Wait, brothers! This is Prince Yin Hong!"

The men all kowtowed to the prince. Yin Hong said to them, "You are all very brave. I am going to join the king of West Qi in his fight against the king of Shang. Please join me."

One of the men asked, "But you are the prince of Shang. Why would you fight against your own father?"

"He may be my father but he is an evil tyrant. He has been cruel to the people and gone against the will of heaven. Now, will you come with me to West Qi?"

The men agreed. They told their three thousand men that they were joining West Qi. The men burned their camp, made banners with the West Qi symbol, and headed towards West Qi.

Soon they saw a man in the road in front of them, riding a black tiger. He had a long white beard and wore a Daoist robe. The men were afraid of the tiger, but Yin Hong rode up to the man. He asked, "What is your honorable name, sir?"

"I am Shen Gongbao. And I believe you are Prince Yin Hong."

"Yes. My master has ordered me to go to West Qi to offer my help to their king."

"But you are the son of the king of Shang! Why would any son be so unfilial as to fight against his own father?"

"Even filial sons cannot go against the will of heaven."

"Oh, you are a young fool!" said Shen Gongbao. "No son should ever attack his own father. And what about you? If your father is defeated, you will never become king. You will lose the throne, and for a thousand years people will talk about Yin Hong, the unfilial son."

Yin Hong said nothing. He thought about it for a while. Then he said, "You are right. But I gave an oath to my master."

"What was the oath?"

"That I be burned to ashes."

Shen Gongbao laughed. "That is a crazy oath. How can your flesh turn to ashes? You must decide what path you will take. But if you want to help your father, go to West Qi and join up with Su Hu."

"But Su Hu's daughter killed my mother!"

"Let go of your anger, young man. Once you are king, you can get your revenge any way you like."

With that, Shen Gongbao mounted his tiger and rode away. Yin Hong ordered the men to change the banners from West Qi to Shang, and they continued towards West Qi.

When they came near to the Shang camp, a messenger ran to Su Hu and told him, "His Highness the Prince has arrived. He wants to see you immediately."

Su Hu said, "But both princes are dead."

The messenger replied, "This is Yin Hong, the second prince. You must come right away."

Zheng Lun said, "Commander! You remember that the two princes were taken away by a magic wind. I think they were rescued by some immortals, and now Yin Hong has returned to help us. You'd better go and see him."

Su Hu agreed. He and Zheng Lun went to see Yin Hong. Su Hu said, "Your Highness, would you please tell me how you came to be here?"

Yin Hong replied, "My father ordered my brother and I to be killed. But we were rescued by some immortals. Now I am here to help you."

Su Hu told the prince of the situation. Then the prince's army joined the Shang army in their camp.

The next day, Yin Hong came out of the Shang camp to challenge the Zhou. Huang Feihu came out to meet him. Yin Hong had not seen him in ten years and did not recognize him. He said, "I am Prince Yin Hong. Who are you, and why are you rebelling against your king?"

"I am Prince Huang Feihu."

The prince replied, "I know a man named Huang Feihu, but you are not him." Then Yin Hong attacked Huang Feihu, and the two of them began to fight fiercely.

Chapter 60
Ma Yuan Helps the Shang Army

Ma Yuan trained a long time under the purple gate
He is angry and cruel

He is full of the five evils
Though he looks like three flowers and good fruits[1]

The Shang king's reign is coming to an end
King Wu's army is powerful

Ma Yuan goes away to study Buddhism
But West Qi remembers how it was afraid of losing its heart

≡ ≡ ≡

As the two men fought, more generals came from both sides, until at last ten men were fighting, using both ordinary and magic weapons. Yin Hong could not win against so many enemies, so he ran away. Then suddenly he turned around and flashed the white side of his mirror at Huang Feihu. Huang Feihu fell from his horse and was taken prisoner. Then the prince flashed his mirror at Huang Tianhua, and he was also taken prisoner.

When they returned to the Shang camp, Yin Hong flashed the red side of his mirror at the two prisoners. They opened their eyes. Huang Feihu saw the prince and said angrily, "You say you are Yin Hong, but why don't you recognize me? I am Prince Huang Feihu. I saved your life at the palace gate back in Zhaoge, and I helped you escape from your father."

"Oh, it's you!" cried Yin Hong. He jumped up and untied the two prisoners. "I am so sorry! But tell me, why are you fighting for the Zhou?"

"Your Highness, I must tell you, your father is a very evil man. He killed

---

[1] The expression "three flowers, good fruits" describes someone who is good from the inside out, and appears to be of good character, healthy and kind.

my wife and my sister."

Yin Hong ordered that the men's armor and weapons be returned to them. Zheng Lun was unhappy about this, but Yin Hong said, "This man saved my life. I must do the same for him." Then he took the two men to the camp gate and made sure they could leave the camp safely.

The next day, Yin Hong rode out of the Shang camp and called for Jiang Ziya. When the prime minister came out, the prince said to him, "You were once a high minister at Zhaoge. Now you are a rebel. How can you be so ungrateful to your king?"

Jiang Ziya bowed and replied, "Your Highness, a king must love his people and listen to his ministers. But the king of Shang has become the enemy of the people, and he listens only to his evil queen. The king of West Qi has the blessing of heaven and controls two thirds of the country. I think you should not go against the will of heaven."

Yin Hong did not want to hear this. He shouted, "Who will kill this man for me?" Several of his generals rode forward, waving their swords. Several Zhou generals rode forward to block their attack. The fight began. Two Shang generals were killed, one by Nezha's spear and one by Yang Jian's dog. Their souls flew to the Terrace of Creation.

Seeing that the fight was going badly, Yin Hong took out his mirror and flashed the white side at Nezha. But of course it did nothing, because Nezha was made of lotus flowers instead of flesh and bone. While he was busy doing this, Deng Chanyu threw a stone at Yin Hong, hitting him in the face. Bleeding badly, he turned to flee. Nezha saw this and slashed at him, but Yin Hong's magic robe protected him. The Shang fighters returned to their camp, and the Zhou fighters returned to the city.

Back in the city, Yang Jian told Jiang Ziya, "I recognize that magic mirror. It belongs to Master Pure Essence. I must go and talk with him about this."

He flew off to see Master Pure Essence in his mountain cave. He entered the cave, bowed, and said, "Master, we are having difficulty fighting against the Shang army. Jiang Ziya has asked me to come here and borrow your magic mirror."

The master replied, "Yin Hong has the mirror. I told him to go and help Jiang Ziya. You should ask him for it."

"I'm afraid that Yin Hong has joined the Shang side."

Master Pure Essence sighed. "I gave him all of my treasures. Now he has turned his back on me. All right. Go back to West Qi. I will be there soon."

Three days later, Master Pure Essence arrived in West Qi. He met with Jiang Ziya and explained the situation. Then he went outside the city and called for Yin Hong to come out.

When Yin Hong came out, he was surprised to see Master Pure Essence. "Master," he said, "your disciple cannot give you a full bow because he is wearing armor."

"Yin Hong!" said Master Pure Essence. "Don't you remember your oath? Do you want your body to turn to ashes? Turn away from this path before it is too late."

"Master, how can I turn against my own father? You know what the ancients say, 'Before you try to become an immortal, first be a good person.' How can I be a good person if I kill my own father?"

"Your father has turned his back on the nation. He has killed many loyal ministers. He drinks and lusts without end. He is hated by men and by heaven. If you continue to support him, it will be the end of the Shang dynasty. Now get down from your horse."

"I cannot do that."

"How dare you oppose the will of heaven!" shouted the master, and he struck at Yin Hong with his sword.

"Master, please control your anger," said Yin Hong, blocking the blow. The master struck at him again. Now Yin Hong was angry. He shouted, "Master, now I must strike back!" The two of them began to fight. Yin Hong took out his magic mirror, but the master saw it. Quickly he escaped on a beam of golden light.

Yin Hong returned to the Shang camp. He was talking with Su Hu when a strange man came in to see them. The man was eight feet tall, had green skin, and a mouth full of long fangs. He wore a red robe and a necklace of skull bones. Fire came from the places where his eyes, ears and nose should have been. Yin Hong's generals were terrified.

The man bowed and asked, "Which of you is Yin Hong?"

"I am," said Yin Hong. "Who are you?"

"I am Ma Yuan from Skeleton Mountain. Shen Gongbao asked me to come and help you."

Yin Hong gave the strange man dinner and a place to sleep. The next day the man went out of the camp gate and called for Jiang Ziya. When Jiang Ziya heard of this, he said, "I know that I am fated to meet thirty-six different enemies. So, I must go and see this man." He walked out of the city gate, with his generals walking on both sides of him.

Jiang Ziya saw the tall Daoist and said, "What is your honorable name, sir?"

"I am Ma Yuan. Shen Gongbao asked me to come here to help the prince defeat you and your rebels."

Jiang Ziya replied, "I think that Shen Gongbao does not like me, and that's why he asked you to fight against me and my army. But tell me, why don't you listen to the will of heaven and the wishes of the people?"

Ma Yuan laughed. "Yin Hong is being filial to his father, that is all. Jiang Ziya, you do not respect the king, and you do not respect a son's filial duty to his father. Now it's time for me to kill you."

Ma Yuan attacked, slashing at the prime minister with his sword, and the battle began. Jiang Ziya and his generals fought against Ma Yuan. Suddenly a large hand appeared behind the Daoist. It reached forward, lifted up one of the generals and threw him on the ground. Ma Yuan put his foot on the general's leg so he could not move.

Then he opened the man's chest, pulled out his heart, and ate it in front of Jiang Ziya and his generals.

Everyone was terrified. But suddenly, little Earth Traveler Sun shouted, "I'm coming for you!" and ran forward, swinging his cudgel and hitting the Daoist on the legs. At first, Ma Yuan laughed, but then he became angry because of the blows to his legs. He tried to use his magic third hand to grab Sun and throw him to the ground. But Sun simply disappeared into the ground.

As he stared at the ground, Deng Chanyu threw a stone at his face, hitting him in the nose. He started to bleed. Yang Jian ran forward and attacked him. Ma Yuan could not fight him, but he used his magic third hand to pick up Yang Jian and throw him to the ground. Then he opened up the general's chest, pulled out his heart, and ate it.

Seeing this, the Zhou generals retreated back to the city. Ma Yuan returned to the Shang camp. But soon he was sweating and feeling terrible pain in his stomach.

Zheng Lun said to him, "My friend, you just ate two human hearts. Try drinking some warm wine, it will help your stomach."

But the pain became even worse. Soon Ma Yuan was rolling around on the ground, grabbing his stomach and crying in pain. He did not know that Yang Jian could do transformations. So, when he thought he was eating Yang Jian's heart, he was actually eating a poison that would make him very sick for three days.

Back at West Qi City, Master Pure Essence and the Heavenly Master of Outstanding Culture arrived at the prime minister's palace.

Heavenly Master said, "Jiang Ziya, we have come to help you deal with Ma Yuan."

"Thank you!" replied Jiang Ziya. "How will you do this?"

Heavenly Master told him what to do. Later that afternoon, Jiang Ziya rode out to the gate of the Shang camp. He did not call for Ma Yuan, but he just looked around.

A guard ran to Ma Yuan and told him that Jiang Ziya was outside the camp gate. Ma Yuan ran to the gate and shouted, "Don't leave, I am coming for you!"

Chapter 61
The Death of the Second Prince

There are secrets hidden in the map of eight diagrams
But only a few people know them

The transformations and magic are mysterious
Repent your mistakes and thoughts of the past

Yin Hong regrets his oath but the teacher will not save him
The will of heaven is clear, he cannot still walk on earth

The evils of the Shang king are known all around the world
How can one piece of wood save someone from their fate?[1]

☰ ☰ ☰

Ma Yuan tried to catch up to Jiang Ziya, but he was on foot while Jiang Ziya was riding his horse. After a while he stopped to catch his breath. Jiang Ziya turned and shouted at him, "Ma Yuan, I dare you to fight me!" Ma Yuan started running towards the prime minister again, but Jiang Ziya rode away. This continued throughout the day until evening. As the sun was going down, Ma Yuan found himself in a strange place. He was on a mountain. Dark clouds were all around and dangerous large birds flew overhead.

He was tired and it was getting dark, so he sat down to rest against a tree. He stayed there for several hours, not moving. Around midnight he looked up and saw a fire on the mountain top. Jiang Ziya and King Wu were there, sitting and drinking. He jumped up and climbed up to the mountain top, but when he got there the two men were gone.

He looked down and saw soldiers all around the bottom of the mountain. Angry, he ran down to fight them, but they all disappeared. Now he was angry, tired and hungry.

He walked slowly along a mountain path. He heard a sound. Looking

---

[1] A "piece of wood" means something small or insignificant, when compared to the fate of the entire world.

down, he saw a woman lying in the grass. "Help me, master!" she cried.

"Who are you? What do you want?" he asked her.

"Sir, I am a married woman. I was going to visit my husband's family but I had a heart attack. Would you please go to the village and get me some hot water? It will save me from death."

"Dear lady, the village is too far away. I think you will die before I get back. I am very hungry. Please let me have a meal."

"Of course, if you help me, I will be happy to give you a meal."

"No, that's not what I mean. Please let me eat you."

"How can you eat me?" cried the woman. But Ma Yuan stepped forward. He put his foot on her chest and cut her body open with his sword. He reached inside, trying to find her heart. But he could not find it. The woman had no heart or any other internal organs.

As he was thinking about this, the Heavenly Master of Outstanding Culture walked up to him. Ma Yuan tried to pull his hands out of the woman's body. But her chest wound closed up, trapping his hands inside her body. He looked up and saw Heavenly Master raising his sword. "Oh Master," cried Ma Yuan, "please don't kill me!"

Just as Heavenly Master was about to bring down his sword, a man with a yellow face and a short beard came up. Heavenly Master turned to look at him. The man said, "Sir, I am a Buddha from the west. Please do not kill Ma Yuan. His name is not on the List of Creation because he is fated to become a Buddhist. If you give him to me, I will teach him the ways of the Buddha."

Heavenly Master said, "Sir, you are a great master of heaven. Of course you may take this man." He released Ma Yuan's hands from the woman's body.

The Buddha walked up to Ma Yuan and shaved his head. He said, "My son, you have spent your life foolishly. Now it is time for you to become a new man. Come with me to the Forest of Seven Jewels." Ma Yuan agreed, and the two of them left.

Heavenly Master returned to West Qi City and told the others what had happened.

In the Shang camp, Yin Hong was worried about Ma Yuan because he had not returned. In the morning, while cannons roared and soldiers shouted, he walked to the city wall and called for Jiang Ziya to come out. Jiang Ziya rode out of the city gate. The two of them fought for a few rounds. Then Jiang Ziya rode away to the southeast, with Yin Hong chasing after him.

They came to a golden bridge. Jiang Ziya rode across the bridge and called to Yin Hong to fight him. Yin Hong rode onto the bridge. He did not know that this was a magic bridge created by Master Pure Essence, using Laozi's magic map.

When Yin Hong rode onto the bridge, he became very confused. He thought he was in Zhaoge with his father, the king of Shang. He thought he saw Concubine Huang, and then Concubine Yang. He spoke to them but they did not hear him. Then he saw his dead mother. She said, "My son, you have gone against your own master. You are standing on Laozi's magic map. In a few minutes you will be turned to ashes!"

"Help me, Mother!" he cried. But it was too late. Master Pure Essence rolled up the map with Yin Hong inside it. Yin Hong and his horse turned to ashes. When the wind blew, the ashes flew away. Yin Hong's soul flew to the Terrace of Creation.

Master Pure Essence began to cry. He said, "I have just killed my own disciple. Now who will want to study with me?"

Merciful Navigation said, "Don't worry, my friend. This was his fate."

Back at the Shang camp, Su Hu was still trying to figure out how to cross over to the Zhou side. He wrote a letter to Jiang Ziya. In the letter he told Jiang Ziya to attack that night, and said that Su Hu and his family would cross over to the Zhou side during the battle. He tied it to an arrow, and told his son to shoot the arrow into West Qi City.

Jiang Ziya read the letter. He prepared his army, and they attacked at the second watch. The Shang army was not prepared, and they put up only a little fight. During the battle, the Zhou army captured Zheng Lun and tied him up.

After the battle was over, Su Hu entered the city with his family. He was taken to see Jiang Ziya. He kowtowed and said, "Prime Minister, I have committed serious crimes. By letting me live, you have been too kind."

"Please stand up," replied Jiang Ziya. "You are a great hero. We all look up to you."

Then Zheng Lun was brought in. He refused to kneel. Jiang Ziya said,

"Take him outside and cut off his head."

Su Hu rushed forward and said, "Prime Minister! You are correct that Zheng Lun deserves to die. But he is a very good general. We can use him. Please let him live."

Jiang Ziya smiled and said, "I was hoping you would say that! Go and talk with him."

Su Hu went outside. He told Zheng Lun, "General, can't you see what is happening here? Two thirds of the country have already joined the Zhou side. Soon Jiang Ziya and his army will go to Zhaoge and bring down the old king. Please, remember the old saying, 'A good minister chooses a good master.' You must choose the right side!"

Zheng Lun listened. He felt like he was just waking up from a dream. He replied, "Thank you, my friend. Your words are true. I would like to come over to the Zhou side, but I don't think the Prime Minster will have me."

"Don't worry about that," replied Su Hu. Together they walked back inside. He said to Jiang Ziya, "Zheng Lun wants to come over to the Zhou side, but he is afraid that you and your generals don't want him."

"We are no longer enemies," replied Jiang Ziya. Turning to Zheng Lun he said, "General, you are a good man and a great general. Let's forget the past!" Then he ordered a great banquet to be held for the newcomers.

Chapter 62
The Arrival of Winged Celestial

Chaos and war, not a single peaceful day
The people suffer, as lonely as stars in the sky

Bodies of the dead lie in piles on the ground
The king uses their money to pay for feathered arrows

Soldiers are still willing to serve their ruler
But heaven doesn't want the palace gate to stand

Great disaster brings great suffering
Death and blood in West Qi

☰ ☰ ☰

Back in the capital city of Zhaoge, the old king was told that his father-in-law, Su Hu, had crossed over to the Zhou side. He was surprised and angry.

Daji heard this. She said to the king, "Your Majesty, you have been so kind to me, and now my father has done this terrible thing. His family must be punished. Please, cut off my head and hang it on the city wall. This will show the people that you follow the law. As for me, I am happy to die for you."

She put her head softly on the king's lap and cried. Her tears fell like rain. The king felt lust rising in his body. He lifted up her head and said, "My dear, there's no way you could have known what your father was thinking. Please don't worry about it. I don't want this to make you less beautiful."

The next day he ordered Zhang Shan, the commander of Sanshang Pass, to be the new leader of his army in West Qi. Orders were sent to Zhang Shan. He took a hundred thousand soldiers and headed towards West Qi City.

The army traveled for several days. When they arrived at the Shang camp outside West Qi City, the generals greeted Zhang Shan. One of them said, "Remember the old saying, 'An army that travels for 100 *li* is too tired to fight[1].' Please rest. We can attack tomorrow."

Meanwhile, Jiang Ziya was preparing to bring his army to Mengjin, where he would meet with the other marquises and begin the final battle at Zhaoge. He ordered his men to change all the flags to red. One of his generals did not understand this. He said, "Sir, the flags are like the eyes of our army. They tell us what to do and how to move. If they are all the same color, the men will become confused. Why are you doing this?"

Jiang Ziya replied, "Red is the color of fire. The weather is cold now, and the soldiers need to fight like fire. Don't worry, though. We will put a small piece of colored cloth – green, yellow, pink, white or black – on each flag, so our soldiers know what to do."

Just then, a messenger came in. He told Jiang Ziya that the new leader of the Shang army, Zhang Shan, wanted to meet him. He sent Deng Jiugong out to meet him. Deng Jiugong had been the commander of Sanshang Pass before crossing over to the Zhou side.

When Zhang Shan saw this, he sent one of his own generals out to meet Deng Jiugong. The two of them shouted at each other, then began fighting. But Deng Jiugong was the stronger fighter, and he soon struck the other man with his sword, killing him instantly.

Zhang Shan was furious when he saw this. The next day he came out himself, demanding to see Deng Jiugong. He shouted, "You traitor! How dare you kill a general sent here by your king? You deserve to die. But I will take you prisoner and bring you back to Zhaoge to face your king."

Deng Jiugong replied, "You are just a dog wearing the clothes of a man. You serve the king of Shang even though you know he drinks and lusts and cares nothing for his people. Don't throw away your life. Join us and save the people."

"You should be cut into a thousand pieces!" shouted Zhang Shan, and he rushed at his enemy. They began to fight. Deng Jiugong was having trouble. His daughter Deng Chanyu saw this. She threw a stone and hit Zhang Shan in the face, causing him to bleed badly. He almost fell from his horse, but managed to return to the Shang camp.

---

[1] He is quoting Chapter 7 of The Art of War, where Sunzi says, "Therefore, if you pick up your armor and rush off, not stopping day or night, marching doubletime for a hundred *li* and then fighting, your commanders will be captured by the enemy."

He sat down and tried to stop the bleeding. A strange man, a Daoist, came up to him and bowed. The man had bright eyes and a mouth like an eagle's beak. He wore a black robe, straw shoes, and carried a gourd on his back and a sword at his side. "How did you hurt yourself?" he asked.

"A female general hit me in the face with a stone," he replied.

The Daoist took out some elixir, mixed it with water, and put it on the general's face. The wound healed.

"Thank you!" said Zhang Shan. "Who are you?"

"My name is Winged Celestial. I come from Penglai Island and I am here to help you if I can."

Zhang Shan thanked him, then closed his eyes to rest. The next day, Winged Celestial went outside the camp and called for Jiang Ziya to come out.

Jiang Ziya said, "We are fated to have thirty-six invasions, and we have had only thirty-two so far. Four more to go. I'd better go out and meet him."

He came out of the city gate, with his huge army in five square formations. All his generals rode out with him. He said to the Daoist, "May I know your honorable name?"

"I am Winged Celestial from Penglai Island. Why did you tell people that you would pull off my feathers and break my bones?"

"I never said anything like that. Perhaps someone is trying to cause trouble between us. Please think about this."

Winged Celestial thought about it for a minute, then he said, "Perhaps you are right. Let's forget about this. But be careful what you say from now on."

The Daoist turned to go back to the Shang camp. But Nezha shouted, "Cruel Daoist, how dare you insult my uncle!" He raced up on his Wind Fire Wheels and slashed at the Daoist with his sword. Other generals joined the fight. Thunderbolt used his golden cudgel. Earth Traveler Sun struck at the man's legs. Yang Jian's dog bit his neck. Huang Tianhua stabbed his arm with his magic nail. Unable to fight them all, the Daoist ran away back inside the Shang camp.

Bleeding from many wounds, he took out some elixir, mixed it with water, and put it on his own wounds. They healed instantly. He said to Zhang Shan, "I did not want to fight, but they attacked me first. Now they all must die. Bring me some wine. Later tonight I will turn their city into a great sea."

In the city, Jiang Ziya felt a powerful wind. He did a divination and learned what the Daoist was planning to do. Quickly he took a bath, put on clean clothes, and bowed towards Mount Kunlun. Then he unbound his hair and let it fall across his shoulders. Waving his sword, he picked up the North Sea and put it on top of West Qi City to protect it.

Seeing this, Heavenly Primogenitor took some magic water from his vase and spread it on top of the North Sea.

Late that night, Winged Celestial changed into a huge golden bird. He flew over the city, blocking out the moon and stars. He saw the North Sea hanging over the city and laughed. "Jiang Ziya is a fool. Does he think he can stop me?" He began to flap his wings, trying to turn the water into clouds. But the more he flapped his wings, the deeper the water became.

Finally, he gave up and flew away. He flew for a long time, until he came to a great mountain. At the foot of the mountain was a cave. Inside the cave was an immortal, thousands of years old.

Winged Celestial was very hungry. He wanted to eat the immortal. But the immortal saw him and pointed with his finger. The great bird crashed to the ground.

Winged Celestial said, "I am sorry, great immortal. I wanted to eat you because I am so hungry. But I didn't know you had such great powers. Please forgive me."

"You should have just asked me for food, you foolish bird. I will help you this one time. About 200 *li* from here is Purple Cloud Cliff. Many Daoists go there to eat delicious vegetarian food. Go there and they will feed you."

Winged Celestial thanked the immortal. He flew to Purple Cloud Cliff and turned back into human form. He saw many Daoists eating food given to them by children. He walked up to one of the children and asked for some food.

"I'm sorry, but the food is all gone," the child replied. "Please come back tomorrow."

Winged Celestial became angry and started shouting at the child. A Daoist in a yellow robe came up and said, "Please let go of your anger. I think we have some rice cakes."

The child ran off, and returned a short time later with eighty rice cakes. Winged Celestial ate all of them. The child got twenty-eight more, and Winged Celestial ate them too. He thanked the Daoist and the child, then flew back to the cave to thank the immortal. But the immortal just pointed his finger, and Winged Celestial crashed to the ground again.

Chapter 63
Yin Jiao Returns

Shen Gongbao wanted to cause trouble
This led to the death of the king's sons

First he convinced the younger son to rebel
Then he brought disaster to the elder son

He has caused much trouble
His smooth words have brought much suffering

Although this is heaven's will
Is there really a need for all this talk?

≡ ≡ ≡

As Winged Celestial lay on the ground, the immortal walked up to him. "Are you having a problem?" he asked.

"I ate some rice cakes," the Daoist replied, "but now my belly really hurts."

"Ah, that's too bad. Try vomiting. That should help."

Winged Celestial vomited. But the rice cakes did not come out. Instead, a string of white eggs came out of his mouth. He pulled at the string, but found that the string was wrapped around his heart. When he pulled, it caused great pain in his heart. Frightened, he jumped up and tried to run away.

"Where are you going?" shouted the immortal. "You should know, my name is Burning Lamp. How dare you try to harm Jiang Ziya! He has been ordered by the gods to end the rule of the king of Shang, so the people may live in peace." Then Burning Lamp said to his genie, "Hang him from a tree!"

"Please, Master!" cried Winged Celestial, "let me live. I won't cause any more trouble."

"It's too late. You have studied the Way for a thousand years, but still you cannot tell right from wrong." Then he thought for a minute and said, "All right. If you accept me as your master, I will let you live."

"Certainly. You are my teacher now," said Winged Celestial. Burning Lamp nodded his head. He waved his hand to release the string of eggs. Then the two of them left together to return to Burning Lamp's home.

Meanwhile, Master Grand Completion was meditating in his cave on Nine Immortal Mountain. He decided that it was time to send some help to Jiang Ziya. He called for Yin Jiao, the elder son of the king of Shang.

When the young man arrived, Master Grand Completion told him, "Soon King Wu will lead his army to Mengjin. The time of your revenge is coming near. I want you to serve in that army as a general. Will you go?"

Yin Jiao replied, "Yes. My father is the king of Shang, but his concubine Daji is my enemy. She killed my mother and tried to kill my brother and me. I will go and have my revenge on her."

"All right. Go and find some weapons." Then he told the young man where to find a cave that had the weapons. Yin Jiao found the cave. It was in a beautiful meadow, surrounded by lovely trees and flowers.

He walked up to the cave doors. They opened by themselves as soon as he got close. Walking inside, he saw a stone table. On the table was a bowl of hot soup. "This soup smells good!" he said to himself, and he ate all of it.

A few moments later, he felt strange. His body began to shake. Four new arms and two new heads appeared on his body. His face turned dark blue and his hair turned bright red. His teeth grew long, and a third eye appeared in the middle of his forehead.

He walked slowly back to Master Grand Completion. The master clapped his hands and said, "Wonderful!" Then he gave the young man three magic weapons: a pair of swords, the Heaven Overturning Seal, and the Soul Dropping Bell. Then he said, "Now you have a powerful body and three magic weapons. You must help King Wu and his army get through the five passes. Don't forget to do this!"

"Master, don't worry. My father is a tyrant and King Wu is a saint. If I ever forget to help King Wu, may my head be cut off with a hoe!"

He jumped in the air and began to travel on a dust cloud towards West Qi City. He grew tired after traveling for a while, so he stopped at the base of a beautiful mountain to rest. As he sat on the ground, a man rode towards him on a horse. He wore a red robe covered in gold chain. He held two wolf tooth clubs, one in each hand. Right behind him rode another man, wearing a yellow robe and carrying a long sword. Both of the men had three eyes, just like Yin Jiao.

The men shouted at Yin Jiao, "What are you doing on our mountain?"

"I am Yin Jiao, son of the tyrant, the king of Shang. My father has gone against the will of heaven and committed many terrible crimes. By order of my master, I am going to West Qi City to join the army of King Wu. You look like strong and brave men. Will you join me?"

They talked for a while, then they stopped to eat. When the meal was over, the two men, who were bandits, agreed to join Yin Jiao and the Zhou army.

They continued on their journey. Soon they met a Daoist riding a large black tiger. Yin Jiao said to him, "Sir, may I know your honorable name?"

"I am Shen Gongbao, a disciple of Mount Kunlun. May I ask where you are going?"

"By order of my master, I am going to help Jiang Ziya in his battle against my father, the king of Shang."

"Why would a son attack his father? And why would you want to end his dynasty? If your father dies a natural death, you become the king. But if he is killed by the Zhou, the dynasty ends and you are nothing. Think about it. It's better for you to use your strength and weapons to help your dynasty and your people."

"You may be right. But this is the will of heaven and the command of my master."

Shen Gongbao saw that this was not working. He said, "You say you are going to help Jiang Ziya. Did you know that he killed your brother?"

"Is that true?" asked Yin Jiao.

"Yes, it's true. Your brother also was sent to help King Wu. But Jiang Ziya used a magic map and turned the poor boy into ashes. Have you no love for your own brother?"

"How can I know if your words are true?"

"Go to the Shang camp at West Qi. You will find General Zhang Shan.

Ask him what happened to your brother." Then Shen Gongbao turned and rode away on his black tiger.

A few days later, Yin Jiao arrived in West Qi. He went to the Shang camp and asked to see Zhang Shan. He entered the general's tent. Zhang Shan looked up and saw Yin Jiao standing before him, with three heads and six arms. On his left and right stood the two bandits.

"How may I help you?" asked Zhang Shan.

"I am Yin Jiao. Do you know anything about my younger brother?"

"Yes. He was turned to ashes on Laozi's magic map."

Yin Jiao roared with anger. He turned and rode out to the West Qi City gates and called for Jiang Ziya. The two bandits rode with him.

A short time later, Jiang Ziya rode out to meet him, with his generals by his side. Nezha looked at the three men facing them and laughed. He said, "How strange for three men to have nine eyes. That usually is enough for four and a half men."

"Jiang Ziya! Why did you kill my brother?" shouted Yin Jiao.

Jiang Ziya replied, "He caused his own death. I had nothing to do with it."

"How dare you!" shouted Yin Jiao, and he attacked. Nezha rode forward and blocked the attack, but he was knocked off his Wind Fire Wheels by the Heaven Overturning Seal. Then several other generals attacked Yin Jiao, but he struck his Soul Dropping Bell and captured Huang Tianhua. Huang Feihu rushed forward to help his son, but was also captured using the Soul Dropping Bell. The rest of the Zhou generals retreated back to the city.

In the Shang camp, Yin Jiao looked carefully at Huang Tianhua and Huang Feihu and recognized both of them. "Long ago, you rescued me," he said to Huang Feihu. "Because of your kindness, I will set both of you free."

"Thank you, Your Highness," said Huang Feihu. "But tell me about that day long ago. What happened when you were carried away by the magic wind? Where did you go?"

Yin Jiao did not want to say too much, so he replied, "An immortal helped me. I stayed with him to study the Way. But now I have returned to avenge my brother. I will let you go this one time, but be careful. If I capture you again, you will die."

Huang Tianhua and Huang Feihu returned to West Qi City, and told Jiang Ziya what happened.

The next day, one of the three-eyed bandits, a man named Ma Shan, came out of the Shang camp. Deng Jiugong went out to face him. The fight was over quickly, and Ma Shan was carried back inside the city to face Jiang Ziya. Ma Shan did not kneel. He just said, "No need to talk. Just kill me."

"All right," said Jiang Ziya. He told one of his generals to cut off the man's head. But the general's sword passed through Ma Shan's neck as if it was going through water. He tried two more times, but he could not kill Ma Shan.

"What kind of magic is this?" asked Jiang Ziya. He told another general to smash the man's head with a huge club. The club came down on Ma Shan's head, but it passed right through his head without hurting him at all.

"Burn him with magic fire!" said Jiang Ziya to several of his generals. Nezha, Jinzha, Muzha and several others all shot magic fire towards Ma Shan, but the man just stood and laughed at them.

"That's enough," Ma Shan said to them. "I have to go now." He turned and walked out of the city.

After he left, Yang Jian said, "We need to learn what is going on here. First, I must go to Nine Immortals Mountain and find out about Yin Jiao. Then I will get a Demon Exposing Mirror so we can see what kind of demon this Ma Shan really is."

Yang Jian jumped in the air and flew to Nine Immortals Mountain. He found Master Great Completion and asked him why Yin Jiao was attacking the Zhou instead of helping them.

"That fool," said Master Great Completion. "I told him to help you, not attack you. And he has all my magic weapons!" He sighed and said, "Go back to your city. I will come soon."

Next, Yang Jian went to Master of the Clouds and asked him for his Demon Exposing Mirror. The master gave it to him, and he returned to the city.

The next day, Yang Jian went out of the city gate and called for Ma Shan. When the man came close, Yang Jian turned away from him and looked backwards, seeing Ma Shan in the mirror. He did not see a man, he saw a burning lamp wick. Then he put away the mirror, fought a few rounds, then rode back to the city. He told Jiang Ziya what he saw.

Jiang Ziya said, "So, he is actually a burning lamp. That's why we cannot hurt him with swords or clubs. As far as I know, there are only three magic lamps in the world. One is at Mount Kunlun, one is in the palace at Mount Xuandu, and one is on Mount Divine Hawk. He must be one of those three. Go and find out!"

First, Yang Jian went to Mount Kunlun. He had never been there before, and he was pleased to see what a beautiful place it was. The place was covered with large maple trees. Golden sunlight shone through the trees. He could see colorful birds flying through the trees. In the distance, high towers rose through the clouds.

He saw a young man in a white robe. "Brother, please tell me, is your master's magic lamp still burning?"

The young man smiled and said, "Of course it is."

Yang Jian thanked him and flew off to Mount Divine Hawk. This was the home of Burning Lamp.

Yang Jian knelt on the ground and kowtowed to Burning Lamp. "Uncle," he said, "please take a look at your magic lamp. Is it still burning?"

Burning Lamp looked at the lamp. It was dark. "Oh, no!" he cried. "How did you know?" Yang Jian told him everything that had happened.

"Thank you. Go back. I will be there shortly." Said Burning Lamp.

Yang Jian returned to West Qi City. Soon after he got there, Master Great Completion arrived. The master stood outside the Shang camp and shouted, "Yin Jiao! Come out here now!"

Chapter 64
The Burning of West Qi City

Luo Xuan, the master of fire, left his home
It was the year of fire

The burning mountain flowed like liquid gold
The sky was like a sea of flame

Even King Wu was frightened by the fire in the sky
He fell to the ground and prayed to the gods

Not because of the trouble caused by Luo Xuan
But because the immortals were all coming to the west

≡ ≡ ≡

Yin Jiao looked outside the camp and saw his master, Grand Completion, standing at the gate. He rode out on his horse and said to his master, "Master, I am sorry that I cannot bow to you. I am wearing too much armor."

Grand Completion was angry. He said, "You beast! Don't you remember what you said to me before you left the mountain?"

"Master, please listen to me. As I traveled here, I met a man named Shen Gongbao. He tried to make me change sides and help the Shang, but I would not do it. Then he told me that my brother had been killed by Jiang Ziya. That is when I decided that I could not serve that man. I must kill him."

"You should not believe Shen Gongbao. Your brother caused his own death."

"What? Are you saying that my brother was so foolish that he walked onto a magic map and killed himself? That cannot be true. Master, please go back to your mountain. I must have revenge."

Grand Completion roared in anger and slashed at Yin Jiao with his sword. Yin Jiao said, "Master, why are you attacking me? I don't want to fight you."

"Give up this foolish plan now, or you will bring your own death!" shouted Grand Completion.

Yin Jiao's face turned red. He said, "Master, if you continue to attack me, I will have to fight back." He struck at his master. They fought for several rounds. Then Yin Jiao threw his Heaven Overturning Seal. The immortal saw it. He flew away on a ray of golden light.

Grand Completion returned to the prime minister's mansion. He told Jiang Ziya, "My disciple was told by Shen Gongbao that you killed his brother. We fought. He tried to kill me with the Heaven Overturning Seal. I had to flee."

Burning Lamp said, "So, my own lamp wick is causing trouble. This is a serious matter. Let's deal with Ma Shan first." He told Jiang Ziya his plan.

The next day, Jiang Ziya rode out alone and demanded to see Ma Shan. Yin Jiao did not understand why the prime minister was doing this, but he told Ma Shan to go out and meet him.

Ma Shan rode out of the camp, his sword held high in his hand. He slashed down at Jiang Ziya, who turned and rode away towards the southeast. Ma Shan chased him. Before long, they came to an old Daoist sitting under a large tree. The Daoist let Jiang Ziya ride past. Then he jumped up and shouted, "Ma Shan! Don't you know who I am?"

Ma Shan swung at the Daoist with his sword, but missed. The Daoist, who was really Burning Lamp, took a lamp out of his robe. He threw it in the air. It came down on Ma Shan, trapping him inside. Instantly Ma Shan changed back to his original form, a wick burning inside the lamp. Burning Lamp gave the lamp to one of his disciples, then he returned to the city.

Yin Jiao heard that Ma Shan had been turned into a lamp wick and taken away. Furious, he rode out of his camp and shouted a challenge to Jiang Ziya.

"Go ahead," said Burning Lamp to Jiang Ziya. "Meet him. Use the Yellow Apricot Flag if you run into trouble."

Jiang Ziya rode out, with his generals on his right and left. Yin Jiao shouted at him, "You beast! You turned my younger brother into ashes! You and I cannot live under the same sky!" They began to fight. Other generals from the Zhou and Shang armies also joined the fight. Yin Jiao threw the Heaven Overturning Seal, but Jiang Ziya covered himself with the Yellow Apricot Flag. The seal flew around in the air but it could not come near the flag. Jiang Ziya hit his enemy with his staff, knocking him off his horse. Jiang Ziya's generals tried to kill Yin Jiao while he was on the ground, but some Shang generals grabbed him and carried him back to their camp.

Just as they returned to the Shang camp, two strange Daoists came to the camp. One had a dark red face, red hair and a red beard. He wore a red robe and rode a red horse. He said, "I am Luo Xuan from Fire Dragon Island. Shen Gongbao asked me to help you."

The other Daoist also wore a red robe, but he had a yellow face and a long beard.

Yin Jiao welcomed them and gave them a place to sleep. Early the next morning, the two Daoists rode out of the camp and called for Jiang Ziya.

Jiang Ziya looked out and saw them. "That man is red all over," he said.

"There are many strange looking people in that camp," said one of his disciples.

Jiang Ziya and his generals rode out to meet the two Daoists. They fought a few rounds, but the Zhou generals were too strong, and the Daoists had to flee back to their camp. Luo Xuan had several injuries from the fight. He took some pills from a gourd, mixed them with water, and ate them. The wounds healed quickly.

He said angrily to Yin Jiao, "We must destroy West Qi City. There is no other way."

That night, the two Daoists rode their red horses close to the walls of the city. They shot flaming arrows over the walls. Wherever the arrows fell, fire started. Soon the entire city was burning. Men, women and children ran through the streets, crying, but there was no place safe for them to go.

King Wu saw the fires. He knelt down and prayed to heaven, "We have angered the gods and brought this disaster to our people. Please, burn our houses but don't burn the houses of the people."

But things got worse. Luo Xuan opened a magic bottle. Ten thousand fire birds flew out of the bottle. They flew over the city, spitting fire. Everything in the city was burning.

Just then, Princess Long Ji arrived. She helped Yang Jian earlier. She was the daughter of Haotian, the Supreme God of Heaven and the Golden Mother of Jade Pond. She had been ordered to serve wine at the Peach Festival but did it poorly, and as punishment she was sent to live on a lonely mountain.

Now she saw the fires that were destroying West Qi City. Quickly she threw a net of magic mist over the city. The net was cool and wet. It put out all the fires. It also captured all the fire birds.

Luo Xuan was in the city, trying to start more fires. He saw what she did. He shouted at her, "How dare you put out my fires!"

But the princess just smiled at him and said, "You are going against the will of heaven and trying to harm the future king. I am here to help him. Now leave this place, or you will be sorry."

Luo Xuan threw a flaming dragon wheel at her. She pointed her magic Four Seas vase at him, and the dragon wheel disappeared inside it. The great waters of the four seas extinguished the fire of the dragon wheel.

Angrily, Luo Xuan shot fire arrows at the princess. She held the vase out. All the arrows went inside the vase and disappeared. He attacked her with his sword, but she waved her hand. A great sword appeared in her hand. She slashed at Luo Xuan, cutting off his head. But quickly he changed his form, and now he had three heads and six arms. He threw more fire weapons at her, but they all disappeared into her vase. With no weapons left, he turned and rode away as quickly as he could.

The princess met Jiang Ziya on the stone courtyard outside his mansion. She said, "I am Princess Long Ji. I used some little Daoist skills to put out the fires. Now I will help you defeat the Shang king."

In a field not far from the city, Luo Xuan sat on a rock, trying to catch his breath. He heard a man coming up from behind him. The man sang this song:

> "I am just a poor scholar
> I have no money, I just eat vegetables
> I do not want fame or high rank
> I only want to live in the forest
> I fish in the stream
> I read books in my cave
> I sing poems and drink wine

*Now I will help the new king
Luo Xuan must die!"*

Luo Xuan said, "Who are you?"

"My name is Li Jing." This man was the father of Nezha, Muzha and Jinzha. He had been the commander at Chentang Pass, then he became a disciple of Burning Lamp. "I am going to West Qi to help the new king. I have no gifts for him. But now I will make you a prisoner. That will be my gift to the king."

Chapter 65
The Crown Prince is Captured

The war drums have started, the sun has gone down
This is the day that Yin Jiao will be killed

Even with the magic seal, Yin Jiao will fail
If you leave the earth without a flag, can you rest?

Good wishes will not help them
But their names will be remembered

What a pity that both sons paid for their vows
Their souls flew away with the wind

☰ ☰ ☰

Li Jing's words angered Luo Xuan. He attacked. The two fought, sword against sword. Li Jing threw his golden pagoda in the air. Luo Xuan tried to run away but it was too late. The pagoda came down on his head, killing him instantly. His soul flew to the Terrace of Creation.

Li Jing continued on his way to West Qi City. He met with Jiang Ziya and the other immortals and generals, and told them what happened to Luo Xuan.

Burning Lamp said to them, "It's good that Luo Xuan is dead. But Yin Jiao still has the magic seal. It is very powerful, and we need a way to fight it. We need to gather all four of the magic flags: the Soaring Flame Flag, the Green Lotus Flag, the Yellow Apricot Flag, and the White Cloud Flag. Right now, we only have the Yellow Apricot Flag. We must get the other three."

"I will get the Soaring Flame Flag," said Grand Completion. "Laozi has it."

He flew away on a ray of golden light, and soon arrived at Mount Xuandu. He was greeted by one of Laozi's disciples. "Brother," he said, "would you please tell Laozi that I am here to see him?"

The disciple went away, and came back a few minutes later. "Laozi says you do not need to see him. He will give you the flag. Here it is." He handed the Soaring Flame Flag to Grand Completion. The immortal thanked the disciple, then took the flag back to West Qi.

Next, he flew to the west to see the Buddha. The Buddha was sixteen feet tall, with a round yellow face like the moon. The Buddha said, "Brother, I am sorry we have not met before. We are honored to have you visit us today."

Grand Completion bowed and replied, "As you know, Jiang Ziya is preparing to remove the tyrant and bring a new wise king. But the tyrant's son Yin Jiao is causing trouble. We need the Green Lotus Flag to stop him."

"I am sorry. Our way is different from your way. I do not want our flag to become dirty in the human world."

"Yes, our religions are different, but we are one family and we live in one world. We both agree that the human heart should obey the will of heaven."

"That may be true, brother, but the Green Lotus Flag must not touch the dust of the human world."

As they were discussing this, Zhunti[1] walked in. She said to the Buddha, "Brother, we have both looked to the southeast and seen red light rising thousands of feet up to heaven. This means that it's time for Buddhism to spread to the southeast. To do this, we must work together with other religions. Please give him the flag."

Buddha nodded and gave the Green Lotus Flag to Grand Completion. The Daoist thanked the two Buddhas, then he returned to West Qi.

Burning Lamp said, "All right, now we have three of the four flags. We can hang one in the south, one in the east, and on in the west. That will make Yin Jian flee to the north. We can capture him there."

"But where is the fourth flag, the White Cloud Flag?" asked Grand Completion.

None of the other immortals knew where it was. But Princess Long Ji was in the other room. She heard them talking, and came in to join

---

[1] This male immortal, Zhunti Daoren ("Person of the Way"), is loosely based on Cundi, a multi-armed female bodhisattva. She brought the Buddha's wisdom and laws from the West and enlightened the people of the Shang Dynasty. She is sometimes considered a manifestation of Guanyin.

them. She said, "I know where the flag is. My mother has it. Whenever there needs to be a conference at the Jade Pond, she raises the White Cloud Flag to call the immortals."

"Can you get it for us?"

"No. The only one who can get it is the Immortal of the South Pole."

Hearing this, Grand Completion jumped up and flew to Mount Kunlun. He waited there until he saw the Immortal of the South Pole. He told the immortal about the flag. The immortal replied, "Of course, I will help you. Go back to your home and wait for me."

Dressed in his official robe, his jade necklace, and holding a white stone tablet in his hand, Immortal of the South Pole flew to Jade Pond. He arrived there. Looking around, he saw jade palaces all around. They were covered with jewels and their floors were made of beautiful colored bricks.

He approached Golden Mother of Jade Pond and kowtowed to her. He said, "Golden Mother, you know that the wise king has appeared, and the phoenix has sung in West Qi. Recently the leaders of the three religions met. They decided that new gods will be created from ones who die in this great war. Now Yin Jiao, son of the tyrant king and disciple of Grand Completion, is fighting against the will of heaven. We must stop him. I am asking you to give us the White Cloud Flag, so we can capture him."

Golden Mother looked at him said nothing. But a moment later two golden doors opened. Four pairs of young maids came in, carrying the White Cloud Flag. They said, "Her Highness Golden Mother commands, 'The tyrant king must die, and King Wu must take the throne in Zhaoge. You are acting according to the will of Heaven, so I will give you this flag.' You may go now."

Immortal of the South Pole thanked them and returned to West Qi. He gave the flag to Jiang Ziya. Then he said goodbye and returned to his home in the South Pole.

Burning Lamp said to the immortals, "We cannot wait any longer. Heavenly Master of Outstanding Culture, take the Green Lotus Flag and wait on the east side of Mount Qi. Pure Essence, take the Soaring Flame flag and wait at the south side. King Wu, if he agrees to help us, will go to the west side with the White Cloud Flag. Jiang Ziya, you go with the king. I will go to the center of the camp with the Yellow Apricot Flag."

Then Burning Lamp called his generals. He said, "Huang Feihu, you will attack the front gate of the Shang camp. Deng Jiugong, attack the left side. Nangong Kuo, the right side. Nezha and Yang Jian, wait at the left side. Thunderbolt, wait at the right side. Huang Tianhua, follow me. Li Jing, Jinzha and Muzha, wait and see how the fighting goes, and help where you are needed."

The immortals, the generals, and many thousands of soldiers began to prepare. In the Shang camp, Yin Jiao's generals saw this. They said, "Your Highness, this looks bad. Perhaps we should withdraw to Zhaoge and wait for help from the king."

"Don't worry," replied Yin Jiao. "I have the Heaven Overturning Seal. Even my master fears it."

At first watch the cannons roared, and the battle started. Huang Feihu and a huge army attacked the front gate. The Shang army was having trouble fighting so many immortals and soldiers. Yin Jiao used his magic weapons but they did not work as he hoped. He used his strongest weapon, the Heaven Overturning Seal, to attack Yang Jian. But Yang Jian knew transformations and was not hurt by the magic seal.

Several Shang generals died in the fighting. Yin Jiao was surrounded by generals on all sides who attacked him with swords, lances and clubs. He rode away towards Mount Qi. Huang Feihu chased him for thirty li, then turned and returned to the city.

The battle was over. It was a great victory for the Zhou. Yin Jiao spent the night outdoors, not knowing what to do next.

The next morning, Heavenly Master of Outstanding Culture appeared on the East side of Mount Qi. He said, "Yin Jiao! Today you will die!"

Quickly, Yin Jiao threw his magic seal at Heavenly Master of Outstanding Culture. But the immortal waved his magic flag. The seal floated in the air, unable to come down past the flag. Yin Jiao called the seal back, put it in his robe, and rode away to the south.

Soon he saw Master Pure Essence. The master shouted, "Yin Jiao! You broke your oath. Now you will see the same fate as your brother!" Yin Jiao threw the magic seal at him, but the immortal waved his magic flag. Again, the seal floated in the air and could not come down. Yin Jiao fled towards the center.

Burning Lamp was waiting for him there. He shouted, "You damned fool! You made an oath and then you broke it. Now you will meet your death!" Yin Jiao attacked the immortal with his sword. Then he threw his seal, but it could not come near Burning Lamp's flag. He fled to the west.

Jiang Ziya and King Wu were there with a large army. Dragon and phoenix banners flew all around. King Wu was frightened when he saw the thing with three heads and six arms. But Jiang Ziya said to him, "Don't worry, Your Majesty. This is just the crown prince."

"Oh," said the king, "We must get down from our horse and bow to him."

"No, please don't do that. He is our enemy. I will deal with him."

Yin Jiao attacked Jiang Ziya, but the prime minister waved his flag and the magic seal could not touch him. Angry, Yin Jiao rode away to the north. The Zhou army chased him.

As he rode northward, the path became more and more narrow. Soon it was too narrow for his horse. He got off the horse and continued running on foot. He looked back and saw the Zhou army close behind him. He raised his hand and threw the magic seal at the mountain. There was a loud crash, and the mountain split in two. Between the two halves was a road, just wide enough for him to run through.

The Zhou army came towards him from all sides. Yin Jiao flew up on a dust cloud. But Burning Lamp clapped his hands together. The two halves of the mountain slammed together, trapping Yin Jiao's body between them. Only his head could be seen rising up from the ground.

Chapter 66
The Sorcerer Hong Jin

Strange magic and escape tricks
Generals lose their heads, flags are captured

Black fire calls to souls, covering the sun
Green flags are thrown down into the dust

Great ones are at the three mountain pass
A man with five breaths[1] stands before the cliff

The goddess princess does not know
That the matchmaker god has already made a plan

☰ ☰ ☰

King Wu and Jiang Ziya rode to the place where Yin Jiao was trapped in the mountain. King Wu jumped down from his horse and kowtowed to the young prince. He said, "Your Highness! Your minister Ji Fa is your poor servant. I would never do a thing like this to you. What my prime minister has done will harm my name for ten thousand years!"

Jiang Ziya took the king's elbow and lifted him up. He said, "Yin Jiao has gone against the will of heaven. He cannot escape his death."

"Please, prime minister, let the prince live!"

Burning Lamp said to the king, "Your Majesty, you don't understand. The prince has gone against the will of heaven. There is nothing you can do."

King Wu knelt down, burned incense, and said to the prince, "I've tried my best, Your Highness, but the masters all say that you must be punished. I'm sorry."

The immortals led the weeping king down the mountain. Then Grand

---

[1] The "five vital breaths" is a term from Daoist inner alchemy. It refers to the vital breath, or qi, in the five viscera. Each one corresponds to one of the five elements: the heart (fire), liver (wood), kidneys (water), lungs (metal), and spleen or stomach (earth). Daoists practiced inner alchemy to control and refine these breaths during meditation.

Completion went back to the top. He picked up a hoe and swung it. Yin Jian's head rolled onto the ground.

Yin Jiao's soul flew to the Terrace of Creation, but it was not yet ready to enter. It flew to the king's palace in Zhaoge. A great wind blew, turning day to night. The king was drinking with his concubines when he heard a voice calling him. He became very tired. He went to bed, falling asleep immediately. His concubines also joined him in the royal bed.

In his dream, a strange man came to him. The man had three heads and six arms. The man said, "Dear father, I am your eldest son, Yin Jiao. My head was cut off with a hoe. Please change your ways. Become a good king. Select a good man to be prime minister. If you don't, Jiang Ziya will bring his army to Zhaoge and your dynasty will end. Now I must go, or I will not be able to enter the Terrace of Creation. Good bye."

The Shang king woke up, confused. "How strange!" he cried. Daji, Hu Ximei and Concubine Wang woke up and asked him what happened. He told them about the dream.

"This dream comes from your mind. Don't believe it," said Daji. The king agreed, and he put the dream out of his mind.

A few days later, he heard that Yin Jiao and the commander of the army Zhang Shan were both dead. He needed a new commander. He selected Hong Jin, the commander of Sanshang Pass and a powerful sorcerer. Hong Jin took a hundred thousand soldiers and marched to West Qi. His army joined the rest of the Shang army.

The next day Hong Jin went to the city gates and demanded to see Jiang Ziya. Soon the cannons roared and the city gates opened. A great army marched out in formation. There were generals who looked like tigers, and Daoist immortals who looked like gods. In the center, dressed in Daoist robes, was Jiang Ziya.

"Are you Jiang Ziya?" asked Hong Jin.

Jiang Ziya did not answer this, but just said, "What's your name, General?"

"I am Commander Hong Jin. You oppose the will of heaven and of our king. His Majesty orders you to get down from your horse and come back to Zhaoge as my prisoner."

Jiang Ziya just laughed. He said, "If you are a great general, you must know that all 800 marquises and the entire kingdom are already on the Zhou side. Soon we will march together to Zhaoge and pull your tyrant king off his throne. Come over to our side now, or you will meet disaster."

Hong Jin shouted and attacked Jiang Ziya. They fought for a few rounds. Then Hong Jin stuck a black flag in the ground. The flag turned into a black door. Hong Jin rode through the door and disappeared.

One of the Zhou generals, a young man, raced through the door and was instantly killed by Hong Jin's sword. Then Hong Jin walked back through the door and picked up the flag. "Does anyone else want to die?" he asked.

Deng Chanyu shouted, "Damn you! Here I come!" and attacked him. Hong Jin stuck the black flag in the ground again and rode through the black door. But Deng Chanyu did not follow him. She threw a small stone through the door, hitting the sorcerer in the face. Screaming in pain, he closed the door, picked up the flag, and ran back to the Shang camp.

During the night, Hong Jin used some elixir to heal his wounded face. And the next day, he came out again and called to Deng Chanyu to fight him again.

But Princess Long Ji stopped her from going out to face him. She said, "I know this trick. There are two doors. The black flag is the inner door, but there is also a white flag which is the outer door. Let me handle this."

She borrowed a horse from Jiang Ziya, and rode out to meet the sorcerer. Hong Jin asked her name. She replied, "You don't need to know my name. Get down from your horse and prepare to die."

Hong Jin attacked her, then he stuck the black flag in the ground and rode through the black door. But Long Ji stuck a white flag in the ground. It turned into a white door. She rode through the white door and appeared just behind Hong Jin. She slashed at his back with her sword, hitting his armor. Crying in pain, he rode away.

The princess followed him, shouting, "I will chase you through the sky or under the earth until I hold your head in my hand!"

Hong Jin jumped off his horse and tried to fly away on a dust cloud. But the princess jumped onto a wooden cloud. She knew that wood can conquer earth.[1]

Now very frightened, Hong Jin threw something into the sea. It turned into a giant sea dragon. Hong Jin jumped on its back and rode it out to sea, creating giant waves that crashed like thunder. But the princess threw a small object into the sea. It became a huge creature, a dolphin.

She jumped onto the dolphin's back. The dolphin swam up to the sea dragon. The sea dragon lost its strength and stopped swimming. The princess easily captured Hong Jin, tied him up and carried him back to West Qi.

---

[1] Each of the five elements conquer another. Wood conquers earth, earth conquers water, water conquers fire, fire conquers metal, and metal conquers wood. But as the historian Pan Gu pointed out in the second century A.D., fire comes from wood, metal comes from earth, water comes from metal by melting, wood comes from water through plant growth, and earth comes from fire as ashes.

Chapter 67
Jiang Ziya, Commander of the Army

A general is named at the golden tower, many gods are present
Large pieces of gold hang in the sleeve[1]

The dream of the flying bear is now coming true
He is very old but now he meets his fate

Extend the Zhou dynasty, pass on the work
People not yet born will speak of the people here today

Good fortune or long life, very few have both
This story will be told for a very long time

☰ ☰ ☰

Princess Long Ji brought Hong Jin, bound with ropes, back to West Qi City to face Jiang Ziya. The prime minister ordered General Nangong Kuo to cut off the sorcerer's head. The general led Hong Jin outside. One of his soldiers raised his sword and was just ready to cut off the sorcerer's head. But just then, a strange Daoist ran up and shouted "Stop! Stop!"

Nangong Kuo told the soldier to wait, then he walked inside with the Daoist to talk with Jiang Ziya.

The prime minister asked, "Where do you come from, brother?"

The Daoist replied, "Prime Minister, my name is Heavenly Matchmaker[2]. I must tell you that Hong Jin and Princess Long Ji are fated to be man and wife."

Jiang Ziya was surprised to hear this. He asked Deng Chanyu to go and talk with the princess about this. She told the princess. She replied, "I was sent to this mortal world as punishment. Now it seems that things

---

[1] Robes in ancient China did not have pockets, so valuables were placed in the sleeve behind the elbow.
[2] This is Yuè Xià Lǎorén, literally "The Old Man Under the Moon" and sometimes just called Yue Lao. He is the god of marriage and love. He lives in the underworld, and appears at night to tie predestined couples together with a red cord, after which nothing can prevent their union.

are getting even worse. But Heavenly Matchmaker has power over marriages, so who am I to say no?"

Jiang Ziya and Heavenly Matchmaker were happy to hear this. The prime minister set Hong Jin free. He returned to his camp and gathered his army. Then he brought back the army and joined it to the rest of the Zhou army. He and Long Ji were married on the third day of the third month of the thirty-fifth year of the Shang king's reign.

Finally, after years of fighting, the West Qi army was ready to march east. Jiang Ziya went to King Wu's court and told him all the reasons why it was time to move against Zhaoge.

King Wu sat silently for a long time. Then he said, "Prime minister, you are right that the Shang king is evil and has harmed his people. For that, we should attack him. But remember what our father Ji Chang said. He said that no matter what, no one should attack his king. If we allow you to attack the king in Zhaoge, we will be disloyal to our own father. We think we should just wait. Give him time and see if he changes his ways. What do you think of that?"

Jiang Ziya replied, "I cannot forget your father's words. But all the marquises and their armies will be at Mengjin waiting for us. What will happen if we do not come?"

"They may do as they wish. We must do what is right."

"But Your Majesty, we cannot just watch the people suffer. We must obey the will of heaven!"

San Yisheng, the supreme minister, stepped forward. He said, "Your Majesty, please listen to your prime minister. The Shang king has attacked us many times. Let's march to Mengjin and meet with the marquises. Together we will wait for the king to change his ways. In this way, the people of the kingdom will have peace and the marquises will trust us."

King Wu agreed to this. He decided that it was time to name Jiang Ziya to be commander of the Zhou army. The next day, workers began to build a high terrace. It was to be used to offer prayers to heaven, earth, the rivers and the mountains. The workers finished the terrace in just ten days.

The king wrote the following regulations for the army:

These are the rules for all soldiers in the Zhou army.

First, you must advance when you hear the sound of drums, retreat when you hear the sound of gongs, not run away from the enemy in battle, and act quickly when commanded. If you violate this rule, you will be put to death.

Second, you must treat other soldiers and officers with respect, return to camp on time, and obey all camp rules. If you violate this rule, you will be put to death.

Third, you must not get drunk, you must report bad deeds immediately to your commander, and you must not tell lies. If you violate this rule, you will be put to death.

Fourth, you must speak well of the generals, not complain, and obey orders. If you violate this rule, you will be put to death.

Fifth, you must not make loud noises or fight with others. If you violate this rule, you will be put to death.

Sixth, you must not steal money or grain from the army. If you violate this rule, you will be put to death.

Seventh, you must not believe in ghosts and demons, or use dreams as a way to spread lies, or say anything to cause trouble. If you violate this rule, you will be put to death.

Eighth, you must never mix up right and wrong, or fight with other soldiers, or cause soldiers to fight each other. If you violate this rule, you will be put to death.

Ninth, you must treat the local people well, and never do anything to sexually harm women. If you violate this rule, you will be put to death.

Tenth, you must not steal money or things from other soldiers, or speak badly of others. If you violate this rule, you will be put to death.

Eleventh, you must not try to listen to secrets told by officers. If you violate this rule, you will be put to death.

Twelfth, you must never tell the army's plans to the enemy. If you violate this rule, you will be put to death.

Thirteenth, you must always do what you are told, even if it means a change in your job or rank. If you violate this rule, you will be put to death.

Fourteenth, you must not run around making noise or disobey orders. If you violate this rule, you will be put to death.

Fifteenth, you must never pretend to be sick, wounded or dead in order to avoid battle. If you violate this rule, you will be put to death.

Sixteenth, if you are in charge of money or food, you must never give extra money or food to your friends, or sell food for money. If you violate this rule, you will be put to death.

Seventeenth, if you spy on the enemy, you must be careful and report exactly what you see. If you violate this rule, you will be put to death.

On the 15th day of the third month, San Yisheng went to Jiang Ziya and brought him to see the king in his mansion. Jiang Ziya wore his Daoist robes. He approached the king. The king bowed and said, "Commander! Please ride with me." The two of them got into the royal carriage.

Together they rode from the city to Mount Qi. Red flags were flying on both sides of the road. Thousands of people watched them.

They arrived at the terrace. The king and the prime minister got out of the royal carriage and got into the royal sedan chair. Servants carried the sedan chair into the terrace.

The terrace was thirty feet high and square. It had three floors. They entered the first floor and saw 125 guards. Twenty-five of them wore yellow robes and stood in the center. Twenty-five more wore green and stood in the east. The same number wore white in the west, red in the south, and black in the north.

They went up to the second floor. There they saw 365 guards standing in a large circle.

They went up to the top floor. They saw seventy-two generals, each holding a weapon.

On the top floor, San Yisheng helped the king get down from the sedan chair. The king turned and said to Jiang Ziya, "Commander, please come down from the sedan chair and face south."

San Yisheng said to everyone, "The king has sent this poor minister to pray before the gods of the five mountains and the four rivers. Heaven is kind, but the king in Zhaoge has no love for heaven. He makes the people suffer, he drinks and lusts with women, he has forgotten his filial duty, he removed the heart of a loyal minister, he put a loyal grand duke in jail, and he only listens to the minions. For that reason, the gods have turned away from him. Our wise King Wu now names Jiang Ziya as commander of the army, to attack the tyrant so that all can live in peace. May all the gods bless us and help us to victory."

More ministers spoke, saying similar words. Then while music played, one of the ministers gave Jiang Ziya the yellow royal axe, the white scepter, and the dragon and phoenix seals of office. They gave him a golden helmet covered with jewels, and Jiang Ziya put it on his head. Someone gave him a jade belt, and he put it on. Finally, someone gave him the royal sword, and he put it on.

Jiang Ziya turned to King Wu and said, "Thank you, Your Majesty. I am just an old servant. But I know that every servant must do his duty, otherwise the country will not have peace, the ministers will not serve their king, and the army will not see victory. You have named me commander and given me this power. I will do this job as best as I can."

Then Jiang Ziya said, "Tell the generals that I will meet with them in three days. First, I must go and speak with my immortal brothers." He left the terrace and went to the south side of Mount Qi. There he met with Nezha and the other immortals. As they talked, the sound of music came from the sky. They looked up, and Heavenly Primogenitor floated down. They all knelt and said, "Long live the grand master!"

Heavenly Primogenitor smiled and said, "Jiang Ziya, you have studied on Mount Kunlun for forty years. Now you are a powerful leader!" He said to his servant, "Bring the wine!"

Jiang Ziya drank the first cup as the master said, "May this cup help you serve your king!" He drank the second cup as the master said, "May this cup help you rule the country in peace!" He drank the third cup as the master said, "May this cup help you lead the marquises!"

After drinking the three cups of wine, Jiang Ziya knelt before the master. The master asked, "Why are you kneeling, Jiang Ziya?"

"Master, I have questions about the future."

"You don't need to worry about that. Here is a poem for you to remember:

> *A trap to kill immortals at Jiepai Pass*
> *Sickness at Chuanyun Pass*
> *Watch out for Da, Zhao, Guang, Xian and De*[1]

---

[1] These are the five sons of General Yu Hualong of Tong Pass, where Jiang Ziya is fated to fight the Shang army. They are, from oldest to youngest: Yu Da, Yu Zhao, Yu Guang, Yu Xian, and Yu De.

After the Ten Thousand Immortal Trap there will be peace."

"Your disciple will remember this," said Jiang Ziya. Then the master flew away on a gust of wind.

Heavenly Master of Outstanding Culture was also getting ready to leave, but the disciples gathered around him to ask about their future.

Jinzha asked, "Please, master, what will happen to me in the coming battle?"

Heavenly Master replied, "You will become an immortal."

Nezha asked, "What is my future?"

"You will do great things at Sishui Pass."

Muzha asked, "What about me?"

"Be sure to use the magic tricks that I have taught you."

Thunderbolt asked, "What will happen to me?"

"You will bring peace to the country with two apricots."

Yang Jian asked, "What is my future?"

"You are not like the others. That is all I can tell you."

Li Jing asked, "What is my fate?"

"You will rise up to heaven in your mortal body and become the guardian of Mount Divine Hawk."

Finally, Huang Tianhua asked about his fate. The master said nothing for a minute. Then he said, "My dear disciple, I cannot tell you your future. But I have some words for you to remember."

Chapter 68
Two Daoists Stop the Army

For trying to stop the rebellion
They will be remembered for years

The king listened
He remembered his father's words

Good people live in goodness
Brave people live in bravery

I read the story and cry alone
Tasting my own tears[1]

≡ ≡ ≡

The generals of West Qi watched the immortals fly away to their mountain homes. Huang Tianhua was still thinking about what one of the immortals had said to him,

You must avoid a man named Gao
Bees fly together above the Golden Chicken Mountains
Do great things and people will remember you for a thousand years
But if you forget my words, you will suffer

Earth Traveler Sun was also thinking about the words spoken to him,

You can travel quickly underground
But you must be very careful!
Watch out for a pool of blood near a cliff
A beast will bite you and you will die

The generals and their armies began preparing for the battles to come. After three days, Jiang Ziya climbed to the terrace on Mount Qi. He looked down and saw six hundred thousand soldiers ready to march. He

---

[1] This poem is about Boyi and Suqi, the two Daoists who are met by King Wu and Jiang Ziya on the road to Mengjin. King Wu recalls his father's instructions to remain loyal to the Shang king, no matter what. In Chinese folklore, Boyi and Suqi are revered for their loyalty, however misguided it may have been.

divided the huge Zhou army into four smaller vanguards. He ordered Huang Tianhua to lead the front, Nangong Kuo the left, Wu Ji the right, and Nezha the rear.

To make sure the armies had enough food and supplies, he told Yang Jian, Earth Traveler Sun and Zheng Lun to take care of that. He drank three cups of wine with them, and put red flowers on their chests.

There were over a hundred generals in the Zhou army, including thirty-six sons of King Wen.

Jiang Ziya called Huang Feihu to meet him on the terrace. He told him, "The Shang Dynasty will fall. But we must still be very careful. Some of their generals are powerful magicians. General Huang, you must train our soldiers and make sure they are ready for the coming battles."

King Wu went to see his mother and say goodbye to her. He said, "Mother, we have been asked to go with Jiang Ziya to meet the other marquises at Mengjin. We will not be gone for long."

"You should go," she said. "Make sure you listen to Jiang Ziya's advice." They had one last dinner together.

The next day, the army began marching towards Mengjin. It was the twenty-fourth day of the third month of the thirtieth year of the reign of King Di Xin of Shang.

Soon after they left West Qi City, they met two Daoists standing in the middle of the road. They disliked the Shang king, but they did not want the army to attack him. "We want to speak to your commander!" they said.

King Wu and Jiang Ziya rode forward to meet the Daoists. They tried to bow, then they said, "We are sorry we cannot bow to you because of our armor. Tell us, why are you stopping us from marching?"

"Where are you going?" the Daoists asked.

"We are going to Mengjin, and from there to Zhaoge. The king is evil, and it is the will of heaven that he be punished. All the marquises agree on this."

"A son should never speak of the faults of his father, and a minister should never tell others the evils of his master. Yes, the king is evil, but we should help him to change his ways. The ancients say, 'Great good can touch the hearts of evil people, and great love can win the hearts of bandits.' You should remain loyal to the king, and try to change evil into good."

King Wu said nothing. But Jiang Ziya replied, "I understand your words, but you do not see the truth. The sky is falling, the earth is breaking apart, the seas are burning. Heaven is angry and wants us to do this job."

Now the other generals were becoming impatient and angry. The two Daoists saw this. They grabbed the reins of King Wu's horse and shouted, "You are not a filial son!"

Other generals rushed forward to kill the Daoists, but Jiang Ziya stopped them, saying, "Don't kill them. They are holy men."

The two Daoists turned and walked away. They did not want to see the battles to come, and later after the war was over, they refused to eat food made by the new dynasty. They went to live in the mountains, eating wild vegetables and grasses. Nobody ever saw them again.

The Zhou army continued towards Mengjin. When they reached the Golden Chicken Mountains, they saw another army on the mountain. Red flags fluttered in the wind. Jiang Ziya told Nangong Kuo to go and speak with them. Nangong Kuo rode his horse towards the army, while Zhou cannons roared behind him.

Soon he came to another general on a black horse, a man named Wei Ben. "Who are you and why are you stopping us?" asked Nangong Kuo.

"Who are you and where are you going?" replied Wei Ben.

"We are going to the capital to kill the Shang king!" said Nangong Kuo, and he attacked the other man with his sword. They fought for thirty rounds.

The enemy general was a very good fighter. Nangong Kuo was soon tired and covered with sweat. Wei Ben rushed forward and captured Nangong Kuo. He said, "I will not hurt you. Go back to your army and tell Commander Jiang to come see me."

Nangong Kuo returned to the army and reported to Jiang Ziya. Jiang Ziya was furious. "You are the general of one fourth of my army. You lost the fight. And now you dare to return here and tell me to go see that enemy?" He ordered his men to tie up Nangong Kuo and cut off his head.

Watching from the Shang side, Wei Ben saw and heard this. He shouted, "Don't hurt him! Let me talk with Commander Jiang. I have important words for him."

Jiang Ziya rode forward slowly, surrounded by two dozen generals. Soldiers rode beside them holding red banners. Wei Ben got down from his horse and knelt in front of Jiang Ziya. He said, "Commander, I can fight, I can ride, and I can lead an army. But I have never found a good master until now. I want to join you in your battle against the Shang king. Please accept me."

Jiang Ziya replied, "We are lucky to meet you. We are happy to have you join our army." Then he turned to Nangong Kuo and said, "I should kill you for what you did. But I will forgive you because Wei Ben has joined us. He will take your place as leader of the left vanguard. You will stay with me." Nangong Kuo thanked him for sparing his life.

In Zhaoge, the Shang king heard that the Zhou army was marching. He ordered Kong Xuan, a powerful magician who was the commander of Sanshan Pass, to attack the Zhou army.

Kong Xuan took a hundred thousand soldiers and marched to Sishui Pass. When he arrived, he found that the Zhou army had already left there. He marched for two more days and arrived at Golden Chicken Mountains. He set up camp and prepared for battle.

Chapter 69
Trouble at Golden Chicken Mountains

Punish crimes and kill tyrants
This is Yuxu Palace's plan

It is fated by heaven
But still has never been easy

Only a foolish peacock fights heaven
Barriers fall at Golden Chicken Mountain

No need to talk about tricks
All the disciples will go to the west[1]

≡ ≡ ≡

Jiang Ziya sat in his tent, thinking about the army that had just arrived. He thought, "This is strange. Heavenly Primogenitor told me there would be thirty-six invasions. And we have had all thirty-six." But then he counted them on his fingers, and realized that there had only been thirty-five. So, this must be the last one.

He ordered Huang Tianhua to ride out on his jade unicorn to meet the other army. He shouted, "I am Huang Tianhua, a general under Jiang Ziya. Tell me your name, so I can write it down later after I kill you."

"You are just a little chicken," replied the Shang general. "How dare you fight me?" He attacked Huang Tianhua with a halberd. Huang fought back with two hammers, then he rode away. The Shang general followed him. Suddenly Huang Tianhua turned and threw his Fire Dragon Javelin, knocking the other man from his horse. Huang Tianhua cut off the man's head and returned to his camp.

Jiang Ziya picked up a brush and was getting ready to write something about Huang Tianhua's victory. But as he dipped the brush in ink, the end of the brush broke off. Jiang Ziya did not say anything about this,

---

[1] Yuxu Palace on Mount Kunlun is the home of Heavenly Primogenitor, the leader of Chan Daoism. In the last line, "go to the west" refers to the Buddhist traditional belief that souls go to die in the west.

but he knew what it meant. Huang Tianhua would soon lose his head.

The next day, Kong Xuan sent another general out to fight. This man was dressed in pink robe and golden armor, and held a cutlass in his hand. Jiang Ziya sent Wu Ji, the woodcutter. The Shang general shouted, "Who are you?"

"I am Wu Ji, a general under Commander Jiang Ziya."

"Jiang is just an old fisherman, and you are a poor woodcutter. You make a good pair!"

Wu Ji shouted angrily and tried to stab the Shang general. The Shang general blocked him. They continued to fight. The Shang general grew tired. Wu Ji stabbed him in the chest, killing him.

Now Kong Xuan had lost two of his generals. He sent another general, a man named Gao Jineng who had a bag full of centipedes and bees. Jiang Ziya sent Nezha. Gao Jineng was afraid of Nezha and his powerful weapons. As soon as Nezha took out his Universal Ring, the man fled back to his camp.

The next day, Kong Xuan rode out himself. He wore golden armor and rode a red horse. Bright colorful lights of green, yellow, red, white and black shone from his back. He called for Jiang Ziya.

Jiang Ziya rode up on his horse. Kong said, "You were once a Shang minister, but now you are a rebel. If you stop now, you may keep your lands. Otherwise, I will destroy all your cities."

Jiang Ziya replied, "Why do you fight for such a cruel king? Every heart has turned against him. Join us now and we will welcome you, General."

Kong shouted angrily and attacked. Hong Jin, the sorcerer who had married Princess Long Ji, rode up to help his commander. He shouted, "All eight hundred marquises have joined us. Why do you fight alone?"

Hong Jin had several magic flags. He pushed one of the flags into the ground. When he waved his cutlass at the flag, it turned into a door. But when he tried to enter the door, Kong just laughed. He turned around so his back was facing Hong Jin. Yellow light came from his back and hit Hong Jin, who disappeared, leaving only his horse behind.

Jiang Ziya retreated back to his camp. He thought about Kong Xuan and the light that came from his back. He knew that the five lights had something to do with the five elements, but he did not know what. He decided to attack that night, hoping to surprise his enemy.

Later that night, in the Shang camp, Kong Xuan flashed his lights. Hong Jin fell to the floor and was taken prisoner. A powerful wind blew through the camp. Kong Xuan did a divination with his fingers, and learned of the attack coming that night. He ordered his generals to prepare for the Zhou attack.

When the Zhou came, the Shang were ready for them. Thunderbolt was taken prisoner by Kong Xuan's yellow light. Nezha was captured by his white light. Huang Tianhua was met by Gao Jineng and his cloud of centipedes and bees. They stung his jade unicorn, who reared up and threw Huang Tianhua to the ground. Gao Jineng killed him with his sword.

Hundreds of soldiers from both sides fought through the night. Dead bodies covered the mountain, the grasses were red with blood.

After the battle, Huang Feihu cried when he learned that his son was dead. Jiang Ziya said to him, "General, your son's name will be remembered for a thousand years. Now we have to get rid of those centipedes and bees. Go find Chong Heihu. Tell him to use his hawks to get rid of those dangerous insects."

Huang Feihu left immediately. He rode on his ox to Flying Phoenix Mountain. When he got there, he saw three generals fighting each other. But looking more closely, he saw that they were laughing and joking at each other. The three men stopped fighting when they saw him. One of them said, "Prince Huang Feihu, we are pleased to meet you!"

"How do you know me, General?" asked Huang Feihu. "And why are you fighting?"

"We recognize you. And we are fighting just to have some fun."

Huang Feihu said, "I am in Jiang Ziya's army. We are traveling to Mengjin to meet the other marquises and begin the battle against the Shang king. My son was killed by a cloud of centipedes and bees. I need help from Chong Heihu's hawks to get rid of them."

"We can take you to see him. He is training his troops for the coming battle, but he cannot begin the fight yet. He must wait for King Wu to arrive. Let's go see him tomorrow." They invited Huang Feihu to stay overnight.

The next day, the four of them rode to Chong City to meet with Chong

Heihu. Huang Feihu greeted him, then explained that they needed his help. Chong Heihu agreed at once. Together, they rode to the Zhou camp and met with King Wu.

"Your Majesty," said Chong Heihu, "how dare Kong Xuan try to stop you. You are acting according to the will of Heaven!"

King Wu replied, "We think Heaven is not with us right now. Why else would we face such problems? Do you think perhaps we should withdraw and ask the Shang king to forgive us?"

"No, Your Majesty! All the marquises are depending on you, as are the generals, the soldiers, and the common people."

King Wu agreed. The next day, Chong Heihu and several other generals rode out towards the Shang camp. He was met by Gao Jineng, who said, "You are all rebels and traitors! Why have you come all the way here to cause so much trouble?"

"You damned fool!" replied Chong Heihu. "Did you kill Huang Tianhua?"

Gao Jineng smiled and said, "Yes, and we have captured Nezha and Thunderbolt. What can you do about it?" He attacked Chong Heihu, who fought back with his two axes.

More Zhou generals joined the fight. Huang Feihu rushed forward, shouting, "I will kill you!"

Chapter 70
The Mystery of the Five Lights

Zhunti came from the west
His virtue is deep and powerful

Lotus leaves blow in the wind
Lotus flowers are untouched by rain

Kong Xuan is defeated by the golden bow
And the silver halberd

Under a swaying tree
He becomes Zhunti's peacock[1]

≡ ≡ ≡

Now Gao Jineng was fighting against five Zhou generals. He opened his bag. Thousands of centipedes and bees flew out. The Zhou generals were frightened, but Chong Heihu opened a gourd he was carrying on his back. Black smoke poured out. The black smoke turned into thousands of hawks. They flew into the sky and quickly ate all the centipedes and bees.

Gao Jineng shouted, "How dare you kill my magic insects!" He fought against the five Zhou generals, but there were too many for him. Huang Feihu stabbed him in the ribs. When he fell off his horse, Huang Feihu cut off his head.

Kong Xuan saw his general die. He rushed towards the five Zhou generals. Huang Feihu laughed and said, "You really are a fool!"

But Kong Xuan was ready for them. He shot five lights towards the five generals, and they all disappeared. He returned to his camp, waved the lights again, and all five generals fell to the ground. They were tied up and taken prisoner.

---

[1] This is about the downfall of Kong Xuan, the commander of Sanshan Pass, who is defeated by Zhunti's many weapons. He is transformed into his original form, a peacock, and is ridden away by Zhunti at the beginning of the next chapter. The lotus referenced in the second line is a metaphor for Buddhism.

Back at the Zhou camp, the generals met to discuss the problem of the five lights. Yang Jian said, "We need to understand what kind of demon this Kong Xuan is. I still have the Demon Exposing Mirror that I got from Master of the Clouds. I will use it tomorrow when Commander Jiang meets with Kong Xuan."

The next day, Jiang Ziya went out to talk with Kong Xuan. Yang Jian was standing nearby, under the banners. He took out his mirror and looked at Kong Xuan. Kong Xuan saw him. He laughed and said, "Yang Jian! A warrior must not sneak around like that. Come here and look at me!"

Yang Jian came closer and looked at Kong Xuan in the mirror. He saw something with many colors, rolling around. He did not understand what he saw.

Kong Xuan attacked him. The two of them fought for thirty rounds. Yang Jian released his heavenly dog, but the dog disappeared in Kong Xuan's lights. Quickly, Yang Jian rode away before the light could hit him too. "Come back and meet me again!" shouted Kong Xuan.

Next, Li Jing approached the magician. He threw his golden pagoda into the air, but it disappeared in a yellow light. Kong Xuan captured him. Two of Li Jing's sons, Jinzha and Muzha, rushed forward but were also captured by the red light.

Jiang Ziya saw many of his best generals captured by the colored lights. He rushed forward. Kong Xuan tried to hit him with green light, but Jiang Ziya wrapped himself in his Yellow Apricot Flag. It protected him from the lights.

While they were fighting, Deng Chanyu grabbed a small rock and threw it, hitting Kong Xuan in the face. The magician tried to flee back to his camp. As he rode his horse, Princess Long Ji stabbed him in the left shoulder. He cried out in pain and almost fell off his horse.

In the Zhou camp, Jiang Ziya sat down with his generals. "What can we do?" he asked them.

King Wu sent a messenger, asking Jiang Ziya to meet with him in the royal tent. When he arrived, King Wu said, "Our soldiers have left their families to come and fight for West Qi, but we have lost many battles. We are also worried because we are an unfilial son, going against the wishes of the late king. Do you think it is time for us to withdraw?"

"Your Majesty," replied Jiang Ziya, "that would be going against the will of heaven."

"But if heaven is with us, why are we having so much trouble?"

Jiang Ziya thought about this. Perhaps, he thought, it was time to return home. He gave an order for the army to prepare to move out in the morning. A few minutes later, Lu Ya came running into the tent. Breathless, he said, "Sir, you cannot retreat. That would put all of us in danger. It is the will of heaven that we fight."

Now Jiang Ziya did not know what to do. He told the army to stay in camp until he gave more orders.

The next day Lu Ya went out to fight Kong Xuan. He was almost captured. He just managed to turn into a rainbow and flee. He said to Jiang Ziya, "I don't know what he is. But he is very powerful."

Earth Traveler Sun arrived, bringing food and supplies for the army. He heard what had happened. "I will fight this magician!" he shouted.

He ran out and attacked Kong Xuan with his cudgel. Kong Xuan looked down at the little man and laughed. "Oh, so this little man has come to play with me!" He tried to strike Earth Traveler Sun with his cutlass, but he could not reach him. He thought, "It's time for this little man to die. I will just get off my horse and kick him to death."

Kong Xuan dismounted. He was used to fighting on horseback, not on foot, so it was difficult for him to fight Earth Traveler Sun. The little man hit him several times, and danced away whenever the cutlass came near. While they were fighting, Deng Chanyu threw another stone, hitting Kong Xuan in the face. Kong Xuan, bleeding heavily, ran away.

The next morning, Kong Xuan demanded to fight Deng Chanyu again. But Jiang Ziya would not let her fight the magician. He ordered a sign of truce to be hung on the camp gate.

Just then, Burning Lamp arrived, saying, "I know this man very well. I will meet him." Jiang Ziya took down the sign of truce, and Burning Lamp went out to meet Kong Xuan.

"Lay down your weapons and surrender!" shouted Burning Lamp. But Kong Xuan did not lay down his weapons. They began to fight. Burning Lamp threw his magic pearls in the air, but Kong Xuan made them disappear. Burning Lamp threw up his Purple Begging Bowl, but it also disappeared.

Burning Lamp shouted, "Disciple, come here!" A huge eagle flew towards them and attacked the magician. A red beam of light shot into the sky. There was a great sound like thunder. The eagle fell to the ground.

Burning Lamp turned into a beam of light and flew away. Later, he asked the eagle what it saw. The eagle replied, "I do not know. His body is protected by colorful light. He has two wings, so he is probably a bird, but I don't know what kind."

A messenger arrived, saying that a Buddha had come to see them. Jiang Ziya and Burning Lamp went out to greet him. It was Zhunti, a bodhisattva who brought the Buddha's wisdom from the west. Zhunti said, "I am a Buddha from the west. I see that Kong Xuan is blocking your path. I am here to take him back with me, so he can live happily in the Western Region."

Burning Lamp said, "We are so glad you are here!" Zhunti went out to see the magician.

Chapter 71
The Battle of Three Passes

The prime minister commands chariots
And brave soldiers

Lords drink and play
The people sing outside their homes

Swords shine in heaven's light
Army flags flutter in the sunlight

Heaven on their side
They come like ocean waves on the sand[1]

≡ ≡ ≡

"Please come out, I want to talk with you," said Zhunti.

Kong Xuan came out of the Shang camp. He saw a strange looking Buddha, holding a small branch in one hand. He said, "Who are you and what do you want?"

Zhunti replied, "Kong Xuan, please stop all this killing and come with me. We will go together to the Western Region. You can remove all the dirt that is on your feathers, and become an immortal."

Kong Xuan swung his cutlass at Zhunti, but he just waved his small branch. The cutlass sliced through empty air. Kong Xuan attacked again with a golden staff, but the Buddha waved his small branch again and the staff fell to the ground. Then he tried hitting Zhunti with red light. But the Buddha just smiled. There was a bright light like lightning, and a loud sound like thunder. When Kong Xuan could see and hear again, Zhunti was behind him. Now he had twenty-four heads, eighteen hands, and held many different objects in his hands. He sang,

> *"Golden light comes from the sun*
> *The great way comes from the west*

---

[1] This poem contrasts the decadence and complacency of the Shang nobles and common people, with the immense power of the approaching Zhou army.

> *Thousands of necklaces, thousands of gems*
> *Many lights are born one by one*
> *The divine staff is not often seen*
> *How can you hold the cup of seven jewels?*
> *Let us go together to the lotus terrace*
> *We will see the completion of the great path."*

Zhunti tied a piece of silk around Kong Xuan's neck and said, "Now, please show us your original form."

Kong Xuan changed into a beautiful peacock. Zhunti climbed on the bird's back, and said to Jiang Ziya, "We must go now. Your friends are waiting for you in camp. Goodbye." They flew into the air and headed west.

Jiang Ziya and the other generals went to Kong Xuan's camp to allow his army to surrender. Then they returned to the Zhou camp, where all the people captured by Kong Xuan were waiting for them. The army marched to Sishui Pass and rested there for three days.

Han Rong, the commander of Sishui Pass, stood on the wall and looked out at the great West Qi army. He sent an urgent message to Zhaoge, asking more soldiers to be sent immediately.

Jiang Ziya decided to attack three passes at once. He ordered Huang Feihu to attack Good Dream Pass, and Hong Jin to attack Green Dragon Pass. He would lead the attack himself against Sishui Pass.

At Good Dream Pass, the commander rode out to meet Su Quanzhong. "You damned rebel," he shouted, "Your own sister is the queen of Shang. How can you be so evil as to fight against her?" But Su Quanzhong was the better fighter, and after a long battle he killed the commander of the pass.

At Green Dragon Pass, Hong Jin ordered Nangong Kuo to ride forward and do battle with Hu Lei, one of the generals guarding the pass. He defeated the general and captured him. Nangong Kuo brought him back to his camp, but Hu Lei refused to kneel before Hong Jin, saying, "You think you are a great general, but in my eyes, you are just a pig. I wish I could eat your flesh and drink your blood." Hong Jin did not reply. He just told his soldiers to cut off the man's head.

But a few minutes later, a messenger came in to report that Hu Lei was waiting outside the camp, ready to fight. "Cut off the head of that messenger," shouted Hong Jin. "How dare he give such a false report?"

But before they did that, they looked outside. Sure enough, Hu Lei was standing there, sword in hand. Nangong Kuo fought with him, and again they took him captive. This time, though, they did not know what to do with him. They did not want to just cut off his head again. They asked Princess Long Ji to come and give them some advice. She smiled and said, "He is using a very simple kind of magic. I can easily deal with it." She took a needle from her robe and pushed it into the middle of Hu Lei's head. "Go ahead, cut off his head now," she said. They did, and Hu Lei died.

The commander of the pass knew his army could not win against the Zhou. He ordered the flags of Shang taken down, and the flags of Zhou raised. But as he was getting ready to surrender, a female Daoist came to see him. "What can I do for you?" asked the commander.

"I am Mother Fiery Spirit. Hu Lei was my disciple. I heard he was killed by the Zhou, and I want my revenge. Tell me, why are you not fighting these rebels?"

"There are too many of them, Master. I have only twenty thousand soldiers and just a few generals. I must surrender to save the lives of my army and my people. If you are angry with me, please go ahead and kill me."

"That will not be necessary. Raise the Shang flags again. Put up the sign of truce. And give me three thousand soldiers. I have a special job for them."

She ordered the three thousand soldiers to take off their shoes, dress in red, and wear their hair loose on their shoulders. Each of them wrote the words "wind" and "fire" on the bottoms of their feet. Each one carried a cutlass in one hand, a flag in the other, and a paper gourd on their back.

She trained them for seven days, then she ordered the sign of truce be taken down. She rode out of the pass on a golden-eyed camel, with her soldiers behind her. Hong Jin was waiting for her. She shouted, "Hong Jin, here I come!" and rushed towards him, waving two ancient swords. "Get down from your horse or you will die."

Hong Jin tried to use his magic gate, but Mother Fiery Spirit took off her golden hat. Immediately a ray of golden light shot from the top of her head. Hong Jin could not see her, but she could see him. She stabbed him with her sword. Wounded, he rode away on his horse.

The three thousand soldiers rushed into the Zhou camp. Everywhere they went, they brought wind and fire. The entire camp was burning.

Princess Long Ji saw her husband riding away but she had no time to go and help him. She ran around the camp, reciting magic spells to put out the fires. She did not see Mother Fiery Spirit come up from behind her and stab her in the back.

Chapter 72
The Immortals Argue

Three bows to honor the great immortal
In his palace

Phoenixes dance in pairs
Deer sing before the green fence

This is the beginning of endless conflicts
And many deaths

The Zhou are strong
They receive wisdom from the west[1]

≡ ≡ ≡

Princess Long Ji screamed in pain. She rode to her husband, who was also badly wounded. The two of them returned to the Zhou camp and put medicine on their wounds. They sent a messenger to Jiang Ziya, telling him of their defeat and asking for more soldiers.

Jiang Ziya heard the news and was worried. He immediately rode to Good Dream Pass with Nezha and three thousand soldiers. "What happened?" he asked when he arrived.

Hong Jin replied, "We were winning, but then Mother Fiery Spirit came. We could not see her behind her golden light. And she had three thousand soldiers who set everything on fire."

Soon after, Mother Fiery Spirit came out and called out, "Jiang Ziya, is that you?"

"Yes," he replied. "Why are you helping the Shang king continue his evil ways? This is against the will of heaven. Please come over to our side and join us."

---

[1] This poem describes Grand Completion's three visits to the palace of the leader of Jie Daoism, Grand Master of Heaven. The disagreement between Grand Completion and Grand Master's disciples leads to a war between the Chan and Jie sects, resulting in endless bloodshed until it's settled by Hong Jun in Chapter 84.

"You are just a foolish old fisherman!" she shouted, and slashed at him with her sword. He fought back. She took off her golden hat and a bright golden light came from her head. Jiang Ziya could not see her, so she was able to slash him across the chest. Badly wounded, he rode away to the west.

Her three thousand soldiers ran into Jiang Ziya's camp, setting it on fire. Many Zhou soldiers were burned to death. Black smoke filled the air.

Mother Fiery Spirit ran after Jiang Ziya. He was old and slow and badly wounded, so she easily caught up to him. She threw a hammer at him, hitting him in the back. He fell off his horse and onto the ground.

As she approached her enemy, she heard someone singing. She looked up and saw Master Grand Completion. She yelled at him, "Master, you should not be here!"

"My master ordered me to come. I have been waiting for you," he replied.

They fought. Mother Fiery Spirit tried to hide in her golden light, but the master wore a magic shirt that collected the light. He could see her clearly. She tried to stab him but missed. He took out his Heaven Overturning Stamp and threw it in the air. It came down on her head, smashing it. Blood, hair, and pieces of bone flew everywhere. She died, and her soul flew to the Terrace of Creation.

Master Grand Completion walked over to a nearby stream. He gathered some water and mixed it with some elixir, then put it in Jiang Ziya's mouth. He said, "Jiang Ziya, my master ordered me to come and save you. I must leave you now. Be careful."

Jiang Ziya watched him go. He began riding slowly back to his camp. A powerful wind came. It was so strong that trees fell down all around him. A black tiger appeared in the road in front of him. On the tiger was Shen Gongbao, his old enemy.

"How are you, my brother?" said Jiang Ziya.

Shen Gongbao replied, "It is your bad luck to meet me today. You are alone. No one can help you this time."

"Brother, why do you hate me?"

"Don't you remember that day on Mount Kunlun? I called your name, but you ignored me. Then you told that young man to grab my head and carry it to the South Sea, to kill me. I will never forget that. Now it's your turn to die."

"Brother, it wasn't me. The Immortal of the South Pole ordered the young man to carry off your head. I saved your life. And this is how you repay me?"

"I know that the two of you both wanted me dead. Don't try to trick me."

He attacked Jiang Ziya, who was too old and tired to fight him. He rode away on his horse, with Shen Gongbao close behind. Shen Gongbao threw a magic pearl, hitting Jiang Ziya on the back and knocking him off his horse again.

Just then, Krakucchanda appeared. He had been sent to protect Jiang Ziya. "Stop!" he shouted. Shen Gongbao turned and tried to run away. "Where are you going?" he shouted. He threw a magic rope, capturing Shen Gongbao.

Krakucchanda told his genie to bring him to the Unicorn Cliff and hold him there. Then he helped Jiang Ziya to stand up, and gave him some magic elixir.

"Thank you, my brother!" said Jiang Ziya. "It must be my fate to be attacked like this." He got on his horse and rode back to camp.

Krakucchanda rode on a beam of light back to the palace on Mount Kunlun. He saw Heavenly Primogenitor, who was just leaving the palace and was surrounded by eight attendants holding pennants, incense burners, and feather fans. Krakucchanda knelt on the side of the road.

"What can I do for you?" asked Heavenly Primogenitor. Krakucchanda explained what had happened. Heavenly Primogenitor went to Unicorn Cliff. He ordered a genie to pick up the cliff and put Shen Gongbao inside, trapping him. "Keep him there until after Jiang Ziya creates the gods," he said to the genie.

"You can't do this!" shouted Shen Gongbao.

"I must. If I set you free, you will only try to hurt Jiang Ziya again."

"Master, I give you my word. If I give Jiang Ziya any trouble again, may my body be thrown into the North Sea."

"All right," said Heavenly Primogenitor. "You may go." He told the genie to release Shen Gongbao.

Meanwhile, Grand Completion brought the golden hat to the beautiful palace of the Grand Master of Daoism. He saw ancient cypress, peach and pine trees. Songs of white cranes and yellow birds filled the air. He waited outside the jade gates until a young man greeted him. "Young man," he said, "would you please tell your master that Grand Completion is waiting outside the gates?"

Soon after, the young man returned and led Grand Completion inside the palace. The Grand Master of Heaven said, "Why have you come here today, Grand Completion?"

"Master, the war against the Shang dynasty has begun. But Mother Fiery Spirit has joined the Shang side. She has badly wounded Hong Jin, Princess Long Ji and Jiang Ziya. My master ordered me to see her, but she tried to kill me also. I had to use my Heaven Overturning Stamp to defend myself. Unfortunately, she was killed. I have come here to beg you to forgive me, and to return her golden hat to you. I wait for your orders."

"Many of my disciples are named on the List of Creation, and many will die. Please tell Jiang Ziya that if any of them oppose him, he has my permission to hit them with his Staff for Beating Gods. Now you may go."

Grand Completion bowed and left the palace. Outside, he saw almost all of Grand Master's disciples waiting for him. They heard what the Grand Master had said, and they were angry. One of them shouted, "The death of Mother Fiery Spirit is an insult to all of us. This is Grand Completion's fault, and now our master is on his side!" They waved swords and shouted at him.

Grand Completion just smiled and said, "Brothers and sisters, what can I do for you?"

One of them, a goddess named Spiritual Tortoise, shouted, "How dare you insult us! I will get revenge for my sister now!"

"Sister," he replied, "Mother Fiery Spirit's name was on the List of Creation. Her death was fated by heaven, and brought by her own actions. It would be stupid for you to seek revenge against me."

Spiritual Tortoise screamed at him again, and attacked with her sword. Grand Completion blocked her blows. Then he threw his Heaven Overturning Stamp. She knew this weapon could kill her, so she changed into her original form, an ancient tortoise from the beginning of time.

The others were even more angry now. They all rushed at Grand Completion, waving their swords and shouting at him. He knew he had no chance against this crowd of immortals. He turned and ran back into the palace. He rushed into the room where Grand Master of Heaven was, and knelt before him. "Master, please help me. I cannot fight all of them!"

Grand Master of Heaven ordered Spiritual Tortoise to come before him. "Why did you attack Grand Completion?" he asked.

She replied, "He killed my sister, and now he insults our religion by coming here."

"How dare you! Grand Completion did nothing wrong. He honored us by coming here to return the golden hat. You are the one who insults our religion. From now on, you will not be allowed to come here and listen to my lectures."

Grand Completion left the palace. But all the disciples were still there, and now they were even angrier than before. They all roared, "Catch Grand Completion! Don't let him escape!"

Having no choice, Grand Completion ran back into the palace for the third time.

Chapter 73
The Earthworm

The water flows day and night
Not knowing the sun and moon

The ocean becomes dry land
Chaos becomes calm ocean

Great generals eat with their swords
Heroes drink the wine of war

Early or late, it's all fate
Blood and tears fall to the ground[1]

≡ ≡ ≡

The Grand Master of Heaven was becoming a bit annoyed. "Grand Completion!" he said, "Why have you come back here again?"

"I tried to leave," replied Grand Completion, "but your disciples were waiting for me outside. They shouted and waved their weapons at me. I beg you, please let me leave in peace."

The Grand Master of Heaven ordered his disciples to come into the palace. He said, "You beasts! How dare you cause trouble for Grand Completion. It is the will of heaven that he should help King Wu. You have no business trying to stop him." The disciples all bowed their heads and said nothing. Turning to Grand Completion, the master said, "You may leave now. Pay no attention to them."

Grand Completion kowtowed to the master, and returned quickly to his cave on Nine Immortal Mountain.

After he left, the Grand Master spoke to his disciples. He said, "All three religions agree that the Shang Dynasty must end and Jiang Ziya must begin the Zhou Dynasty. Mother Fiery Spirit's death was her own fault, no one else's. You must not try to stop Grand Completion anymore."

---

[1] Here, the poet tells us that everything is written and happens according to the will of heaven, so all the actions of humans, all the bloodshed and tears, are in vain.

"But Master," said Many Treasures, one of the immortals, "Grand Completion has insulted you, and us, and our religion."

"How so?"

"I am sorry to have to tell you this. He has said that our religion is worthless. He said that your disciples were born from eggs, with hair and horns and feathers all over their bodies."

"Grand Completion always tells the truth. He would not say such things."

But all the disciples, speaking as one, said that they had heard Grand Completion say these words.

Grand Master grew angry. "What a beast he is, to say these things. Many Treasures, go into the back room and fetch me the four Immortal Killing Swords. Hang them over the main gate of the palace. They will stop any evil immortal from entering. Then, go to Jiepai Pass and set up an Immortal Killing Trap. We will see who goes inside."

Jiang Ziya returned to the Zhou camp. He told his generals what happened to him. The Zhou army had lost five thousand soldiers, but they won the battle. They had a feast to celebrate their victory, then they marched back to Good Dream Pass.

In the Shang camp, the commander did not know what to do. "We planned to surrender to Jiang Ziya," he said, "but then Mother Fiery Spirit came. She won several battles, but now she is dead. What should we do now?"

"We should surrender, as we planned before," said his generals.

The commander agreed. He sent a message to Jiang Ziya, saying they were ready to surrender. Jiang Ziya thought he was telling the truth, so he told the messenger that the surrender must happen the very next day.

The next day, the Zhou army approached Good Dream Pass. They saw that the Shang flags had been replaced again by Zhou flags. The commander came out and greeted Jiang Ziya. He said, "I wanted to surrender, but my brother would not allow it. Then I tried again, but Mother Fiery Spirit stopped it. We beg your forgiveness for our crimes."

Jiang Ziya replied, "You are only surrendering because your generals are all dead. You change your mind too easily. We cannot trust you." He ordered his men to cut off the commander's head. He appointed one of his own generals to command Good Dream Pass. Then he returned to the main camp and told King Wu everything that had happened.

The next battle was at Green Dragon Pass. Huang Feihu took a hundred thousand soldiers there. The commander of the pass, a man named Qiu Yin saw them. He said, "The enemy has arrived. We must defeat these rebels!"

"We will fight to the death!" shouted his generals.

One by one, generals from the Zhou army rode out to meet their enemies. First was Deng Jiugong. He fought one of the Shang generals and killed him. Next was Huang Tianxiang, only seventeen years old and as brave as a calf before a tiger. He fought another of the Shang generals and stabbed him through the heart.

Angry at losing two of his generals, Qiu Yin rushed out on his horse, holding a long lance and wearing a silver helmet and armor. Two of his generals rode out with him, one on either side. Huang Tianxiang killed both of the generals almost right away. Then he stabbed Qiu Yin in the leg. The commander was badly wounded and had to return to the fort in defeat.

Qiu Yin was not a true man. He was an earthworm who had taken human form, and he had great magic powers. He used his magic to heal the wound in his leg.

After three days the wound was fully healed. Qiu Yin rode out again to fight Huang Tianxiang. The young man saw that the commander was wearing some kind of mirror on his chest. Realizing that he was fighting a sorcerer, Huang Tianxiang hit him in the chest with a silver club. It smashed the mirror which protected the sorcerer's heart. Blood came out of Qiu Yin's mouth and he almost fell off his horse. He managed to ride away back to the fort.

Now that the commander was wounded and several of his generals were dead, Deng Jiugong decided it was time to attack. The Zhou army attacked the fort. But the fort was protected by deep ditches and high walls, and the soldiers could not enter the fort. Huang Feihu ordered the army to retreat.

Qiu Yin felt that his army now had the advantage. He sent several thousand Flying Tiger soldiers to attack the Zhou camp and capture Deng Jiugong. There was a great battle. Deng Jiugong fought bravely, but Qiu Yin blew out some yellow smoke from his mouth. Deng Jiugong breathed some of it. He fell to the ground and was captured.

When Deng Jiugong was brought before Qiu Yin he said, "You are no brave warrior. You used evil magic to capture me. Go ahead and kill me. I can't eat your flesh when I am alive, but I will find you after I die and kill you!" Qiu Yin ordered his men to cut off Deng Jiugong's head.

When news of Deng Jiugong' death reached the Zhou camp, many of the generals wanted to go out and avenge his death. Huang Feihu selected three of his sons, Huang Tianlu, Huang Tianjue, and Huang Tianxiang. All three of them rode out to fight the Shang army.

Chapter 74
The Battle of Green Dragon Pass

Two great generals meet at the pass
Deciding victory or defeat

Five elements are used
Ten thousand lives lead up to this day

Yellow smoke makes a general fall
White light captures an enemy

The greatest magic cannot change fate
As your life slips away[1]

≡ ≡ ≡

The Shang commander sent one of his generals, a sorcerer named Chen Qi. The three Huang brothers surrounded Chen Qi. One of them stabbed him in the right leg. But the Daoist could still fight even with an injured leg. He waved his staff. The Flying Tiger soldiers attacked, yellow lights coming from their bellies. They captured Huang Tianlu and put him in jail.

Chen Qi used his own elixir to heal his leg. The next day he came out to seek revenge. With spear in hand he rode towards the Zhou camp, shouting for Huang Tianxiang to come out and fight him.

After a brief fight he captured Huang Tianxiang and brought him back to the fort. But the young man would not kneel. He said, "You demon! You used magic instead of fighting like a real man. I want to stab you with my spear, smash your soul, and shoot an arrow into your heart. But I cannot. So, go ahead and kill me. I will become a ghost and come back to kill you." Furious, Qiu Yin ordered the young man's head cut off, and his body hung on a pole on the wall.

Huang Feihu saw his son's body and cried. He said this poem,

> *Giving his life for his country*

---

[1] The poet reminds us yet again that everything happens according to heaven's will.

His heart is as bright as the sun
He fought many battles and many enemies
Only to fall at the hands of an evil sorcerer

Then he sent a messenger to Jiang Ziya, asking for more soldiers. When the message arrived, Deng Chanyu said, "Commander, please let me go and avenge my father." Jiang Ziya agreed, and sent Nezha to go with her. Deng Chanyu rode her horse swiftly, but Nezha used his Wind Fire Wheels to travel to Green Dragon Pass in just a few seconds.

The next day, Nezha saw the body of Huang Tianxiang hanging from the wall. Furious, he shouted for Chen Qi to come out and fight him. The Shang general came out a few minutes later, saying, "Oh, is this Nezha?"

Nezha replied, "You demon! Why did you have to kill Huang Tianxiang? I will crush you!" Then he attacked. Their two horses crashed into each other; their spears hit each other. Chen Qi rode away, Nezha chased him.

Chen Qi sent white light from the top of his head, and a large red pearl appeared. "Look at my treasure!" he shouted.

But Nezha, who was not made of flesh and bone, just laughed and said, "This is just a little red stone. Why are you showing it to me?" He used his Universal Ring to smash Chen Qi's shoulder, knocking him from his horse. The sorcerer fled back to the fort, and Nezha returned to the Zhou camp.

Earth Traveler Sun heard that his father-in-law was killed. He asked Jiang Ziya for permission to seek revenge. Around midnight, he traveled underground into the Shang fort. He saw Tai Luan and Huang Tianlu in jail, and told them that they would be free soon. Then he grabbed the corpse of Huang Tianxiang and brought it back to the Zhou camp.

Huang Feihu cried when he realized that two of his four sons were now dead, and another in jail. He told his last son, Huang Tianjue, to bring the corpse back to West Qi. This was his way of keeping his last surviving son safe.

The next day, Earth Traveler Sun and his wife Deng Chanyu went out together, to avenge her father. When they saw Chen Qi, Earth Traveler Sun shouted, "You killed my father-in-law. I have come to capture you and avenge him!"

The sorcerer just laughed and replied, "You people are nothing but dead wood. If I kill you, it will only make my hands dirty."

Chen Qi tried to slash the little man, but could not reach him. He sent his Flying Tiger soldiers into battle. Then he blew some yellow smoke from his mouth. Earth Traveler Sun fell to the ground and was captured.

But the sorcerer did not see Deng Chanyu. She threw a stone, hitting him in the mouth. It knocked out some of his teeth and caused him to bleed heavily. He tried to run away, but she threw another stone, hitting him in the back and smashing the magic mirror he wore.

In the Shang fort, Qiu Yin ordered Earth Traveler Sun to be brought to him. He looked at the prisoner and said, "This little man is no use to us. Cut off his head." But Earth Traveler Sun just touched the ground with his foot and disappeared into the earth. "That was a very strange man," said Qiu Yin. "We must be careful. Guard the pass day and night."

Later that day, Zheng Lun arrived at the Zhou camp, bringing food and supplies. Earth Traveler Sun said to him, "My friend, there is a Shang general named Chen Qi. He has the same ability as you. He can emit yellow gas from his mouth, just like your ability to emit white gas from your mouth."

"That is interesting," replied Zheng Lun. "My teacher told me that nobody else in the whole country had this ability. I must meet him!"

The next day, Zheng Lun and his three thousand Black Crow soldiers rode out. They saw Chen Qi. "Who are you?" demanded Zheng Lun.

"I am Chen Qi. I am the general who brings food and supplies to the army guarding this pass. Who are you?"

"I am Zheng Lun. I have the same job as you, but for the Zhou army." He rushed forward, waving his staff, and the two of them fought. What a battle!

> *Two generals meet on the battlefield*
> *Neither will run, each wants to win*
> *One is a lion coming from the mountain*
> *The other is like a roaring tiger*
> *One wants to bring order to the world*
> *The other wants to save the king*
> *Heaven brings these two together today*

Their swords meet in battle

All the Zhou generals went out to watch the battle. The Black Crow army advanced like a large black snake, attacking the Flying Tiger army. Zheng Lun shot two white lights from his nose, while Chen Qi shot two yellow lights from his nose. They both fell from their horses. Their armies dared not capture the enemy general, but they each grabbed their own general and retreated back to their camps.

Earth Traveler Sun and the other generals laughed. But Zheng Lun said, "It is strange that such a man is in this world. I must fight him again tomorrow."

When they met the next day, Chen Qi said, "There is no need for magic. Let's fight man to man, using only our fighting abilities. Will you agree?"

Zheng Lun agreed. They fought all day, but neither could win. When the fight was over for the day, Nezha said to the other Zhou generals, "This is a good time for us to attack. Tonight, Earth Traveler Sun should travel underground and free the prisoners. I will open the gates of the fort."

When it was dark, Earth Traveler Sun traveled through the earth, came up inside the Shang fort, and freed the two prisoners. Nezha used a golden brick to knock out the gate guards, then he smashed the lock and opened the gates. The Zhou army rushed in and captured the city. The people fled for their lives.

In the darkness, Qiu Yin found himself surrounded by several Zhou generals. Earth Traveler Sun hit his horse, knocking him to the ground. But before anyone could stab him, Qiu Yin flew away in a cloud of dust.

Chen Qi was not so lucky. He was hit by Nezha's Universal Ring. When he fell to the ground, his own sword stabbed him in the chest and he died.

The battle for Green Dragon Pass was over. Jiang Ziya, hearing the news, named a new commander for the pass. He was happy that his army won the battle, but was deeply unhappy about the deaths of Deng Jiugong and Huang Tianxiang. He said, "It is too bad that these great warriors will not be able to see the birth of the Zhou Dynasty."

The next battle was at Sishui Pass. The commander at that pass, Han Rong, heard that the other two passes were taken by the Zhou army.

Then a messenger arrived with this letter from Jiang Ziya.

To the commander of Sishui Pass,

The Shang king is an evil tyrant, and the people suffer. Heaven is unhappy. It is our duty to obey Heaven's will. Wherever we go, the people greet us and Shang armies surrender. Two passes have already surrendered. Now you must decide whether to fight or surrender. I wait for your reply.

Jiang Ziya, Commander of the Zhou Army

Han Rong read the letter. He wrote on the bottom, "We will see you in battle," and gave the letter back to the messenger.

When they met on the battlefield the next day, Han Rong said, "Commander Jiang, how can you lead a rebel army against our king?"

Jiang Ziya replied, "General, heaven loves a virtuous king and lets him stay in the throne. But surely you know that long ago, King Jie of the Xia Dynasty became a tyrant and was removed from the throne by King Tang, first king of the Shang Dynasty. Your king is far worse than King Jie. Every marquis is against him. That's why we have come to punish him."

One of Han Rong's generals rushed forward but was killed by Nezha. Han Rong rode back to the pass. The Zhou army chased close behind him.

Just then, Yu Hua arrived at the Shang fort. He was called the "seven-headed general." He had a golden face, red hair and beard, and golden eyes. He wore a tiger skin robe under his armor, and a jade belt. He said, "Several years ago, I was defeated in battle by Nezha. I asked my master for a magical weapon. He created the Blood Transforming Dagger and gave it to me. This weapon is so powerful, it can destroy an entire army."

When he went out the next day, his old enemy Nezha was waiting for him. Yu Hua brought out the Blood Transforming Dagger. It moved so fast that Nezha could not see it. He could not die, but he was badly injured. He could not ride his Wind Fire Wheels. His soldiers carried him back to the Zhou camp. They called his name, but he did not speak.

Chapter 75
The Little Man Steals a Camel

Yu Hua is strong but lost his life; Master,
Why waste your power?

Burning the little man brings trouble,
Anger provokes Krakucchanda

Escaping from the North Sea,
How can Yu Yuan be captured again?

Yu Yuan is on the List of Creation;
Don't try to understand fate[1]

≡ ≡ ≡

After his victory, Yu Hua went out again the next day ready for battle. Thunderbolt went out to meet him. "Are you Yu Hua?" he asked the man with the yellow face and red beard.

"Traitor!" shouted Yu Hua. "You don't recognize me?"

Thunderbolt leaped into the air, slashing down with his golden staff that was as heavy as Mount Tai. Yu Hua fought back with his spear, as swift as a flying dragon. Desperately, Yu Hua used his Blood Transforming Dagger to cut Thunderbolt's wings. But the wings were made from two immortal apricots, so the injuries were not serious. Yu Hua returned to camp, defeated.

Jiang Ziya hung the sign of truce while he tried to decide what to do next. Yang Jian came to see him. "It's been almost ten months, but we have not moved forward an inch. Please take down the truce sign and let me see what's going on."

As they were discussing this, a young Daoist came in. He said, "I am a disciple of Fairy Primordial. He sent me to bring Nezha back to him, for

---

[1] This poem touches on several events in the chapter. First, Yu Hua is captured, placed in an iron box, and dropped into the North Sea. He escapes and continues to cause trouble. Next, Earth Traveler Sun is nearly burned alive but is rescued by Krakucchanda. And finally, Yu Yuan is killed by Lu Ya.

treatment. He is quite sick." Jiang Ziya looked at Nezha, and saw he was looking very pale.

"Of course," replied Jiang Ziya. The young Daoist left with Nezha.

As soon as the truce sign was taken down, Yu Hua rode out of the Shang fort, ready for battle. Yang Jian rode out to meet him, saying, "Yu Hua! I am the nephew of Commander Jiang!" The two began to fight. Yu Hua attacked with his magic dagger.

Yang Jian let himself be cut in the shoulder, then he flew to Mount Yuquan to meet his master, Jade Tripod. He said, "Master, one of the Shang generals has a strange dagger. He cut Nezha with it, and now Nezha is quite sick. He cut me also, but thanks to your teaching I was not badly injured. Can you please look at the wound and tell me what kind of poison it is?"

Jade Tripod looked at the wound. He said, "I know this poison. It causes immediate death. Nezha is immortal and you have been trained well by me, so you both are still alive."

"How can we cure this poison?"

"I cannot cure it. This dagger comes from Yu Yuan, an immortal from Penglai Island. When the dagger was made, three pills were also made. Only those pills can save you."

Yang Jian flew to Penglai Island and changed his appearance so he looked like Yu Hua, the seven-headed general. The island was surrounded by a vast ocean, with huge waves crashing onto the rocks. Dragon spirits moved the winds, phoenix and qilin walked among the trees, cranes and other colored birds flew through the air. The ground was covered with colorful flowers and green grasses.

Seeing Yu Yuan, he bowed and said, "At my master's command, I guarded Sishui Pass. Jiang Ziya's army arrived. I injured Nezha and Thunderbolt. But then Yang Jian fought me. He used some magic to turn the dagger against me, and it cut my shoulder. I ask for your help."

Yu Yuan replied, "What? When I made this dagger, I used fire to separate dragon from tiger, yin from yang. At that time, I also made three pills. I have no use for them now, so you can take them."

The immortal who looked like Yu Hua bowed and left the island, returning to the Zhou camp. Soon after he left, Yu Yuan began to wonder what he had just seen. He did a divination with his fingers and learned that he had been tricked by Yang Jian. Furious, he flew after him on his golden-eyed camel. Yang Jian looked back and saw the master chasing him. He released his heavenly dog. The dog used its teeth which were as sharp as steel swords, biting Yu Yuan on the neck. Yu Yuan was badly injured and had to return to Penglai Island. But he said, "I will come back and punish you, Yang Jian!"

Back at the Zhou camp, Jiang Ziya used some of the pills to treat Thunderbolt. He sent the rest to Mount Qianyuan to treat Nezha.

The next day, Yang Jian went out to fight Yu Hua again. He shouted, "Yu Hua, you hurt me yesterday with your dagger. But I have the elixir, so your dagger cannot harm me."

They began to fight again. By now, Thunderbolt was completely cured. He rushed out and joined the fight. Together, the two Zhou immortals defeated Yu Hua. Yang Jian killed him with his sword.

Han Rong was very unhappy to hear about Yu Hua's death. But just then, Yu Yuan arrived. He was nearly seven feet tall, with a blue face, red hair and very long teeth. Han Rong greeted him, saying, "Sir, who are you and what famous mountain do you come from?"

The visitor replied, "I am Yu Yuan from Penglai Island. Yang Jian has gone too far this time. He stole my elixir and killed my disciple. I am here to get my revenge."

Han Rong gave the visitor food and wine. The next day, he went out and shouted to Jiang Ziya, "Commander! Tell Yang Jian to come out and face me!"

"Sorry," replied Jiang Ziya, "he is not here. He is busy getting food and supplies for our army. Sir, it has now been six hundred years since Chen Tang took the throne. The king of Shang has done evil things and caused heaven to become angry. Now it is the time of the new Zhou Dynasty. How can you go against the will of heaven? Join us or die!"

"We can't stop these problems if I don't end your life!" replied Yu Yuan, and he rode forward on his five-cloud camel and attacked. Jiang Ziya blocked the attack with his sword. Two other Zhou generals joined the fight. Yu Yuan threw up his Golden Light File. Jiang Ziya blocked it with his Yellow Apricot Flag. Then he hit his attacker with his staff, causing Yu Yuan's divine fire to shoot out ten feet from his mouth. Another general stabbed Yu Yuan in the leg. Badly injured, Yu Yuan rode away on his camel.

Earth Traveler Sun saw Yu Yuan riding away on his camel. He liked the camel and wanted it for himself. His wife, Deng Chanyu, told him what just happened in the battle. Earth Traveler Sun decided to go out that night and steal the camel.

At the second watch, he traveled underground to Sishui Pass. He waited underground, listening to Yu Yuan. But Yu Yuan did a divination and learned what was happening. He pretended to be asleep, his breath as loud as thunder.

Earth Traveler Sun was delighted to hear his enemy sleeping. He came up out of the ground, untied the camel, and stepped on a large rock to climb onto its back. Then he dismounted, walked over to Yu Yuan, and hit him on the head with an iron rod. Yu Yuan did not move. Earth Traveler Sun hit him again. Still the man did not move. "Oh, well," said Earth Traveler Sun. He got back on the camel and started to fly away. But the camel could not fly through the wall.

Yu Yuan jumped up and grabbed Earth Traveler Sun by the hair. He shouted, "I have caught the thief!"

He brought the prisoner to Han Rong. "I can't put him down," he said. "If he touches the ground, he will disappear."

"How should we deal with him?" asked Han Rong.

"Let's put him in a bag. We will build a fire under him, and burn him to death." Han Rong agreed to this.

Earth Traveler Sun started to burn. He screamed. Far away, Krakucchanda heard his screams. He rushed to Sishui Pass and grabbed the bag away from the fire. He flew away holding the bag, while Yu Yuan shouted, "Krakucchanda, damn you, I will get you tomorrow!"

Krakucchanda brought Earth Traveler Sun back to the Zhou camp and dropped him in front of Jiang Ziya. The commander was very angry. He wanted to cut off the head of the little man, but Krakucchanda asked him to show mercy. Jiang Ziya agreed.

The next day, Yu Yuan came to the Zhou camp and shouted that he wanted to fight Krakucchanda. But Krakucchanda captured him with his magic rope, and brought him back to the camp. Jiang Ziya ordered that he be killed, but the soldiers could not cut off his head. Their swords just bounced off his neck. Yu Yuan smiled and said,

> *"I have reached the Dao, I am immortal*

The five elements do as I command
I have traveled all over the world
I have learned the secrets of gold and jade
The immortal fire burns in my furnace
You cannot kill me now
Since ancient times, a sword for a sword
All your words will not work."

"What should we do?" asked Jiang Ziya.

Krakucchanda said, "Make an iron box. Put him in it, and drop it into the sea."

They put him in an iron box and carried it to the North Sea. They dropped it in the water. The box sank down to the bottom. But Yu Yuan used the elements of metal and water to escape from the box. He flew to the mountain where his master, Mother Golden Spirit, lived. She was furious when she learned what had happened. She flew to see the Grand Master of Heaven.

The Grand Master of Heaven was angry, but as the ancients say, 'A saint cannot show his anger.' So, he just waved his hand, causing the ropes to fall off of Yu Yuan. Then he told Yu Yuan, "Go and find Krakucchanda. Bring him back to see me, but don't hurt him."

Yu Yuan returned to Sishui Pass. He went out and shouted for Krakucchanda to meet him. Krakucchanda saw the Daoist standing there. He said to Jiang Ziya, "I don't know how he could escape from that iron box. He must have some new and powerful weapon. You should go and meet him. I will grab him when he is not looking."

Jiang Ziya went out. Yu Yuan shouted, "Jiang Ziya, this is the moment of truth. Your fate will be decided today!" He rode his camel forward and attacked but did not see Krakucchanda, who captured him again with his magic rope.

But the Zhou did not know what to do with him. "How can we kill him?" asked Jiang Ziya.

But just then, Lu Ya arrived. Yu Yuan was very frightened to see him. His face turned yellow. "Brother Lu," he said, "please have mercy on me! I have studied the Way for a thousand years. If you show mercy, I will never cause problems for the Zhou again."

But Lu Ya said, "You have gone against the will of heaven, and your name is on the List of Creation. I must punish you." He burned incense, bowing to Mount Kunlun. He picked up a small gourd and placed it on the table. He took off the lid. A white light shone from inside the gourd. The end of the light was a dagger, with eyes and wings. "Turn around!" said Lu Ya. The dagger spun around three times. Then it flew towards Yu Yuan and cut off his head. His soul flew to the Terrace of Creation.

Jiang Ziya wanted to hang the head on the wall of the camp, but Lu Ya said, "Please don't do that. Yu Yuan was an immortal. It would not be right to show his head. Just bury his corpse." Then Krakucchanda and Lu Ya left to return to their mountains.

Han Rong called his generals together for a meeting. "We are in trouble. Yu Yuan is dead, and we have no one to fight the Zhou magicians. The passes on our left and right have both been taken by the Zhou. We cannot win, and I will not surrender. What can we do?"

"It is time to bow to Zhaoge and leave this place," said the generals. Han Rong agreed. They gathered all their personal things, loading them onto carts. Then they prepared to leave the pass and go into the mountains.

But as they all prepared to leave, Han Rong's two sons heard about it. They rushed in to see their father.

Chapter 76
The Zhou Army Captures Sishui Pass

You cannot stop a thousand knives
And attacking chariots

If your flags burn,
Your generals and soldiers will all face disaster

You can't protect half your army during the day,
What about night?

Two sons die
When they meet the general in charge of supplies[1]

≡ ≡ ≡

When his two sons came to Han Rong, they said, "Father, why do you want to give up this pass?"

He replied, "You two are too young to understand. Pack up your things. We must avoid war."

Han Sheng, the elder son, said, "Father, don't let anyone hear what you just said! You have a high post and good pay. You wear purple clothes and a gold belt. Is this how you repay your king and country? We are not afraid. We have been trained by an immortal since we were very young. We are ready to fight to the end for our country!"

Their father replied, "You are loyal. I understand. But our king is stupid and evil, and the Zhou army has many powerful magicians. I must go to the mountains to save the people. You should come with me."

"This unworthy child will give up his life for his country. Let me show you something." Han Sheng went into the back room and came back holding a small toy. It looked like a windmill. It had a piece of paper in the center which could spin. There were four small pennants on the

---

[1] Zheng Lun is in charge of supplies for the Zhou army, along with Earth Traveler Sun and Yang Jian. But he is also a powerful magician and a fierce fighter who kills the two sons of Han Rong, the commander of Sishui Pass.

four corners of the paper, with the characters "earth," "water," "fire," and "wind" written on it.

Han Rong looked at it. "This is just a toy for children."

"No, father. Come and see." They led him to the courtyard. The two boys let their hair fall loose onto their shoulders. They said some magic words. Instantly the air filled with clouds and fog. Strong winds blew fire through the courtyard. Millions of flying swords flew in the wind.

Han Rong was frightened. "Who taught you this?" he asked.

"A few years ago, we were in Zhaoge. We were playing in front of our house. A strange monk came, begging for food. We gave him some food. Just before he left, he said, 'Jiang Ziya will come and attack your father's pass. Here is a weapon to use against him.' Then he showed us how to use this weapon. Now, we can win this war and capture Jiang Ziya."

Han Rong thought about it. He said, "How many soldiers do you need to fight the Zhou?"

"We need only three thousand soldiers on horseback. That will be enough to defeat six hundred thousand Zhou."

Han Rong gave three thousand soldiers to his sons. They trained the soldiers for twenty-seven days. Then Han Rong and his sons led them out of the pass to fight.

Jiang Ziya ordered his generals to go out and meet the enemy that was waiting for them. "Who are you?" asked one of his generals.

A young man replied, "I am Han Sheng, eldest son of Han Rong. Today you will meet your death!" He waved his hand, and the three thousand soldiers rode forward on horseback. Their hair was loose on their shoulders, and their feet were bare. As they rode forward, Han Sheng waved his sword. A thick fog came, the air turned dark, and fire rode on the wind. The Zhou soldiers could not see anything. Thirty million swords flew forward in a great cloud and attacked the Zhou army. More than eight thousand Zhou soldiers and generals died. The rest retreated back to their camp.

Back at Sishui Pass, Han Rong said, "This is a great victory. But we cannot defeat the entire Zhou army now, in daylight. We will attack them tonight."

At the first watch, Han Sheng led his three thousand soldiers in a surprise attack. High winds came, turning the sky black. Fire came, filling the air with smoke. The attackers had no lamps, only knives and swords. They entered the Zhou camp like great waves. Nothing could stop them. Even the weapons of the immortals could not stop the attackers' flying swords. The green grass of the camp turned red with blood. Many soldiers died.

King Wu escaped, protected by several generals. The rest of the army escaped, with Jiang Ziya using his magic flag to protect them. They rode as fast as they could towards Golden Chicken Mountain. When they got to the mountain, they saw a great army. Jiang Ziya was happy to see that it was Zheng Lun's army of Black Crow soldiers.

Zheng Lun was a very powerful magician. He led his soldiers back towards the Shang army. He sent two bright white lights out of his nose. The Han brothers fell to the ground and were easily captured by the Crow soldiers.

As soon as the brothers were captured, their three thousand soldiers lost their magic power. They dropped their weapons and ran away.

Zheng Lun ordered the two brothers tied up and brought to Jiang Ziya. Jiang Ziya rode to the wall of Sishui Pass and shouted, "Han Rong! You tricked me once, but now we are here to take the pass. We have both of your sons."

Han Rong saw his two sons. They were tied up, barefoot, and dirty. He said, "Commander, I will give you Sishui Pass if you give my sons back to me."

But his son Han Sheng shouted, "No, father! Don't give up the pass! Wait for more soldiers to come from Zhaoge. Then you can capture Jiang Ziya and cut him into a thousand pieces. We are happy to die for our king."

Jiang Ziya waved his hand. Nangong Kuo stepped forward and swung his cutlass twice. The two sons' heads were cut off. Han Rong saw this, cried out, and jumped off the wall to his death.

Later, this poem was written,

> *The river flows day and night*
> *Han Rong died for his country*
> *The lonely monkey cries when his father was a minister*
> *The old crane is sad when the son is loyal*

> *One death rewards the country*
> *Three souls are proud of the king*
> *Now I have no regrets*
> *But I remember laughing with my wife and children*

The Zhou army entered the city. The people opened the gates and welcomed them. King Wu ordered a formal burial for Han Rong and his sons. The army rested for three days.

Far away on a mountain top, Fairy Primordial called Nezha to see him. He said, "Nezha, your wounds are healed. Go back to your army. I will follow later, and break the Immortal Killing Trap for you." Then he poured three cups of wine for Nezha, and gave him three fire dates to eat. Nezha drank the wine and ate the dates.

He turned to leave. Suddenly there was a loud noise, and an arm grew from his left shoulder. "What was that?" cried Nezha. There was another noise, and another arm appeared. More noises, more arms, until he had eight arms instead of two. Then he grew two more heads.

He ran back to see Fairy Primordial, who laughed and said, "How wonderful!"

Nezha waved all of his arms and said, "What do I do with all these arms and heads? I look like an ugly tree."

"Nezha, your army has many immortals with magic powers. Some can fly, some can travel underground, some can change their shapes. Now you have some special powers too. You can change from your regular form into this form whenever you want."

Nezha used five hands to pick up five weapons, the Universal Ring, the Sky Muddling Damask, the gold brick, and two fire tipped lances. His master gave him the Nine Dragon Divine Fire Coverlet and two yin yang swords for the other three hands. Nezha thanked his master and rode back to Sishui Pass.

At the pass, Jiang Ziya was thinking about how to deal with the Immortal Killing Trap. Just then, Yellow Dragon Immortal arrived and said, "Brother, be very careful. Do not attack the trap yet. Wait until the immortals and Buddhas arrive to help. Prepare a pavilion for them."

Jiang Ziya told two of his generals, Nangong Kuo and Wu Ji, to go and prepare a pavilion for their guests.

Nezha returned. He had some difficulty getting inside the camp, because the guards did not recognize him with eight arms and three heads. But Li Jing came, and Nezha explained to his father what had happened to him.

The next day, the pavilion was ready. Jiang Ziya, King Wu, and all the generals walked forty *li* to the pavilion to wait for their visitors. Soon the visitors began to arrive. Over the next two days, twelve of the greatest immortals gathered at the pavilion.

The last to arrive was Burning Lamp. He sat down and asked, "Have any of you seen this trap yet?"

"No," they answered, "we have not seen it."

"What about that red cloud?"

They all turned to look. Far away, they could see a huge red cloud in the sky. One of the immortals clapped his hands. This pushed the red cloud away, and they could all see the trap. It was surrounded by gray clouds, thick fog, and cold winds. Yellow Dragon said, "Well, there's the trap. Let's go take a look."

But Burning Lamp said, "Remember what the ancients said, 'Look at good places a thousand times, don't look even once at a place of evil.' " But the other immortals wanted to go see it. Burning Lamp could not stop them.

Chapter 77
Laozi Brings Three Immortals

Three gods from a single breath
Powerful magic from Mt. Sumeru

Born from moving a piece of wood
Don't let them wander off

Killing the gods shows
How shallow the roots are

Heaven decides who rises and falls
Jie's efforts are for nothing[1]

≡ ≡ ≡

The twelve immortals approached the Immortal Killing Trap. They saw four swords hanging, one each in the east, south, west and north sides. They heard someone singing,

> *We cannot avoid killing immortals when we fight with swords*
> *The emotions of the heart stir the unknown fire*
> *I am sad because life and death depend on me*
> *The Jade Emptiness Palace brings nothing but trouble*
> *When I look back, I see the past has been corrupted*
> *Danger is close, how can you escape?*
> *Rely on your own skills and your end will come soon!*

Burning Lamp heard the song. He said, "Do you hear his words? This is not a good man. We should wait to see what our master says."

Just then, an immortal named Many Treasures rushed out of the trap. He had been sent earlier by the Grand Master of Heaven to set up the

---

[1] This poem is about the battle between Laozi and Grand Master of Heaven. In this chapter, Laozi removes his hat to release his aura and summon the Three Pure Ones. They are the highest gods in Daoism, associated with the underworld, earth and sky. "Shallow roots" refers to a lack of commitment to the Dao, as discussed by Heavenly Primogenitor in this chapter. "A piece of wood" is an insignificant thing, so moving it means performing an easy task.

trap, to get revenge against Grand Completion. He shouted, "Grand Completion, where are you going? Your end is near!"

The two immortals began to fight, while a powerful wind blew dust and sand. Grand Completion threw his Heaven Overturning Stamp. It hit Many Treasures in the back. Badly hurt, he ran back inside the trap.

The immortals returned to the pavilion. They heard music in the air, and they knew that Heavenly Primogenitor was coming soon. A few moments later, the great immortal came down from the sky in his carriage, pulled by nine dragons.

At the trap, Grand Master of Heaven arrived around midnight. Many Treasures welcomed him. He sat down and greeted his disciples, who gathered around him.

The next day, the fighting began. Heavenly Primogenitor sent his disciples, two at a time, to approach the trap. The Grand Master of Heaven came out of the trap. He bowed and said, "How are you, brother?"

"Dear brother," said Heavenly Primogenitor, "why did you build this evil trap? You and I were both at the meeting when the List of Creation was written. You know that there are three levels. Those with deep roots will gain immortality; those with middle roots will gain the heavenly way; those with shallow roots will stay in the human world to suffer births and deaths. Why are you now going against the will of heaven?"

"Don't ask me, brother. Ask Grand Completion."

Heavenly Primogenitor did not understand this. He looked at Grand Completion, saying, "Tell me what is going on here." Grand Completion told him about the meeting he had with Grand Master, and the lies that were told by Grand Master's disciples.

Grand Master of Heaven said to Grand Completion, "How can you say that our disciples have feathers and horns? Don't you know that the three religions come from the same place? We all have the same master. We are really all one body. If I am a beast with feathers and horns, so are you!"

Heavenly Primogenitor said, "Brother, many of your disciples speak like people but act like wild animals. You let them cause trouble. How can you feel good about this?"

Grand Master became angry. "And your disciples never cause trouble? It is clear that you do not see me as your brother. All right, then. The trap is ready for you. Try and break it!"

Heavenly Primogenitor sat down in his carriage. Four immortals picked it up, each one holding a leg of the carriage. Light surrounded it, and thousands of lotus flowers grew from it. As they walked through the gate, Grand Master made a thunderclap with his hands. A sword came down. It cut off a lotus flower near Heavenly Primogenitor's head, but the immortal was not injured.

Heavenly Primogenitor finished looking at the trap. He returned to the other immortals and said, "I cannot break this trap on my own. I must wait for my elder brother. Ah, here he comes now."

They looked up and saw a man riding a blue ox. It was Laozi. All the immortals bowed to him. Laozi said, "Grand Master of Heaven is our younger brother. Why has he set this trap for the Zhou army?"

Heavenly Primogenitor replied, "We do not know. I have looked at the trap, but I did not try to break it yet."

Laozi said, "Tomorrow we will break this trap. If Grand Master asks for forgiveness, we will let him go. If not, we will take him to see our master at Purple Heaven Palace."

They rested that night. Bright red clouds filled the sky. The next morning, Laozi rode his blue ox towards the trap. Grand Master of Heaven was there to greet him, saying, "How are you, dear eldest brother?"

Laozi replied, "Dear younger brother, the three of us made the List of Creation, to make gods of the ones who will die in this war. All of us agreed to this. Why are you now trying to stop the Zhou army?"

"Grand Completion came into my palace three times. He insulted me and said terrible things about our religion. If you want to solve this problem, just send Grand Completion to my palace and let me deal with him."

"Grand Completion would not say such things. Why do you believe the lies told by your disciples? And even if he did say these things, this is not the way to deal with it. Do not go against the will of heaven. You must remove this trap immediately. If you don't, I will take you to see our master at Purple Heaven Palace. He will change you into an ordinary human, and you will be put on the Wheel of Birth and death."

Grand Master was furious. His face turned red and smoke came from his eyes. "Laozi, how can you insult me like this! Do you think I am less of an immortal than you? I dare you to break this trap!"

Laozi replied, "That's no problem. Get the trap ready. I will enter it soon." Grand Master turned and entered the trap.

A little while later, Laozi rode his blue ox towards the west gate. Purple and red clouds filled the air. White light came from the ox's feet. He took out his magic map and unrolled it, using it as a bridge. He crossed the bridge and passed through the gate. Grand Master released thunder from his hand and sent a magic sword flying, but Laozi only laughed. "Dear brother," he said, "you know nothing. Watch out for my walking stick."

He hit Grand Master with his stick. Grand Master fought back with his sword. The leaders of the two religions fought for over an hour. What was it like?

The wind howls, the world shakes
Thunder moves mountains and rivers
Lightning flies through the clouds
Fog obscures the sun and moon
Sand and dust covers the world
Tigers and lions hide in the forest
Fog makes the trees disappear
Thunder makes the ground shatter
Lightning confuses the immortals
Fog makes them lose their way
The wind moves rocks and knocks down trees
Smoke covers the Nine Layers of Heaven

Some of Grand Master's disciples joined the fight, but Laozi easily kept them away by using a golden pagoda.

Laozi said to himself, "He knows a little bit of Daoist magic, but he has not studied the Way. I will show him some new things!"

Suddenly, Laozi jumped away from his enemy. He pushed his hat to the side. Three columns of smoke came from his head. They turned into the Three Pure Ones, the greatest gods in Daoism[1].

---

[1] In Daoism, the three Pure Ones are manifestations of pure qi, the primordial celestial energy.

Grand Master looked at them. He said to one of them, "Who are you?"

The first one was the Daoist of Upper Purity. He wore a crown of nine clouds, a red robe, and he rode a white horse. Attacking Grand Master with a sword, he said,

> "In the beginning, the Dao was one
> There is something, but there is also nothing
> Purple air from the east passes through Han Pass
> For the first time in five thousand years."

The second was the Daoist of Jade Purity. He was a man with a long beard and a yellow robe. He said,

> "I am the founder of Jie Daoism
> I came to Mount Kunlun from Han Pass
> My body is immortal, like heaven and earth
> Even if Mount Sumeru falls, I will live."

The third was the Daoist of Extreme Purity. He wore a purple robe and held a Dragon Beard Fan in his hand. He rode a lion. He said,

> "I cannot count the years since my life began
> I was the first to be separated by Hongmeng[1]
> I know all about heaven and earth
> You can look through the door and see."

Grand Master was confused. He did not know who these three Daoists were, but now he was being attacked on all four sides. His disciples watched the battle but did not interfere.

They are formless but are often represented as elderly men. The first is heavenly qi, the second is human qi, and the third is earth qi.

[1] Hongmeng, literally "vast mist," is the primeval chaos that existed in the world before Pangu created the world and separated heaven and earth.

Chapter 78
Breaking the Trap

The trap has four doors
Smoke, wind, fire and thunder

Grand Master is gone
Like a feather in the wind

The swords can kill gods
But now they just leave black smoke

Powerful magic won't help you
If it's time to meet the great leader[1]

≡ ≡ ≡

The Three Pure Ones inside the trap were made from qi and were not real people. They could not hurt Grand Master but they could confuse him. Laozi rang a bell to make the three immortals disappear. Then he struck Grand Master three times with his walking stick. Many Treasures tried to help his master, but he was captured by Laozi's genie. The genie carried him out of the trap and put him in the peach garden.

Laozi left the trap. "What happened in the trap?" asked Heavenly Primogenitor when Laozi returned.

"There are four gates," he replied. "You and I can break two of them. But none of our disciples are strong enough to break the other two."

Just then, Zhunti arrived from the western region. Laozi greeted him, and thanked him for arriving at just the right time. "Brothers," he said, "I live in the western region, where flowers bloom and people are happy. Recently I saw some red light in this region, so I have come to see if you need my help. I saw four swords hanging in that trap nearby. What are they?"

---

[1] This poem is about the battle at the Immortal Killing Trap, where Laozi defeats Grand Master of Heaven. The four swords in the trap can kill gods ("swallow gods' bones"), but against these great ones they can only leave a harmless trail of smoke.

Laozi replied, "A long time ago, our master gave those four swords to Grand Master of Heaven. He was told to use the swords to fight monsters and demons, but it was fated that he would use the swords to cause trouble for us. Now he has built a trap with those swords. We must break the trap. We need one more powerful person to help us."

"Let me invite the religious leader of the western region. Then the three religions will work together to tell jade from stone. We will break the trap."

Zhunti flew to see the Buddha of the western region. He told the Buddha, "I saw hundreds of red lights in the southeast. I went to see what was going on. I found a very dangerous trap. It has four gates. Four powerful immortals are needed to break the trap. We have three, but need one more. This poor Daoist asks you to come and help us."

The Buddha replied, "My friend, I know very little about the human world. I may not do the right things to help you."

"Don't worry," said Zhunti. "We will do this together."

Heavenly Primogenitor was waiting with Laozi near the trap when Zhunti and the Buddha arrived. He told Jade Tripod, Heavenly Master of Divine Virtue, Grand Completion and Pure Essence to hold out their hands. He wrote a spell on each of their hands. He said, "Wait until you see fire in the sky and you hear thunder from the trap. Then rush to the gates. Each of you must take down one sword. Then wait for me." He said to Burning Lamp, "You will wait in the air above the trap. Use your magic pearls if you have to."

At dawn the next day, the four religious leaders rushed up to the trap, shouting, "Grand Master of Heaven, come out now!"

Grand Master came out. He looked at Zhunti and the Buddha and said, "You two should be living happily in the western region. We live in the east. We are like fire and water that cannot be in the same place at the same time. Why did you come here to cause trouble? You cannot harm me. I was born at the beginning of time, and I know the five elements."

Zhunti smiled and said, "Brother, you should not brag like that. The Dao is as deep as the sea, we cannot talk about it. Now it is time for you to break this trap."

Grand Master just said, "We will see who comes out on top," and he went back inside the trap.

The four masters rode towards the four gates. Grand Master sent out a thunderclap from his hand. The sword above Heavenly Primogenitor fell down, but a cloud of flowers and pearls protected the immortal's head as he passed through the gate.

Another sword came down towards the Buddha, but three Buddhist relics came from the top of his head, pushing the sword into a wall. He also entered the trap.

Laozi used his gold pagoda to protect himself from the falling sword. The sword hung in the air while Laozi entered the trap with no trouble.

Zhunti lifted his small lotus branch to stop the falling sword. He entered the trap and waited for the others.

When all four were inside the trap, Laozi shouted, "What will you do now, Brother?" He spread yellow fog everywhere. Zhunti changed into a creature with twenty-four heads and eighteen arms. He held many weapons in his hands. Grand Master attacked, but the four immortals surrounded him and fought back with their magic weapons.

Grand Master could not win the battle. Laozi hit him in the back, knocking out his magic fire. Zhunti hit him with his club and he fell off his ox. He tried to fly up and away, but Burning Lamp was waiting for him and hit him with magic pearls. He fell to the ground.

Now the other four immortals ran into the trap and pulled down the four swords, breaking the trap. The battle was over.

Grand Master ran away. He was badly wounded and had lost all four of his magic swords. He did not want to face his disciples. He went alone to a nearby mountain. There he built a terrace. He built a tall flagpole and placed a large flag on it. The flag had six tails on it. The tails had names written on them, Buddha, Zhunti, Laozi, Heavenly Primogenitor, King Wu and Jiang Ziya. Every day he wrote magic spells on them, and shook them to try and destroy the souls of the six people. He also planned to use the flag later in another trap, to be called the Ten Thousand Immortals Trap.

The four religious leaders returned to their homes. Before they left, Laozi told Jiang Ziya that he could now attack Jiepai Pass.

The commander of Jiepai Pass was a man named Xu Gai. When he learned of the destruction of the trap, he wrote a letter and sent it by messenger to the Shang king, asking for help.

When the message arrived in Zhaoge, a minister brought it immediately to the king. The king read it. He said, "We did not know that Jiang Ziya was rebelling and attacking the five passes. We must stop him."

The minister replied, "Your Majesty, Jiang Ziya and King Wu now have six hundred thousand soldiers. They have taken three passes already. I beg you, please stop drinking and save the kingdom."

Daji and the concubine Hu Ximei asked the king why he was unhappy. "My queen," he said to Daji, "Jiang Ziya's army has captured three passes. This is a serious problem. We are worried about the country and our ancient temples."

Daji smiled and said, "Don't worry, my love. Those generals at the passes only want to get rich. They are telling lies, hoping that you will send more men and supplies to them. They are just lying to you."

"What should we do, my queen?"

"Cut off the messenger's head. That will send a message to them, telling them that you are wise and are not fooled by their lies."

The king ordered that the messenger be killed, and his head hung on the city wall. Some of his ministers rushed in to ask why he killed the messenger. "Don't worry!" said the king. "Jiang Ziya is just an old fortuneteller. We still have four strong passes, and we have the Yellow River and Mengjin. That old man can't do anything." The ministers went away, sadly, thinking that the dynasty's end would come soon.

Jiang Ziya went to see King Wu. He told the king that he was preparing to attack Jiepai Pass, the next pass east of Sishui Pass. The army traveled to Jiepai Pass. Jiang Ziya selected one of his generals to go out and challenge the Shang army.

Xu Gai had just heard that his messenger was killed by the king. He was very unhappy, and did not want to fight for the king. But one of his generals, a magician named Peng Zun, said, "We all are subjects of the king. We eat his food and live on his land. How can we turn away from him now? I am willing to serve as a dog and a horse to repay the king's kindness." He rode out of the pass to meet the challenge.

Peng Zun fought with the Zhou general. Peng Zun could not fight as well as the general, so he turned and rode away. But as he rode away, he threw something on the ground. A small trap appeared. Peng Zun disappeared into the trap. Thunder roared, and the Zhou general died, turned into black smoke.

The next day, Thunderbolt went out and challenged Peng Zun. Peng Zun attacked, but he did not know that Thunderbolt could fly. Thunderbolt flew into the air and tried to knock Peng Zun off his horse. Peng Zun turned to ride away. Thunderbolt remembered what happened the previous day, so he knew what Peng Zun was planning. Before Peng Zun could use his magic, Thunderbolt knocked him off his horse with his golden cudgel, then he cut off his head.

Chapter 79
Four Generals Are Captured

One pass is crossed, another comes
Magic treasures bring danger

Fa Jie's soul is in the past
Long Anji's bones bring chaos

Many dangers
But Western Qi still has heaven's blessing

Xu Fang is a fool
To fight against them[1]

≡ ≡ ≡

Xu Gai, the commander of the pass, was very upset when he saw Peng Zun killed in combat. He was thinking about how to surrender to Jiang Ziya, so that more of his people would not be killed. But just then, a Daoist monk came to see him.

The monk said, "Commander, my name is Fa Jie[2]. I am a poor Daoist monk from Mount Penglai. My disciple, Peng Zun, was killed in combat by Thunderbolt. I have come to get revenge."

"My friend," said Xu Gai, "that may be difficult. Jiang Ziya is very powerful. He has already taken three passes and five mountains. I don't think we can defeat him."

"Of course we can. I will capture Jiang Ziya and bring him to you."

Xu Gai gave the Daoist a vegetarian dinner and a place to sleep. The next day, Fa Jie walked out of the pass, alone. He had a bright gold ring on his head, and he wore a black robe with a picture of a white crane looking up at clouds in the sky. He called for Thunderbolt to come out

---

[1] This poem mentions three of Shang's fighters: Fa Jie, a Daoist monk; Long Anji, a general at Chuanyun Pass; and Xu Fang, the commander of Chuanyun Pass.

[2] It's not clear who Fa Jie ("dharma law") is, as his name does not appear in the historical records. This character might be inspired by Dharmaratna, an Indian Buddhist monk who introduced Buddhism to China in the 1st century A.D.

and fight him.

Thunderbolt flew out of the Zhou camp on wings of wind and thunder. They fought for a few rounds. Then Fa Jie waved a flag. Thunderbolt fell to the ground. The Shang soldiers grabbed him, tied him up, and took him prisoner.

Nezha saw this. He shouted, "How dare you use sorcery to capture my brother!" He ran out to fight. Fa Jie waved his flag, but it did not bother Nezha at all. Nezha threw his Universal Ring. It knocked Fa Jie to the ground, but he escaped on a cloud of dust.

When he returned to the pass, Xu Gai asked him what happened. He replied, "I could not hurt Nezha because he has no soul." He was very angry, so he ordered some soldiers to cut off Thunderbolt's head.

Xu Gai did not want to see this happen, because he still wanted to surrender to the Zhou side. So he said, "No, we should not kill him. After we win the battle, we will take him to Zhaoge and let the king decide what to do with him."

The next day, Fa Jie went out and fought Jiang Ziya. He could not defeat Jiang Ziya, but he did succeed in capturing his magic staff. Then more Zhou generals joined the fight. Li Jing used his sword and Earth Traveler Sun used his iron rod. Zheng Lun and Yang also attacked him. Fa Jie could not win against the four immortals. He fell to the ground and was captured by the soldiers. They brought him before Jiang Ziya.

When Fa Jie saw Jiang Ziya, he shouted, "Jiang Ziya! You don't need to say anything to me. I had bad luck today. The ancients say, 'The storms on the sea are huge, but I was caught by a small magic trick.' This is my fate. Just do what you have to do."

Jiang Ziya was just about to order the man killed, when a Buddha came to see him. It was Zhunti. He sang this song,

> *Forget what is good and what is bad*
> *Don't worry about wealth or fame*
> *Eat when you are hungry*
> *Drink when you are thirsty*
> *Sit quietly and meditate*
> *Devils may come to visit you*
> *If you think evil thoughts*
> *You will die by the sword in this world*

Then he said, "Jiang Ziya, don't kill this man! He is not on the List of Creations. His fate is to become a Buddhist."

Jiang Ziya smiled and said, "I would not dare to disobey you!" He ordered his soldiers to set Fa Jie free. Zhunti took Fa Jie by the arm and led him away, singing,

> Young man, come with me to the west
> The moon is bright, the air is sweet, the wind is soft
> White clouds dance in the sky
> Water flows down the mountain
> A wonderful land of seven treasures
> A quiet pond of eight virtues
> Buddhist relics shine brightly everywhere
> Mount Kunlun has many wonderful things
> But in the west, ours are even better!

Fa Jie followed Zhunti to the west and became a Buddhist. Many years later, he came back to China and helped to bring Buddhism to the people.

Now Xu Gai was able to surrender. He left the pass and walked to the Zhou camp. He waited outside the gate. After a little while, Jiang Ziya invited him to come in and meet with him and King Wu. They both welcomed him to their side. The Zhou army marched into the pass and took control of it without a fight.

The next pass to the east was Chuanyun Pass, about eighty *li* away. Jiang Ziya marched his army east like a tiger hungry for a meal.

The commander of Chuanyun Pass was a man named Xu Fang. He was the brother of Xu Gai. When he heard that his brother had surrendered, he was so angry that smoke came from his nose. He said to his generals, "My brother is a fool! He does not care about the safety of his parents, his wife and his children. Now our entire family might be put to death, and he will be known as a traitor for a thousand years. We must do our best to capture the rebels, then we will ask His Majesty to forgive us."

One of his generals, Long Anji, shouted, "Don't worry, my lord. We will defeat the Zhou army and take their leaders as prisoners to Zhaoge. That will show the king that you are loyal to him."

When the Zhou army arrived at the pass, Xu Gai told Jiang Ziya there was no need for fighting. He would just go and talk with his brother.

Jiang Ziya replied, "If you can do that, your name will be famous for a thousand years."

Xu Gai approached the gate and shouted, "Open the gate!" But as soon as he entered, his brother's guards grabbed him and tied him up.

"You fool!" said Xu Fang. "You are a disloyal minister. You have brought shame to our family. Our ancestors have brought you here today, so I can save our family from death."

"You are the fool," replied Xu Gai. "Can't you see that the whole kingdom has joined the Zhou? If you want to see a loyal minister, look at Su Hu, look at Huang Feihu, look at Deng Jiugong. They are loyal to the country."

Xu Fang threw his brother into jail.

The next day, Nezha rode out on his Wind Fire Wheels for the first combat. The Shang general blew a cloud of black smoke out of his mouth. But Nezha just flew up into the sky. He shook his body and changed into his other form, with three heads, eight arms, and a blue face. The Shang general was terrified. Nezha threw his Nine Dragon Divine Fire Coverlet over the general, burning him to ashes.

On the third day, Huang Feihu rode out on his divine ox. Long Anji rode his horse out of the pass and shouted, "Huang Feihu! You are a rebel and have caused too much trouble. I will take you prisoner today!"

The two of them fought for a long time, almost fifty rounds. Long Anji took a small thing from a silk bag and threw it into the air. It made a sound like small bells. He shouted, "Huang Feihu! Look at my treasure!" Huang Feihu foolishly looked up. His muscles became weak. He fell from his horse and was captured by the Shang soldiers. Xu Fang ordered his soldiers to put him in jail with Xu Gai.

On the fourth day, Hong Jin rode out from the Zhou camp. Long Anji was waiting for him. Many years earlier, Hong Jin was a commander and Long Anji was a general under him. Now he shouted, "Long Anji, it has been a long time! Please get down from your horse and surrender to your old master!"

"You talk too much," replied Long Anji.

Hong Jin fought with his sword and his ax. Long Anji threw two rings into the air. They flew around each other in circles, like yin and yang. They were called Paralyzing Rings, because anyone who looked at them would lose the use of their muscles. Hong Jin looked at them, and immediately fell to the ground. He was thrown in jail with the other prisoners.

On the fifth day, Nangong Kuo went out to fight. He was captured the same way that the others were.

Nezha said, "We must stop this, we are losing too many generals. I will find out what kind of magic this is."

Chapter 80
Breaking the Plague Trap

Plague umbrellas use dark magic
They can kill everyone in the world

The trap is difficult to break
The people are afraid

It enters every home
It brings death

Ziya will see more disasters
He must suffer at Chuanyun Pass[1]

≡ ≡ ≡

Nezha rode out towards the pass, shouting, "You on the left! You on the right! Tell Long Anji to come out and fight me!"

Long Anji rode out to meet Nezha. First, he tried to stab Nezha with his lance. Then he threw his Paralyzing Rings up in the air and shouted, "Look at my treasure, Nezha!"

Nezha looked at the two rings, yin and yang. He was not harmed by them at all, because he was made from lotus leaves instead of flesh and bone. The rings fell to the ground.

Nezha changed into his other form, with eight arms and three heads. He threw his Universal Ring into the air, saying, "Your rings are not as good as mine!" Long Anji could not do anything to stop the Universal Ring. The ring hit him on the head. He fell, and Nezha killed him.

Xu Fang, the commander of the pass, saw the defeat of his general. He did not have any more generals to send into battle. He did not know what to do, other than writing another letter to the king asking for help.

Just then, a Daoist came to see him. It was Lu Yue, the powerful

---

[1] The trap they encounter in this chapter has 21 plague umbrellas used to spread smallpox through the Zhou camp. Jiang Ziya is caught in the trap because he is fated to suffer there for 100 days.

magician. He had three eyes, a blue face, red hair, and long fangs coming out of his mouth. He said, "I am Lu Yue from Nine Dragon Island. Jiang Ziya killed four of my disciples. I am here to seek revenge!" Xu Fang gave him food and wine, and they talked long into the night.

The next day, Lu Yue demanded to see Jiang Ziya. Jiang Ziya came out. He laughed when he saw Lu Yue. "My friend, you don't know when to advance and when to retreat. You escaped alive once already, why do you now come and seek your own death?"

Lu Yue flew into the air and slashed at Jiang Ziya with his sword. Several of Jiang Ziya's generals came to help him. They surrounded him and fought against him. What a battle! The earth shook, the seas boiled, the rivers danced.

Thunderbolt was injured in the fight and had to return to camp. But the others continued to fight. Lu Yue could not stand against them, so he turned and rode back to the pass. He said to Xu Fang, "That was a difficult fight. Now I must wait for my friend to come and help me."

Three days later, a Daoist arrived at the pass. Lu Yue said to the commander, "Please meet my younger brother, Chen Geng. Together, we will defeat the Zhou and take their king prisoner."

The next morning, Lu Yue came out of the pass with Chen Geng and three thousand soldiers. He shouted, "Jiang Ziya! You and I cannot live under the same sky. I have built a trap. Let's see if you can survive it!"

Jiang Ziya said, "My friend, no good Daoist would build an evil trap like this. But since you have gone to the trouble of building it, I am happy to take a look at it. Please do not use any hidden weapons when we go inside to look at it."

"Of course not, I would never do something like that."

Jiang Ziya and several of his generals walked into the trap. They looked around for a while, then they went outside again. "Well?" asked Lu Yue. "What do you think of it?"

Yang Jian answered, smiling, "It's nothing for us to worry about. It's got a little bit of Daoist magic in it. It looks like some kind of plague trap. But you have not finished it yet. Tell us when you are done, and we will take another look at it."

Lu Yue heard these words. They were like stones thrown into the sea. He could not say anything. He just returned quietly to the pass.

In the Zhou camp, Jiang Ziya was pleased with the words that Yang Jian had said. But he added, "We don't understand much about this trap. We must be careful."

Master of the Clouds walked into the room. He said, "I have come to help you break this plague trap. It is not a powerful trap, but still, you must suffer for one hundred days. Then someone will be able to break it. Please let me be the commander of your army for a while."

"Of course," said Jiang Ziya, and he gave his seal and sword to Master of the Clouds.

Lu Yue and Chen Geng continued to work on the trap. They added twenty-one plague umbrellas, placing them according to the nine palaces and eight trigrams[1]. In the center was a platform made from dirt.

While they worked on the trap, Lu Yue's friend Li Ping came in. Lu Yue said, "Wonderful! You can help us build the trap."

"No," said Li Ping. "I heard you were building this trap, and want you to stop building it. You know that the king of Shang is evil, and the entire country is rising up against him. But King Wu is a good man, as good as Yao and Shun. Please listen to me. Stop building this trap. Let King Wu and Jiang Ziya take the pass. Join with the Zhou and help save our country."

But Lu Yue did not listen to his friend. He continued working on the trap. Li Ping said, "My brother, listen to me. Jiang Ziya has already broken ten traps. You know what the ancients say, 'The cart in front has overturned, the cart behind should learn from it.'"

Still, Lu Yue continued to work on the trap. Li Ping tried five times to get his friend to stop, but nothing worked. When the trap was finished, Lu Yue sent this letter to Jiang Ziya,

"Lu Yue, a Daoist from Nine Dragon Island, tells this to Commander Jiang Ziya. If you go against the will of heaven, you will be punished. Now heaven is angry. It has asked me to build this trap. It is not too late for you to join us and support your king. If you do not, then you will

---

[1] This is a famous arrangement, said to be invented by the legendary emperor Fu Xi who lived around 1500 B.C. Each trigram consists of three stacked lines, each line solid or broken, taken from the I Ching. The eight trigrams are arranged in a circle, with a ninth trigram placed in the center.

soon beg for death."

Jiang Ziya read the letter and just said, "It is time for me to break this trap." Master of the Clouds put charms on his chest, back and head, and placed a pill of elixir in his shirt. Jiang Ziya rode his huge horse out, shouting, "Lu Yue! I've come to break your evil trap!" King Wu and all the ministers and generals watched from behind the camp walls.

Lu Yue rode out on his golden-eyed camel, waving his sword. Jiang Ziya met him. They fought for a few rounds, then Lu Yue turned and rode into the trap. Jiang Ziya followed him inside.

What was the trap like?

> *The air is evil, sad wind surrounds you*
> *The darkness is filled with cries of ghosts*
> *The sky is full of thunder and lightning*
> *It's so cold you cannot breathe the air*
> *It's so cold you cannot let the wind hit your face*
> *From afar, it looks like flying sand and rocks*
> *From near, it looks like rolling fog and clouds*
> *The plague comes, also water and fire*
> *The gods are afraid*

Lu Yue walked over to the platform and picked up one of the plague umbrellas. He opened it. The air turned dark, a fog rolled in, and plague surrounded Jiang Ziya. He held his yellow apricot flag and moved forward, slowly.

Lu Yue rushed outside and shouted, "Jiang Ziya is dead!"

But Master of the Clouds said to the others, "Lu Yue does not understand. Jiang Ziya must suffer for a hundred days inside the trap. Don't worry about him."

The Zhou generals were angry. They rushed forward and used all their magic weapons and abilities to attack Lu Yue and Chen Geng. The Shang generals could not fight so many powerful immortals, so they rode back to the pass.

A hundred days passed slowly. To King Wu, every day seemed to last for a year. Master of the Clouds said to him, "Your Majesty, please don't worry. Do you remember that once before, Jiang Ziya was trapped for a long time inside one of the traps? No harm will come to one who is blessed by heaven."

Lu Yue went inside the trap three times a day. Each time he waved the plague umbrellas at Jiang Ziya, trying to make him sick. Each time, Jiang Ziya protected himself with the yellow apricot flag.

Xu Fang was worried. He said to Lu Yue, "I think we should bring our four prisoners back to Zhaoge. We should beg the king for mercy, and we can ask him for more soldiers." Lu Yue did not like this idea, but Xu Fang was the commander of the pass. He put the four Zhou generals in a cart and told his soldiers to take them to Zhaoge, a distance of about eighty li.

Meanwhile, the immortal named Master Pure Void Virtue was on Mount Green Peak, meditating on his green cloud. He called to his disciple Yang Ren and said, "It is time for you to go down to Chuanyun Pass. You must rescue Jiang Ziya and the four generals."

"But Master," said Yang Ren, "I am a minister, not a soldier. I know nothing about weapons or fighting."

The master smiled and said, "That's not a problem. If you want to learn how to use a weapon, you can learn. But if you don't want to learn, you won't be able to use it." Then he taught Yang Ren how to use the Flying Lightning Lance. He said, "This weapon is sharp enough to stab through armor and bone. It can kill a tiger and defeat a dragon. It brings male energy and female energy together. It can fly, it can fight, and it can help you save the Zhou commander and his generals. Now I will show you how to use it."

The master also gave Yang Ren a flying beast and a Five Fire Heavenly Fan. Then he told Yang Ren to fly away to Chuanyun Pass.

Yang Ren looked down and saw the prisoners and some soldiers, about thirty *li* from the pass. He came down in front of the soldiers and said, "Where do you think you are going?"

The soldiers looked at Yang Ren. He was very strange looking. He had two small hands growing from his two eye sockets, and he had two eyes in the palms of his hands. Yang Ren continued, "I am the supreme minister. This country already belongs to the new king. There is no need for you to act against the will of heaven."

Yang Ren was not a soldier, his voice was soft. The Shang commander thought he was weak, so he shouted, "Taste my lance, you rebel!" and rushed forward.

Yang Ren took out his Five Fire Heavenly Fan and waved it at the Shang general. Instantly the general and his horse were both turned to ashes. A powerful wind came and blew away the ashes. Terrified, the Shang soldiers turned and ran in all directions.

Yang Ren walked over to the prisoners' cart. He said, "My name is Yang Ren. I was once the supreme minister for the king of Shang. When the king began to build the Deer Terrace, I told him it was a bad idea. He became angry and had my eyes gouged out. Master Pure Void Virtue saw this. He saved my life by putting elixir in my eye sockets."

He freed the four generals. They all returned to the Zhou camp near Chuanyun Pass. He told his story to King Wu. The king said, "You have come at a very good time. Jiang Ziya has been in the trap for ninety-seven days. Wait three more days, then you can save him."

Three days later, Yang Ren approached the trap. Lu Yue rushed out to meet him. "Who are you?" he shouted.

"I am Yang Ren, disciple of Master Pure Void Virtue. I am here to break your trap and destroy your army."

"You are nothing but a little baby!" replied Lu Yue. He attacked Yang Ren, then turned and ran into the trap. Yang Ren ran inside after him.

Chapter 81
The God of Plague

Smallpox is a terrible disease
Much worse than other injuries

Purple pox can save lives
But it can also kill

Nobody can travel
Every family suffers

If not for King Wu's blessings
The army would be destroyed[1]

≡ ≡ ≡

Lu Yue ran into the trap, running fast to keep away from Yang Ren. Quickly he grabbed one of the plague umbrellas. But Yang Ren waved his fan. The umbrella burst into flame and burned to ashes. As Yang Ren continued to wave his fan, all of the plague umbrellas burned.

Lu Yue tried to extinguish the fires, but it was magical fire created from the five elements so there was nothing he could do. He tried to run away. Yang Ren waved his fan again. Lu Yue's body became hot, then it began to burn. He died and his soul flew to the Terrace of Creation.

Jiang Ziya was still in the trap. He had wrapped the apricot flag around himself for protection. His face was the color of pale gold and he was very weak. Wu Ji carefully picked him up and carried him back to the Zhou camp.

When they got back to the camp, Master of the Clouds poured some elixir in Jiang Ziya's mouth. The commander opened his eyes and said, "Thank you for saving my life!"

---

[1] Smallpox was probably introduced into China around 49 A.D., when soldiers fighting barbarians came down with the disease. Since the Chinese did not know about viruses, it was believed to be caused by excessive heat in the internal organs. There were many treatments but no cures. However, by 1022 A.D. a method was developed to inoculate against the disease by inserting powdered pox scabs (the "purple pox" mentioned in the poem) into the nose.

Master of the Clouds said, "You must rest for a few days. I must go now. But I will return when you arrive at the Ten Thousand Immortal trap." Then he flew back to his home in the mountains.

Yang Ren said, "Our four generals have been rescued and we have broken the trap. This is a good time to attack the pass!"

Jiang Ziya agreed. He ordered all his generals and his entire army to attack the pass from both sides. Thunderbolt flew to the tower that guarded the pass, and he smashed it with one blow from his cudgel. Nezha broke the lock on the gate. The Zhou army rushed in and surrounded the pass commander Xu Fang. One of the generals tried to kill Xu Fang with his sword, but the sword cut off the head of the Xu Fang's horse instead, throwing him to the ground.

Jiang Ziya led his army into the fort. He spoke to the people, telling them that they had nothing to fear from the Zhou army. Then the soldiers dragged Xu Fang forward to stand before Jiang Ziya.

Xu Fang would not bow. Jiang Ziya said to him, "You captured your own brother and put him in prison. How dare you do such things to your family!" To the soldiers he said, "This is not a man, this is a beast. Take him out and cut off his head."

King Wu held a banquet to celebrate the great victory. The next day, the Zhou army marched about eighty *li* to Tongguan Pass. They set up a camp and fired their cannons to tell the soldiers inside the fort that they had arrived.

The commander of the pass was a man named Yu Hualong. He had five sons. From oldest to youngest, their names were Yu Da, Yu Zhao, Yu Guang, Yu Xian, and Yu De. They all heard the cannons. The commander was worried about the battle that was to come. But the sons all said, "Father, don't worry. This commander has very little talent. He cannot defeat us, so he cannot take the pass."

The next day, Tai Luan from the Zhou army asked to take the first battle. He went outside and saw a general on a big silver horse. The general wore silver armor over a red robe. "Who comes out to meet me?" shouted Tai Luan.

"I am Yu Da, the eldest son of Commander Yu," came the reply. "We have heard many stories about your commander. We have heard that he is a rebel who has forgotten his duties as minister of the king. How dare you fight us now!"

Tai Luan replied, "My commander has been sent by heaven. He has already taken several passes. You cannot fight us. It's best for you to surrender now. If you don't, you will be very sorry."

Yu Da attacked. Tai Luan was a good fighter but he could not win against Yu Da. He saw he was losing the battle, so he turned and tried to ride away. But Yu Da hit him with his Heart Smashing Club, killing him. Yu Da cut off his head and brought it back to the fort to give to his father.

Su Hu saw this. He became angry and asked Jiang Ziya for permission to go and fight. Jiang Ziya agreed. Su Hu rode out on his horse. He saw someone on horseback and shouted, "Who are you?"

The reply came, "I am Yu Zhao, the second son of commander Yu. And who are you?"

"I am Su Hu, the marquis of Jizhou."

"Old man, you are the father-in-law of the king, you should be fighting to protect our king. But you have forgotten your duty to your king and have become a rebel. Soon King Wu will be captured and killed. Give up now and save yourself!"

Su Hu was furious. He attacked the young man. But Yu Zhao took out a yellow flag. Waving the flag, he and his horse both disappeared in a golden beam of light. Su Hu could not see him. Suddenly Yu Zhao stabbed him in the ribs. Su Hu fell off his horse and died. Yu Zhao cut off his head and brought it back to give to his father.

When Su Quanzhong saw his father killed in battle, he begged Jiang Ziya to let him go and get revenge for his father's death. He rode out towards the fort. He saw a young man coming out. He shouted, "Are you Yu Zhao? Come out and meet your death!"

The young man said, "No, I am Yu Guang, the third son of the commander."

"I don't care who you are, I will kill you!" shouted Su Quanzhong. They began to fight. After twenty rounds, Yu Guang took out a javelin and hit Su Quanzhong with it three times, almost knocking him off his horse. Su Quanzhong held on to his horse and rode back to the Zhou camp.

Yu Hualong was feeling good about the three victories. The next day he and his four oldest sons rode out of the pass and called for Jiang Ziya to come out.

Jiang Ziya wanted to frighten his enemies, so he fired the Zhou cannons and rode out of the camp. All his generals surrounded him on his left and right sides. He said, "I am sorry I cannot bow to you. I am wearing too much armor. Heaven has sent me to punish the evil king. We have won many battles, and many commanders have come over to join us. You were lucky three times, but your luck will not last forever. Please think twice before fighting us."

Yu Hualong smiled and said, "I see that you know nothing, and you do not understand heaven or earth. You are rebelling against your king. You are trying to trick the people with your evil words. Today you will die, and there will be no one to bury your body." Then turning to his sons, he shouted, "You on the left, you on the right, who will help me defeat this fool?"

The commander and his sons rode forward. They were met by four Zhou generals. The armies rushed together like two ocean waves. Spears smashed against spears, knives against knives. The sky turned dark, ghosts cried, gods shouted. Dead bodies fell to the ground, the grass turned red with blood.

The Shang commander and one of his sons were badly wounded. The next day, the youngest son, Yu De, rode out to get revenge against Jiang Ziya. He wore a Daoist robe and straw shoes. He shouted, "Yesterday my father was attacked by a dog, and my brother was hit by a ring. Today I will get my revenge!" He was quickly surrounded by several of the Zhou generals. He fought against them. Then Yang Jian threw a golden ball that hit him on the head. Crying in pain, he rode away.

Jiang Ziya said, "I remember my master told me, 'Beware of Da, Zhao, Guang, Xian and De.' Now I know what he was talking about!"

Yu De was even more angry than before. He told his brothers that he was going to destroy the Zhou army. "Take a bath tonight," he told them. "Tomorrow I will use magic against our enemies. We don't need to use swords or arrows. Within seven days they will all be dead."

The brothers all took baths and put on clean clothes. Yu De took out five colored handkerchiefs – green, yellow, red, white and black. He put them on the ground. Then he gave each brother a small gourd full of a strange liquid. He told them to turn the gourd over and pour a little bit of liquid on their handkerchief, and then stand on it. He walked around them, saying magic words. A strong wind came. It was so strong that large trees crashed to the ground.

That night, Yu De picked up the five handkerchiefs and flew into the air over the Zhou camp. He shook the handkerchiefs, causing the strange liquid to rain down onto the ground. Soon all 600,000 men were sick, and so were the horses. Some of them had their skin turn black. Others had their skin turn green, yellow, red or white. The only ones not sick were Nezha because he was made of lotus flowers, and Yang Jian who had left the camp earlier.

Yu Da, the eldest brother, saw that nobody was moving in the Zhou camp. He wanted to attack. But Yu De said, "Elder brother, no need to fight them now. Let's just wait a few days. They will all be dead and we won't have to lift a finger."

If they attacked that day, it would have been the end of the Zhou rebellion. But the Shang army waited.

Yellow Dragon Immortal and Jade Tripod arrived at the Zhou camp. They told Yang Jian to fly immediately to Fire Cloud Cave to get some help.

What did he see when he arrived at the cave?

> *Green pine trees, tall bamboos with phoenix tails*
> *Soft green grass with dragon whiskers*
> *Rocks like crouching tigers*
> *Old vines on the trees like brown snakes*
> *Golden shadows on the red wall*
> *Lotus flowers in the flowing stream*
> *Green mountains covered with heavy fog*
> *Heaven is no more beautiful than this place*
> *Fire Cloud Cave is better than Xuandu*

A disciple led Yang Jian into the cave. Emperor Fuxi[1] was sitting there. Yang Jian bowed low to him and said, "Your disciple wishes you ten thousand years of life!"

Then he gave Fuxi a letter. The letter said that the Zhou army was attacked and poisoned by the sorcerer Yu De. It asked Fuxi to take pity on them and save their lives.

---

[1] Fuxi is known in Chinese mythology as the "original god," born around 2600 BC. He and his sister Nuwa created humanity and invented music, hunting, fishing, cooking, and domestication of animals. He is sometimes shown as a snake-like creature, or a man clothed in animal skins.

"King Wu is the next king, chosen by heaven," said Fuxi after reading the letter. "He is fated to suffer, but I think we should help him. What do you think, Brother?"

Emperor Shen Nong[1] was standing nearby. He said, "You are right, Brother." He gave three pills to Yang Jian, saying, "Give one of these to King Wu and one to Jiang Ziya. Put the last one in the camp's water supply. This will save the lives of your people."

"What is this plague?" asked Yang Jian. "And if it comes again, what should we do?"

"This plague is called smallpox. I will show you how to cure it." He led Yang Jian out of the cave. They walked around looking down at the ground. Shen Nong reached down and picked up an herb[2] and handed it to Yang Jian. "When you return, tell your people to use this to cure smallpox."

Yang Jian bowed and thanked the two emperors. Then he flew back to camp and gave the pills to Yellow Dragon Immortal and Jade Tripod. They did what the emperor had told them.

The next day, everyone was cured of the plague, though many had scars on their bodies. Jiang Ziya said, "We must conquer the pass today. We will not stop until we have beaten them all."

---

[1] Emperor Shen Nong is another mythical Chinese emperor. He came to power after the reign of Fuxi. He invented the plow, the hoe, the axe, and established the first farmer's market.
[2] The herb is cimicifuga foetida, known as black cohosh or in China as hēi shēngmá. It's used by Native Americans and in traditional Chinese medicine to treat several disorders, including smallpox and monkeypox.

Chapter 82
The Last Trap

Entering the evil trap
Cold wind hits their faces

Lights cover the sky
The spirit of death fills the heart

Now you can tell dragons from fish
And jade from stone

Years of study are gone
But now there is a path to the west[1]

≡ ≡ ≡

At Tongguan Pass, the commander and his sons waited for seven days, hoping that everyone in the Zhou camp would die from the plague. They drank wine and talked and waited. On the eighth day, they climbed to the top of the wall and looked over at the Zhou camp. To their surprise, they saw thousands of soldiers busy working and preparing for battle. Yu Da said to his brothers, "You should have listened to me and attacked the Zhou when they were sick. Now it might be too late."

Yu De replied, "They are still weak. Let's attack today." They all rushed out of the pass and approached the Zhou camp. The attack came like high winds and heavy rain, the soldiers shouting loudly and waving their weapons.

The Zhou saw them coming. They rushed out to meet them, with Nezha leading the attack. It was a terrible battle. Six Zhou generals surrounded Yu Hualong and fought against him. The four older Yu brothers were all killed one by one. The youngest brother, Yu De,

---

[1] This poem is about Black Cloud, who was originally a turtle. At the end of the battle, the Buddha Zhunti could "tell dragon from fish" (that is, see his true nature) and "tell jade from stone" (that is, the valuable from the worthless), and he brings Black Cloud to the Pure Land of the western region.

screamed and rushed at Jiang Ziya. But Li Jing jumped in front and stabbed him to death.

Yu Hualong saw all his sons were dead and his army was defeated. He looked up at the sky and said, "My king, I am sorry I cannot defeat these rebels. I will give up my life to repay you for what you have given me." Then he cut his own throat and died.

The battle was over. Jiang Ziya entered the pass and spoke to the people, telling them that they had nothing to fear from the Zhou. Then he ordered that Yu Hualong and his sons be given a proper burial. Injured soldiers from both sides were given treatment.

Yellow Dragon Immortal and Jade Tripod said to Jiang Ziya, "There is only one trap left. It is the Ten Thousand Immortals trap. It is very dangerous, so King Wu should stay away from it. Many immortals will work together to destroy the trap. Build a pavilion for the immortals when they come. This is the last time we will kill in this world."

When the pavilion was ready, Yellow Dragon Immortal said, "All the disciples should come with me to the pavilion. The rest of the generals should stay here."

All the Chan Daoist immortals came down from their mountains. One by one, they arrived and entered the pavilion: Master Grand Completion, Pure Essence, Heavenly Master of Outstanding Culture, Universal Virtue, Merciful Navigation, Virtue of the Pure Void, Fairy Primordial, Spiritual Treasure, Heavenly Master of Divine Virtue, Krakucchanda, Master of the Clouds, and finally Burning Lamp. Jiang Ziya joined them, and they talked about how to destroy the last trap.

Yellow Dragon Immortal said to the others, "Recently the Jie[1] Daoists have been teaching their religion to bandits and thieves. They are fools, and it's too bad that they are fated to remain on the Wheel of Rebirth." They began walking towards the trap.

At the trap, Mother Golden Spirit saw the Chan Daoist immortals coming. Using wind and thunder, she pushed away the fog that surrounded the trap.

Another Jie Daoist named Ma Sui came out of the trap. He said, "Ah,

---

[1] The Shang are supported by immortals of the Jie sect which favors spiritual cultivation, while the Zhou side are supported by the Chan sect which favors charms and incantations. According to the scholar Shi Changyu, the friction between the fictional Jie and Chan sects is based on conflict between the Quanzhen and Zhengyi sects during the Ming Dynasty.

have you come to take a look at my trap? Come closer!"

Yellow Dragon Immortal replied, "Ma Sui, you have no great abilities. We will not enter your trap now. We will wait until our leaders arrive, then we will come back and break your trap." As he turned to leave, Ma Sui threw a golden hoop around the immortal's head. The hoop caused Yellow Dragon Immortal great pain, but the others carried him back to the pavilion.

As he sat in the pavilion holding his painful head, Heavenly Primogenitor arrived. He just pointed his finger at the golden hoop, and it fell to the ground. He said to all the immortals, "We will break this trap. But afterwards, you all must return to your caves. You must work to give up your desires, and you must never cause trouble in the human world again."

They all heard beautiful music coming from the sky. Looking up, they saw Laozi himself coming down. They all went out to greet him. Laozi said, "I have come to the human world one more time, to help the birth of the Zhou Dynasty. It is difficult to avoid fate, even for Buddhas and immortals."

At the trap, more Jie Daoists arrived. Grand Master of Heaven arrived with his disciples. He wrote a letter to the Chan Daoists and told one of his disciples to take it to Laozi.

Laozi read the letter. He said to the disciple, "We will meet you at the trap tomorrow."

The next day was the day of the great battle of the last trap. Laozi and Heavenly Primogenitor walked towards the trap. Behind the trap were the two Jie immortals and three thousand of their disciples.

Fog was in the air, and a cold wind was blowing. Inside the fog were lights of many colors. There were Daoist monks at the front and rear, and other immortals at the north, south, east and west gates. Colorful flags fluttered on the roof of the trap. The air was filled with the ringing of golden bells and jade chimes.

Grand Master of Heaven came out of the trap, riding on a huge bull, to greet them. He said, "How do you do, Brothers?"

Laozi said angrily, "Brother, do you have no shame? How can you be the leader of Jie Daoism? After you built the Immortal Killing Trap, you should have begged for forgiveness. But instead, you built another trap to kill more people. How can you be so evil?"

"Don't think you are better than me!" came the reply. "We are one. When the Buddha Zhunti hits me with his stick, don't you feel pain? How can you be so angry with me, when I am really you?"

Laozi said to the other Chan immortals, "This trap is not difficult to break. Who will break it for me?"

Pure Essence stepped forward. He approached the trap. A Daoist with a long black beard walked out of the trap. Pure Essence said, "I know you. You are Black Cloud. You will die right here!"

They began to fight. Black Cloud used a magic hammer to knock Pure Essence to the ground. But before he could kill him, Grand Completion ran up to join the fight. Black Cloud swung his magic hammer, but Grand Completion turned and ran away. Black Cloud chased him. Just as he was about to catch him, Zhunti stepped forward.

Zhunti smiled and said, "Black Cloud, how are you today?"

Black Cloud roared, "Buddha Zhunti! You hurt my master once. How dare you try to stop me today!" He slashed his sword at Zhunti.

But Zhunti opened his mouth. A green lotus flower came out of his mouth and blocked the sword. He said, "We are fated to be friends. Come with me to the western region[1]. You will become a Buddhist."

"You damned Buddha! You've gone too far this time!"

Zhunti pointed his finger, and a white lotus flower came out. "My friend, don't you see that the lotus flower can easily stop your sword? Come with me to the western region!"

This made Black Cloud even more angry. He swung his sword down at Zhunti, but he just waved it away with his hand.

"Where is my disciple?" he called out. A young man appeared, carrying a bamboo fishing pole.

---

[1] This story takes place about a thousand years before Buddhism comes to China. So, there are several places in the story, like this, where a Buddha comes from the western region (presumably India) to stop the killing of someone who is fated to become a Buddhist later.

Chapter 83
Lion, Elephant and Tiger

The crescent moon becomes a half-moon
Three stars are in the sky

Lion and elephant stand together
Merciful Navigation rides the tiger

Greed, anger and fear
They can keep you from gaining wisdom

No matter if you wear fur or horns
You will find peace[1]

☰ ☰ ☰

The Buddha Zhunti said to Black Cloud, "Show us your true form!"

Black Cloud shook his head. He turned into a huge turtle with a golden beard. He lifted up his head and bit the hook on the fishing pole. The young man climbed up onto the back of the turtle and rode it to Eight Virtue Pond.

Grand Master of Heaven saw what happened to Black Cloud. He shouted, "Zhunti, come into my trap. You will never escape!"

But Zhunti replied, "Black Cloud is very happy now. He is living in the western region, free from the troubles of this human world."

Another immortal named Dragon Head ran out of the trap, ready to attack Zhunti. But Zhunti called out, "Heavenly Master of Outstanding Culture, please take care of this one. He is yours!" Then he pointed a finger at Outstanding Culture's head to cover it with an auspicious light.

The two started to fight. Dragon Head saw that he was losing the fight. He ran back inside the trap, surrounding himself with thousands of

---

[1] This poem is about two of the three defeated Jie fighters who are revealed to be animals: Dragon Head, a lion ridden by Outstanding Culture, and Spiritual Teeth, an elephant ridden by Merciful Navigation. The third, Black Cloud, is revealed to be a turtle and is ridden by one of Zhunti's disciples.

swords that flew in circles through the air inside the trap. Outstanding Culture waved his magic flag to block the flying swords. Then he captured Dragon Head with a magic rope and dragged him out of the trap.

Immortal of the South Pole was waiting there. He shouted, "Change into your true form!" Dragon Head shook his head twice. He changed into a green-haired lion. Outstanding Culture climbed on the lion's back and rode him back and forth in front of the trap.

Laozi smiled at this. He called out, "Grand Master of Heaven, you say you are a great master, but your disciples are nothing but animals!"

Another immortal rushed out of the trap. This was Immortal Spiritual Teeth. He had a purple face and long fangs. He attacked Universal Virtue, then ran back inside the trap. Universal Virtue followed him into the trap. He changed his form so he had three heads, six arms, and rode on a lotus flower. He threw a magic rope which tied up Immortal Spiritual Teeth. Then he ordered his genie to drag the immortal outside the trap. Laozi ordered the immortal to change into his original shape. Instantly the immortal changed into a white elephant. Universal Virtue climbed onto the elephant and rode it around in front of the trap.

Another immortal was waiting inside the trap. This was Immortal Golden Light. He ran out of the trap and was met by Merciful Navigation. Just as before, the immortal ran back into the trap. Merciful Navigation followed him, protected by an auspicious cloud and a golden turtle. He captured the immortal and dragged him out. He ordered the immortal to change into his original form. Golden Light changed into a golden tiger. Merciful Navigation climbed on its back and rode him around.

Inside the trap, Grand Master of Heaven heard a voice behind him saying, "Don't be angry, my dear. I am here!" He turned and saw it was one of his disciples, the goddess named Spiritual Tortoise. She attacked Krakucchanda. He fought her, defeated her, and ordered her to change into her original form. She changed into a large female tortoise. One of Krakucchanda's disciples, a young man, rode her back to the pavilion.

No more immortals came out of the trap. Zhunti and the other Chan immortals returned to the pavilion. Just as they reached the pavilion, a huge cloud of mosquitos appeared in the sky. There were so many that the sky turned black. The mosquitos attacked the tortoise and sucked her blood. The poem says,

> *Their sound is like thunder*
> *Their mouths are like needles*
> *Hungry for blood, they attack the body*
> *The heat becomes more powerful*
> *The cold wind becomes more deadly*
> *The Turtle Spirit dies*
> *As the mosquitos gather together*

Soon there was nothing left of the tortoise except dry bones and a shell. When the devil mosquitos were finished eating the tortoise, they flew to the western region, where they ate the lotus flowers in three of the ponds there.

Grand Master of Heaven was furious. He saw Zhunti, Laozi and Heavenly Primogenitor standing together. He cried, "You broke my trap once before, now you are trying again. I will show you how good you are!"

He attacked Zhunti with a sword, but Zhunti just waved his hand, using three Buddhist relics that came from his head to block the blows. The relics danced in the air, spreading golden light.

Then he attacked Zhunti with a fishing drum[1], but Zhunti blocked it easily with a golden lotus flower.

Laozi turned to the other two and said, "Brothers, I think we are finished here today. Let's go back to the pavilion and rest a while."

When they returned to the pavilion, Heavenly Primogenitor said, "We must go back tomorrow and kill these creatures."

Zhunti replied, "Yes, there are many evil ones in that trap, and only a few good ones. I cannot go against the will of heaven."

Heavenly Primogenitor said to the other Chan immortals, "Tomorrow, look for a pagoda to rise into the air. When that happens, use these swords to destroy them all." Then he handed out several swords that had been taken earlier from the Immortal Killing Trap at Jiepai Pass.

The Chan immortals and generals were excited about the coming battle. Princess Long Ji and her husband Hong Jin also wanted to join in the

---

[1] A fishing drum (鱼鼓) is a percussion instrument used in traditional music. It consists of a long bamboo tube with a dried fish skin stretched over one end. The character 渔 is a verb, meaning "to fish."

fight. They asked King Wu, and he agreed that they could go. They drank a cup of wine with the king before leaving for the pass.

The next day, Heavenly Primogenitor ordered his disciples to ring the golden bells and the jade chimes, to let everyone know that it was time to break the trap.

Inside the trap, Grand Master of Heaven ordered the Six Soul Flag to be waved. He shouted, "I will fight you to the end!"

Long Ji and Hong Jin rushed forward. Jiang Ziya watched them go. He was sad to see them go, because he knew they were fated to die in the trap.

The two of them rode their horses into the trap, waving their swords. They killed or wounded several Jie disciples. Mother Golden Spirit saw this. She rushed over and began fighting with Long Ji. After a few rounds, Golden Spirit stabbed the princess in the neck, killing her instantly.

Hong Jin saw his wife killed. He screamed and rushed at Golden Spirit. She threw her Jade Dragon Tiger weapon at him. It hit him in the head, smashing it. Their two souls flew together to the Terrace of Creation.

Now it was time for the twenty-eight constellations to come out of the trap and fight for the Jie. They were all disciples of Grand Master of Heaven, and they were all fated to become the gods of the twenty-eight constellations in the future[1].

Waving a green flag and dressed in green, four future constellations came out. They were Wood Insect, Wood Dragon, Wood Wolf, and Wood Elk.

Waving a red flag and dressed in red, four more future constellations came out. They were Fire Tiger, Fire Pig, Fire Snake, and Fire Monkey.

Waving a white flag and dressed in white, four more future constellations came out. They were Golden Ox, Golden Goat, Golden Dog, and Golden Dragon.

The Grand Master pointed to each of the four directions with his sword. Four more future constellations came out. They were Water Leopard, Water Ape, Water Worm, and Water Beaver.

---

[1] These are 28 of Grand Master's disciples, each fated to be transformed into one of the Twenty-Eight Mansions (èrshíbā xiù), similar to the zodiac constellations in Western astronomy.

Heavenly Primogenitor sighed and said, "It's too bad that none of these have any understanding of the Dao. They will all lose their lives."

Waving a black flag and dressed in black, four more future constellations came out. They were Earth Bat, Earth Pheasant, Earth Buck, and Earth Jackal.

Laozi looked at them and said, "Look at them! They call themselves immortals but they know nothing of the Way."

The trap opened again, and four more constellations came out. They were Sun Horse, Sun Rooster, Sun Rat, and Sun Rabbit.

Finally, the last four future constellations came out under a white flag. They were Moon Crow, Moon Swallow, Moon Fox, and Moon Deer.

Grand Master of Heaven ordered the twenty-eight future constellations to stand in a circle around him. Everywhere there was red fog, purple lightning, and green light. An air of death hung in the sky.

Chapter 84
Two Religions Come Together

Monkeys cry under the Six Soul Flag
Soldiers beat the drums

Black fog comes, souls run away
The stars grow dim

Strike the cooking pot
Ring the bell of victory

Heroes fall to bloody knives
Grass grows thick at the city's walls[1]

≡ ≡ ≡

Laozi looked at the twenty-eight future constellations surrounding Grand Master of Heaven. He said, "Ten thousand immortals will suffer today, and you are the one who has caused it." Grand Master did not reply. He just waited for the attack.

Heavenly Primogenitor shouted at his disciples, "Today is the day of the final battle. Today you will be able to teach the ten thousand immortals. Don't fail!"

Hearing these words, the immortals from the Zhou army rushed into the trap. The battle began. The trap filled with black clouds. Hundreds of Jie immortals died, cut down by flying swords and magic weapons.

Three of the Chan immortals, Outstanding Culture, Universal Virtue and Merciful Navigation, changed into strange shapes with many heads and many arms, and surrounded Mother Golden Spirit. Their bodies were covered with bright lights, golden lanterns, white flowers, and colorful necklaces. Golden Spirit tried to fight against all three of them. Her gold coronet fell off and her hair flew wildly around her. Burning

---

[1] The Six Soul Flag is a powerful weapon that Grand Master of Heaven plans to use against his enemies. The third line speaks of a copper cooking pot, called a *diaodou*. In ancient times, sentries would carry a diaodou and strike it softly to warn each other at night.

Lamp joined the fight, threw his magic pearls at her head, and she died.

Grand Master of Heaven fought against Laozi and Heavenly Primogenitor. Seeing his disciples falling all around him, he shouted to Immortal Long Ears, "Quick, give me the Six Soul Flag!"

Long Ears looked at the fierce battle all around him. He saw the Chan immortals were much more powerful than his own Jie brothers. He grabbed the Six Soul Flag but did not give it to his master. He wrapped it around himself and ran out of the trap into the pavilion.

Grand Master shouted, "Where is my flag?" He was furious when he saw that Long Ears had run away with it. He also thought about running away, but he did not want his disciples to see him defeated by fear. So, he kept fighting.

Laozi struck him with a large stick. Grand Master dodged the stick and threw his purple hammer at Laozi. Laozi saw the hammer coming towards him it. A beautiful pagoda rose up from his head and blocked the hammer. Grand Master watched this and did not see Heavenly Primogenitor coming up behind him. Heavenly Primogenitor hit him with a club, almost knocking him off his ox.

Now Buddha Zhunti joined the fight. He opened his bag and gathered up three thousand Jie disciples to bring to the western region. Then he changed his form. Now he had twenty-four heads and eighteen hands. Grand Master tried to attack him with a sword, but Zhunti just waved a tree branch to block it. Seeing no way to win the fight, Grand Master rode away quickly on his ox.

Back at the pavilion, Laozi saw Long Ears. He said, "You are a Jie Daoist. What are you doing here?"

Long Ears kowtowed and replied, "Uncle, my master made this flag to hurt you, King Wu, Jiang Ziya, and the others. I did not think that was right, so I did not give it to him."

Heavenly Primogenitor smiled and said, "You may be a Jie Daoist, but you understand the Way. You may stay with us. Now, let's see what this flag can do."

He told Long Ears to open up the flag. Long Ears thought that the flag would kill the immortals, but he opened it anyway. It had no effect at all. Auspicious clouds hung over Heavenly Primogenitor, a pagoda hung over Laozi, and three Buddhist relics protected Zhunti. Seeing this,

Long Ears fell to the ground, kowtowed, and begged to join the Chan Daoist religion.

The battle was nearly over. Some immortals died and their souls flew to the Terrace of Creation. Some became Buddhists. Some ran away. And some died but did not fly to the Terrace of Creation. Shen Gongbao saw the battle was lost and ran away. And Grand Master rode away to a mountain, taking two hundred immortals with him. He said, "I must go and see my master. Then I will know what to do."

Just then, he looked up and saw an elderly Daoist walking towards him. There is a poem about this,

> Sleep in the Ninth Heaven
> Find truth on a bed of straw
> Beyond the black and yellow sky and earth
> I am known as master of the Way
> Daoism has divided into two ways
> I am the leader of all leaders

Grand Master saw that the old Daoist was Hongjun, his master. He kowtowed and said, "Master, I did not know you were coming. May you live for ten thousand years!"

Hongjun was angry. He asked, "Disciple, why did you make this trap which caused so much suffering?"

"My Chan brothers said terrible things about me. They tried to destroy our religion and kill my disciples. Please have mercy on me!"

"You are a liar. You are the one who caused all this suffering, all because you were angry over such a small thing. These brothers did nothing to you. It's a good thing I have come here today, or else this fight would continue forever."

Hongjun ordered the other immortals to go into their caves and not cause any more trouble. Then he said to Grand Master, "Now we will go together to the pavilion to meet the others."

Grand Master thought to himself, "How can I stand in front of them, after what I have done?" But he dared not disobey. So, he and Hongjun walked towards the pavilion.

In the pavilion, Nezha and the others were talking about the battle. They saw Grand Master walking towards them. With him was an old

Daoist who used a walking stick. They heard Grand Master shout, "Tell Laozi and Heavenly Primogenitor to come and meet my master!"

Nezha ran to tell Laozi and Heavenly Primogenitor about the visitors. Laozi said, "I know. Hongjun has come to make peace between the Chan and Jie."

Laozi and Heavenly Primogenitor went to meet Hongjun. They bowed to him, but Hongjun said, "You don't need to bow to me. There is no need to be afraid. Now, I must tell you. I did not think that Grand Master would cause so much trouble. This was not your fault."

"You are right," said Zhunti.

"There must be no anger between us anymore. Many people have suffered, but that must end. Jiang Ziya has important work to do. And you must continue to study the Way."

Then he reached into his sleeve and took out a small gourd. He turned it upside down, and three small pills fell out. He said, "Take this medicine. It will not bring health or long life, but it will help you live together in peace. If you ever decide to fight among yourselves, it will turn to poison in your belly and cause your immediate death."

Laozi, Heavenly Primogenitor and Heavenly Master all bowed to Hongjun. They each ate a pill.

Hongjun stood up to leave. He said, "Grand Master, please come with me." He left. Zhunti and Heavenly Primogenitor also left. As Laozi prepared to leave, Jiang Ziya knelt and said, "Thank you for helping me and my army. I don't know what will happen next."

Laozi said, "Here is a poem to help you understand,

> *We have passed through many dangers*
> *No need to ask about the future*
> *Eight hundred marquises are watching*
> *They wait for the gods to sing*

Laozi left. Grand Completion and the other immortals also said goodbye and left to return to their mountains.

Lu Ya said to Jiang Ziya, "There are still many dangers ahead. Many people will help you if you need it. For now, please take this treasure. You will need it." He handed Jiang Ziya a small gourd. Inside the gourd was a small flying knife.

Shen Gongbao was hiding in the nearby mountains. Heavenly Primogenitor flew towards him on his carriage. He said, "Shen Gongbao! You swore that you would be thrown into the North Sea if you caused any more trouble. Now it is time for you to pay!"

Shen Gongbao just lowered his head and said nothing. Heavenly Primogenitor told his genie to tie him up and throw him into the North Sea. That was the death of Shen Gongbao.

After the immortals had all left, Jiang Ziya marched his army eighty li, making camp just outside Lintong Pass. The commander there was a man named Ouyang Chun. The commander saw the great Zhou army and sent messengers to the king to ask for more soldiers and supplies.

Chapter 85
The Rebellion of Two Generals

The sun sets in the western mountains
A great building is held up by one stick

Bian Ji died for nothing
Ouyang's hot blood covers the pink sky

The tyrant destroys the peoples' lives
The kingdom shakes while evil grows

Cheng Tang began a great dynasty
But now the tide carries it into the past[1]

☰ ☰ ☰

Jiang Ziya said to his disciples, "The fighting between Jie Daoists and Chan Daoists is now finished. The great master Hongjun came. He spoke to me, Heavenly Primogenitor, and Heavenly Master. He told us to stop fighting and work together. Then he told each of us to swallow a pill, and told us that if we ever started fighting each other again, the pill would turn to poison in our bodies. Now it is time for us to all work together to defeat the King of Shang and bring peace to our country."

He marched his army eighty li, making camp just outside Lintong Pass. The commander there was a man named Ouyang Chun. He saw the great Zhou army and sent messengers to the king to ask for more soldiers and supplies. He knew it would take time for help to come from Zhaoge, so he had to buy time by having his generals fight the Zhou generals one at a time.

The first day, he sent one of his generals out. Huang Feihu came out from the Zhou camp. They fought for thirty rounds, then Huang Feihu used his sword to cut off the head of the general.

The general's family heard about this. His son, a young man named

---

[1] Cheng Tang was the founder of the Shang Dynasty. Bian Ji is the son of a slain Shang general and Ouyang Chun is the commander of Lintong Pass. Bian and Ouyang both die in this chapter.

Bian Ji, became angry and asked, "Who killed my father?"

"It was Huang Feihu," replied the commander.

"Then I will go out and get my revenge!" cried Bian Ji. The next day he rushed out of the fort and called for Huang Feihu to fight him. But the big general Nangong Kuo came out instead.

"You are just a small child," said Nangong Kuo. "You cannot fight me."

Bian Ji shouted back, "How dare you speak to me like that! I will let you live, but you must tell Huang Feihu to come out and fight me!"

This made Nangong Kuo angry. He attacked with his cutlass. Bian Ji rode away on his horse. When Nangong Kuo followed him, the boy ran under a huge pennant, more than fifty feet long. Nangong Kuo rode under the pennant. Suddenly he fainted and fell off his horse. Shang soldiers captured him and brought him before Ouyang Chun.

Ouyang Chun wanted to cut off the head of his prisoner. But his generals said, "Commander, it would be better to keep him here as a prisoner. We have heard the king has killed messengers sent to Zhaoge. Let's defeat the Zhou army, then bring this man and the other generals back to Zhaoge. That will show the king our loyalty." Ouyang Chen agreed with this.

The next day, Bian Ji came out of the fort again, calling for Huang Feihu to fight him. When Huang Feihu came out, the boy shouted, "I will cut you into a hundred thousand pieces, to get revenge for the death of my father!"

They began to fight. Again, the boy rode away. When Huang Feihu rode under the pennant, he also fell off his horse and was taken prisoner. Bian Ji wanted Huang Feihu's head cut off, but again the commander refused, saying he wanted to return all the Zhou prisoners to Zhaoge. Bian Ji turned away so the commander would not see his tears.

Jiang Ziya was worried about the loss of two of his best generals. He sent a magician out to get a better look at the pennant. The magician returned and said, "I have seen the pennant. Magicians call it the White Bone Pennant because it is made of human bones. It is surrounded by black smoke and cold fog. There are magic words written in cinnabar on each bone. If anyone goes under the pennant, they faint and can be taken prisoner."

The pass commander Ouyang Chun wanted to meet Jiang Ziya and talk with him face to face. The commander rode out, being careful not to come too close to the pennant. Jiang Ziya saw him. He rode forward and asked, "Are you the commander of this pass?"

"Yes," replied Ouyang Chun.

"My brother, don't you understand the will of heaven? This is the last pass before we march on Zhaoge. You cannot defend it against us."

This made the commander angry. "Who will capture this fool for me?" he shouted. Bian Ji rode forward to attack Jiang Ziya, but Thunderbolt blocked him. Thunderbolt tried to smash the flagpole to bring down the pennant, but when he came close to it, he also fainted and was taken prisoner.

Nezha rushed forward, showing his enemy his three heads and eight arms. He hit Bian Ji with his magic ring. The boy was hurt in the fight and had to return to the fort.

Jiang Ziya decided it was time to end the fight. He ordered his men to beat the war drums. All his generals rushed forward. They formed a circle around Ouyang Chun. But the commander managed to fight his way out of the circle and flee back to the fort. He immediately wrote a letter to the King of Shang, asking for more soldiers.

The king was drinking with his concubines when a messenger brought the letter to him. Greatly alarmed, he called a meeting of his ministers to discuss the situation. He told them, "Jiang Ziya's army is now at Lintong Pass. How can we stop him?"

One of his ministers replied, "Your Majesty, I know several people who can deal with this situation. But they will not help you, because you have not helped them or this kingdom for a long time. I can only think of two men who might have the ability to do this job, and who would also be willing to do it. They are Deng Kun and Rui Ji."

The king agreed with this. He ordered the two men to come to the king's court. They received their orders, thanked the king, and left for Lintong Pass the next day.

The king did not know that Deng Kuo was the brother-in-law of Huang Feihu.

Around this time, Earth Traveler Sun arrived at the Zhou camp, bringing supplies. He heard what happened, and went immediately to see the White Bone Pennant. He came too close, fainted, and was also taken prisoner.

When he was brought before the commander, Ouyang Chun said, "Who are you, little man?"

"I saw a gold cudgel on the ground," Earth Traveler Sun replied, smiling. "I wanted to take it home to play with it."

This made the commander angry. He ordered his men to cut off Earth Traveler Sun's head, but the little man easily escaped by touching his foot to the ground and disappearing into the earth.

The next day, the new Shang generals sent by the king arrived from Zhaoge. They asked Ouyang what the situation was. The commander told them that they had used the White Bone Pennant to capture Nangong Kuo, Huang Feihu, and Thunderbolt.

"Is Huang Feihu a general in the Zhou army?" asked Deng Kuo.

"Yes," replied Ouyang Chun. He also did not know that Deng Kuo and Huang Feihu were brothers-in-law.

The next day, the two new generals led the Shang army out of the pass. They rode towards the Zhou camp, making sure to avoid the White Bone Pennant. They called for Jiang Ziya and King Wu to come out.

"Jiang Ziya!" shouted Deng Kuo. "You are a criminal. This is the king's country. How can you fight against him?"

Jiang Ziya smiled and said, "You two are servants, but you do not know your master. It is time for you to leave the darkness and come into the light. Join us!"

There was a short fight, but Deng Kun was frightened by Nezha and told the army to return to the pass.

That night after dinner, Deng Kuo sat in his room and thought, "King Wu is a great man. He is like a dragon or phoenix, as bright as the sun. He should be our new king. And Jiang Ziya is a wonderful leader of his army. I want to join them, but what about Rui Ji?" He decided to talk with Rui Ji, so he sent one of his men to invite him over for a drink.

Deng Kuo told him, "We have only a few men, but Jiang Ziya has a huge army. What should we do?"

Rui Ji replied, "We still have the White Bone Pennant. I don't know any way that Jiang Ziya's army can get past it."

"My friend, let's speak truth to each other. What do you think the future will bring? Who will rise and who will fall?"

"Dear elder brother, I would like to tell you my thoughts. I am afraid to speak freely to you, but also I do not want to say half-truths and lies."

"Your words will not leave this room. Please tell me what you think."

Rui Ji said, "All right. I believe we are acting against the will of heaven. Our king is a tyrant, and every duke is now against him. Everyone wants a good ruler. King Wu is a good man and could be a great king. As for us, we must serve our nation until the very end."

"Yes, it's too bad we were born in this time, and cannot serve a good master. We should be ready to die when the King of Shang meets his end."

Rui Ji smiled. "I can see that you want to join the Zhou side. I have the same thought. If you go, I will follow you, even if I have to be your horse boy, running behind you."

Deng Kun stood up and said, "The ancients say, 'Two people with one mind are like a sharp sword that can cut metal.' Let's talk about how we can join the Zhou."

While they were talking, Earth Traveler Sun was just under the floor, listening. Jiang Ziya had sent him to visit the prisoners, but he could not enter the jail because there were Shang soldiers there. So he decided to listen to Deng Kun's room.

When he heard this, he jumped up out of the earth and said, "Hello! Don't be afraid. I am Earth Traveler Sun, I am an officer in Jiang Ziya's army. I know you want to join our side. If it is all right with you, I will speak with my commander and tell him what you have said. He is a good man, and will welcome you with open arms. Quick, write a letter. I will bring it to Jiang Ziya."

Deng Kun and Rui Ji quickly wrote a short letter. Earth Traveler Sun took it in his hand, twisted his body, and disappeared into the earth. The two generals watched him go.

Earth Traveler Sun brought the letter to Jiang Ziya, who said, "Good work. His Majesty will be pleased."

The next day, Deng Kun and Rui Ji led the Shang army out of the pass. They stopped when they got to White Bone Pennant. "General Bian Ji," they said, "please move that pennant out of the way."

"But if we do that, the Zhou army can take the pass!" replied Bian Ji.

Deng Kun said, "We are generals sent by the king himself. It is dishonorable for us to have to ride around the pennant, while you ride straight under it."

Bian Ji thought about this. Then he said, "We don't need to move the pennant. Come with me. I will give you something to protect you from its magic." They went back to the fort. Bian Ji wrote magic words on three sheets of paper. He gave one to Deng Kun, one to Rui Ji, and one to Ouyang Chun. He told them to put the paper under their helmets. Now they were able to ride directly under the pennant safely.

Jiang Ziya saw the three generals ride under the pennant. He told Earth Traveler Sun to return to the Shang fort that night, and find out how the three generals were able to do that.

Earth Traveler Sun came out of the ground in Deng Kun's room. Deng Kun told him about the magic words on the paper. He gave one of the papers to Earth Traveler Sun, who brought it back to the Zhou camp.

Jiang Ziya looked at the paper and quickly understood the magic. Using a brush and ink made from cinnabar, he began writing the words again and again, in preparation for the coming battle.

Chapter 86
Generals and Princes Fall

Mianchi is small but defends Shang
Its general is a hero

The horse breathes out black smoke
Traveling underground is truly amazing

Two young kings die because of it
The five great mountains also died for you

Clever Yang used his body magic
He kills the old mother[1]

☰ ☰ ☰

Jiang Ziya called a meeting of all his generals. He gave each of them a piece of paper with the magic words on it, and told them that this would protect them from the White Bone Pennant. Then they all rushed out, surrounding Bian Ji.

Bian Ji rode under the pennant. He expected the Zhou generals to fall like flies at his feet. But he saw that they had no trouble at all with the pennant. Frightened, he returned quickly to the Shang fort.

The pass commander Ouyang Chun asked him how many generals he captured. When Bian Ji replied that he did not capture any generals, Deng Kun became angry. He said, "It is clear to me that Bian Ji ran away from the Zhou army, refusing to fight. No good soldier or general would do this. Take him outside and cut his head off."

Before Bian Ji could say anything, soldiers tied him up, took him outside, and cut off his head.

---

[1] this poem talks about three kinds of magic. Zhang Kui's horse, Black Smoke Single Horned Beast, has magic powers and kills two younger brothers of King Wu. Zhang Kui himself travels underground (in the following chapter). And Yang Jian used his transforming magic to kill the beast as well as Zhang Kui's elderly mother. The "five great mountains" are the five Zhou generals who are killed but are later (in Chapter 99) deified as Gods of the Five Mountains.

Ouyang Chun was shocked. He shouted, "What did you do?"

Deng Kun replied, "I must tell you the truth. We are seeing the end of the Shang dynasty. All the nobles have joined Zhou, and all the passes have fallen except this one. Let's join the Zhou, and attack the tyrant together."

Ouyang Chun looked up at the sky and shouted, "Your Majesty! Why did you send these two traitors to me?" Then he raised his sword and tried to kill Deng Kun and Rui Ji. But he could not fight both of them at once. He was killed by Rui Ji.

The two generals ordered the prisoners freed. The generals went out and met with Jiang Ziya, who said, "You are wise to join us. Good ministers always find a good master."

The Zhou army entered the pass. The people all waved pennants and shouted greetings to the soldiers. King Wu gave a great banquet for the generals, and gifts for all the soldiers.

The Zhou stayed at the pass and rested for a few days. Then they marched to Mianchi , a region close to Zhaoge. The commander of the pass was a man named Zhang Kui. He told his generals, "The Zhou army has taken all five passes and is getting close to Zhaoge. Only the river stands between them and the city. But don't worry, I will stop them here."

For the first battle, Nangong Kuo went out to fight one of the Shang generals. After only twenty rounds, he killed the Shang general, cutting him in two with his sword. The next day, Huang Feihu went out to fight, and stabbed his enemy to death.

Zhang Kui was worried. He talked over the matter with his wife, but she told him that he should not worry, because he was a good magician and rode a wonderful animal called the Black Smoke Single Horned Beast.

Just then, he heard the sound of drums, cannons, and shouting men. He rushed to the wall and saw the Zhou army attacking the city wall. In the middle of the army was Jiang Ziya, surrounded by his generals.

Jiang Ziya rode forward. He said, "Greetings, General Zhang! The will of heaven is with us. Look at what happened at the five passes. You cannot win against us. A single stone cannot support a huge building that is about to fall. Think about this. Join us now."

Zhang Kui became angry. He rode his horse forward to attack Jiang

Ziya. Two of King Wu's younger brothers blocked him, and the three of them began to fight. The two brothers turned and rode away, hoping that Zhang Kui would chase them. But they did not know that about the Black Smoke Single Horned Beast. The beast ran as fast as lightning. The two princes did not even have time to turn around to fight, as Zhang Kui cut them both to death.

Jiang Ziya saw this, and told his men to withdraw. He was discussing the matter with his generals when Chong Heihu, the Grand Duke of the North, arrived. He said, "We won a battle at Chentang Pass, then set up camp at Mengjin. We have been waiting for you for several months. We want to join with you to attack the tyrant."

The next day, Zhang Kui came out again. Jiang Ziya invited Chong Heihu to fight him. Chong Heihu, Huang Feihu, and three other generals rode out and surrounded Zhang Kui.

Even the five of them could not defeat Zhang Kui. Suddenly, Chong Heihu rode away and started to release his hawk. But before he could release the hawk, Zhang Kui caught up with him on his Black Smoke Single Horned Beast. Using his cutlass, he cut Chong Heihu in two.

The battle continued. A woman general appeared. It was Zhang Kui's wife. She took a red gourd out of her robe and took out forty-nine Sun Needles. She threw them in the air. The light was so bright that the Zhou generals could not see. Zhang Kui easily killed them with his cutlass.

Zhang Kui had killed five Zhou generals. Their souls flew to the Terrace of Creation, and later they became gods of the five great mountains in China.

Jiang Ziya did not know how to fight this magic. But Yang Jian arrived with supplies. He said, "I have been bringing food to the army for a long time. I really want to fight!"

Just then, Zhang Kui came out of the city again, wanting to fight. Huang Feibao begged his commander to let him fight to get revenge for the death of his older brother. Jiang Ziya agreed, but asked Yang Jian to go with him.

Huang Feibao fought against Zhang Kui, but he soon became tired, and was killed.

Yang Jian saw the beast that Zhang Kui was riding, and knew that the beast was the real enemy. "You bastard!" he shouted, "I will cut you into a hundred thousand pieces for killing our generals!"

They began to fight. Yang Jian allowed himself to be captured. Soldiers carried him into the city and chopped off his head. Zhang Kui ordered his head put on a pole outside the city walls.

But then, Zhang Kui's horse boy came running in, saying, "Sir, your beast's head just dropped to the ground. The Black Smoke Single Horned Beast is dead!"

Zhang Kui did not know what happened. But then someone told him that Yang Jian was standing outside the city wall. "He tricked me!" shouted the commander. He found a horse and rode out to fight Yang Jian.

They fought a second time, and again Yang Jian allowed himself to be captured. Zhang Kui spoke to his wife, saying, "I captured him again, but I don't know what to do with him."

His wife replied, "I know what to do. Kill a black rooster and a black dog. Mix their blood with human urine and feces. Then tie up the prisoner, write magic words on his body, and pour the dirty mixture over his head and body. He will not be able to escape, and you can really cut off his head."

Zhang Kui told his men to do these things. A soldier raised his sword and cut off Yang Jian's head. The commander and his wife smiled, then returned to their home.

Just then, a servant ran up to them and said, "General, terrible news! Your mother was just resting in her home. Suddenly blood, urine and feces rained down on her. Her head fell off, and she died immediately."

Zhang Kui kneeled down and cried. "First my magic beast, then my dear mother. Both dead!" Then he ran out of the city and challenged the Zhou camp again.

Chapter 87
Death of Earth Traveler Sun and Deng Chanyu

One can travel underground,
Who knew that Zhang Kui could do it even better?

In front of the mountain the beast is already dead;
Under Mianchi city the wife also dies

So much success, what use is it?
So much fame, is it all for nothing?

He gets two lines in the history books,
But heaven has already written everything[1]

≡ ≡ ≡

When Zhang Kui called for battle, Nezha came out to meet him. They began fighting. Nezha threw his Nine Dragon Divine Fire Coverlet over the enemy and his horse, then touched it with his hand to start a fire under it. Zhang Kui's horse was burned to ashes, but Zhang Kui could travel underground. Nezha did not see him escape.

Zhang Kui returned to the city and told his wife what happened. She told him, "Don't worry about fighting all those generals. Just go inside the Zhou camp and kill King Wu. That will end the war."

Zhang Kui liked that idea. That night, he picked up his dagger and traveled underground to the Zhou camp. Yang Ren had magic eyes in his hands that could see everything, so he saw Zhang Kui under the ground. He shouted to the guards, "Be careful! There is an assassin in the camp!" Every guard drew his sword, and all the lamps were lit.

Zhang Kui saw that he could not kill King Wu or anyone else, so he returned to the city. Yang Ren used his magic eyes to watch him leave.

The next day, Yang Jian rode out to do battle with Zhang Kui. Zhang Kui shouted, "You bastard! You killed my mother! I cannot live under

---

[1] A recurring theme in this story is fate. Everything has already been written; all you can do is live, but know that the end of your story is already foretold by heaven.

the same sky as you. You must die!"

They began to fight. When Yang Jian sent his heavenly dog, Zhang Kui jumped into the ground and disappeared. Yang Jian saw this, and reported it to Jiang Ziya. He said, "He can travel underground just like Earth Traveler Sun!"

Zhang Kui was starting to think that he could not win against the Zhou. But his wife said, "Let me see what I can do." The next day, she rode out of the city and was met by Deng Chanyu.

"I am Gao Lanying," she said, "wife of Zhang Kui. Who are you?"

"I am Deng Chanyu, wife of Earth Traveler Sun."

"The king ordered your father to fight the Zhou, but you married one of them! How could you?"

Deng Chanyu roared, and attacked with her two cutlasses. Then she ran away. Gao Lanying chased her. Deng turned and threw a small rock, hitting Gao in the face. Blood poured from her wound. She ran back to the city, hands on her face.

Soon after, Earth Traveler Sun arrived at the camp, bringing supplies. He told Jiang Ziya that he wanted to fight, not just bring supplies. Nezha told him about Zhang Kui's ability to travel underground.

"My master told me that I was the only person in the world who could do that," he said. He begged Jiang Ziya to let him go fight Zhang Kui. The commander agreed.

The next day, Earth Traveler Sun went out of the camp. His wife Deng Chanyu was with him, and also Yang Jian and Nezha.

Zhang Kui saw him and said, "Who are you, little man?"

"I am Earth Traveler Sun," he replied, and they began to fight. Zhang Kui jumped off his horse and into the ground. Earth Traveler Sun followed him. They fought underground, hand to hand and sword to sword. Earth Traveler Sun was smaller and faster. Soon Zhang Kui grew tired and had to retreat to the city.

Earth Traveler Sun returned to the camp and told Jiang Ziya what happened. Jiang Ziya said, "Remember when your master captured you by turning the earth into steel? Perhaps you can do that trick also."

Earth Traveler Sun immediately set off for the mountain cave where his master lived. But he did not know that Zhang Kui had rushed ahead of him underground and was waiting for him. When Earth Traveler Sun arrived at his master's cave, Zhang Kui jumped out from behind a rock. He swung his cutlass, cutting off Earth Traveler Sun's head.

Earth Traveler Sun's head was brought back to the city and hung on a pole. Deng Chanyu cried bitterly when she saw her husband was dead. She begged Jiang Ziya for permission to go and fight Zhang Kui. He agreed. She rode out of the camp, crying and shouting, "Zhang Kui, come out and die!"

Gao Lanying came out instead. She had a cutlass in one hand and a red gourd in the other. When Deng Chanyu came near, Gao Lanying threw forty-nine Sun Needles in the air. They were so bright that Deng Chanyu could not see anything. It was easy for Gao Lanying to cut off her head.

Jiang Ziya cried when he heard that both were killed. He decided to finish the fight by having his entire army attack the city. The Zhou soldiers used cannons to break down the city walls and ladders to climb over the walls. But even after two days they could not capture the city.

Meanwhile, Zhang Kui's messenger arrived in Zhaoge and delivered a letter to the king, asking for reinforcements. The king was drinking with his queen and concubines. When he heard that the Zhou army was only five hundred *li* away, he became worried. "We will go and fight them ourself!" he shouted.

But his ministers said, "Your Majesty, there are five hundred nobles waiting at Mengjin. if you go to Mianchi, they will let you pass, then they will block your retreat. You will be attacked from all sides."

"What do you think we should do?"

"Offer a big reward for generals and soldiers to go and fight for you."

The king agreed. Soon, many men stepped forward and said they wanted to fight. Three of them were actually water demons. One was an ape demon, one was a centipede demon, and one was a snake demon. The three demons went to see the king.

"How will you defeat Jiang Ziya?" asked the king.

"We don't need to defeat the entire Zhou army," said the ape demon named Yuan Hong. "We only need to capture Jiang Ziya. Then you can forgive the nobles and bring them back to your side. The war will be over."

The king agreed, and told Yuan Hong to prepare for war. The other generals saw that Yuan Hong did not know anything about how to be a general, and knew nothing about war. They decided to watch him closely.

"What will you do?" asked the king.

Yuan Hong replied, "It is too difficult to attack the Zhou army in Mianchi. Instead, we should attack Mengjin. It is closer, and has a smaller army. If we win there, the Zhou army will be blocked and cannot attack Zhaoge."

The king agreed, and gave 200,000 soldiers to Yuan Hong.

Chapter 88
Crossing the Yellow River

The white fish is a sign of good things to come
For the Zhou family

Eight hundred lords praise them
Generals and ministers will serve for a thousand years

Prepared for battle
In groups of three and rows of six

The people welcome the master in the rainy season
Cheng Tang's works are already gone[1]

≡ ≡ ≡

Zhang Kui, the commander of the Shang forces at Mianchi, was surprised and worried. He just found out that the king had not sent any reinforcements to him. Instead, the king had sent a new general, Yuan Hong, to Mengjin with 200,000 soldiers. He said, "If the king sends no reinforcements, how can we defend the city? Zhou troops are coming, with four hundred princes. Has the king given up on us?"

With no reinforcements available, he decided not to attack the Zhou army. He and his wife would stay and try to defend Mianchi.

In the Zhou camp, a young Daoist came to see Jiang Ziya. He brought a letter from Krakucchanda. The letter read,

Earth Traveler Sun was fated to be killed by Zhang Kui. I could not help him. I have cried for him. Now it is time for you to defeat Zhang Kui, but it will be difficult to take him down. Here are some magic words. Give them to Yang Jian and tell him to wait at the Yellow River. You are the one who must lure the tiger away from the mountain. When Zhang Kui leaves Mianchi, your army should attack. You will win a great

---

[1] King Wu arrives after crossing the Yellow River and having an auspicious white fish jump into his boat. His army is arranged in a majestic array, and the people welcome him, knowing that the dynasty founded by Cheng Tang is coming to an end.

victory.

That night, Jiang Ziya ordered all the cannons to fire. His army attacked Mianchi but they could not get past the city walls. He ordered the army to withdraw.

The next day, Jiang Ziya tried something different. He went out alone with King Wu. The two of them rode close to the city wall. They discussed different ways to attack the city. Zhang Kui saw this and became angry. He said, "How dare they do this! They act like they own this place! I will go down there and kill both of them."

He rushed out of the city to attack Jiang Ziya and King Wu, shouting, "You two will not escape death today!" The king and the commander rode away. Zhang Kui chased them west for twenty li. Suddenly he heard the sound of cannons, gongs, and drums. He realized that the Zhou army had begun an attack on the city.

Gao Lanying led the city's defenders. Nezha flew over the city wall and attacked her. She fought back with two cutlasses. While she was fighting, Thunderbolt smashed the city gates with his golden cudgel, letting the Zhou army enter.

Gao Lanying tried to use her Sun Needles, but they did not work against Nezha. He stabbed her and she died at once, her soul flying to the Terrace of Creation. The poem says,

> *The lonely city was defended to the death*
> *Too bad she died today*
> *Her name will never die*
> *She will be praised for thousands of years*

The Shang soldiers saw her fall. They all dropped their weapons and surrendered. The battle was over. Nezha rushed westward on his Wind Fire Wheels to chase Zhang Kui.

At the Yellow River, Jiang Ziya shouted, "Zhang Kui, your city has fallen. Surrender now!"

Zhang Kui tried to return to the city, but Nezha blocked him. They fought for about twenty rounds. Nezha threw his Nine Dragon Divine Fire Coverlet, but Zhang Kui jumped down into the earth and disappeared. He ran underground all the way back to the city. He ran as fast as the wind and the lightning. When he got there, he saw that the city had fallen to the Zhou. He turned around and ran back underground to the Yellow River.

As Zhang Kui ran underground, Yang Ren watched him with his magic eyes and followed him closely. If Zhang Kui turned right, Yang Ren turned right. If Zhang Kui turned left, Yang Ren turned left. As soon as Zhang Kui reached the Yellow River, Yang Ren shouted to Yang Jian, who used Krakucchanda's magic words to turn the earth in front of Zhang Kui into steel. He was trapped. He tried to turn around, but the earth behind him turned into iron. Wei Hu threw his magic club into the air. It crashed down on the steel earth and turned Zhang Kui to dust. His soul flew to the Terrace of Creation.

The battle was over. The Zhou army took over Mianchi. Jiang Ziya ordered the army to rest for two days. Then they marched to the banks of the Yellow River. It was a cold winter day:

> *The leaves are heavy with ice*
> *The pine trees carry frozen bells*
> *The ground breaks from the severe cold*
> *The pond is flat because of the ice*
> *The fishing boats are empty, the temple is deserted*
> *The soldier's beard is like iron, the poet's pen is like cold water*
> *The old monk is stiff on the bed, the traveler's soul is frightened*
> *Don't be fooled by the cold, the army's orders are like thunder*

They paid each of the local people five silver coins to use their boats to cross the river.

King Wu and Jiang Ziya were in a large dragon boat. The wind was strong, the waves were high, and the dragon boat rocked back and forth wildly. Suddenly a huge white fish leaped out of the waves and landed on the ship's deck. It jumped around on the deck, trying to get back into the water.

"Your Highness," said Jiang Ziya, "this is a good sign! It means the days of the Shang king will soon pass. Tell the cook to prepare this fish for eating."

"Oh, no!" replied King Wu. "This fish has done nothing wrong. Throw it back!"

"It's already here. You know what the ancients say: 'Do not ignore the gifts of heaven.'" The cook prepared the fish, Jiang Ziya invited all the generals to come onto the dragon boat and eat with the king.

After the storm ended, all the boats arrived at the western bank of the river. Jiang Ziya led them to set up camp outside Mengjin. All four hundred nobles came to greet them. Jiang Ziya asked them to not discuss any plans to attack the Shang king, and they agreed. He also asked them not to use the words "Your Majesty" when speaking to King Wu.

King Wu entered the camp. All the dukes, marquises and other nobles greeted him. They said, "Thank you for coming here. You are wise and the people love you. Please save us from our suffering."

He replied, "My friends, I am no leader, just a poor servant. I have come here to better understand what is happening in our capital."

"Please, we beg you to punish the tyrant. Heaven will be happy if you do!"

"Our king has been listening to bad ministers. If we get rid of them, we can help the king return to the right path."

But they said, "Remember the story of Yao and Shun. Yao did not have a good son, so he gave the throne to Shun. Shun also did not have a good son, so he named Yu as the next king. And so it went, until Jie, the last emperor and an evil man. Heaven and earth were against him, and his dynasty was destroyed by Tang, first ruler of the Shang dynasty. Now we have another evil king. You must punish him!"

King Wu did not know how to reply to this. Jiang Ziya said, "My friends, please, let's not talk of such things. We can discuss it later when we reach Zhaoge."

The next morning, Jiang Ziya led his huge army towards Mengjin. He wore Daoist robes and rode at the front of his army. King Wu and six hundred nobles were with him.

Yuan Hong was waiting for him, wearing a silver helmet and white armor, sword in his hand. "Are you Jiang Ziya?" he shouted when the army came near the walls of Mengjin.

"I am. The Zhou army has taken every pass, every city. All the nobles are with us, and so are the people. If you try to stop us, you will be like a cup of water trying to put out a burning building. Surrender immediately!"

"Jiang Ziya! You are nothing but a poor fisherman. You can catch fish at a small stream, but you do not know how deep the water is here. Your words mean nothing!" Then, turning to his generals, he asked, "Who will kill this fool for me?"

Chang Hao, the snake demon, shouted, "I will!" and rushed forward.

He rode his horse straight towards Jiang Ziya. One of the Zhou generals rode up, swung his axe, and shouted, "Come on, man, I'm here!" The two horses met, and the fight began.

The Zhou general was too strong, so Chang Hao turned and rode away, looking like he was too tired to fight anymore.

Chapter 89
The King Cuts Open Pregnant Women

No king was as evil as King Zhou
He loved wine, sex, and fine living

Pregnant women were killed by evil
Walking men met their death

History books call him a cruel tyrant
The people know him as an evil king

Heaven is hard to understand
It's easier to drink wine with beautiful servants[1]

≡ ≡ ≡

When Chang Hao saw the Zhou general pursuing him, he created a cloud of black smoke that was so thick that the general could not see him. Then he changed into a giant snake. He spat poison gas from his mouth. The Zhou general fell off his horse and was killed by the snake.

Another Zhou general rushed out, shouting, "How dare you!" The centipede demon, named Wu Long, met him in battle. Six hundred nobles watched the fight. The general and the demon fought for a few rounds, then Wu Long changed into a giant centipede, surrounded by black clouds and wind. The general fainted, and Wu Long killed him with a sword.

Nezha saw this. He changed into his three-head and eight-arm form and attacked Wu Long on his Wind Fire Wheels. He threw his Nine Dragon Divine Fire Coverlet over the demon, but the demon changed into a beam of green light and disappeared.

---

[1] this chapter tells of how the King of Shang carelessly tortured and killed his subjects. The king's name in his lifetime was Di Xin. After his death he was mockingly referred to as King Zhou, because zhòu (紂) is Chinese for "crupper," the rear strap on a saddle that goes under the horse's tail and is most likely to be soiled by the horse. For this reason, many translations refer to him as King Zhou. Note that the this use of Zhou (紂, zhòu) is not the same as the Zhou (周, zhōu) Dynasty that succeeded Shang.

Nezha turned and fought against Chang Hao, the snake demon. But the demon changed into a beam of red light and also disappeared.

Yuan Hong shouted, "Jiang Ziya, let's see who the winner is now!" He rushed forward. Yang Ren met him and tried to burn him with his magic fan, but the commander ran away, leaving his horse to be burned to death.

"Enough!" shouted Jiang Ziya when he saw that his generals could not win against the demons. He called for his army to withdraw.

In the Shang camp, Yuan Hong was feeling good. He sent a report to Zhaoge. A messenger brought the message to the king. The king was very pleased. He said, "We will give Yuan Hong a beautiful robe, gold, pearls, a hundred rolls of silk, and ten thousand coins. Give him wine and meat to feast with his generals and soldiers. Tell him to kill all the rebels."

Daji was listening. She said, "Your Majesty, this is a great victory. The war will be over soon. Let's go up to the Deer Terrace and drink wine together."

The king agreed, and ordered a great nine-dragon feast. He sat with Daji and two concubines on the terrace, eating and drinking. It was winter. Heavy snow began to fall. "My dear," said the king, "you are a wonderful singer and dancer. Would you sing us a song about the dancing snow? I will toast you with three cups of wine."

Daji began to sing a beautiful song. The music floated out from the terrace. She sang,

> *The birds fly over the land and outside the city gate*
> *They cross the jade bridge and float in the air*
> *They carry the jade of heaven and earth upside down*
> *Fishes sink and geese disappear in the frozen river*
> *Tigers roar and monkeys cry in the empty forest*
> *Six flowers fall, they pile up on white jade steps*
> *The palace is cold, but the warm sun shines overhead*
> *Dark clouds fly away, revealing the blue sky*
> *Auspicious air and auspicious light come out*

The king smiled and drank the three cups of wine. The snow stopped falling and the sun came out from behind the clouds.

The king and Daji looked out from the terrace. Far below there was a ditch, left over from when the terrace was built. It was deep and difficult to cross. They saw an old man come to the ditch. Even though he was old, he was strong. Barefoot and wearing just a little bit of clothing, he ran across the ditch with no trouble. Following him was a young man. He had heavy clothes and walked slowly. He could not cross the ditch and had to be helped by the old man.

"How strange!" said the king. "The old man ran across the ditch quickly, but the young man had trouble."

"Your Majesty," replied the fox demon queen, "can't you see? The old man was born from parents who were young and strong. The father's sperm was strong, and their lovemaking was hot. That's why his bone marrow is strong. But the young man was born from parents who were old and tired. His father's sperm was weak. That's why his bone marrow is weak even though he is young."

"My dear, everyone is strong when they are young, and weak when they are old. How can this old man be stronger than the young one?"

"Order your guards to bring them here," she replied. "You can see for yourself."

The king sent his guards to bring the two men to the terrace. They cried, "Don't arrest us! We did nothing wrong!"

The guards said, "Don't worry. You will get to meet the king. Maybe he will give you some gifts." The two men went with the guards, up to the terrace where the king and Daji waited.

The king said to the guards, "Cut off their legs and bring them to us." When the legs were brought to him, the king looked at them and saw that the bone marrow was different in the two men. He told Daji, "My dear, you are like a goddess. You know everything!"

She said, "I am just a woman, but I know about yin and yang, and I can see everything. In fact, I can tell you whether an unborn baby is male or female, and which way they are facing in their mother's womb."

The king thought this was interesting. He told his guards to take away the bodies of the two men, and find some pregnant women to bring them to the terrace. The guards searched Zhaoge and found three pregnant women. They dragged the women to the palace. They cried bitterly, and their husbands and children tried to hold on to them, but it made no difference.

A group of ministers was sitting and talking in the palace when they saw the women dragged past. One of them, Ji Zi, asked the women what was going on. "We live in Zhaoge," they said. "We have done nothing wrong. Why are we here? You are a high minister, we beg you to save us!"

Ji Zi asked the chief guard what was going on, and the guard told him. Ji Zi became very angry. He and the other ministers went to the terrace to see the king. Ji Zi knelt on the ground and cried out, "Your Majesty! How can you let the dynasty end after twenty generations? You are acting like a criminal. How can you face your ancestors in heaven?"

The king explained, "The war is almost over. We have killed many of their generals and soldiers, and victory will come soon. My queen says that she can tell the sex and position of unborn babies in their mothers' womb. I want to see this for myself. We will cut open their bellies and see if the queen is correct. Do not dare to argue with me!"

"Your Majesty!" cried Ji Zi, "as king, you are the father of the people. How can you cause your people to suffer? This is why the people are rising up against you. Don't you know that eight hundred nobles are gathered in Mengjin with a huge army? Once they come to Zhaoge, they will not need to fight. The people will throw open the gates of the city and let them in!"

The king became furious. "Take him out and beat him to death!" he shouted to the guards.

The other ministers ran forward and fell to their knees. They said, "Your Majesty, Ji Zi is a loyal minister. He has served you well for many years. We beg you to think about this. You have already cut out the heart of Bi Gan. How can you kill another faithful minister? Please, forgive him."

"All right," said the king. "I will let him live. He will not be a minister anymore, just a common man."

Daji heard this. She said, "Oh no, you can't do that! If you let him live, he will cause great trouble later."

"What should we do with him, then?"

"Shave his head and throw him in prison for the rest of his life." The king agreed to this. The other ministers walked out. They decided to remove the spirit tablets of all twenty generations of rulers from the great temple and hide them far away. They went to live in caves and never returned to Zhaoge.

The king turned to Daji and said, "Now, dear, tell us about these unborn babies."

Daji pointed to one and said, "She has a boy, facing left." Pointing to another, "She also has a boy, facing right." And to the third, "She has a girl, facing backwards."

The king told his guards to cut open their bellies, killing the women and showing the unborn babies inside their wombs. All were just as Daji had said. "Dear queen, you really are wonderful!" said the king, and he drank another toast to the fox demon. But outside, the sky became dark, and the sun and moon lost their light.

A few days later, two demons came to Zhaoge. One, Gao Ming, had a blue face, two golden eyes as large as lamps, a wide mouth with long teeth, and huge muscles. The other, Gao Jue, had red skin, a face like a melon, teeth like swords, and two horns on his head.

They came to the palace, saying, "We heard that Jiang Ziya has taken our passes and our lands. We want to fight for our king. We do not care about rank or money."

The king liked them, thinking that they looked like real warriors. He made both of them generals and sent them to Mengjin. They took large barrels of wine with them, to give to the generals and soldiers there.

Chapter 90
The Defeat of Two Demons

Their eyes are bright, their ears are sharp
They can reach out a thousand li

Plans are created but heard right away
No secrets, all in vain

Xuanyuan Temple is taken by ghosts
Mount Qi is full of beautiful peach trees

Their names are on the List of Creation
No way to avoid the magic weapon[1]

≡ ≡ ≡

Gao Ming and Gao Jue arrived at Mengjin, bringing gifts from the King of Shang. They were met by the commander, Yuan Hong. The commander knew these two were really a peach demon and a willow demon from Mount Chessboard. He himself was really a white ape demon. So the three demons laughed, talked, and had a great time.

A few days later, the peach demon and willow demon went out to the Zhou camp. They shouted, "Jiang Ziya! Come out and meet us!" Jiang Ziya sent Nezha to meet them.

"Who are you?" shouted Nezha, standing on his Wind Fire Wheels.

"We are Gao Ming and Gao Jue. By order of the King of Shang, we are here to arrest the rebel leader. Don't dare to stop us!"

"You evil beasts!" shouted Nezha. He transformed into his three-head and eight-arm form. The two demons fought against him. Nezha smashed one of the demons, and threw his Nine Dragon Divine Fire Coverlet over the other. It looked like both were dead. Nezha returned

---

[1] this describes the two demons Gao Ming and Gao Jue who can hear and see over a distance of a thousand *li*, eavesdropping on the Zhou plans. It then contrasts the fox demon nest at Xuanyuan Temple with the lovely peach groves of Chessboard Mountain (Mount Qi). The weapon in the last line is Wei Hu's Demon Subduing Pestle.

to camp and reported to Jiang Ziya.

But the next day, the two demons returned, demanding to see Jiang Ziya. "What is this?" asked Jiang Ziya.

Nezha replied, "They must know a little bit of magic. Please come with us today, maybe you can tell me what is going on."

Jiang Ziya went out the next day, surrounded by dozens of Zhou generals. All three demons were there, as Yuan Hong had joined the other two. Gao Ming laughed and said, "Jiang Ziya, you have never seen anyone like us." There was another big battle. The poem says,

> Generals fight in Mengjin
> Who is real, who is human, god, or ghost?
> Disasters are always determined by heaven
> Even the most brilliant plans can fail
> The cold wind rises, the evil air arrives
> The white ape uses the iron rod; the demon-subduing club is powerful
> Give your life to protect the world, fight for peace

Yang Ren used his magic fan, but one of the demons turned into a beam of black light and disappeared. Li Jing threw his gold pagoda, but the other demon disappeared also. Thunderbolt hit Yuan Hong on the head, but Yuan Hong turned into a beam of white light and disappeared. All three demons were gone.

Jiang Ziya sounded the horn, calling the Zhou generals back to camp. He told them, "We cannot use our strength to defeat these demons. We must think of a better way." He told four of his generals to set up pillars in four places, spread dog blood on them, and write magic words. Then he told Wei Hu to make a special poison from black chicken blood, black dog blood, and a woman's urine and feces, and be ready to throw it at the demons when they entered the trap.

Unfortunately, Gao Ming and Gao Jue were in the Shang camp listening to every word, using their magic eyes and magic ears. They laughed at Jiang Ziya, saying "What a fool! You call yourself a great general, but you are just an ordinary person. Why do you play with chicken blood and dog blood? Wait until tomorrow, you will see how powerful we are!"

The next day, Jiang Ziya went out, surrounded by his generals. The demons came out and said to him, "Jiang Ziya, you are a stupid fool. Because you are a scholar, you should know how to fight us. Instead, you build a trap. But we are not afraid of your stupid trap and your poor magic."

The battle began. Zhou generals surrounded the demons. Jiang Ziya pretended to ride away in defeat, hoping the demons would follow him into the trap. But the demons just laughed, turned into beams of green light, and disappeared.

Jiang Ziya was angry. "There must be spies in our camp!"

But Yang Jian replied, "I don't think so. Our generals and soldiers have been with us through many battles, and many have died. Nobody would tell the enemy our plans. Please, let me find out what is going on."

"All right. How will you do that?"

"I'm sorry, but the enemy is listening to every word we say. I cannot tell you," said Yang Jian. Then he flew away to the cave of his master, Jade Tripod. He knelt before his master and told him what was going on.

Jade Tripod said, "I know those two. They are the peach demon and willow demon from Mount Chessboard. Both have deep roots in the ground that spread for thirty li. They have been capturing the qi of heaven and earth, of the sun and moon, for thousands of years. They are now extremely powerful.

"There are two clay statues in the temple at Mount Chessboard. One is the Thousand Li Eye, and the other is the Good Wind Ear. The two demons can use these statues to see and hear for a thousand li. Beyond that, they cannot see or hear anything.

"Tell Jiang Ziya to send his men to Mount Chessboard. They must dig up the tree roots and burn them. Then they must go to the temple and destroy the two statues.

"Finally, make sure you cover your camp with fog, so the demons won't know what you are doing."

Yang Jian returned to camp, but he would not tell Jiang Ziya what he was planning to do. He ordered two thousand soldiers to wave red flags. He told another thousand soldiers to beat drums so loudly that the earth shook. When the flags were waving and the drums were roaring, he shouted in Jiang Ziya's ear, "The red flags make it impossible for Gao Ming to see us, and the drums make it impossible for Gao Jue to hear us." Then he told Jiang Ziya his plan.

Jiang Ziya sent soldiers to Mount Chessboard to dig up the two trees and smash the statues in the temple. The poem says,

> *Tigers fight dragons in the deep mountains*
> *Wise ones can see evil plans*
> *If the immortal master had not given help*
> *It would have been difficult to extinguish the two ghost winds*

The soldiers burned the temple to the ground. They returned and told Jiang Ziya what they had done.

Just then, Zheng Lun, the Grand Duke of the East, arrived.

In the Shang camp, Yuan Hong was tired of waiting. He ordered a surprise attack for that night. Jiang Ziya noticed a strange wind blowing through the camp. He did a divination and saw what the enemy was planning. He called his generals to tell them to prepare for an attack. He told them to set up another trap. Then he took a bath to cleanse his body and his heart. He went to a terrace to wait for the attack.

The attack began at sundown. In the first wave, Gao Ming and Gao Jue smashed the door of the Zhou camp and rushed in with thousands of soldiers. Jiang Ziya was waiting for him. His hair was loose on his shoulders and a sword was in his hand. Looking to the sky, he spoke prayers to bring clouds, wind, and fog.

Chapter 91
The Giant Attacks

His strength is great
He moves mountains and drags trees with one hand

Pushing a boat on land, how can he do that?
Defeating enemies, who else can do it?

He made a name for himself
By capturing tigers and eating cows

Blood spills for nothing
Heaven has always been with the Zhou[1]

☰ ☰ ☰

The battle started. Black clouds and thick fog filled the sky. Thunder and lightning crashed all around. The sound of the drums was deafening. The two Gao's attacked first and were quickly surrounded by a dozen Zhou generals. Jiang Ziya came forward and smashed them on the head with his Staff for Beating Gods. They both died instantly.

The three other demons – the ape demon Yuan Hong, the centipede demon Wu Long, and the snake demon Chang Hao – were met by Nezha and Wei Hu. Seeing that they could not win, the centipede demon and snake demon changed into beams of light and disappeared. But Yuan Hong hid behind a white light. Then he came out and smashed Yang Ren on the head, killing him.

At dawn, Jiang Ziya sounded the horn to call his army back to camp. He was very unhappy about the death of the former minister Yang Ren. "We need to learn what these demons are," he said. "Yang Jian, go to Mount Zhongnan and see Master of the Clouds. Get the Demon Exposing Mirror from him."

Yang Jian flew away and soon arrived at the master's cave. He bowed low and said, "Master, I have come to ask to use your magic mirror. Our

---

[1] this poem describes the giant Wu Wenhua, who has great size, strength, and fame, but his efforts are all in vain because heaven supports the Zhou.

army has been stopped by some demons, and we need to know what they are."

Master of the Clouds gave him the mirror. Yang Jian quickly returned to the Zhou camp.

They did not have to wait long to use the mirror. Early the next day, Yuan Hong and his demons rode out of their camp. Jiang Ziya shouted, "General, you must know that heaven favors the Zhou Dynasty. How can you fight us? Surrender now or die."

Yuan Hong laughed, "Surrender to you? You are nothing more than a common fisherman." Then, turning to Chang Hao, he said, "Take him!"

Chang Hao rushed forward on his horse. Yang Jian rushed forward to meet him. They began to fight. Yang Jian turned around and looked in the magic mirror. He saw that he was fighting a huge white snake. He quickly changed into a giant centipede. His wings fluttered like a cloud, his black body and yellow feet were like fire. He flew onto the snake's neck and bit off its head. The snake rolled on the ground. Then Yang Jian changed back to his human form. Using his sword, he chopped the snake into pieces. Finally he brought down lightning from the sky, burning the snake to ash.

Yuan Hong and Wu Long both rushed up to help the snake demon. Nezha met them. Yuan Hong escaped back to his camp, but Wu Long attacked Nezha with two cutlasses. Yang Jian watched the fight through the magic mirror and saw that Wu Long was a centipede. He changed into a giant five-colored rooster and pecked the centipede to pieces.

After the fight was over, Yuan Hong said to his generals, "I did not know that those two were demons."

His generals replied, "The ancients say, 'It is too late to dig a well when you are thirsty.' We should withdraw back to Zhaoge and defend the capital."

"No," replied Yuan Hong. "Our king told us to defend this place. If we retreat to Zhaoge, we will be fighting the enemy at our own door. Be patient, my friends. Jiang Ziya's army is a long way from home. Soon they will run out of food. Then they will be weak and we can defeat them."

The generals left Yuan Hong's tent. One of them said, "We all see the current situation. Our country will soon belong to West Qi. If we use evil spirits as generals, how can we succeed? But how can we not be loyal to our country? If we die, let's die in Zhaoge. We cannot die here with evil spirits. It is better to go to Zhaoge, even if we die there."

Yuan Hong's army was also running low on food. They only had enough for five days. He sent a messenger to the King of Shang, asking for food.

Meanwhile, a giant had come to Zhaoge. He was so big, he could eat an entire cow in one meal. He could pick up a bunch of trees with one hand and use them as a weapon. He could push a boat up onto land without working hard. His name was Wu Wenhua, and he wanted to help the King of Shang. The king's ministers sent him to see Yuan Hong.

"General," said Yuan Hong, "I am happy to see you. Do you have a plan for defeating our enemy?"

"No sir," said the giant. "I am a simple man. I have no plan. I will be happy to obey your orders."

"All right. Go out and fight the Zhou."

The giant walked out towards the Zhou camp, dragging behind him a tree that had long metal spikes. His beard was ten feet long, and his feet were as big as small boats. He shouted, "Jiang Ziya! Take a bath and prepare to die!"

Dragon Beard Tiger went out to meet the giant. "What is this little shrimp?" laughed the giant. "You don't look like a human."

"You fool! Tell me your name so I can write it down after I kill you."

"My name is Wu Wenhua. And you are nothing more than a brainless little beast. Go away and tell Jiang Ziya to come out."

Dragon Beard Tiger threw a stone at him, hitting him in the thigh. The giant lifted his tree trunk and tried to hit the tiger, but he missed. A spike in the weapon went three feet into the ground. Dragon Beard Tiger threw stones one after another, hitting the giant on the thighs and crotch. The giant was in so much pain, he had to run away. He ran twenty li, then he sat down and waited for the pain to go away. Then he returned to Yuan Hong.

Yuan Hong was not happy with the giant. But Wu Wenhua said, "Don't worry, commander. Let me attack the enemy camp tonight. I will smash them all."

"Good!" said Yuan Hong. "I will use a little magic to help you."

At second watch that night, Wu Wenhua rushed towards the Zhou camp, shouting and waving his tree trunk weapon. Nobody knew he was coming. Yuan Hong sent a demonic cloud to cover the Zhou camp, making it too dark to see. The giant broke down the front gate, jumped over four wooden fences, and began smashing soldiers left and right. Their blood flowed to the ground, turning it red.

Jiang Ziya jumped on his horse and escaped the camp. King Wu also got away, protected by four generals. A few other generals also escaped.

The giant walked towards the building where the food was stored. Yang Jian saw him. Quickly he threw a bit of grass into the air and said magic words. The grass changed into a giant the size of a mountain. Its head reached to heaven. Its eyes were as big as water jugs, its front teeth were as big as bamboo poles, and its head was as big as a city gate. Golden light came from its mouth. It shouted, "Wu Wenhua, come fight with me!"

Wu Wenhua looked up and saw the giant, much bigger than he was. "My father is here!" he shouted, and ran away as fast as he could. Yang Jian and his giant chased after him but could not catch him.

When the fighting was over, 200,000 Zhou had died, including thirty-four generals. Jiang Ziya said, "It is all my fault. I should have been more careful with that giant."

Yang Jian rode all over the countryside outside of Mengjin. He found a deep ravine between two great mountains. The people who lived there called it Coiling Dragon because of shape, which looked like a dragon. He returned to camp and told Jiang Ziya his plan.

Jiang Ziya ordered two thousand soldiers to go to Coiling Dragon and hide on both sides. He told them to prepare dry grass and firewood, and wait.

Then Jiang Ziya and King Wu went out on their horses to look around outside the city. Yuan Hong ordered the giant to go out and attack them. As soon as the giant appeared, Jiang Ziya and King Wu rode away to the southwest. The giant was close behind them. "O great warrior," shouted Jiang Ziya, "please let us go home. We will not trouble you again!" This only made the giant angrier. But he was on foot and could not catch up to the other two on their horses. He became tired and slowed down. Jiang Ziya turned and shouted at him, "Wu Wenhua, are you afraid to fight me?" The giant began to chase them again.

When they reached Coiling Dragon, Jiang Ziya and King Wu rode down into the ravine. "Ha!" said the giant. "Now they are just like fish swimming in a cooking pot!"

Chapter 92
Yang Jian Defeats Demons

Seven monsters of Meishan block the Zhou army
They feel they cannot lose

The dog demon is fierce but he dies
The buffalo demon is evil and brings its own death

The pig demon loses his head
The goat demon loses his life

The foolish white ape demon causes trouble
He loses a thousand years of study[1]

≡ ≡ ≡

The giant ran into the ravine. He stopped and looked around. He did not see Jiang Ziya or King Wu. Just as he was getting ready to leave, he heard the sound of cannon fire and the shouts of soldiers. He saw that he could not leave the ravine because it was blocked by a huge pile of rocks and logs.

Up above, soldiers at the edge shot burning arrows and cannon balls down into the ravine. Fires started all around. Then the soldiers threw dry grasses and dead tree branches onto the fires. Black smoke filled the air. The poem says,

> *Fires burns, smoke rolls*
> *Mountains fall, thunder and lightning flash*
> *Green trees are stained red*
> *Even a wide river will turn dry*
> *From burning rocks and liquid metal*
> *The wind shows its power, the fire fights with anger*
> *Not just the body of Wu Wenhua*

---

[1] the seven monsters of Meishan are the snake demon Chang Hao, the centipede demon Wu Long, the pig demon Zhu Zizhen, the dog demon Dai Li, the goat demon Yang Xian, the buffalo demon Jin Dasheng (not named in this chapter), and their leader, the thousand-year-old white ape demon Yuan Hong.

All the mountain creatures will die

The Zhou army had buried mines in the ground. When the fire grew hot enough, the mines exploded. Rocks came crashing down on the giant. He was smashed to death and his body was burned to ash.

The generals and soldiers returned to the Zhou camp. Jiang Ziya said, "I am glad that the giant is dead. But what do we do about Yuan Hong?"

Yang Jian replied, "We know now that he is a white ape demon. He has great power. I don't know what to do. Let's wait and see what happens."

The next day, a new warrior came out from the Shang camp. He had arrived recently to help the Shang. He had a black face, a short beard, big ears, and eyes that shone like the sun. He wore black clothes, and there was a cold air around him.

Jiang Ziya came out to face him. "Who are you, monk, and why are you here seeking your own death?" he asked.

The man replied, "My name is Zhu Zizhen. Surrender now or I will cut you into a thousand pieces." Not waiting for an answer, he rushed at Jiang Ziya. One of the Zhou generals ran forward to block him. They fought for twenty rounds, then Zhu Zizhen turned and ran away. He was faster than any horse. The general chased after him. Suddenly Zhu Zizhen turned and spat out a cloud of black smoke. The general fell off his horse and died.

Yang Jian looked in the magic mirror and saw this fight. He could see that Zhu Zizhen was really a big pig. He ran towards the pig-man. Zhu Zizhen opened his mouth and swallowed Yang Jian. Then he returned to the camp, where the commander Yuan Hong gave him food and drink.

As they were eating and drinking, a strange man walked into the camp. He had a white face, a long beard and two horns. "My name is Yang Xian," he said. Yuan Hong knew him and knew he was a goat demon, but he pretended to not know him. He gave food and drink to the goat demon.

Just then, a voice came from Zhu Zizhen's belly. It said, "Hello! This is Yang Jian. I am in your belly now. I know you have killed and eaten many people. It is time for you to pay. I am going to grab your heart and liver." Then he squeezed the pig demon's heart and liver, causing him great pain.

"Oh, please stop!" cried the pig demon.

"If you want to live, change into your pig form, go to the Zhou camp, and kneel at the front gate. If you don't, I will squeeze your heart until you die."

The pig demon had no choice. He walked slowly to the Zhou camp gate, and kneeled in the dust. Nangong Kuo was on guard. He thought it was just a pig that had wandered away from its farm. Then a voice came from inside the pig. "General Nangong!" it said, "go tell Jiang Ziya that this is the pig demon. It swallowed me, and now I am in its belly."

Nangong Kuo went to tell Jiang Ziya. The two of them went back and saw the pig kneeling on the ground. Yang Jian called from inside the pig, "Kill the pig at once, before it causes more trouble!" Nangong Kuo lifted his sword and cut off the pig's head. Yang Jian swam out through the blood that poured out from the pig's neck.

Yuan Hong watched this and became angry. "We cannot let Jiang Ziya live!" he shouted. Just then, yet another strange person came into his camp. This was Dai Li, a dog demon. He was a friend of Yuan Hong and the other demons, but he pretended to not know them.

Soon afterwards, Dai Li went out to fight. Nezha met him. During the fight, the dog demon spat out a large red pearl. It hit Nezha on the face, giving him a bloody nose. Nezha had to leave the fight. Yang Jian rode forward. He sent his heavenly dog against Dai Li. The heavenly dog bit the demon dog. Then Yan Jian cut the demon's head off.

The next strange person to come into the Shang camp was a huge man, sixteen feet tall and extremely strong. He was a buffalo demon, and a good friend of the other demons. He went out and fought with Zheng Lun. The buffalo demon spat out a huge hairball that hit Zheng Lun in the face. The general fell off his horse, and the buffalo demon killed him.

Yang Jian saw this. He rushed forward to fight the buffalo demon. The demon spat out another hairball that just missed his head. He turned and rode away quickly. As he was riding away, he saw colorful clouds and smelled flowers. Looking around, he saw four lovely girls holding yellow flags. "Come with us, Yang Jian!" they called.

He followed them. Soon he saw a beautiful woman riding a green phoenix. He bowed to her.

"Yang Jian," she said. "I am Nüwa. Several years ago, the King of Shang insulted me, so I decided to bring down his dynasty and allow the new Zhou dynasty to rise. Now I will help you defeat the demons who are trying to stop you." She turned to one of the girls and said, "Please bring that beast to me."

The girl walked up to the buffalo demon and said, "The lady Nüwa has ordered me to arrest you. Come with me." The buffalo demon lifted his sword to attack her, but she threw a magic rope around his head and hit him on the head three times with a bronze hammer. He stopped fighting. The girl led him back to Nüwa.

"Yang Jian," said Nüwa, "take this demon back to your camp and deal with him. Later, I will help you defeat the white ape demon."

Yang Jian led the buffalo demon back to the Zhou camp. Nangong Kuo killed the prisoner.

Jiang Ziya said, "Now we have killed all the demons except the white ape demon. Tonight we will attack. Yang Jian, you and Nezha must go after the demon."

That night, the Zhou army attacked. Two hundred nobles led their armies, attacking the left, right and center of the Shang camp. The Zhou army quickly defeated the Shang, killing thousands of soldiers.

Yang Jian and Nezha fought against the white ape demon. The demon rose into the air and tried to smash Yang Jian with his cudgel. Yang Jian changed into a beam of golden light, escaped, then tried to hit the demon with his cutlass. The demon blocked it with a beam of white light.

They fought all night but neither one was able to win. At dawn, Yuan Hong decided to flee back to his mountain. He flew away on a beam of light. Yang Jian chased him on his horse. Yuan Hong quickly changed into a rock by the side of the road. Yang Jian used his magic sight to recognize this. He created a hammer and smashed the rock, but Yuan Hong turned into a cool wind and flew to his mountain.

Yang Jian chased him to the mountain. There he was attacked by thousands of little monkeys, each one holding a small cudgel. Yang Jian could not fight them all. He turned and escaped on a beam of golden light.

As Yang Jian rode away, he saw Nüwa. He kowtowed to her.

She said to him, "You are a disciple of Jade Tripod, but you are not powerful enough to defeat the ape demon. I will give you this weapon. It is a magic map of the kingdom. It will help you. You must hang it from a large tree."

Yang Jian did as she ordered. Then he went looking for Yuan Hong. He found the ape demon. He said, "Yuan Hong, you won't live much longer today!"

Furious, the ape demon rushed at Yang Jian, who rode away. The ape demon followed him. Yang Jian rode up a mountain path, and the demon followed him. But the path was not real, and the mountain was not real. Both were produced by the magic map. Yuan Hong looked around, but he could not see Yang Jian, and he could not see any way out of the ravine. He was trapped inside the map and could not escape.

Chapter 93
Jinzha Captures the Pass

The Dipper points east again
Even though Dou Long tries to be a hero

Jinzha's clever plan helps the Zhou
Madam Dou could not stop him

Floating clouds cover the morning sun
Deadly air fills the mountains

Even the greatest general belongs to his master
Spirits cry out on the path of death[1]

≡ ≡ ≡

Yuan Hong was lost inside the magic map. His mind became confused, the world around him became like a dream. If he thought of something, it appeared. He thought of a river, and a river appeared. He thought of a mountain, and there it was. If he thought of the past, he saw the past. If he thought of the future, he saw the future.

In his dream, he forgot that he was supposed to look like a man, and he changed back to a white ape. He saw a peach tree nearby. There was a big red peach on a branch. He could smell its sweetness. He climbed up, grabbed the peach, and ate it. Then he sat down on a rock to rest.

A little while later, he looked up to see Yang Jian coming towards him, sword in his hand. He tried to get up to fight, but he had no strength. The red peach had taken all his strength.

Yang Jian tied him up with a magic rope. He knelt towards the south to give thanks to Nüwa for her help. Then he carried the ape back to the Zhou camp.

When Jiang Ziya saw the ape, he said, "This monster has caused too much trouble, and hurt too many people. Cut off its head immediately."

---

[1] When the handle of the Big Dipper faces east in the spring, it heralds the beginning of a new era.

Yang Jian lifted his cutlass and brought it down, cutting off the ape's head. But no blood came out, just green smoke. A white flower grew where the head had been, then the flower turned into a new head. Yang Jian cut it off, but it grew back. He cut it off again, but it grew back again.

"What is going on here?" he asked.

Jiang Ziya replied, "This ape has too much qi from heaven and earth, the sun and moon. But don't worry, I have Lu Ya's weapon, the Flying Dagger. He told me that I would need to use it one day. It can defeat any demon. Watch."

Jiang Ziya picked up a red gourd and placed it on the incense table. He picked up the lid. A white light rose up from the gourd, thirty feet high. He bowed and said: "Please come, treasure!" A strange object appeared, seven and a half inches long, with eyebrows and eyes. Two white lights shot out of the eyes and pushed the white ape against a wall. Jiang Ziya bowed again and said, "Please turn around, treasure!" The weapon turned two or three times in the air, and the white ape's head fell to the ground. Blood was everywhere. Yuan Hong was dead.

Two messengers rode away to Zhaoge to see the king. They told him, "Your Majesty, all of our demons are now dead: the snake demon, the centipede demon, the pig demon, the dog demon, the goat demon, the buffalo demon, and the white ape demon. Our soldiers are nearly all dead. The Zhou army is at Mengjin with all the nobles, and soon they will march on Zhaoge. Please, do something to help us!"

The king called a meeting and asked his ministers what he should do. One of them told the king, "We have a general named Lu Renjie who might be able to help. Give him the rest of your army. Tell him to defend Zhaoge. Don't attack the enemy. Just wait until they run out of food, then we can defeat them." The king had no other ideas, so he gave his army to Lu Renjie and told him to defend the capital city.

Now there was just one mountain pass between the Zhou army and the capital. It was called Youhun Pass. The commander was a man named Dou Rong. Jiang Ziya ordered Nezha's two brothers, Jinzha and Muzha, to find a way to defeat the army at the pass. They decided to dress like Daoists and meet with the commander, to trick him into opening the gates of the pass. They flew near the pass, then walked up to the gate. They asked to see the commander.

"Dear Daoists," said Dou Rong, "what can I do for you?"

Jinzha replied, "Sir, we are two hermits from the Eastern Sea. We know that the East Grand Duke is leading part of the Zhou army here, on his way to attack the king and the capital city. We want to help you. If you defeat the army, the king will be pleased and will give you great rewards."

Dou Rong said nothing to this, but one of his generals shouted loudly, "Don't believe him, sir! Jiang Ziya has sent them to trick you. If you trust them, you will fall into their trap."

Jinzha heard this and laughed. He said to the commander, "It is right for you to be careful. At times like this, dragons and snakes are mixed together and it is hard to tell right from wrong. But here is the truth. Our master is dead, killed by Jiang Ziya at the Ten Thousand Immortal Trap. We want revenge. But if you don't want our help, that's fine, we will leave." Jinzha and Muzha walked out.

Dou Rong sent his men after them, to ask them to return. But Jinza said it was impossible for them to return after being insulted by the commander. "Please, come back with us!" said one of the soldiers, grabbing Jinzha's arm. "If you don't, our commander will punish us!"

Jinzha and Muzha agreed. They returned to the commander's house. Dou Rong said, "I am so sorry. Please, stay and help us." He ordered a great feast for them, but Jinzha refused, saying that they were vegetarians and could not eat meat or drink wine. They went out into the hall, sat down, and spent the night in meditation.

The next morning, one of the Zhou generals came out to challenge them. He was a big man, wearing a red robe and gold armor. "Come out, Daoist, and taste my sword!" he shouted.

"What should we do now?" asked Dou Rong.

"I will go out and fight him," said Jinzha. He went out and shouted to the general, "I am a Daoist hermit from the East Sea. If you put down your weapons, I will let you live. If not, I will smash you to dust."

The Zhou general attacked him. They fought for twenty rounds. Then Jinzha used his Invisible Dragon Stake to capture the general. Seeing this, Dou Rong told his army to attack. They defeated the Zhou army.

Afterwards, soldiers brought the Zhou general to Dou Rong. The general refused to kneel. He shouted, "You used evil magic to capture me. Why should I kneel before dogs and pigs? Kill me if you want. I don't care."

Dou Rong ordered the man killed, but Jinzha held up his hand. He said, "No, wait. Let's capture the East Grand Duke. Then we can bring them both to the king in Zhaoge and show him what we have done." Dou Rong agreed.

The next day, the East Grand Duke, a man named Jiang Wenhua, came out to challenge the Shang. He was the son of Jiang Huanchu, the previous East Grand Duke. He was also the brother of Queen Jiang who was killed by the Shang king.

Jinzha and Muzha, still dressed as Daoists, ran out to meet him.

"Who are you, evil sorcerers?" shouted Jiang Wenhua.

"You don't need to know our names. We are hermits from the Eastern Sea, here to help our king. How can you rebel against your own king?"

"You are demons!" replied Jiang Wenhua. "I will cut you into pieces!" They began to fight. After only a few rounds, Jiang Wenhua turned and rode away quickly on his horse. Jinza and Muzha followed close behind. Jinzha said quietly, "Dear Duke, attack tonight at the second watch. We will do our best to open the gates for you."

Jiang Wenhua turned and shot an arrow at Jinza, who knocked it down with his sword. Jinza shouted, "How dare you try to kill me! I will take you prisoner tomorrow!" Then he and his brother turned and rode back to the pass.

That night, Dou Rong gathered his generals to discuss things. His wife, Madame Dou, came to the meeting. She pointed to Jinza and Muzha and asked her husband, "Who are those two Daoists?"

"They are hermits from the Eastern Sea, here to help us. They have already captured one Zhou general and chased another away."

"Be careful, dear old husband. They may not be who they say they are."

Jinzha smiled and said, "Dear general, your wife may be speaking the truth. We will leave and not trouble you anymore."

The commander replied, "Please forgive me, dear Daoists. My wife is only a woman, but she has studied war and is wise. She does not know you are loyal to our king. Please stay and help us. I will give you a big reward when we have defeated our enemy."

"All right," said Jinzha. We will stay tonight. Tomorrow, we will show you our loyalty when we defeat your enemy."

At the second watch, the air was suddenly filled with the roar of cannons, gongs and drums, and the shouts of attacking soldiers. It was Jiang Wenhua's army, attacking the pass with cannons and high ladders.

Dou Rong and Madame Dou climbed the wall to fight them. Jinza told them that he and his brother would go outside and fight on the ground. Madame Dou said to her husband, "I don't trust those two!" So Dou Rong decided to go outside with them. The three of them led a great army out the gate to battle with the Zhou.

It was a great battle as the Zhou and Shang soldiers fought fiercely. It was nighttime, but the sky was bright with torches, lanterns, and fires. In the middle of the battle, Jinzha threw his Invisible Dragon Stake, capturing Dou Rong.

Chapter 94
Death of the Messenger

Armies approach the city while lords talk peace
How can they stop the weapons?

Tang's great works are now finished
King Wu's works are now sung to the four seas

The great tower is about to fall; who can stop it?
The wound is about to open, who can cure it?

In the end, what is evil?
It leads nowhere, flowing east into the ocean[1]

≡ ≡ ≡

Dou Rong was a loyal servant of the king of Shang. He had guarded the pass for twenty years and fought in hundreds of battles, but now he was captured by Jinzha's magic rope. He could do nothing. Jiang Wenhua walked up to him and cut him in two with his sword.

Madam Dou was standing nearby. Muzha threw his magic sword in the air and said, "Please turn around, treasure!" The sword turned around three times and cut off Madam Dou's head.

The battle was over. Muzha called out from the top of the city wall, "By order of General Jiang Ziya, we now take control of this pass. Surrender now or die." All the remaining soldiers knelt down in surrender. Muzha sent soldiers to open the main gate. The main army entered the pass. They freed the general who was in prison, checked the treasure house, and comforted the people.

Jinzha and Muzha said goodbye to Jiang Wenhua and traveled on a dust cloud to return to the main army. Several days later, Jiang Wenhua also arrived, with all the nobles from the east. Now the main army had over

---

[1] The second line compares the passing of the great Shang Dynasty (founded by Cheng Tang) with the benevolence and kindness of King Wu. In the fourth line, "flowing into the ocean" is equivalent to "going down the drain."

1,600,000 soldiers, eight hundred nobles, and hundreds of other lords. Jiang Ziya and King Wu took time to pray to the gods, then they began marching towards Zhaoge. The poem says,

> *Clouds of war hide the distant valleys*
> *The spirit of death shakes the distant lands*
> *Swords and spears are like mountains of snow*
> *Swords and halberds are like mountains of ice*
> *Banners cover the green fields*
> *Gongs and drums shake the empty trees*
> *The army marches like heavy rain*
> *The horses run like a pack of wolves*

Messengers rushed to the King of Shang to tell him of the situation. The king climbed to the top of the city wall and looked out. He saw a huge army camped outside the city. It was so big that he could not see the far side of it. He met with his ministers and said, "Dear ministers, all the nobles of the country are at our gates. The enemy's army surrounds us. Who has a plan for defeating the Zhou?"

Lu Renjie, the general who was in charge of defending Zhaoge, said, "Your Majesty, you know that if a house is ready to fall down, a single log cannot hold it up. Our treasure houses are empty, the people are unhappy, and our soldiers do not want to fight. We cannot win. I think we should send someone to talk with Jiang Ziya, to tell him to withdraw his army."

The king said nothing to this. After a minute, another minister stood up and said, "Your Majesty, this is not the time to show weakness. The ancients say, 'Brave heroes will appear when there are great rewards.' You can ask for heroes to come and help save the city. We still have 100,000 soldiers and plenty of food. We should not give up without a fight!"

The king liked this plan.

About thirty *li* outside the city lived three hermits. One of them, Ding Ce, heard about the army surrounding the city. He said, "Many nobles have received rewards from the king, but now they rebel against him. Why are they not helping the king now? I want to help the king, but I am just one man. A single log cannot support an entire building!"

Just then, another hermit, Guo Chen, came to see him. He said,

"Brother, I hear that our king is looking for heroes to fight the enemy. You know all about war, I think you can help the king in this fight. And if we win, you will become rich!"

Ding Ce smiled and said, "Brother, the king does not have the hearts of the people. What can we do? Can we put out a burning building with just a cup of water? We cannot hope to win against a hero like Jiang Ziya."

"No, Brother, we must help our king, even if we die. Our blood is hot, now is the time to fight for our king and country!"

The third hermit came in, a tall man named Dong Zhong. He said, "Brothers, I have heard that the king is looking for heroes to save the city. I have told one of his ministers that we will do as he asks. The minister ordered us to see His Majesty tomorrow. The ancients say, 'When you know everything about war, it is time to serve your king.' We cannot just sit and watch as our king dies."

"What?" said Ding Ce. "You didn't ask us first?"

Dong Zhong replied, "You are not the kind of man who sits under a tree waiting for a rabbit, so I just went ahead and acted without speaking with you first."

Ding Ce had no choice. He gave food and wine to his two sworn brothers, and they ate, drank, and talked through the night. The next morning they went to see the king. They kowtowed before him. The king asked them if they had a plan for defeating the huge Zhou army.

Ding Ce said, "This kingdom is like a pile of eggs that may fall and break at any moment. We have no choice, we must defend our king and our country."

This was not really a plan, but the foolish king liked to hear words like this. He made the three men generals in the Shang army, and gave them silk robes and jade belts. Then he sent them to see Lu Renjie. Together, they led their army out of the city, setting up camp outside the city walls.

They saw Jiang Ziya riding his strange horse. "How do you do, Jiang Ziya!" called Lu Renjie. "I am Lu Renjie, commander of His Majesty's army. How dare you attack your own king? He is a kind man. He will let you withdraw your army, so you can live in peace. If you do not, we will smash you like a rock smashes an egg."

Jiang Ziya laughed loudly. "Why do you act against the will of heaven?" he asked. "Your army is small and weak. How long can you fight against us?"

The three hermits all rushed forward, waving their spears. Guo Chen was met by Nangong Kuo. Ding Ce was met by Wu Ji. Dong Zhong was met by the South Grand Duke. Other generals rushed in from both sides. Soldiers beat the war drums and gongs. In just a few minutes, all three hermits lay dead on the ground.

The Shang king was unhappy when he learned that the three hermits were killed. One of his generals, Yin Pobai, said that he would go and meet with Jiang Ziya. The king agreed. The general went out and called out to Jiang Ziya, "Commander, we have not seen each other for a long time. I am happy to see you are now the head of this army and leader of the nobles. May I speak with you?"

"Of course," said Jiang Ziya.

Yin Pobai sat down. He said, "We all know that 'A king's honor is as high as heaven.' Anyone who attacks a king is a rebel, and must be put to death. Any minister who plots against the king is a traitor and must be put to death along with his entire family. You know this, but yet you rebel. People will call you a traitor for ten thousand years. Please, beg His Majesty to forgive you, so you can live."

Jiang Ziya smiled and said, "You have it wrong, General. A kingdom does not belong to the king, it belongs to all the people. And heaven will always help the virtuous. Now heaven has walked away from your king. It is up to us to do heaven's will."

"General, your mind is too small. Think about it. If a ruler or father does something wrong, a minister or son should talk to him and try to lead him towards the right path. A loyal minister would never fight against his king, just as a filial son would never fight against his father. You remember that when Ji Chang was a prisoner in Youli for seven years, he never spoke a word against our king. But here you are, rebelling against your king, a traitor to your country."

The Zhou generals were listening to this and growing more and more angry. Finally one of them rushed forward, pointing his sword at Yin Pobai. He shouted, "If you are such a good minister, why have you failed to lead your own king in the right path? You are lower than a pig or a dog! Leave now or I will kill you."

Jiang Ziya stepped between them, saying "My friend, when two countries are at war, messengers are always treated with respect. We should not threaten this man."

But now Yin Pobai was getting angry. He shouted at the general, "Go ahead and kill me! I will turn into a ghost and drag you through hell!"

The general lifted his sword and cut Yin Pobai in two. The other generals were pleased to see this, but Jiang Ziya was angry. He said, "Yin Pobai was sent here to discuss peace. We should not have killed him. Well, there's nothing we can do about it now." He ordered his men to bury Yin Pobai with respect.

Chapter 95
The King's Ten Crimes

King Zhou is as evil as a Qionqi
His ten crimes are known for generations

He cuts bones and wombs while people suffer
He uses the snake pit and burning pillars while gods mourn

The Xuan sings while the night wind blows
The cuckoo cries as the night rain falls

The past brings great sadness
Even today the history books cannot hide it[1]

≡ ≡ ≡

After Yin Pobai was buried, Jiang Ziya ordered his generals to prepare to attack the capital city again. While he was meeting with his generals, a young man rushed into the room. It was the eldest son of Yin Pobai.

The young man shouted, "How dare you kill my father! He was a messenger of the king. The law says that messengers are protected and should not be harmed. I cannot live under the same sky as the man who killed him! I must cut you into a thousand pieces." Then he rushed at Jiang Wenhua. It was a long fight, lasting over thirty rounds. But in the end, Jiang Wenhua slashed the young man with his cutlass, killing him instantly.

Soon the Zhou army was at all four gates of the capital city. They saw the city was defended by Lu Renjie and a large number of soldiers, so Jiang Ziya ordered his army to withdraw. "What should we do?" he asked his generals.

"Let's use magic to enter the city," said one of them. "That way, we can fight from the inside of the city. That will be easier."

---

[1] The Qionqi ("thoroughly odd") is one of the Four Perils in Chinese mythology, a malevolent creature that instigates wars and enjoys human suffering. The third line paints a picture of the end of an empire: the Xuan, a type of swallow, once sang to give life to the people of Shang, while the cry of the cuckoo is associated with sadness.

"No," replied Jiang Ziya. "There are too many people there. If we fight inside the city, too many citizens will die. They have already suffered too much. We have come to rescue them, not harm them."

"What should we do?"

"I think we should tell the people we are here to rescue them. We can write notes and put them on arrows, then shoot the arrows into the city. The people will read the notes and rise up against the tyrant."

Everyone thought that was a good idea. Jiang Ziya wrote this note:

"Long ago, the great ruler Tianbao crushed the Tang Dynasty. He told the people of Zhaoge that heaven loves the people, and the ruler is the parent of the people. Now we see that your king is evil and cruel. He has sex with demons, he ignores the law, he kills loyal ministers, tortures people, and angers people and gods. He cuts off the legs of men, cuts open the bellies of women, and eats the kidneys of boys. It is so sad! Now heaven orders me, the commander of the Zhou army, to punish this tyrant. I wanted to attack the city, but I am afraid that everything will be destroyed. This will not help the people. So I ask you to quickly surrender the capital, to avoid death and suffering. Do this quickly."

He ordered his secretaries to make hundreds of copies of this note. Then his soldiers attached the notes to arrows and shot them into the city. The notes fell on walls, buildings, and streets. Many people read the notes. And that night, the people rushed to the city gates and opened them wide. They shouted, "Come in and save us!"

Jiang Ziya saw this. He ordered a small army of 50,000 men to enter the city. He told them that killing and stealing were forbidden, and any soldier who harmed a citizen would be executed. The army marched slowly into the city from all four gates. They reached the palace gate and set up camp. They fired cannons, beat drums, and shouted for the king to come out.

The King of Shang was drinking with his concubines when he heard the news. He put on his yellow-gold armor and golden helmet and rode out of the palace on his horse. Soldiers rode in front of him, carrying dragon and phoenix banners. Lu Renjie and other generals rode alongside him, and they were all surrounded by the royal guards.

The Zhou army came out to meet him. Jiang Ziya was in the front, riding in a four-horse carriage under a large red umbrella. Behind him were the four Grand Dukes, then dozens of generals and disciples, then hundreds of thousands of soldiers.

The Zhou army halted. Jiang Ziya rode forward slowly. He said, "Greetings, Your Majesty. I am sorry that I cannot bow to you, as I am wearing armor."

"Are you Jiang Shang, also known as Jiang Ziya?" asked the king.

"I am."

"I remember you were my minister. Then you fled to West Qi and became a rebel. Now you kill my messenger and attack my city. I will not leave until I have your head."

"You have not been a proper ruler. Why should we honor you as our king?"

"I have done nothing wrong. Tell me, what are my crimes?"

Jiang Ziya raised his voice so everyone could hear him. "Princes and generals, disciples and soldiers, hear my words! These are the crimes of the King of Shang.

"Number one: the king should be the parent to the people. But you spend all your time drinking and playing with women. You ignore heaven, harm loyal ministers, and do not take care of your duties as king. You have said, 'I hate the people.' You have been the most evil king since ancient times. This is your first crime.

"Number two: the queen is the mother of the nation. Yet you listened to Daji's lies. You gouged out the queen's eyes, burned her hands, and killed her. How could you take Daji as your queen, and have sex with her day and night? This is your second crime.

"Number three: the crown prince was next in line for the throne. The people loved him, but you listened to lies about him. You sent two men to kill the crown prince and his brother. This is your third crime.

"Number four: loyal ministers are the trunk and branches of the nation, but you treated them badly. You burned them to death on red-hot pillars, or made them slaves. When ministers tried to give you good advice, you treated them worse than animals. This is your fourth crime.

"Number five: the king must always speak truth to the people. But you lied to the Grand Dukes to make them come to you so you could kill them. You listened to Daji and her minions, even though you knew they were speaking lies. This is your fifth crime.

"Number six: the king must always follow the law, and treat the citizens fairly. But you did not do this. You built burning pillars to cruelly kill your loyal ministers. You dug a large pit and filled it with poison snakes. Then you threw palace maids into the pit to feed the snakes, ignoring their cries for help. This is your sixth crime.

"Number seven: the king must take care of the kingdom's treasure and not use it for foolish things. But you built high towers and terraces. You built a pool filled with wine, and a meat forest. You allowed your evil minister Chong Houhu to steal money from the people. Now stealing is common in Zhaoge because the people do not have enough money to buy food. This is your seventh crime.

"Number eight: the king must never try to have sex with women who do not want it. But you tricked Huang Feihu's wife into coming to the Star Picking Mansion, then you tried to have sex with her. She jumped to her death to get away from you. Then Concubine Huang came up, but you threw her off the balcony, killing her. This is your eighth crime.

"Number nine: the king must treat the citizens well. But you killed many people for your own pleasure. You cut off the legs of men, you cut open the bellies of pregnant women. Why should these people die for your pleasure? This is your ninth crime.

"Number ten: the king must not forget his duties and spend all his time seeking pleasure. But you have spent far too much time drinking and having sex with the demons Daji and Hu Ximei. You even drank soup made from the kidneys of young men, to make your sex drive stronger. This is your tenth crime.

"In all, you have caused the death of millions of people. Now, by order of heaven, we have come to punish you."

As the King of Shang listened to this, he grew more and more angry. Then Jiang Wenhua rushed at the king. He wore golden armor and red robe, and rode a white horse. He shouted, "You killed my father. You gouged out the eyes of my sister, the queen. I will punish you with death!"

The South Grand Duke also rushed forward, shouting, "You killed my father! How can heaven allow you to live another day?"

The two of them both attacked the Shang king, but the king fought back fiercely. King Wu watched this sadly. He said to Jiang Ziya, "Ah, it is too bad that His Majesty acted so badly. Now everything is mixed up. It is as if a person wore shoes on his head and a hat on his feet. Why are the dukes fighting him? They should help him return to the right path."

Jiang Ziya replied, "Did you not hear me telling of the king's ten crimes? He is a tyrant. Heaven has turned its back to him." Then he shouted, "Beat the drums!"

The war drums started. Fifty nobles rushed forward, surrounding the King of Shang in a large circle.

Chapter 96
Daji Flees

Her smile can bring down a palace
Her love can capture a king

Her slim waist will take your life
Her lovely body will take your soul

The pheasant sings to the moon
The jade lute ignores the sound of the drum

They have reached their goal of ending the Shang
But they die covered with blood[1]

≡ ≡ ≡

Dozens of Zhou generals and nobles surrounded the King of Shang, all waving swords and shouting at him. The king fought back, slashing with his sword. Lu Renjie rushed forward to help him, joined by other Shang generals.

What a battle! This poem tells everything:

> *The air is filled with dust, the mountains are covered with smoke*
> *Eight hundred nobles are here, the earth is upside down*
> *The drums beat like thunder, the king's guards wave flags*
> *The disciples are like tigers, the Shang King is destroyed*
> *The nobles are everywhere, the sky is filled with swords*
> *Jiang Wenhuan is powerful, the South Duke is like a tiger*
> *Under the green flag of the east, the nobles are like rock*
> *Under the white flag of the west, the generals are like ice*
> *Under the red flag of the south, the disciples are like fire*
> *Under the black flag in the north, the guards are like clouds*
> *The thunder phoenix on the right blocks the left*

---

[1] this poem is about the three fox demons. The first two lines describe Daji's uncanny power over humans. The third line is about the pheasant fox demon Yu Ximei and the jade lute demon Concubine Wang.

> the thunder phoenix on the left protects the right
> The King's generals attack from front and back
> The weapons are like ice, their swords are like snakes
> All you can hear is ding-dong, ding-dong
> Swords chop, souls go left and right
> The King is as strong as grass in spring
> He becomes stronger as he fights
> The princes are angry like thunder, they shout and kill
> The King was strong but now he becomes tired
> Why should we hold on to life for the sake of the country?
> Why do we cherish our lives for fame?
> The princes shout, "Capture!" The generals shout, "Hit!"
> The King's sword is like a flying dragon
> He cuts down generals and wounds soldiers
> He slashes marquises like a child at play
> He kills generals and makes ghosts cry
> Yang Jian is furious, he shouts, "Don't run away!"
> The crying shakes heaven and earth, soldiers eyes fill with tears
> Heroes die for their country, blood flows red on the ground
> Crying generals run around, throwing away broken drums
> Many soldiers are dragged away, injured
> The King fights, the generals are frightened
> The king is evil, his country is ruined
> The snow melts, the spring brings rushing water
> The wind blows red across the ground

After a long battle, Jiang Wenhuan hit the King of Shang on the back with a heavy staff, almost knocking him off his horse. The king turned and rode quickly back to the palace. His men closed the gate behind him.

Twenty-six Zhou generals and nobles were killed in the battle, including the South Grand Duke. King Wu said sadly, "Today the relationship between king and ministers is broken. This causes me much pain."

Jiang Wenhuan replied, "No, Your Highness! Heaven and the people hate the Shang king. Even death is too good for him."

In the palace, the King of Shang took off his armor and sat down to rest.

He said, "We should have listened to our loyal ministers. Now they are all gone, and we are injured. How can we fight again?"

"Don't worry, Your Majesty," said Fei Lian, one of the king's minions. "Victory and defeat are both common in war. You should rest for a few days, then we can fight them again."

But then Fei Lian turned to his friend E Lai and said quietly, "There is no way we can win this battle. Let's get the national seal. When the enemy enters the palace, we will give them the seal. They will reward us, and we will live!" They both laughed.

The Shang king did not hear this. He slowly walked into the inner chamber. He met with his three fox demon lovers: Daji, Hu Ximei, and Concubine Wang. He said sadly, "We never thought that Jiang Ziya could bring all the nobles together to fight as one. The Shang Dynasty has lasted for twenty-eight generations. Now all is lost. How can we face our ancestors in the underworld when we die?"

The three fox demons knelt and wept at his feet, saying, "We can never forget your love! Where will you go? What will you do?"

"We don't know," he replied. "Daji, please sing for us." Then he wrote this poem, and Daji sang and danced for him while he drank more cups of wine.

> We sang and danced on the Happy Terrace
> Who knew that Jiang Ziya would come with his army
> Today we part like birds, we may never see each other again
> Our heroes are ashes, new ministers seize power
> This cup of wine helps me forget
> When I wake up, the world will be new

Then Daji said, "Don't be sad, Your Majesty. I was born in a general's family. I can fight. And Hu Ximei and Concubine Wang know some magic. Let us fight for you!"

"That would be wonderful," replied the king.

The three fox demons put on armor and picked up weapons. The king thought they looked cute dressed for battle.

That night, the three fox demons attacked the Zhou camp. Daji held two cutlasses, Hu Ximei held two swords, and Concubine Wang held a long knife with a phoenix on the blade. They rushed past the guards and began killing soldiers in the camp.

Jiang Ziya woke up when he heard the shouting. Quickly he told his disciples to fight back. Nezha, Jinzha, Muzha, Yang Jian, and Thunderbolt attacked the demons. Jiang Ziya stayed in his tent, reciting prayers. Thunder and lightning crashed all around the fighters.

With no way to win the battle, the three demons turned into three winds and flew back to the palace. They told the king what happened. Sadly, he said, "It's finished. We cannot win. We should all go our separate ways, so we do not all die together." Then he turned and walked up to the Star Picking Mansion.

Daji said to the other demons, "His Majesty is going to kill himself. Let's get out of here." They flew quickly to their old home, the cave at Emperor Xuanyuan's grave.

But Jiang Ziya did a divination and learned of their plan. He sent Yang Jian, Thunderbolt and Wei Hu to wait in the sky above Emperor Xuanyuan's grave. When the three demons arrived, they rushed down to attack them.

Hu Ximei saw them coming. She said, "Why do you attack us? We have done our best to destroy the Shang Dynasty. You should thank us!"

"Shut up!" replied Yang Jian. "By order of Jiang Ziya, we are here to arrest you."

Hu Ximei, the pheasant demon, fought against Yang Jian. Daji, the fox with nine tails, fought against Thunderbolt. And Concubine Wang, the jade lute demon, fought against Wei Hu. But after only a few rounds, they flew away on beams of demon light. The three disciples chased them.

The three disciples chased the three demons for several li. Then suddenly, two large yellow pennants appeared in the sky, and there was a sweet fragrance in the air.

Chapter 97
Death of the Tyrant

The Shang king is cruel
He plays with women while the common people suffer

He drinks fine wine
While the blood of the people runs dry

Like a monster, he throws his servants Into the snake pit
And he burns loyal ministers

His punishment will come in the bright light
It is written in the morning star[1]

≡ ≡ ≡

Yang Jian was chasing the pheasant demon when he saw the two yellow pennants in front of him. Beautiful young women were standing on the left and right. In the middle was Nüwa, riding a green phoenix.

The three fox demons stopped when they saw Nüwa. They dared not run from her. They knelt down and greeted the goddess. "Dear Lady," they said, "please save our lives. Yang Jian and the others are chasing us. They want to kill us."

Nüwa told her servant, Blue Cloud Boy, to tie them up with magic demon-binding ropes and hand them over to Yang Jian.

"Dear Lady!" cried the demons, "we have only done what you asked of us. You ordered us to seduce the King of Shang and lead his kingdom to destruction. We did that. We gave him every pleasure we could think of. We killed all his loyal ministers. Now the Zhou army wants to kill us! Please save our lives."

---

[1] In the third line, we call the king a monster, but the original poem refers to him as a tiger salamander, a huge creature known for its ferocity. The fourth line talks about divine retribution which will come "in bright light," that is, as plain as day. This Chinese concept of retribution is similar to the Indian idea of karma. Even before Buddhism arrived in China, the people believed that good deeds are rewarded and bad deeds punished by the invisible hand of fate. Thus, the king's punishment is "written in the morning star."

Nüwa replied, "Yes, I ordered you to help the King of Shang lose his kingdom. But I did not order you to kill and torture people, or to be so cruel. How could you waste the kingdom's treasure on foolish things like the Happy Terrace? Heaven cannot forgive you. You must pay with your lives." Then to Yang Jian she said, "Take these three to your camp and have them executed by Jiang Ziya. Today the Zhou Dynasty will have its victory and the world will be at peace again. Go now."

Yang Jian and the other disciples brought the fox demons to the Zhou camp and led them before Jiang Ziya. Daji said, "Commander, you know me. I am the daughter of Su Hu. I know nothing of the things of this world. I was sent to the palace to be the king's concubine. When the queen died, His Majesty kindly chose me as the new queen. The king and his ministers made all the decisions. As a woman, I was kept busy cleaning, managing the palace maids, and giving pleasure to His Majesty. How could I, an ordinary woman, tell His Majesty how to rule his kingdom? Please, send me back to my homeland in Jizhou, so I may live the rest of my days in peace."

Jiang Ziya smiled. He said, "You are a liar. You are not the daughter of Su Hu. You are a nine-tailed fox demon. You killed Daji and used her body to seduce the king. You told him to create the meat forest, the snake pit, and the burning pillars. I have told the king of his ten crimes, but all of those crimes were caused by you." Then he turned to his disciples and said, "Yang Jian, execute the pheasant demon. Thunderbolt, execute the fox demon. Wei Hu, execute the lute demon."

Daji was kneeling on the ground, tied up with magic rope. But she was as beautiful as a flower in spring. She looked up at the soldiers who surrounded her. Her face was as lovely as the morning dew, her eyes were like autumn water, her teeth were as bright as jade. She said in a voice as sweet as song, "I have done nothing wrong. Please let me live."

The soldiers' bones and muscles became weak, their eyes grew wide, and they lost the ability to speak. They could not move, much less pick up a weapon. "Soldiers, execute her!" shouted Thunderbolt, again and again, but the soldiers could not move.

Yang Jian and Wei Hu killed the other two demons, but Thunderbolt's soldiers could not kill Daji. He went back to see Jiang Ziya.

"Where is the head of the fox spirit?" asked Jiang Ziya.

"She spoke to the soldiers, and they could not kill her," Thunderbolt replied.

"Then cut off their heads and get new executioners!" shouted Jiang Ziya. But when a new group of soldiers was brought before Daji, they saw the beautiful woman and could not kill her. They stood still, like clay statues.

"I will deal with this myself," said Jiang Ziya angrily. He ordered the soldiers to leave. He told his attendants to set up an incense table and burn incense. Then he brought out Lu Ya's gourd, put it on the table, and removed the cover. A white light rose up. A creature with eyebrows, eyes, wings, and feet appeared. It turned slowly inside the white light. Jiang Ziya bowed and said, "Please turn around, my treasure!" The creature turned around three times. Daji's head fell into the dust, and blood splashed all over the ground. This was the death of the thousand-year-old fox demon.

In the palace, the king's attendants told him that the heads of three women were hanging outside the Zhou camp. He rushed to the palace wall and saw that it was his three lovers. His heart was broken, and tears ran down his face. He wrote this poem:

> How sad
> Jade is broken, beauty is gone
> Your beautiful faces hang there
> Where are your wonderful songs and dances now?
> Our love is gone forever
> Just like that, ten thousand years of love are gone

The king knew his life was almost at an end. He walked to the top of the Star Picking Mansion. He felt a strange, cold wind. Looking down, he saw the snake pit was full of ghosts. Their faces were dirty and their eyes were empty. They grabbed at the king, shouting, "Give us back our lives!" Mei Bo, the former Supreme Minister, shouted, "Tyrant! Today you will go to hell!"

The ghost of Queen Jiang appeared. She grabbed his arm and said, "You tyrant! You killed your wife and sons. You destroyed the dynasty. How will you face your ancestors?"

The ghost of Concubine Huang came to him. Her body was covered with blood. She said, "Tyrant! You threw me from the balcony to my death. How could you be so cruel? Heaven and earth will be happy when you are dead."

The ghost of Lady Jia slapped him across the face, saying, "To stop you from taking my body, I had to throw myself off the balcony. Today I will get my revenge!"

After a while, the ghosts went away. The king called his chief of guards. He said, "We cannot win this war. We will not be taken prisoner. And if we kill ourselves with a sword, the enemy will take my body. We must burn ourselves to ashes. Bring firewood and pile it up. Burn the mansion, with us in it."

The chief of guards cried and said, "Your Majesty, how can I do this?"

"Long ago, Ji Chang said that we would die by fire. This is heaven's will. Do it."

The chief of guards sadly went away to gather firewood. The king wrapped himself in his royal robe, and put on pearl and jade. Then he sat down with a piece of green jade in his hands. The chief of guards came in and kowtowed to the king. Then he lit the fire. Soon, the palace was full of thick black smoke. Ghosts cried and gods screamed. Palace maids ran outside, shouting in terror. The wind grew stronger, making the fire bigger and hotter. The chief of guards shouted, "Your Majesty, I will give my life for you!" and jumped into the fire.

Someone looked at the fire, here is what they saw:

> *Smoke and fog float, golden light blazes across the sky*
> *Flames come from clouds, strong winds blow like rain.*
> *If everything turns to ashes, why build a tower to the sky?*
> *If the tower turns to dust, who cares about rain and clouds?*
> *Now pearl and jade are all like dirt, who knows the cost?*
> *Six palaces and three halls burn, the pillars collapse*
> *Eight concubines' heads are burned*
> *All the palace maids suffer; all the evil eunuchs die*
> *This Shang emperor!*
> *No more talk of fine clothes and food*
> *Golden bowls and altars all turn into a raging flood*
> *He cannot speak of his beautiful eyebrows, clear voice, white teeth*
> *All are transformed into death and dreams*
> *The king turns to ashes, the country is in flames*

Jiang Ziya saw the huge fire. Quickly he rode to the palace with King Wu and other nobles. In the middle of the fire, a man was sitting. He wore a yellow dragon robe and a crown, and held a piece of jade in his hand.

King Wu could not watch. He covered his face with his hands.

The fire became bigger and hotter. Soon the flames reached the top of the Star Picking Mansion. The pillars collapsed, and the whole building came down on the king of Shang, killing him. His soul flew to the Terrace of Creation.

Jiang Ziya ordered the fire be put out. The gates of the palace were opened, and King Wu entered, riding the imperial carriage. Palace guards, attendants and maids welcomed him. They burned incense and threw flowers at his feet.

Chapter 98
The New King Gives Food

King Zhou takes the people's wealth
He forgets the story of Jie

Grain cannot last a thousand years
Wealth cannot last a hundred

You must know that now is the time
For the true king

Today everything is returned to the people
The will of heaven is never about oneself[1]

≡ ≡ ≡

Jiang Ziya's first order was to extinguish the fire. King Wu heard this and said, "Tell your men to be careful around the palace maids. They have suffered too much already. Any soldier who harms them must be punished." Jiang Ziya agreed, and issued the order.

After the fire was extinguished, Jiang Ziya and King Wu walked around the palace. "What are those?" asked the king, looking at the copper pillars.

"Those were used by the Shang king and Daji to burn people alive," replied Jiang Ziya.

The king replied, "Oh, my heart breaks!"

Jiang Ziya led him around. He showed the king the Star Picking Mansion, the snake pit filled with white bones, and the wine pond and meat forest where so many palace maids were killed.

---

[1] Jie was the 17th and last emperor of the Xia Dynasty, ousted by Cheng Tang of Shang around 1600 B.C. He was a corrupt man lacking in virtue, and infatuated by his concubine Mo Xi, who convinced the king to give her a lake filled with wine and naked men and women. She ordered 3,000 men to drink the lake dry, then laughed when they all drowned. This is a clear parallel to the King of Shang (again, called Zhou here instead of his real name Di Xin). The rest of the poem refers to King Wu coming and distributing stored grain and treasure to the common people.

"How terrible," said King Wu. "The King of Shang lost every bit of human feeling."

They looked at the ashes of the Star Picking Mansion, where many palace maids were killed in the fire. King Wu ordered that they receive a proper burial. And he ordered that the bones of the King of Shang be put in a coffin and buried with a proper funeral.

They walked through the Happy Terrace and looked at the carved jade railings, golden beams and pillars, the coral, jade and other jewels. King Wu said, "How foolish. How could he protect the kingdom if he used the treasury to build this?"

Jiang Ziya replied, "It has always been like this. When kings empty their treasury, the dynasty falls. The ancients tell us, 'Always treasure virtue instead of jade.' "

King Wu agreed, and ordered that the storehouses of grain be opened and given away to feed any people who were hungry.

Just then, some soldiers ran up to them, saying that they had found Wu Keng, a son of the Shang king, hiding in the harem. Jiang Ziya said, "Bring him here!"

When the boy was brought to them, some nobles said, "The Shang king was evil. We should kill his son to please heaven and earth."

But King Wu said, "Oh, no. Even great ministers like Bi Gan could not stop the king from doing evil. What could a young boy do? The law says that the family of a guilty man are themselves free of guilt and should not be punished. Give him land and a house, so he can live his live in peace."

Jiang Wenhuan said to King Wu, "Your Highness, we need a new king. Everyone knows you have great virtue. The people and the nobles all want you to be our king. You should sit on the throne."

"No," said King Wu. "You should select someone who is more virtuous than me. I must return to West Qi and do my best to serve as a good minister."

"Your Highness, no one is more virtuous than you!"

"What virtue do I have? You must look for someone better than me."

"But remember, the phoenix sang on Mount Qi, showing us that this is the will of heaven. Your virtue is like that of Yu and Tang."

King Wu smiled and replied, "Duke, you are virtuous, perhaps you should get the throne."

Now all the nobles shouted as one, "Why do you still refuse, Your Highness? We want the country to be at peace. If you do not take the throne, the country will be in trouble again."

Jiang Ziya stepped forward and said, "My friends, please calm down. I will talk with His Highness about this." Then he said, "Let's build a terrace, and write a prayer to heaven asking for His Highness to take the throne."

Everyone thought this was a good idea. In a short time, the terrace was finished. It was three stories high and shaped like the eight diagrams that represent heaven, earth, and humans. In the center were seats for heaven and earth. Around the outside were seats for the gods of mountains, rivers, and lands. There were twelve banners for the twelve vital gods, ten banners for the ten heavenly stems, and four seats for the four gods of the seasons. There was a long table with many kinds of food and drinks. Incense was burned, and flowers were in vases.

Jiang Ziya asked King Wu to come to the top of the terrace. Eight hundred nobles watched him. A minister read this prayer:

On the third day the first month of the first year of the Great Zhou Dynasty, Ji Fa offers this prayer to the gods of heaven and earth: Only heaven will benefit the people, and only heaven will be obeyed. The Shang Dynasty is finished. I, Ji Fa, accept the will of heaven and will correct the sins of the Shang Dynasty. Day and night I am afraid of falling into the shoes of the heroes before me. However, the princes, soldiers and civilians have repeatedly requested that I do this, and I cannot go against them. I have followed their advice and chosen an auspicious day. Today I agree to accept the throne. I hope you will bless me and comfort the people.

More incense was burned, and the sweet smell drifted over the crowd. The people of Zhaoge all shouted with joy. King Wu took the royal seal, and took the throne as His Majesty the King. Nobles came forward, each holding a piece of ivory, and said, "Long live our new king!"

King Wu ordered that all prisoners in the kingdom be given their freedom. Then he ordered a grand feast, and they all ate and drank far into the night.

The next day, King Wu ordered that the riches of the Happy Terrace be distributed to the people. He ordered the dukes and nobles to return to their homes, and make sure their people learned the five virtues, worshipped their ancestors, and lived a good life.

He released all animals used in the war and let them live the rest of their lives in the Peach Forest, to show the people that there would be no more fighting.

King Wu stayed in Zhaoge for ten months. The people were happy, grass grew, and phoenixes appeared. Jiang Ziya told him, "We should appoint a commander to guard Zhaoge. I think it should be Wu Keng." King Wu agreed, and appointed two of his own younger brothers to assist Wu Keng in his new job.

Then he knew it was time for him to return to West Qi. Thousands of people came out into the streets to cheer him and beg him to stay in Zhaoge.

They reached Mengjin and crossed the river in a dragon boat. The king remembered crossing the same river a year earlier, when a huge white fish had jumped into his boat. They got to the other side, and continued marching through the five passes.

Just as they were approaching Golden Chicken Mountain, two Daoists appeared. Jiang Ziya recognized them as Boyi and Suqi, two uncles of the Shang king.

"What can we do for you?" he asked the two men.

"We are happy to see your army returning to your native land," they replied. "But may we ask what happened to our nephew the king?"

Jiang Ziya replied, "The old king was evil and the entire world had turned against him. Our army entered the five passes and were victorious. We marched north while blood flowed. The Shang king burned himself, and now the world was at peace. My master King Wu has given away all the wealth of the Deer Terrace, distributed the grain, and brought peace to the country. All the princes are happy and respect King Wu as the new king. The Shang Dynasty is no more."

Boyi and Suqi shouted, "How sad! How sad! Replace evil with more evil? This is not for us!" They turned away and went into the mountains, where they wrote the poem, "Picking Wild Vegetables." They refused to eat food grown within the Zhou Dynasty, and they both died of hunger in seven days.

After a long journey, King Wu reached West Qi. He entered the palace to greet his mother and grandmother. Then he ordered a grand banquet for all the ministers and generals.

The next morning, King Wu held a conference with his ministers and generals. "Does anyone have anything to say?" he asked.

Jiang Ziya stepped forward. "Your Majesty," he said, "by your order, this old minister led an army to kill the Shang king and establish the Zhou Dynasty. Now we have peace. But those who died have not yet been deified. I ask your permission to return to Mount Kunlun and discuss this matter with my master."

"Of course, you may go," replied King Wu. "Please return to us soon."

Before we learn what happened to Jiang Ziya on Mount Kunlun, there is the matter of Madame Ma. She was Jiang Ziya's wife, but she divorced him, thinking he was a worthless husband, and married another man in her village. But now, everyone in her village knew the story of how Jiang Ziya led the Zhou army to victory.

One day, her neighbor came to visit her. She said, "Don't you know your former husband is now a famous man? He is Prime Minister and commander of the army. You should never have divorced him! Now instead of enjoying wealth and power, you are poor just like the rest of us."

Madame Ma was angry with herself. She thought, "Why could I not see his greatness when he was my husband? What good are my eyes? I cannot stand being so foolish and poor. I should just kill myself." But then she thought, "Wait. What if there is another man also named Jiang Ziya? I should not kill myself until I know for sure." That evening, she asked her husband about it.

"Oh yes," he told her, "Jiang Ziya is a great leader now! I was thinking about going to see him to ask for a job as a low-rank officer. But I was afraid of him, so I did nothing. Anyway, now it's too late. He has returned to West Qi."

This made Madame Ma even more unhappy. Later that night, she asked her husband to go to bed before her. When he was asleep, she hung herself from a ceiling beam. Her soul flew to the Terrace of Creation.

Chapter 99
The Naming of the Gods

The mist clears, colorful clouds appear
The streets are filled with people singing songs of peace

Light of blessing comes from the north
Purple clouds come from the south

Today the gods finish their journeys
The saints return to heaven

Incense smoke travels far
From now on, may the nation remain clean forever![1]

≡ ≡ ≡

Jiang Ziya flew to Mount Kunlun and waited outside the palace until a disciple arrived to lead him in. He knelt down before Heavenly Primogenitor and said, "May you live ten thousand years! It is now time for me to deify all the souls at the Terrace of Creation. I have come to beg you to give me the jade talisman and the golden words."

Heavenly Primogenitor replied, "Of course. Please go back and wait for me." Jiang Ziya quickly kotowed and returned to West Qi.

A few days later, several messengers arrived at West Qi, bringing with them the jade talisman and the golden words. Jiang Ziya took them. He bowed to Mount Kunlun before flying to the Terrace of Creation. He placed the jade talisman and the golden words on an altar. He ordered Nangong Kuo and Wu Ji to put up pennants all around to keep out evil spirits. And he ordered 3,000 soldiers to guard the terrace.

When these things were finished, he bathed and put on a clean robe. He burned incense, poured wine, and walked three times around the terrace. Then he read the golden words aloud, including this:

"I have ordered Jiang Ziya to deify you according to your abilities. You

---

[1] this poem paints a picture of the day when 365 souls are deified on the Terrace of Creation. Purple clouds are considered a blessing from heaven.

will be in charge of every part of heaven, to keep an eye on the good and evil in the world, and to report what happens in the three realms. You will be free from the wheel of life and death from now on. You must follow the great rules and never act for your own interest. I now give you this command!"

Now it was time to begin. Jiang Ziya put the golden words on his desk, picked up the Yellow Apricot Flag, and called out, "Bai Jian! Hang up the List of Creations! Let all souls come, one at a time."

Bai Jian put up the list on the wall. All the souls rushed up to read it. The first name on the list was Bai Jian himself.

"By order of Heavenly Primogenitor," said Jiang Ziya, "I deify you as God of Pure Happiness." Bai Jian kowtowed and left the terrace.

"Huang Tianhua! You gave your life for your country. I deify you as the God of Three Sacred Mountains.

"Huang Feihu, I name you God of Taishan, the East Mountain. You will be chief god of the five mountains, with power over the eighteen hells. All deceased souls are under your command." Huang Tianhua and Huang Feihu kowtowed and left the terrace.

"Let the Gods of Mountains come forward. Chong Heihu, I deify you as God of Hengshan, the South Mountain. Wen Pin, you are the God of Songshan, the Middle Mountain. Cui Ying, you are the God of Hengshan, the North Mountain. And Jiang Xiong, you are the God of Huashan, the West Mountain." They all kowtowed and left the terrace.

"Let the Gods of Thunder come forward." They approached him, but Grand Tutor Wen refused to kneel. Jiang Ziya shouted, "All kneel down to hear the orders from Mount Kunlun!" Grand Tutor Wen knelt.

"Wen Zhong, I deify you as Chief of Thunder Gods under the Nine Heavens. You will gather clouds, give rain, and grow grains for the people. You will have twenty-four gods under your leadership. They are Deng Zhong, Xin Huan, Zhang Jie, Tao Rong, Pang Hong, Liu Fu Gou Zhang, Bi Huan, Qin Wan, Zhao Jiang, Dong Quan, Yuan Jue, Li De, Sun Liang, Bai Li, Wang Bian, Yao Bin, Zhang Shao, Huang Geng, Jin Su, Ji Li, Yu Qing, Mother Golden Light, and Fairy Lotus. You are all deified as Thunder Gods." All twenty-four kowtowed and left the terrace.

"Let the six Gods of Fire come before me. Luo Xuan, I deify you as

Chief of the Fire Gods. You must watch over the people and control their good or evil deeds. The five gods under you are Zhu Zhao, Gao Zhen Fang Gui, Wang Jiao, and Liu Huan. All are now Fire Gods." They all kowtowed and left the terrace.

"Bring the Gods of Plague to the Terrace! Lu Yue, I deify you as Chief of the Plague Gods. The six gods under you are:

> Zhou Xin, God of Plague in the East
> Li Qi, God of Plague in the South
> Zhu Tianlin, God of Plague in the West
> Yang Wenhui, God of Plague in the North
> Chen Geng, Grand Instructor for Goodness
> Li Ping, God for Destroying Plague

"Let the Gods of the Constellations come to the terrace!" Bai Jian led Mother Golden Spirit and the others to the terrace. They knelt. "Mother Golden Spirit, you are now Honorable Goddess of the North Pole Dippers, with 84,000 stars under you. You are leader of the constellations. The gods under you are:

> Su Hu, Jin Kui, Zhao Bing, and Ji Shuming: Gods of the Eastern Constellations
> Huang Tianlu, Long Huan, Sun Ziyu, Hu Sheng, and Hu Yunpeng: Gods of the Western Constellations
> Lu Renjie, Chao Lei, and Ji Shusheng: Gods of the Central Constellations
> Bo Yikao: God of the North Pole, the Great Emperor
> Zhou Ji, Hu Lei, Gao Gui, Yu Cheng, Sun Bao, and Lei Kun: Gods of the Southern Constellations
> Huang Tianxiang, Bi Gan, Dou Rong, Han Sheng, Han Bian, Su Quanzhong, E Shun, Guo Cheng, and Dong Zhong: Gods of the Northern Constellations

"These are the Star Gods:

> Deng Jiugong: God of the Green Dragon Star
> Yin Chengxiu: God of the White Tiger Star
> Ma Fang: God of the Red Sparrow Star
> Xu Kun: God of the Mysterious Martial Star
> Lei Peng: God of the Gone-with-the-Old Star
> Zhang Shan: God of the Snake Star
> Xu Gai: God of the Solar Star
> Queen Jiang: Goddess of the Lunar Star

Shang Rong: God of the Jade Hall Star
Ji Shuqian: God of the Heavenly Precious Star
Hong Jin: God of the Dragon Virtue Star
Princess Long Ji: Goddess of the Red Phoenix Star
King Di Xin: God of the Heavenly Happy Star
Mei Bo: God of the Heavenly Virtue Star
Xia Zhao: God of the Lunar Virtue Star
Zhao Qi: God of the Heavenly Amnesty Star
Lady Jia: Goddess of the Upright Behavior Star
Xiao Zheng: God of the Metal Mansion Star
Deng Hua: God of the Wooden Mansion Star
Yu Yuan: God of the Water Mansion Star
Mother Fiery Spirit: God of the Fire Mansion Star
Earth Traveler Sun: God of the Earth Mansion Star
Deng Chanyu: Goddess of the Six Combinations Star
Du Yuanxian: God of the Doctorate Star
Wu Wenhua: God of the Power Star
Jiao Ge: God of the Admonishment Star
Huang Feibiao: God of the River Leading Star
Madam Chedi: Goddess of the Moon Leading Star
Jiang Huanchu: God of the Imperial Coach Star
Huang Feibao: God of the Heavenly Inheritance Star
Ding Ce: God of the Imperial Chariot Star
E Chongyu: God of the Heavenly Horse Star
Li Jin: God of the Imperial Grade Star
Qian Bao: God of the Heavenly Medical Star
Concubine Huang: Goddess of the Earthly Queen Star
Ji Shude: God of the Domestic Dragon Star
Huang Ming: God of the Dragon Taming Star
Lei Kai: God of the Station Horse Star
Wei Ben: God of the Yellow Pennant Star
Wu Qian: God of the Leopard Tail Star
Zhang Guifang: God of the Mourning House Star
Feng Lin: God of the Lamenting Visitor Star
Fei Zhong: God of the Pulling-Twisting Star
You Hun: God of the Rolled Tongue Star
Peng Zun: God of the Throat Control Star
Wang Bao: God of the City Planning Star
Ji Shukun: God of the Flying Curtain Star
Chong Houhu: God of the Great Spending Star
Yin Pobai: God of the Minor Spending Star

Qiu Yin: God of the Linked String Star
Long Anji: God of the Railing Star
Tai Luan: God of the Head Spreading Star
Deng Xiu: God of the Five Devils Star
Zhao Sheng: God of the Goat Cutlass Star
Sun Yanhong: God of the Bloody Light Star
Fang Yizhen: God of the Official Seal Star
Yu Hua: God of the Single Morning Star
Ji Kang: God of the Heavenly Dog Star
Wang Zuo: God of the Sickness Spell Star
Zhang Feng: God of the Bone Boring Star
Bin Jinlong: God of the Death Spell Star
Bai Zianshong: God of the Heavenly Defeat Star
Zheng Chun: God of the Floating-Submerging Star
Bian Ji: God of the Heavenly Slaying Star
Chen Geng: God of the Yearly Killing Star
Xu Fang: God of the Yearly Punishment Star
Chao Tian: God of the Yearly Breaking Star
Ji Shuyi: God of the Lonely Fire Star
Ma Zhong: God of the Blood Light Star
Ouyang Chun: God of the Lost Spirit Star
Wang Hu: God of the Monthly Breaking Star
Lady Rock: Goddess of the Monthly Touring Star
Chen Jizhen: God of the Dead Air Star
Xu Zhong: God of the Salty Pond Star
Yao Zhong: God of the Monthly Disgusted Star
Chen Wu: God of the Monthly Punishment Star
Gao Jineng: God of the Black Killing Star
Zhang Kui: God of the Seven Murders Star
Yin Hong: God of the Five Grains Star
Yu Zhong: God of the Avoiding Murder Star
Ouyang Tianlu: God of the Heavenly Punishment Star
Chen Tong: God of the Heavenly Net Star
Ji Shuji: God of the Earthly Net Star
Mei Wu: God of the Heavenly Space Star
Ao Bing: God of the Parasol Star
Zhou Xin: God of the Ten Evils Star
Huang Yuanji: Goddess of the Silkworm Breeding Star
Gao Lanying: Goddess of the Peach Blossom Star
Lady Ma: Goddess of the Broom Star
Li Gen: God of the Great Calamity Star

Han Rong: God of the Scattering About Star
Lin Shan: God of the Mourning Dress Star
Dragon Beard Tiger: God of the Nine Ugliness Star
Sa Jian, Sa Qiang and Sa Yong: Gods of the Three Corpses Stars
Jin Cheng: God of the Yin Mistake Star
Ma Chenglong: God of the Yang Error Star
Gongsun Duo: God of the Cutlass Slaying Star
Yuan Hong: God of the Four Wastes Star
Sun He: God of the Five Poverties Star
Mei De: God of the Earthly Space Empty Star
Concubine Yang: Goddess of the Red Lovely Star
Wu Rong: God of the Flowing Star
Zhu Sheng: God of the Odd Star
Jin Dasheng: God of the Plague Star
Dai Li: God of the Desolate Star
Ji Shuli: God of the Fetus Star
Zhu Zizhen: God of the Hidden Broken Star
Yang Xian: God of the Reverse Yin Star
Yao Shuliang: God of the Hidden Chant Star
Chang Hao: God of the Anvil Star
Fang Jingyuan: God of the Lost Star
Peng Zushou: God of the Ancient Hate Star
Wu Long: God of the Broken Star

"Next, there are the Gods of the 28 Mansions. The 7 gods of the Azure Dragon of the East are:

Bai Lin: Wood Dragon of Horn
Bai Lin: Golden Dragon of Neck
Gao Bing: Earth Badger of Root
Yao Gongbo: Sun Rabbit of Root
Su Yuan: Moon Vixen of Heart
Zhu Zhao: Fire Tiger of Tail
Yang Zhen: Water Leopard of Winnowing Basket
"The 7 gods of the Black Tortoise of the North are:
Yang Xin: Wood Insect of Dipper
Li Hong: Golden Ox of Ox
Zheng Yuan: Earth Bat of Girl
Zhou Bao: Sun Rat of Emptiness
Hou Taiyi: Moon Swallow of Rooftop
Gao Zhen: Fire Pig of Encampment
Fang Jiqing: Water Pangolin of Wall

"The 7 gods of the White Tiger of the West are:

Li Xiong: Wood Wolf of Legs
Zhang Xiong: Golden Dog of Bond
Song Geng: Earth Pheasant of Stomach
Huang Cang: Sun Rooster of Hairy Head
Jin Shengyang: Moon Bird of Net
Fang Gui: Fire Monkey of Turtle Beak
Sun Xiang: Water Ape of Three Stars

"The 7 gods of the Vermilion Bird of the South are:

Shen Geng: Wood Dog of Well
Zhao Baigao: Golden Sheep of Ghost
Wu Kun: Earth Deer of Willow
Lü Neng: Sun Horse of Star
Xue Ding: Moon Deer of Extended Net
Wang Jiao: Fire Serpent of Wings
Hu Daoyuan: Water Earthworm of Chariot

"These are the 36 Gods of the Heavenly Gallant Stars:

Gao Yan: God of the Heavenly Leading Star
Huang Zhen: God of the Heavenly Gallant Star
Lu Chang: God of the Heavenly Planning Star
Ji Bing: God of the Heavenly Leisure Star
Yao Gongxiao: God of the Heavenly Courageous Star
Shi Gui: God of the Heavenly Heroic Star
Sun Yi: God of the Heavenly Fierce Star
Li Bao: God of the Heavenly Mighty Star
Zhu Yi: God of the Heavenly Courageous Star
Chen Kan: God of the Heavenly Honorable Star
Li Xian: God of the Heavenly Rich Star
Fang Bao: God of the Heavenly Full Star
Zhan Xiu: God of the Heavenly Lonely Star
Li Hongren: God of the Heavenly Injured Star
Wang Longmao: God of the Heavenly Mystic Star
Deng Yu: God of the Heavenly Healthy Star
Li Xin: God of the Heavenly Dark Star
Xu Zhengdao: God of the Heavenly Safety Star
Dian Tong: God of the Heavenly Empty Star
Wu Xu: God of the Heavenly Swift Star
Lu Zicheng: God of the Deviance Star

Ren Laipin: God of the Heavenly Different Star
Gong Qing: God of the Heavenly Demon Star
Shan Baizhao: God of the Heavenly Minute Star
Gao Ke: God of the Heavenly Retreating Star
Qi Cheng: God of the Heavenly Longevity Star
Wang Hu: God of the Heavenly Sword Star
Bu Tong: God of the Heavenly Level Star
Yao Gong: God of the Heavenly Criminal Star
Tang Tianzheng: God of the Heavenly Damage Star
Shen Li: God of the Heavenly Defeat Star
Wen Jie: God of the Heavenly Imprisonment Star
Zhang Zhixiong: God of the Heavenly Clever Star
Bi De: God of the Heavenly Violent Star
Liu Da: God of the Heavenly Weeping Star
Chen Sanyi: God of the Heavenly Skillful Star

"These are the 72 Earthly Fiend Stars of the Dipper:

Chen Jizheng: God of the Earthly Leading Star
Huang Jingyuan: God of the Earthly Evil Star
Jia Cheng: God of the Earthly Courageous Star
Hu Baiyan: God of the Earthly Heroic Star
Lu Xiude: God of the Earthly Gallant Star
Xu Cheng: God of the Majestic Star
Sun Xiang: God of the Earthly Mighty Star
Wang Ping: God of the Earthly Strange Star
Bai Youhuan: God of the Earthly Fierce Star
Ge Gao: God of the Earthly Literature Star
Kao Ge: God of the Earthly Upright Star
Li Sui: God of the Earthly Secluded Star
Liu Heng: God of the Earthly Closing Star
Xia Xiang: God of the Earthly Strong Star
Yu Hui: God of the Earthly Dark Star
Bao Long: God of the Earthly Helping Star
Lu Zhi: God of the Earthly Gathering Star
Huang Bingqing: God of the Earthly Assisting Star
Zhang Qi: God of the Earthly Safety Star
Guo Si: God of the Earthly Spirit Star
Jin Nandao: God of the Earthly Beast Star
Chen Yuan: God of the Earthly Minute Star
Che Kun: God of the Earthly Clever Star
Sang Chengdao: God of the Earthly Violent Star

Zhou Geng: God of the Earthly Silent Star
Qi Gong: God of the Earthly Mad Star
Huo Zhiyuan: God of the Earthly Rampant Star
Ye Zhong: God of the Earthly Flying Star
Gu Zong: God of the Earthly Walking Star
Li Chang: God of the Earthly Skillful Star
Fang Ji: God of the Earthly Bright Star
Xu Ji: God of the Earthly Progressive Star
Fan Huan: God of the Earthly Retreating Star
Zhuo Gong: God of the Earthly Full Star
Kong Cheng: God of the Earthly Successful Star
Yao Jinxiu: God of the Earthly Round Star
Ning Sanyi: God of the Earthly Disappearing Star
Yu Zhi: God of the Earthly Different Star
Tong Zhen: God of the Theory Star
Yuan Dingxiang: God of the Earthly Gallant Star
Wang Xiang: God of the Earthly Happy Star
Geng Yan: God of the Earthly Adroit Star
Xing Sanluan: God of the Earthly Swift Star
Jiang Zhong: God of the Earthly Suppressing Star
Kong Tianzhao: God of the Earthly Detaining Star
Li Yue: God of the Earthly Devil Star
Gong Qian: God of the Earthly Sprite Star
Duan Qing: God of the Earthly Tranquil Star
Men Daozheng: God of the Earthly Submitting Star
Zu Lin: God of the Earthly Secluded Star
Xiao Dian: God of the Earthly Space Star
Wu Siyu: God of the Earthly Lonely Star
Kuang Yu: God of the Earthly Complete Star
Cai Gong: God of the Earthly Short Star
Lan Hu: God of the Earthly Corner Star
Song Lu: God of the Earthly Imprisonment Star
Guan Bin: God of the Earthly Treasure Star
Long Cheng: God of the Earthly Level Star
Huang Wu: God of the Earthly Damage Star
Kong Daoling: God of the Earthly Slave Star
Zhang Huan: God of the Earthly Examining Star
Li Xin: God of the Earthly Wicked Star
Xu Shan: God of the Earthly Soul Star
Ge Fang: God of the Earthly Counting Star
Jiao Long: God of the Earthly Punishment Star

Qin Xiang: God of the Earthly Torture Star
Wu Yangong: God of the Earthly Strong Star
Fan Bin: God of the Earthly Inefficient Star
Ye Jingchang: God of the Earthly Healthy Star
Yao Ye: God of the Earthly Spending Star
Sun Ji: God of the Earthly Theft Star
Cheng Menggeng: God of the Earthly Dog Star

"These are the Nine Luminaries of the Dipper Division:

Chong Yingbiao, Gao Xiping, Han Peng, Li Ji, Wang Feng, Liu Jin, Wang Chu, Peng Jiuyuan, and Li Sanyi: you will all have the title God of the Nine Brightly Shining Stars.

"Lu Xiong, you are God of the Water Virtue Star of the Northern Dipper. The four gods under you are:

Yang Zhen: God of the Water Leopard Star of the Ji Constellation
Fang Jiqing: God of the Water Crocodile Star of the Bi Constellation
Sun Xiang: God of the Water Monkey Star of the Can Constellation
Hu Daoyuan: God of the Water Earthworm Star of the Zhen Constellation

"Now, bring the Gods of the Year to the terrace! I declare Yin Jiao as God of the Year. Your duties are to watch over everything that happens, whether good or bad. And Yang Ren, you are God of the Sixty-Year Cycle. The ten Gods under your command are:

Wen Liang: Day Patrolling God
Qiao Kun: Night Patrolling God
Han Dulong: God of Increasing Fortune
Xue Ehu: God of Decreasing Fortune
Fang Bi: God of Manifesting the Way
Fang Xiang: God of Opening the Way
Li Bing: God of the Year
Huang Chengyi: God of the Month
Zhou Deng: God of the Day
Liu Hong: God of the Hour

"Next, I deify Wang Mo, Yang Sen, Gao Youqian and Li Xinba, giving each of you the title of God to Guard the Precious Spiritual Firmament. You will serve the Great Saint Commander in Chief and help to guard the spiritual worlds.

"Zhao Gongming, I deify you as Genuine God of the Profound Dragon

Tiger Altar. You have followed the Way and entered the land of the immortals, but you are still trapped in the world of delusion. Once you fall into evil, you cannot return to good. The four Gods under your command are:

> Xiao Sheng: God of Welcoming Treasures
> Cao Bao: God of Storing Valuables
> Chen Jiugong: Envoy of Welcoming Wealth
> Yao Shaosi: Fairy Officer of Good Market

"Now, I call on the four Mo generals. Come forward. I name you Great Heavenly Kings. You will guard the western religion of Buddhism and protect the nation with earth, water, fire, and wind. Your new titles are:

> Mo Liqing: Developing Heavenly King. You hold the green light sword and are in charge of the wind.
> Mo Lihong: Wide-eyed Heavenly King. You hold the green jade lute and also manage the wind.
> Mo Lihai: Literature Heavenly King. You hold the magic umbrella and are in charge of the rain.
> Mo Lishou: National Protection Heavenly King. You hold the ermine, and you also manage the rain.

"Now, Zheng Lun and Chen Qi, because of your great strength, I deify you as God of Heng and God of Ha. You will guard the gate of the western mountain gate of the Buddha.

"Yu Hualong, I deify you as Green Haze Prime King Controller of Smallpox. Your wife, Lady Jin is the Saint Queen to Protect Sickrooms. The five gods under you are:

> Yu Da: God of Smallpox in the East
> Yu Zhao: God of Smallpox in the West
> Yu Guang: God of Smallpox in the South
> Yu Xian: God of Smallpox in the North
> Yu De: God of Smallpox in the Center

"High Firmament, Jade Firmament and Green Firmament, your crimes were serious, but you are forgiven and are deified here today. You will all have the title of Goddesses of the Golden Bowl of the Primordial Chaos. Everyone who is born must first pass through the Golden Bowl. Do your jobs carefully!

"And now we come to you, Shen Gongbao. You were once a member of Chan Daoism, but you went against your religion. You were trapped in the North Sea because of your crimes. But we forgive you. You are deified as Water Dividing God of the East Sea. You must watch the sun rise in the east and go down in the west, year after year. You should be grateful for this gift, and do your job carefully."

Shen Gongbao was the last god to be deified. He kowtowed and left the terrace. All the new gods left Mount Qi to begin their work. Jiang Ziya ordered all the ministers and generals to meet with him the next day.

The next morning, Jiang Ziya ordered two prisoners to be brought before him. The guards brought in Fei Lian and E Lai. Jiang Ziya said, "You two lied to the emperor to make trouble. You caused the death of many loyal ministers, and you worked to destroy the kingdom. But as soon as the old king died, you come here to offer us treasures, hoping to save your lives and become safe and wealthy. How can we let you live and cause more trouble?" He ordered, "Take them out and cut off their heads!"

Chapter 100
King Wu Gives Gifts

Zhou begins its dynasty
The king gives land to many who fought in the war

Three emperors are named
Five levels of nobles are rewarded

Copper contracts and golden books are put away
The flag is wrapped around the stone

From now on, lords will scatter like stars to protect the country
The people come alive[1]

☰ ☰ ☰

Guards cut off the heads of Fei Lian and E Lai, and their souls flew to the Terrace of Creation. Jiang Ziya returned to the Terrace of Creation. He walked up to his desk, shouting, "Where is Bai Jian? Bring the souls of Fei Lian and E Lai!"

The two souls were brought to Jiang Ziya. He said, "These two were minions from the time they were born. They cheated the king, harming him and the country. However this was all caused by fate. I now deify both of them as Gods to Melt Ice." The two minions, now gods, kowtowed and left the terrace. Jiang Ziya left the terrace and returned to West Qi.

At court the next day, it was time for the first meeting with the new king. Fragrant mist filled the air and the sun was bright in the sky. The bells were run three times, and everyone shouted, "Long Live His Majesty!"

King Wu sat on his throne and asked, "Who has anything to report?"

Jiang Ziya stepped forward. He said, "Your Majesty, by order of my

---

[1] the second line refers to the three ancestors of King Wu who were named emperors, and the five ranks given to their descendants: duke, marquis, earl, viscount, and baron. "Copper contracts" were used as verified communications, usually in two halves that must fit together.

master, I have deified 365 souls of ministers, generals, good people and bad people killed in the war. However, many others are still alive who fought bravely in the war. They should be rewarded."

King Wu replied, "I agree. We have waited until the deification was complete. Now you may reward these people as you wish."

Next, seven immortals came forward: Nezha, Jinzha, Muzha, Li Jing, Yang Jian, Wei Hu and Thunderbolt. They told the king that they left their mountain homes to help the Zhou, but now that the country was at peace, they all wanted to return to their homes to live quietly. They did not want fame or wealth.

The king said, "Thanks to you, the sun shines brightly again. The people and the kingdom are grateful. How can you leave us now and go back to the mountains?"

"We beg you to allow us to return," they replied.

"All right. But please let us hold a feast for you tomorrow." They agreed.

The next day, the king held a great feast a few *li* outside West Qi City. The seven immortals walked through the city streets to the city gate, accompanied by Jiang Ziya, King Wu, and all the ministers and generals. Crowds of people watched them and shouted greetings.

When they all reached the place of the feast, the king took their hands. He told them, "After you return to your homes in the mountains, you will no longer be subject to my rule. For now, though, let us eat and drink together!" After the feast, the immortals said goodbye to King Wu, Jiang Ziya, and the ministers. They returned to the mountains and never got involved with the affairs of men again.

The next day, the king gave land and titles to hundreds of people who fought in the great war. The king's father, grandfather and great-grandfather were all given the title of Emperor.

The king was not finished giving gifts. He granted land to seventy-two people and made them nobles. He opened the kingdom's treasure houses and gave away gold, silver, and jewels.

The king decided to move the capital city to Fengjing. This was just north of Chang'an, near the center of the kingdom. He ordered his ministers to transfer of the capital from West Qi to Fengjing.

A few months later, the king said to Jiang Ziya, "Prime Minister, you are becoming quite old. If it is not comfortable for you to continue serving us at court, you might be happier relaxing at home." Jiang Ziya thanked him, accepted gifts, and traveled to the state of Qi where he had received the title of duke. He lived there for the rest of his life. He married a woman named Shen Jiang and had fourteen sons and one daughter. His daughter, Yi Jiang, married King Wu and had two children, including King Cheng of Zhou.

Jiang Ziya remembered his sworn brother Song Yiren, who had helped him long ago when he first left Mount Kunlun and arrived in Zhaoge. He sent a messenger to Song Yiren with a gift of a thousand catties of gold. He received a reply saying that Song Yiren and his wife were no longer alive, but his son had taken over the family business and was doing quite well.

After Jiang Ziya's death, his descendants took over as rulers of the state of Qi, through the Spring and Autumn period of the Zhou Dynasty.

In the capital city, King Wu was a good ruler. The people were happy and the kingdom was at peace. After his death, King Cheng took the throne. In all, the Zhou Dynasty lasted for eight hundred years from the days when Jiang Ziya fought and won the great war against the last King of Shang.

About the Authors

Jeff Pepper is President and CEO of Imagin8 Press, and has written dozens of books about Chinese language and culture. Over his long career he has founded and led several successful computer software firms, including one that became a publicly traded company. He's authored two software related books and was awarded three U.S. patents.

Xu Zhonglin (1567 – 1619?) was a Chinese novelist who lived during the Ming Dynasty. He is believed to be the original author of *Investiture of the Gods*. The only direct evidence for his authorship is an original copy of the book in the Japanese Library of the Grand Secretariat, which is inscribed with the words "edited by Xu Zhonglin, the Old Recluse of Mount Zhong."

Printed in Poland
by Amazon Fulfillment
Poland Sp. z o.o., Wrocław